COR
AMARE

COR AMARE

Book Two
The Luna Duet

by

NEW YORK TIMES BESTSELLING AUTHOR

PEPPER WINTERS

Cor Amare
Book Two
The Luna Duet
Copyright © 2023 Pepper Winters
Published by Pepper Winters

Published: Pepper Winters 2023: **pepperwinters@gmail.com**
Cover Photo: Cleo Studios
Cover Design: Cleo Studios
Edited by: Editing 4 Indies (Jenny Sims)
Proofread by: Christina Routhier
Translation & Authenticity Reader: Betül Silence is Read
Sensitivity Reader: Sedef

OTHER WORK BY PEPPER WINTERS

Pepper currently has close to forty books released in nine languages. She's hit best-seller lists (USA Today, New York Times, and Wall Street Journal) almost forty times. She dabbles in multiple genres, ranging from Dark Romance, Coming of Age, Fantasy, and Romantic Suspense. She has won awards for best Dark Romance and is a #1 Apple Books Bestseller.

For books, FAQs, and buylinks please visit:

https://pepperwinters.com

Subscribe to her Newsletter by clicking here or following QR code

To grab three of Pepper's books for free (Tears of Tess, Pennies, and Debt Inheritance) Please CLICK HERE or use the QR code

SOCIAL MEDIA & WEBSITE
Facebook: Peppers Books
Instagram: @pepperwinters
Facebook Group: Peppers Playgound
Website: www.pepperwinters.com
Tiktok: @pepperwintersbooks

**Digitally Signed
By
Pepper Winters**

Thank you so much for reading.

*Love,
Pepper*

Letter from Author

This book is a tale of blended culture, languages, and love that overcomes every obstacle. Sensitivity readers have been enlisted for authenticity and translations, and research has been conducted to provide as accurate and as respectful tale as possible. Creative license has also been used as the characters are their own person and their evolution is unique to them.

This book is intended for audiences who enjoy graphic sexual descriptions, intense emotional challenges, and are familiar with my darker work. This is a life story, a coming-of-age story, and ultimately, one of the most poignant love stories I have ever written, but it does deal with topics such as torture, mutilation, loss, grief, and other mental health challenges.

Please read responsibly.

Pepper

x

Dedication

To Soulmates.
Human and animal.
Family and pet.
Long term or short.
Known or not.
To every special bond and unexplainable connection.
We have loved before.
We have lost before.
But now we are found.

Prologue

NERIDA

(*Love in Latin:* Amare)

I'VE KNOWN PAIN.

Exquisite pain. Devastating pain. Ravaging pain.

But no matter the abuse on my body or the torment in my mind, nothing could've prepared me for the savaging of my heart.

They say a heart needs love to survive, and love needs a heart to exist.

But what if both are stolen?

What if both are broken?

What if, by the end of everything, all that's left are fragments and pieces, hope and unhappiness…an emptiness that swallows everything?

Chapter One

NERIDA

AGE: 17 YRS OLD

(*Love in Welsh:* Cariad)

I DIDN'T TURN AROUND AS THE TWO policemen tumbled into my room.

I didn't look back at my unconscious father on my favourite cream rug. I had no interest in those men when the only man I wanted, the only boy I would live and die for, tripped and stumble-sprinted out of our garden and down the street.

The coral pink sunset etched Aslan in glowing warm splashes, staining the ridiculous Hawaiian shirt Dad had made us wear for Christmas. I'd worn a matching shirt, before the strain of the day's festivities and the haunting in my mind made me lock myself in the bathroom.

I'd hurt myself.

I'd put on makeup to hide that hurt and tried to dress up my pain with a little black dress.

Both my attempts had failed at healing me.

But Aslan?

God, *him*?

He'd given me the perfect brand of medicine.

Not quite a cure but enough of an antidote that I felt stronger than I had in so very, very long. More myself. More brave. More accepting than ever before.

In an act of love wrapped up in violence, he'd proven to me that I didn't have to be afraid of the world.

The world needs to be afraid of me.

I clung to that conviction as Aslan vanished into suburbia, running from the police my parents had called, bolting from a rape charge that wasn't his to bear.

Balling my hands, I turned from the window with my teeth bared and fury flowing swiftly in my veins.

It burned so bright, so hot, so *sharp* that I pitied anyone who got in my way.

My attention fell on the two policemen.

The slender, leaner one with short brown hair tripped to my father. Speaking into the radio hooked to his chest pocket, he barked, "Unconscious male. Requesting ambulance immediately."

Guilt panged. My hand still throbbed from the vibration of hitting my beloved dad over the head with the very same mermaid lamp he'd bought me for my thirteenth birthday.

Tears pricked but then my hackles rose as the other cop, the shorter, stockier one with black hair, marched into me and shoved me away from the window. "Where is he?" Folding himself over the windowsill, he peered at the garden with its ferns, boulders, and sandy-bottomed pool.

Using his radio, he barked, "Male running on foot. Requesting a unit to patrol the streets around Helmet and Reef." His gaze lingered on the sala-bedroom where Aslan had hidden for almost six years.

With a huff, he pushed back into the room. "You let him go? After what he did to you?"

My chin tipped up. "He didn't do anything to me."

Crackle of radio chatter as the cop tending to my father checked his vitals.

My mother stepped into the room, wringing her delicate hands, her pretty pink dress dancing around her calves.

I stiffened as our eyes met.

The guilt inside me swarmed thicker.

And then she noticed why I was guilty as her dark blue gaze landed on my father.

"Jack?" Her eyes popped wide in horror. "Oh my God, *Jack!*" Running to his side, she dropped to her knees and grabbed my father's suit lapels. "Jack. Honey. Wake up!"

"Mrs Taylor, I must request that you don't shake him," the taller officer muttered. "He might have spinal injuries that we're unaware of—"

"*What?*" Tears streamed from her eyes. "Spinal injuries. W-What happened? H-How could Aslan *do* this? After everything we did for him!" Rage thickened her voice. Her fingers clawed at my father. "Get out there and find Aslan Avci, right now!"

I winced at the hate in her tone. At the awful, *awful* belief that the boy she'd welcomed into our family wasn't the kind, loyal, and hardworking illegal immigrant she'd grown to love as her own, but was somehow a complete stranger. A stranger who'd become a daughter molester, father hitter, and criminal.

He's none of those things.

How could she believe them when she *knew* him?

How could she question his loyalty after he'd given every part of himself to us?

Another gush of anger heated my blood, followed by panic rippling down my spine.

I'd ruined everything.

Every mistake and consequence was my fault, and I refused to let Aslan pay.

Not even for a second.

My kneecaps bounced as I stepped around the shorter cop. "It wasn't Aslan, Mum."

Her frantic stare ripped to mine. With her hands still on Dad's chest, she narrowed her eyes. "Of course, it was him. He hurt you, and then he hurt Jack to get away. We had him so wrong." More tears coursed over her cheeks. "We didn't know him at all—"

"You know he adores us," I hissed. "To doubt his integrity and devotion to our family is just plain wrong, Mum."

"But he *hurt* you—"

"No. *He didn't.* If everyone had stopped for a damn fucking second and *listened* to me, you'd see the truth instead of making up lies."

Her lips thinned. "Nerida, you're in shock and—"

"It was me," I snapped. "I hit Dad when he went to hurt Aslan again."

Everyone froze.

The two police officers glowered at me with matching condemning stares. "I think you better explain."

For a moment, I stared at the four people in my ramshackle bedroom. My mosquito net, that I'd yanked from the ceiling by accident when Aslan had tackled me, lay bunched by the end of the bed. Pillows were strewn all over the floor, and my rumpled blankets shared a tale of despair. It painted a scene of a man forcing me down and touching me against my will.

I understood why my dad had jumped to conclusions. I could see why the police had condemned Aslan before they'd even talked to him.

But what they didn't know was *why.*

Why Aslan had 'attacked' me. Why he'd put his entire life on the line to save mine. Why he'd done whatever he could to take me back to that awful night.

I couldn't stop thinking about it, despite all my promises to forget.

Aslan had made me hurt him.

He'd willingly worn the pain I needed to inflict.

He'd shown me that I wasn't helpless or weak, and I'd let him, even though every intuitive nudge had screeched not to do this. Not to be so stupid. So *reckless.* Not to play with such dangerous fire when my parents were just down the corridor.

I'd tried to stop him.

I'd snapped and fought him—fiercely and genuinely—trying to snap him out of his drunken stupidity. But the longer we battled, the more I lost myself to memories of Ethan touching me, not Aslan. Of a stranger pinning me down, tying me up, and entering me against my will.

I forgot where we were.

I forgot who I fought.

I let all my unresolved trauma and repressed pain blind me, and the war between us became far, far too real.

But then we'd crashed to the floor.

Aslan had sprawled amongst the fallen pillows, tonguing the blood I'd drawn on his lips, wincing at the pain I'd delivered between his legs, and…something happened.

Something snapped free inside me.

The drowning darkness that'd steadily been smothering me these past few weeks cracked.

Just a sliver.

Just a splinter.

But it was a crack full of *me*.

The girl I'd forgotten. The girl full of power and tenacity.

A girl who'd let a monster do his best to smother her light all while the son of a true monster struck a match and relit that flame inside her.

I shivered with strength.

I felt reborn.

I'd pounced on Aslan in gratefulness.

I'd been the one to beg him to fuck me, right there, without a thought to the consequences. I'd needed him with desire bordering on violent.

He'd tried to stop me.

I'd argued and cajoled.

And because he lived and breathed to keep me safe and happy, doing whatever it took to deliver what I asked, he didn't say no again.

In one colossal mistake, we'd grabbed our fragile future and torn it into smithereens.

No.

Just no.

I wouldn't let him wear the blame on this. I wouldn't let my parents hate and judge him when he'd been nothing but good and kind.

Fuck that.

Fuck Ethan.

Fuck fate.

Aslan wasn't going to be deported and killed because of me.

No way.

Sucking in a breath, choking on words I never wanted to utter, I glowered at my mother and said, "The night I went to Zara's to patch up our friendship, I was drugged and restrained. I was raped in a house full of people, and no one heard me screaming because the music was so deafening."

Mum froze beside my unconscious dad.

I had front-row seats to the shattering devastation in her stare. For the longest time, she couldn't speak. She choked on a sob, her face blanching white. But then she found her tongue and so many awful tears. "Oh, Neri…baby. No." Scrambling to her feet, she charged me and wrapped me in the tightest embrace.

A groan came from the carpet as my dad rallied. Sirens once again echoed in the thickening twilight, either police hunting Aslan as he ran or the ambulance here to help my father.

I struggled in my mum's arms, my thoughts fleeing through the streets with Aslan. Was he hiding? Could I prevent them from deporting him if they caught him?

I have to stop this.

Now.

Squirming in her hold, I stepped back. "I'm fine."

"You're not fine. How the hell could you be fine?" Mum cupped my cheeks with shaking hands. "Why didn't you say anything?"

"Because I didn't want you to know."

"But, Neri—"

"Aslan knew." I pulled her hands away and embraced a fresh wave of anger. "He knew. He's the only one who knew. He was trying to help me, Mum. It was stupid and looks far worse than it is, but he's never *ever* hurt me. Never done anything against my will." Stepping away from her, I braced my spine and became the hurricane that my father had always likened me too.

A hurricane that'd petered out for a time.

A hurricane that'd become a tepid frightened breeze.

But now, that force was back.

I wasn't meek, I was howling and snarling and ready to tear cities apart, uproot trees, and destroy anyone and everyone who got in my way from protecting Aslan the same way he'd protected me.

Glowering at the police, I hissed, "Aslan Avci didn't hurt me. But I'll tell you who did. Call off the hunt for him and take me down to the station. I'll make a statement. I'll answer any questions you want. But if you try to prosecute Aslan for something he didn't do, so help me God, I will go to every media outlet and tell them you racially profiled him based on his origins."

The shorter cop scowled. "You're threatening us?"

"I'm merely telling you that Aslan *did not do this*. My parents are incorrect. You were called here for no reason. It's my body and my life. I didn't want to tell anyone, but I will. I'll tell you who truly hurt me if you promise you won't go after Aslan."

"Neri," my mother said quietly. "Aslan still needs to be questioned."

"No, he doesn't."

"But he was hurting you, sweetie. He hurt your father."

"He was saving me from myself, Mum!" I bared my teeth. "He knew I was struggling to put what happened behind me. He offered to help. That's what he was doing tonight. He was saving me. He *always* saves me." Tears latched around my throat, but I swallowed them down with fresh anger. "And I was the one who hurt Dad. I told you that. I whacked him around the head with that lamp." I toed the forgotten mermaid light on the floor. "*I* hit him. Not Aslan. Aslan would never. You *know* him. You know he'd never hurt us. Trust that. Trust the past six years, for goodness' sake!"

Mum shook her head, stubbornness and horrified disbelief all over her face. "But...I saw what happened with my own eyes. His shorts were undone. You have...you have teeth marks on your neck, Neri, and your wrists are welted—"

"I undid his shorts, Mum. He tried to tell me to stop. It was my fault you found us in such a compromising position. And the truth is...the truth is we've been sleeping together for months."

"*What?*" she gasped.

The two policemen shared a look.

"He bit me yes, but I wanted it. And my wrists..." I held up my fresh bruises. "I did that. I hurt myself to try to stop the memories of Ethan tying me to Joel's bed with his belt. He bound me, and I struggled. I struggled so damn much, I broke the skin and had to cover up the bruises for weeks afterward. I-I hoped by recreating the pain, I could heal my heart this time and not just my skin." Silent tears I couldn't stop streamed down my cheeks. "Aslan is the only reason I haven't completely lost my mind these past few weeks, and I fucking refuse to stand here and let you think less of him! This was my fault. All of this is *my* fault. So give me the chance to fix it before anything else goes wrong."

"Ethan?" the tall cop asked from the floor beside my rallying father. "Ethan who?"

"I'll answer every question you have if you vow you won't go after Aslan."

"We have to talk to him, Ms Taylor." The short cop moved closer to me. "If what you say is true, then his story will align with yours and there will be nothing to fear."

My heart buckled.

If they knew what Aslan had done to Ethan?

If they knew he was here illegally?

He'd be thrown on the first plane back to Turkey and his father waiting to murder him.

I'd already put him in so much danger.

Not just with what happened in my bedroom but what happened on *The Fluke.*

What if they figure out Ethan's missing and find his blood all over our boat?

My heart raced sickeningly fast. "I'll only speak if you call off the chase for him." I crossed my arms, doing my best to hide my trembles at the thought of all of this blowing up spectacularly in my face.

"We'll have to talk to him eventually," the tall cop said softly.

And by then, I'll have come up with a plan to keep him safe.

Tipping up my nose, I snapped, "But not tonight. Not on Christmas. Tonight is already ruined because of me. All I'm asking is for a chance to fix it."

The two police looked at one another.

Sirens stopped outside our house.

Someone pounded on the door.

My dad groaned again, slipping from sleep. He winced and smacked his lips, his eyes feathering open. "W-What happened?"

In a daze, Mum went to him.

The taller cop bent over him, pressing a hand on his chest as he tried to sit up. "Easy there. Take your time. Don't move if anything hurts."

My dad blinked and groaned, touching the back of his head where I'd struck him. "Ow." Struggling to sit up again, he grunted as the tall cop kept him down.

"Sir, best not to move. The ambulance is here to—"

"Ambulance?" Dad scoffed. "I don't need a damn ambulance." Pushing the officer away, he slowly sat up and reclined against my bed with another wince.

"Jack. Are you…are you okay?" Mum dropped to her haunches, pressing her hand to his forehead.

Dad smiled softly, love blooming in his eyes.

The touching moment broke my heart because I'd caused this disaster. I'd hurt my darling dad because he was hurting my soulmate. And that soulmate was now running through the streets, most likely terrified, hopelessly trying to stay hidden, all while an armada of police was after him.

God, what a mess.

"I'm fine, my love." Dad cupped Mum's cheek before his fingers strayed to the back of his head again, tracing where I'd struck. "That's a decent bump."

"You might need a scan. Just to make sure nothing's fractured." The tall cop stood, his knees popping.

Dad shook his head. "It's just a bruise, nothing more. I've been concussed enough times in my youth from sports to know the headache will go. I'll be fine." His eyes danced over the chaos in my room before finally settling on me. "Neri…" The way he said my name wasn't full of anger like I'd expected but soft with aching betrayal.

I couldn't stop my shakes this time. Or my guilt. Oceans and oceans of it. "I'm so, *so* sorry, Dad."

He dropped his hands into his lap with a sad shrug. "You struck me."

"You were hurting him."

"Because he was hurting *you*."

"He wasn't." I stepped toward him but stopped as he held up his hand with a wary scowl.

"I failed you, little fish. He's well and truly brain washed you and—"

"No, you're wrong." Fury blew through me, and despite my guilt and fear, I couldn't play *nice* anymore. "You didn't fail me. *No one* failed me. Aslan thought the same thing, and that's why we're in this bloody mess. He didn't fail me just because he wasn't at that party to save me. And you didn't fail me just because you failed to kill a boy who never deserved your fists. He was trying to *help* me."

Drifting forward, I struggled to keep my temper under control. "He's only ever tried to keep me safe, Dad. And if you forget what you saw and listen to what I'm saying, you'll know I'm speaking the truth."

"I saw him on top of you, Neri. He was between your legs and—"

"*Consensually*," I hissed.

"They've been sleeping together for months, Jack," Mum murmured.

"*What?*" Dad scrambled to his feet, swaying a little. "Is that true?"

The two police shared another look as they shuffled on the spot. Their obvious discomfort thickened the air. They'd been called to a domestic violence incident on Christmas night and ended up witnessing teenage drama and miscommunication.

And I'd well and truly had enough.

Marching into my dad, I stabbed a finger into his chest. "I'll tell you what I just told Mum, and then we're leaving. All of us. We're all going down to the station, and you're going to help me straighten this out." Inhaling, I prepared to hurt my father for the second time.

He would never look at me the same way again.

I would lose the closeness with him because he'd always see me as his damaged little girl, not the feisty fish that drove him up the wall.

I mourned for that.

I cried for that.

It was why I didn't want to tell them in the first place.

But I loved Aslan more.

And I no longer cared what anyone thought of me, including my own parents. "I was raped, Dad. By a boy named Ethan. At Zara's almost a month ago. The only person who knew was Aslan. By *my* choice, not his. Without him, I wouldn't have coped. You owe him your thanks, not your hate. You owe him for all the nights he's held me while I cried and for all the days he made me feel strong when I wasn't."

Tears shot to his eyes. "Nerida, I…" He couldn't finish, choking on a cry.

I turned to the police and snapped, "Tell them to stop searching for Aslan. Right now. And let's go. I wish to make my statement."

Grabbing a grey cardigan from my wardrobe, I marched out of my room without another word.

I stomped down the corridor.

I opened the door and found two worried EMTs on the doorstep.

I wrapped my arms around myself as I drifted to the front gate and looked into the falling night.

Nightmares crowded my mind that Aslan was already caught and detained.

Hope did its best to fill my heart that he was hiding and safe.

And tears stung hotly as my mother and father joined me on the garden path. Without a word, they hugged me tightly as a policeman spoke into his radio. "Stand down on the search. We're heading back to the station to make a statement."

I kept my spine straight as the ambulance drove away unneeded and the police escorted us to our trusty old Jeep. They waited until my mother took the steering wheel, my dad winced in the front seat, and I'd buckled my seatbelt in the back.

"We'll meet you there. You know the way?" the short cop asked through the open window.

My dad nodded. "Yes. One of our neighbours is a detective. We share a beer every now and again."

"Is that Wayne Gratt?"

"That's him." Dad rubbed his temples, revealing the headache I'd given him hurt worse than he wanted to admit.

"He was called in earlier today. He should still be at the station. He can take Ms Taylor's statement, if you want. I'll radio ahead."

"That would be good. Cheers." Jack forced a smile and glanced at my mum who shoved the rickety Wrangler into gear.

"See you there." The cop tipped his chin and stepped away.

"See you soon." Mum nodded tightly, her eyes catching mine in the rear-view mirror as she reversed off our driveway.

Neither of us spoke but tension tightened, along with aching grief.

Once on the road, she stomped on the accelerator and took off.

I stiffened as I peered down darkened streets, my heart pounding painfully.

I looked for shadows.

I searched for signs.
Nothing.
No nudges that Aslan was safe.
No knowing that he was okay.
Just emptiness and bone-chilling fear.
Aslan...where are you?

Chapter Two

NERIDA

(*Love in Turkish:* Aşk)

"WAIT A MINUTE. YOU GAVE THE POLICE the identity of the man who raped you, all while knowing that Aslan had brutally chopped off two of his fingers, almost cut off his cock, and then tossed him overboard while still alive?" Margot sat back on my quaint wicker furniture, her eyes wider than moons. "Are you...are you *mad?*"

I laughed under my breath. "Oh, I'm entirely mad. I'm seventy-two years old. I've lived a life that's almost killed me through heartbreak multiple times. I've done things I never thought I would be capable of...all in the name of love."

"But you had to have known how risky that was? Admitting that Ethan was the one who hurt you? A crime you admitted that no one else knew about but Aslan? A rapist who suddenly went missing on the same night you were hurt?" Dylan scratched his bearded cheek with his pen. "I mean...you had to have guessed where the police's suspicions would've instantly led them."

"I did. But...all I was thinking about was saving Aslan that night. Tomorrow night didn't matter if I couldn't save him. One day at a time. One problem at a time."

"I can't imagine how hard that would've been, confessing what Ethan did to you in front of your parents."

"I didn't let them into the room with me when I told Detective Gratt. Apart from my confession that it wasn't Aslan who raped me, I never told my parents exactly what happened. It was enough for them to know I'd been abused in that way. More than enough." I rubbed at the chills on my arms and wished for a shawl. The sun had gone to bed, sinking like it always did into the horizon, cooling the tropical heat.

"Did it set you back emotionally? Answering such graphic questions?" Margot whispered, her notebook completely ignored at this point, her gaze locked on mine.

"No. It helped actually." I gave her a smile. "The thing with trauma is you can say you're done living in its shadow and pretend that you're okay, but until that trauma is done with you...you can't be free."

"What do you mean?" Margot whispered.

"I mean, you can choose to be free and still be trapped. You can convince others with words that you're okay, but those words won't save you. Until you can prove to your trauma that you're ready to do *whatever* it takes to truly be free and not just desperately cling to words that have no strength to make it so, then it won't stop. I didn't know that at the time. I was only seventeen, after all. I thought the power of my mind and the repetition of positive words would eventually heal me, but...Aslan was right. Until I stopped running and accepted it, I kept giving away my strength with denial."

I spun my wedding ring, remembering the surge of that strength. "Who would've thought that the best cure for my trauma was to fight for the life of another? To realise that everything I'd endured only carved me into who I was meant to be? And I *liked* who I was meant to be because that girl would do *anything* to protect those she loved."

"So...you told the police everything?" Dylan asked.

"Everything about the rape? Oh, yes. I held nothing back. I ensured they hated Ethan as much as I did by the time I finished. Of course, I told them nothing about what happened afterward. I'm not *that* mad."

"And then what?" Margot whispered.

"And then fate ensured that my decision to accept what Ethan had done was right."

"What do you mean?" Dylan frowned.

"I mean, Zara turned up later that week and mentioned the police had been round to talk to her boyfriend, Cooper."

"Shit, wouldn't he say that he hadn't seen Ethan since the night of the party?" Margot gasped.

"You'd think that. But no." I smiled and leaned back, hugging a lacy pillow to ward off the early evening chill. "I'll tell you how serendipitous luck stepped in and everything that happened next, but I'm getting ahead of myself. Let's go back to the police station and the night where I shattered Ethan's hold over me, once and for all. I grew stronger than I'd ever been, and I not only accepted what Ethan had done but I was also...strangely grateful."

"Wait, *what*? You can't be saying you're grateful for what he did?" Dylan scoffed, his face twisting with disgust. "That's just wrong on so many levels."

"Oh no, sorry, that came out incorrectly. I didn't mean to say I was grateful for the abuse. I meant I was grateful for the lesson of overcoming it. Grateful to learn, early on, that I was stronger than I thought. Thankful to learn how to find myself, to trust myself, to be ready to fight when it mattered, because when that last domino fell, I didn't buckle and die. Even though I begged for death and fully believed I would die from a shattered, haemorrhaging heart, I survived. Barely.

"Without Ethan teaching me my own power, I would never have lived past the worst day of my life. I know that without a shadow of a doubt. That adversity gave me the strength to survive because no matter the pain Ethan gave me, it was nothing, absolutely *nothing* to what came next. He was a mere thorn, a sting, a silly little splinter."

"Oh God." Margot shook her head. "I don't think I can take much more. You know…it's getting late. I think. I think we should stop and—"

"I'm not stopping until it's over." I picked up my phone to text Tiffany to bring another tray of drinks and some food, along with a cosy blanket or two. Once I'd sent the request, I settled back and studied the faces of the reporters who were no longer strangers.

Their features blurred and blended, spinning with the dark, the beach, and the sky until the stark walls of an interrogation room and the detective I'd seen throughout my childhood filled my mind's eye.

Chapter Three

NERIDA

(Love in Finnish: Rakkaus)

"YOU'RE SURE THIS STATEMENT IS AS TRUE and as accurate as you can make it? I know you said you don't know Ethan's last name, but you made sure his description is as detailed as possible?" Wayne Gratt, my father's friend and our next door neighbour four houses down, steepled his hands on the cold metal table and gave me a forlorn look.

"It's true and accurate, and yes, I don't know his last name."

He rolled his shoulders. "As a cop, I shouldn't say this, but as a friend of your father's, I'm so sorry, Nerida. What he did to you. What you've told me here tonight." He shook his head, his lips curling into a snarl. "I want to murder him myself."

You're too late.

I hung my head, clinging to the performance I'd given of a distraught, abused little girl who hadn't watched her soulmate beat Ethan within an inch of his life and then toss that life overboard.

"Thank you, Detective Gratt."

He shuddered and squeezed his nape. "You know, you should tell your parents everything he did. It might help. I know Jack will be going out of his mind. The 'what ifs' will drive him more mad than the actual knowing."

His weathered face and salt-and-pepper hair made him look older than his sixty years. What a shame he was here, working on Christmas night, when his two older children were staying with their toddlers, filling his house with the newest generation. I knew he worked a lot because he'd lost his wife two years ago. I knew Dad went around to his place fairly often for a beer and to keep an eye on him. And I knew the way he watched me with a bone-deep pain and remorse wasn't faked, it was genuine.

And that hurt because if he watched me in such a terrified, horrified way—a man who'd only existed on the outskirts of my childhood—how on earth would my own father look at me?

I stiffened. "Can I trust you not to tell him? It's my choice to keep this from them. They know it happened. That's enough. I did something I never thought I'd ever do by hitting Dad around the back of the head. I've already hurt him enough without making him hear what Ethan did as well."

"We should probably talk about that." He raised an eyebrow. "You know you can't go around knocking your parents out just because you don't agree with them, right?"

"He was hurting Aslan and not listening to me. I couldn't stand by and let Aslan bleed for something he didn't do."

"Yes, well. I'll be talking to your father about that too. Aslan is fully within his right to charge him with assault." He licked his lips, taking his time before adding, "Aslan Avci...he's lived with you guys for a while now, hasn't he?"

My legs locked under the table. "Six years in a couple of months."

"And...you're sure he hasn't touched you inappropriately in that time? Not once. Not a single moment where you've felt uncomfortable?"

My spine stiffened. "You've met Aslan a number of times, Detective Gratt—"

"Call me Wayne, just like you do when I pop round."

"Do you think Aslan could touch me inappropriately...Wayne?" I asked quietly, watching his every move. "Do you truly think he'd be capable of hurting me?"

He contemplated my question like a good police officer before shaking his head. "In all honesty, no, I can't see him hurting you. He's always been very respectful and courteous. If what you say is true and he was merely trying to help you deal with what that bastard did, and if you're in a consensual relationship like you mentioned, then...I accept he's done nothing wrong." Leaning over the table, his voice dropped to a quiet murmur. "I have to ask though. When did you two, eh...?"

"Sleep together?"

He cleared his throat with an awkward nod.

"Why?" I glared. "So you can charge him with underage sex? Are you going to say what my father did?"

"What did your father say?"

"That Aslan groomed me. Which is ridiculous. If anyone groomed someone, it was *me* grooming *him*. The poor guy endured years of me promising I'd marry him. Of dodging my kisses and keeping boundaries firmly in place between us." Temper burned through my veins as I crossed my arms. "So if you're thinking of investigating that angle, I suggest you don't because we're going to have a problem."

Easy, Nee.

My goal was to stop the cops sniffing around Aslan, so he remained unseen directly beneath their bureaucratic noses. Not yell at high-ranking officials and cause suspicion.

"Just tell me how old you were the first time—"

"Seventeen," I snapped. "Not that it's any of your business. Sixteen is the consensual age, as you well know. He might have lived with my family for years, but he's been nothing but dutiful and loyal. He broke no laws. Aslan is innocent on any and all charges you might conjure up."

Apart from being illegal, that is.

He scowled. "I'm not trying to condemn an innocent man, Nerida. Just trying to get all the facts straight."

"The only facts you need to know is…I'm in love with him. He's in love with me. We met young, but we already know it's forever. You can think that's stupid fancy coming from a teenaged girl, but it's the truth. I will stand by him. I will do whatever it takes to keep him safe. So—"

"*Whatever* it takes?" Wayne Gratt's hazel eyes narrowed, slipping from family friend to detective.

Shit.

Sucking back my temper, I leaned forward and did my best to play the part I was supposed to. Meek and damaged, confused and young. "Please. All I'm saying is, it wasn't Aslan. What my father saw in my bedroom was wanted and invited. The boy who raped me was *Ethan*. He used a condom and is friends with my…" I swallowed hard, forcing myself to finish. "My ex-best-friend Zara Lancet's boyfriend. It's all there in the report. Can I go home now?"

Holding my eyes for a moment longer, he sighed. "You can put your hackles down, you know. I accept what you're saying. You don't have to hit me around the head like you did your dad."

I flinched with fresh guilt.

He smirked. "Sorry, bad joke."

"I need to apologise to him. A-Are we done here?"

He nodded. "Sign your statement and you're free."

"And no one will go after Aslan?"

"Not tonight. Not unless he does something that warrants our attention."

I hid my second wince.

Overstaying definitely warrants attention.

Snatching up the pen, I skimmed the typed-up piece of paper printed off from the tape recorder as I'd recounted everything Ethan had done. I'd held nothing back. I'd told Wayne everything, right from Ethan refusing to let me leave the party to drugging me with a mug of Coke and restraining me on Joel's bed. I even mentioned how he'd let me go afterward with a pat on my butt and a promise to put in a good word with Zara, as if what we'd done was mutually shared and not straight-up rape.

I signed with a flourish, no longer hiding my bleeding pain. For the first time in a month, I had nothing to hide. No need to repeat a useless mantra that I'd be okay if I could just stop thinking about it. I'd spoken about it for the past two hours. I'd relived every moment, and I was still alive, still breathing, still functioning. In fact, I was functioning better than I had in weeks, all because I'd finally moved on.

It'd happened.

It was over.

And I had much more important things to worry about than a rapist who'd already been dealt with.

Aslan…

Where are you?

The pen scratched over the paper as I dated my statement, my concentration turning inward as I sent all my hope and love toward Aslan. I waited for an echo. Some soul-deep echo hinting he'd heard me, just like he claimed he had when I'd screamed for him as Ethan hurt me.

But there was no answering nudge. No sign that we were so connected, we could sense each other over time and space.

We had no magic.

No magic except our everlasting bond and the undying knowledge that we belonged to one another.

Shoving back the signed piece of paper, I looked up.

Wayne hadn't taken his eyes off me.

I felt mean for being so snappy with him, but I'd meant what I said. I'd do *anything* it took to keep Aslan here, alive, with me.

With a weary sigh, Wayne took my signed statement and tucked it into the new file that'd been made on me. He didn't speak for a long moment before finally shifting in the metal chair and pulling out a business card from his trouser pocket. "Here." Stabbing it into the table, he slid it to me with his finger. "If you don't want to talk to Jack and Anna, then talk to this woman. She's very good at her job. Helps all manner of people overcome all manner of things."

My initial instinct was to refuse as a tiny piece of me cursed him for thinking I was weak. But I balled my hands and scolded that egotistical part of me. I wasn't weak by accepting his goodwill gesture. I wasn't weak if I needed to talk to someone.

Nodding once, I snatched the card and slipped it into my bra—the only place I could store it in my little black dress.

His eyebrows rose but he didn't mention my strange pocket. His steely hazel eyes met mine. "Do you want to tell me anything else about that night? Anything at all?"

Yes, you'll probably find Ethan at the bottom of the ocean.

If you searched The Fluke, *you'll find Ethan's blood all over it, regardless that we bleached it down.*

If you knew what Aslan did to him, all because I asked him to, you'd deport him to his death without a second thought.

I shook my head. "I've said everything you need to hear."

Glancing at the closed door, he leaned closer across the table. "You know, Nerida, sometimes the people we love the most are the ones most capable of doing bad things."

I froze. "What? Why are you saying that?"

"Because, in my experience, where there's smoke there's usually a fire. If you and Aslan have managed to hide your relationship from your parents until tonight, the real question is…what happened for him to throw all caution to the wind and attempt…sexual intercourse…on Christmas? Knowing the chances of being caught were extremely high? What would make him not care about that? What would drive him to do something so out of character?"

My eyes dropped to my bruised wrists. I circled the fresh discolouration with my fingers, cursing myself all over again for wrapping the cord of my hairdryer around and around, then yanking and pulling as hard as I had when Ethan had tied me up.

My heart fisted all over again at the memory of Aslan's face as he'd noticed. At the sharp glisten of horror in his eyes. At the awful way he tripped forward as if I'd driven a dagger into his chest.

To tell the truth or not?

To share what pushed Aslan over the edge or hope that Wayne just let it go?

But if I can make him see how caring Aslan is…it will prove he's so good and kind and incapable of doing what my father thinks he did.

Pressing on a self-inflicted bruise, I murmured, "I…hurt myself. Aslan noticed. He's been trying to get me to talk to someone ever since it happened. When I shut down and he saw I'd damaged myself, he…got scared." I looked up. "He let his worry for me overflow."

I shrugged and smiled sadly, telling my dad's friend far more than he should know. "We were only an hour away from telling them, you know. He was going to propose to me in front of my parents after we'd eaten Christmas dinner and were opening our presents." I laughed under my breath, not that it was a laughing matter. "I have no idea why we're the only family to open our presents at night, but that's how it goes in our household. Think Dad made the rule just to annoy me. It's freaky to think that none of this would've happened if we'd just opened our gifts like normal people the moment we all crawled out of bed. Dad and Mum would've known we were together. Aslan wouldn't have been wound up and worried about me. And I probably would never have…"

Dropping my fingers from my bruises, I shivered in the cold, stark room. "Can I go now? I would really like to go."

"Of course." He gave me a fatherly smile. Standing, he waited for me to do the same before hugging my folder to his chest and saying, "The way you talk about him makes me grateful you have someone who cares so deeply for you, but also…scares me a little."

I stiffened.

His eyes locked on mine. "Don't you see, Nerida? You've just proven my point. I asked what would drive Aslan to do something so out of character, and it was *you*. You hurting yourself drove him to breaking point. Just like watching your dad hurt Aslan drove you to yours. I bet you didn't think you could strike your father and I bet Jack didn't think he could beat the son of his family friend. But you both hurt those you love to *protect* those you love. If you could do that to someone you care for, imagine what you could do to someone you hate."

I tried to think up something to say. Some way of protecting Aslan from Wayne's far-too-insightful evaluations, but I couldn't. My brain was a gasping fish, flopping for air and utterly useless.

"You know…I watched a show on Netflix the other night called the *Inside Man*. My favourite actor, Stanley Tucci, plays a character on death row who helps out with criminal investigations, and you know what he said?"

I shook my head, not wanting to hear but knowing he'd tell me regardless.

"He said…'*Everyone is a murderer. You just need a good reason and a bad day.*'"

I froze.

Wayne shrugged and patted my shoulder on the way to the door. "That line has really stuck with me, not because it's morbid but because it's *true*. Everyone has that switch inside them, Nerida. And if that switch gets pushed…we're capable of monstrous things, regardless of the consequences."

I followed him blindly out of the interrogation room and down the bleak linoleum-floored corridor to the waiting room where my parents paced anxiously for my return. With every step, what Wayne had said echoed in my heart.

It affected me.

It woke me.

And I knew without a shadow of a doubt, I was a murderer.

Just because I hadn't spilled blood yet didn't mean I wouldn't. I'd kill Cem Kara, Aslan's biological father, if he ever came for him. I'd kill any bureaucrats who tried to deport him. I'd kill any police who tried to arrest him.

Deep in my loving heart and gentle soul, a violence lurked, swimming in the depths of despair, snapping with jaws of fury. An entire brutal, black ocean existed within me, housing monsters of the deep, monsters ready to tear and claw and devour.

I just hoped I never had to unleash them.

"How did it go? Was Wayne nice to you?" Dad asked quietly, twisting in the front seat to stare at me.

I held his eyes, flinching at the tight, wary way he watched me.

My voice was small as I ignored his question and said, "I'm so, *so* sorry, Dad. I didn't mean to hit you. I never wanted to hurt you. But you didn't listen and Aslan…" I sat taller, swallowing down my choking regret. "Are you okay? Is your head still hurting? Perhaps, we should go to a doctor and—"

"My head is fine. I'm fine. You don't need to apologise, and I don't want to talk about me." The wariness in his eyes morphed into self-hatred that he hadn't been able to stop what'd happened. His face twisted and he suddenly exploded with everything he'd been suffocating on. "Neri, *I-I'm* the one who's sorry. So unbelievably sorry. I'm so sorry I wasn't there to protect you. So sorry you felt like you couldn't tell me. So sorry I didn't know in the first place. I feel like I should've *known*. How did I not know? How did I not see how much you've been hurting? I'm your goddamn father and my baby girl was fucking raped and I—" A sob cut him off. Twisting back around, he rested his hand on my mother's thigh. "Anna. Stop the car. *Now.* Stop the fucking car."

Mum threw him a look but seemed to understand. Flicking on the blinker, she pulled onto the small verge. Before she'd even stopped, Dad shoved open his door, leaped out, and threw himself into the backseat with me.

"Neri. Baby." He grabbed me in the tightest, hardest embrace of my life. The moment he touched me, I was his little girl again.

I buried my face into his chest and let my dad give me safe harbour…just for a moment. A single moment before I fought for Aslan.

His strong, comforting arms wrapped fiercely around me as Mum slowly veered back onto the empty streets, taking us home while everyone else was in a food coma, safe in their homes celebrating Christmas.

Dad pressed kisses all over the top of my head as he cradled me close, his voice breaking as tears wet his face. "I want to kill that bastard for what he did to you. I hate him and I've never even met him. All you've given me is a name. A name that's on a loop inside my head. I can't stop thinking about what you went through. Why didn't you tell me, huh? I would've killed that motherfucker for you. I would literally do anything for you, Neri. *Anything*, do you hear me? I'd kill for you, little fish, and the fact that you kept it from me—"

"Jack…" Mum murmured from the front seat, her knuckles whitening around the steering wheel. "Give her some space to breathe, darling."

"Crap, sorry." Unwrapping his arms, Dad pulled away and cupped my cheeks. The way he watched me, with tears falling and grief glowing, I couldn't do it.

I hated that I'd hurt him in so many more ways than just a bump on the head. That I was the reason he felt such remorse. Gripping his wrists and cursing the way his eyes went to the fresh bruises around mine, I whispered, "It's okay, Dad."

"None of this is okay," he gasped around his sadness. "Nothing will be okay again. He hurt you. He hurt my baby and—"

"And Aslan kept me safe."

"Aslan?" Dad stiffened and pulled away from me, his hands dropping into his suited lap. "That's right. *Him*. The bastard I found on top of you. You say it wasn't him who raped you, but he was hurting you just the same. I saw the state of your room. Saw him about to—"

"I'm in love with him. I have been since the day we found him."

A black cloud darkened his face. "You mean to tell me he's been touching you since you were *twelve?*"

"No. He didn't lay a finger on me until I was seventeen. The night I broke up with Joel was the first night he kissed—"

"That was almost six months ago!" Dad raked both hands through his hair, pressing himself against the door. "Bloody hell, Nerida—"

"We were only fooling around. We didn't sleep together until the night I was raped."

Wow, you're really laying it all out there.

"*What?*" Fury carved deep tracks through his forehead. "You mean to tell me he made you sleep with him the very same night some bastard raped—"

"It was *me* who asked *him*."

Dad grunted as if I'd punched him in the gut.

I winced at how many private secrets I was telling my parents. I'd had no intention of sharing any of this, but…I would fight with whatever weapon I had to ensure Aslan still had a home with us. That Mum and Dad treated him no differently than they had before. They loved him just as much as I did. I needed them to remember that.

"He didn't want to, Dad. He tried to refuse. But I begged him. And just like you would do anything for me, he would tear down the sky and gift it to me if I asked him." Tears pricked my eyes. "He's so respectful, Dad. So kind and good and *pure*. I-I needed him to make it all go away. And…he did." I sighed and linked my fingers, willing the drive home to end so I could breathe air that wasn't throbbing with tension.

"Wait a minute." Dad held up a shaking hand. "I thought you said you slept alone on *The Fluke* that night. That Aslan didn't join you until the next day. You guys returned home together—in my borrowed Wrangler no less—

gushing with stories of Aslan going diving for the first time." His brow furrowed. "I just assumed Aslan left to meet you that morning before we were out of bed, but now you're saying—"

"She lied, Jack," Mum murmured, seeing between the lines of what I wasn't saying, just like any intuitive mum would. "He never came home that night. You called him from the party, didn't you? Aslan went to get you. That's why he asked to borrow the Jeep, darling. He didn't go grocery shopping at freaking ten p.m. He went to get our daughter. And we went to bed not long after, so we didn't hear if he came home or not."

"Is that true?" Dad strangled. "Did you call Aslan instead of me?"

I shifted in my seat and faced him, preparing to hurt him all over again, and perhaps, offer a tiny shred of salvation. "I didn't have to call him," I whispered. "He knew. He knew I was hurt and came after me." The tears that'd tickled the back of my throat slowly dripped down my cheeks. "He said he *felt* me, Dad. He felt that something was wrong. He found me as I stumbled from Zara's. He thought I was drunk and told me off, but then...he went quiet as if he sensed something had happened. I told him I couldn't go home; I wouldn't have been able to hide what happened, and it wasn't until we were on *The Fluke* together that he saw my bruises."

A cry caught in my throat as I recalled how he'd looked. How his gorgeously handsome face had shattered. How his knees had buckled. How he'd fallen at my feet with crystal tears spilling over his dark lashes as he kissed my feet and wrists.

As quickly as his despair had killed him, demon-lashing fury had resurrected him. The power billowing off him as he stood and asked who did it. The way his black eyes glowed with coal-fire. The way his lips had thinned with war and the tears on his cheeks glittered like battle paint.

He'd made my stomach swoop and stumble. Made my heart crack and crumble. And my soul bowed at his feet, just like he'd bowed at mine, curling into a safe little ball, knowing that he'd always protect me, avenge me, and tear apart every monster in the world for me.

"He—"

Hurt for me.

Likely killed for me.

I couldn't tell him what Aslan had done. I couldn't give my dad peace by sharing the bloodbath that Aslan had delivered. All I could say was a simple, "He saved me, Dad."

"But that wasn't his duty to do, Nerida." Dad grimaced. "It was mine."

Temper dried up my tears. "You made it his duty the day you assigned him as my bodyguard when I was fourteen. The day he brought me back to life with CPR was the day you put my life in his hands. You made him shadow my every move. You made him responsible for my well-being. And he obeyed you with every cell in his body. He's been my guardian angel ever since that day, and everything you know about him—every honourable, sweet, and noble part of him—is *real*. The only thing you don't know is, he's loved me like I was *his* instead of his responsibility. So don't you dare get angry with him for protecting me when you gave me to him years ago."

Dad's mouth hung open, his wet eyes wide.

Using his stunned silence, I added, "He was going to tell you today. About us, I mean. He's been planning it for weeks. He wanted it to be just right, so you'd accept him like the son you always proclaim he is. He wanted to prove to you that this is real. This isn't a fling. It isn't a stupid crush or teenage lust. He *loves* me, Dad. He loves me enough to—"

I cut myself off.

Silence was sharp after my outburst.

Finally, Mum asked softly, watching me in the rear-view mirror. "Loves you enough to what?"

Torture and kill for me.

Licking my lips, I shook my head. "It doesn't matter. All that matters is—"

"I knew he was in love with you," Dad muttered, wrenching my eyes to him.

"Wait…you did?" My mouth fell open.

He chuckled sadly. "I only figured it out recently, but…you'd have to be blind not to see the way he looks at you. Then again, I've been blind for years, so what do I know? All I know is, his heart beats for you and only you. Good God, Neri, he worships the very ground you walk on."

"So…what's the problem then?" I shrugged. "If you knew—"

"I knew he was in love with you. But I didn't know he'd done anything about it. I trusted him *not* to do anything about it. You practically grew up together. He knew his place—"

"Knew his *place*?" I bared my teeth. "What the hell does that mean?"

"It means…he knows how fragile his existence is here, and I figured he wouldn't risk it by giving in to temptation. But then I saw him on top of you with his pants undone and his mouth on yours, and…I lost it. I figured all that longing coupled with the beer he'd drunk had made him do something unforgivable. In turn…*I* did something unforgivable."

I didn't know what to say.

Dad reached across and grabbed my hand, squeezing it when I went to pull away. "If it's true that he didn't hurt you, Neri. That he's never hurt you in the past six years he's lived with us, then…I owe him the biggest apology. You're right that I forced the closeness to build between you. I asked too much of him to watch over you the way I did. If I'd seen what's so obvious now, I never would've done it. But it's too late for that."

"When…" I swallowed hard. "When did you know he loved me?"

"The day you flinched from me. A couple of weeks ago when I tossed you in the pool." He hung his head, tracing his thumb over my knuckles. "It broke my heart. I didn't know why you acted as if I'd terrified you. Of course, it all makes sense now, but…at the time, I couldn't understand why you wouldn't play like usual. And when I looked at Aslan standing by the pool edge, it was as if he knew how sad I was. He mirrored my pain and looked away. His eyes landed on you stepping out of the water, and I swear…all the pain I felt was a thousand times worse for him. He acted as if you'd just cut out his heart and set it on fire, adding a bucket of gasoline to make it burn faster."

I curled my fingers around Dad's. "He hated that I was letting what Ethan did affect me. He begged me to get counselling. It was eating him up inside each day I refused." My voice turned quiet as I confessed. "I used him to make it all go away. I went to him to make me forget. That's what you walked in on. He was *helping* me, Dad. Nothing more. He would literally do anything I asked if he thought it would help me, and I was stupid to think you and Mum wouldn't find us."

"If that's true, then he's still the guy I thought he was. He's still looking after you. Still protecting you."

"All of it is true."

"It still doesn't change the fact that he lied to us, Neri. You both did."

"I know."

"If he comes back, we all need to sit down and have a serious chat to figure out this mess."

"You mean you won't report him if he comes back?"

"No." Dad winced. "If he doesn't report me for battery, of course." Glancing at Mum as she turned into our street, he added, "We should go and try to find him. I hurt him pretty badly. I don't want him running around in the dark, fearing he'll be deported when he's black and blue."

"I know how we can find him," I said, catching my mum's eyes as she pulled into our driveway and killed the engine.

"You do?" She raised her eyebrow, turning to face me. "How?"

"There's an app on his phone. I installed it there a few nights before you guys went to Whitsundays on that research trip. He's kept it on ever since so we can track each other."

"Bloody hell, there is so much we don't know, isn't there?" Mum sighed, glancing at the house with its shabby fence, faded grey roof, and all the lights still on, just as we'd left it a few hours ago.

Turning back to face me, she murmured, "How about we make a deal? No more secrets or lies, and your father and I promise to do our best to understand. To accept that you're no longer our little girl. To see you as a woman in your own right, on the cusp of turning eighteen. I trust you enough to accept that if your heart is set on Aslan, then…we're okay with that."

My heart skipped as I nodded. "No more secrets."

"Alright then." Opening her door, she climbed out. "Now, let's go get your phone so we can find Aslan. It's our turn to save him."

Chapter Four

ASLAN

(*Heart in Latin:* Cor)

I WINCED AS THE THUD OF SLAMMING car doors set my heart racing.

Three hours.

Three unbearable hours where I'd run in fucking circles around suburbia, hiding in shadows, and listening for sirens, only to give into my pain and return to Neri's street. I'd waited by the beach for a long time, watching the house where I'd lived for six years, waiting for signs that the police had set up an ambush.

But only soft silence reigned, punctured occasionally by the happy squeals of children playing with new toys and the quiet babble of Christmas movies.

I'd taken the risk and hobbled back home.

The house was quiet and welcoming as I stepped in through the back door. It was eerie being here without anyone else. My skin itched with wrongness. My heart beat pathetically.

What if I never see Neri again?

What if Jack and Anna took her far away from me and this was the last time I walked through their home as a free man?

With my heart in my throat, I raided the medicine cabinet for a fistful of painkillers, then did my best to mop up the oozing blood along my hair line and wipe away the dried rust painting my jaw. The image in the bathroom mirror revealed a haunted man who'd fought every day of his existence, doing his best not to succumb to inherited violence only to wear that violence from someone else.

From Jack.

My chest panged.

Regardless that my life hadn't been easy since losing my family, I'd fallen for Jack and Anna as if they were my own. I loved him. I thought he loved me too. Yet as I poked at my black eye and ran my cut tongue over my split lip, I had to face the facts.

He didn't love me.

Not really.

He would've killed me if Neri hadn't knocked him out.

Fuck.

My hands gripped the sink as a crest of nausea struck me.

She loves me.

She *chose* me.

Over her own father.

My hands curled around the cold porcelain.

I don't deserve her.

But I can't live without her.

I wanted to leave this place but how could I without her? How could I survive a single day without her smile, her touch, her love?

I'd returned to this house that was both my prison and sanctuary with intentions to pack a bag and leave. To slink into the dark and figure out a way to live in this country without being seen or caught.

But…what would be the fucking point?

I didn't want to hide when I had nothing to hide for.

I didn't want to scrape out a living when the only thing that made sense was already stolen from me.

I'd rather be caught and sent back to my father than exist another day in this country without the one girl I would die for.

So…that's what I'll do.

Raising my head, I stared into my bloodshot eyes. Every part of me hurt. My ribs blazed every time I breathed, my cheekbones felt as if they'd shatter at the gentlest touch, my head throbbed, my ears rang, and the bruises down my legs where Jack had repeatedly kicked me threatened to buckle me to the floor.

I couldn't run.

I *wouldn't* run.

I'd wait for whoever walked through that door and put the rest of my battered and bruised life into their hands because…I was done. Jack had effectively shown me that physical pain was *nothing* compared to the pain of never seeing Neri again.

I couldn't breathe without her.

I wouldn't survive a day without her in my life.

I'm done hiding how I feel—

My left leg gave out, and I crumpled to the floor.

Tiredness swarmed me.

My blood-dirty forehead rested against the edge of the sink.

I'll rest...just for a minute.

I think I passed out because I was stiffer than ever when I rallied round—finding myself curled into a painful ball on the damp bath mat.

I had no idea what the time was, and the painkillers barely took the edge off, but urgency crawled through me.

Wherever Jack, Anna, and Neri had gone with the police, they might be back any moment. Which meant I was running out of time to figure out how to tell her that I'd always love her, even as they dragged me away. I needed her to vow to me that she would never follow me. That the moment I was taken, that was it. She had to forget about me because the very idea of my father getting his hands on her made me dry retch on the turquoise bath mat.

Shuffling to my feet, I groaned with agony as I forced my despairing body into a stumble. Limping into the lounge, I grabbed the ring box on top of the presents I'd bought for Jack and Anna, bit my bleeding lip as I almost rolled my ankle stepping out of the slider and onto the deck, and barely avoided falling face first into the pool as I cursed the uneven steppingstones to my sala.

I eyed up the three stairs to my door.

I swayed and blinked at the room where I'd slept for so long. The shingles were weathered. The plywood in need of replacement. The Perspex windows were now foggy and sun-damaged, but I'd never been so grateful for it.

I never stopped to truly see what Jack and Anna had put on the line for me when they kept my secret and hid me. They were good people. Good, wonderful people who loved their daughter enough to do whatever it took to keep her safe—

Footsteps sounded in the kitchen, ripping me around.

Vertigo scrambled my beaten brain, and I sat heavily on the wooden steps where Neri had found me eating a stolen carrot from her veggie garden all those years ago.

Cursing under my breath, I fisted the ring box. A ring that I'd give anything to slip onto Neri's finger.

Sweat prickled my back as Jack headed to the sink in the brightly lit kitchen, poured himself a glass of water, and drank it down in one go. Anna hugged him from behind, her arms slinking around his waist as he put the glass down on the draining board and twisted in her embrace to hug her.

My chest squeezed where I sat hidden in the dark.

Why were they allowed a long and happy marriage, and I wasn't?

Why did fate hate me so much to give me my soulmate and then do whatever it could to prevent me from claiming her?

Furious tears pricked my eyes as I cracked open the box and looked at the ring inside. At the golden waves crashing over the band, the crest of each sparkling with diamonds until they smashed together in the centre, splashing into one solitaire that wasn't as big as I would like but was the greatest symbol of my commitment.

My commitment to Neri.

My absolute desperation to bind her to me for eternity.

Quiet footsteps stepped outside the slider and onto the deck, pulling my head up.

Time stood still as Neri fumbled with her phone, quickly swiping through apps, her entire focus on the bright screen in her hands. The darkness of the garden shrouded me. The solar lights around the pool had faded in recent years, failing to spread their light to where I sat in the shadows.

My heart picked up its beat, thundering to the same song it always did around her. Quick and sharp, hard and sure. She was mine. I'd known it from the moment she first touched me as I broke beneath raw grief. That same grief lapped at my ankles now, whispering of goodbyes.

I would give anything to just sit here. To always watch over her. To never be away from her. Fuck, I'd be happy to die and stay as a ghost, just so I never had to lose her.

How much longer before the police returned?

How much longer could I stare—

My phone vibrated in my pocket, making me flinch.

Had she text me?

Was she looking for me to keep me hidden or to say what she knew we had to say? Were the police inside the house, inspecting her bedroom again and seeing the chaos I'd unleashed? Fuck, they'd wrap me in chains and never let me free.

With a sharp cry, Neri suddenly lifted her head.

The blue glow of her screen etched her throat and chin, shadowing her eyes as if she'd sold her soul to step into the underworld to find me.

"Aslan," she breathed as our eyes locked across the garden.

I couldn't speak. Could barely move.

"He's here! Dad, Mum, I tracked his phone, and he's here!"

I flinched at how loudly she announced my location.

Perhaps she'd gone through all the scenarios I had and realised I would eventually be caught. That there was no point delaying the inevitable. Perhaps she was doing me a kindness by revealing where I was to the police so we could get it over and done with.

Neri…

Fuck. I didn't want to say goodbye.

I didn't think I could.

I'd vomit and break and get on my fucking knees.

I'd beg. I'd murder. I'd hide under a rock if only I could stay.

If only I can keep her…for just a little longer.

A wash of heated despair and sickening nausea clutched me around the throat as she tossed her phone onto the glass-topped outdoor table where we'd eaten so many meals as a family, leaped off the deck, and bolted toward me.

Her black dress billowed around her thighs. The rose gold stitching on her torso glinted like bleeding stars. And I grunted with every trapped and savaging emotion inside me as she soared into my arms, crunching my back against the steps, burrowing her face into the crook of my neck and hugging me so damn hard.

"You're here. God, I was so worried. So, *so* worried." Her voice was wet with tears and sharp with love. "Aslan. God, I'm so sorry. All of this is my fault. I'm so, *so* sorry."

"Nerida." My arms snapped around her. I hoisted her higher on my lap. "I was so afraid I'd never see you again." My voice broke. My soul shattered. And I didn't care if police were about to pour through the door and arrest me. I didn't care that Anna and Jack were in the kitchen, able to see every touch, every kiss, every promise.

I had no control as I let loose the agony, the misery, and all the heavy black depression that I'd never truly mastered and broke spectacularly in her arms.

A silent sob wracked my spine as I pressed my forehead to her frangipani-scented hair.

Loss.

Longing.

Desire.

Desperation.

It was too much. Too hard. Too painful.

I can't lose her.

I can't fucking do this.

I buried myself into her as she burrowed into me, both of us clinging for life, suffering such fucking heartache, such motherfucking anguish. "I'm so sorry, Neri," I growled. "So sorry for pushing you, *canim*. I didn't mean to hurt you. I didn't mean to ruin this. I didn't mean to—"

"You have nothing to apologise for. It was me. All me. I should *never* have shut you out. I should never have thought I could do this on my own." Pulling away, she nudged her nose with mine. "I can't do any of this without you, Aslan. None of it. I don't want to. You're it for me."

My chest caved in on itself as wretchedness wrung me dry. "But the police—"

"Have been dealt with. They're gone and not coming back."

"What?" I froze, hissing between my teeth as bruised muscles sent agony through me. "H-How?"

"I told them about Ethan. I made sure they know it wasn't you. Dad knows it wasn't you. Everyone knows."

"Everyone?" I sucked in a breath. "How…how *much* do they know?"

Sitting back, she ran her hands through my hair, finding injuries and bumps I hadn't been aware of. Jack hadn't held back. For a marine biologist in his fifties, he was as vicious as my crime lord of a father.

"Everything," she whispered. "They know everything." Looking over her shoulder, she smiled softly. "Hi, Dad. Hi, Mum."

I shot to my feet—or as fast as I could with my bones screeching and protesting. Placing Neri carefully on the ground, I stumbled to the side as my pounding head made my vision feather with grey before solidifying back into night. "Jack. Anna."

Swiping at the wetness on my cheeks, I stood before the two people who'd kept me alive far longer than I should've been permitted, and I had no idea what to say.

Jack stood with his hands balled on either side of his thighs. The suit he'd changed into, to enjoy a fancy Christmas dinner, shimmered in the fading solar lights. His nostrils flared and it took all I could not to cower away from his fists.

His knuckles were bloody and swollen from striking me, and instincts warned me to run before he could pummel me again.

But then I glanced at Anna, and my heart stopped.

The older version of Neri—with her shorter brown hair, darker blue eyes, and pretty pink dress—looked at me as if I wasn't her mortal enemy but her golden son.

I-I don't understand.

My heart flopped around in my chest as I looked between the two Taylors, then back at Neri who hadn't left my side. "What exactly do they know?" I whispered under my breath so they couldn't hear. "Tell me. Quickly."

Turning her back on her parents, she grabbed my hand even though I tried to pull out of her grasp. I shot a look at Jack. To watch his reaction at his daughter so blatantly touching me, laying claim to me, but he didn't say a word. He just stood silent and condemning on the steppingstones.

"I haven't told them in detail what Ethan did to me, but they know it happened at Zara's and you've been trying to help me through it. They know you came to get me and we slept together for the first time that night."

"*What?*" I whisper-hissed. "You told them that?"

"I needed them to see what I do. That you will do whatever it takes to save me. That you are the exact opposite of Ethan. They know everything about us, apart from what you did to him—"

"Aslan." Jack cleared his throat. "I think…if you're done whispering with my daughter, we should talk. Don't you?"

I froze.

A fork opened up before me.

A crossroads in my life that was so blatant, so black and white, that I shivered at the awful sensation that this was *the* moment my entire happiness hinged on. A life of fervent happiness, always hidden, always illegal, but a happiness I was willing to do anything for because the alternative was death. Not because my father would eventually get his hands on me but because I'd never get my hands on Neri again.

And that…just can't happen.

Untangling my fingers from Neri's, I gave her a soft smile and pushed her away slightly. My mind raced with ways to fix this. To repair the rift between Jack and me because no matter his willingness to talk, his body language said he'd rather throw me in the pool and drown me.

He could say he forgave me for walking in on me seconds away from mounting his daughter. He could have Neri tell him how I did my best to save her mind from cracking the night she was raped.

But what he truly needed to know was how far I would go for her.

How far I *did* go.

How far I would *always* go.

To deserve her, protect her, love her.

The insane decision settled like a glacier in my stomach, and I turned back to the ring box that'd fallen onto the sala steps when Neri leaped into my arms. Fisting it, I swallowed a groan of discomfort as I straightened abused bones, then walked toward Jack.

You sure?

You positive you want to do this?

I shut down that worried little voice.

I held Jack's stare.

I marched directly toward him.

And then, I dropped to my knees, unable to stop the grunt of pain as I landed on the injuries he'd given me.

Anna sucked in a sharp breath beside him.

Neri drifted toward me.

And Jack didn't move as I plucked the ring out of the box and held it up to him. The golden waves glistened, the tiny diamonds glimmered, and I licked my split lip with my still bleeding tongue and confessed all my darkest parts. Every secret. Every coveted piece of me.

I tore myself wide open, all to earn a single thing in return.

One precious, wonderful thing.

Her.

"The day you dragged me onto your boat was the day you saved my life, just like my father, Emre Avci, was trying to do. I've been lying to you ever since. I deliberately didn't tell you much about my past because…the less you knew, the fewer lies I had to spin, but…here's the truth. Every shred of fucking truth. My real name is Aslan Kara. If you research my father, Cem Kara, you'll find a shady businessman with rumours of darkness, but nothing proven. To the world, he's crafted a careful story that hides what he truly is, but Emre told me everything. Kara is the worst bastard alive. He's killed people. Maimed people. Trafficked minors. Peddled drugs. Raped women. And done a hundred other terrible things. He is ruthless, cruel, and pure fucking evil.

"He found out my parents had me—after a lifetime of searching for me after I disappeared when I was eight months old. He found out my uncle stole me and gave me to his brother to raise. He killed my uncle and aunt. He would've killed every person in my family just to get to me. And that's why my adoptive father and the best man in the world, left the country we all loved more than anything. To give me a chance. To give my sister and cousin a chance. And when they died, I knew it was my fault. I've lived with their death ever since, knowing that if he'd just told me *why* we ran, I could've prevented it all and taken their place. I would've marched to Cem Kara and let him kill me if he'd promised to leave them alone.

"But it's too late for them now. They're gone, and I was lucky enough to be given a second chance by you, Jack. You and Anna cared for me like they did, and I'm so fucking sorry for betraying your kindness. But…what I'm about to tell you will hopefully show that the loyalty I had to my mother and father, sister and cousin, now belongs to you."

I shot a glance at Neri.

Her blue eyes glowed.

She was so beautiful, so perfect, so *mine*.

My voice twisted with every drop of love I had for her as I said, "I love Neri with all my miserable heart. I think I always have. I know I always will. I love her with the same violence I've always hidden from, inherited by a man I want nothing to fucking do with…but…the night Neri was raped, I couldn't hold back that violence. I need you to know, Jack, Anna…I did what was needed. I felt Neri calling to me—"

My voice broke, but I gulped and carried on, catching Jack's unreadable stare. "I *felt* her. How or why, I can't explain, but I knew something was wrong, but…I was too late. I was too fucking late. When I found her slurring and sick from that bastard drugging her, I thought I'd found her in time. I thought I was there to prevent her from doing something stupid and reckless, so I yelled at her. I will *never* fucking forgive myself for that. When I took her to *The Fluke* and saw what that bastard had done to her, well…"

I shrugged and looked at Neri again.

She stood with tears pouring down her cheeks. Her arms crossed so tightly as if she could contain her heart from leaping out and joining mine, smoking and splattering behind my very bruised ribs. The energy between us. The chemistry. The magic. It made my skin prickle and pulse quicken, and I fell all over again as I looked back at her father and embraced the fury that'd infected me that night. "I grabbed a diving knife, left Neri on your boat, and then I returned to that party."

"Aslan...don't." Neri pressed her lips together, shaking her head.

I ignored her. "I found him pissing on weeds and knocked him out. The police were there. They stopped me with Ethan mumbling incoherently in my arms. I thought for sure I would be arrested, but...they let me go. They watched me toss Ethan into your Jeep and drive away and, right then, I knew I'd been given permission to do what was needed to be done."

"Aslan...stop," Neri gasped.

Jack swayed on the spot, his face as white as Anna's. He grasped her hand for support, choking, "Go on."

"I tied him up and drove him out to sea. I saw Neri's pain in the way she watched him. I saw her agony in the way she cut up her favourite dress that she was wearing when he—" I shook my head, my voice thick with murderous rage. "I stopped the boat, grabbed the speargun, and shot that cunt in the leg."

Jack sucked in a breath.

Anna clamped a hand over her mouth.

And still, I kept going, my voice as dark as the night. "While the bastard was bleeding and screaming, he said things that made me become a monster. I lost myself. I beat him harder than you beat me. I hacked off two of his fingers for touching her. I would've cut off his cock for defiling her. But Neri..." My head snapped toward her; I drowned in her gorgeous sea-glass eyes. "Regardless of what that prick did to her, she still wanted to let him go. She's so much better and braver and kinder than me, and...she made me stop."

Jack shot a tear-streaming look at Neri. Heartbreak carved all over his weathered face.

He didn't speak, couldn't speak, as I dropped my hand and ran my thumb over the diamond engagement ring. "I obeyed long enough for her to start the boat. I obeyed as long as I could before I lost myself to rage again. I yanked him to his feet. I pressed him against the railing, sobbing and bleeding, begging and shitting himself, and then...I tossed that motherfucker overboard."

Jack stumbled, his legs folding in slow motion, dropping him to his knees before me until our eyes were level. He never looked away from me, seeing what I'd done as if I'd projected every gruesome, cruel, and merciless thing into the night sky between us.

A morbid movie.

The worst kind of hologram.

We stared at each other as two animals, not people, two beasts that would do anything to protect their mates.

Anna stayed standing, her hand still in Jack's as I held up the ring and confessed, "I married your daughter that night. As she rinsed away his touch in the sea, I told her what I just told you. I told her the truth about my origins. I stood before her as a murderer and the son of a monster, and asked her to accept me. I married her with every fucking part of me, Jack. The vows we uttered that night, with just the moon and stars as our witnesses, were the most binding vows of my life. I will never be with anyone else. I will never love anyone else. I was born for your daughter, sir, and if a single shred inside you would accept me, I promise to you, here and now, there is *nothing* I wouldn't do, no law I wouldn't break, no man or beast I wouldn't kill to keep her safe. It isn't a choice; it's a necessity. An absolute necessity because I love Neri with all my useless soul, and I wholeheartedly mean it when I say I would die if I had to live a single day without her."

I turned the ring, spinning it in the moonlight. "You have enough to call the police and have me thrown away for life. If they figure out who I truly am, they'll deport me, and my father will ensure I'm killed the moment I step foot on home soil. I've put everything I am into your hands, and all I'm asking for, all I'm *begging* for, is your mercy. Your mercy and the chance to keep loving your daughter. In my heart, she's already my wife. I promised my entire being to her that night, and yes, I did sleep with her like she told you. She was my first and my fucking only because I don't want anyone else. I don't *need* anyone else. I only want her, and if you can't forgive me for what you saw tonight, if you can't trust me that I would lay down my own life for her, then…"

I shrugged and sniffed back aching waves of grief. "Then I suppose I have no choice but to let fate deal with me. I won't run as there's nowhere else I want to be. I won't fight if I'm arrested. I'll accept my death sentence from my father, all because I'm too selfish to stop loving your daughter. I tried to let her go, I truly did. It was my fault she went to Zara's that night because I told her I wished I didn't have this need for her or her for me. I called what we had a mistake and—"

My voice cracked again, but I balled my hands and let anger siphon through me. "It was a mistake to think I deserved her when I've done nothing but cause her pain. It was a mistake to think I could survive without her when I can't take a single breath without her near. I'm condemning her to a life of misery and grief if I get caught. And I hate myself for that. I hate that I have nothing to offer her. I hate that our future won't be easy. I hate that I've stolen her heart, and I know you'll hate me too. Hate me all you want, but I can't give her back. I *won't*. She was mine the moment she found me, and I wish…I wish…. Fuck, I *wish* I'd come to you sooner. I wish I'd told you the night Neri came to me with hurt in her heart. If I had, she never would've gone to Zara's. Ethan would never have been near her, and I…I would never have destroyed everything you love."

Breathing hard, I hung my head, feeling the cold kiss of an executioner's blade on my nape. Jack could slaughter me with how much I'd told him. In a way, I wanted him to.

That awful fog of despair that never let me go was unbearably thick and heavy. Without Neri, that cloud would swallow me whole. I wouldn't survive. But how could I ask her to keep giving me her light? Forever putting her in charge of my happiness when all I gave her in return was stress and worry and pain?

I looked at Anna. At the tears raining down her cheeks.

And then I looked at Jack. At the stony glower on his face.

My ribs turned crimson as my heart bled all over them. I struggled to speak. "I love Neri with every fucking part of me, but I love you too. I love this family. I love who I am when I'm with you. I'm so grateful to you for every day you've given me. And I'm kneeling before you, not as a shipwrecked orphan or the son of a monster, but as the boy who fell in love with your daughter. I want this ring on her finger. I want you to know how deeply committed I am to her, not just for now but for *always*. And I want you to accept me as the son you always said I was, not because you fished me from the sea but because my heart belongs entirely to Nerida…and that…well that, as much as you probably don't want it to…makes me…*yours*."

Silence fell as I finally stopped speaking.

My lungs hurt from Jack's kicks.

My heart palpitated with fear.

Neri cried quietly a few feet away.

And Anna groaned softly, tore her hand from Jack's, then dropped to her knees beside me. With a sob, she wrapped her arms around my shoulders and hugged me so damn tight. "God, Aslan. I-I don't know what to say. I had no idea how much you struggled. I'm so sorry. So, so sorry." Kissing my cheek, she cried quietly, "Thank you for taking care of my baby. Thank you for being there for her. Thank you for loving her so damn much. *Thank you*, Aslan. I love you too. I'm so honoured and humbled by your dedication, and…I'm so, so sorry for what happened here tonight. For what Jack did. For what I did in return. For thinking badly of you when you've been nothing but the kindest, most wonderful guy."

Her perfume of flowers and sunshine wrapped around me as I sat frozen. Not knowing if Jack would let me hug his wife. Not knowing if I was forgiven or if this was goodbye.

But then Jack swiped at the tears rolling down his horror-drawn cheeks and choked around the rocks in his throat. "You killed him?"

I held his stare and nodded, ferocity roaring through me. "He was in pieces and bleeding. I didn't take his last breath, but I hope to God the ocean did."

His hands balled on his thighs. "And you went to Neri because you felt her. She didn't call you. You had no way of knowing she was in trouble apart from…sensing her?"

I nodded again, this time with utmost conviction. "I don't understand it myself, but yes. I did."

"How?" He shook his head, his forehead furrowing.

My heart slowed as I looked at Neri, standing in shadows and moonlight.

I sank into her, calmed because of her, and a worshipping smile tipped my lips as I breathed, "Because she's my other half."

Jack flinched.

Anna hugged me harder, crying into my neck.

And every part of me stiffened as Jack cleared his throat and grunted, "You've said your piece. Now…it's my turn."

With a sniff, Anna pulled away and shifted back to kneel beside Jack, her eyes on the ring in my fingers.

"You have lied to me for months. Snuck around behind my back. Touched my daughter without our consent. And gone out of your way to assure me that nothing was going on. You tell me you've loved her for six years, and I honestly don't know if that makes me feel sick or strangely grateful. You expect me to trust that you didn't do anything inappropriate with her until a month ago when you *married* her without telling any of us, and you don't even have the gall to be angry with me for hurting you."

"Dad—"

Jack ignored Neri, snapping, "You speak of yourself as if you're worthless. You have the audacity to *kneel* before me and give up your life as ammunition against you. You tell me you have nothing to offer my daughter. No future that she could want. No prospects or hopes or riches." His mouth twisted as he spat, "You watch me as if I'm going to kill you myself, and what's worse is…you'd fucking let me. You'd honestly let me murder you with my bare hands because you truly think you don't deserve to be here. With us. Happy. Free. In love.

"Fuck, Aslan, for a guy who has an eidetic memory, you're so fucking *stupid*."

Anna touched Jack's bunched thigh. "Jack—"

He ignored her just like he ignored Nerida. "You think you have nothing to offer my girl? *Look* at yourself. Look at what you did. You *killed* for her. You did what I would've done in a fucking heartbeat. You felt her screaming for you, for God's sake. You're so wrapped up in my daughter that I believe you would commit mass genocide if it kept her safe. And bloody hell, that alone puts me in your debt. What you did to that bastard is *exactly* what I would've done, and the fact that you did it for *her*…" His finger shot to Neri, shaking just as much as I did. "That you did it for the girl you love?

That you did it for my daughter? Shit, Aslan, that shows me you are *exactly* the man I thought you were. The man I'm honoured to have in my home. The man who I asked to look after my baby because I trusted him to care for her above himself. You did that and more, mate. You did what any man in love would do. And you need to stop hiding from who you truly are because you are a good man. A great man. A man I owe fucking everything to because you protected my baby when I couldn't. You avenged her when she was wronged. You put your life on the line to help her. And that kind of dedication—"

His voice cracked as he dropped his arm. "I'm sick to my fucking stomach for laying a single finger on you, Aslan. I will *never* forgive myself. Not now that I know what you did. You've saved me from a lifetime of hunting for him. You saved my life because I would've gone to prison if I'd ever gotten my hands on him. All the secrets and sneaking around you two did—they don't even come close to my mistakes."

He rubbed his nose and sniffed back his tears, his voice firmer. "The first mistake was pushing you to watch over Neri. I blamed myself for seeing you on top of her tonight. I should never have asked you to watch over her because without that permission, you might never have had the chance to get so close. But that's a lie, isn't it? It had nothing to do with me. Neri didn't lose herself in you. You didn't groom her or molest her. You fell hook, line, and sinker for her and instead of going over all the things I should've done differently and all the moments I should've seen coming, you know what I see?"

He paused and pinned me with a stare.

I shook my head, not speaking.

"Neri never lost herself in you. You found yourself in *her*. Hearing the way you talk about her. Hearing the raw devotion in your voice and watching the way you look at her." He pinched the bridge of his nose with a slight shake of his head. "It's terrifying."

My heart stopped beating.

He's going to deny me.

He's going to kick me out and—

"You've been honest with me, so I'll be honest with you. I told Neri in the car that I knew you were in love with her. I saw it in the way you watched her when she flinched from me in the pool. Now that I look back, I might have always known and used that love for my own advantage. I trusted you not to do anything about it. I knew how careful you were not to rock the boat—excuse the pun. You had the most to lose out of everyone. You wouldn't touch her. You wouldn't hurt her. And that was my fault, my sin, because…I didn't have a fucking clue the true depth of what's been going on under my nose."

"Dad…stop. Enough." Neri stepped forward, but Jack held up a hand.

"Let me finish." His eyes locked back on mine. "I don't care who you were born to, Aslan. I don't care how precarious your future here is. I don't care that I'm breaking all kinds of laws keeping you hidden. All I care about—" His voice cracked, and a fresh tear rolled down his cheek. "All I care about is my little girl, and frankly, no one deserves her…but you…" He exhaled heavily. "You love her enough to kill for her. And that? Damn, that alone means you have my blessing."

I froze.

Hope ricocheted agonisingly through my bones.

He rubbed his palms on his trousers, fighting another sob. "I give you my daughter, Aslan, not because you asked for my mercy but because I'm so fucking grateful to you. I owe you a thousand apologies for what happened tonight. I can't tell you I won't still question you sometimes. I can't tell you it will be easy. And I can't tell you I can snap my fingers and solidify your status here. But…if that ring you're holding is an engagement ring, and if what you said about marrying her that night was true, then…" Giving me a watery smile, he climbed stiffly to his feet, pulled Anna to hers, then held out his hand to me. "Do us the courtesy of seeing your commitment for ourselves."

Neri made a suffocated little noise, her eyes blazing bright.

I looked from her to Jack's outstretched hand, trembling with so many things.

I blinked. I blinked again. My head was woozy. My heart manic.

Is this…is this real?

Looking up the length of his body, I breathed, "A-Are you sure? Are you saying what I think you're saying because if you're not, then—"

"I'm saying you were my son the day we found you. I don't care that we aren't blood. I don't care you would've left us eventually and made your own mark on the world. No matter where you went, you would have always had a home here with us. But now…you're one of us. And…if you have the decency to propose to my daughter in front of us, and she truly wants you in return, then it's my absolute honour to welcome you to the family, not just as my sea-given son but as a man I will never stop being grateful for. A man I would be fucking honoured to call my son-in-law."

Fucking hell.

I struggled to stand.

I swayed and fell back to my knees. Fear lashed through me, even as hope burned bright. "You know I can't marry her. Not truly. Not here. And I can't go back home, even though I'd give anything to show Neri my country. I wish I could show you all how stunning it is. I wish I could explain how much I miss it by showing you everything there is to miss. But…I can't. I can't even offer Neri my last name because I doubt I have a legal birth certificate stating me as Aslan Avci—"

"Are you trying to get me to change my mind?" Jack cracked a smile. "Because I hate to tell you, after that speech, after knowing what you've done for her, no one else will ever compare. I might as well throw her in a nunnery because if you don't take her off my hands, no one will. I'll forbid it."

"Bloody hell, Jack." Anna swatted him in the belly. "Now is not the time for your warped sense of humour."

He chuckled, holding out his arm for Neri to go to him. "Come here, little fish. I think Aslan has something he wants to ask you." His smile widened. "He's already kneeling and seems to be struggling to stand—which probably has to do with what I did to him. I truly am so sorry about that." Flicking me a look, he added, "The moment you've asked my daughter your very important question and she's given you her equally important answer, I will do whatever it takes to put you back in one piece. After all, I can't have Neri hating me for hurting her future husband, can I?"

He suddenly laughed, transforming the strange night of tension and stress. "Fuck me." He shook his head as Neri drifted into his outstretched arm, cuddling close. "You told me this would happen, Nerida. You warned me, and I didn't listen."

"When I was twelve, in the corridor?"

"You said you'd end up marrying him."

Wiping away her tears, Neri glanced up at her father with a grin. "Believe me now?"

"I believe I still need to get you tested. All those nudges and knowings. If I didn't know any better, I'd say you were a witch."

"Not a witch," I murmured. "A siren."

Anna sucked in a breath, and Jack stopped chuckling.

The world fell away.

Jack and Anna faded.

The only person I saw was her.

Neri bit her bottom lip as I raised onto my knees and presented the ring I'd hunted hours for. Living in a coastal town made it relatively easy to find ocean-inspired jewellery. But this one? This almost hummed with the salty power of the sea, the waves forever destined to crash over her fingers, bringing us together like it did that fateful day, again and again, always returning us to one another.

I didn't care that I'd already done this part.

If I added up all the times I'd asked this girl to marry me, I'd guess this was the fifth or sixth attempt.

But I couldn't deny having Jack and Anna witness this, knowing they accepted me, after everything? It made my very marrow vibrate with joy that'd been so elusive to me, so hidden beneath grief and worry and endless, awful fear.

Kneeling before the three Taylors, a smile of pure happiness cracked my bleeding lip, and my breath caught as I murmured, "Nerida Taylor, Nerida Avci, I think I was born already falling in love with you. I was halfway fallen before we'd even met, and the moment we did, I crashed at your feet and never got up. I married you a month ago, but you've been mine for far longer than that. If I have to propose to you every day for the rest of my life to somehow make a true marriage happen, then I will. I will never get sick of loving you. Never get sick of being so in awe of you. You know my life is yours, *canım*. You've stolen every shred of my heart, and I'm asking you to take the rest of me. Take my bones, my breath, my every last piece because I'm nothing without you. Will you…will you marry me?" A small smirk lifted my lips. "Again."

Anna pressed her hands to her mouth as Neri stepped out of Jack's arm and dropped to her knees before me. Both her parents backed up, giving us space, but I only had eyes for Neri.

I couldn't look away from her.

From the starlight in her hair and the endless sparkle of her soul in her eyes…she'd never been more beautiful.

Never been so stripped back and spirit-bare, never opened herself so fully. She gave every piece of herself, right there in her parents' garden, and I gathered up every fragment and hoarded them.

She'd never get them back.

I would keep her heart safe, all while she kept mine.

A trade.

A bargain.

A promise.

It was her and me now.

For life.

Forever.

Her eyelashes glittered with unfallen tears as she held out her left hand.

Gritting my teeth so I didn't embarrass myself with another sob, I cradled her shaking fingers. We both flinched, gasping at the sting, the zap, the bone-throbbing *snap* of home and heart, forever locking us into place.

This felt different.

This felt so unbelievably *real.*

"I took you that night, and I take you again," she whispered, making me shiver. "I promised to love you until my last day. I vowed to keep you hidden in plain sight. None of that has changed. No amount of time will ever stop how I feel about you, Aslan. This is us, giving in to fate."

Looking over her shoulder, she smiled at Jack and Anna. "Thank you, Mum, Dad. I can't tell you how grateful I am that you see what I do. That you aren't telling me I'm too young to know my own heart. That this is too sudden or wrong. Thank you for accepting *us.*"

Anna couldn't speak, shaking her head as tears cascaded.

Jack's eyes locked on Neri's hand in mine. He didn't say a word, giving her a tight smile and a sharp nod, waging war on his own emotions.

Neri's gaze met mine again, twinkling with tears. "For the final time, yes, Aslan. Yes, I will marry you. I'm already yours. Here, there…everywhere."

I groaned as her words struck me right in the chest, reminding me of our first kiss. That heartsick moment in Jack's Jeep when she told me she'd broken up with Joel after I'd kissed her in the bar. I'd spoken those words to her. I'd meant them with every part of me.

"*Seni seviyorum*," I breathed. "Here, there, everywhere." With trembles that made my entire body rattle, I placed the ring on her wedding finger. I went to push it into place—

"Wait." Neri tugged softly in my grip, making my heart crash and burn.

"What's wrong?" Blazing, black-dripping fear billowed through my veins. "Don't you like it?" Perhaps, she'd changed her mind, after all. Maybe she'd had a premonition about our future and decided she couldn't survive the pain.

Not answering me, she took the ring from her shaking finger and held it closer to the solar lights. With narrowed eyes, she studied the inside of the golden band. "Something's written there."

I stiffened. I didn't think she'd notice. I'd hoped it would rest against her skin for the rest of time—a binding spell. An incantation that I'd asked the jeweller to inscribe to keep her safe, keep her mine.

"It's Latin." I looked past Neri to Anna, to the woman who'd sparked my love of learning so many tongues, including ancient ones. "*Per lunam tuus sum, per mare meus es. Aeternum.*"

Anna sucked in a breath. "It means, 'By moonlight I am yours, by sea you are mine. Forever.'"

Neri froze.

Her eyes snapped to mine.

And with a grin that only a siren could give, knowing full well she'd entrapped her prey, she shoved the ring onto her finger, crawled into my arms, and kissed me square on the mouth.

In front of her father.

In front of her mother.

In front of the moon that had married us.

Chapter Five

ASLAN

(*Heart in Welsh:* Calon)

WE ENDED UP HAVING A VERY LATE Christmas dinner.

Everything was a little overcooked and a tad soggy, but I'd never tasted a better meal. I didn't care that I ached all over or that I desperately needed to rest. My body and emotions had been put through the wringer, but I couldn't stop pinching myself that this was real.

Somehow, all my wishes had come true.

I sat at the dining room table, openly holding Neri's hand on the holly embroidered tablecloth, fighting the familiar urge to hide. To tuck our linked hands where they couldn't be seen. To keep my distance. To keep my smiles reserved. To keep the love inside me as secret as possible.

The fact we didn't need to hide anymore. The fact Neri scooted her chair until our thighs kissed and rested her head on my shoulder. The fact everyone was okay with our affection...blew my fucking mind.

It made me tremble with thankfulness, and I wished I'd done more to deserve this gift. I needed an even bigger gesture to show Jack just how much this meant to me.

The darkness inside me didn't tolerate this newfound blistering joy. It sulked in my chest and slithered around my heart, dusting me with fear that something was coming, something bad, because how could I deserve all this good?

Frankly, it terrified me.

I kept glancing at the door, expecting the police to charge in and arrest me. For life to laugh in my goddamn face and say, *'You thought this was for you, you silly fool? You thought you were safe now? That everything you've been running from and everything that's been hunting you is just...gone?'*

I wanted a beer to drown out those whispers, but after what'd happened earlier today, I never wanted to drink again. Alcohol amplified my despair and was why I wore so many painful bruises.

I did my best to stay present and not succumb to exhaustion and fear.

I marvelled at how quickly things could change. Six hours ago, Jack had been beating me to death for abusing his daughter. And now, he nodded in my direction with respect and awe, willingly giving me the same daughter he'd beaten me for.

If something that profound could change that quickly, then…why couldn't everything else in my life?

Why couldn't I believe I was safe now? That I'd paid my dues and deserved this? Deserved *her*.

As the night wore on, Anna caught my eyes each time Neri leaned into me, whispering something sweet in my ear. I braced for a scowl and blinked in surprise when Anna swooned instead. And when Jack stood at the head of the table, the top button of his pants undone from the indulgence of rich food, he raised his sweating beer glass and toasted me.

Me.

He saluted me with his drink and made my heart fucking burst with a simple but perfect welcome into his family.

"To Aslan. To Neri. To love and belonging."

Anna stood and wrapped her arms around him, and Neri sighed with utter happiness beside me. And I'd almost broken into fucking tears again, because how lucky was I that Jack was a romantic at heart? For all his gruffness and sternness, beneath his shell, he believed in love as much as I did.

He didn't judge me for my circumstances.

He didn't question Neri's choice to be with me or belittle our convictions because of our tender age.

He accepted that fate had intervened, and…there was no stopping it.

He let me propose to her.

He let her accept me.

He knew this was for life because he'd found his ever after with Anna.

It was a testament to him as a man that he understood that I'd found my ever after with Neri.

I didn't care that I'd lived with them for years—that this was my fifth Christmas with the Taylors. In that moment, in that delicious, *wonderful* moment, I felt truly at home for the first time since I'd left Turkey.

Boxing Day arrived, and no one got out of bed until ten o'clock.

Well, that wasn't technically true.

Neri slept in her room; I slept in mine. After everything I'd been given last night, I hadn't dared broach the subject of sleeping arrangements. I didn't care if Jack never let us share a room, just as long as we could share a house. But just as she'd been sneaking into my sala since she was thirteen, I woke at dawn to my door creaking open. The first rays of sunshine shone shyly as she darted to my bed.

I groaned as her warm, delicious body wriggled under my blankets.

I scooted against the wall, making room for her.

She lay on her side and let me spoon her.

I cradled her close and tried to go back to sleep, to give the stiffness and pain from my endless injuries time to heal, but Neri slipped her night shorts down her legs and arched her lower half deeper into mine.

I sucked in a harsh breath.

The feel of her silky bare thighs. The heat radiating from her core. The way she teased my rapidly hardening erection with her ass.

Fuck.

All the familiar forbiddenness between us and the sneaking around that'd become second nature made my heart lurch with fear that we'd be caught. Jack could march in at any moment and see the blankets moving as I thrust into his daughter.

But then my ring on her finger flashed in the dawn as Neri whispered, "I didn't tell you last night how much I love my ring. You couldn't have chosen a more perfect one. And that inscription? If I wasn't already head over heels for you, I'd be in trouble of becoming obsessed. But…I do have a tiny problem."

My eyebrows drew together. "Oh? What problem is that?"

"You proposed again."

"I did."

"I accepted. Again."

"Thank everything holy."

A smile painted her voice. "But then we went to separate beds."

"Out of respect to your parents."

"Yes well, they're still sleeping. And it's the perfect opportunity to bind yet another proposal."

My brain still clung to dregs of sleep. "Bind?"

"Consummation, Aslan. Stay with me, sleepyhead." Twisting in my arms to look over her shoulder, she drowned me with all her affection. "We should consummate all over again, don't you think?"

"Consummation comes after the wedding, not at the start of an engagement."

"Fine. Forget the wording and obey me, husband. Your wife is asking you to—"

"Fuck her?" Winding my arm tighter around her middle, I hooked my boxer-briefs with my spare hand and shoved them down just enough to free myself.

"Unless you're too sore from what Dad did?" True concern filled her tone. "You should probably see a doctor. I wonder if Jedda would—"

"Jedda? Who's Jedda?"

She stilled and bit her lip. "Just a family friend. She's, eh…she's a nurse."

I froze. "I can't see anyone official; you know that." I kissed her ear. "I think our engagement has gone to your head. Just because we're not forbidden anymore doesn't mean I'm suddenly legal, *canım*."

"I know, but you might be seriously hurt."

"I don't care. I'd rather hurt than be taken away from you. Especially now I have you." I shuddered with terror. "No way could I lose you after this."

She melted in my arms. "I feel the same. It would tear out my heart if I lost you." Sighing heavily, she paused for a moment before whispering, "At least let me go and grab you some painkillers. I'll be right back." She went to leave, but my arm snapped tight around her.

"You crawl into my bed, wriggle your tempting ass against me, call me your husband, command I fuck you, and then think you can…*leave?*" I tutted and bit the shell of her ear as I pulled her closer. "I would've thought you knew me better than that by now, Nerida Avci."

Her soft chuckle did painful things to my belly as she crooked her ankle over my calf, opening herself up to me. "I should've known you wouldn't let silly things like bruises stop you."

"You thought right." Splaying my hand on her lower belly, I kept drifting down and down until my fingers found her centre. She gasped in welcome, but it was eerily close to a flinch. Slicing worry dampened my desire. "Are you okay, Neri? Did you have a nightmare again and that's why you're in my bed?"

For the longest moment, she didn't answer. My pulse steadily sped up while she gave my question the seriousness it deserved. Finally, she murmured, "Something happened to me yesterday. Something rather profound."

"Oh?" I feathered my fingers through her folds, touching her but not going any further. "What?"

"When I was giving my statement about what Ethan did, I had no choice but to relive every awful detail—"

"I hate that you had to do that." Fury flowed hotly. "That you had to tell a stranger—"

"I'm not," she whispered. "By facing it, instead of running from it, I did what you've been telling me to do all along. I *accepted* it. I'm not saying I won't relapse, and I'll probably reach out to the therapist Wayne Gratt recommended, but…I'm okay, Aslan. Truly. I faced it and found it has no power over me if I don't want it to. I hate that I was stupid and thought we could get away with fooling around while my parents were down the hall. I hate that you were hurt, that I hit my dad with a lamp, and that you came face-to-face with the real terror of being deported, but…I'm also kinda glad it all happened."

I stiffened, my fingers barely inside her. "*Glad?*"

"The only thing I cared about yesterday, the only thing I care about now, is *you.*" She caught my stare over her shoulder, her eyes glowing with passion. "Fighting for you made me heal enough to say, *I'm going to be okay.* And sitting in that stark little room with a detective taught me a valuable lesson that only *I* have the power to cripple my mind with memories and tragedies. If I decide they don't have a power over me anymore, then…they don't."

I tripped into her, tumbling, falling, crashing into yet another layer of love. This layer was gentle and billowy, full of awe and devotion. "Stop making me fall for you, *aşkım.* I won't be able to survive much more."

She sighed and arched her hips into my hand. "Promise me you'll never stop because I won't. We can crash and burn together."

Her wetness seared my fingers as I sank my touch a little deeper. My panic over her mental state faded the longer her body twitched against mine, seeking connection, begging for touch. "Tell me again why you're here, wife…I'm fully awake and willing."

She giggled under her breath, rocking back against my aching erection. "I can feel that. Something is *very* awake."

"Do you want it?"

"God, yes." Her head tipped back, revealing the elegant line of her neck. "I want you to give it to me as hard as you want."

A full-body shudder quaked through me. "And what would you do if I took you brutally hard? If I wanted to punish you for making me run last night? If I wanted to make you feel a tenth of the pain I did at saying goodbye?"

"I'd say…do your worst." Her teeth snapped close to my nose. "Show me. Fuck me."

"*Fucking hell*, you're going to kill me."

"Aslan…"

I licked her curved neck. "Your wish is my command. I only live to serve my hot little siren. And if she wants to be fucked? Well then…I better obey."

"Good God, I love it when you speak filthy." She jerked in my arms as I sank two fingers inside, curled and possessive, testing how ready she was for me.

I groaned in her ear, finding how slippery she was. "Dammit, *karıcığım*, do you finger yourself before coming to me, knowing how hard I take you, or do you get into this state the minute I touch you?"

She moaned as I rocked my hand deeper between her legs. Her hips thrust with my rhythm, lazy and sleepy, sexy as fucking hell. "What can I say, Aslan? Your touch is magic."

Withdrawing my fingers, she whimpered in annoyance as I dragged my wetted touch under her pale pink camisole and fisted her breast. Shifting a little, I angled my cock between her thighs, thrusting, seeking, using instinct and her cues to find her.

"I think you're the one with the magic touch," I hissed. "You have a power to make me painfully hard with a single look."

"Good job I'm wet and you're hard then, because…I don't know if you've figured it out yet, but I didn't come here to talk or be teased."

"Oh, I'm sorry…am I moving too slow for you?" I chuckled into her hair, relishing the ease between us, the joy at playing.

"Well, I did tell you I came here for a reason."

"Remind me, I forgot." I inhaled her mouth-watering frangipani scent. "What was that reason again?" My hips rocked, slotting me into place on the cusp of claiming her. My eyes snapped closed at the branding heat pumping from her body. I swallowed a feral groan as I sank just an inch inside her.

She shivered and arched into me, trying to push herself deeper but cursing when I withdrew until barely anything linked us. "Aslan, stop it."

"Neri, tell me what you want." I teased her, dipping inside, then pulling away. Making my spine tingle and breath catch.

"I want…" She opened her legs wider. "God, I want…"

I licked her neck from collarbone to ear, tasting her, branding her. "Go on…you won't get what you want unless you tell me." I bit her, sinking my canines into the vulnerable part of her throat.

She cried out, her nails landing on my hip, trying to pull me into her. "Give it to me."

"Give *what* to you?"

"You *know* what."

"No…I don't. And if this is a legally binding activity between us, I need to know *exactly* what you expect me to *give you*."

She made a tortured little noise that sent my heart pounding. "If you don't stop teasing and fuck me, Aslan, I want a divorce."

I chuckled and bit her again, sucking hard, not caring if I left a hickey. "I'll never give you a divorce. Ever. You're bound to me for life."

"You're going to kill me if you don't stop."

"Good. We can die together."

"I'll only find you again and torture you all over."

"You torture me every damn day, Neri. I only find a cure by sinking inside you."

"Yes. That. I want that. I want you to sink inside me." Her forehead scrunched as I slipped my tip back inside her. "I want to be fucked by the guy I'm madly in love with." Her arms came up, pushing her breast into my hand as she grabbed handfuls of my hair and tugged. "I want your cock inside me. I want you to ride me. I want you to remind me that I'm yours and you're mine, and if you don't stop teasing me, Aslan, I'll—"

"Beg?" I rolled my hips, withdrawing again. Lust and obsession spasmed in my lower belly as I fondled her nipple. "What would you say if I asked you to beg?"

She moaned as I teased her again, thrusting an inch inside, driving both of us mad. "I never said I'd beg. I'd much rather threaten."

"Violence now?" I gritted my teeth as the games between us grew to a fever pitch.

"If you don't put me out of my misery, I will scream and wake up the entire neighbourhood. If you don't fuck me with your big, hard—"

"Here." I shut her up with a quick, savage thrust. "Fucking take it."

She grunted with pleasure as I sank to the hilt.

"Take all of me." I stabbed into her with every inch. "You've already taken everything else." I skated my hand from her breast to her throat, wrapping my fingers around her fragile neck. Every inch of her clenched around every inch of me as I drove home and held still, trembling, panting, fighting waves upon waves of mindless bliss. "Happy now?"

"Oh *god,* you feel good."

"I think that's my line," I groaned, dark and gruff.

My cock pulsed inside her, cursing me all over again with how sensitive I was. How much this woman pushed me over the edge. I could come just like this. No rock. No dance. I could bury my face in her neck and let go of the slicing, sparkling fireworks that'd already gathered at the base of my spine.

"No, your line is that I make you crazy and that you're going to snap any second and fuck me like the lion you're named after."

I nuzzled the soft, tender skin behind her ear. "Is that what you want, *canim?* You want me to fuck you as if I can't breathe without you? Fuck you as if I'm going to die if I don't come inside you? Fuck you as if I hate you?"

"God, yes. That one. Fuck me like you hate me."

"What a shame that that's a physical impossibility."

"I bet I could find a way to make you snap."

I stabbed inside her without warning, making her shudder and moan. "You always do. You truly will be the death of me, Neri. One of these days, my heart is going to give out with just how much I need you."

"That heart of yours better keep beating forever, Aslan, because you're not going anywhere." She held up her hand, wriggling her wave-crashing diamond ring. "I have your promise right here. Inscribed with Latin and very firmly, very willingly worn until my dying day."

Her tone remained flirty and coy.

But my desire to play mutated into something black and desperate. Seeing my ring on her finger, remembering how it'd felt to kiss her and leap out of her window, never knowing if I'd see her again. How heartsick I'd been, tripping through the neighbourhood, running because she told me to, not because I wanted to.

It all roared back with a vengeance.

My back snapped with unresolved panic.

I shook my head as the terror of losing her made me turn as primal as the lion she joked about. My hand clamped around her neck, my thumb on her fluttering pulse, my palm against the delicate lines of her larynx. My arm siphoned around her like a snake, not caring I squeezed too hard, unable to stop myself from lashing her to me until she squirmed with discomfort.

"Aslan…?" Her whisper lost all echo of games as true worry gilded her words. "Are you…are you okay?"

"Give me a minute," I grunted into her hair, doing my best to remind myself that she was here, with me, in bed. My body was inside hers; her heart was tucked safely with mine, and nothing could tear us apart. So why did everything inside me scream and howl at the very thought of losing her?

At the very real terror that one day I *would* lose her, and I wouldn't fucking survive it.

Yesterday's brief taste of separation was only going to get worse.

The police had my name.

They had suspicions.

They'll come back.

Despair dropped over my mind. Fury made me rough. And I barely clung to humanity as I hissed into her ear, "Hold on, *hayatım.* Use the safeword. Say seahorse if you need me to stop."

"Aslan?"

"I can't. I-I'm drowning, Neri. Running from you yesterday, when every bone in my body was snarling not to…it's…it's twisted me up inside and—"

"I know. Me too." Her ass shoved back, drawing me even deeper inside her. "I feel it too. That panic at being apart. The terror of losing you. The horror of never seeing you again. It's all I can think about. I can't stop fearing that one day you won't be there, that you won't be inside me, that you'll be gone and—"

"*Fuck.*" I buried my face into her hair and let go.

My hips rocked with a primitive beat, pumping and taking, relentless and cruel.

She gasped in my hold as I pulled her head back and turned her chin. "Kiss me." Dragging my hand up her throat to capture her jaw, I held her prone, forcing her to obey.

Our eyes locked as my mouth crashed down on hers.

An awkward, vicious kiss with our tongues duelling and our bodies twisted and locked in such prehistoric fashion.

We were nothing more than animals, writhing to an ancient song. A ritual that bound her to me in this life and the next, drawn in blood, summoned by sex, signed with every grunt and gasp as we punished each other.

I bit her bottom lip as I pistoned harder, faster inside her.

She moaned as her breasts bounced and my blankets fell away, revealing swathes of her glorious skin.

I well and truly lost myself.

Lost myself to her, in her, for her.

I snarled into the kiss and took every part of her that I could. I thrust as deep as I could get. I bruised her. Marked her. Didn't stop drilling inside her until she stiffened in my violent hold then shattered around my pounding cock.

My tongue silenced her cries. Our lips locked. Our breath shared as I rode her through her orgasm, sending her higher, wringing her dry, committing to memory just how incredible she looked, spread on my cock, trapped in my hold, giving me everything all while it would never be enough.

I would never get enough.

Never stop needing her, craving her.

Missing her.

She bit my bottom lip as the last wave of her release made her twitch and moan. Her vicious teeth caught the cut that Jack had delivered and I entered another realm of mania.

Lightning bolts replaced my bones.

Thunder rumbled in my blood.

I was light and dark, good and evil, human and monster, and as the metallic splash of my blood tainted our kiss, I fucked her so goddamn hard.

I punished her for making me need her this way.

I hated her for asking me to run.

I loved her for choosing me.

And I sacrificed myself with every pumping, pounding, thrusting madness as I made sure she'd feel my punishment forever.

I came on a grunt, unable to catch a breath as my spine broke apart, cord by cord, vertebrae by vertebrae. Pure, crucifying energy tore from my body in a pulsing, spurting storm, splashing into Neri, coating her with every monstrous surge.

My ears rang as I shuddered and jerked, my cock rippling with instinct to fill up my chosen one. Jet after jet of my cum, ensuring she might be able to wash that part of me away, but she'd never erase the spiritual connection. The part of our union that only burrowed ever deeper, sinking into our blood, scribing permanent promises into our souls.

Only once I'd endured the final throes of my climax did I blink back stars and realise what I'd done.

"Shit." With a wince, I let her jaw go, and just like every time I lost myself in Neri, I buckled beneath horrendous shame for being so rough. *"Iyi misin?"*

She stretched and practically purred in my stranglehold of a hug. "I love when you talk to me in Turkish. I'm going to learn everything about your heritage and language. I want to be fluent. And one day, when your asshole of a father dies—hopefully tomorrow by some helpful twist of fate—you're going to take me home with you."

I groaned and nuzzled into her hair. "I would love nothing more than to take you there, safely."

"Then we'll make it happen. One day. You'll see."

She snuggled against my pillow, my cock still inside her even as her eyelashes danced on her cheeks and sleep crept back into bed with us.

"Neri…" I shook her gently. "Do we need to talk about what we just said? The fact that we're still messed up from yesterday?"

"We lost each other for three hours, Aslan." She shuddered and buried closer. "That's the longest I ever want to go. And, as long as we make smart choices and look out for each other, then there's no reason it can't be the only separation we'll endure."

I did my best to trust her.

I did my damnedest to believe that the loss we felt would be a one-time thing. But as I relaxed behind her, those nasty black whispers were back.

I couldn't stomach the thought of withdrawing from her. I didn't have the strength to separate. While I was still inside her, we were linked and joined as one.

"I love you, Nerida."

She gave me a sated moan. "How do you say 'I love you with all my heart'?"

"Seni bütün kalbimle seviyorum."

Snuggling against me, she whispered, *"Seni bütün kalbimle seviyorum."*

I smiled and kissed her neck. "I'm keeping you forever, Neri. I hope you understand that."

"I understood it the moment I found you." She yawned and closed her eyes. "Rest now. Then we'll go for a swim."

I watched over her as she drifted back to sleep.

I closed my eyes, chasing her into dreams that I hoped were happy.

But those black whispers found me again.

They twisted dreams into nightmares.

We were together.

We were officially engaged with her parents' blessing.

Nothing would go wrong.

It wouldn't fucking dare.

So why did my nightmares scream that something terrible was coming?

Chapter Six

ASLAN

(Heart in Vietnamese: Trái tim)

"NEE...ARE YOU HOME? OH, CRAP! SORRY."

Nerida launched out of my arms, pushing me away as she dove under the water, her body rippling with crimson and sunlight as she swam to the other end of the pool and grabbed her towel from one of the boulders.

My ribs still ached from Jack's kicks and parts of me remained stiff with healing, but the cut on my lip and temple had thankfully knitted together enough that swimming felt good instead of stinging.

"Zara?" Neri leaped out of the pool, raining droplets everywhere as she quickly snapped her towel around her blood-red bikini—the same bikini she'd worn when we'd slept together for the first time on Low Isles.

Quit it.

Remembering fucking Neri on that beach definitely did not help deflate my erection.

The erection Neri summoned by kissing me when she should've been practicing her breath hold.

"Hi, Neri." Zara hunched her shoulders.

Wringing out her hair, Neri blinked as if she couldn't believe her eyes. "Wh-what are you doing here?"

Zara folded deeper into herself, her blonde hair catching bright sunshine, her sunglasses huge and round, hiding most of her face. "I-I didn't mean to interrupt." She threw me a look, standing stiff and furious in the pool. "Hi, Aslan."

If I had a knife, I'd probably throw it at her. "Zara," I snapped.

She flinched and looked away.

Neri marched bravely toward her ex-best-friend who stood on the threshold of the garden, her hands wrapped firmly around the handlebars of Neri's bike.

The bike that Neri had been clinging to, fighting nausea and the aftermath of rape, when I'd found her at the party. The bike she'd completely forgotten about as I'd yelled at her for being drunk, then taken her to *The Fluke*, not knowing what she'd just endured.

She'd replaced her phone from losing it that night but had never mentioned going back to get her bike, almost as if the thought of returning to where Ethan had hurt her wasn't worth it.

"You came to return my bike?" Neri asked.

Zara tucked loose blonde hair behind her ear nervously. "I figured it was about time I gave it back. It's just been sitting in our garage, and Joel said—" She winced and cut herself off. "Anyway, here you go." Yanking Neri's lost phone from her pocket, she held it out. "This too. I found it under our couch. I know your password, so I took the liberty to ensure it hadn't been tampered with and then I shut it down. It's been safe in my bedside drawer ever since."

"I wondered where that'd gone." Neri stepped closer and accepted the phone. "You...didn't read any messages or anything?"

Zara flicked me a guilty glance before shaking her head. "No. I mean...I saw one from Aslan, but I didn't invade your privacy. I'm sorry I didn't bring it back sooner. I just...I couldn't face you."

I'd always thought Zara was pretty in a wholesome Australian girl kind of way but after what she let happen? After she'd been in the same house while Neri was raped and didn't hear her screaming...

Fuck, now I couldn't stand to look at her.

My hands fisted as Neri put the phone into the drink holder of her bike then wheeled it from Zara's grasp. "Thanks." Pushing it to the side of the house, she rested it against the cream-painted bricks, then turned back to face her frenemy. Crossing her arms over her towel-wrapped chest, she tipped up her chin. "Anything else?"

I'd never been prouder.

Her body language said 'fuck off' and I was beyond fucking grateful that seeing Zara hadn't regressed her to what'd happened the last time they were together.

Awkward silence fell between the two girls as Zara shoved her hands into her denim short-shorts, her floaty flower top dancing in the muggy breeze. "I, eh...how have you been?"

Neri's eyes widened. "You're asking me how I've *been*?" She shot me a look full of hurt and confusion. "I-I don't know how to answer that."

Fury scalded my blood. I couldn't permit this to go on.

"You've delivered her bike and phone," I snarled, wading out of the pool to the sandy shore. Ice frosted my bones as I wrapped a spare white towel around my waist, grateful my cock no longer tented my black boardshorts. "Now *go*."

Zara sucked in a breath, her nostrils flaring. "I only meant…"

"Have you forgotten what you said to me that night?" Neri asked coldly.

"No, I—"

"You were *awful* to me, Zara."

"I know. I was drunk and hurt and—"

"That's no fucking excuse," I hissed, going to my wife's side, curling my arm around her and tucking her ever so close. "You were a cold-hearted bitch."

Neri sighed in relief as she leaned against me, drawing strength from my embrace. "You really hurt me, Zar."

"I know. I've felt terrible about it for weeks."

"Yet you only come by now?" I glowered at her. "You're not worth Neri's time."

Zara stiffened, looking from Neri to me and back again. "I said bad things, I know. But…it was only because I was hurting. I miss you, Nee. So much."

My hackles shot to full bristle. "Fuck off, Zara. You're no longer welcome here—"

"I know I hurt you," Neri said softly, cutting me off. "I meant what I said, Zar: that we'd grow old together and have our children grow up as cousins, but I was wrong to let you think I would have those kids with Joel. I led you on in that way. I led both of you on, and I'm sorry for that."

Tears shot to Zara's eyes. "I was protecting my brother. I let him tell me who I could and couldn't be friends with. I can't stop thinking about what I said to you at that party. I didn't mean it. I—"

"Did you hear me?" Neri interrupted, shivering in my hold. "Did you hear me screaming?"

Zara's entire face crumpled. That one question set off a torrent of confessions. "Nee, you have to believe me, I had *no* idea what happened. None. Not until that detective visited us this morning. He was searching for my boyfriend. My parents have been allowing Coop to stay with us while he finds his own place, now that he's decided to move here permanently for me, and when Cooper stepped outside to talk to the detective, I hid by the open window and listened. Fuck, Nee. The detective asked such awful questions. He said there was an allegation about Ethan Karlton. That he'd raped someone at my house the night of my party when my parents were in Singapore. He said Ethan was missing, and his family in Adelaide hadn't heard from him in over a month. He…he said the alleged rape occurred around ten p.m. and that got me thinking which then got me horrified,"

Tears poured down her cheeks. "You were there then. We fought—"

"You called me a brother fucker and a whore," Neri murmured.

"You did *what?*" I roared, stepping forward, fully intending to wring Zara's neck. "Fuck, how could you?"

How could Neri not tell me that? I'd just assumed Zara had said the typical bitchy things, not such vile, abhorrent slurs.

Zara scrambled backward, raising her hands. "I did. I won't deny it. I said those awful things, but even as I said them, I didn't mean them. I'm so sorry. You have to believe me, Neri. I was heartbroken. I missed you so damn much. And Joel, he told me if I ever talked to you again, he'd disown me as his sister. I said those things so I never had the chance to be your friend again. I knew you'd never forgive me."

"Ethan overheard you," Neri breathed. "He took it as an invitation to see just how much of a whore I was."

A tortured groan escaped me as Zara sucked in a sob and wedged both hands into her lower belly. "Did…did he hurt you? Is what the detective said true? That you were—"

"When you went upstairs with Cooper, Ethan grabbed me and wouldn't let me go. He drugged me in your kitchen, tied me to Joel's bed, and raped me." Every muscle in Neri's body snapped to stone. "I screamed for you, Zara. Fuck, I screamed. And even though you were only a room away, you never came. You never heard me. But Aslan…" She looked up at me with blue fire in her stare. "*He* heard me. He wasn't anywhere near that party, but he heard me because he *loves* me. Because he cares for me. He came for me and—" She pursed her lips, cutting herself off and sighing heavily. "I'll always be sorry for lying to you about how I felt about Joel. And I accept your apology for how you acted toward me, but…I'd like you to go away now."

Zara nodded repeatedly, tears plopping off her chin. "I'm so, so sorry, Nerida."

"It's over. We're over. Just—"

"I hope Ethan is dead," Zara blurted, shooting me a look. "I hope his guts were ripped out, and he's crab bait somewhere. I never liked him. He scared me. Something in his stare was empty and cold. Cooper warned me to stay clear of him if he wasn't with me. He didn't invite Ethan to visit him. I need you to know that. Cooper's been trying to shake Ethan for years—"

"Why are you saying this?" I growled. "You heard Neri. *Leave.*"

"Let me….Please let me finish." Sucking in a breath and swiping at her tears, Zara lowered her voice. "The detective asked Cooper if he'd heard from Ethan since the night of the party. I know he hasn't. He was worried the first few days because when Ethan goes missing, bad shit happens. It's not the first-time allegations of assault have swirled around him. As the weeks passed and he didn't show up, Cooper confessed he hoped he'd messed with the wrong person and had finally been *dealt* with. He hoped he was gone so he couldn't hurt anyone else."

Stepping closer to us, she braved my wrath and removed her sunglasses, revealing bloodshot eyes. "Cooper knows how much I love you, Nee. He's had front-row seats to my mourning over you, so when the cop asked him again if he'd heard from Ethan, I dashed outside and went to his side. He hugged me like Aslan is hugging you now and, in that moment, I knew Cooper chose me. He might've tolerated that sociopath, but he chose me over him. And you know what he did?"

Neri began shaking in my hold.

I squeezed her closer, sticking us together with pool water and skin.

"What?" she whispered. "What did he do?"

"He lied," Zara breathed ever so quietly. "He lied to the police and said he'd heard from Ethan the day after the party. That Ethan hopped on a plane for Borneo, ready to disappear into the jungles of Malaysia before starting his O.E."

"But that's not tru—"

I pinched Neri. Hard.

She wasn't supposed to know what wasn't true. She wasn't supposed to know a damn thing.

Zara glanced at me, her eyebrows drawn, her eyes hiding secrets I didn't like.

Why is she looking at me like that?

Neri licked her lips, anxiety rippling down her spine, infecting me. "I mean...how is that lying? Ethan could very well be overseas—"

"I think he's *under* the sea," Zara whispered.

I turned ice cold. "H-How would you know that?"

"Because a few days after he went missing, when he didn't return to grab his stuff to catch his flight back to Adelaide, Cooper managed to get his service provider to tell him where Ethan's last phone location was."

"Jesus fucking Christ," I hissed under my breath, borrowing a well-used Australian curse. No other words were vicious enough for the rip-roaring terror inside me.

I was going to jail.

No matter what Neri had told the police last night, if Ethan's *friend* could figure out his last location, I was fucked.

"His phone pinged in the middle of Trinity Bay before it went dark," Zara said, throwing a furtive look at the kitchen window behind us. "I guess...I came here to tell you, Nee, that...I know I failed you as a friend. I know I hurt you unforgivably. And I know you'll curse me until the end of your days for not hearing you screaming. But...I wanted you to know that I did my best to fix this. Cooper's pretty savvy with tech and managed to clone Ethan's phone with his number and all the stuff in his cloud. There's software that you can use to plug in a phone number, and it pings that location all over the world, leading anyone searching for it on a wild goose chase."

My ears pricked.

My panic paused.

Is that truly possible?

Zara's face blanched. "I made the mistake of scrolling through Ethan's content and…" She shook her head. "Let's just say, I hope to God he's dead because the images on there? The sick shit he was into? The dead animals that I'm pretty sure he murdered and mutilated—?"

Wiping her mouth, she stood taller and locked eyes with Neri. "Whoever Ethan pissed off did the world a favour by making him disappear, and as far as Cooper and I are concerned, we will do whatever it takes to ensure the police believe Ethan is off living his best life far, *far* away."

Her brown eyes locked onto mine again, pinning me to the spot. I never thought Zara was anything more than an easy-going girl. A girl who'd somehow befriended Neri thanks to the convenience of school, but as our eyes tangled and my nape prickled, I wondered, just briefly, if the reason Zara and Neri were friends was because they had a lot more in common than I thought.

A knowing kind of similarity. An otherworldly connection to things not many people could sense.

Sudden fear crawled up my spine.

Could Zara know?

Had I left evidence behind when I'd knocked Ethan out?

Fuck…are there cameras?

An insidious chill spread through me as Zara said, just to me, "Along with Ethan's phone, I made sure all the home security footage of the party was taped over." Bracing herself, she whispered, "Thanks for taking the rubbish out that night, Aslan. I'm very glad Neri has you. Keep her safe for me, okay?"

Darting forward, she placed a quick kiss on Neri's cheek before bolting from the garden.

I couldn't move.

I couldn't swallow.

She saw.

She'd seen me hunting Ethan in the shadows of her house. She'd seen me hiding behind her rubbish bins.

She knows.

"Aslan…" Neri squeezed me. "Hey…what's wrong?" Turning in my hold, she reached up and cupped my clammy cheeks. "Speak to me. You're scaring me."

I looked down.

I drowned in her worried stare.

I sucked in a breath to say—

"Ah, great, you're finally out of the pool." Jack chuckled, ripping my gaze to his as he stepped out of the house and grinned in the bright afternoon. "How long did you hold your breath for, little fish?"

Neri scowled at my taut silence, smiling unwillingly at her dad. "Only four minutes and forty-three seconds. I got…distracted."

"I can see that." Jack raised his eyebrows at how close Neri and I were.

I didn't even have the power to step away from her, regardless that our closeness was now permitted.

She knows.

All it would take was for Zara to pick up the phone and tell—

"We have a guest. Hey, Aslan? Come have a quick beer with us. Wayne wants to personally apologise for what I did to you."

Fuck.

My insides smothered beneath icy avalanches as Wayne Gratt—Jack's friend and neighbour from down the street—stepped onto the deck. I knew he was a cop. It was why I always found tasks that needed doing when he was around or made myself scarce if he stayed longer than usual.

Shit.

SHIT.

"Aslan?" Jack asked, stepping toward Neri and me. "Everything okay, mate?" He winced. "It's been five days, yet those bruises I gave you only seem to be getting more colourful."

She knows.

What the fuck was I supposed to do with that information?

Was Wayne here to arrest me?

Was this what my nightmares had been so afraid of?

I'd been lucky enough to be officially, legally engaged to the love of my life, only for it to last less than a motherfucking *week.*

"Aslan?" True worry filled Jack's eyes as he stepped off the deck and approached us.

I tripped backward, colliding with Neri's bike, sending it smashing to the ground. "*Lanet olsun.*" (Damn).

"It's okay," Neri whispered, quickly grabbing the handlebars and righting the tangle of wheels. "I think Aslan has a touch of heatstroke, Dad. Perhaps a beer might not be best."

"Have a lemonade then," Anna said, coming to join the disaster in the garden. "I just squeezed some." She held up a dewy carafe, smiling so kindly, so happily.

My mind spiralled. My heart suffocated.

Too many people.

Too many moving parts and secrets and fears.

"I think I know what's going on here," Wayne muttered, placing his hands on his lean hips, puffing up his chest beneath a short-sleeved, lime-coloured shirt. His kneecaps were knobbly beneath neatly-ironed black shorts. "You're afraid I'm here to interrogate you, aren't you?"

My heart did its best to keep me alive as I forced myself not to shatter beneath panic. "I, eh…" I cleared my throat.

Get a goddamn grip.

I couldn't break in front of this man.

I couldn't show any weakness.

Because she knows.

"I'm just…tired, that's all. Still healing."

"I'll never apologise enough for hurting you so badly, mate," Jack muttered. "You sure nothing is seriously wrong? I didn't break anything, did I?"

"I'm fine." I balled my hands, never taking my eyes off the cop.

"You can press charges, you know," Wayne said with a quirked lip. "Jack, for all his good intentions, committed assault on you."

"Wayne's not kidding that he's here on your behalf, Aslan. Not ours," Jack said. "If anything, he's come to give me the third degree." He chuckled but his eyes were slightly wary.

I would never lay charges against Jack, even if I could.

"It's all good," I muttered.

"That's a relief to know," Wayne said with a smile. "In that case, have no fear, Aslan. After my chat with Nerida the other night, I know you could never do such a heinous thing. She's lucky to have you in her corner." He grinned at Jack as he placed a beer bottle into the detective's hand. "Cheers."

"I told Wayne that we've buried our differences." Jack clinked his bottle with Wayne's, beckoning me to join them. "I made an awful mistake hitting you, but it's all good now. So good, in fact, you've forgiven me enough to become my future son-in-law."

"Congratulations, by the way." Wayne saluted me with his bottle. His smile warmed as it landed on Neri. "To both of you. I met my wife young too. When you know, you know."

"Thanks." Neri grinned. "We're both very happy."

Wayne studied her for longer than I was comfortable with. Finally, he nodded with another smile. "I can see that. And I'm glad."

"Will you stay for dinner, Wayne?" Anna asked. "We're still working through Christmas leftovers, so it will just be a simple fare of roasted chicken, some salads, and the last pieces of chocolate cake Neri and I made."

"That wouldn't be too much trouble?" Wayne asked, his face far too eager. "My kids and their kids left yesterday. I returned to work this morning to stay busy even though I'm meant to be off until next Monday. If I'm honest, an empty house doesn't sound all that appealing."

I know you worked today.

You were in the house where I dragged a man away to be murdered.

And Zara knows.

But she didn't tell you.

My hands fisted as I looked at Neri, and all my fear and panic solidified into a glacier, seeping with icy death in my belly.

74

Should I tell her? Should I tell her that Zara might have been an utter bitch to her, but she'd done something that well and truly redeemed herself?

Or should I keep Zara's secret, just like she was keeping mine?

Before I could decide, Neri grabbed my hand and tugged me toward the outdoor table where Jack, Anna, and Wayne had made themselves comfortable. "Later," she whispered. "We'll talk later."

And that was how I found myself sharing a beer with the goddamn detective hunting for the guy I'd brutally beaten and most likely slaughtered. How that same cop reached across the table and patted my hand, saying, "Welcome to the Taylors, Aslan. Any member of Jack's family is a good egg. You have nothing to worry about from me, okay?"

I wished I could believe him.

I wished I could shut up those mocking, black whispers.

I wish I could trust that everything would be exactly what the cop said…

Okay.

Chapter Seven

NERIDA

(*Love in Greek:* Agápi)

"CAN I GO TO THE BATHROOM AGAIN?" Margot's question ripped me from the past, making me blink with disorientation.

My headache was back, softly pounding in the base of my skull, steadily getting worse the closer I got to the awful crux of our story.

"You went like twenty minutes ago," Dylan groaned, grabbing another cod slider from the platter of finger food that Tiffany had brought down for us. "Do you have bladder problems?"

"Not that it's any of your business, but I have *anxiety* problems." Margot stood, brushing away the crumbs from the wedges she'd been snacking on while I spoke. "I can't take much more of this." Wincing in my direction, she added, "No offense, Nerida, but…the foreshadowing is turning my stomach into knots, and all the alcohol you're plying me with is just going right through me."

I smiled softly. "No offense taken. I feel the same way." I stood too, pushing aside the blush-coloured blanket Tiffany had brought me. I stretched out the many kinks in my ancient spine.

Seventy-two wasn't that ancient.

If the genes in my family were to be believed, I could live another twenty years with ease. But just because I could, didn't mean I wanted to.

"Come," I said. "I'll escort you to the pool house. I need to go myself."

"Fine." Dylan rolled his eyes. "If you're going, I might as well join you. I have a feeling once you begin the next part, Nerida, I'll be suffering enough without needing to piss too."

I laughed under my breath as Margot drifted to my side and Dylan fell in behind us. The solar lights in the sweeping gardens were so much brighter than the cheap ones I'd had in my family home. These were bright spotlights, angled to spear into the canopy of the many palm trees, stencilling the night sky with ever-watchful sentries, revealing the flitting shadows of moths and other night insects.

"I have a question, if I may." Margot slipped her hands into the pockets of her pretty burnt-yellow dress.

"Of course." I moved carefully over the steppingstones that reminded me so much of the garden where Aslan and I had fallen in love. "That's the whole purpose of this interview, is it not?"

She nodded, nibbling on her bottom lip before blurting, "I'm obviously gleeful that your parents accepted you and Aslan. That speech Aslan gave to your dad was out of this world. So, *so* romantic. And the fact that he admitted what he did to Ethan? That your father dropped to his knees with gratefulness that Aslan defended and avenged you? That he never revealed Aslan's secret even though he was friends with the cop searching for Ethan is something you only read about in fairy-tales, but..."

"But?" I raised an eyebrow.

"Well, you were seventeen—"

"Almost eighteen. I turned eighteen on the second of April."

"And Aslan was twenty-one—"

"He was twenty-two. His birthday fell on the eighth of December."

"Okay...he was more of an acceptable age for a committed relationship I suppose, but not many parents I know would be happy their daughter had already cut herself off to other experiences and—"

"Other experiences being other men?" I scowled. "Isn't it good to find love early and avoid sleeping around, running the risk of sexually transmitted diseases, unwanted pregnancies, and heartbreak?"

"Of course, but...those experiences also make us grow."

"Aslan made me grow. We evolved together."

Margot stopped walking. I copied her. Dylan paused behind us, his head volleying between us as we took turns speaking.

"All I'm wondering is...were your parents *truly* okay with you two getting engaged, or are you perhaps remembering the past with rose-coloured glasses?"

I linked my fingers and studied her. I appreciated her question. I liked that she was thinking about everyone's point of view and not just accepting my own as gospel, but she wasn't there. She didn't know my parents, and she didn't know *me*.

Smiling at Dylan as he scratched his short beard, staying out of this particular line of questioning, I said quietly so as not to disturb the stars, "You have to understand, Margot, I was a wild child. An intuitive, rebellious little thing. I'd been raised with freedoms and trust. I could test certain boundaries and become my own person, as long as I obeyed my parents' scant rules to keep me safe. So...by the time I was an adult, good luck to anyone who tried to stop me from doing what I wanted to do."

Dylan chuckled. "You wouldn't have taken no for an answer."

"Not for a second. I loved my parents. I still do even though they're gone. They gave me the best childhood I could've imagined. But even they knew my love for Aslan was different, just like his love for me. They knew they wouldn't be able to stop me. They knew I'd had sex with Joel, so I wasn't a delicate little virgin. They knew Aslan couldn't truly get married, not unless we performed a visa miracle…so…what was the harm in indulging us?"

I ran my hand through my time-whitened hair, long and breeze-teased by decades of salt and sun. "After hearing what Aslan did to Ethan. After seeing first-hand the depth of loyalty Aslan had for me…why *wouldn't* they agree to let him protect me for the rest of my life? And if our relationship petered out, what was the harm? A ring was just a ring. A promise was just a promise. I can't say if they truly believed we'd last the distance, but I can tell you that they believed in our fantasy. And that was what they allowed us to have."

"You were fortunate to have such open-minded folks," Dylan said. "I'm not sure if I'd be okay with my boy getting engaged so young, but then again…" He shrugged. "If he mutilated a rapist, all for the girl he loved, then…I guess that's a pretty big flag that they're rather deeply involved, and I've lost all say in the matter as his father."

"Exactly." I grinned. "Better to support than deny. Time always has a way of taking care of things, despite your opinions on the matter."

Margot caught my eyes with a worried smile. The nerves she claimed made her bladder overreact, glowed in her kind stare. "Please, *please* tell me you did get married, Nerida. Tell me that the ring you keep spinning truly did bind you in the eyes of the law, and you had the ceremony, cake, and happily ever after."

I wasn't prepared for the way my heart faltered. Or the way my bruised soul flinched with a typhoon of agonising memories.

I swayed on the steppingstones before rubbing my bleeding heart and forcing a smile. "There are questions I can answer now and questions I cannot. That is one I cannot. Not yet at least. How about we find that bathroom?"

"*God.*" Margot tipped her head back to the velvet-dark sky and groaned. "I'm going to die. I think I need to go home. Hearing about the rape almost did me in. I don't think…I don't think I can listen to any more tragedy."

Tears pricked my eyes, but I swallowed them down. "But doesn't tragedy make true love all the sweeter?"

"As long as there's a happily ever after, sure." Margot stepped into me, clutching my hand with her slightly clammy one. "But not if you're going to break my heart."

I squeezed her fingers, shooting Dylan a look. "If it gives you peace of mind, there are still two years to discuss before I break you," I said. "Before *I* was broken. You don't have to be in pain…just yet."

"Oh God, two *years*?" Margot untangled her hand from mine and placed her delicate wrist to her forehead, swooning dramatically. "I won't be able to cope. Two more years of falling in love with your husband through your eyes? Two more years of worrying that any day now, Zara will announce her dirty secret and that Wayne character will rip Aslan out of your arms and deport him for murdering Ethan…" She scowled. "By the way, what was his last name? Ethan's?"

"Don't tell us," Dylan muttered, his eyes scanning the gorgeous moon-glowing garden with its fairy lights swaying from the frangipani trees and the turquoise glow of the infinity pool up ahead. "The less information we have on him, the better. Especially as you don't want us to redact that from the finished interview."

"Fine." I nodded, striding back into a walk, dragging the reporters with me. "I do know his last name, but you're right. It's probably for the best that we leave that part out."

"Wise." Dylan caught my eyes and smiled, falling into step. "Anyway, you were saying…we have two more years before the 'incident'."

I winced. "It wasn't an 'incident', Dylan. It was the day my world collapsed."

"You could just tell us now; put us out of our misery," Margot whined. "I'm not lying when I say I truly don't know how much more of this I can take."

Stopping by the pool house where the changing rooms and luxury bathrooms were, I turned and looked at both journalists. They'd already sacrificed so much for me. They'd come here expecting to spend an hour or two interviewing me before returning to their own lives and forgetting all about me and Aslan. Yet they were still here, twelve hours later, dedicating their time to knowing how our love story ended.

"I'm very grateful to you both. I hope you know that," I whispered. "I had no intention of revealing all of this when you arrived this morning. I feel rather guilty for taking you down a long and twisting memory lane when you came for the simple version of Lunamare's creation but…it means a lot to be able to share him with you."

Margot smiled, her young, pretty skin glowing in the darkness. "And it means a lot that you're willing to share him with us too. I feel as if I know Aslan. As if he's mine. I'd prefer to hear about the more kinky exploits than the fade-to-black commentary you've been doing, but…I'm head over heels for a man I've never met." Her eyes narrowed, peering into the darkness surrounding us as if searching for something, someone. "Are you sure we can't meet him? It would be so great to get his side of the story. To learn more about his culture and how he found being thrust into an Australian way of life."

Dylan stood quietly, his shrewd gaze never leaving my face.

And I think…some part of him knew.

Some part of him guessed why I kept avoiding that question.

Swallowing hard, he brushed past me and looped his fingers around Margot's wrist. "Come along, fellow reporter. Let's pee so we can return to Nerida's world."

"But I—"

Margot's voice cut off as Dylan dragged her into the pool house, leaving me alone in the blossom-perfumed night.

I turned on the spot, putting my back to the pool and my face to the sea.

My heart tugged me to go home.

Soon.

Soon…

Chapter Eight

NER¹DA

AGE: 17 YRS OLD

(*Love in Zulu:* Uthando)

TEDDY: SO I FEEL A LITTLE STRANGE messaging a complete stranger just because my sister told me to, but she assured me that you're cool and I wouldn't come across as creepy. So...if you're cool and don't find this creepy, message me back sometime. I have questions about your comment to Honey about living under the sea.

"Oh my God!" I looked up from my phone, shoving it under Aslan's nose. "Read this."

"Bloody hell, not so close, Neri." He winced and pushed my arm away, focusing on the text from a readable distance. His eyes scanned the message before closing again as he reclined against the beach towels we'd spread over the deck of *The Fluke*.

"Have I told you how sexy I find you using our local curses?"

He smirked. "You like it, huh? How about I start using the word strewth?" He chuckled. "Or how about fair dinkum and dipstick?"

I fanned myself dramatically. "Crikey, you better stop. I'm burning up over here."

He laughed loudly. "You're insatiable."

"For you...absolutely."

He grinned and tossed a vein-roped forearm over his eyes. His carved belly flexed as he held in another chuckle. The bulge between his legs filled his black boardshorts far too temptingly, and the little trail of darkness running from his belly button and disappearing below made my mouth water. His dark-brown hair had given up fighting the sun, turning bronze tinted on the ends, making his coal-black eyes all the more intense.

"So...what do you think?" I asked, rereading Teddy's message. "He sounds super lovely."

"I think you probably shouldn't show me texts from other guys." He raised his arm, glowering at me. "Are you forgetting that I have a minor problem controlling my temper when it comes to keeping you safe, *canım*? How do you know he's not going to hurt you?"

"He's Honey's older brother. I've mentioned him before. He's gay."

"Doesn't mean he won't still fall in love with you."

"Oh, that's almost certainly going to happen."

"Wait, what?" He sat up, his forehead furrowed. "Does he have a death wish?"

"According to Honey, he falls for people all the time. As *friends*, Aslan. It's his thing. It's his and Honey's thing. They're both adorable and love to love. What can I say? He sounds like he has a big heart and likes to use it."

"A heart I'll wrench out of his chest if he suddenly decides to steal you from me."

"Pretty sure he's mostly married. Honey mentioned his boyfriend is called Edmund."

Aslan's lips turned up, fighting a smile. "Unfortunate."

"What? Why?" I frowned. "What's wrong with—"

"Teddy and Eddie? They sound like a two-person boy band."

"Oh my God, you're seriously bad." I snickered, opening a new screen to text Teddy back. "You're going to hell."

"Only if you're coming with me." He lay back down again. "Because even the devil himself won't be able to keep me down there if you're floating around in heaven."

Forgetting all about my phone, I crawled over him, straddling his hips and sitting down in the perfect spot.

I grinded against his cock, making his eyes fly wide. "Fuck." Wildfire blazed through his stare. His tongue shot out, licking his bottom lip, making it glisten in the sun. "*Again*, Neri?"

"Again, Aslan." I kissed him.

His hands clamped onto my bikini-clad hips, pulling me down even harder on his rapidly swelling erection. "You're draining me dry."

"I don't care." I sucked his tongue into my mouth, shutting him up.

Flipping me over onto my back, he wedged his hips between mine, rocking against me indecently. "How will we go back to being respectable when your parents come home?"

Wriggling my hand between us, I undid one side of my golden bikini and tore the Velcro of his boardshorts apart. "We might as well just stay naked and avoid everyone. I think we're ruined for life."

"*Beni mahvetmekten fazlasını yaptın, beni bedenen ve ruhen tükettin.*" He hissed like a viper as my hand dove into the dark heat of his boardshorts and fisted his thick, impressive length.

Licking his bottom lip, I murmured, "What did you say?"

"You expect me to remember words when your hand is around my cock?"

"Tell me." I pumped him, brushing my thumb over his pre-cum slippery crown. "You can't whisper something naughty in Turkish and then not tell me. That's like denying me an orgasm."

He groaned so low, so black, the sound rumbled through my bones, making me wetter than the sea all around us. "It wasn't naughty. But I can oblige if you want."

"What. Did. You. Say?" I fisted him harder, making his muscles twitch.

"I think…I think I said…you've done more than just ruin me, you've consumed me body and soul."

"My evil plan is working then." I smiled as he kissed me deep. I moaned as his tongue plunged inside, hunting mine, forcing me to yield and submit. We lost ourselves to the kiss for a while, our bodies undulating, our tongues tangling, our hearts smoking with unquenchable fire.

When I pulled away, the tendons in his neck were stark as he fought to stay in control. "Your evil plan isn't just working, Neri, you've corrupted me completely. Would I have willingly gone diving with you this morning otherwise?"

I palmed him, stroking slowly, relishing in the beauty that was my moon-given husband and basking in the sparkling, tingling connection between us. "You liked it. Don't try to deny it."

This morning had been insane. It was partly why my blood flowed with passion and my body wasn't sated, even though Aslan had fucked me the moment we'd climbed out of the ocean an hour ago.

He'd been ruthless and unforgiving, taking me over the table where he'd sat for so many years, inputting all the data my mum and dad had gathered.

I honestly couldn't believe he'd agreed to go with me when I suggested diving this morning. There weren't many things we could do without risking his freedom or putting us both at risk. At least spending time on *The Fluke*— where the sea didn't care he wasn't papered and I was secure in my nautical skills—gave us somewhere to go that wasn't our pool or garden.

For once, I'd willingly donned a tank and regulator to spend more time with him without having to return to the surface. We'd explored the seabed as I showed him the patches of seagrass and coral that my parents had been painstakingly replanting when Sapphire had come to say hi.

Her latest calf had darted and spun, showing off for us, swimming beneath my legs before nudging Aslan in the chest and blowing bubbles at her mother.

It'd been one of my favourite days, and I kept twisting my left hand under the water, staring at the diamond-encrusted wave ring Aslan had given me, fearing my heart would burst from overflowing.

So lucky.

I was so damn lucky.

83

Four glorious weeks since Christmas.

Four wonderful weeks of sun, sand, sea, and sex, and not necessarily in that order.

Just because my parents knew about us now, and the taboo factor was no longer an aphrodisiac, didn't mean Aslan and I had gotten any better at keeping our hands off each other.

We might not share a bedroom, but bloody hell, we made sure to get our fix in other ways. We'd become absolute deviants the moment Mum and Dad had gone away for a week, heading to Fiji for a quick romantic getaway before returning to work.

Dad had sat us down, pointed at our faces, and barked, "No sex on the table, the couches, or any other areas where we eat or hang out. Got it?"

Aslan had groaned and turned bright red with embarrassment. Silly boy had delusions that my father was naïve to what we got up to.

We were engaged.

We're engaged.

I would never get tired of saying that.

But just because I had a ring on my finger and my parents' approval, didn't mean they weren't highly aware of the kinky-fuckery we got up to when they weren't watching.

Mum had even pulled me aside and checked I was still diligently taking my pill, giving me a hug and saying, "Out of anyone you could've chosen, Neri, I'm glad you chose him. I know he'll always keep you safe and love you with every piece of his heart, but…he's still only twenty-two and you're only seventeen. You do *not* want a surprise before you've figured out how to get legally married and have solid careers sorted."

I agreed with her.

Just because I'd fallen for my soulmate when I was twelve didn't mean I wanted a child before I was thirty. I had far too much to conquer. And besides, I was too obsessed with Aslan to share him with anyone.

When I'd driven my parents to the airport with Aslan in the front seat and my parents in the back, he'd planted his hand on my thigh as if it was the most natural thing in the world to always be touching me.

I'd caught Mum and Dad sharing a look in the rear-view mirror.

And my heart had swelled to four times its size because they didn't get angry or look at us with worry that we were too young for the depth of feelings between us. They merely kissed each other and shared a smile. A smug smile as if they were personally responsible for bringing us together and were content with their life's work at finding their wayward daughter a suitable mate.

That wayward daughter was a terrible person because even though I loved them, I'd practically kicked them out on the curb when I'd pulled up outside the airport, giving them a hasty goodbye before driving a little too fast home and dragging my sea-wed husband inside a blissfully empty house.

We'd broken Dad's rules within ten minutes of being back. I barely made it to the couch before Aslan flipped up my silver skirt, yanked off my bikini bottoms, and sank inside me over the arm of the very same settee where I'd snuggled in Dad's embrace while watching *The Little Mermaid* for the first time.

We'd broken another rule that night after I'd returned home from picking up Italian takeaway. Aslan and I behaved and sat at the table instead of on the couch, doing our best to stop our hands from wandering.

We hadn't even finished before my fork clattered to my plate as Aslan curled his arm around my waist, pulled me from my chair and laid me on the table where my mother usually sat.

His hands spread my thighs as he dropped to his knees, and I'd choked on a scream as his mouth found my core and his tongue speared indecently deep inside me. He'd snarled and bit, tongue-fucking me to a release with his teeth on my clit and his hands on my breasts, kneading me, pawing me, drinking down my cries before standing up, shoving down his shorts, and dragging me to the edge of the table.

With a look drowning with love, he'd stabbed inside me so savagely, so possessively, my body had tangled with my heart, feeling both adored and used, worshipped and defiled.

That first week my parents were in Fiji had passed in a blur of sex, and I had absolutely no regrets. None. Okay, maybe one. The fact that I'd probably have to buy them new furniture was a very real thing.

When they'd returned, sun-kissed and more relaxed than I'd seen in a while, they'd announced they were only back to change the tropical clothes in their suitcase for thicker cardigans and wetsuits. While away, they'd received an urgent request for data from the University of Auckland on the native orcas down in the South Island of New Zealand.

Apparently, the pod was the only orcas who ate manta rays, and it'd been proven that, thanks to their remote location and different cultures within the matriarch-commanded group, they'd come up with their own chirps, trills, and songs, morphing into an entirely different whale language compared to the orcas in Norway, Falkland Islands, and Antarctica.

The university wanted recordings of those songs to prove it.

As Mum had packed their bags to go, I'd sat on their bed, jealousy pinching just a little. I'd travelled with my parents to New Zealand when I was eleven to help study the native Hector's Dolphins. The water had been crisp and the weather temperamental, but I'd never forgotten what it'd felt like to have the smallest dolphin in the world stare right into my soul.

Mum had waited until Dad left the room before asking quietly, "Do you want to come, sweetie? You don't start uni for another six weeks."

My heart had leapt, and if life was just about me, I would've started packing immediately.

But it was no longer just about me.

I had Aslan.

And he couldn't step foot in an airport, let alone a plane.

The thought of leaving him alone, not knowing if something would happen while I was away, that I might never see him again?

No.

Just no.

I would never be able to leave him, and I didn't care if that made me stupid or lovestruck. I would rather enjoy every moment with Aslan, tucked up in our garden and hidden on the sea, than travel the world without him.

Eventually, you'll get your own research assignments.

You'll be sent overseas for work.

I shuddered.

"Hey…" Aslan whispered, brushing hair away from my sun-pinked cheeks. "What are you thinking about? You suddenly look sad."

"Sad?" I kissed him. "Not sad."

"Tell me what you were thinking."

I hadn't kept anything from him. I'd always been so honest—sometimes *too* honest—yet…how could I tell him that I'd happily spend the rest of my life never stepping foot out of this town again if it meant I got to keep him forever?

All my other dreams of travelling the world: of visiting the Narwhals in Greenland and the monk seals in the Mediterranean Sea were incomparable to the biggest dream of all. The dream of marrying him (for real) and creating a world with him.

"I'm fine, Aslan." I wrapped my hand harder around his erection.

His nostrils flared. His hips rocked into my palm. But his eyes remained worried. They stayed worried as I shoved his boardshorts down just enough to free him, brushed away my untied bikini, and angled him to pierce inside me.

My mouth fell open as he pushed the moment he sensed my heat.

His jaw worked as he claimed me, stretched me, didn't stop taking me until he'd given me every inch of himself. Only once he was fully seated and our short, shallow breathing matched each other did he bend his neck and kiss me.

He kissed me as he thrust into me, sending coils of need and crackles of electricity through my blood. He kissed me as if he knew where my thoughts had gone and felt the same agony of separation even though we were still in each other's arms.

He swallowed a growl as he hitched my leg over his ass, widening my hips for him to rock a little bit deeper. "I'll always love you, Neri. Always."

"I know." I blinked back sudden tears. "There will never be a moment where I don't love you."

He kissed me again, his hips thrusting in time with his tongue in my mouth.

The towel beneath us bunched and gathered as we forgot we were people with words and reverted to animals that only spoke a language of lust and tongues.

I moaned as he buried his face against my neck, his spine rounding to pump into me. "How am I still so sensitive when it comes to you? I could fuck you a million times, and each time, it feels as if you're pouring lightning into my veins."

"How quickly could you come?" I whispered, crying out as he drove particularly deep.

"I could come right now," he groaned. "I could come just from being inside you. It's a daily battle not to embarrass myself."

I stilled beneath him, forcing him to look at me. "Show me."

His eyebrows raised. "Show you?"

"Come right now. Come without moving. Come with nothing but my wet heat around you."

He bit his bottom lip, his bronze-tipped hair flopping deliciously over his forehead. "But…what about you?"

My inner muscles clenched around him, surprising me as he sank deep and held punishingly still. "You never know…I might be able to follow you."

"It goes against every instinct I have not to pleasure you first." His gorgeous face twisted with refusal. "Let me make you shatter and then—"

"No." I banded my legs around his hips, deliberately squeezing my core around his penetrating length. "Now. Like this. When we're plastered together and ever so close."

His eyes snapped closed. Every bone in his spine went rigid. "Neri, I—"

"Show me how much you need me, husband."

Darkness clouded his eyes as he spread his legs between mine, slid his fingers through my hair, then stabbed his elbows into the towel on either side of my ears.

He didn't speak.

Didn't even breathe.

He looked into me as if he'd never seen me before. He swept me up, captured me with black fire and aching fevers, dragging me into him, binding our souls, knotting our hearts, and braiding everything we were into one.

His lips pulled back from his teeth as lust carved over his face, highlighting his sharp cheekbones and the fine sun-given lines around his eyes.

Time stood still as the waves rocked *The Fluke* beneath us. The sun blanketed us in its golden warmth, and Aslan kept staring, staring, staring into me. Stripping me bare, giving me no place to hide. I became his idol, his goddess. He turned devout in my arms, praying to me with his silence, turning a simple request into one of the most spiritual moments of my life.

"Neri…" His mouth parted with a shallow gasp that was somehow the most erotic thing I'd ever heard. It tumbled around my heart and fed into my blood, and my body reacted.

It hummed in his stillness.

It vibrated beneath his reverence.

And I moaned as I lost all control.

My clit throbbed against the base of him.

The lightning in his blood crackled into mine, and when every muscle in his back rippled with his impending release, I tripped with him.

It took me by surprise.

The softest, quietest orgasm tore through me. It felt like gentle laps of the sea, silky petals of a flower, and the brightest gilded sunrise.

His eyes flared as he felt me flutter around him.

His soul-deep groan made my heart stop.

And the first splash of his silent climax only added another element to my release. He grunted quietly as his body spurted into mine, primal and carnal, gifting me what I'd asked for, conjured by nothing more than the endless trust and aching connection between us.

"*Sana hiç bu kadar bağlı hissetmemiştim Nerida Avcı. Seni sadece sikimin etrafında hissetmiyorum. Seni her lanet hücremde hissediyorum.*" Burying his face into my neck, he sighed with a final jerk. "Before you ask, I said, I've never felt more connected to you. I don't just feel you around my cock. I feel you in my every fucking cell." Kissing my throat, he exhaled heavily. "And if I'm honest, that petrifies me because you're in my very essence, in every drop of my lifeblood, and that…surely, that can't be right."

Rising up on his elbows, he cupped my face with slightly trembling hands, his cock still twitching inside me. "Is it normal to feel this way? Please tell me it's normal because I feel like I'm going out of my mind with how much I feel for you."

I held his stare.

I gasped at how big my heart expanded and merely whispered the truth. "I think, if someone is as lucky as we are and finds their soulmate…then yes, this is normal. But to others who are not as lucky, I think to them…we're probably wonderfully strange and worryingly besotted."

His lips quirked as he kissed me. "Who are you calling strange?"

"You." I laughed softly, sticking our sweat-slicked bodies closer together. "You did just perform a magical act of coming without any stimulation."

He chuckled, sending his cock shifting deliciously between my legs. "Oh, I had stimulation, *aşkım*. I have you in my arms and your heart in my hands. That's all I'll ever need to find euphoria." Dropping his head, he found my mouth and kissed me.

A kiss of gratefulness, promises, and belonging.

I kissed him back, slinking my fingers through his hair and holding on tight.

His cock swelled inside me.

My clit sparked.

Our hips rocked to a time-worn rhythm.

As we lost ourselves and found each other, I thanked the empty ocean around us and the sun cloaking us in gold.

This wasn't just the place where we'd met.

The sea wasn't just my playground or backyard.

The day I'd met Aslan in its salty cradle, it became so much more than that. It became our shrine and our sanctuary, a house of prayer and benediction.

"Neri…" Aslan groaned as our thrusting dance became heated and hungry.

I felt it too. Felt the spindling and spinning, the gathering and colliding.

It turned out, we could come just by being inside one another.

That hearts could explode as spectacularly as our physical forms.

And it irrevocably changed me because up until now, I'd fucked Aslan, made love to Aslan, teased and played and seduced Aslan, but this was the first time we'd fallen into a different realm of emotional belonging.

A soul bondage.

A spirit enthrallment.

A silent form of transcended enslavement that could never be undone.

Chapter Nine

NERIDA

AGE: 17 YRS OLD

(*Love in Filipino:* Pag-ibig)

ME: *HI, TEDDY! YEP, HONEY WAS RIGHT. I am cool, and you're not creepy. What did you want to ask about living under the sea?*

Teddy: *Hey! Nice to officially 'meet' you, even if it is through a screen. My sister won't stop going on about you. I've had your number for a while, but she's only just browbeaten me enough to make me use it.*

Me: *Honey might be tiny, but she's mighty.*

Teddy: *No truer words have been spoken….Anyway, my partner and I (to give some backstory, my business partner and husband-to-be, Eddie Blackstone, is an architect like me). We finished our degrees and are busy deciding what legacy we want to be remembered for. I'm sure Honey has told you about my goal of creating a sustainable community that's impervious to disasters, natural or otherwise, and I have to say, I'm intrigued with the idea of building in a different world entirely. Do you think it would be possible?*

Me: *You're the architect. You tell me.*

Teddy: *I think we need to meet and discuss this over a copious number of cocktails.*

Me: *Sounds great! I should warn you, though, I have an overprotective fiancé who isn't afraid to make sacrifices to the sea in the form of men who might hurt me.*

Teddy: **Snicker. Did he ask you to write that?*

"Oh my God. He totally just called you out." I laughed, looking at Aslan as he finished cleaning the kitchen after we'd made a taco bowl for dinner. We were due to head to the airport in ten minutes to collect my parents from their research trip in New Zealand.

To be honest, I was looking forward to the change of scenery.

I was sick of being inside.

I was sick of Aslan dictating how I spent my holidays, even if it was a necessary chore.

The past few days had been hellish: spent indoors (bleh), on a laptop (double bleh), scrolling through rental listings for somewhere to live in Townsville. I should've sorted accommodations *weeks* ago. I should've done it the moment I earned my enrolment for my Bachelor in Marine Science…yet something had been holding me back.

Something named Aslan because it went without saying he would come with me. He'd already given me every dollar my parents had paid him over the past six years, telling me to put it toward our new home.

The amount he'd saved would keep us sheltered for a while.

It was enough to buy his own place (something small and modest with a mortgage), but just like we couldn't go to many places, he couldn't do most things others could.

We'd had to come face-to-face with that awful conclusion more times than I wanted to admit as we applied for studios and one-bedroom apartments, knowing we'd have to head to Townsville earlier than I wanted to go house-hunting.

I don't want to go.

I didn't want to leave this home where we'd been safe.

I didn't want to be responsible for Aslan living in a bigger city where the locals weren't used to him being part of the community, so familiar and protected by a well-spun lie, keeping him invisible right beneath their noses.

Here, he was mostly safe to drive, shop, and exist.

But there?

God, it's so risky.

Just because he had enough money to keep us housed while I studied, didn't mean he'd stay sane not doing anything with his days while I was off at school.

What would he do while I studied?

Where would he go? How would he fill his days?

He wasn't safe doing anything.

Which meant he had to do *nothing*.

And I couldn't ask that of him.

I couldn't trap him in a stuffy apartment and deny him the minuscule amount of freedom he had.

A terrified part of me whispered that it would be kinder to let him stay here. So what if it was almost a six-hour drive? So what if the separation would kill me? At least he could continue working for Mum and Dad and not risk his life.

"Let me see that." Aslan held out his hand, his fingers strong and tanned.

My cheeks flushed, remembering where those fingers had been an hour ago as I placed my phone into his grip.

His eyes skimmed the message thread, a smile quirking his lips. "I actually rather like this guy."

"Good. Because you're probably going to meet him soon if he's true to his word about coming to visit."

"May I?" Waggling my phone, he pressed both thumbs on the screen and replied to Teddy under my account.

I did ask her to write that, and it's true. You're welcome to be friends with my girl, but if you ever hurt her, you'll quickly learn how ill-equipped a human is to live under the sea, regardless of fanciful ideas of making it your home. I'll give you the keys to your new place for free.

"All yours." Tossing my phone back, he smirked and snatched the Jeep keys. "We better go pick up Anna and Jack."

I laughed under my breath as Teddy's reply pinged.

Teddy: *Oh, I like him. And I like you. Right, Nerida and her rather violent fiancé, I'll talk to Eddie and make a date happen. I have a feeling we're gonna do great things together.*

I replied as Aslan dragged me out the door and down the front path to the old Wrangler.

Me: *Honey said something very similar, and you know what? I think so too. I'm glad you messaged.*

Teddy: *Me too. Look forward to getting to know you!*

Me: *Keep in touch!*

Teddy: *Quick question before you go, if we did hypothetically try to design a house under the sea (crazy to even ask that. Like WTF, right?) Where would you suggest we put it?*

Me: *Oh, that's easy. Here in Port Douglas. The Great Barrier Reef.*

"Seatbelt," Aslan barked, turning the Jeep on and nursing the growling vehicle down the driveway and onto our street.

I blew him a kiss, strapped myself in, and grinned as Teddy's message came in.

Teddy: *In that case, I suppose Eddie and I are moving to Port Douglas. LOL. I did tell you I might come across as creepy. Talk to me for all of ten minutes and I'm already moving in with you.*

"What's he saying?" Aslan muttered, his hands firmly on the steering wheel, his eyes scanning the streets with sheer-minded determination like always. He acted as if he could see around corners when driving, doing his very best to spot police cars before they saw him.

"He said he's moving in with us."

"What?" His eyes shot to mine. "You can't be serious."

"Relax." I laughed and dropped my phone onto my lap. "It just means we can get a bigger apartment, that's all. Win-win."

Aslan groaned, sounding genuinely tortured. "The guy's spoken to you for all of four seconds, and I now have to commit murder for the second time if he dares to lay a finger on you."

"And possibly a third." I laughed harder. "There are two of them, remember? The boy band? If you're murdering one, you'll probably have to murder the other. It's only fair, seeing as they sound as if they can't live without each other." I bit my bottom lip, doing my best not to burst into hysterics.

Aslan glowered at me, his hands strangling the steering wheel. I was surprised the Jeep didn't cough and die with his death grip. He looked so protective, so beastly, so swoon-worthily gorgeous that I couldn't hold it in anymore.

Bursting into giggles, I reached across the console and placed my hand directly between his legs.

He almost swerved into the other lane as I rubbed the bulge in his shorts.

"Neri…fucking hell. Are you trying to make me crash?"

Unbuckling, I shifted in my seat.

"Put your belt back on," he snarled.

I didn't obey. Instead, I popped his button, unzipped his denim shorts, and wriggled my hand into his boxers to pull his rapidly hardening erection free.

His left hand snapped around my wrist, stopping me mid-stroke. "Is this you trying to kill me so you can move in with two other guys, or are you trying to apologise for making me irrationally obsessed with you?"

I fisted him, making the tendons in his neck appear as he gritted his teeth.

"This is me showing you that I could live with a hundred men, and the only one I want to touch…to lick…to *fuck*…is you."

His fingers twitched around my wrist. "Once we pick up your parents, you're going to behave, right? No more making me fuck you against the sink with your dishwashing fetish. No more shower sex. No more doggy-style in the shallows of the pool at two in the morning."

I licked my lips, drowning beneath the heat pumping off his cock and the way it kept swelling larger and thicker in my hold. "You have my word, Aslan. The moment we bring them home, we'll go back to humping secretively against your bedroom door…until we move into our own place. And then…well, you better drink a lot of water."

His eyebrows raised. "Why?"

"Didn't you complain that I was wringing you dry?" I smirked and bowed over his lap, dragging my tongue over his sensitive tip, licking up the salty pre-cum that tasted like the ocean I loved so much. "It's only going to be worse when we have our own place," I breathed on his crown.

His head fell back; he let out the feralest groan. "I'm going to have a heart attack."

"No, you're going to come so you relax." I licked him again, deep and long.

Almost mindless, he swiped on the blinker, swerved into a darkened street where lit-up houses revealed families having dinner, then slammed into park.

His hand sank firmly into my hair.

I froze in his hold as his fingers feathered around my head possessively, almost threateningly. I shivered as every inch of me prickled for touch.

Glancing down the cul-de-sac, making sure no one walked their dogs or peered into our dark little cocoon, he growled, "Open. Open wide and suck me."

I gasped at the black-dripping command.

I obeyed.

My mouth encircled him, my tongue slid down his thick length, and my hand stroked him hard and fast, just the way he liked it.

His thighs bunched. His right hand buried deeper into my hair, pushing me farther into his crotch, being rough with me, losing control with me. "Make me come, *hayatım*." His voice was stone and gravel as his harsh breathing filled the car. "Fucking hell, *please* make me come." His left hand stole across the gear stick, diving between my legs.

Finding my phone on my lap, he tossed it to the floor, shoved aside my underwear, and speared two fingers deep inside me.

My mouth opened wide at the invasion, moaning at his vicious penetration.

He took full advantage, thrusting his cock deeper past my lips.

His fingers plunged into me, ruthless and desperate as if we'd be caught at any moment.

I lost myself to a cocktail of making him break apart and his brutal touch making me shiver and sparkle.

His thumb ground hard against my clit, pushing me up the cliff quickly, expertly, using my own body against me as he tugged my hair to make me suck him faster.

The sounds of my wetness as his fingers plunged over and over inside me and the slurps of my mouth around his huge, hot cock sent me over the edge.

I cried out as I came all over his hand.

Wave after shattering wave, fast and furious, naughty and needed.

Only once my final spasm faded did he withdraw his arousal-wet fingers, sink both hands into my hair, and grunt, "*İyi misin?*"

I nodded, almost choking on his thickness.

"I'm going to come. Tell me now if that's a problem."

I shook my head, deliberately scraping my teeth over his sensitive flesh.

He bucked and cursed. "Hold your breath, Neri. Put all that talent to use while I fuck your sinful mouth."

I wasn't ready for him to let loose completely.

I moaned as he shoved my head down, holding me there as his hips surged upward, feeding me as many inches as he could, grunting as his belly clenched and his cock spurted with bliss.

His ragged breathing echoed in my ears as he climaxed, splashing hot, salty seed all over my tongue.

I drank down every drop. I fought the urge to choke. I did as he said and held my breath so I didn't have to fight my body's attempt at removing the pulsing obstruction in the back of my throat.

Slowly, he stopped shoving me down, and the dominating hold he'd trapped me in turned apologetic and full of shame. "*Fuck*," he whispered.

Pulling me upright, the *pop* of his cock leaving my encircled lips made my cheeks heat and him flinch. His erection speared upright, smearing my saliva and his release all over the hem of his light-grey t-shirt. Anyone who'd ever been frisky in a car would know exactly what that stain meant and why it was in direct line of Aslan's zipper.

Sucking in a breath, I went to suggest turning around and changing, but Aslan grabbed my cheeks and attacked me.

He kissed me with nothing held back.

Our teeth cracked, our tongues warred. I held his wrists as he devoured me with reckless devotion.

Only once he'd successfully raised my heart rate to that of a sprinter running for her life did he pull away, let me go, and wedge the back of his head against the seat rest. "You make me lose control every time you touch me. I hate that I bruise you. I hate that I take you so hard." His blazing dark eyes met mine. "But I can't help it. I can't stop myself from losing myself in you, and…I'm so sorry, Nerida."

"Sorry?" I rubbed my swollen-stinging lips. "I'm not. Never have I ever thought you were too rough. I love being with you. And you say you lose control, but you don't. You still asked if I was okay. You still let shame affect you." Cupping his cheek, I whispered, "One of these days, I want you to let go fully, and I'll tell you if it's too much or not."

"The day I let go fully is the day I break both of us." He smiled sadly, nipping at my palm as he arched his hips, shoved his still-hard cock into his boxers, and flinched as he zipped up. "We better go. We're late now."

"But was it worth being late for?" I smirked, catching his gorgeous stare.

He kissed me again, breathing into my mouth. "Being with you is worth absolutely-fucking-everything, Nerida Avci. Every breath, every heartbeat, I'd give them all to you just to keep you."

I threw my arms around his powerful shoulders and hugged him tight. When I pulled away, I smiled, utterly love drunk, star struck, and goofily grateful. "In that case, let's go get my parents so we can somehow control ourselves and not spend the rest of our lives playing with each other."

He laughed as he pulled back onto the main road, heading toward the airport. "I will never get tired of playing with you, *canım*. You're the best toy I've ever had." He winked.

I giggled.

Life was good…

Chapter Ten

ASLAN

(*Heart in Zulu:* Inhliziyo)

"SO...I HAVE SOME NEWS."

My head shot to where Jack sat on the couch with Anna tucked in beside him. They'd been back from New Zealand for over a week, and Neri and I had had to embrace some much-needed discipline. We slipped every now and again with a quick kiss that turned a tad too passionate in the kitchen or a straying touch that definitely wasn't appropriate for parental eyes in the pool, but for the most part, our three weeks of uninhibited fucking on every surface of their house had been curtailed.

It didn't help that I had those memories, though.

Every inch of Jack and Anna's home now held some erotic fantasy of my fingers or my cock in their innocent little daughter, all while she screamed my name loud enough to wake the nosy neighbours.

"What news, Dad?" Neri asked from where she was sprawled on the shaggy rug in front of the coffee table. She'd made herself a little nest, wrapping herself up in a peach sherpa blanket. The two colours of peach and cream reminded me of the spiky shell she'd given me that never left my pocket.

It was a good luck charm at this point.

A talisman of *us*.

My fingers strayed to run over the smoothed spikes as Jack turned his head toward Anna. "Do you have the envelope, sweetheart?"

"Oh, no. I left it in the kitchen. I'll go get it." She went to move, her blue sundress caught under Jack's thighs they sat so close.

"I'll go." I shot to my feet from the La Z Boy where I'd been sitting, nursing a beer as we'd all convened in the lounge after a big meal, a great conversation of what they'd been up to down south, and now planned on some mindless entertainment on TV before we all went to separate rooms.

That part was my least favourite of the day.

I hated heading out to the garden alone.

Honestly, I wasn't sleeping well.

Ever since Neri had started sleeping in my bed, the night her parents went away, it'd felt like she'd always slept cocooned in my arms where I could protect her through the night. Not having her there made my bed and heart tragically lonely.

"That's lovely of you, Aslan, thanks." Anna smiled. "You'll find a manila envelope on the sideboard where all the junk lives."

"Be right back." Catching Neri's piercing blue eyes as she blew me a kiss from her nest, I rubbed at my heart as it skipped with love, then headed to the kitchen. I found the envelope straight away, bringing it back and tossing it into Jack's lap before sitting back down and toeing Neri on the floor.

She grinned and grabbed my bare ankle, making my skin tighten and body do unmentionable things.

"*Behave*," I mouthed, flicking Jack and Anna a glance to make sure they were looking elsewhere.

Jack muttered something as he pulled the papers out and inspected them.

Neri rolled her eyes, blew me another kiss, then pinned her attention on her father. "So…what did you do, Dad? Are you going to tell us or make us guess?" Rolling onto her back, she fanned her delicious chocolate hair all over the rug. The sunshine had been particularly sneaky with her strands, thanks to all the swimming and sunbathing we'd done while on holiday. Instead of one depth of colour, Neri's hair now mimicked an earthy rainbow of cinnamons, coppers, and even a few shades of gold.

"Here." Jack grinned and tossed her the paperwork. "See for yourself."

Sitting upright, Neri's blanket fell away, revealing a dark purple dress she bought last time we were in town together. "What is it?" She scanned the document, flicking to the next page as her eyes widened. "Oh my God."

"What?" I bent forward, doing my best to see what had made her shoot to her knees and clutch the paper as if it'd solved world peace. "What is it?"

"Read for yourself." She waddled toward me on her knees and passed over the document. Resting against my legs, she didn't move away as I read quickly.

"A rental agreement?" I frowned, locking eyes with Jack. "To where?"

"To a two-bedroom apartment in Townsville." Jack grinned smugly, snaking his arm around his wife. "Don't worry, it's close enough to James Cook University but not on campus. The bus system is good there. It's in a quiet six-floor high rise with a total of twenty-four apartments. No pool but…it does have a bath, which not many places do."

"Where did you find the listing?" Neri asked, peering at the weekly rent. "And how on earth did you find a two-bedroom place for only three hundred and sixty dollars a week?"

"Serendipitous really."

"How?" I let Neri have the contract back as she skimmed the fine print.

"Well, you know we were in New Zealand. Another group of biologists were there, doing their own data gathering and we got talking. Turns out this guy, Griffen Yule, is a lecturer at James Cook. I said how my daughter is following in the family footsteps and he said you'd left it a bit late to find anything decent to rent. He's been savvy with investing and owns that apartment complex. He's been holding on to the last apartment as it needs a refresh, but he hasn't gotten around to it. He gave me his card."

"A total stranger offered you an apartment for less than market value?" Neri asked suspiciously.

"He wasn't a stranger by the end of two weeks, let me tell you that." Anna laughed. "The amount of beer your father and Griffen drank almost put the cubic litres in the ocean to shame."

"Hey!" Jack chuckled. "We had to celebrate. That orca invited us to eat with them! She dropped that mangled manta ray right in our faces and hung around as if inviting us to tea. She posed for photos, for goodness' sake. I mean…I swear she even smiled!"

"Anyway…" Anna chuckled. "Griffen showed us photos of the place. It's very airy and bright. It does need a bit of a renovation, like Jack said. The walls need a fresh coat of paint, the kitchen is outdated, and the bathroom is frankly stuck in the eighties, but…" She flicked me a glance. "We mentioned that you're skilled at almost everything, Aslan. That you're a number whizz and know almost as many languages as I do at this point. He knows that you'll be unemployed most of the time Neri is studying, and…he, eh…" Anna glanced at Jack, pursing her lips as if not quite sure how to announce the rest.

Jack took over. "He mentioned he needed a handyman. Someone who lives on-site. Someone who isn't afraid of hard work. I personally vouched for you, mate. Gave you a glowing recommendation. He's willing to reduce the rent in return for you taking care of things for him. You'll spruce up the place you'll be living in and do the odd maintenance jobs around the complex."

I went still as Neri shot me a worried glance.

"I can't work, Jack," I said quietly. "Remember?"

"Yeah, yeah, I know. He's happy to pay you under the table. No questions asked. You'll have the same gig as you do with us. Cash in hand every week."

"Why would he do that?" Neri asked. "Why not hire someone else? Someone with a tax number?"

"Because hiring people to look after your investments when you're too busy to oversee them yourself is always a risk. We got friendly. He gave me his trust. And I convinced him that Aslan is the man for him." Jack pouted dramatically. "Even though I'm now down the best employee I've ever had and have no idea how I'll survive without your help."

I gave him a tight smile. "I'm sorry to leave you in the lurch."

"I'm just glad you're going with Neri to keep her safe." His eyes flashed, remembering what I'd confessed about Ethan. The darker side of him spoke to the darker side of me, grateful that I wasn't afraid to get my hands dirty to keep Neri protected.

I reached for my beer and took a healthy sip.

"You didn't tell him about his visa status, did you?" Neri croaked. "Please tell me you didn't tell this guy that Aslan is an illegal immigrant, Dad."

Jack scowled. "Do I look like a moron? Of course, I didn't."

"We merely said that for now, Aslan is working on getting his residency," Anna said, doing her best to calm her daughter.

"How? Through work?" I asked, taking another drink, doing my best to school my nerves.

"No, through marriage." Jack puffed up. "I've protected you, Aslan. Believe me. He's okay with this. It's not unusual for people to hire under the table here. Mostly in trades but sometimes in bars and backpackers too. As long as you treat him right, he'll treat you right. And I intend to stay friends with the bloke, so the chances of him ever waking up one day and thinking *'Oh, I know, I'll call the tax office about my awesome employee and dob him in'* just won't happen. I swear, you're safe. Both of you. I promise this will work. I've even ensured your name is not on the lease, see?" Jack leaned forward, tapping the paper in Neri's hands. "It's only in your name, little fish. I doubt you could find another two-bedroom place that would allow just your name on the agreement, especially being a first-year uni student."

"Seems you've thought of everything," I murmured. I didn't know why my hackles had gone up. Jack had done us a massive favour. He'd given us a place to live. A place to call home. A place where I could be as safe as possible when heading to a city with over one hundred and fifty thousand people instead of the close-knit community of three and a half thousand in Port Douglas.

More chance for anonymity but less community.

Less familiarity of a small town and the fact that I'd been seen around this place for the past six years.

I was somebody here.

The guy at the dive shop knew me, the manager at the local supermarket always asked about my day.

I was a local here, but there…I would be a nobody. Which was both a good and a bad thing.

"Say you'll sign and accept it," Jack muttered. "Please don't go to Townsville next week. It's too soon."

"Jack, sweetie, they're going to have to leave eventually," Anna said.

"Yeah, I know." He gave Anna a sad smile before looking back at me.

"But not yet. I've watched you guys trawling the listings online. I've seen you applying for studios and one-bedroom places, and I wasn't going to interfere, because this is your life now, not mine, but when Neri said you guys would have to leave early to find a home before the term started, I decided enough was enough."

"Oh my God, the lease starts two days before I begin classes!" Neri waved the papers. "How am I supposed to move in, get settled, and go to class within forty-eight hours of moving there?"

Jack grinned. "That's Aslan's job."

"Excuse me?" I coughed on my final mouthful of beer. "What do you mean?"

"I mean…you will leave here together—at the last possible moment, mind you—so I can milk all the remaining time I can with you both. You'll take a few essentials so you're not sleeping on the floor, and then it's your job, Aslan, to renovate and furnish the apartment. It's Neri's job to go to uni and learn."

I held his stare, knowing what he'd done and trying to curse him for it but finding I was utterly unable to. "You've ensured I stay busy."

"Not busy." He grinned. "Sane." He saluted me with his beer. "I know you, Aslan. You can only do so much sudoku or math papers online before you go stir-fucking-crazy. You need a job. Neri isn't going to be around much while she studies. If you don't have something to fill your days with, you'll get into mischief and probably be deported." He laughed.

I forced a laugh too.

I knew he meant it as a joke, but it was a little too close to home.

I'd been fearing the same thing.

Wondering how long I could sit in a tiny apartment, kissing Neri goodbye each morning and desperately waiting for her to return to me in the evening.

I was already half insane with missing her, and we weren't even there yet.

My half-hearted laughter faded as I grabbed the contract from Neri.

"Do you have a pen?" I asked Jack.

"I do indeed." Whipping a ballpoint out of his short pockets—ever the scientist to record important data and numbers—he tossed it to me. "Make my daughter sign that, start a list of what you need to take with you, then tomorrow, we're all going to Mark Blythe's house two streets over for lunch."

"What? Why?" Neri asked, accepting the pen and nodding as I tapped the blank box for her to sign.

Only her.

I would once again hide behind her, desperate never to be seen.

"Because he's selling a Jeep Cherokee, and I want you to test-drive it."

"You're buying me a *car*?" Neri's eyebrows shot to her hair. "I-I can't let you do that."

"We want to," Anna said. "We want to know you have reliable transport to visit us whenever you want. The apartment has its own carport, so you don't have to worry about parking."

Neri finished signing and gave me a smile just for me—a smile full of love and every day of our unfolding future—before standing and launching herself at her parents.

Pressing kisses to both their cheeks, she grinned. "Have I told you how awesome you guys are?"

"Not lately. You've been far too obsessed with your shiny new fiancé to even spare me a second glance. I've been demoted." Jack pouted again, his eyes drooping like a sad, demented beagle. "I'm heartbroken and ever so jealous."

"No, you're not. You're ecstatic that I picked him. This way, you don't have to murder a new boy I might hook up with far away from home."

"You know what?" Jack grinned, glancing at me with seriousness. "I am. I'm so glad you picked him." Patting Neri's behind, he announced, "Now go to the fridge, get your man another beer, your father another beer, your mother a gin tonic, and whatever you're drinking these days—seeing as you're only a few weeks from being legal to drink—and then we're all going to celebrate."

"Celebrate me leaving home?" Neri laughed. "Who are you, and what did you do with my father who never wanted me to leave the nest?"

He grinned. "I was lucky enough to put you into the hands of a guy I trust with all my heart. It helps knowing he'll be with you, even when I won't be."

Neri rolled her eyes and skipped to the kitchen, all while Jack met my stare, and everything he didn't say swirled around us.

Keep her safe.

She's yours now.

I gathered up his silence and gave him my own.

I'll guard her with my life.

You have my word.

Chapter Eleven

ASLAN

(*Heart in Croatian:* Srce)

"THIS IS ALL OURS?" I ASKED, PIVOTING in my black flip-flops, drinking in the lounge with its white tile floor, patchy and stained walls, rickety glass sliders leading to a weed-filled communal garden, and an open-plan kitchen with some cupboards missing while doors hung haphazardly off their hinges on others. The grimy cream countertop had burn marks and the forest-green cabinets did nothing for the rest of the space, soaking up the late afternoon sunshine like greedy haunted trees.

"I can't believe it," Neri breathed, kicking off her own silver flip-flops to drift over the grout-stained tiles and down the short dark corridor to the small bathroom, complete with a showerhead that was so calcified that I doubted water could rain, and the ugliest pink vanity and matching bathtub full of spiderweb cracks and soap scum.

I followed her as she headed toward the bedrooms, peering into each, noticing the slightly mouldy plaid curtains, equally grout-grotty tiles, and the suspicious holes in the wall from either a rowdy party or an angry tenant.

Both bedrooms were a similar size, both with sliding windows with bars over the exterior. Bars that didn't exist on the apartments above but had been gifted to the ground floor homes only.

"I mean…it's a little dirty, but it's ours." Neri spun on the spot, her hands clasped together over her heart, her turquoise-and-navy ombre maxi dress floating around her ankles. "I never thought we'd get a place this big and on the bus route to uni. I was happy to settle with a studio where our bed was practically in the fridge, but this?" She spun again as if this was a mansion and she was its lady. "Wow."

I went to her, wrapping my arms around her stunning body and resting my chin on the top of her head. "It needs work, but I'm glad. It gives me something to do. Something new to learn while you're off playing with microscopes and being a lab geek."

She chuckled in my embrace. "I think that's the part I'm going to curse the most." Tipping her head back, dislodging my chin so she could look up at me, she said, "I'll miss you, of course. That goes without saying. But I'm going to struggle not being on the sea. My parents have their mobile lab in the spare room and are perfectly capable of their own analysis, but the fact that they made a business gathering data for other firms, rather than being stuck in a lab most of the time was genius."

"The curriculum for this degree definitely sounds like you'll be spending far more time in a classroom than on the ocean."

"And that's going to suck big octopus balls."

I chuckled, my heart panging for the past few weeks that'd passed far too quickly. We'd all returned to work on *The Fluke*. Neri had spent most of her days diving with her parents while I manned things above. Twice, I'd been coerced into diving with them as a family, and I had to admit, it'd been fun.

Pretty fucking cool actually, to finally see the humpback whales that Neri sketched and spoke about. The grace with which they swam and danced, their huge bulk effortless in the salt. Their songs swirling around us, echoing in our bones.

We'd all been rather quiet that night at dinner, reliving the majesty of nature and all its beasts. Neri had snuck into my sala when her parents were asleep, and we'd kissed and writhed with a primordial desperation that felt both light with love and heavy with loss.

We were so insignificant compared to such giant creatures. Yet the way I felt about Nerida made me feel both immortally invincible and terribly breakable.

Each day, as we counted down to leaving, had been a rush of emotional addiction, sexual gratification, and I'd been lucky enough to reach another level in my relationship with Jack.

Something had changed between us.

He no longer saw me as a boy he'd protected with lies and kindness but a man in my own right. A man who'd done such violent things, all in the name of love. Anna looked at me differently too, her eyes catching every touch and kiss Neri and I shared. I did my best not to slip in front of them, but when I did, Anna seemed to hoard our affection, tears twinkling in her eyes, watching us like we were her favourite Hallmark movie.

She'd pulled me aside the night before we left and hugged me as if I was her own son. I had no idea who my biological mother was, I'd lost the woman who'd raised me, and now I had a third mother who I would always be so grateful to because she gave me Neri.

It fucking hurt to leave them.

Hurt to pack up Neri's new Jeep and say such awful goodbyes.

It wasn't forever.

But as Jack hid his tears and Anna stood on the street waving farewell, it'd felt like it.

And standing in this apartment, on the cusp of a new adventure, I was both torn by the past and teased by the future. I just prayed that we'd be as safe and happy here as we had been back there.

Hugging Neri tighter, I sighed as I let her go. "Only three years. Then you'll be qualified and can either work for Jack and Anna or open your own research team."

"Would you work with me?" she asked softly. "Would you be okay returning to the ocean after a three-year break from it? It might be impossible to get you back in once you've been away from it for so long." She pouted adorably. "I didn't think about that. What if you get stubborn again and refuse to put your big toe in? Let alone go diving with me."

Her eyes held genuine worry, and I pressed my finger beneath her chin. "I'll go wherever you go." Lifting her face to kiss her, I captured her mouth. "Always."

The moment we touched, all our tiredness from the long trip and the weight of what we were now facing faded. I only meant for it to be a quick peck, a flurry of affection and acknowledgement that we were in this together, but she moaned against my mouth and stepped into me, her arms lashing tight and lips parting.

My mind swirled; my body reacted. Cupping her jaw, I kissed her deeper, plunging my tongue between her strawberry-tinted lips and—

"Oh, good. You figured out how to get in."

"Shit." I jerked away from Neri and shoved her behind my back. My eyes locked on the stranger standing in our bedroom. "Who the fuck are—"

"Griffen Yule," Neri snapped quickly, giving me a wide-eyed look to behave. "Hi, Mr. Yule. Thanks so much for sending us the keys. And for letting us lease this place." Marching in front of me, she extended her hand politely. "Sorry about him. He's just—"

"Protective." Griffen Yule, our new landlord, held out his hand and shook Neri's offered one. "And please, call me Griffen." His green eyes met mine as he grinned. Bald head, weathered face, stocky build, and a face covered in three-day-old whiskers. His skin was most likely meant to be white, but he'd spent so much time on the ocean and in the sun that he'd turned a little leathery. "I did knock, but no one heard me. I was driving past on the way home and wanted to welcome you to the building. Make sure you know how everything works, that sort of thing, settle you in before night falls and you can't figure out the power and water."

"Thanks." I stepped forward and shook his hand, clearing my throat. "I'm sorry for what I said. I wasn't expecting company."

"Not at all. My fault for barging in. Technically, I'm breaking the law by being in this apartment now you've signed the lease. I have to request a meeting if I want to see you guys, but…" He winked. "If you're as easy-going as Jack Taylor is then I feel as if we're friends already. But of course, if you'd rather keep things strictly by the books, then…boundaries."

"You're giving us the place below market rent and offering work to my fiancé while we arrange for his visa. I think we're beyond boundaries," Neri said with a respectful smile. "We're super grateful for the apartment. And for everything else you're doing for us. I can't believe the space for the price and how close it is to James Cook."

Griffen smiled. "Your dad and I bonded over a matriarch orca who practically made us part of her pod. I feel like he's been a mate for life, so it's no trouble to help out his daughter."

He glanced around the bedroom, his forehead furrowing a little at the state of it. "I bought this block about ten years ago when the market retracted. Best thing I ever did with my money. I'm sure I don't need to tell you that we spend our lives learning about sea beasts and discovering the secrets of the deep, not for the money, but for passion. My advice?" He held up his finger like a sage. "Take the pittance amount you earn from your career as a marine biologist, and put it into something that will turn a profit. That way, you can keep doing what you love but also have money to retire with."

"Wise words." Neri grinned. "I'll remember that."

"Now." Griffen cracked his fingers, making me flinch as his knuckles popped. "I'm guessing you figured out the keycode system outside, found your carport, spied your letterbox, and worked through the jumble of keys to find the one linked to this place."

"We did." Neri grinned. "When Dad said you were sending the keys, I assumed it would just be one. Not an entire envelope full."

"Yes, in hindsight, I should've waited to see you before handing over every key in the building. My mother always did say that when I got an idea, I went all guns blazing…sometimes with good consequences and sometimes with bad. But…" He laughed, his eyes crinkling. "I believe when fate drops a solution into your lap to a problem that's been irking you for ages, you don't procrastinate. This happened quick, but…" His eyes landed on mine. "If you're as good as Jack says you are, Aslan, then I'm very excited to let you loose on my building."

I shot Neri a glance and did my best to seem knowledgeable about all things renovation. "I-I'll do my best not to let you down. I can start tomorrow—"

"No, no. Take a week to settle in. This place needs a good scrub down—my apologies for the state of it. In fact, I won't charge you the first week's rent—put that money toward cleaning supplies. I'm embarrassed by the state of it, to be honest. I had bad tenants who did a number on the place. Still chasing them up on unpaid rent. I've been busy with research and overseas commitments and haven't had a chance to do the hard yards myself."

"You oversee the building yourself?" Neri asked. "You don't use a company?"

"Not anymore." Griffen shook his head with an exaggerated cringe. "I fired my last rental agency for negligence. They're the reason I'm seventeen grand out of pocket for unpaid rent. They weren't keeping track of payments and failed to do police checks. I lost all faith in them, hence why I'm in this mess."

He rocked back on his heels, his tan shorts, cream shirt, and camo-coloured Birkenstocks looking as if he'd come off a cruise ship, not from lecturing at the local university. "In fact, the whole palaver with the rental agency is why I got so excited when Jack told me about you, Aslan."

"Oh?" I frowned, keeping one eye on Neri out of habit. "How come?"

"He said you're a math nerd. That you have a real gift with numbers."

"He's the best." Neri placed her hand on my forearm proudly. "He tries to pretend he's not, but I swear he's a genius. He said numbers feel good in his brain. That he—"

"I like math, but I'm definitely not a genius." I shot her a look, scowling. No one liked a bragger. My gift with numbers filled me with pride to stay linked with my father, the math professor, but also scared me shitless that the synesthesia I suffered was yet another tie to my biological father, who I wanted nothing to do with.

"Well, I'm hoping...if you were interested, of course...that you could help me with rent collection, depreciating new appliances and upgrades, and work out how to reduce my tax bill. I've been meaning to do it for so long, but..." Griffen shrugged. "There aren't enough hours in the day."

My ears perked up. Playing with numbers appealed to me a lot more than pretending to be a proficient handyman. "I'd be happy to. To be honest, it would probably be safer to let me sort your books than your properties." I smiled, even as the strangest sensation of hope siphoned through my veins. Hope that was usually buried beneath cloying concern.

This guy, this job, this home...they all seemed too good to be true.

But I trusted Jack...

Which meant I had to learn to trust this guy too.

Perhaps the next stage of our lives wouldn't be so bad, after all.

Neri gave me a dreamy look, probably feeling the same hope I did.

Just because we'd left Jack and Anna. Just because we'd driven to Townsville in Neri's brand-new, second-hand Cherokee, and we were all alone in a city that could potentially destroy us as easily as reward us, didn't mean we had to fear everything about the future.

With a bit of luck and a lot of love, we might be able to thrive here...as a couple. As independent adults who'd committed, promised, and were ready to face our entwined lives head-on.

"I'd still appreciate if you did the renos too," Griffen said. "That would be a huge help."

I nodded, unable to let him down. "Sure. I'll do my best."

"Great!" Griffen clapped his hands. "How about you focus on getting this apartment into better shape? Then, over the next few weeks, I'll bring over the books and go over the rent for each place, the dates of payments, and lists of expenditures, and we'll see if you can do both. Handyman and accountant? I'll pay, of course. The rental agency was charging twelve percent of rent plus incidentals. I'm happy to pay you eight…cash in hand. And then an hourly rate for your labour."

My eyes bugged. "But you don't even know me."

"I know, but I have a good feeling. And what's the worst that can happen?" He shrugged as if he honestly went through life trusting every stranger he ever met. "You suck at bookkeeping and can't use a hammer to save your life? Oh well, I rented out an apartment that was just sitting empty and helped look after the daughter of a new friend." He winked. "Still a good deal. But…if you do prove to be a savant with sums and can figure out how to tackle a building as well as you tackled Jack's boat, then I have no doubt I'm gonna be the lucky one in this scenario."

"Aslan single-handedly ran Mum and Dad's research operation. They passed almost everything over to him so they could spend as much time under the waves as possible," Neri said with awe. "He can do anything."

My nape prickled with embarrassment. I really didn't like being the centre of attention or being spoken so highly of. I wanted to stay in the background, surrounded by shadows that kept me safe. "Neri, enough—"

"I'm excited." Griffen smacked his hands together again. "Right, the day isn't getting any younger, and I promised my wife, Millie, that I'd take her out for dinner, so…how about a quick tour? I'll show you the electrical mains for the twenty-four apartments, the maintenance shed with all the tools, and the shut-off valves for water, gas, etcetera. That way, you can get familiar with how things work, so it won't be quite so terrifying when I send through the list of issues that need addressing."

I held the man's stare. He seemed friendly, trustworthy, and had an ease about him that soothed my stress just enough for me to relax. A little.

"Sounds good," Neri said on my behalf, throwing me a wide-eyed look, no doubt trying to remind me to be polite and not shut down.

"This way then," Griffen announced, sweeping out of the room, expecting us to follow.

Neri gave me another piercing scowl as she padded toward the living room. I chased after them, my eyes locked on the sway of her stunning hair as Griffen's voice sailed from up ahead. "Not sure if you've ever gutted a kitchen, Aslan, but I've already ordered a new flatpack. It'll be delivered sometime next week. If you're okay with ripping this one out and installing the new one, that would be great. It's just like Ikea furniture, really, anyone can do it. Once you've got the new cabinets and Formica countertop in, I'll give you the number for the sparky and plumber to wire in the new stove and sink. Sound good?"

My ears buzzed. My brain ached.

"I, eh—"

"Sounds perfect," Neri said, falling back to pinch me. "He'll figure it out. Like I said, he always does."

"Great. Come along then." Griffen opened our front door, stepping into the ground floor corridor.

I followed my new landlord and moon-wedded wife as they headed past other apartment doors and didn't stop until we reached the maintenance rooms.

Music played in one home above me.

A baby screamed in another.

The pressure of life existing all around us made my back prickle with warning.

So many people.

So many eyes and mouths.

Too many eyes to see that I didn't belong and too many mouths to share my secret.

The black whispers did their best to twist my guts with worry.

Could I do this?

Could *we* do this?

Were we *safe* to do this?

I did my best to listen to what Griffen said. I balled my hands and told my ever-present anxiety to shut the fuck up.

This was just another sala.

This complex was just another garden.

As long as I didn't do something stupid, and no one figured out I didn't belong…I'd be fine.

Three years.

It wasn't that long.

And then Neri and I could go back home to the reef, the rainforest, and a town that didn't threaten me.

"Apartment 1A. Yes, that's right. Ground floor. Buzz the intercom when you're here, and I'll come right out." Neri nodded to whatever the pizza guy said before hanging up and sliding her phone back into the pocket of her oversized light-grey hoodie she'd slipped into an hour ago.

The sun had set, the lights had been turned on—revealing more pockmarks and stains—and we'd spent the last two hours unloading the Cherokee and dragging in the bare essentials we'd brought from Port Douglas. A blow-up mattress was now covered in blankets and pillows in the largest bedroom. Our towels hung side by side in the monstrosity of a bathroom, the kitchen held scant knives, forks, and glasses, and we'd set up the camp chairs in the living room along with the lamp and side table that Jack had told me to take from my old room.

Tomorrow, Neri and I would engage Google's help to find the local thrift stores to buy a bedframe, couch, and coffee table. We'd purchase a new mattress from the cheapest store we could, and anything else we needed we could buy online when we realised what was missing.

At least, I could do that now.

Up until recently, buying anything online was impossible for me as I didn't have a credit card. But…not only had Jack arranged this apartment for us, a job for me, and a car for Neri, he'd also kindly opened a new bank account linked to Neri's. He'd put some of my cash into it, ready to be used with a supplementary credit card number.

It didn't matter that the card had Jack's name on it, all the incomings and outgoings were mine.

I didn't think having a piece of plastic would give me such a strange peace of mind, but it did. Yet another layer of camouflage while I hid in plain sight.

"Dinner will be here in thirty minutes or so." Neri came toward me, a smile I was all too familiar with teasing her lips.

I stopped fiddling with a light switch that didn't seem to turn anything on and spun to face her. "Neri…stop with the look."

"What look?"

"You know what look."

"The look that says I'll be on my knees for you in about two seconds?"

I groaned as she rested her palms on my chest, gathering my white t-shirt in her fists. "We need to christen our new home, Aslan."

"Our new home needs a fire hose and buckets of bleach before I fuck you on any of its surfaces."

"Germaphobe."

"And proud of it."

She chuckled. "Tell you what. We can postpone sex in every room until tomorrow. I'm knackered from the long drive and really just want to have a shower, stuff copious amounts of three-cheese pizza in my face, and then crash into bed with you, but…we have to do one thing first."

I brushed gold-glittering chocolate strands off her gorgeous cheek. "And what's that, *hayatım*?"

Linking her fingers with mine, she tugged me into the centre of the living room. The two camping chairs that we'd used in Daintree flanked us. Back then, when we'd camped in a jungle and I'd almost had a panic attack at the crocs and spiders and everything else waiting to kill the love of my life, she'd been fifteen and I'd been nineteen. We'd been hot with hormones, broken by boundaries, and desperate to be together.

Now…we not only were together, but we *lived* together.

Holy fuck…we're living together.

I blinked as the reality chose that moment to slam into me.

This wasn't us messing around playing house while her parents were at a conference or research trip. There was no reason to hide and a shit ton more responsibility to pay the rent, keep ourselves fed, bathed, and properly attired to function in society.

My existence in this borrowed country might not be what I'd envisioned when I was fourteen before my world imploded. I might once have dreamed of a stone house in Foça, Izmir, following in the footsteps of my father.

But I was…happy.

Grateful.

Awestruck and frankly terrified at how much I *wanted* this.

Wanted *her*.

I would never get over my father's death. Never be able to fully hide from the nightmares of my sister and cousin being ripped from my arms or my mother's screams as she drowned.

But right here, right now, I wouldn't change a single thing because I had Neri.

She would always come first.

Always.

And I just had to trust myself that I deserved this. That my new life wouldn't just vanish like my old one. That this was where I was supposed to be.

"Kiss me, Aslan Avci. Prove to me that our life together begins now. That this is just our start, and what an exciting start it is." Raising her chin, Neri smiled softly as I stepped into her and pressed my mouth to hers.

"Your wish is my command, *aşkım*."

Her lips parted, and I groaned as her arms looped around my waist, tucking herself against my hips, pressing her belly to my rapidly hardening erection.

Fuck, this girl.

She had a spell permanently woven over me.

She had to.

There was no other explanation for how quickly she turned me on and how connected we were on every level. Spiritually, sexually, steadfastly, *eternally*.

Our tongues danced. Our noses nudged. And when she nipped my bottom lip, I grabbed the hem of her hoodie, ready to rip it off her—dirty apartment or not—but she broke our kiss and grabbed my hand. "Next room."

Dragging me dazed and aching into the falling-down forest-coloured kitchen, she whispered, "Kiss me."

I obeyed.

Losing myself in her all over again, I backed her against the damaged cutlery drawer and ground my cock against her belly.

We were both panting when she pulled away and took my hand again.

She didn't speak as she dragged me down the corridor and into the abhorrent pink bathroom. "Kiss me."

I smiled. "*Öp beni.*"

"What's that?"

Cupping her cheeks, I backed her against the vanity. "Kiss me."

Her crystal-blue gaze dove into mine as she breathed, "*Öp beni*, Aslan."

My mouth crashed on hers, making her spine arch toward the grimy tap as I kissed her exquisitely hard. Hearing her speak my tongue did things to me. Violent things.

Her right leg hooked over my hip as she rocked against me. I dry-humped against her, remembering all the times this friction was all we permitted ourselves and all the moments I'd come in my shorts just because I couldn't control myself.

She cried out as my zipper rubbed against her clit.

I lost another piece of my sanity, ready to yank up her dress and sink inside her, soap scum be damned.

Breathing hard, she pushed me away, took my hand, and guided me down the corridor.

I could barely walk with my hard-on.

My eyes were hazy. My ears ringing.

I needed more.

I needed everything.

Dragging me into the spare bedroom, she threw her arms around my shoulders, kissing me before I could kiss her. I lost another shred of my humanity as I slammed her against the dirty wall and fisted both hands in her hair.

Our kiss got dirty.

Filthy and wet and hungry.

I bit her lip. I licked her tongue. I drove both of us to breaking point.

She mewled and whimpered as I clamped both hands around her ass and hoisted her from the floor. I rocked my cock right between her legs. "I want to fuck you. Right here."

"One more room," she panted. "Have to kiss-christen one more room."

"But I need you, you tempting little siren. I said I wouldn't do this and look at the state you've put me in. Again."

She sighed with a soft giggle. "One more room and then, if you behave, I'll let you fuck me."

My stomach swooped. "Do you honestly think I need your permission when you've teased me this much? When I know how wet you are beneath that dress?"

Her stare narrowed, flashing with fire and heat. "Want to hear another fantasy, Aslan?"

I trembled. "I don't know. Do I? Will it make me come right here before I get inside you?"

"Maybe." Shrugging too innocently, she pressed her mouth to my ear and whispered, "I want you to take me without my permission one day. Just pounce on me and take me. Hard. Wild. Tie me up. Make me beg. Just like the books I read."

Slicing lust carved through my heart, chased quickly by ever-present worry. "But wouldn't that remind you too much of *him*?"

Her eyes flared. We didn't often talk about Ethan anymore. I trusted that whatever she'd accepted the night I'd run and she'd told Wayne Gratt what Ethan had done, she'd found some form of healing.

But I still worried.

Still wondered if she had nightmares like I did.

I supposed I'd soon learn if she was truly coping, seeing as we were now defacto man and wife, sharing a hearth and heart.

My thoughts turned black thinking about Ethan.

Whatever Zara had told the police and whatever software her boyfriend had used to bounce Ethan's phone number all over the world had seemed to work.

For now.

Zara hadn't shared my secret.

No threat arrived in the post or ransom to pay for her silence.

No one hammered on our door to arrest me.

There was no mention of Ethan mysteriously missing in gossip around the town.

He was an outsider.

A visitor.

He meant nothing.

"It's you, Aslan," Neri breathed. "You could never hurt me. You could do anything to me, and I would love it. I refuse to let what Ethan did steal a hot fantasy that I want to share with you. I told you...I want you to fully let go with me. I want to know how rough you'll get."

Images of how far I'd go bled through my mind, making my cock lurch and balls tighten.

There were some things I could tell my moon-given wife and some things I couldn't.

How far I truly wanted to take her was not one of those things.

I would bruise her, even bite her, but I would never give in to the black monster prowling inside me. The monster I'd inherited from another monster—a bastard who'd donated my genetic code.

Not answering her, I gathered her against me and staggered into the corridor. I kissed her as I carried her into our bedroom.

"The last room," I growled into her mouth. "And then this damn place is christened."

"Thank God," she moaned as I marched to the air mattress. "I'm going to explode."

"Let me inside you before you do. I want to feel you break." Dropping her on the bouncy bed, I crawled over her.

With one hand digging into the blankets for balance, I rucked up her dress until her white cotton knickers flashed me. With a growl, I tore them down her legs, rolling out of the cradle of her hips just long enough to remove them entirely.

We didn't say a word as I trapped her beneath me. In a rush, I unbuttoned, unzipped, shoved down my shorts and boxers, then mounted her in one quick impale.

She went rigid beneath me; her head tipped back, her well-kissed mouth wide. "God, Aslan…" She vibrated hotly around my length, fighting the explosion fizzing in our veins.

She sank into the electrical blaze between us, all while her body fought my penetration.

My eyes snapped shut as her tightness slowly gave way to invitation, letting me sink a little farther and causing Neri to melt with a seducing moan.

My cock rippled with a release.

Ever since I'd given in and come inside her without moving—ever since we'd shared the most connected, intense moment of our lives on *The Fluke*, I'd had a terrible time of controlling myself.

The moment my body joined with Neri's, lust became unbearable and the very primal, very brutal urge to spill inside her ensured every muscle locked with need. Gritting my teeth, I refused to become a one-thrust wonder.

I hissed under my breath as Neri's inner muscles milked me.

"Fuck, you're as close as I am," I growled.

I fucking loved she was as sensitive and responsive as me. It was yet another sign we were destined. Another truth that her blood sang to my blood and her body vibrated with the same knowledge that we belonged.

Her teeth sank into her bottom lip as I withdrew and thrust back into her.

She cried out.

Her pussy clenched.

Her forehead furrowed as she tried to fight off bliss. "Let me calm down. I don't want to—"

"Give in. I don't want you to stop." I bit her throat as she arched again. "I love having you on a knife-edge. I love that my kisses turn you on just as much as my fingers and cock."

"Aslan, stop that."

"Neri, stop what? Talking dirty?"

"Yes, that. You know what it does to me." She squirmed beneath me as I ground her deeper into the air mattress.

"I know it makes you wet. I know it makes you desperate. I know it turns you mindless. I could do whatever I wanted to you, and you'd let me."

She gasped as her entire body jerked. "Aslan—"

"My cock is deep inside you, *aşkım benim*. Can you feel me? Stretching you? Throbbing inside you? I can feel every ripple and every flicker of your pussy. I own you, Nerida. I own every part of you when you're wet and spread for my pleasure."

I drove inside her. "I fucking love being inside you. Watching my body vanish into yours, riding you, fucking you, marking you as mine."

"Ah, fuck..." She bowed in my arms, her fingernails digging into my shoulders.

"Come, *canım*. I want to feel you explode."

She scratched my upper back, biting her bottom lip like a siren-turned-vampire. "But I want to last—"

"I'm not going to give you a choice." Folding over her, I took her mouth again, all while my hips pistoned into hers. My back rolled, using my height to pump ruthless and determined, plunging my body into hers, again and again, driving us both fucking wild.

"Oh God. Oh *God*." Her breathing turned shallow as I drilled her into the bouncy, jiggling air mattress, not giving her a chance to fight me.

"Come for me. Come, Neri. Fucking come all over me so I can." My head fell forward; my teeth found her neck. I bit her as I fucked her like an animal and groaned with spine-cracking pleasure-pain as she screamed and let go.

This time, it wasn't a ripple but a lashing earthquake that fisted me.

Her moans became heinously erotic as I thrust and pumped, nailing my young wife to the unstable mattress.

"*Fuck*, Aslan!"

I clamped my hand over her lips. "Quiet. You'll scare the neighbours."

Her eyes widened, then shot with blue wildfire as I rode her through the rest of her orgasm before giving in to the lightning crackling up my length.

Only once I knew she was sated. Only once I knew her body was completely accepting of my punishment did I let go.

I growled and turned feral.

Driving again and again, pumping, fucking, treating her roughly in bed when in every other aspect, I bowed before her. While I had her like this, legs spread, pussy wet, whimpers in her throat and lust in her eyes, I stopped treating her like my queen and fucked her right into the gutter where we belonged.

I roared as my release broke every bone in my body.

The jerks of my cock made me see fucking stars.

Hot splashes.

Blistering spurts.

Pouring into her.

Marking her.

Branding her so that pieces of me would be with her when she started school the day after tomorrow. I wanted her to smell like me. I wanted her skin to reek of sex and her aura to scream to every guy that she was well and truly claimed.

The last shudder of my release made me breathless. Neri moaned as I drove a final time into her, my ears ringing as the intercom buzzer went off and the tinny voice of a delivery man shouted, "*Pizza's here!*"

I sucked on air as Neri wriggled beneath me, her legs trying to scissor closed even while my cock stayed locked deep inside her. She kissed my nose with fleeting affection that broke my miserable heart all over again.

"Our first sexy times in our new house." She beamed. "And now our first dinner! Best night *ever!*" Planting another adoring kiss on my five o'clock-shadowed cheek, she shoved me, trying to push me off her. "Now disengage, my lusty lion. I need to go get our food."

I nipped her throat, thrusting once more for good measure. I loved her when she was like this. So young and free. She reminded me of her twelve-year-old self. The little sea sprite who'd stolen my heart with a single look.

"*Seni çok seviyorum,* Nerida Avci."

She stilled and fell back. Her pussy clenched around me; our eyes locked with so much more than just passion. She looked at me with eternity, and I looked at her with perpetuity, both of us knowing this wasn't just the beginning of this life. It was the beginning of all of them. An infinite number of existences that always ended up with her inside me and me inside her.

"*Seni çok seviyorum,* Aslan Kara. I love you so, *so* much." She reached up to kiss me, soothing the shock of her using my true name. Her tongue entered my mouth. I grew drunk on her—

Buzz, buzz, buzz of the intercom. "*Pizza! Anyone coming or what?*"

Neri laughed against my lips then, with a sharp shove, she pushed me onto my back. "Dinner's calling. Get off me, you oaf." My unwilling body withdrew from hers, and I groaned as she shot to her feet, snatched up her underwear from the dirty floor, shimmied back into them, and skipped down the corridor.

I glanced down at my arousal-glistening cock, wincing at the oversensitivity still stinging in my blood. A sated smirk twisted my lips. We'd only been in this place a couple of hours, and Neri had already made me snap.

I took her warning from when she'd sucked me off in the car seriously.

If she planned on making me take her as often as we'd fucked when Jack and Anna were away…I definitely needed to drink more water.

Chapter Twelve

ASLAN

(*Heart in Thai:* Hạwcı)

IT TOOK ME A MONTH TO COMPLETE the kitchen renovation.

An embarrassingly long time but, in my defence, I'd literally never used a crowbar, drill, or hammer in my life. The first week, I did what Griffen had suggested and took time to get our life sorted before work became my top priority.

I bussed with Neri to the university on her first day, kissed her goodbye, waited until she'd vanished into the sprawling campus, then hopped back on a bus to head to the closest supermarket.

We'd both agreed I wouldn't drive her Jeep unless necessary. Not having a license already put me at risk, but couple that with the whole illegal thing, and it just wasn't worth it. The buses would do, and the Cherokee could hang out in its carport until we returned to Port Douglas for a visit.

At the huge supermarket, I bought as many cleaning supplies as I could carry and got to work disinfecting the apartment. By the time Neri had finished her first week, going through orientation, meeting her professors, and getting the feel of how her life would be for the next three years, I'd ensured our home was clean enough to fuck on every surface and even eat off if we were so inclined.

The second week, Griffen paid me a visit one afternoon as I raided his shed of tools in the corner of the small communal garden and did my best to dismantle the forest-drab kitchen.

I'd ripped off the doors, the drawer fronts, and somehow managed to remove the sink and countertop by the time he popped his head in, carrying a massive box of paperwork. He'd laughed at my misuse of his tools, given me a crash course on what did what, then helped me remove the rest of the cabinets and gross linoleum from the floor.

It'd been nice working side by side.

Nice to meet another guy who seemed just as kind and friendly as Jack.

Once most of the mess was in the skip he'd hired outside, he'd patted me on the back, cracked open two beers, then dragged me to the dining table Neri and I had bought at a local thrift store for a hundred bucks. He'd sat on one of the mismatching chairs that needed reupholstering and upended the box of papers.

For three days, I'd gone through each tenant's contract, stolen one of Neri's empty workbooks, and made my own notes on renewal lease dates, payable rent, overheads of rates and insurance, and all the maintenance issues that needed attending to.

To think I'd been afraid of being bored moving here...

Fuck me, I missed Jack and Anna's dawn starts and long days at sea. That was hard work but this? This responsibility of learning how to run payments, budgets, and oversee a building that needed a fair bit of work was both brain-taxing and body-breaking.

My mind finally had something to wrangle.

I found myself sinking into the joy of playing with numbers, working out depreciation, and how much it would save Griffen on his tax bill if he installed a new roof this year instead of next.

Neri had bought me a calculator, but I didn't use it.

I preferred the colours in my brain and the satisfaction of an answer given to me through whatever gift I'd been born with.

The days apart from Neri went blessedly fast, and the separation didn't hurt too much as she shared her nights with me and I shared mine with her. We ensured we ate dinner together every evening—sometimes I cooked, sometimes she did, and sometimes we got takeaways and broke all our rules to eat it in bed. We'd indulge in pizza and watch a shitty movie on the second-hand TV we'd hung on our bedroom wall after I'd patched the holes and painted the room a nice calming grey. The paint was called Seafog, and I liked to think it reminded Neri of the early dawn starts as mist shimmered in the rising sun, making the entire ocean glimmer with water magic.

At least we'd deflated the air mattress on our third night here, trading it in for a king-sized dense piece of foam that fit perfectly on the teak bedframe with elephants carved into the headboard that we'd found behind a bunch of other unwanted furniture in a local Sallies.

I'd never been more content.

Hard work kept me sane.

Numbers kept me happy.

And having something to do while Neri went off to study gave me something to think about without worrying too much about her.

After that first month, once I'd reassembled the kitchen with white glossy cabinets, brand new oven, stainless sink, and matte black tap, I'd felt like I'd accomplished something.

Jack and Anna drove down to check out our place, and we'd spent the weekend exploring Townsville. I'd almost managed to forget that even though I was a part of this amazing Australian family, I wasn't truly one of them.

Despite my ring on Neri's finger and all the vows we uttered late at night, we couldn't get married or buy a house in my name.

Those reasons used to prevent me from being with Neri.

Now they were just things to ignore.

Just like my dead family and the reason we'd fled Turkey.

If I ignored them, they left me alone, but I was never truly free of them.

Jack and Anna opted to stay in a hotel rather than in our second unfinished bedroom, and we all went out for brunch on Sunday before they headed back to Port Douglas.

For the rest of the day, I watched Neri carefully, waiting to see if she'd be sad or homesick, but she merely kissed me a little harder, snuggled a little closer, and sighed into this new journey we were on.

By month two, I'd torn out the bathroom, getting quicker with my demolition skills and savvier with my rebuild. I watched a shit ton of YouTube videos, saving countless building channels on my phone and sitting in the cracked pink bath for far longer than I'd admit, trying to figure out how to remove the caulking and rip out the offending tub.

Griffen ordered a new wooden vanity with a porcelain bowl, brand-new toilet, and boxes full of tiles resembling mermaid scales. He'd tasked me with replacing the bath for a large walk-in shower and glass screen.

Neri hadn't been happy that I'd removed the bath, but...I would've had a fit if she'd wallowed in that cesspit. I compromised with her and fucked her in the newly tiled shower. I kneeled between her legs as she stood with water streaming over her head and plunged my tongue inside her, tasting her desire, my cock agonisingly hard, her hands buried in my drenched hair to keep herself from falling.

After I'd given her two orgasms and claimed two of my own, I took her swimming at The Strand. We went to the beach as many times a week as we could. And if I'd ever been under the impression that Neri wasn't part sea creature herself, it became glaringly obvious whenever we headed to the ocean.

The way she'd step into the lapping waves as if they were old friends. The longing kind of sigh that echoed with homesickness for the sea rather than her parents. The way she'd shiver with delight as she'd walk deeper into the brine, almost as if the salt changed the acidity of her blood, giving her back a piece of herself that she lost while on land.

I'd wait for her on our towels, heart hurting, mind whispering, bones cracking beneath everything I refused to deal with and all the feelings I drowned with. I'd once become a master of pushing aside my grief and barricading myself off from loss. But now, Neri was the master of me, and my every thought, my every need, wish, and desire all centred on her.

If I ever lost her…

Balling my hands, I shoved aside that black, depressing thought. I'd become a master of that too. A master of ignoring the heavy fog inside me that suffocated at the oddest moments.

I was happy.

Far happier than I'd been for years, yet…something inside me refused to heal. It sat sulking in darkness, hissing filth that I didn't deserve this, didn't deserve her, didn't deserve this life I'd been given because of where I'd come from.

I probably overcompensated in my worship of Neri, not because I'd lost every part of me to her, but because I used her to hide from the pieces I didn't want to acknowledge.

What I did to Ethan…

The ease with which I'd cut off his fingers.

The sick satisfaction that'd run through me as I kicked him overboard…

That part of me was dangerous, cold-hearted, and disgustingly violent.

I hated that it existed but was grateful for it too.

Grateful that I would happily sink to any level to protect Neri, all while terror filled me that the more I embraced that side of myself, the harder it would be to stay good.

By the third month of our new life, we found a rhythm that worked for both of us. She settled into her studies and shared stories of her fellow students and teachers. She complained about the number of hours spent in a lab and moaned that her eyes were sore from peering into microscopes.

Some days, she'd be given lab work that meant she had to stay past class time, using the equipment on campus to get her work done.

Those nights were the worst.

I loved that she was so diligent and dedicated to her calling, but I couldn't settle if the sun was down and Neri wasn't safely in our apartment. I turned to numbers on those nights, losing myself in setting up automatic payments for Griffen's tenants and teaching myself the tax software that was said to make paying GST easier.

True to his word, Griffen dropped an envelope of cash into our letterbox every Monday morning on his way to the university, paying me for my time. When the first money came in for a full month of gathering his rent, sending reminders to those behind, and figuring out a depreciation avenue that he hadn't been using, I'd almost dropped to my knees at the amount.

Eight percent of all the rent gathered, plus my time renovating.

Fuck me.

I'd never held so much in one pay packet.

And just like before, I had nothing I wanted to spend it on.

Nothing but Neri.

As I'd tripped in a daze back to our rapidly improving apartment, I'd been struck with an idea. Once Neri had gone to uni for the day, I ignored the risk of going out in public and headed downtown. The cash burned a hole in my pocket as I hunted through every electronic and science shop I could find before I stumbled on what I was looking for.

I'd taken the chance of paying cash so Neri wouldn't see the transaction on our shared card and spent almost all of my earnings on my wonderful wife.

I'd gotten home before Neri and carried the many bags into the spare room that I'd painted, disinfected, and hung new silver drapes in. It wasn't furnished as we had no need for a second room, but now…I had a plan.

Hiding what I'd bought in the wardrobe, I'd made Neri her favourite meal—pesto pasta with mushrooms and parmesan—then went online and found a perfect desk while she did her homework at our battered dining room table.

The next day when she went to uni, I distracted myself with chores around the complex, keeping an eye out for the delivery. The van turned up just before three p.m., giving me enough time to assemble the glass desk and set up the spare room with a brand-new microscope, glass slides, beakers, droppers, storage vials, labels, and a drawer full of litmus tests.

It wasn't a full lab.

The microscope wasn't nearly high-end enough for most of her studies.

But I wanted her to have a space to work, like her parents did in their house.

She'd leaped into my arms as I dropped my hands from her eyes and showed her what I'd done.

To say that I got lucky that night was an understatement.

Neri took one look at the home lab—as rudimentary as it was—dropped to her knees, yanked my shorts down, and had me down her throat before I'd even grasped the doorframe for balance.

It didn't matter how many times we touched, licked, fucked, or kissed, we couldn't get enough of each other.

I kept waiting for our need to simmer, but it never did.

It stayed just as hot, just as needy, and the daily separation meant I'd get instantly hard at the sound of her key in the door, and she'd get instantly naked as she found me scribbling down numbers or dripping in sweat from renovating.

By the time six months had rolled around, our apartment was fully done, and I'd begun work on the place two levels above us, I stopped on the stairs on the way to sign for yet another hardware and timber delivery and froze.

Somehow, life had lulled me into believing I was free.

That my signature on the deliveryman's paperwork was as legitimate as Griffen Yule's. That my ring on Neri's finger made her mine in the eyes of

Australian law. That the cash I was paid gave me permission to live and work here.

But none of that was true.

I might be anonymous.

No one might care that I wasn't one of them.

The amount of work Griffen gave me might leave no free time to think about the day when this incredible fairy-tale blew up in my face.

But in that stairwell, the black whispers came back with a vengeance.

All the worry I'd been too exhausted to notice or too skilled at suppressing roared back into existence.

All the questions I'd refused to ask about how long I could remain hidden in this city crushed my heart like a six-tonne killer whale.

I couldn't shake the feeling that something was waiting, just out of sight.

Something was coming.

Something was hunting.

Something was after...me.

Chapter Thirteen

NERIDA

AGE: 19 YRS OLD

(Love in Thai: Rạk)

TEDDY: *WHAT DO YOU THINK OF THESE schematics? I took your sketches of the underwater spheres and looked into what material they could be made from. The glass would have to be thick enough to withstand water pressure and the seals reliable enough to stay waterproof. But that doesn't address how they could be secured to the reef, how they could be linked to other spheres, or even how oxygen could be circulated. This is a lot fucking harder than I thought. We've been at this for months and still have no idea how we can make it happen.*

I paused chopping capsicum for our spaghetti bolognese and replied.

Me: *I recently rewatched my favourite TV show as a kid,* Ocean Girl. *They have an entire research lab beneath the water attached to a rig on the surface. They have different water locks in case of flooding and different purification systems for waste, water, air, etc. I know it's fantastical, and the special effects are old school now, but it has merit. You should watch it with Eddie. It'll probably give you guys some ideas.*

I smiled as I added another message.

Me: *Plus, the main character is called Neri, and her best friend is a humpback whale called Charlie. My parents swear they didn't call me after that character, but I always made up that I was an alien like her from a water planet and that I could sing whale songs.*

Teddy: *You are the biggest dork I've ever met. And if you want to be an alien, congratulations, you're an alien. Never met anyone as odd.*

Me: *Hey! I'm the coolest person you know.*

Teddy: *Pfft, says who?*

Me: *Honey. My soul sister.*

Teddy: *Hands off my sister. Mine. Not yours. I heard about your past of stealing siblings.*

Me: *Don't worry. I'll just borrow her from you. Besides, pretty sure she loves me more than she loves you at this point.* *snicker

"Teddy again?" Aslan asked, padding barefoot into the kitchen, running a hand through his longish, wet hair from a shower. He'd dressed in a pair of track pant shorts that hung off his trim hips, teased with his happy trail, and clung to the mouth-watering bulge between his legs.

"Yep." I couldn't take my eyes off him. "He's still moaning about the lack of suitable building supplies."

"Tell him he'll have to design something himself if he truly wants to do this. Nothing in today's building supplies will work." He scratched his five o'clock shadow. "Believe me, plywood, Gib board, metal, glass—none of it will be strong or durable enough. Tell him to put his fancy degree to work and design the materials before the structure."

"God, I find you so sexy when you talk like that."

He chuckled. "Like what?"

"So assured. So confident."

"Glad you find me sexy, *aşkım benim.* I suffer the same affliction whenever I look at you." His teeth dug into his bottom lip as he looked me up and down. "Sexiest woman I've ever met."

Liquid heat flushed between my legs.

God, when would I stop falling into a lusty stupor around this man?

When would my heart stop kicking and my stomach stop clenching?

Never.

That was the answer.

Never.

Even the therapist Wayne Gratt recommended was pleasantly surprised that my desire for Aslan had never waned, even after what Ethan had done to me. My libido was well and truly healthy, even though I could've shut down all forms of intimacy.

We'd had a few sessions via Zoom, and she'd given me some visualization techniques for those sneaky moments that made me doubt myself. I hadn't told Aslan, but sometimes, just sometimes, bussing home at night—if I'd stayed longer than normal at uni—brought back unresolved fear.

On later nights, Aslan offered to pick me up in the Cherokee, but I had mild panic attacks of him driving around Townsville without me. What if he was stopped again? What if they realised who he was, and I came home to an empty house and no idea where they'd taken him?

I'd rather take the bus, even in the dark.

Besides, nothing had ever happened on those bus rides, and my fellow students were nothing but nice. All of us shared a love of animals, the desire to make the oceans a better place, and the ethics to work hard to complete our life's purpose.

It annoyed me that I couldn't control those pesky day terrors that could pounce from nowhere for no reason. But thanks to my therapist, Maureen, and her expertise and kind ear, I'd learned it would take time for my psyche to fully let go.

A full year we'd lived here.

A year that had been one of the best of my life.

Aslan had fully embraced becoming a building manager. Griffen regularly stopped by with awe in his eyes at how neat and improved his complex was. Aslan had muscles that he'd never had before from hauling heavy timber and using a sledgehammer to break apart kitchens and bathrooms, and he'd even bought a cheap pair of reading glasses when we were last in town as he complained his eyes were getting tired looking at numbers late at night.

There hadn't been a single moment of my life that I didn't think Aslan wasn't the hottest man alive. Yet when he'd put on those black-framed glasses?

Fuck me sideways, I was *not* responsible for the way I jumped him.

It was his fault the chair legs broke beneath him as I launched myself into his lap.

His fault that we crashed to the floor in a tangle of limbs and heat, and somehow ended up with him behind me, me on my hands and knees, and him riding me painfully hard amongst the rubble of the broken chair.

We hadn't even closed the drapes. Anyone in the communal garden would've seen.

But I didn't care.

And by the way he'd roared as he came inside me, he hadn't cared either.

It was a nightly effort for me not to pounce on him whenever he put those glasses on. I knew he probably needed a proper check-up and visit an optometrist, but without ID or a Medicare number…I didn't know if he'd be asked uncomfortable questions or if records of his test would be saved on systems that could ruin his secret life on our shores.

He'd never once seen a dentist. Never needed a doctor (thank God), and it was getting to the point where we stopped thinking about all the things he couldn't do because we were lucky enough to find things he could.

He was a valued employee.

He'd made us a beautiful home.

He saved almost every penny, so we were financially comfortable even while I was a poor student. He paid all the bills by giving me his cash. I'd deposit it into our joint account that my dad set up for us. Internet, rent, and power came out automatically, and we usually did a large grocery shop each week on a Sunday.

I didn't care I might one day be audited and asked where the lump sum payments came from. I'd rather get in trouble for tax evasion than have him deported back to Cem Kara.

Aslan sniffed the air, dipping his finger into the sauce simmering on the stove. Sampling the flavours, he sucked his finger clean. "Yum. Need any help?" Coming toward me, I shivered as he kissed me, placing his large, hot hand on my lower back, stinging me with the crackle of energy that always flowed between us, branding me through my floaty yellow sundress.

"Nah, I'm good. Go sit down and relax. My turn to cook." I smiled, completely forgetting what I'd been talking about with Teddy and even forgetting how to freaking cook.

He gave me another kiss, sending my pulse quickening.

"*Teşekkürler*, Neri. Thank you for feeding me."

The gruff gratefulness in his tone. The overwhelming love in his eyes.

It made me ravenous for other things.

My gaze shot to the sauce.

I'll turn that off. It'll be fine for twenty minutes while I feast on—

"Don't even think about it." Aslan tapped the end of my nose with his finger. "You had me when you came home from uni. You didn't even let me have a shower first, and I was fucking filthy from crawling all over the roof. You made me hungry, and now it's your turn to sate that hunger. And in case you're thinking dirty things, I mean food, *hayatım*."

"But I'm hungry too. For you."

"You'll just have to be patient."

"Spoilsport," I whispered. "Saying no to your horny wife? Shame on you." I pouted. He had no defence against me when I fluttered my eyelashes and stuck out my bottom lip. "*Lütfen*, Aslan."

"Say please all you want. You can beg me in Turkish all night long, and I'll still make you wait."

"What if I showed you how hot I get hearing you speak to me in Turkish?" I slowly gathered the material of my dress.

His eyes flashed. His hands balled. Tension exploded between us.

With a groan, he backed away and pinched the bridge of his nose. "You're insatiable."

"I thought we'd already established this."

He laughed under his breath as he dropped his hand.

I went to him, grabbed that hand, and brought it beneath my dress.

I shivered as his fingers grazed over my wet underwear.

His legs almost buckled. His eyes turned black. "*Her seferinde, karıcığım. Her seferinde bedeninle, gülümsemenle, öpücüğünle bana sahip oluyorsun.*" His lips found mine as he rubbed my clit.

"What did you say?" I parted my legs, encouraging him to take more.

With a snarl, he pulled his hand away and stepped back. "I said...every time, wife. Every time you own me with your body, your smile, your kiss." Licking his fingers from my taste, he groaned. "Thanks to you, I now drink copious amounts of water, yet somehow, I'm still thirsty."

My gaze dropped to his shorts, my heart racing with need. "Then you probably shouldn't wear workout shorts that provide a full view of what you're refusing to give me."

His eyebrows raised as he dropped his chin down his bare, droplet-glittering chest. It should be illegal how toned he was. How the ridges and valleys, shadows and etches carved his flesh from mortal to myth. "You can't see anything."

I laughed. "I can see that you're tucked to the right with a semi. I can see the outline as clear as day. So if I ever catch you wearing those shorts around anyone else but me, we're gonna have a problem."

His eyes flared with crackling heat, making the kitchen blaze. "No one else would know how I'm tucked, Neri. Only you because you're obsessed with it."

"More than obsessed." I picked up the knife and waved it in the air. "Stabby if anyone else touches what's mine."

He groaned again and chuckled. "I shouldn't find that as hot as I do."

"Have a fetish for knives, Aslan?"

"I have a fetish for you." Sucking on his bottom lip, he went to the fridge, pulled out a beer and a Sprite for me, then stalked back toward me. Placing the ice-cold can beside the chopping board, he leaned in and blew the softest stream of air on my neck.

I shivered as if an earthquake tore through my body.

"Cook me dinner, çiçeğim, and perhaps I'll give you dessert."

I jumped as my phone danced around the counter, buzzing with an incoming FaceTime. The lust in my system scratched through me, making me itch and twitch.

Aslan glanced at the screen, a soft smile teasing his lips. "Should I get jealous of how often you guys talk?"

"I mainly talk about you, so no." I kissed his lips, schooled my aching needs, and accepted the call. Leaning my phone against the saltshaker, I blew Aslan another kiss as he went to the sun-faded grey couch and flopped down.

I returned to chopping capsicum. "Honey. Hi!"

"Why is Teddy messaging me demanding to know where my loyalties lie?" She rested her chin on her hands, leaning into the camera with a wrinkled nose.

I laughed at her attempt to be serious, grinning as Billy appeared on the screen and kissed Honey on the top of her head.

"You again?" He rolled his eyes. "I swear there are three people in my relationship."

"Try four," Honey said. "Me, Neri, you, and Aslan."

"Isn't it more like six, though?" I chuckled. "Can't forget Teddy and Eddie."

"Are you riling him up again, Nee? He said that I like you more than him, and now he's packed a sad."

"He knows I love him just as much."

Honey grinned. "Silly boy gives his heart away to everyone and then expects to hoard everyone's heart in return."

"He can have a tiny piece of mine on loan." I looked up, catching Aslan's endless stare. "Aslan owns all of it. Always has. Always will."

"Don't start." Billy groaned. "I can't deal with you two." He rolled his eyes again. "I feel like I know more about your relationship than I should with how Honey prattles on about you guys."

"Same here!" Aslan shouted from the couch. "Hi, Billy!"

"Hi, mate." Billy held up his hand, his plaid shirt stained on the cuffs from working. Picking up my phone, I shoved the screen toward the living room, letting the boys see each other.

Aslan toasted Honey's boyfriend with his beer.

I didn't know how it'd happened, but we'd gotten into the habit of having drinks together over FaceTime. Honey and Billy had come to visit us a few months ago, sleeping on the air mattress in the second bedroom-turned-lab that Aslan had so wonderfully made for me, and Honey and I had been beside ourselves that our significant others got along so well.

For the first time in his life, Aslan had a male friend who wasn't old enough to be his father. We'd spent most of their visit in bars that didn't ask for ID, eating fried foods and sharing jugs of slightly flat beer, chatting about everything and anything.

The ease between Honey and me was unexplainable.

I'd loved Zara.

I still did, even though I flatly refused to rekindle our friendship.

But Honey was different.

She seemed special.

Just like Aslan was special.

"How was work?" Aslan asked, sitting taller and shifting on the couch to face my phone.

"Yeah, okay. Keep thinking the commissions will dry up from selling expensive tractors, diggers, and farm equipment with the state of the world right now, but nope. Farmers are still spending big bucks. Gotta feed the masses somehow, I guess."

"That's good." Aslan smiled, taking a drink. "Gets you one step closer to your own farm."

"That it does, mate. Can't wait for that day." Billy smacked a kiss on Honey's head. "Can't wait to knock this one up and have her making me little worker bees. She can be barefoot and pregnant, and I'll work the land. Don't care that I'm not supposed to say that with all this political correctness bullshit. Honey wants kids, and I want to provide. We'll be in our version of heaven."

Aslan's coal-dark gaze shot to mine.

His intense look fisted my heart, and I didn't understand it. Was he envisioning our future? One where I was barefoot and pregnant on a boat somewhere, or perhaps living under the sea?

With a swallow that flexed the tendons in his neck, Aslan cleared his throat but didn't say anything.

Was he thinking of all the things that could go wrong? Fearing that a typical dream for others might not happen for us?

If I did have his child, what name did I put under 'father' on the birth certificate?

Could his be listed, or would that put him at risk?

You're nineteen.

By the time you're both ready for children, he'll be legal, and everything will be fine.

An awkward silence fell; my pulse skittered. "Anyway…" I turned my phone back to face me, resting it against the saltshaker again. "I need to finish cooking, so you'll just have to watch me while we chat. I want my dessert and can't get it unless I feed my man."

"Is dessert code for cock by any chance?" Honey giggled.

"Oh, Jesus, and this is where I leave." Billy backed away, waving at me. "Bye, Neri. Bye, Aslan!"

He vanished from the shot, and I slipped into a happy evening of cooking, talking to my best friend, and stealing stares at my delicious sexy man as he put his glasses on, pulled up a math problem on a second-hand tablet we'd bought together, and settled into the numbers he loved so much.

What a wonderful night.

What a wonderful life.

What a shame that soon, it would just be a memory.

A memory with the power to kill me.

Chapter Fourteen

ASLAN

(*Heart in Swahili:* Moyo)

TWO YEARS.

On the one hand, time shot by in a whirlwind of study, renos, work, parental visits, and sex that never failed to draw us closer. On the other, time had turned into my enemy, aging me from twenty-two to twenty-three to twenty-four, ensuring the more years I lived in Australia overshadowed the years I'd lived in Turkey.

I spoke my language often.

I shared my culture with Neri regularly.

But I couldn't help feeling that a part of me that belonged to a different country, a different life, was slowly dying the longer I lived in Australia. The sun and salt were a part of me now. I might not ever earn a passport or call myself an Aussie, but I felt at home here.

A home that we'd made, just the two of us.

For two years, we lived together in wedded bliss. We hardly ever fought; we supported one another, looked after one another, and kept falling into deeper levels of love.

Each day, Neri took me by surprise—bringing home a matching shell to the one she'd given me when she was fourteen. Or waking me up with her lips trailing kisses down my belly. Or feeding me painkillers when I rolled my ankle after a stupid mistake on the stairs.

Each little, caring thing she did made me fall a little more.

There was no bottom.

No end.

If I was ever taken away from her or she was taken away from me, I wouldn't fucking survive it.

Luckily, we were safe for now.

We had no enemies to fight and no murderous fathers to run from. Our biggest stresses were grocery shopping when neither of us wanted to do it, and whose turn it was to do the laundry.

Griffen kept our rent ridiculously low and continued paying me a substantial amount for my time. He no longer guided me in how he wanted things to be run but trusted that if I implemented a new system, it was because it was better than the old one. I learned how to order police checks on new tenants, arrange bonds, and even organised taking a tenant to tribunal for wilful damages to a newly renovated apartment.

I did everything under his name.

Nothing under mine.

He gave me his logins to business bank accounts so I could track payments and set up direct debits for his tax. Considering I wasn't legal, I knew more about Australian rental laws and tax obligations than most of its citizens.

Jack and Anna popped down to visit when they could.

Billy and I grew friendly enough to share a few messages in the odd times that we didn't have all-night calls with our two girls monopolising most of the conversation. Those nights, alcohol would be consumed, a movie shared on Netflix, and the sense that our little life of two had expanded to include friends.

Fuck, I had a friend.

My own age.

I honestly didn't think I'd get close to anyone apart from Neri. It wasn't easy confiding in someone who might say the wrong thing to the wrong person and be the reason everything crashed and burned.

I'd grown used to guarding myself, and regardless of how close Honey and Neri became and how much I valued Billy's friendship, and even Teddy and Eddie as they became regular visitors in our apartment—thanks to the ease of internet and smart-phones—I never told them the truth.

No one asked.

Why would they?

Like most people I dealt with—the tenants, the tradies, and the outside world—no one ever looked at me as if I didn't belong. The endless fear I'd always had that somehow a stranger would be able to look at me and just *know* that I wasn't permitted faded as I grew older.

I did my best to say goodbye to depression and hello to optimism. Most days, I succeeded. When I felt pride for a job well done and bliss as I came brutally hard in Neri's arms, I didn't have to choose to be happy.

I *was* happy.

That kid inside me who'd always been worried, always grieving, always guilty for living his life when his family was dead had healed enough to enjoy every moment.

Neri had a magic that never failed to get me out of my head and into my heart. With her, I was wholly present and wonderfully grateful.

She was the one.

Not because of coincidence or convenience.

But because she was born for me and me for her.

She was *mine.*

I was so proud of how hard she worked on her bachelor's degree. How many nights she sacrificed to homework and how often she put up her hand for extra learning. In her second year, she spent more time on the sea with her fellow students, travelling on the university's research vessel to Magnetic Island to study the reef, and farther out where the coral dropped away and bigger creatures lived.

By night, she studied heavy books full of chemistry and biology, learning the makeup of plants and ecosystems, gradually transforming from the eager-eyed child who wanted to be like her parents into a fully-fledged scientist in her own right.

Her hair changed colours with the tides, depending on if she spent time in the salt and sun, and she grew ever more beautiful every year.

For her nineteenth birthday last year, we'd gone out for a nice dinner and rented a hotel for the night that had an indoor pool.

We'd snuck inside once it was closed to guests and swam until one a.m., reliving those wonderful evenings in her back garden where I'd craved her, wanted her, but never touched her.

Now I touched her so often it was borderline obsessive.

Our need for each other hadn't tamed. If anything, it grew more poignant between us as we left behind the last remnants of youth and stepped into the adults we were destined to become.

I loved growing with her.

I loved maturing with her.

I loved who we grew into *because* of each other.

On the night of her birthday, after we'd swum and petted beneath the water, I timed her breath-hold like old times.

She'd sunk to the bottom like a fallen starfish, and I'd dangled my legs off the edge. She'd only lasted four minutes and had been distraught that for all her practicing, the past two years of uni and not having a bath to practice in robbed her ability of going over six minutes.

I'd hated the despair in her eyes. That loss.

And I'd made it my mission to make her remember that all things came in balance. The more energy you put into something, the faster you got what you wanted. She could get her freaky ability to hold her breath again once she'd graduated.

For now, her focus was studying.

But that night, I made sure her only focus was on me.

We hadn't slept.

And if the hotel staff knew what we got up to in that room, I had no doubt they'd burn the loveseat, bleach the carpets, and wipe down the windows. Neri's handprint on the glass as I'd pumped into her from behind while we'd looked down at the city below was still smeared when we left the next morning, returning to the perfect life we'd carved out for ourselves.

I expected Neri home in an hour or so.

She thought it would just be a typical Friday night for us, but I planned on enacting a scene from one of her dirty romance books tonight in honour of her third and final year at university.

She'd been back at classes for one week.

We'd been back in town since last Sunday after spending the holidays in Port Douglas with her parents. It'd been an idyllic month of sex, sun, and sand. Neri had slept with me in my sala-bedroom, cuddled close on my old double bed, hidden from parental eyes in a gazebo that'd seen better days.

Almost eight years since I'd become an honorary Taylor and four years since I first kissed Neri at the Craypot. My ring on her finger hadn't magically permitted us to get married, but our wedding beneath the moon was enough for now.

One more year and we could return to Port Douglas for good.

I shared Neri's excitement at going home. As grateful as I was to Griffen for his faith in me, his generous payments, and the full-time job of running his tenants and property, I missed being outdoors. I missed being on the water—not because I'd finally forgiven the ocean, but because I preferred Neri sun-drenched and sea-dripping.

She belonged out there, and I belonged with her.

According to Neri, Teddy and Eddie had actively started looking for houses to buy in Port Douglas to be closer for when she finished her degree. They'd all been getting steadily frustrated with the lack of progression on their joint venture of underwater living, and Teddy decided he needed daily inspiration from the Great Barrier Reef if he and Eddie were ever going to come up with the building materials necessary to turn the impossible into possible.

Even Billy and Honey were looking at farms on the outskirts of Cairns, dabbling with the idea of leaving Sydney behind so they could be closer to Honey's brother, brother-in-law, and us.

Neri and I weren't the only committed ones in this strange six-some. Teddy and Eddie had gotten married last year, and Billy had proposed to Honey three months ago when he'd earned enough for a downpayment on a decent-sized property.

So much to celebrate.

So much to be thankful for.

Including my kinky wife.

Stepping into our apartment after spending the day installing yet another kitchen, I dumped my keys onto the bashed-up dining table that we still hadn't bothered replacing.

Rolling out the kinks in my spine, I pulled out my phone and checked the time.

Neri would be finishing class by now and coming home to me.

I better hurry.

I'd ordered a few toys.

I'd hidden them in our wardrobe.

I'd been trying to get up the guts to give her what she wanted for months now, still terrified of letting myself fully go in case I couldn't stop. But last night, I'd read the book she'd been devouring, and had to admit, some of those scenes were fucking hot. As long as I could keep the monstrous part of myself tamed, I could give her what she wanted.

I could tie her up.

I could bind her, blind her, and treat her as if she was nothing more to me than a wet, willing possession.

I gritted my teeth as my cock reacted.

Heading toward the sliding doors, I yanked the curtains tightly, blocking out the darkening twilight. I needed to set up a few things before she got home. I wanted all the curtains closed, all the windows locked, and candles lit for illumination.

I needed a shower and to attach the cuffs to the ceiling in our bedroom.

If she wanted to be fucked by a lion, she would get mauled by one tonight.

My cock thickened again, picturing Neri with her arms up and bound, tethered in place with leather cuffs in the middle of our bedroom. Naked and begging, skin flushed and legs parted—

Fuck.

Grabbing myself through my work-dirty shorts, I hissed between my teeth.

You better jerk off in the shower.

I wouldn't have the stamina to give the full bondage experience if I didn't. I was on the cusp of coming just thinking about her ass blooming red and my cock sinking inside her wet, tight—

Fuck, shower.

Now.

Unbuttoning and unzipping, I stalked down the corridor to the bathroom.

Wrenching down my shorts and boxer-briefs, I yanked off my t-shirt and opened the glass door to turn on the water—

Ring, ring. Ring, ring.

"Fuck," I huffed as my phone had a meltdown where I'd left it in the lounge.

The temptation to ignore it was strong. The images of what I'd do to Neri tonight made me slightly insane. But the ever-present fear of something happening to her dampened my lust with ice, making me march back, butt naked, to the table and snatch up the vibrating device. "Yeah?"

"Aslan, hey. Was worried you weren't going to pick up."

I pinched the bridge of my nose. I didn't have time for this. I needed to deal with my hard-on, prepare the apartment, and ensure I pounced on my hot little wife the moment she stepped through the front door. "Griffen. Hi. Everything okay? I'm a little pressed for time at the mo—"

"I'm not calling about rents or tenants. I, eh—" He cleared his throat. "I'm at the hospital."

My head snapped up. "Shit, are you okay? What happened?"

"It's, um…it's not me who's hurt."

"Nerida." The ice in my veins turned into a raging blizzard. "Please tell me she's not—"

"I was on campus when her class returned from a research trip on the reef. She was stung by a *glaucus atlanticus*."

My knees wobbled as adrenaline drenched me. I had no idea what that was, but if it lurked in Australian waters it was fucking deadly. "*Kafami sikeyim,* is she okay? What hospital? I'm coming right now." Racing to our bedroom, I yanked open the wardrobe.

"She's coherent and doing much better. She, um…she told me to tell you not to come. That it's probably best you don't—"

"What hospital, Griffen? Tell me, or I'll waste my entire fucking night looking for her."

"Shit, okay, fine. But just…be careful. She'll kill me for letting you—"

"*Where the fuck is she?!*"

"Townsville University Hosp—"

I hung up before he'd finished.

Not wasting time with underwear, I yanked on a pair of jeans, shrugged into a black t-shirt, and bolted out the door.

Chapter Fifteen

ASLAN

(Heart in Filipino: Puso)

"NERIDA..."

My heart finally stopped smashing itself against my ribs as I found her. Striding into the private room where she lay on a bleached-white bed, I stumbled a little in sheer fucking relief.

Her crystal-blue eyes found mine. "Aslan. Oh my God, what are you doing here? You shouldn't have come." Her gaze shot to Griffen, who stood beside her, his bald head gleaming with the fluorescents above. "I told you not to let him come. He can't be here. It's not safe."

Griffen shrugged with a grin. "You told me not to call your father too, but I did. And besides, we both know Aslan would've found you, with or without my help."

"You called my dad?" Neri scowled. "This has all gotten completely out of hand. I'm fine!"

"You weren't fine when I drove you here. Professor Mazen told me you threw up six times on the voyage home. You were doubled over in pain and passed out—"

"She passed out?" I choked as I stopped by the side of her bed, drinking her in. She looked pale and drawn; shadows existed under her eyes, and she kept wincing as her legs moved beneath the sheets.

I didn't know what possessed me, but I grabbed the sheets and yanked them away, almost as if some sixth sense alerted me to what was hurting her, what dared hurt my fucking soulmate.

"Aslan, stop—" Neri tried to catch the sheet but failed.

I swayed on the spot as my eyes fell on her left leg.

The worst fucking rash I'd ever seen covered her from hip to knee. The hospital gown she'd been dressed in was split over her thigh, revealing the remnants of white cream that'd been spread over her blistered skin.

I couldn't tear my eyes away.

I couldn't speak.

I felt like I'd failed her all over again.

I wanted to kill whatever had hurt her.

Red haze fell over my eyes, and my hands fisted.

"Aslan…it's okay," Neri murmured, shifting on the bed and resting her hand on my flexed forearm. "It was a silly mistake on my part. I'm okay. Truly."

"*Bu nasıl oldu?*" I groaned as nausea rushed up my throat. "*Ne yapabilirim. Söyle bana. Bunu nasıl daha iyi hale getirebilirim?*"

Griffen shot me a look. "What did you say?"

I winced, noticing my slip from English. I went to translate, but Neri surprised me by saying softly, "He wants to know what happened and how he can make it better."

My eyes widened.

I knew she'd been spending more time on her language app. That she listened each day on the bus and practiced with me at night, but I hadn't stopped to understand what that would one day mean.

That one day, she would be bilingual…just like me.

My abhorrent fear tangled with shattering love, and I snatched her to me.

I wrapped my arms around her so fiercely, so violently, Griffen sucked in a breath. "Easy, mate. She's still a little fragile."

"*Seni çok seviyorum Neri. Yaralandığın için çok üzgünüm. Yaralanmandan ve yardım etmek için orada olamadığım için nefret ediyorum.*" (I love you so much, Neri. I'm so sorry you got hurt. I hate that you got hurt, and I wasn't there to help).

I kissed her cheek. I inhaled her sterile scent from being treated by doctors and nurses. I struggled to keep my heart in my chest when all it wanted to do was splat at her feet and beg her to take it wherever she went, so I never had another phone call like this. Never suffered this level of panic.

She hugged me back, her arms not her usual strength and her skin a little feverish, but her voice was steady and soothing as she whispered, "*Seni çok seviyorum.* And don't be sorry I got hurt. It's just one of those things. It wasn't your fault."

Pulling away, I brushed away her sea-tangled hair, begging to know everything. "Tell me."

She sighed and looked at Griffen. "We were diving for core samples to take back to the lab to study. A blue fleet washed in on the way back to the surface."

"Blue fleet?"

"She means a group of blue dragons."

"Dragons?" My eyebrows shot up. Thanks to all my years working with Jack and Anna, I knew many aquatic beasts used the name dragon. Most were cute frilly things that floated around at the mercy of the ocean's currents, but it still didn't stop my heart from lurching at the danger she'd put herself in.

"They're sea slugs," Neri said quietly. "I've seen them before, but Dad was adamant about never getting close."

"Rightfully so." Griffen crossed his arms. "They might be stunning blue sea-fairies, but they're carnivorous, cannibalistic little monsters that feed on their own species and Portuguese man o' war. All that venom they ingest becomes even more potent. You know better than to let one touch you, Nerida."

My mind raced as I stood taller. I pulled my hands away from her. I didn't trust myself not to wring her neck. Anger hazed my vision again as my voice turned dark. "You swam with a creature that eats jellyfish? Jellyfish that has the potency to kill a human?"

"I didn't swim with it. The current wafted it into my leg on the way to the surface."

"Why weren't you wearing a wet suit?"

"I had my long-sleeve surf-suit on. My torso and arms were covered, but my legs were—"

"Fucking *poisoned*."

"They're venomous, not poisonous," Griffen said.

My eyes snapped to him. Fury bristled through my entire body.

He winced and rolled his shoulders. "Not that that's important of course." He shrank back and crossed his arms. "Anyway, it's over now. Professor Mazen did all the right things. She was rinsed in hot water, doused in vinegar, and brought straight here. Her nausea has subsided, and the rash has been treated. She's showing no allergic reactions, so the chances of the sting becoming fatal are—"

"*Fatal?*" My heart stopped. "Fucking hell." I pinched the bridge of my nose as my vision shot black.

Fatal.

I never wanted that word anywhere near Neri.

It just...*no*.

No fucking way could she ever die under any circumstances, anywhere, any time.

"Aslan..." Neri's soft fingers landed on my wrist, tugging my hand down. "I'd tell you if I wasn't feeling well. I'll admit it hurt like a bitch when it first touched me. It really packed a punch for such a tiny little nudibranch, but the effects are fading now. I'm even feeling a little hungry, which is a good sign after all the throwing up I've done."

"Ah, I see there's a party going on in here." A female doctor appeared behind me, smiling at Neri and nodding at me and Griffen. Her brown eyes scanned all of us, her dark hair in a neat bun. "You family?"

"Friend of the family." Griffen pointed at himself. "Fiancé." He pointed at me.

I stiffened as she looked my way.

It'd been a while since I'd been in a place of authority. In a place where they could legally ask for identification and report me to whoever they felt like. I'd had my hackles up since stalking through the hospital searching for Neri. My instincts prickled, and my urge to stay unseen drained me, but I'd gotten this far. I gave them no reason to suspect me. They didn't need to know a single thing about me.

But what would I do if they started asking questions?

Calm the fuck down.

It was Neri they cared about. Not me.

"Hello." I nodded politely. "Thank you for taking care of her so well."

"My colleague first tended to her, but I'm glad she's doing okay." She pulled out an e-tablet from her white coat pockets. Scanning whatever notes were on Neri, she said, "Wow, you're the second person this month to get stung by a blue dragon. No sightings for ages, then boom, they're back in town."

"Think they've been hunting jellyfish." Neri grinned. "Rising ocean temperatures threaten their food source and screw up their usual locations."

"I'll keep that in mind next time someone asks why we had to have a refresher on venomous creatures and protocols." The doctor laughed kindly. "For now, how are you feeling?"

Neri shot me a look before licking her lips and admitting, "I'm a little weak and still feel a bit sick, but I'm much better."

"Least the antihistamines have kicked in, and it sounds as if the paracetamol has as well." Consulting the notes, the doctor added, "We can keep you overnight if you feel like you're getting worse, or you can go home with the strict proviso that you'll come back if you get light-headed, feverish, struggle to breathe, or—"

"She's staying here," I snapped. "In case any of the above happens."

"No." Neri crossed her arms. "I want to go home." Her eyes flashed blue fire. "I'm not spending a night here. I'm fine."

"I can't be responsible if you get worse, Neri." Rocks tumbled into my stomach. "What if you can't breathe in the middle of the night? What if I can't get you here in time? What if you—"

Sour sickness splashed on my tongue.

I couldn't even say the word.

Her name and the mere mention of dying was as forbidden as the word fatal.

"I understand your fear, Mr…" The doctor raised her eyebrow in my direction.

"Taylor," Neri said quickly, shooting a look at Griffen before she took my hand and squeezed. "Aslan Taylor."

"Oh, so you're already married? He's not your fiancé but your husband?" The doctor frowned at Neri's notes. I assumed your maiden name was Taylor."

I froze.

Fuck.

My tone was thick as I struggled to do damage control. "I—"

"My mistake," Griffen said quietly. "I'm going senile in my old age. They got hitched last month. I missed the wedding, hence why I keep calling him her fiancé."

The doctor chewed on her cheek for a moment before shrugging and slipping the e-tablet back into her pocket. "No problem. I've confirmed your discharge papers and will have a script for you to collect on the way out for some more antihistamines and a topical cream for the rash."

"How long will the rash last?" Neri asked. "Can I go swimming?"

"I'd stay out of the ocean for a week at least. If the blisters become open wounds, it's best not to swim in water that could be contaminated. Hopefully, the redness will fade within a few days, but it's not uncommon for it to reoccur as the venom leaves your system."

"Is it painful?" I winced, hating that she was hurting, and I couldn't do a damn thing about it.

"It won't feel nice." The doctor winced in commiseration. "How does it feel, Mrs Taylor?"

Neri flashed me a look as if she didn't want to be entirely honest. "It's just prickly and sore. It's fine."

Bullshit.

She flinched each time the sheets touched her.

"It will most likely start to itch in a week or so. Use ice to numb it or one precent hydrocortisone cream. Try not to scratch." Nodding at all of us, the doctor smiled. "If that's everything, I'll go. But please don't hesitate to return to the emergency department if your symptoms worsen."

With another professional smile, she swept from the room.

Only once her footsteps faded did Griffen inch closer to the bed, his gaze flicking between Neri and me.

My chest tightened at the questions in his eyes.

Questions brought about thanks to Neri using her surname as mine. Questions that I had no answers for.

I trusted him to keep my secret that I had to be paid under the table while working my way through an imaginary visa process, but I didn't trust him to know I'd arrived illegally and was most likely being hunted, even now.

Neri stiffened in bed. Her shoulders went back with a familiar battle cry, getting ready to defend me. Before she could make matters worse, I placed my hand on hers and murmured, "The less you know, the better, Griffen. I'm still the guy looking after your apartments. Nothing's changed."

He gritted his teeth but finally nodded. "I trust you both. I like you both. We have two years of history between us, and I'm not about to throw that away." He rubbed his hands over his face. "But…there will come a time when this arrangement needs to be legal. If my books ever get audited, they'll question where the eight percent of my rental income is going. I'll need to give them an answer."

"I know." I bowed my head. "And I'm sorry to put you in that position."

"Don't be. I'm glad to do it. Jack has become a great friend as have you, Aslan. I'm not about to betray anyone." Leaning over, he kissed Neri on the cheek. "Get better quick, you hear? If you need anything, Millie and I can drop by tomorrow." Walking around the bed, he stopped beside me. "Did you want me to take you guys home?"

"We're good. I drove the Jeep."

"Aslan." Neri grumbled under her breath. "You know why that's a very bad idea."

"She's right, you know." Griffen shrugged. "I always wondered why that vehicle just sat in the carport doing nothing, but I'm beginning to understand now. My suggestion is to get home quick. It's Friday. They'll be breath testing tonight, I'm sure. Along with a few more patrols for drunken idiocy."

I shivered, remembering the night I'd been breathalysed. The night I'd broken and kissed Neri. If I hadn't come face-to-face with how much I wanted her, thanks to the very real panic of being deported, I didn't know if we'd be here, together.

I might have always fought my feelings.

And that was both a depressing thought and a strangely regretful one.

If I hadn't given in, she wouldn't have to live in the shadows with me, restricted in what she could and couldn't do, always having to weigh up the risks.

"Night, Griffen. Thanks for staying with her and calling me." I put out my hand.

He shook my hand firmly. "Anytime."

He left, leaving a heavy silence between Neri and me that clogged my lungs.

For the longest moment, we didn't speak. Finally, she whispered, "Let's go, Aslan. Take me home where it's safe."

I did what she asked.

I drove her home and helped her limp over the threshold.

I showered with her, rubbed cream into her red-welted leg, gave her more painkillers, then put her to bed.

And as she drifted off to sleep beside me, my fingers tracing over her back like they always did, I clutched my shell with my free hand.

I clutched it so fucking hard the spines threatened to puncture my palm.

I clutched it because somewhere along the line, the shell Neri had returned with from the land of the dead represented luck, freedom, and *us*.

I rubbed its peach spikes as if it were a genie's lamp, wishing for just another few years of luck. Another few years of safety. Another few years of *this*.

But as sleep came for me, the nightmares swarmed.

Only this time, the nightmares weren't about losing my family...

I lost her instead.

Chapter Sixteen

NERIDA

(Love in Swahili : Upendo)

"IF I COULD TURN BACK TIME, I'D never put my hand up to be on the data-gathering team that day. I would've opted to stay onboard the university's research vessel. If only I hadn't been stung by that stupid sea slug, Aslan wouldn't have slipped into dark, depressing thoughts that never truly stopped stalking him."

"I'm guessing he struggled seeing you hurt again." Margot blew on the steam rising from her coffee mug. Tiffany had kindly brought us a tray of caffeine as the clock kept ticking and the night kept passing.

"He did." I nodded, sipping my almond latte. "At least with Ethan, he had an enemy to destroy. With this, he didn't have anything to direct his fear and fury at. Each time he looked at my rash, the shadows in his coal-black eyes would gather and swarm. Each time he heard me hiss with discomfort, he'd withdraw a little as if he couldn't cope with the depth of worry he had for me.

"I took a few days off from classes to get over the worst of the nausea and dizziness. Aslan stayed by my side. Frankly, he suffocated me with care. He never let me out of his sight. He leapt to his feet each time I shifted on the couch as if he could personally deliver everything I needed to heal and heal swiftly.

"He brooded while I spoke to Teddy and spent the afternoon sketching up another biosphere concept, and practically jumped down Honey's throat when she called to check on me.

"Everyone saw the overprotective man at his wit's end to keep me healthy and alive, but only I saw the floundering boy who'd never dealt with his grief. Grief that drowned him in a terrible way the moment he heard the word *fatal.*

"He tortured himself with researching *glaucus atlanticus.* He snapped at my parents when they called to discuss my recovery. He punished himself for not being there to protect me, when really, it wasn't his duty to protect me. Not from life itself. It was his duty to love me. To be faithful and caring and supportive, but it wasn't his responsibility to stop me from existing. To prevent things from happening just because sometimes those things hurt."

"Let me guess…he didn't agree," Margot said. "He'd rather burn the world to ash than risk losing you."

I sighed sadly. "Some might say that was unhealthy."

"Undoubtedly unhealthy." Dylan nodded. "But also, understandable."

I looked at the swirling coffee in my cup. "I really did try to free him from his pain. I was there for him if he wanted to talk. I was there to wake him from his nightmares with kisses and sex, using our physical connection to bring his mind back to me. But ultimately, he had to be the one to stop running from his demons and accept them."

"His demons being his blood?"

My eyes shot to Dylan and his very poignant remark. "You've been listening closely."

He half shrugged, swallowing a hot mouthful of espresso. "Like I said, I'm good at reading between the lines. You mentioned that Aslan never got over his family's death because of his guilt. He carried their death all his life. He believed he was the reason they were fleeing in the first place, which meant he never fully embraced who he truly was because in order to do that, he had to embrace the parts of himself that came from his true father. The very man who was the reason for all that loss and guilt and grief."

Goosebumps darted down my arms as my heart grew heavier than I could bear. "You're right. About everything. If only Aslan had trusted himself as much as I trusted him, then he might finally have been free."

Free.

That word mocked me the moment it fell from my lips.

He'd been free.

For eight wonderful years, he'd been free with me.

But that freedom was almost at an end.

Tears welled, bruising my eyes like they always did whenever I thought back to that night in the hospital, the many nights after when Aslan would wake, roaring with misery and mayhem, fighting off ghosts, seeing a nightmare where I was gone, and he had nothing.

I'd grown used to his unconscious outbursts.

My veins had bled dry on multiple occasions when his nightmares caused him to scream my name and not his dead sister's.

In his sleep, he showed me the depth of how much he loved me and how much that love destroyed him. His dream-terrors revealed how tragically entwined we were, and I hated that we weren't playing a game when we said our hearts beat as one.

It was undeniably true.

When his hurt, mine hurt.

When his thundered, mine galloped.

When his stopped, mine never restarted.

Oh God...

I wasn't ready.

I'm not ready...

Goosebumps scattered down my entire body.

My chest collapsed in on itself.

My bones throbbed with tears I'd swallowed back, year after year, slowly filling up my body with a salt of my own making until I fermented in sadness.

I-I don't think I can do this.

My hands trembled, spilling my coffee all over my soft pink blanket.

"Hey. Nerida. Hey, it's okay." Dylan leapt to his feet and plucked the cup from my trembling fingers. Placing it on the mango wood coffee table between us, he inched around it and sat beside me. We sat in my favourite place in this house—surrounded by glass and scrolled metal work of the huge conservatory. A seahorse fountain babbled in the corner and lush tropical plants seasoned the air with sweet blossoms. This room was a paradise, yet it seemed like an absolute travesty as I struggled with what came next. What Aslan was about to endure. What I was about to endure. What had ultimately destroyed us.

I hunched and did my best to gather my strength, but a keening noise escaped me.

Dylan sucked in a worried gasp. He hesitated a moment before wrapping his arm around my fragile shoulders. "It's okay. Everything is okay."

My temper flared, igniting my sadness like a steaming cauldron. I finally understood why sixteen-year-old Aslan had hated that word when he'd first been found.

It was an empty word.

A word that promised nothing and had the power to grate on your nerves and make a mockery of everything you hoped for.

Sitting taller, I did my best to collect myself.

I thought I could do this.

I thought I'd been prepared to do this.

When I'd started sharing my love story, I'd promised myself that by the time we got to this part, I wouldn't shed a tear. I would stay cool and collected. It was in the past, after all. It'd already happened. It couldn't hurt me now.

And yet...

I'd never felt older.

Never been more breakable.

Never craved the sweet oblivion of death more than I did in that moment of confession.

You can't stop now.

Finish it.

Images of Aslan's handsome face swirled in my mind's eye. The rakish sable hair tumbling over his forehead with sun-bronzed tips. The wide, fathomless ebony eyes where dark monsters roamed. The perfect kissable lips that I'd tasted a million times. And the body that embodied power and longevity, only to prove that as immortal as our love made us, his bones could break, his blood could flow, his heart could stutter and splutter and…stop.

Wrenching my head up, I blinked and swiped at the torturous tears on my cheek.

Dylan withdrew his arm but didn't leave my side.

Margot forgot all about her coffee.

The sleepy haze of conversation turned into painful sharpness of what came next.

I'd warned them.

I'd told them again and again that this tale had torture and pain and loss.

I was about to find out if they believed me.

They winced as I caught their eyes.

They stiffened as I inhaled.

Margot even shook her head as if denying what I was about to tell her.

They knew.

They remembered.

My chin tipped up; I said almost coldly, "I told you I'd give you two more years of happiness. I warned you that the end of our happiness would come the day I turned twenty. Two years have passed and—"

"Don't," Margot whispered. "I don't want to know."

Holding her hurting stare, I muttered, "Six weeks after the blue dragon sting, when my leg was all healed and life had returned to somewhat normal, Aslan decided to celebrate my birthday with every part of him. Three things. Three memories—"

My voice cracked.

I bowed my head as forbidden tears tumbled down my paper-thin cheeks. My heart bled all over again as I rubbed my left arm beneath the long sleeves of my seafoam green dress. I still wore one of his presents. It'd kept me alive. In some serendipitous way, my tattoo had kept me fighting even while ripping out my heart.

My lonely, lovelorn heart.

It'd haemorrhaged until there was nothing left inside it. It'd seeped and oozed and gushed every lifeforce until it'd become nothing more than a desiccated organ with no magic, no spark, no soulmate.

The headache that'd slowly been getting worse as my story crept closer to this pinnacle throbbed in my temples.

It was almost midnight.

My throat was hoarse.

If I was a better woman, I'd tell them to go. I'd take them to the door and send them back to their own homes.

But I had to finish.

I had to tell them tonight or not at all.

Sucking in a breath, I rubbed at my empty chest.

I braced my shoulders.

I fought so damn hard for strength.

Dylan cleared his throat and leaned nearer. Taking my hand, he squeezed my brittle bones. "Just remember you survived it, Nerida. Whatever happened, you survived it."

Margot gasped quietly, tears rolling silently down her cheeks. Her skin had whitened, and her fingers shook as she clutched her coffee mug. "You might have survived it, but...he didn't, did he?"

I winced.

My headache pounded.

And all I could give her was the weakest, saddest smile as I whispered, "I'm sorry. I'm sorry for what I'm about to share. Endlessly sorry that I wasn't able to protect him. Eternally sorry that I wasn't able to find him. And I-I—"

My voice cracked with tears.

An ocean roared through me, splashing up my ribs, wetting all my pieces. The salt stung, the cold weight crushed, and the sharks swimming in the tide chewed me alive, all while I silently *screamed*.

"Nerida...it's okay." Dylan shifted until our thighs touched, wrapping his arm around my shoulders again.

I shouldn't draw comfort from him.

But I did.

I let myself be held by a man all while I sank into the tale of another.

A man who was my soulmate.

My always.

My ever after.

A man who suffered.

A man who broke.

A man who I lost forever...

Chapter Seventeen

ASLAN

(*Heart in Swedish:* Hjärta)

DID ANYONE EVER TRULY KNOW THEIR LIVES were about to end?

What sort of intuition did you need to be able to sense death sneaking ever closer, breathing down the back of your neck, sharpening its axe, all while waiting for the perfect moment to strike?

Whatever skill it took, I did not have it.

For all of Neri's nudges and knowings, she didn't have the necessary sight.

We were both as blind as the other as I woke her up on her twentieth birthday with my mouth on hers and my hand slipping between her silky thighs.

I had an itinerary planned for today.

Three things I wanted to do to celebrate the twenty incredible years my wife had been alive. I'd been lucky enough to share eight of those years and planned on sharing a thousand more.

Starting with today.

What a shame I didn't have a fucking clue that those three things were the only things standing between me and death. Three little events that were over so fast and fleetingly, passed by in a single day and gone.

If I'd known they would be my last with Neri, I would've paid more attention. I would've hoarded every second. Clung to every moment. I would've imprinted every one of her breaths, recorded every sound of her laughter, and engraved her every touch upon my out-of-time heart.

I supposed it was good that I didn't know what was coming for me.

If I had, I wouldn't have been able to move.

Unable to breathe.

Unable to accept that our life together was over.

Dreams clung to my thoughts as I rolled closer to Neri and kissed her. My blood hummed with the crackling connection flowing between us. She moaned in her sleep as I licked her lips then parted them gently with my tongue. She shifted a little under the blankets as I inserted the tip of my finger inside her, claiming her sleep-shrouded body for my own.

She sighed as I kissed her harder all while my finger sank deeper.

Her eyes flew open and locked with mine.

Her lips quirked into a sexy smile as I kissed her softly.

Her legs fell open, unashamedly welcoming me to take whatever I wanted.

A gruff groan rumbled in my chest as I pressed a second finger inside her, stretching her, preparing her, waking her up with lust and love.

Her hands landed in my hair, tangling and tugging, bringing my mouth harder against hers. Her tongue touched mine, and I shuddered as she licked me back. Licked me slow. Licked me like she owned me.

My cock reacted.

My morning erection grew impossibly harder as I rolled on top of her, pushing her legs wider to make enough room to settle between them. Her back arched as I removed my fingers and reached between us, angling my cock at her entrance.

Our eyes locked as I found her heat and hovered on that delicious, piercingly sharp moment of mounting her.

Sex with Neri never failed to wrench open my heart and chain me to her, body and spirit. It didn't matter if we were rough or violent, soft and silent, or barely moving in each other's arms as we came—each time we joined, it felt as if we tangled our souls even more, knotting us together never to be undone, binding us in every way that mattered.

We didn't speak as I pushed.

Her eyes snapped closed as I claimed her, sinking slowly, parting her wetness, notching deep. Only once I'd fed every inch of my length did I take a breath and allow the shiver of pure fucking bliss to crackle down my spine.

Moaning under her breath, she raked her fingernails down my back and grabbed my ass, pulling me into her as I rocked. We lost ourselves to the primal motion, fighting against each other to get closer, getting harder and quicker the more we lost ourselves.

The urge to come shot between my legs, but I smothered it.

I wasn't nearly done with her.

I wanted her wet and willing, ready to writhe all over my cock as I gave my filthy wife one of her fantasies…not that I would, just yet.

She still wasn't one hundred percent from that venomous sea slug.

The toys I bought were still in their box in the wardrobe. The night Neri got stung and I'd rushed to the hospital to find her had ensured a month of healing. The rash faded and returned multiple times over six weeks. She'd returned to the doctor to ensure her recovery was normal and had to take antihistamines daily to keep it in check. She claimed she suffered light-headedness for weeks afterward, so any thought of being rough with her flew out the fucking window.

Not that that'd stopped us from having sex. She'd pounced on me the very next day, making me pump into her while she lay resting on the couch. She'd come, flushed with fever, then snoozed the rest of the afternoon.

I'd been utterly useless, staring at her, making sure she continued breathing as day became dusk and time slowly healed her.

I'd hoped for her birthday, I could've let loose. That she could've handled what I wanted to give her. To prove to both of us that I wasn't afraid of who I truly was. To use the toys I'd bought and the cuffs ready to bind her.

At least the rash on her leg was now nothing more than a pink blush.

"Aslan…" She begged beneath me, her eyes still closed, her head tipped back as I rode her. "Harder…please."

Her pussy fluttered around my invasion. I knew her body as well as I knew my own. All it would take was my thumb on her clit and my tongue in her mouth and she'd shatter.

But…she'd have to wait.

With gritted teeth, I tampered my own impatient release and withdrew.

Her eyes flew wide as a scowl furrowed her forehead. "W-Why did you stop?"

Pushing away from her, I kneeled between her spread legs and was stunned fucking silent at how beautiful she was. How open she was. How ready.

She'd read a fantasy book this week called *The Sea Dragon*. I'd thought it was a non-fiction text—something she had to read for class—before I'd skimmed a few chapters and found the filthiest romance full of forced marriages, brutal conquests, and a race of people who could breathe both water and air.

I couldn't take her like the mermen in that book, but I could take her like a beast.

A beast that would restrain himself until she was fully healed.

Grabbing her hips, I flipped her onto her belly and hoisted her onto her hands and knees. Her sun-faded chocolate hair draped around her face, the ends kissing the mattress as her hands dug into the sheets and her back arched with carnal invitation.

My breathing came shallow and quick as I dragged my hands over the perfection of her bare ass. We slept naked. Ever since we'd moved into this place, we preferred no clothes so we could wake up like this. Wake up and roll over and fuck each other while still hazy with sleep.

Pity for her, I was well and truly awake now.

Tracing my fingers down her crack, I slipped them inside her wetness.

She jolted and pushed backward, forcing me to touch her deeper.

"Easy, *canım*. You don't want to rush your birthday treat too quickly, do you?"

She shivered. "What do you have in mind?"

Pumping my fingers inside her, I grabbed her hip with my other hand. "Lots of things. Starting with completely ruining you, followed by totally worshipping you, then utterly seducing you."

"Oh…I like the sound of that."

"Good." I bit my bottom lip as I withdrew my touch and smeared her arousal on my cock. "I like the sound of it too." I rose up behind her. "I like the look of you on your knees, *hayatım*." Lining myself up with her heat, I growled, "You look so submissive. So greedy for something only I can give you."

She hung her head, her spine arching like a cat. "Give me what I need then, husband."

My heart thundered with black yearning. "Tell me what you need, wife."

"You. Inside me. *Now*."

"Ask nicely."

"Please, Aslan. Please give me—"

"Happy birthday, Neri." Slamming inside her, my vision shot black. She screamed as I speared to the hilt, her body fighting my invasion before welcoming me, fisting me, drowning me with delirious pleasure.

I looked down at where we joined. "Fuck, you look good with my cock deep inside you."

She moaned as I drove in deeper.

"You're mine, Nerida. Say it."

Her voice was pure eroticism as she obeyed. "Yours. I'm yours."

"*Her şeyin bana ait. Vücüdun. Kalbin. Düşüncelerin, hayallerin ve geleceğin.*" I thrust explicitly hard, driving my words inside her. Would she understand what I said? How advanced was her vocabulary these days?

With a frustrated little noise, she pleaded, "Tell me. Tell me what you said."

Tipping my head back, I clamped both hands on her hips and yanked her onto me. No space existed between us. Her ass pressed against my belly. My balls slammed against her clit. "I said everything belongs to me. Your body. Your heart. Your thoughts and dreams and future."

Her entire body flexed around me, rippling with want. "All of me. Every last piece is yours."

My back locked with power and disgusting relief that her promise gave me. Today was meant to be about her, yet…somehow, I'd stolen every part of her.

And I'm never giving it back.

Her core fluttered again, making my eyes hood. Desire to reward her blazed through me. "Does it turn you on when I speak to you in Turkish, *aşkım?*"

"God, yes."

I chuckled as I withdrew, then sank back in, an endless pulling and pushing, feeding and receding. "How *much* does it turn you on?"

"I get so wet," she panted. "When you call me between lectures and whisper dirty things, I spend the rest of the day in a constant state of need."

I rode her slowly, deeply. "Is that why you leap on me the moment you walk in the door?"

"I thought you knew." She grunted as I thrust. "You only have to say a single word, and I melt."

"*Bana sadece bakman gerekiyor ve ben sertleşiyorum.*"

She convulsed. Her skin broke out in shivers.

"You know what I said?" I pumped into her, staying at a mind-breaking rhythm.

"You said you just have to look at me and you get hard."

"Fuck, I love that you're becoming so fluent, *canım.*" Palming her ass, I squeezed a perfect handful as I lost control and gave in to need.

"Yes. God, yes." Neri spread her legs and dropped to her elbows, bowing her head onto the sheets. "Faster. You're driving me insane."

"*I'm* driving *you* insane? You make me senseless, wife. I can't imagine a day of not being with you. I can't picture my life without you in it. You are *everything* to me, Nerida. I don't think you fully understand that."

Her fingers clawed at the sheets as I thrust harder, sharper. "Tell me then. Show me."

Letting go, I embraced the monster in my blood and dug my fingers into her hipbones. She couldn't escape. Couldn't run. I leaned back, pressing my thighs to the back of her legs and forcing every last inch of my body into hers.

I obeyed her command.

I gave her deep.

I gave her hard.

I gave her punishment for every spell she'd cast over me and every leash she'd tightened.

"*Sen Benimsin.*" (You are mine). I embraced the feral desire to fuck her ruthlessly hard. "*Kanının her damlası ve aldığın her nefes bana ait.*" (Every droplet of your blood and every breath that you take belongs to me).

The lightning that always forked and sizzled between us arced and sparked. "*Her iç çekişin, her yalvarışın, her iniltin.*" (Every sigh, every beg, every moan). I lost myself to savage rutting, taking her straight to hell with me. "*Her orgazmın, her öpücüğün, her okşaman.*" (Every orgasm, every kiss, every stroke).

Neri moaned with each of my punishing thrusts. The bedhead smashed against the wall, adding to the dents we'd left from previous lovemaking. Her core clenched around me, hinting she was close, so close.

Sweat beaded on my temples as I continued to fuck her like I couldn't survive without her. Just the way we liked it, needed it. "*Sensiz ben yokum. Sensiz var olmak istemiyorum.* (I don't exist without you. I don't want to exist without you).

She cried out as every part of her tensed. She shook and trembled. Panted and whimpered.

"*Ve bu benim, sana her şeyimi veriyorum çünkü zaten senin her şeyini aldım.*" (And this is me, giving you my everything because I've already taken everything of you).

I drove us to breaking point, harder and harder, faster and deeper and—

"Aslan…God…I'm going to. I'm going to—"

"Come, Neri. Fucking come all over me."

She screamed as she broke.

Her core fisted me in hot, wet waves, not giving me a chance.

I broke with her.

I snarled and growled and couldn't catch a breath as my body took over, and I came in the thickest, tightest rush.

Spurt after agonising spurt.

Pleasure ricocheted like thunder, throbbing in my bones, splashing into the only girl I ever wanted.

We spent the entire day in bed.

After our first round of sex, I went to make her breakfast. The ingredients I'd bought the day before were easy to turn into freshly grilled french toast, maple-baked bananas, and a bowl of sugar-dusted strawberries.

We ate.

We watched a movie with the sun bright outside with no guilt whatsoever.

We fell together again as the credits rolled and morning switched to afternoon. We moved slower, softer, wrapped up in each other and unapologetically obsessed. Once we came, our satedness turned to sleepiness, and Neri drifted off in my arms. My cock remained deep inside her, our limbs tangled as heartbeats slowed into dreams.

We woke as afternoon slipped into dusk, and I dragged my cosy-sleepy wife into the mermaid-tiled shower I'd renovated. I pushed her against the wall, commanded she grab the caddy holding her delicious frangipani shampoo, then drilled her hard and fast as hot water rained over us.

By the time we'd come for the third time and washed each other with soap and lingering kisses, I was ready to deliver the second part of Neri's birthday gift.

One, two, three.

Three simple things stood between me and the death inching ever closer, unseen, unheard, unknown.

I'd enjoyed the first part of her birthday immensely. We'd never been lazy enough to spend an entire Saturday having sex and sleeping in. And now, it was time for another thing she'd never done.

Something linked to the dirty fantastical books she read.

I wanted her permanently.

I wanted others to see that permanence.

"Get dressed." I patted her towel-wrapped ass as I strode out of the steaming bathroom. "Wear that sunset dress you bought last week from the night market."

Neri stilled and looked at me in the foggy mirror. Her shoulders tensed as she turned around and continued brushing her damp hair. "You went quiet when I bought it. I didn't think you liked it."

I scowled, annoyed that she'd seen how much it'd affected me.

The dress was an almost replica of the one she'd hacked into ribbons. The dress she'd been wearing when Ethan raped her. The vibrant orange bleeding into bruised midnight had been one of my favourite dresses on her—a representation of her as the Australian sun and me as the Turkish night—yet after what Ethan had done to her in that dress?

Fuck.

I was grateful she'd strewn it all over the sea…

So I was shocked fucking silent when she'd bought a twin dress that would undoubtedly bring back memories.

Maybe that's why she did it?

Raking a hand through my hair, I asked softly. "Did you buy the dress to prove you've moved on from what he did or because you haven't?"

She stopped brushing, her mouth parting a little. "You see so much more than I give you credit for."

I smiled sadly. "I see everything about you, *hayatım*."

Padding barefoot toward me, she pressed the softest kiss on my mouth. "I bought the dress because it was one of my favourites before what happened. And don't think I didn't notice the way you'd look at me when I wore it either." She laughed under her breath. "Your eyes would physically burn me. Your need would cover me like a cloud, and I'm not afraid to admit I wore it often to make you want me."

"You're a minx."

She grinned. "That dress was mine before Ethan tainted it. I've moved on enough to reclaim it as mine. And I couldn't think of a better night to wear it than going out to dinner with you on my birthday."

"I love you, Neri," I whispered against her lips.

"*Seni seviyorum*, Aslan."

I headed into our bedroom to get ready.

My eyes never left Neri as she came to join me and slipped into her stunning sunset dress.

My heart tripped all over again as we left our home and summoned an Uber to take us to town. The entire time we drove there, I couldn't stop looking at her. Couldn't stop touching her flawless skin or kissing her perfect mouth.

I loved that she was so brave.

I loved that she'd healed enough to wear something that made her happy.

I loved that she knew just how much that dress affected me.

And I loved that we were together.

Happy.

The dress symbolised a new beginning.

But really, it marked our ending.

If only she hadn't worn it.

If only we realised how cursed that dress truly was.

Perhaps, if she'd worn something else, we might've avoided what happened next.

Chapter Eighteen

NERIDA

AGE: 20 YRS OLD

(Love in Italian: Amore)

"WHAT ON EARTH ARE WE DOING HERE?" I laughed in surprise as I spun in the foyer of a tattoo parlour.

Aslan smirked, looking divine in a black long-sleeve shirt that he'd rolled up his forearms, revealing the powerful muscles from working with tools all day, along with the hint of ropey veins beneath his honey-dark skin. His hair was a tad too long, teasing with his collar in a perfect brown-bronze mess, and his acid-wash jeans hugged him just enough that I was constantly aware of how well endowed he was.

"Happy birthday, *canım*." Capturing my chin with his calloused fingers, he kissed me sweetly. Shooting a look at the heavily tattooed, pink-haired receptionist, he pressed his lips to my ear and whispered, "I can't mark you like the fantastical alphas in your filthy books. I have no power to inscribe your flesh with magic or bind us with joining ties. I can't even marry you in the eyes of the law. So…this is the next best thing."

I shivered as he pressed a kiss to the sensitive skin behind my ear, pushing aside my loose hair and making my nipples pebble beneath my sunset dress. I'd bought this for me—to give the final finger to Ethan as he receded into my past, but knowing how it affected Aslan made the night all the sweeter.

"How is it that I've had you three times today and I want you again?" he murmured.

I choked on a moan.

The receptionist giggled and looked away. I had no doubt she knew exactly how I was feeling. How flushed Aslan could make me with a single word, a single glance, a single graze or touch or look.

"You want to mark me with ink?" I whispered as he pulled away and pinned me to the spot with his stunning ebony eyes.

"If you'll let me."

"I have no idea what design I would get."

"I do," he murmured. "I've already sent it to the tattooist."

"You have?" My eyebrows rose. "What is it?"

He chuckled. "You'll have to wait and see. The women in your books don't get a choice what mark their mates give them. You don't either. But I promise you'll like it."

Goosebumps scattered down my arms at his intensity.

This wasn't just something he'd randomly decided.

He *wanted* this.

He wanted something on my body to say I was his, and that sort of animalistic need made my heart leap with desire.

I didn't care what he'd decided to mark me with.

I didn't care where he wanted it to go on my body.

Every inch of me belonged to him.

And it did hot, delicious things to me to know just how much he meant it when he said I was his.

Dad would probably kill me for getting inked.

He'd had a fit when I'd demanded to get my ears pierced when I was ten. Then again, I was no longer living under his roof. I was, for all intents and purposes, a married woman living with her husband.

A rush of giddy eagerness filled me. My heart raced. "*Ben seninim,* Aslan."

His nostrils flared; he swayed on the spot. A black, ferocious look filled his stare as he towered over me. Bending his head, he hissed in my ear, "Telling me you're mine in my language makes me so fucking hard, *aşkım.*"

I bit my lip and looked down his toned and powerful body. The tightness of his jeans strained, and he balled his hands in front of himself, hiding evidence of his arousal.

"Behave," he growled. "Otherwise, we won't make it to dinner."

"Eh, sorry to interrupt," the receptionist said. "But…if you're booked in with Tate, he's ready now."

With a swallowed groan, Aslan stepped away and looked at the pink-haired girl. "Great, thanks."

"Go right through. His station is the last on the left."

Taking my hand, Aslan practically dragged me around the brown leather couches, past a wall of tattoo sketches, and through the large room where multiple workstations waited to create body art. Two were taken: one with a young girl getting something tiny on her ankle and another with a guy with a beard down to his naval, his beer belly slowly transforming into the roaring head of a tiger.

A slim guy with a purple, blue, and green mohawk smiled as we slowed at the end of the buzzing, music-pumping space.

"You Aslan and Nerida?" He came forward, his hand outstretched.

"We are." Aslan shook it. "You're Tate Rolland?"

"I am indeed."

"I sent the image ahead," Aslan said.

"Yep. Got it. I've printed it off in different sizes. We can have a play around on placement and go from there." Stepping back, he grinned at me then glanced back at Aslan. "So…who's getting inked?"

"She is—"

"We both are," I said at the same time as Aslan.

His eyes whipped to me. "What?"

I grinned and smoothed down my dress. "Every reason you want to mark me, Aslan, is the very reason I want to mark you."

"But…" His forehead scrunched. "What would you want on me?"

"I'm thinking whatever you're putting on me will do."

Tate chuckled. "She's got you there, mate. Can't expect her to wear something for the rest of her life and not share the same commitment." Grinning, he said to me, "I'll show you what he has planned for you and then you can decide. Wait…" His nose wrinkled as if jerking on memories that wouldn't quite come. "Aslan…isn't that the name of the lion in those children's books?"

"*The Lion the Witch and the Wardrobe*, yes." I smiled. "It's Turkish for lion."

"Well, shit, that makes a lot more sense. It also makes the image super cool. I thought it was wicked before, but now I get it." He nodded at Aslan. "Respect, man. I get what you're doing and it's fucking awesome."

"Hang on. What is he doing?" I planted my hands on my hips. "Show me."

Aslan shot me a look. I couldn't tell if it was pride or fear.

"You know this will look awesome on you too, mate," Tate said, reaching for a folder and pulling out a tracing-paper thin stencil. "If you're the lion, then she's the—"

"Siren," Aslan muttered, stepping closer to Tate to peer at the paper in his hands. He studied it critically as if assessing with new eyes now he knew it was going on him as well as me.

"Unfortunately, I won't have time to ink it on both of you tonight." Tate winced. "You only made a booking for two hours, but you can come back next week and—"

"We both have to be done tonight." I drifted closer, needing to see what Aslan had picked. A little nudge inside me chose that moment to pinch rather insistently. If we were doing this, we were *both* doing it. Right now. Together. I didn't know why, but it was important.

"Ah, shit. Um…" Tate passed the folder and stencil to Aslan as he glanced toward reception. "Give me a sec. I think Josephine is due back from her break. I'll check if she has space and see if she could do one of you while I do the other. That work?"

"As long as her fine lines are as good as yours, then that's alright." Aslan nodded. "I like your work on Instagram. I'd appreciate the same quality for both of us. But I'd still like you to do Neri, if that's okay."

"No problem." Tate flashed me a smile. "I'll be right back."

Jogging up the rows of workstations, he left me and Aslan alone. Stepping to his side, I finally looked at the design.

My knees almost buckled me to the floor.

"Oh my God…" My hand shook as I reached out and traced the most stunning, most perfect, most poignant tattoo Aslan could have ever chosen. "W-Where did you find that?"

He sucked in a breath, still a little wary of my reaction. "I found it online, but I amended it to fit us. I've been teaching myself how to use that drawing app on the tablet. I wanted it to be perfect so…I've been tweaking it for a while."

"You made this for me?" Tears pricked my eyes.

"Well, I can't take all the credit. I merely made it personal *for us*," he murmured, passing over the stencil so I could study it.

My heart pounded with every emotion. My skin prickled with how close he stood to me. My blood hummed with the everlasting connection between us.

The image consisted of a fully grown, thickly-maned male lion lying down with his tail wrapped around a girl kneeling and pressed into his side. The look on the lion's face as the girl burrowed into his mane was achingly tender and utterly besotted. The girl had her eyes closed as if there was nowhere else she would rather be than right there, in his protection, surrounded by his crown of fur. His mane was full of flowers and feathers, swirls and stars, while the girl's skin was etched with crashing waves and crescent moons. The detail was exquisite. The story between the girl and her lion blisteringly beautiful.

"I-I don't know what to say."

Aslan carefully tucked my hair behind my ear. His head bent and his height curled around me, just like the lion curled around his siren. "Say you like it—"

"Like it?" My head snapped up. "I *love* it. I've never seen anything more perfect. More…"

"Us?" He smiled.

My heart tumbled from my chest and fell entirely into his paws. It'd been trapped in his claws ever since the day I'd plucked him from the sea, but right there, in that tattoo parlour on an early Saturday night, I gave him everything that I was.

I didn't want any piece of me if I couldn't have him in return.

Take my days.

Take my nights.

Take my entire existence because it's utterly worthless without you.

There were no words.

None.

Only touch.

Flinging myself into his arms, I balanced on my tiptoes and kissed him.

I kissed him with every inch of my soul and heart, and he kissed me back.

His arms wrapped tightly, entwining around my back like the vines and flowers in the lion's mane. His growl of need echoed in every bone, and by the time Tate returned with a pretty girl with long black hair and a nose ring, I was breathless and obsessed and so deeply in love I felt like I could fly.

Fly to the moon that gave me this man.

Swim in all the seas to claim this man.

It was the best night of my life as Josephine, the second tattooist, wheeled her table and chest of drawers full of inks, needles, and sterile equipment toward Tate's, and Aslan sat down.

"Where are you going to put it, *hayatım*?" Aslan murmured.

I looked down my body as I climbed onto Tate's table. It could go anywhere. It was a work of art I would proudly display for the rest of my life, but I wanted to be able to see it every moment I was awake. I wanted to be able to stroke the lion's mane whenever I thought of Aslan. I wanted to be able to stare at our love story every night before I went to sleep.

"Here." I tapped the underside of my left forearm. "I want it here."

"Say halfway between your elbow and your wrist?" Tate asked.

"Sounds good."

"It will wrap around to the front of your arm too, just so you're aware," Tate said, cutting out the right size and wheeling himself toward me on a cling-film-wrapped stool. Placing the stencil on my arm, the size of the lion's mane curled up and over, wrapping around me with its majestic protection.

It's perfect.

"Speak now or forever hold your peace."

I caught Tate's green eyes. "I'm sure."

"Alrighty then."

Holding out my arm, I watched in fascination as Tate squirted me with a gel, placed the paper against my skin and imprinted a purple outline. "How's your pain threshold?" he asked with a wink. "Do I need to teach you how to use your breath to control yourself?"

"She's a master at breathwork." Aslan grinned, holding out his left arm and pointing at the same spot as me. "I'm the one who probably needs the lesson."

"I'll go easy on you." Josephine laughed, running a razor over Aslan's arm to remove any stray hairs. Once his skin held the design like mine, and the tattooists had prepared their guns, I sank back against the table, locked eyes with my moon-given husband, and drifted on pop music and destiny as my virgin skin slowly transformed with the permanent reminder of who I belonged to.

Chapter Nineteen

ASLAN

(Heart in Italian: Cuore)

"OH MY GOD!" NERI MOANED INDECENTLY AS she slipped a spoonful of lamington cheesecake into her mouth.

The sounds she made.

The way her lips wrapped around the spoon.

The way she licked those lips with a glistening wet tongue.

Fuck.

Me.

I was grateful the fancy restaurant had long white tablecloths because there was no way I'd be able to hide my erection otherwise. It threatened to pop out the top of my jeans, pinching painfully as it wedged behind my belt, desperate to thrust back inside her.

My need for her wasn't helped by the lion now scribed on her arm. Every time she took a drink or raised her fork to her mouth she flashed me with evidence of just how much she loved me.

She loved me enough to hit her father over the head with a lamp to defend me.

She loved me enough to share what Ethan had done so the police didn't arrest me.

And now...now she'd permanently inked herself with a design I'd tweaked and sketched. A design that glowed on my own arm.

My eyes dropped to the perfect black lines. Josephine had done an impeccable job. We'd been late leaving as the piece had taken longer than they thought, but beneath the Saniderm see-through bandage, it was worth every penny to share the identical mark as Neri.

It couldn't come off like a wedding ring.

It couldn't be erased like words on a page.

It bound us for life, and my heart had tripled in size, fluttering and kicking, reminding me of all the times it'd tortured me when Neri was younger. All the moments when it'd strayed over the line, falling in love with her when I couldn't have her.

It hadn't cared about appropriate ages or timelines.

It'd known Neri was made for me and was impatient to claim her.

I sighed as a punching epiphany struck me around the head.

I'd been born to know this girl.

To find this girl.

To love this girl.

There was no other explanation for how we'd found each other.

It was fate.

"You have *got* to try this." Neri licked her lips again, making me groan. "It's the best thing I've ever tasted. I really didn't think cheesecake and lamingtons would go together but wow."

"Pretty sure *you're* the best thing I've ever tasted," I murmured as she reached across the table and fed me a spoonful of dessert.

The sugary feast made my mouth water, but it still didn't compare to my wife. "Good." I nodded. "But I still prefer you."

Her cheeks turned a delightful pink. "And you call me insatiable."

"Good job we're equally matched in the desperation department."

"Or you just groomed me to match your sex drive." She winked.

"I know you're trying to get a rise out of me, but it won't work. Not now. Not ever. You're wearing my tattoo, my ring, and I've claimed every inch of you. You're mine, Neri. Every fucking piece."

"Don't forget about my sea lion necklace." She smiled and ran her finger along the silver chain and charm. "My fifteenth birthday present that I've never taken off."

Memories of the beach, the rainforest, and the absolute pain of wanting her clouded my vision.

"I gave you that, and you gave me a kiss." I pinched the bridge of my nose before sighing hard. "I was so close to snapping that night."

"I wish you had," she murmured. "I had fantasies of you taking my virginity in our tent."

My chest panged.

If I had been her first that night, would our paths have been easier? She wouldn't have dated Joel. She wouldn't have been at Zara's that night trying to make amends. I'd thought I was being respectful by not touching her when she was so young, but if I had…perhaps I could've prevented everything that'd happened, all because I'd said no.

"Aslan…" Her hand landed on mine on the table. "Don't. I know where your mind has gone, and there's no point in playing with 'what ifs'."

"You're right." I twisted my hand until our fingers entwined. "If I'd given in that night, you probably would've given nineteen-year-old me a heart attack, and I wouldn't be here with you right now."

"What?" She wrinkled her adorable nose. "How would I have given you a heart attack?"

I squeezed her hand. "If I'd known how good you felt back then, *aşkım*, I don't think I would've had the self-control to stop. You think we're insatiable now? Imagine what we would've been like if we'd given in to the burn between us when we were both so young."

"We would've set fire to that stupid tent."

I chuckled. "We would've put your books to shame."

Our eyes locked.

The empty restaurant with its chandeliers and fancy linen wasn't exactly the right place to seduce each other. We couldn't hide in a crowd of diners because we'd been one of the last couples seated, thanks to our tattoos running overtime, and now we were the last to leave. The night was no longer young and was, unfortunately, almost over.

My chest tightened with contentedness. The night might be nearing an end, but Neri and I were only just beginning. We would go home. Slip into bed. And begin a new day together because we never had to say goodbye. We'd committed to share our lives, which was the greatest gift I could've ever asked for.

If there wasn't a table in the way, I would've grabbed my sea-wedded wife and kissed her.

A black-suited waiter looked our way, then glanced at his watch.

I doubted we had much time before they asked us to leave.

Doing my best to tame my body, I ordered, "Finish your dessert. It's late."

Neri looked me up and down with blue fire. "I'd rather have *you* for dessert."

"Stop looking at me like that," I growled, wincing as my cock hardened to unbearable levels.

"Like what?" she murmured.

"Like you want to fuck me on this table in front of everyone."

She shivered. "That mental image shouldn't be nearly as hot as it is."

"Fucking hell, *canım*. Behave."

She laughed so freely, so happily, I was stunned silent by just how gorgeous she was. How stunning and wonderful and *mine*.

A waitress appeared from the kitchen, shooting us a scowl before she went to the waiter by the bar and pointed at the door.

I got the hint.

Stabbing my own dessert—an Australian-Turkish fusion of baklava and pavlova, I cocked my chin at Neri's plate. "I'm guessing we have five minutes before they forcibly remove us. I suggest you finish what you want before that happens."

165

Huffing, she gathered another forkful.

I chewed on the sweet concoction, pleasantly surprised. I'd ordered the dish as I'd had a hankering for a taste of home. My mind had swum with memories of my mother's delicious baklava and the way she'd smash the pistachios with a rolling pin instead of putting them in a blender. She always said they tasted better pummelled into dust. I'd always joked that the minute she put on her baking apron, she got violent.

"How's the blend of cuisines?" Neri asked, eyeing up my plate as she finished her third mouthful.

We'd shared a four-course meal from breads of the world, a starter that took Vietnamese noodles and twisted them with Greek salads, followed by a main with Indonesian roots and Italian flair.

I'd never had food quite like it.

"It kinda works, actually." I chuckled. Scooping up another spoonful, I leaned across the table. "Try it."

Neri's eyes flashed as her lips closed around my spoon.

She took her time sliding the morsel off, and my cock throbbed as she never looked away from me. White cream smeared her bottom lip as she sat back and moaned. "*So* good."

"You have got to stop driving me insane," I muttered, dropping my eyes to my plate.

"Take me home then, so I can drive you insane in private."

I groaned and pushed my dessert away. "I brought you here so we could keep our hands off each other and talk. I want to know how you're feeling now you're in your last year of your degree. I want to know how your latest designs for the underwater spheres are going with Teddy. I want to make plans with you about what we'll do when we get back to Port Douglas. Are we moving back in with your parents? Are we renting something? Should we try to buy like Teddy and Eddie are?" I looked up. "I want to make sure you know that I love everything about you and not just our insane sex life. It's your birthday and—"

"And you've done exactly what you said you would," Neri breathed. "You ruined me this morning, worshipped me with our incredible tattoos, and now you've seduced me over dinner."

Standing, she placed her napkin down and held out her hand. "I know you love everything about me, Aslan. And I adore you for wanting to ask about my studies and our future. I had similar ideas tonight. I was going to finally make you tell me about your home back in Turkey. I want to know what your house was like, what you did on weekends, what your favourite place was, but…"

Coming to my side of the table in her gold-glittery sandals with her sunset dress dancing around her ankles, she entrapped me in her crystal-blue stare. "We can talk after. We can snuggle and whisper *after*…but only once you take me home and show me why there's a box of toys hidden in the wardrobe."

I froze as the air turned electric. My heart hammered, but I tried to play innocent. "What box?"

She snickered, but her eyes remained hot and sharp. "A box with floggers, cuffs, nipple clamps, rope—"

"Fuck, keep your voice down," I hissed, swooping to my feet.

She laughed with throaty invitation. "Is that part of my birthday surprise too?"

My hands twitched to rearrange myself, to try to find relief from the desperate agony she always drowned me with. But the waiter never took his eyes off us, and the sound of the cash register pinging hinted heavily that it was time for us to leave.

My heart smoked as I stepped into her and nuzzled my nose against her ear. "I was waiting until you were strong enough from that stupid sea slug, but...do you want to play tonight?"

She shuddered and sucked in a breath. "Is that a trick question?"

Pulling away, I captured her stare with mine.

Seriousness filled me.

Deadly seriousness to know that if we did this, if I fully let myself go, she was strong enough to bring me back if I went too far.

"Do you trust me, Neri?"

She frowned a little. "You know I do."

I shook my head, my voice barely louder than a whisper. "Do you truly, *truly* trust me? With your heart, body, and soul?"

She placed her hand on my chest, her fingers burning me through my shirt. "You *own* my heart, body, and soul, Aslan." She flashed me her new tattoo. "I trust you with everything that I am."

Wrapping my hand around hers, I squeezed her hard. "Do you remember the safe word?"

Her eyes widened as if I'd stunned her into silence.

The electricity crackled between us.

Our blood sizzled with connection.

And I very nearly came in my jeans as she breathed, "Seahorse."

I swayed on the spot.

Images of what I would do to her exploded.

Visions of her on her knees, her hands bound, her mouth open—

Urgency choked me.

I grabbed her wrist, careful not to hurt her new ink. "Let's go home, *canım*. I suddenly have the urge for a different kind of dessert."

167

Chapter Twenty

ASLAN

(Heart in Afrikaans: Hart)

"FUCKING HELL, WHERE IS THAT DAMN UBER?" I pressed Neri against the side of the building, dragging my nose down her throat and inhaling her wickedly intoxicating scent.

I kissed her hard.

Long.

Deep.

Pulling away, I struggled to see straight with how much I wanted her.

"I'm guessing the driver is deliberately tormenting us." She ran her hands through my hair, tugging just enough to make me wild.

Fifteen minutes we'd been waiting. The waiter had locked the restaurant doors the moment we left, and the streets were empty. For a Saturday night, the small restaurant quarter where I'd brought Neri had gone to sleep and kicked out all its patrons.

Her deviant hand dropped from my hair and slipped between my legs, rubbing my hard-on.

I growled. Loudly.

Tearing her touch away, I pushed back and sucked in a ragged breath. Pacing, I raked both hands through my hair. "I'm not going to get arrested for public indecency. I'm not touching you again until we're safely in our apartment."

She bit her bottom lip with a smirk. "Always such a spoilsport."

I chuckled even as my heart kicked with torture. "Behave, *canim*. For once in your life." Spinning in place, I stalked back the way I came, pacing, pacing, using motion to keep me sane. "Check your phone again. How far away is it?"

Pulling her phone from her small, beaded clutch, she scowled. "I have no idea what's going on with this driver. It said he was only five minutes away, but now it's back to nine."

"Bloody hell." I looked at the stars. "We could walk home faster."

"It's a lovely night." Neri smiled. "I'd be fine with a walk. Perhaps we can find a shadowy spot and—"

"Stop." I held up my hand. "Not another word out of you."

She laughed. "A bit on edge, Aslan?"

"Your fault. Entirely your fault." I glowered at her tattoo, then my matching one. "Getting inked has made me unbelievably horny."

"I know the feeling," she whispered, her fingers stroking the lion on her arm.

My cock lurched.

Fucking hell.

I resumed my pacing, breathing hard.

I reached the end of the curb and spun to pace again. A group of guys appeared around the corner. Four of them, slightly inebriated by the sounds of the overly loud guffaws, and old enough to know better. Two were slightly overweight with a local AFL shirt covering their middle-age spread, while two were younger and obviously went to the gym. Their tight t-shirts revealed thick arms and egos to match.

My instincts prickled; I marched back to Neri.

She fell quiet as the four guys came toward us. She squeezed my hand as I took hers, stepping closer to her until her dress licked around my legs. Her phone screen glowed in the night as she checked where the damn Uber driver was.

According to the red dot, the car was now even farther away.

Fucking stupid app.

The four guys snickered as they came closer. The younger two did a double take as they looked at Neri. My hackles rose as they elbowed each other and leered in a way that made my knuckles beg to pound into their face.

One of the older ones wolf-whistled.

My teeth ground together.

All four of them looked similar with dirty, sandy blond hair, slightly crooked noses, and the typical righteous air of drunken men. "Hey pretty sheila, aren't you a sight for sore eyes."

"You're a fucking tosser, mate." One of the fatter guys chuckled. "Sore eyes. What sort of expression is that? She's a beauty. That's what she is."

Neri pasted a thin, polite smile on her mouth, but her eyes turned arctic. Her fingers clenched in mine.

I stood taller, willing the group to walk on by and leave us the hell alone.

But then, one of the older guys looked at me. His eyes narrowed as if he could see exactly where I'd come from and found my presence utterly contemptable. "Hey...you. What the fuck are you doing here, fucking foreigner."

I froze.

Neri stiffened.

"Yeah, you! You don't belong here." One of the younger guys studied me closely. "What the fuck are you doing with a girl like her, huh? Fall off the wrong boat, did ya?"

Neri flinched. She swayed forward as if to attack them. I squeezed her hand so hard, I probably hurt her. I shot her a look. A look that screamed not to speak, not to engage.

They were nothing more than drunken idiots looking for a reaction.

They came closer, standing directly in front of us. "Oi, we asked you a question, mate."

One of the younger guys wearing a tight baby-blue t-shirt crossed his bulky arms. "This asshole bothering you, sexy? Want us to teach him a lesson?"

Neri opened her mouth.

I squeezed her hand so hard she winced.

"Did you just fucking hurt her, you cunt?" one of the older guys spat, his eyes locked on our hands hidden in the folds of Neri's dress. "Let her go."

The air suddenly filled with violence and animosity as the other guys shifted, their drunken dawdle tensing with aggression. "Oi, you heard him. Let her go." The fattest of the lot shoved my shoulder. His entire body bristled as if I'd personally offended him just by existing.

I rocked back on my heels, absorbing the strike but not letting it trip me.

The urge to retaliate bubbled in my guts.

The willingness to participate in bloodshed roared through my veins.

But there were four of them.

And two of us.

We're alone.

Neri had already been abused by one Australian bastard. There was no fucking way I'd put her in the position to endure another.

"You don't belong here. And you definitely don't belong with a girl like that." One of the younger guys spat at my shoes. "You're not welcome. And you're definitely not allowed to touch our fucking women."

"Just go away," Neri hissed. "Leave us alone."

My eyes snapped closed.

Fuck.

She'd always been far too ready to defend me. Far too courageous for her own good.

"Ooooo, la-di-daaa…she speaks." One of the older ones waved his arms about like a fucking lunatic. "He tell you to say that, sweetheart? You can tell us if he's scaring you."

"Only one who's scaring me is you," she spat back.

"*Nerida,*" I hissed.

She pressed harder against me. Our palms stuck together with sweat. I swear our heartbeats thundered to the same chaotic beat. She looked at her phone again, sucking in a breath as the red dot of our driver was nowhere to be seen.

"Don't you fucking talk to her like that," one of the older guys barked. "And take your hand off her. We won't ask again."

"I'm with him, you idiot," Neri snapped. "Go. *Away!*"

Fucking hell.

She was determined to destroy me.

"Aww, don't be like that, sweetheart," Blue T-shirt moaned.

"Fuck off." Neri bared her teeth.

"Hey." The older guy with a bald patch scowled. "Don't get mean."

"Fuck. *Off,*" Neri growled. "I'm with him. I'm fine. He's not hurting me. Your concern is not needed. Go. Away."

The other gym buff in a black t-shirt huffed. "Only looking out for you, sexy." He pointed at me. "You really shouldn't be hanging out with trash like this."

"Don't you dare talk about him like that." Neri stepped forward, proud and brave and utterly clueless to the fire she stoked. I held her back, my fingers white around hers.

"Neri…" I breathed, fighting the animalistic part of me that howled and roared to tear these men limb from limb. I barely clung to my humanness. Barely stayed coherent while these assholes threatened my most precious thing.

"Where the hell did you come from, huh?" Bald Spot asked me. "Definitely not from here." He looked at his mate with an ugly fish tattooed on his bicep. "Reckon we should help him find his way home?"

"He belongs with me," Neri hissed.

"Nah, you belong with one of us." Blue T-shirt grinned. "I could make you *real* happy."

My teeth turned to dust in my mouth.

I will not retaliate.

I will not put Neri in danger.

I will not strike.

I will not—

"Cat got your tongue, cunt?" Ugly Fish sneered. "Got nothing to say for yourself?"

Every bone in my body was on fire. The red haze that always fell over me whispered with bloody punishment. I wanted to beat them to a pulp for their slander and disgusting slurs.

But I wouldn't.

Because I would never put Neri in danger.

I would never let my ego choose violence over protecting her.

They could say whatever the hell they wanted about me, but *I*
will
not
react.

"Tell us where you came from. We'll make sure you get back there." The four men chuckled and swayed closer. "We can put you on a boat tonight. How about that?"

Neri shot me a look as if surprised at how calm I was.

I did my best to embrace ice. To become impenetrable to these bastards. My only task was to keep Neri safe. They meant nothing to me. She meant everything.

If I had to look weak, so be it.

If I had to listen to their remarks, fine.

As long as they grew tired of taunting and left us the fuck alone, they could spit on me again for all I cared.

"Fucking rude prick for not responding to us." Black T-shirt snarled. "Hey." He shoved me in the chest. "We're speaking to you."

My vision turned as red as blood.

My free hand balled into stone.

I will not retaliate.

I will not put Neri in danger.

I will not strike—

"If you won't speak willingly, we'll just make ya. Won't we, boys?" Bald Spot grinned.

Fuck.

I braced myself for a punch.

I deliberated how to protect Neri if they attacked.

But then Neri threw a match onto the gasoline these bastards had poured around our feet and stepped in front of me.

Putting herself in harm's way.

Making me lose the final shred of my control.

"Stop being racist pricks and go the fuck away!"

I snapped. I roared. I jerked her back. "*Lanet olsun, Neri. Sus!*" (Damn it, Neri. Shut up!)

All four guys reacted.

Disgust filled their faces.

Neri's wide eyes met mine.

And I realised my mistake too late.

Just like every time when my emotions grew too fierce, my mind slipped into my first language.

The guys bared their teeth. "Bloody immigrant. Can't even speak fucking English."

Fuck.

FUCK.

They stepped closer.

"Let her go, cunt!" Black T-shirt lurched forward, grabbing Neri's arm. He tugged her forward, making her stumble.

My heart stopped beating.

The savagery inside me woke up. The brutality that I'd only embraced once in my life raised its ugly head.

Gritting my teeth, I refused to speak.

I merely stepped forward, tore the bastard's hand off Neri, then shifted her so she was directly behind me. Backing her into the building, I caged her in, trapping her behind me.

"Aslan—"

"*Quiet*," I hissed.

"Fucking bastard. Don't tell her what to do." Ugly Fish tried to grab Neri from the side.

I stepped into his path and snarled. "You touch her, and you're fucking dead."

The two older guys paused and looked at each other.

A slow smile crossed their faces.

The decision I'd wanted to avoid flared cruelly in their drunken eyes.

And I knew.

Just like I'd known what Ethan had done to Neri, I knew what would happen tonight.

I would die defending her.

I would die murdering four Australian idiots who'd ruined one of the best days of my life.

I trembled on the spot, clinging with my final strength not to drown in hate. "I'm asking you nicely to leave," I seethed. "One last chance to continue walking and forget about us."

"You're fucking having a laugh." Blue T-shirt cracked his neck. "Give me the girl. I'll look after her. She'll find out what a real man—"

I hit him.

Square in the mouth.

His teeth split my knuckles, but it was worth it as he stumbled back and tripped off the curb.

The three other guys blinked as if not expecting me to deliver on my promises. I knew I shouldn't have struck first. I wished I could get Neri far, far away from here.

But it was too late

With a roar, the three uninjured men launched at me.

Neri got knocked to the side, landing on her knees as my hand was torn off hers and a punch *thwacked* against my temple.

My vision darted with black spots. Sickness splashed on my tongue. But it wasn't until Neri screamed and the sight of Black T-shirt towering over her, pawing at her, that I lost myself completely.

"Neri!"

She screamed as he tried to catch her swinging fists, his hands somehow tangling in her sea lion necklace. He pushed her to the ground as his fingers broke the silver chain. Neri cried out, more enraged at him for breaking her necklace than him pressing her against the dirty street.

With a chuckle, he threw her necklace into the gutter and trod on her sunset dress, keeping her down as she tried to launch up and fight him.

Another punch landed on my jaw, spinning me around.

I lost sight of her.

I panicked at what that fucking cunt was doing to her.

But all I could see were fists and violence.

Strike after strike landed on my torso, head, and shoulders.

Each one cracked and fissured the man I did my best to be, unlocking the cage, knocking down the bars inside me, smashing through the walls and doors and barriers.

Neri screamed again.

And that was it.

I became everything I always ran from.

I became the monster I was born to be.

Violence *ripped* through me.

Roaring, I launched at the men taking turns to punish me.

I moved faster than them.

I ducked quicker, hit harder, embraced death that always hunted me.

I would give the Reaper a soul tonight.

I'd give him four.

My fists struck.

My legs kicked.

Ruthlessly, silently, I attacked and pummelled, not feeling any pain as they landed their own strikes. They screamed at each other to defeat me. They yelled instructions on how best to win.

But I no longer spoke their language.

Words were useless.

Savagery was everything.

I was free.

The constant suffocation of hiding. The agonising attempt at ignoring who I truly was.

It was as if a pressure valve had opened.

Spilling out my darkness.

Letting loose my brutality.

I attacked them.

Inhumanly, viciously.

I wanted them bleeding.
I wanted them begging.
I want them in motherfucking pieces.

Chapter Twenty-One

NERIDA

AGE: 20 YRS OLD

(Love in Polish: Miłość*)*

I'D ALWAYS KNOWN ASLAN HID FROM A large part of who he was. I felt it each time he drove inside me. I tasted it each time he kissed me, and I heard it every night he snarled in his nightmares.

He treated me like I was his master and queen.

Yet beneath his reverence lurked a darker kind of touch.

A touch that could hurt.

A touch that could kill.

A touch that *had* killed.

Memories of him cutting off Ethan's fingers filled my head. The way his eyes had shot black as he'd lined up the knife against Ethan's cock. The absolute ruthlessness that overcame him as he went to slice.

I'd intervened.

Not because I wanted to save Ethan but because I'd wanted to save Aslan.

I didn't know what that would do to him.

I didn't know if he'd be able to come back from the black pit of violence that'd sucked him so deeply, so quickly, it both thrilled and terrified.

Aslan would do whatever it took to protect me. I'd witnessed it myself. I felt his depravity stalking beneath his devotion. I lived with a man who treated me so softly, so sweetly, but beneath his care existed absolute savagery. The undertones of his love had always been sharp, ready to snap if I was threatened.

And now, he'd snapped.

I wouldn't be able to intervene this time.

Four guys and him.

The one he'd punched and sent into the gutter joined the fray, kicking

Aslan's legs, trying to get him to go down while the other three rained fists all over his head and shoulders.

I stumbled out of the way as the snarling mountain of testosterone crashed against the side of the building. At least the guy who'd pushed me down had forgotten all about me as he chose to help his mates attack the love of my life.

My fingers clutched at my naked neck, my heart racing with loss. My necklace was in the gutter somewhere, but no way would I go and retrieve it. Not while Aslan was being pummelled.

This is my fault.

Why the hell did I talk back?

"Stop it!" I yelled. "Get the fuck off him!"

I kicked the closest guy as Aslan shoved him away. My toes hurt from my stupid glittery sandals. The guy didn't even notice I'd kicked him.

I punched one of the younger guys.

He snarled and backhanded me.

I went flying.

I landed on my ass.

My hands shot behind me to catch my fall, my wrists screaming, palms bleeding.

Leaping back to my feet, I circled them, trying to find a vulnerability to *stop this.*

"*Get off him!*" I yelled.

Nothing.

No one stopped or cared.

I was utterly fucking useless, and I hated it.

I hated that this was my fault.

I hated that I'd let them bait me.

If only I'd held my tongue.

If only I'd done what Aslan had commanded and stayed quiet.

Then they might've harassed us and moved on.

It shouldn't have mattered what these bastards thought of us. They could call us names and slander Aslan with their racist bigotry but who cared? They were nothing more than idiot losers, offended at life and unwilling to be nice.

They meant *nothing.*

So why did I retaliate?!

"GET OFF HIM!" I snarled, kicking someone's ankle. "Stop it!" I slapped someone's cheek.

I was nothing more than a pesky mosquito.

Fists flew, grunts sounded, I ducked out of the way as they crashed to the ground only for Aslan to spring back up and punch with single-minded determination.

I clung to my phone, cursing our stupid Uber driver.

Where the hell was Mazda TYZ129? If only he'd arrived sooner, we wouldn't have even been here when these idiots walked by.

Call the police.

I tripped back as Aslan round-housed a guy, sending one of the older, fatter ones whirling to the ground. The way he moved. The sheer power he possessed. It was awe-inspiring. Heart pounding. A beauty to behold how effortlessly he embraced bloodshed, all to keep me safe.

He groaned as someone's fist crunched against his jaw.

Only for that someone to go flying as Aslan punched him back with a right hook far more vicious. The fight escalated from a drunken brawl into a free-for-all feud.

Grunts and curses.

Blood and bruises.

Aslan was a whirlwind in the centre of the scuffle. A black riptide, sucking them down, drowning them punch by punch.

I swiped on my screen; my fingers poised over the emergency number.

If I called the police, would they question Aslan?

If I begged them to come and stop this, would they arrest Aslan for public brawling?

I looked up and winced as one of the younger guys with his gym-bulging body screamed and flung himself on Aslan.

My heart hurt.

My breath caught.

Guilt roared. Panic stung.

One of the guys cried out as Aslan wrapped his arm around the guy's neck. He twisted and flung himself backward, his eyes blacker than death as the guy scrambled and gagged in his hold.

With a violent twist, Aslan choked the guy into unconsciousness. The floppy body of his enemy tumbled out of Aslan's arms, slumping on the ground in an unnatural way.

Alive.

But…not functioning.

Aslan didn't stop to see if the guy would get up. He hurled himself at the other three assholes who roared with hate for what he'd done to their friend.

Aslan vanished again in the middle of a hurricane of fists and torture.

He absorbed so much pain, yet it never seemed to stop him. His fists landed square and true while the other men were sloppy and drunk. He kicked the ankle of one and sent him crunching to his knees while round-housing another. The guy went soaring backward to trip over the guy already down.

I backed farther away as the fight danced around the footpath, colliding against the building, tripping into the street, becoming increasingly violent.

Once again, I looked at my phone.

Should I call the police?

Think!

Make a damn decision!

Could Aslan actually win this? Or was I condemning him to being broken by doing nothing?

This is all my fault!

One of the younger guys suddenly screamed as Aslan grabbed his arms from behind and yanked him backward onto his uprisen knee. The guy's shoulders wrenched back with a sickening crack.

Aslan let him go the moment his scream turned to pleas, dropping him beside the other man who clutched at his neck and vomited all over himself.

"You fucking cunt," one of the older guys snarled. "You're dead."

Aslan didn't speak. He panted hard. Blood rained down his temple. His hands were a mess of flayed skin, swollen knuckles, and smeared crimson. Not waiting for the two guys still standing to attack, he dropped his shoulder and ran straight into the one with a fish tattooed on his arm.

He drove him hard against the building.

The man snarled.

His head smacked against the bricks.

His eyes rolled back, and he fell face first onto the mound of his mates already writhing and crying on the ground.

Breathing hard, eyes wild, blood dripping, Aslan clenched his fists and turned to face the only bastard still standing. The bald-headed older guy. His face twisted with hate as he looked at his defeated friends, then embraced common sense by raising his hands in surrender. "Fuck you. I'm done. I'm done, alright. Back the fuck off."

I expected Aslan to accept his white flag, but he was too far gone, too deep in that violence that he always ran from.

He stepped toward the guy.

He cricked his neck.

The air turned icy with intention.

"Aslan." I darted forward, clutching my phone. "Don't."

His hands twitched, but he didn't turn to face me. Didn't halt.

A car careened around the corner. A red Mazda with the license plate TYZ129.

My heart leapt as I tried to get Aslan to look at me. "Our ride's here, Aslan. Let's just go home. Okay?" I stepped off the curb, trying to get in front of him as he stalked the guy who did his best to stay out of his way.

They danced around each other until the guy faced the building and Aslan had his back to the street. The Mazda kept driving far too fast, but I was grateful.

At least we could get the hell out of here.

"Aslan, it's okay," I murmured.

His eyes narrowed, but he still didn't look at me.

True panic frosted my blood as the guy flicked me a look of pure fear. He could sense what I could. That Aslan was dangerous. In his current state, I honestly didn't know what he would do—

"*Seni seviyorum,*" I whisper-shouted, willing my brain to turn words I'd learned into a sentence that hopefully made sense. "*Geçti artık. Bitti. Güvendeyim. Artık bana zarar veremezler.*" (It's okay. It's over. I'm safe. They can't hurt me anymore).

Aslan flinched.

His head tipped up; he blinked.

The midnight shadows in his stare faded as he glanced at me and slowly left whatever mayhem he'd existed in.

I held out my hand as the Mazda came flying toward us. "Let's go home, husband."

"*Husband?*" the old guy hissed. "Fucking creep. He has you speaking his language and poisoned you against who you truly belong to." He spat on the ground. "You're both as bad as each other."

I ignored him.

Aslan ignored him.

Our eyes locked, and the frost inside me melted a little. He was still in there. Still the soulmate I knew and loved. The man who wouldn't hurt anyone instead of the murderer who was far too good at it.

I smiled.

I raised my hand.

Aslan swallowed hard and raised his bloody one.

Everything was better now.

Everything would be okay.

"I love you," I whispered.

But then...it happened.

Death that'd stalked Aslan since he'd escaped the shipwreck eight years ago chose that exact moment to pounce.

The older guy charged.

With a war cry, he ran straight into Aslan, arms outstretched, palms smacking against Aslan's chest. He shoved him so fast, so fiercely, Aslan didn't stand a chance.

He went reeling backward.

His ankle rolled as he tripped off the curb.

His arms went flying.

Screeching tyres split the night sky—

Chapter Twenty-Two

NERIDA

AGE: 20 YRS OLD

(Love in Hindi: Pyaar)

I DROPPED MY PHONE AS THE RED car that was meant to take us home drove directly into him, smashing him over the bonnet, crashing him against the windscreen, and flinging him into a broken heap on the street.

No.

No.

NO!

Screams filled my ears, my mouth, my heart. "ASLAN!"

I sprinted to where he lay unmoving in the headlights of the stopped Mazda. The windscreen had exploded into cubes of safety glass, littering Aslan and the road. It crunched beneath my sandals as I bolted to his side and froze.

No.

Please no.

All I could see was blood.

"Aslan..." My stomach eroded with acid, spilling through me, turning my bones into puddles of horror.

"Aslan." I choked on sobs as I dropped to my knees and wedged both hands over my mouth. I couldn't touch him. Couldn't believe this was real.

Open your eyes.

Come on.

Open your eyes.

Please!

I need you to open your eyes!

Any second now, he'd open them, spring to his feet, and gather me in his strong, immortal arms.

"Fuck. Come on!" The guy who'd shoved Aslan into traffic kicked his mates on the ground. "Gotta go. Get up. *Get up!*" The drunken bastard roused his friends, helping them up, pushing them, shooing them stumbling and limping down the street.

I couldn't move.

Couldn't breathe.

I trembled as if a hurricane had replaced my heart as I slowly dropped my hands from my mouth and reached out to touch him.

I did this.

This is my fault.

I shouldn't have stopped him.

I shouldn't have distracted him.

My fault…

My fault!

The guys kept running, lumbering.

They left us.

Left me as I bit my bottom lip to stem my sobs and choked on a breath as I touched Aslan.

The spark between us was missing.

The hum and thrum and everlasting connection was non-existent as I wiped his blood-drenched bronzed hair off his ruby-wet forehead.

"Aslan…please." My heart hammered with an agony I'd never felt before, muted but excruciating, quiet but as loud as thunder. "Please, Aslan…open your eyes."

I didn't know what came over me.

All my life, I'd been strong and brave.

I'd fought for those less fortunate, championed for animals, and never shied away from those in pain, but this?

Him?

I couldn't cope.

Parts of me shut down. My eyes refused to compute that Aslan—the love of my life and my absolutely everything—was unmoving, unbreathing, unblinking in the middle of the road. My mind rejected the images as if this was a horror movie I could turn off and forget. My body refused to accept that the conduit of electricity that always flowed between us was now dull and dead.

Piece by piece, my body folded in on itself as well as my heart and soul.

I hovered in a space of disbelief, distrust, and rejection.

This can't be real.

It just can't be.

It's not.

I rested my palm against his cheek.

He's fine.

See?

He's fine.

On the coattails of denial came the violent need to bargain.

To haggle with angels, negotiate with the devil, and offer up any contract with any entity that somehow had the power to make this all a silly mistake.

Please...

"Aslan..." I ran my fingertips over his closed eyes, smearing blood like a death mask. "Darling, dearest Aslan...please. You're okay. I know you are."

He didn't move.

Didn't do anything.

Just lay there.

Like a corpse.

Like a body that'd lost its soul.

No.

Wrongness flooded my fingers where I touched him.

Hope ruptured inside me.

The worst kind of violation of being left alone and—

No.

With a deep breath, I cupped his cheeks and shifted him onto his back. "You're not gone. I refuse. I won't allow it. It's not possible."

His lips parted as his head fell to the side.

Glass cubes dug into my knees as I bent over him and wedged my ear against his chest.

Come on.

Beat.

Beat for me.

Stay for me...

My ear burned I pressed so hard.

My own heart stopped, waiting for his to reply.

Insidious ice slithered through me, leaving laces of frost in its path. My ribcage glittered with snow. My organs froze solid. I shook my head as sleety fog fell over my mind, whispering that this was just a dream.

Just a silly little nightmare, and I'd wake soon.

I'd wake, and Aslan would be beside me.

I'd wake, and this would all be over.

Wake up.

Wake up.

WAKE UP!

The car door opened.

I blinked from my sickening subspace as a cloud of marijuana smoke appeared, staining the night sky. A skinny guy with short black hair and chains dripping off his jeans tripped from the driver's seat and stumbled to the front of his car. Blood oozed on his temple, and his nose looked broken.

The white pillow of the airbag filled the empty windshield, revealing he'd ploughed into Aslan hard enough to trigger the car's protocols to take care of its driver.

The Mazda had kept him safe with seatbelts and airbags. Cocooned in a bubble of protection. All while Aslan was thrown through the air, launched by metal, propelled by a vehicle driven by someone high as a fucking kite.

Hate soaked into my ice.

Dangerous, treacherous *hate*.

"Oh shit. Oh shit. Oh *shit*." He clutched his short hair, pacing around Aslan and the rubble of his car. "Fuck, is he...?" He toed him, and I lost it.

"*Don't you dare fucking touch him!*" I roared.

"He's dead. Oh fuck, he's dead."

"He's not!" Tears broke loose, pouring down my cheeks. "He can't be. I can't—" I looked back down at Aslan, unmoving and silent by my knees. His cheekbone was swollen from fists, his lip split, his shirt torn. He looked as if he'd been shipwrecked again, only this time by glass and asphalt instead of sea and storm.

I fell on his chest.

Listening, begging, pleading.

Wake up, Aslan.

Please, please wake up.

My breath came too loudly. My heart raced too thickly.

I couldn't hear his.

Couldn't tell if he was here or gone.

I lost my grip on reality as fear of discovery overrode fear of his passing.

I should've let him kill them.

I should never have intervened.

I did this...

My fault.

My fault!

"Aslan, come on, darling. We need to go. We have to go before anyone sees, okay?"

If I could get him back to our place, he'd be fine.

If I could hide him before anyone saw, he'd wake and still be mine.

"Aslan—"

"FUCK!" The guy suddenly bellowed. He bent over and retched, splashing his feet with vomit. He hurled again before tripping backward and fumbling in his pocket. "I-I'm calling an ambulance. I don't care that I'll get in trouble. I can't...I can't live with this. We need help." He yanked out his phone, his fingers flying over the screen.

"No!" I yelled. "You can't."

They'll know who he is.

They'll take him from me.

They'll kill him—

Every bone in my body splintered into pieces.

Guilt crushed me. Killed me. Strangled me.

"Lady, I have to call. If he's not dead already, he's gonna be if I don't." His eyes were overly dilated in the brightness of his headlights. The car motor still ran. The night remained eerily quiet. In the far distance, the four guys who'd beaten Aslan rounded the corner and vanished.

I lost myself.

I lost my grip on reality as urgency flooded me.

Shaking Aslan's shoulders, I commanded, "Come on, Aslan. We have to go." I bent and kissed his forehead, not caring his blood smeared my lips. I shivered, but I wasn't cold. My heart skipped and slipped, but I couldn't get enough air.

I couldn't breathe properly.

Couldn't think.

We need to get home.

Home where I can wash his wounds and tend to his bruises. I'll bathe him and put him to bed, and in the morning, he'll be fine. You'll see. This will all be fine.

"Aslan. Get up!"

The driver never stopped pacing, his phone pressed to his ear. "Yes, hi. There's been an accident."

"You're high," I hissed. "You call for help and they'll arrest you for driving under the influence."

The driver flinched, ignoring me. "Yeah, I, eh...I accidentally ran into someone. He's, eh...he's not moving." His voice cracked as he tipped his head down. "I don't know the street, man. Can't you just track me or something? Please, hurry. There's so much blood."

I blinked and looked at where he stared.

I reared back as truth cut through my fog of disbelief.

Blood.

Everywhere.

I kneeled in it.

Aslan glimmered in it from the headlights.

My hands were covered in crimson.

Noise howled in my ears. White noise. A blizzard. A roaring, snarling—

"Hey. Are you...are you okay?" The guy snapped me back to the worst moment of my life. He balanced on his haunches, reaching to push away my sweaty hair. "They're on their way, okay? They'll fix this."

I shoved away his hand.

This is all my fault.

My fault!

He fell onto his ass, landing in blood. His palm thudded on Aslan's chest. "Fuck." Scrambling away, he shook with uncontrollable tremors. "I'm sorry. I'm so, so sorry. I didn't mean—" Raking both hands through his short hair, tears rained down his cheeks. "I'm so fucking sorry."

I looked back at Aslan, unresponsive and tangled on the street. His legs were spread but didn't look broken. His shirt had rucked up his belly, revealing road rash and cuts from the safety glass. A black contusion spread over his ribcage from being struck by the car.

I waited to break.

To plummet into hysterics.

But all I felt was numb.

Terribly, horribly numb.

Bending over him, I stroked his cheek. "Aslan, baby. Please, open your eyes. We have to go home now."

"Go?!" The driver choked. "He's unconscious. He's probably dead. He can't go anywhere."

My voice was ice and eerily calm. "We can't be here when the ambulance arrives. I need to get him home."

The guy's eyebrows shot up. "He needs a doctor."

"He can't see one."

He shook his head as if he believed he'd run me over as well. Pure panic etched his face. Crawling toward me, he winced as he pressed two fingers to Aslan's blood-smeared throat. He held my stare as he waited for his pulse.

In some foggy part of me, I screamed and tried to shake myself awake.

I should be doing that.

It should've been the first thing I did.

Wake up.

This is just a dream.

WAKE UP!

Exhaling heavily, the guy dropped his hand. "He's still alive."

Pain slashed through me.

Agonising relief.

Blistering guilt.

My dead heart woke up, kicking with renewed hope and lifeforce. "Help me take him home. Drive us."

His mouth fell open. "Did you not hear me? He needs to go to the hospital. This is my fault. I'm not letting him go anywhere unless it's to get medical help. If there's the smallest chance he won't die, then I'll do whatever it takes to ensure he survives." Fresh tears fell. "I can't go to jail for this. I can't."

I felt nothing for him.

Just loathing.

Blocking him out, I curled up beside Aslan on a bed made of glass with blankets made of night. I wrapped my arm around his cooling chest and pressed my face to his neck. His pulse fluttered faintly against my lips, granting an avalanche of love.

He's alive.

He's not gone.

He's alive!

Dread followed that wonderful knowledge, and I sat up again with renewed determination.

All the nudges of my youth. All those knowings I'd listened to when I was younger stabbed me, blade after blade.

He can't go to the hospital.

He's alive.

He's mine.

But if he goes, they'll know.

They'll find out who he is.

They'll take him—

Hysteria chose that moment to infect me, and I did something that seemed so understandable in my smoggy head but most likely looked deranged.

I slapped him.

I slapped him right on the cheek and hissed, "Wake up right now, Aslan Avci. If you don't, you won't wake up at all, do you hear me? They're coming. They're coming for you, and I won't be able to stop them if you don't wake the hell up!"

"Shit, stop that!" The driver launched himself at me. "What the hell do you think you're doing hitting him?"

"Let go of me!"

"No way. Just sit still until help arrives." He looked at Aslan with such remorse. "Hey, Aslan, is it? Mr. Avci. Please, man. Hold on. Help's coming."

"Don't you dare use his name. You're not worthy of using it. You're the reason he's hurt! And it's not help that's coming." I bared my teeth and shoved him away. "It's death."

"What? Of course, it's not. They're going to keep him alive, not kill him."

"Please. Help me get him into your car so I can hide him." I grabbed the guy's sweat-damp beige shirt. "Please, take us home. They'll kill him. I did this. I'm the reason he's hurt. Please help me fix this. Please!"

"You're in shock, lady. That's all this is. You're in shock and—"

"I'm fine. This will all be fine. Everything is fine. It can all remain fine. I just need to get him home where no one will see."

His face contorted with pity. "Look, it's okay. They'll help you too. Just a few more minutes and—"

"A few more minutes and they'll *take him from me!*" Shoving him away again, I tripped to my feet, bent over, and tried to pluck Aslan from the road. His head lolled as I hauled his shoulders. His legs splayed wider as I tried to pull.

I can carry him home.

I'll pick him up and get him far away from here.

My fault.

My fault!

I'll fix it.

I can make it better.

I'll call Mum and Dad, and they can——

"Jesus Christ." The driver snaked his arm around my waist, yanking me back. "Don't move an unconscious man. You don't know what's broken. You're making shit worse!"

I needed help, not a hindrance.

I needed to fix this before it was too late.

Guilt.

So. Much. Fucking. *Guilt.*

Pushing the driver as hard as I could, I wheeled backward, blinded by headlights, ears roaring with the still-running engine.

I fumbled for my phone.

Dad will know what to do.

They've kept him hidden for years.

They can fix this.

Please…please fix what I've broken.

My hands burrowed through my dress and found nothing.

Where is it?

Narrowing my eyes, I glanced at the spot where I'd kneeled beside Aslan. I tripped forward, searching for my phone. Aslan's phone lay smashed into pieces by the Mazda's tyre, and mine lay in a puddle of congealing blood beside my beaded clutch.

I swayed forward to grab it.

I bent——

But my eyes fell on something else dead and unwanted in the sea of safety glass.

Something small and spiky.

Something peach and cream.

Something that belonged in the ocean or Aslan's pocket.

Not here. Not in a city. Not on a dirty street.

The shell.

The spiny frog shell I'd given Aslan when he'd saved my life.

All the ice, all the fog and frost, all the guilt and numbness *shattered.*

I collapsed to my knees.

A wail exploded from my mouth.

And I saw clearly without any film of disbelief or haze of bargaining.

I saw the truth.

And I broke.

No.

No.

NO!

Crawling on my hands and knees, not feeling anything other than the pain searing in my chest, I grabbed Aslan's shell and threw myself over him.

I drove my fist over his heart, over and over again, losing myself to sobs. "Wake up. Please, *please* wake up. You have to wake up. Please, Aslan. Please, *please* don't do this. I can't lose you. I can't. I won't. I'm sorry. I'm so, so sorry. I didn't mean to hurt you. I didn't mean to put you in danger. I—"

Ambulance sirens sounded.

Coming so fast, so quick.

"Wake up!" I rocked over him, clutching his shell, begging it to grant a wish and bring him back to me. "Please!"

Give us one more chance. One more moment where we're unseen and safe.

"Please, Aslan—"

"I'm sorry. So sorry," the driver cried, giant tears rolling down his cheeks as red and blue flashing lights cast over him. A large decal-covered van zoomed up the street: a gallant box on wheels to save the day.

No.

They can't.

I won't let them.

The sirens cut off as the ambulance jerked to a stop behind the ruined car before rolling slowly around to park in front of us.

Headlights from the Mazda and taillights from the ambulance drowned us in illumination.

White light.

Red light.

Heaven and hell.

A woman and man leaped from the van and dashed to the back. Wrenching open the double doors at the rear, the man grabbed a medical bag all while woman muttered something into her radio stuck to her shoulder.

The male EMT took one look at the driver, sniffed the marijuana-pungent air coming from the Mazda, and barked at his colleague, "Tell the police to hurry up." Pointing at the guy, he barked, "Are you hurt?"

The driver shook his head. "Nah. I'm fine. The airbag went off. I-I'm fine." He swiped at his tears. "He's not, though. He's breathing but hasn't moved. Fuck, I'm going to jail, aren't I?" He lost himself in a tangle of sobs. Falling to his ass, he wrapped his arms around his knees, rocking back and forth.

The EMT ignored him, dropping to his haunches beside Aslan and tearing into his bag of tricks.

I just blinked.

I couldn't feel my hands or my body.

The pain was too much.

The loss.

The fear.

The *guilt.*

It choked me, broke me, and the numbness was back.

I dissociated from this life.

I wanted another one.

The one where Aslan surprised me with a tattoo and promised to seduce me tonight with toys and fantasies.

I wanted the one where he was legally allowed to live here. Legally allowed to receive care. Legally allowed to get into that ambulance and come home to me once he was all better.

I floated above my body, looking down on Aslan strewn and still in the middle of the road as the medic worked on him.

I couldn't do a damn thing.

I couldn't breathe.

I couldn't move.

I wanted to steal the ambulance and drive Aslan home myself.

I wanted to stab him with all the needles and patch him up with all the bandages.

If we could be left alone, I'd look after him.

I'd fix him, just like he fixed me.

Please, Aslan.

God, Aslan.

This can't be happening…

I swayed on the spot, fighting the greyness in my vision and the strange stabbing pain in my lower belly. It fluttered and flittered like I'd swallowed a badly behaving bird.

The EMT glanced at me, his eyebrows coming down in worry. "Were you struck too?"

His words were nothing more than static.

A buzzing.

A humming.

Aslan.

Aslan.

I can't lose you.

I'm sorry…

"Hey." The guy snapped his fingers in front of my face. "Are you injured?"

Tears rolled silently down my cheeks.

The female EMT suddenly crowded me, blocking my vision of Aslan and shining a torch in my eyes.

I winced.

I tripped backward.

She caught me and looked at her partner. "I think she's in shock."

I shook my head.

No, I'm fine.

There's nothing wrong with me.

A tearing, slicing pain in my belly.

Aslan.

Heal him here.

Fix him here.

Don't take him anywhere.

Please...

"Call ahead," the male EMT ordered. "Tell them three patients inbound. One will arrive with police and two with us."

The woman obeyed, marching away and relaying the message to dispatch.

Time skipped, and she was suddenly back in front of me, studying me closely as I wrapped my arms around my strangely spasming middle.

"What's your name?" she asked softly. "What's his name?"

Name.

No names.

They can't know names.

Panic poured hotly, coldly, deadly. "H-He's fine," I whispered. "He just needs to go home. Please...just let us go home."

"We're just going to take him to the hospital first, okay?" she murmured gently. "We'll look after him and then you guys can go home."

"No." I shook my head, pawing at her hands. Perhaps she'd be on our side if I could make her understand. She'd protect him. She'd hide him. "He can't go to the hospital. They'll know who he is."

"Know who he is?" She cupped my cheeks, her fingers feathering around my head as if searching for a wound. "Why would that matter? We need to know who he is so we can make him feel better."

I pushed her away. "Please. Just make him wake up and I can do the rest. I can look after him. I was born to be his, don't you understand? You have to understand. If you take him away from me, he'll die and—" A sob cut me off.

My body felt wrong.

My thoughts nothing more than storm clouds.

"I did this, don't you see?" I cried. "He told me not to speak to them and I did. He protected me. He *always* protects me. And I distracted him. If I'd let him kill that bastard, he'd be fine. We'd be fine. I always do this. I make so many mistakes. I don't think. I don't listen. I...I—"

My stomach churned. Guilt slashed at my throat.

"Just ignore all that for now, okay? What's his name, honey? Tell me his name and yours, and we'll call your family to come be with you guys. How about that? You won't be alone to deal with this anymore, okay? You'll have family."

Family.

My family loves Aslan.

Aslan's father wants to slaughter him.

"He has to stay here. *Promise me* you'll let him stay."

The EMTs shared a concerned look. Finally, the man muttered, "Definitely shock." Looking down, he inserted an IV line into Aslan's veins. "No head wounds?"

The woman pursed her lips. "Nothing that I can feel."

"Then it's purely psychological." His voice turned harder as he looked at me. "Climb into the ambulance. We're going to go now. We'll get you both feeling better as soon as possible."

More sirens shredded the night, followed by more flashing blue and red lights.

The empty street became a hive of activity as two police cars joined the traffic jam of Mazda and ambulance.

Car doors slammed as uniformed officers climbed out.

Their buckles glinted.

Their buttons gleamed.

I'm sorry.

I'm sorry.

I'm—

I lost the battle.

Air swirled.

Night crushed.

And the last thing I saw was Aslan, bloody and broken, before I collapsed beside him, and everything went dark.

Chapter Twenty-Three

NERIDA

AGE: 20 YRS OLD

(*Love in Icelandic:* Ást)

MY EYES FLEW OPEN.

I shot upright, dizzy and tingly, completely lost.

W-Where am I?

Organized chaos swarmed around me as nurses drifted from bedsides as patients were assessed and left in different stages of undress, malaise, and distress.

Nausea splashed on my tongue as I slowly sat up, pushing away the hastily spread blanket over me and holding onto the bed railing as the world swam and tilted.

"Easy, easy, just stay down." A middle-aged nurse squeaked toward me in bright pink Crocs. Her head tipped down, her eyes scanning paperwork even as she hustled toward me. Dark-brown hair bordering on black gleamed in a tight bun, while her dusky-olive skin was flawless even under the harsh fluorescents.

Coming to my side, she finished reading whatever she had in her hands then looked up.

She froze and did a double take. "N-Nerida?"

I blinked and urged my useless brain to wake up.

Something wasn't right.

Everything was wrong.

And yet…I couldn't remember what.

But I could remember her, and the relief to see a familiar face made tears prick my stinging eyes.

"Jedda." I swallowed hard as urges inside me did their best to figure out what the hell was going on. "Hi."

"W-What are you doing here?" She scanned whatever notes had been formulated on me. "You fainted at the scene of a car crash?"

And just like that, everything came flooding back.

Every awful, crippling thing.

Aslan!

Oh God.

Where is he?

Panic clutched my nervous system; I swung my legs out of bed, fully intending to go sprinting through the hospital to find him. Only, Jedda placed a calming hand on my uncalmable heart. "Talk to me, Nerida. Tell me what happened."

My eyes flew to her.

It took so much effort, so much self-control to obey her.

Out of every nurse to tend to me.

Out of every hospital.

This had to be fate, right?

Fate stepping in to help me keep him hidden and safe.

"Aslan. He was the one in the car crash. H-He was unconscious. I passed out when the police arrived."

"The police?" Her familiar, pretty face blanched. "Good grief. They don't know who he is, do they?"

I folded in on myself in gratefulness.

Jedda was the only secret my parents and I had ever kept from Aslan.

A secret I'd wanted to tell him but always felt like it would upset him more than offer comfort.

The day after sixteen-year-old Aslan walked on his fractured ankle and begged us for asylum, Jedda had pitched up at our front door while Aslan was in the shower, fumbling with his cast, washing away his grief from losing his family.

I'd stood on the front doorstep with Mum's arms wrapped around me as Jedda shifted on the spot and said...

"The shipwrecked boy...the one you found. He ran from the wards in the night before he could be interviewed by border officials."

Dad had tensed and closed the front door, hustling Jedda toward her small silver Suzuki. "Lovely to see you, Jedda, as always. Tell Coen that we've been meaning to pop by for another night of stories and great food, but now is not the time—"

"He's here. Isn't he?"

Mum gasped, and Dad froze by the gate. "We have no idea where he is—"

"You put your names down as the boy's next of kin. You wouldn't do that if you didn't feel responsible for him."

"We saved his life." Dad puffed up his chest, his eyes flicking to me. "Neri saved his life. The least we can do is—"

"Harbour a refugee?" Jedda crossed her arms, flicking a wary glance down the street as if the neighbours would hear. "You know the trouble you could get into, Jack. This is

dangerous. I admit that he's special. He said he didn't have an eidetic memory, but I have my doubts. The way he remembered the concussion test. How quickly he added up sums. He's unique, and I get why you'd be willing to help—"

"If you understand, then why are you here?" Mum let me go, crossing her arms.

"I'm here because I know how easily he could be caught and how much trouble—"

"You were the one who helped with my water birth, Jedda. You were there when I delivered Neri and have been there every day since. You said she was special. And you just admitted you thought Aslan was special. Don't both deserve a life of safety? Isn't it our obligation to help those in need?"

"Of course, but—"

"He told me he'll be killed if he's sent back home," Dad whispered. "I don't know how or why or who would do such a thing, but…I trust him."

"So he did come here?" Jedda narrowed her eyes. "He's here…right now?"

"The less you know, the better." Dad glowered.

"I already know too much," Jedda muttered. Her hand vanished into her slouchy handbag. She paused for a moment with her fingers inside. "Have you thought this through? Truly? Do you honestly know what you're getting yourselves into?"

Mum shrugged. "We can't let him be deported. And you know they would take one look at him and toss him into a refugee camp or fly him straight back home."

I looked between all three adults, short with my twelve-year-old height and my heart fit to bursting with fear over the boy currently in our shower. With bravery borne from wanting to protect him, I placed my hand on Jedda's arm, remembering all the nights around the bonfire with her people. All the incredible tales of animals that roamed this land before humans existed and all the stories of family, compassion, and connection. Her husband had even tried to teach me the digeridoo last time we'd spent an evening at their place. Apart from the sea, their house was my most favourite place on earth with its open-air living rooms, thatched ceilings, and willingness to share their home with lizards, cockatoos, and the occasional kangaroo.

I wanted to be her when I grew up.

In-tune with the world and driven by destiny to help others in any way I could.

"Please, Auntie Jedda," I murmured. "I found him for a reason. He has to stay for a reason. Please don't tell anyone. Okay? No one else knows we found him. Just you."

Jedda glanced at my parents before reluctantly pulling her hand out of her handbag. Her fingers clutched a file. She shoved it into Dad's hold. "That's the only paperwork on him. Dr Tarn and Dr Cotton will most likely have already forgotten about the teenager with the fractured ankle and wrist. I was the last one to see him, and if they ask, I'll say I saw him hitchhiking out of town." Pointing at the file, she added, "Burn that so no one knows his name."

Mum smiled softly. "You're a good person, Jedda. A wonderful person."

"Not as good as you, it turns out." Jedda shrugged. "I'm not the one adopting a refugee."

"He might only be here a short while to get on his feet, but…if he ever needs medical attention…" Dad said quietly. "Could you help him? He can't go to the hospital after

this."

Jedda flinched. "I can't be a part of this, Jack. Unless it's life or death, my answer is no. I can't risk my position."

"Understood." Dad wrapped his arms around her and squeezed her tightly. "Thank you. For everything. We owe you."

"You owe me nothing. Just...look after him and yourself."

"Neri...Neri, are you okay?" Jedda snapped her fingers in front of my face, dragging me back from a simpler time, a better time, a time when Aslan was safe and unknown.

"Answer me. Do the police know who he is?"

I shuddered as fresh tears spilled. "I-I don't know. I have to find him before they do. I have to get him out of here." Hot terror burned me alive. "If they find out he doesn't have a Medicare number. If they somehow find out he's been hiding here all this time—"

"Easy. One step at a time. Let's find out where he is first. And then we'll figure out what to do."

"You mean...you'll help me?" I gulped. "You'll help me get him out of here?"

"Of course, I will. I love you. I love your parents and don't want them getting into trouble." Her lips pursed. "I didn't cover for him all those years ago for him to be deported now, that's for damn sure." She pulled out a small e-tablet from her scrubs, scrolling quickly. "Are you sure you didn't tell them his name? Before you passed out?"

I froze.

Everything was blurry.

All I could remember was hovering above the road as if I was the one who'd died and lingered as a ghost.

"I-I don't think so...?" I hunched and hugged myself. "I don't remember much if I'm honest. I was petrified."

"Rightfully so." Her ebony eyes softened as they met mine again. "It says you're suffering shock. That you passed out due to witnessing the graphic nature of the crash."

I flinched. "I don't care about me. I just need to see him."

"You'll still need to be checked out now that you're awake. You have a few lacerations on your hands and knees."

"Not until I know he's okay."

"He'll be alright, Neri." She patted my hand with capable urgency. "We'll make sure of it." A smidgen of relief came from her taking control. I wasn't alone anymore. She would help me. She was trustworthy. Aslan never knew he had another guardian angel hiding him in plain sight, but she'd kept his secret just as carefully as we had.

What were the chances?

What was the luck?

"What are you doing here?" I choked. "I thought you said to Mum that you were transferring back to Mossman?"

"I was asked to do another year. I'm the head nurse now, and they're short-staffed." She smiled sadly. "Aren't they always? But I agreed to one more year before I get to go home to Port Douglas." Laying her hand on mine, she murmured, "Anna told me you were studying down here. I never in a million years thought I'd see you in the emergency room. On your birthday, no less."

I gave her a sad smile. "Not exactly how I would've liked catching up. It's been too long, Auntie Jedda."

"I agree. Time has a horrible way of speeding up." She smiled, returning to her scrolling. "You and Aslan will have to come to dinner one night. Coen and I are renting a place not too far from here. We'd love to have you. Just like old times."

"Are you okay if Aslan finds out you've known about him all along? I thought that's why we never brought him around to visit?"

"I don't think I have a choice anymore." She stopped scrolling as her eyes read quickly. "Found him. Unidentified male. Ethnicity unknown. Approx mid-twenties. X-rays show three cracked ribs, possible hip fracture, stable head wound, and twenty-seven stitches on his left shoulder."

Blood.

It flashed through my mind.

There'd been so much blood.

My stomach tore itself apart.

Three ribs? A broken hip? *Stitches*?

Fuck.

"Will he be okay?" I whispered. "Can you take me to him?"

"He's awake and refusing to tell staff his name." Her head shot up, the lines of text she'd read still glowing in her stare. "Good grief, he mentioned you, though. That's not good. Not good at all."

Before I could ask why or what she planned on doing, she bent over me, pressed a quick kiss to my forehead, and whispered, "Don't tell anyone, under any circumstances, that you're looking for him. If someone comes to you asking if you know a man asking for you, deny it."

"But I—"

"Deny it, Nerida. Or you and your parents will be in worse trouble than he is." Patting my cheek, she narrowed her eyes. "Stay here. Don't say a word."

She left in a flurry of pink Crocs before I could stop her.

The temptation to chase after her hit me strong.

But fear over making things worse made me stay.

I always make things worse...

My eyes fell on the small table beside me and the plastic bag holding

Aslan's smashed phone, mine in its glittery blue case, my blood-covered clutch, money-clip, and the spiky shell that I'd been clinging to as I'd collapsed beside Aslan.

My necklace wasn't there.

Most likely still in the gutter and lost forever.

I don't care.

If it were a tax I had to pay to have Aslan returned to me, I'd happily pay it.

I'll sacrifice anything and everything.

Just please…let him be okay…

With tears stinging, I ripped open the bag, grabbed Aslan's shell, and fisted it close.

I stroked it and begged it to fix everything that I'd broken, all while my fingers went to my engagement ring. The ring with the Latin inscription: *Per lunam tuus sum, per mare meus es. Aeternum.* (By moonlight I am yours, by sea you are mine. Forever).

I started to spin the wave-trapped diamond.

Nervous and worried.

Spin.

Spin.

Afraid and terrified.

Spin.

Spin.

Spinning away time until Aslan was mine again.

Chapter Twenty-Four

ASLAN

(Heart in Polish: Serce*)*

THUNDER CRASHED OVER MY HEAD. LIGHTNING FORKED. I clung to the rigging as a wall of water appeared.

The boat screeched as it struggled to stay in one piece. The wave sent us higher, higher up its face.

I turned to grab my sister and cousin.

But in their place sat Neri.

With big sea-blue eyes, drenched hair, and blood smearing her cheek.

"Neri." I reached for her.

She reached for me.

The wave broke.

It slammed between us, ripping us apart, flinging me one way and pushing me down, down, down.

"NERIDA!"

Depths sucked me.

Tentacles lashed around my legs.

I fought—

"Easy there. You're okay." Fingers cupped around my flying fist, absorbing my strike, and planting my arm down.

My eyes wrenched open.

Bright painful lights shone. Sounds of people and beeping machinery filled my ears. Agony tore through every part of me, throbbing in my head, ribs, hip, and shoulder. Even my long-healed ankle twinged, feeding me memories of tripping off the footpath, stumbling, falling—

He pushed me.

That motherfucker pushed me.

I frowned.

Everything was black after that. I had no idea what'd happened or how

I'd ended up here.

Shit.

Where is here?

Pain.

It struck from nowhere.

Everywhere.

Gasping with agony, I glanced around the room.

Wires, monitors, sterile equipment, and a man towering over me in scrubs. His hazel eyes met mine as his lips lifted in a smile. A smile that was supposed to be comforting but merely looked like an executioner's grin.

"Glad you're awake. You slept through all the fun stuff."

I swallowed hard, wincing at the rusty, metallic taste on my tongue. "Wh-Where am I?"

"Townsville University Hospital. You were in a car accident."

Car accident?

I hadn't been near a car.

I'd been fighting the bastards who'd threatened Neri. One of them broke her necklace and pushed her to the ground.

I'd lost myself.

I'd won—

I shook my pounding head as everything went blank apart from one thing.

One excruciatingly important thing.

Neri.

My heart thundered. "Where's Nerida?"

"Nerida?" The male nurse with shaggy brown hair frowned, peering into my eyes as if checking me for concussion. "Who's Nerida?"

"Nerida Ave...I mean, Taylor. She's my wife. They were hurting her. They touched her—" Fury blazed through me. I wanted to kill that bastard for *daring* to lay a finger on Neri.

I'd promised her no one would ever touch her against her will again.

And I'd failed.

I'd fucking failed just like I failed by losing her.

Anger bled deeper than any wound. Physical pain didn't stand a chance. "Nerida. I need to see Nerida. *Right fucking now!*"

"No need for language, sir. I'm here to help—"

"Please," I snarled, remembering my manners. "I need to see her *please.*"

"Just calm down and—"

"I'll calm when I see her." Rage cracked through every limb. Pain burned like wildfire. It felt as if the barrier of good and wrong was broken inside me. My temper was out of control. My fear making me violent.

Neri.

Where the fuck are you?

Shaking my head, trying to get free of the thickness inside, I snarled, "Don't you get it? I'm the reason she was hurt. I'm the reason she's *always* hurt. I need—" Agony stabbed in my skull. "I need to find—" Excruciating pain stole my words. I swayed and gagged on sickness. My fingers went to the back of my head, searching for a way to be free of the blinding discomfort. A bandage was stuck in my hair, thick and padded, covering a wound I couldn't remember.

"Easy," the nurse soothed. "I know you're concerned, and you have every right to be, but you need to calm down."

Tearing my hand away, I fought for stability in a sea of misery. "I need to find Neri."

"Neri being your wife? Nerida Taylor?"

What a waste of time.

What an idiot.

"*Yes*! Take me to her. I can't be here. I need—" The pain was back, pulling me under with suffocating agony.

"Like I said, what you *need* is to calm down. You've suffered a head injury and your ability to regulate your moods might be a little impaired. Just take a deep breath and—"

"It hurts to fucking breathe!" I howled, gasping as my ribs threatened to stab me.

"Yes, well that will be the three cracked ribs you sustained."

"*What?*"

"If you just relax, I can let you know where you are, what happened, and what to expect from here."

Dizziness came for me, twisting me, spinning me.

I drowned beneath confusion, pain, and worry.

I couldn't catch a proper breath. Everything felt ruined and broken.

My heart raced too fast and my rage prowled too hotly.

I felt strange and shaky, and it took all my remaining strength to rein in my fury and do what the nurse commanded.

Raising my head, choking on agony, I grunted, "Please…tell me. Tell me what happened. W-Why do I feel as if I've been run over?"

He chuckled before schooling his face into a more appropriate response. "Sorry. Didn't mean to laugh at that. I know you're not making a joke, but—"

"But what?"

"Well, you *were* technically run over."

The room faded to black before returning. I gritted my teeth to stop myself retching. "I don't…that's not possible."

Taking my confusion as approval to speak, he said, "According to first response, you were struck by a Mazda Axela. You arrived about two hours ago, presenting with open wounds and contusions. You were immediately tended to."

I struggled to focus on him. "Contusions?"

"You have a head injury that didn't require stitches. A shoulder injury that did. X-rays show three cracked ribs and a possible hairline fracture on your left hip. It's hard to tell with the amount of swelling at present, so I'm sure the doctor will discuss that on his next visit."

My mind raced.

My heart hammered.

Fuck.

"Like I said, you might feel out of sorts from the head injury. You might be dizzy and nauseous." Tapping something into a handheld device, he murmured, "I've just added on your file that you're looking for your wife, alright? It's great that you're awake and coherent but before we can treat you any further, we need your name, date of birth, allergies, and Medicare number." His eyebrows rose. "I'll fill in the forms for you if you help me out with the answers."

Snow immediately filled my veins.

I froze.

Name?

Date of birth?

My gaze shot to the door, slipping past a few other patients resting in their matching beds. My head pounded. All I wanted to do was sleep. But…I didn't have that luxury. I didn't have the ability to sink into my pain and let time heal me.

I have to go.

Now.

They'd patched me up. I was no longer on death's door. The sooner I could run, the sooner I could get away from that door. A door I had no intention of knocking on.

"I'm fine. I-I don't need any more treatment." Yanking at the IV in my arm, I muttered, "I want to go."

"*Go?*" The nurse raised his eyebrows. "Hate to break it to you, but you're staying at least the night. You're on concussion watch and—"

"I don't have a concussion." Memories of that stupid test the nurse made me do when I was sixteen came to mind. "Give me that test you guys have. I'll prove it to you." I could remember it even now about a dumb dog, the mouse, and twenty-nine dandelions.

"Doesn't work that way, I'm afraid. The doctor will want to assess your symptoms. If you do have a hairline hip fracture then treatment is the same as your cracked ribs. You'll need to rest, ice, and take anti-inflammatories as and when you require, but—"

"I'm fine." I shifted higher in the starched sheets. "I need to find Nerida."

"Ah, yes. Nerida Taylor. Your wife. Like I said, I've put a note on your file, so if she's in the hospital, someone will alert us. For now, though…" The nurse pulled out a pen from the sleeve of his e-tablet and hovered it over the screen. "How about we answer those questions, hey? What's your name?"

Ah fuck.

Common sense came slamming back.

Self-preservation had kept my secrets intact, but I'd made a colossal mistake.

A life-changing, marriage-ending mistake.

Kafami sikeyim!

What the hell was I thinking?

How could I be so stupid?!

I'd given them Neri's name. Her *full* name.

Groaning, I raked both hands through my hair, ignoring the IV needle, bandages, and road rash. My headache worsened, threatening to drag me down into fog and fuzz.

If something happened to me, I'd implicated her.

Fucking hell!

Get it together!

Think.

You've already fucked up.

Now what?

"Sir…are you okay?" the nurse asked, touching my shoulder gently. "If you're in pain, just let me know your Medicare number and any allergies you may have, and I can administer some stronger pain relief."

My heart fisted as I dropped my hands and sat frozen on the bed. Every part of me bellowed, scrambling all my ability to think.

I'd been too slow.

Far, *far* too stupid.

Perhaps I *was* concussed because there was no excuse for how badly I'd slipped.

Had Neri been as idiotic as me and mentioned *my* name?

If she did…how long did I have before law enforcement came charging through the door?

My aching eyes shot to the double swing doors at the end of the ward. Claustrophobia clawed at me to *run*.

"I need to see Nerida. Right now."

I'd already messed up by giving this guy her name. If by some miracle he could take me to her, then—

"Give me *your* name, and I'll go see what I can find out, how about that? If your wife's name is Mrs Taylor, I'm guessing that makes you Mr. Taylor? Just give me your Medicare number, Mr. Taylor, and—"

"I told you, I'm fine." Rage and terror set my body trembling. I couldn't just sit here anymore.

I need to find her.

We need to run.

Tossing away the sheets, I swung my legs over the edge of the bed. An involuntary cry escaped me as my left hip screeched and my ribs stabbed with agony. Bending over, sharp tears came to my eyes as I tried to cradle the pain in my chest, hip, and the tugging discomfort on my left shoulder.

It all fucking hurt.

It all drove me fucking insane because I couldn't afford to be weak. I couldn't let pain stop me from finding Neri. From running.

"Did you not hear me?" I snarled, gasping through the agony. "I need to find her. *Now.*"

"Look, I know this is all very distressing." The nurse dropped the e-tablet beside me and grabbed my legs. Without warning, he eased them carefully back into the bed, forcing me to lie down. "But you really need to cooperate."

I screamed as my ribs drove their way into my organs.

The pain swelled and suffocated, magnified and morphed into something that made me want to tear out my soul and escape.

Panting hard, I collapsed against the pillow.

Sweat flushed my skin.

I hated this.

I hated being so feeble, so *weak*. I swallowed another scream as my ribs did their best to make me die. Deep breaths killed. Shallow gasps tormented. Images of Neri hurt and lost made me spiral into panic. "Please," I grunted, clutching my chest. "Just let me go to her. I have to make sure she's alright."

"You need to relax, Mr. Taylor. You're going to damage yourself even more if you don't."

My nostrils flared.

Black smog crept over my vision.

No.

Fuck, no.

I couldn't afford to pass out.

Not again.

Not now.

Nerida!

The smog thickened.

The nurse bent over me, his face taking up my entire failing stare.

"Mr. Taylor." He tapped my cheek. "Stay with me, Mr. Taylor. It's okay. You're okay."

I felt nothing.

Nothing but burning, blazing, breaking pain.

I have to run.

I have to—

"Mr—"
The black wave crashed over me.
I drowned.

Chapter Twenty-Five

NERIDA

AGE: 20 YRS OLD

(Love in Croatian: Ljubav)

"I'VE FOUND HIM. HE'S OKAY, OR AS well as could be expected after being hit with a car." Jedda bustled toward me in her pink Crocs and scrubs.

"Oh thank God." Tears sprang and ran down my cheeks before I could stop them.

My entire body broke out in shivers as every emotion bowled through me.

Relief.

Panic.

Elation.

Frustration.

Guilt.

"I need to see him." I leapt from my plastic chair in the busy waiting room. After my consultation and discharge, when the doctor found I wasn't injured, I'd been told to go home.

I'd ignored that suggestion.

And I'd keep ignoring it until I could go home with Aslan.

"Take me to him." The room swam a little. "I have to see him. I have to apologise to him." That strange ache in my lower belly twinged again, full of nausea and worry. "I have to get him out of here."

"Neri, sit down before you fall." Jedda grabbed my wrist as I stumbled, tugging me back to sitting. She folded heavily into the chair beside mine, giving a bone-weary sigh. "You can't see him, and he can't go home. Not yet."

"Why not?" My heart smoked with fear. "Why can't I—"

"You can't see him because no one must know you're together. If he's discovered for overstaying, then I have no idea what will happen to you and your parents for housing him. What laws you've broken. What discipline you'll face." Her hands balled in her lap. "This isn't a trifling matter, Nerida. Promise me you won't go running through the hospital to find him. Let me handle this—"

"Then discharge him and tell him to meet me outside. I'll go home and get the Jeep. I'll swing by and pick him up—"

"He's not in a state to just walk out of here."

"What? But I thought you said—"

"He's mainly in one piece, but he's black and blue. He woke with a rather violent outburst, according to his notes, and fell unconscious again. The nurse was able to rouse him just enough to administer some morphine."

"Morphine?" I rubbed at my tripping, squeezing heart. Panic threatened to overwhelm me. "Jedda, he needs me. He'll be going out of his mind wondering where I am. Please—"

"The best thing you can do for both of you is to stay apart for now. He'll heal, Neri. He's okay. But the cracked ribs and stitches will be overwhelming. Give him time to get over the initial shock of his injuries, and then—"

"He'll be so worried about me." I grabbed her hand. "That will be his worst wound. His concern for me. It'll be his fear over my safety that makes him aggressive. If you just let me see him, I can—"

"No. You're not going anywhere near him while he's being treated here. The less anyone knows about you two, the better."

"But Jedda." Tears rolled again, this time full of remorse. "He'll be frantic wondering where I am. The last thing he saw were those bastards touching me. He won't care about himself. He'll hurt himself trying to find me. I'm the reason he's here. I need to fix what I broke. Please, Auntie Jedda. The best thing for him is for me to go to him, then take him out of here…while I still can."

Jedda rubbed her eyes, her shoulders hunched. She looked frazzled and tired. I had no idea how long her shift had been or what she'd been up to in the past hour since I'd seen her, but her dark eyes were weary, and her skin stretched too tight in the harsh lights. "He'll be asleep for hours due to the morphine. Unfortunately, thanks to his distress and uncooperativeness when he first woke, he's been noted as someone to keep an eye on."

My insides went cold. "What did he do?"

"He woke up trying to punch the nurse—"

"He still has nightmares from the storm. It's not a good idea to touch him when he's asleep."

"Yes, well, no one knew that because there's no file on him, and he refused to tell them his name." She half-smiled. "Least he kept his wits to withhold that information. Not so great that he gave them your name, however." Her eyes sharpened. "We need to get you out of here now you've been discharged. You can't be here if someone starts to question—"

"I'm not going anywhere." I tore my hand from hers and crossed my arms. "Not without him."

"He'll be out for the rest of the night, Neri. You can't stay—"

"Watch me."

"It's dangerous." She scowled. "Due to him refusing to give his name, he's been logged as a suspicious individual. If he's not cooperative when he next wakes up, he'll be interviewed, and his phone could be subpoenaed to learn who he is. He could be detained."

I glanced at the plastic bag between my feet holding the wreckage of Aslan's run-over phone and his slim wallet clip holding some cash and his one and only credit card in my father's name. "I have his phone. And his wallet."

Her eyes lit up. "Oh, that's the first bit of good news I've heard all night." Sitting taller, she slipped back into business mode. "I've called your mum and dad—"

"You did what?" I reared backward. "Why would you do that? It's freaking three in the morning."

She scowled. "I called because you suffered an episode of shock, and your fiancé is in the hospital. The hospital that you're refusing to leave, I might add. You're twenty and all alone in this city. You can't be expected to attend class while you're worrying about Aslan. They could take him back to Port Douglas for a few weeks to rest and heal and then—"

"I'm not letting him out of my sight. I'll look after him." My voice cooled. "I'm not going anywhere, Auntie Jedda. I'll tear apart this hospital brick by brick if I have to."

Temper filled her kind face. Glancing around at the patients, she inched closer and lowered her voice. "Listen to me, Nerida. I agreed to be your godmother, not your best friend. And as your godmother, I am fully within my right to tell you what to do if it keeps you safe. I called your parents to come and get you because I knew damn well that you wouldn't leave without Aslan, and frankly, you need to get as far away from here as possible. They're on their way. They'll be here in five hours. If you're still here by the time they arrive and Aslan is still sleeping off the morphine, you are leaving."

She pointed a finger in my face. "You have my word I'll watch over him. As long as he keeps refusing to say his name, they won't know who he is. By law, we have to provide treatment until such a time as he's well enough to be taken to be interviewed. If it escalates to that point, I'll figure out a way to smuggle him out. I promise you." Her eyes glittered. "You just need to trust me."

I held her stare for the longest moment.

I did my best to be wise about this. To use common sense instead of blind desperation.

But it was hard.

So, so hard to trust someone with Aslan's life when it was all my fault he was here.

Guilt pressed so heavily as I whispered, "He's here because of me. All of this is my fault. I always make the worst choices. I'm so *stupid* sometimes. If only I listened to him. If only I didn't distract him. God, I'll never forgive myself." Stroking my slightly oozy, freshly inked tattoo, I choked, "If only I'd ignored those racist pricks like Aslan did, then we could be home right now and…" I couldn't finish. Tears rolled down my cheeks. "This is all my fault."

Jedda pulled me into an awkward hug with the armrests of the chairs digging into our bellies. "You can't torture yourself with 'what ifs', Neri. And you're not stupid. You're young and passionate, and we all fumble sometimes. All you need to focus on is, he's alive. He's getting care. You're alive, and no one knows who he is. He's just another unfortunate man in the ER. As long as you stay quiet and let me handle this, everything will be okay…you'll see."

Chapter Twenty-Six

ASLAN

(Heart in Turkish: *Kalp*)

"ASLAN? ASLAN, YOU NEED TO WAKE UP."

Something tapped my cheek with annoying repetition.

I floundered on the bottom of my nightmares, swimming in storms, drowning in moonlight. Panic was my only emotion as I searched for everyone I'd lost. My parents, my sister...*Neri*.

My chest exploded as seawater poured in.

My heart tumbled in on itself.

Fuck.

Neri.

What if I never saw her again?

What if I'd lost her for good and I never got to touch her again, kiss her again, love her—

I couldn't.

I can't—

"Aslan. Wake up. We don't have much time." The tapping turned to slapping. It offered me an anchor in a drowned world of salt and pain.

I clung to it. I hauled on it.

My eyes ripped open as I coughed and choked, retching up phantom water, crying out as my ribs stabbed and my shoulder pinched and every bone in my body became my enemy.

"That's it. Easy does it. You're okay. Just breathe slowly and gently."

The blinding lights kept my vision stark white as I slowly adjusted back into a body riddled with agony. Fear from my nightmares chased me into reality and I struggled to sit up.

Neri.

I have to find her.

A gentle but firm hand landed on my sternum.

The white spots organised themselves into pictures, and I frowned as a woman leaned over me.

A woman with a kind smile, brown-black hair, and age marking her pretty face. Her fingers stroked my hair, pushing the unruly strands off my forehead as she willed me to become coherent.

The past slammed into me.

Another hospital.

Another night.

"*You*," I croaked.

For a moment, I couldn't understand. I worried my mind had split and regressed to the past, where I was sixteen and freshly orphaned.

But she was older.

She held secrets in her stare and looked at me as if she knew all of mine in return.

Slowly, she removed her hand from my forehead and stood upright. "So you remember me, then? I did wonder if you would. After all, we only spoke for such a short time."

Wincing, I slowly sat up. My ribs were knives, my lungs their enemy. Memories crowded me. Numbers might arrange themselves in my brain with colours, but so did dates and experiences.

I could recite the time and year of so many events. Every moment I'd spent with Neri. Every stolen touch. Every awful longing. It was all there, filed neatly inside my head. Even with a skull-splitting headache, I managed to tug on one of those recollection strings and pull history to the surface.

Clearing my throat, I threw a glance at the double doors, then back to the nurse. "Of course, I remember you. You know my name. You know Anna Taylor. You were the last to see me in the hospital in Port Douglas."

Her eyebrows rose along with her lips. "I knew you had an eidetic memory."

I might not have known that word when I was newly shipwrecked, but now I did. I went to argue with her, but…the description fit, even if it was proven that most adults didn't have one.

I could vividly recall most things.

I saw in pictures and colours, not words and thoughts.

I was both grateful for the gift and cursed it on a daily basis because it was yet another trait from *him*.

I gritted my teeth. "A-Are you going to tell them who I am?"

Her shoulders swooped back as if I'd offended her. "Of course not."

"Why?" Sluggishness flowed in my veins. A sour aftertaste coated my tongue. At least the pain that'd pushed me under was thankfully duller than before. "What are you doing here?"

"I work here now."

Pressing my hand against my battered ribcage, I looked again at the exit, feeling the unconquerable need to run. "I need to leave."

"I agree."

I froze. "Wait. You're going to help me?"

"Look, we don't have much time, so I'll be brief. The driver who hit you? He's here too. He was treated last night—"

"*Last night?*" My mouth fell open. "How long have I been here?"

"Thirteen hours."

"*Kahretsin.*" I shook my head. "That's thirteen hours too long."

"It's not ideal, I agree. But you were out cold, and I figured nothing could happen to you while you were asleep, especially while no one knew who you were. Unfortunately..." Her eyes tightened as she shifted with worry. "The driver was interviewed this morning by the police. He mentioned that Neri had screamed your name when trying to rouse you. He gave that name to the police. He's been overly cooperative, I'm afraid. Trying to save his own neck, I suppose."

The world narrowed to a pinprick of horror.

"I only found out ten minutes ago," she rushed. "I'm not even supposed to be working anymore but...you can't stay here. The police have your name. They know you were the man the driver hit. I'm sure they're coming—"

"We need to go. Right now." I swung my legs out of bed.

Stars danced over my vision.

My hip flared.

My back pulled where the stitches held my flesh together.

And my ribs were determined to make breathing an impossible task.

"You have morphine in your system, so you need to be careful not to push yourself too far." Her eyebrows knitted together. "You're still injured, Aslan. Fairly badly. You could make things a lot worse if you overdo it."

"I'll rest when I'm far away from here."

Bending down to grab something from the floor, she placed a duffel bag on the end of my bed. "Jack brought you some clothes. He and Anna arrived a few hours ago and have taken Neri back to your apartment to avoid her being questioned." Her lips curled up. "As you can imagine, she did *not* want to leave without you."

I struggled to catch a proper breath. "I-Is she okay?"

"She's fine. Suffered a bad case of shock seeing you so hurt, but...she's okay."

Gritting my teeth, I stood and tested my balance and tolerance.

My hip felt fragile and bruised, but I stayed standing. I could rest later. Heal later. Right now, I'd run a fucking marathon if it meant I could get free and stay free. Jedda turned her back on me as I rifled through the bag of clothes and yanked on a pair of black boxers before ripping off the hospital gown.

Jack had once again given me clothes to escape.

I was already so deeply in his debt I would never be able to repay him, but this? Having him love me enough to risk his own reputation and freedom? Loving me enough to give me his daughter?

It made my throat close up as I shrugged into a white polo shirt and slipped on a pair of cargos—clothes I'd left in Port Douglas after the sun and salt had weathered them.

Glancing over her shoulder, the woman turned back to face me once she saw I was decent. "I'm Jedda, by the way."

"Neri mentioned you a few months ago."

"She did?"

"When Jack found out about us and…" I shrugged. "Doesn't matter." Tipping up my chin, I ignored all my pains from fists, Mazdas, and rotten fucking luck. "It goes without saying that I'm grateful for your help, Jedda, but I'm confused about why you'd give it."

She smiled. "I'm Neri's godmother. Anna and I went to school together before she went into science and I went into medicine."

I swayed a little. "You're Neri's godmother?"

She nodded. "I've known you've been living with them since the first morning you vanished. I know you and Neri fell in love. And I've been assured that I'm invited to your wedding—if it's ever able to go ahead."

"Y-You knew where I was this entire time and never reported me?"

"Of course, I bloody knew." She huffed, dropping her voice to a whisper. "I came to check on you like I said I would. I found the window open and the crushed flowers beneath. Anna put her name as your next of kin, and Jack gave you their address. It didn't take much to figure it out. You put them in a dangerous position, Aslan, and I did what I had to do to protect them and my goddaughter."

"Jack never told me."

"I'm sure there's a lot he hasn't told you." Stepping toward the exit, she added, "Now, if you can walk without passing out, I suggest you leave immediately. Jack's on his way. He'll pick you up outside."

Tossing an old pair of black flip-flops to the ground, I shoved my feet into them and willed my body to behave. The first few steps revealed every bruise, bump, and bash, but I focused on getting the fuck out of here.

Nothing else mattered but seeing Neri again.

The image of her kept me fighting.

The need to be with her gave me strength.

"I won't walk with you." Jedda gave me a worried smile, full of apology. "I'm sure you understand."

"I don't expect you to risk anything more than you already have." I bowed my head, cursing my headache. "I don't know how to thank you."

"Thank me by looking after Nerida." She shot forward, grabbed the empty duffel, squeezed my hand, and whispered, "You and Neri are invited around to dinner next week, okay? It will be nice to finally catch up with both of you, now that secrets are out in the open."

I squeezed her back. "I'd like that."

"Good." Letting me go, she slung the bag over her shoulder and sighed heavily. "Quick healing, Aslan. See you next week."

She rushed out the double doors.

Patients in the rows of beds paid me no heed as I locked down my pain, calmed my panicking heart, and put one foot in front of the other.

Chapter Twenty-Seven

ASLAN

(Heart in Hindi: Dil)

SUNLIGHT TOUCHED MY FACE AS I MARCHED with purpose, doing my best to hide my pain. The warren of hospital corridors had leached what strength I had left, and the faint dullness of morphine was giving way to sharp slicing discomfort.

The sooner I was home, the better.

The sooner I was in Neri's arms, the sooner I could breathe.

I stepped outside.

I was free.

An elderly man pushed a white-haired woman in a wheelchair. The fear in his eyes held aching concern from a husband for his wife. A mother ducked past me with a screaming boy in her arms, and a young woman brushed away tears as she darted toward the ER with a tea-towel wrapped around her bloody hand.

So many maladies.

So many people.

But no one stopped me.

No one cared who I was or that I was leaving without being discharged.

I stood outside the hospital and fought the urge to crumple with relief.

Neri.

My entire nervous system screamed to see her. Anxiety roared through my veins. Impatience cracked my bones.

I moved farther away from the yawning entrance of the hospital.

A silver SUV pulled up in the drop-off zone as I followed the footpath, glancing around the many vehicles for Jack's Wrangler. Four men in black suits stepped out, official and stern.

Instincts prickled to move out of their way, and I cut to the left, scanning the parked cars, wishing I had my phone so I could call Jack and find out where he'd parked.

Is he even here?

Where should I wait if he isn't?

One of the suited men caught my gaze as he headed toward the hospital doors. Dark-brown eyes, neatly styled blond hair, and lips that were so thin they seemed drawn on with a pencil. Our stare held then broke as I continued on my way, and he followed his colleagues toward the sliding doors.

The sound of their footsteps suddenly stopped.

Whispers rose from behind me.

It's nothing.

They're no one.

You're no one.

Just keep walking.

I balled my hands and marched faster, ignoring the screeching in my hip and the stabbing pains of my ribs as I struggled to catch a proper breath.

A glint of sunlight on a windscreen.

The familiar dinged-up sides of Jack's Jeep as he pulled into the hospital drop-off zone, inching toward me.

Relief tried to buckle my knees.

My gaze shot immediately to the passenger side, my heart screaming for Neri.

Had she come?

Is she here?

But it was just Jack.

Just my father-in-law from a marriage witnessed by the moon and sea. A guy who'd probably banished his daughter from coming, just in case something happened.

I couldn't blame him.

I couldn't get mad.

But my heart didn't behave.

It wasn't mad.

It was sad.

Fucking endlessly sad because it missed her so fucking much.

Fifteen minutes and you'll see her again.

Fifteen minutes and you'll be home.

Sucking in a breath, I picked up my pace.

Just a little farther.

Hurry.

Jack spotted me and grinned.

His hand lifted from the steering wheel. He waved as he navigated into a parking spot ten metres away.

So close.

So near.

Keep walking.

Keeping my chin down, I focused on keeping my pain at bay and—

"Excuse me." A solid hand landed on my shoulder, spinning me around.

My stitches yanked, and my ribs poked. But it was my hip that almost made me black out as the man made me twist on the spot. Breathing heavily, I glowered at the guy who'd stopped me, and my heart fucking froze.

Four suited men stood before me.

In the hands of the closest one hung a picture.

My picture.

No…not my picture.

Someone else.

Someone I looked exactly like.

My world narrowed to a single moment, a single breath, a single rip-roaring heartbeat.

I felt as if I was choking, dying, *screaming.*

My nostrils flared as the men glanced at the photo of my father—my biological father—and nodded at each other. "You're Aslan Avci? Or should I say Aslan Kara?"

The sound of Jack's door slamming made me look over my shoulder.

Our eyes connected.

True fear tore between us.

It was tangible.

Alive.

A hot, stinging conduit of disbelief.

One of the men stepped closer, raising the photo of Cem. Planting it in my face, he snapped, "Is this your father?"

Jack stumbled forward; my mind split with so many scenarios.

Of him defending me.

Lying for me.

Implicating himself for me.

My father would learn of his name.

He'd learn of Neri's name.

He'd come for them, just like he'd come for me.

He'll kill them.

I choked on death as I held up my hand at Jack, urging him to stop, then straightened my spine and locked down all my pain. "I've never seen that man before in my life."

The guy with thin lips nodded. "That's because you were kidnapped when you were eight months old. There's been an international missing person's report on you for over two decades."

My heart stopped beating. "I…you're mistaken. I'm Australian. I—"

"We believe you are Aslan Avci, also known as Aslan Kara. Therefore, you are hereby detained for questioning."

"What, why? I didn't do anything wrong—"

"Care to tell us why you're out here and not in the ward where you're supposed to be?"

Anger unfurled. "Because you have the wrong person!"

"We believe otherwise. If you are not who we think you are, a simple chat will confirm everything. Don't be afraid. We are not out to hurt anyone. We merely want to ascertain how you came to Australia, who helped you arrive without any documentation, and inform you that your true family has been looking tirelessly for you since your kidnapping."

"I told you! You have the wrong person."

"We do not believe we do. The resemblance is uncanny."

Jack came closer.

I shook my head at him, desperately trying to figure out how to talk my way out of this. "I know who my true family is. And that man is not one of them."

"Oh? What are their names?" One of the officers ripped out a small notebook. "Where are they currently?"

"They're dead," I snarled.

People glanced at us and scurried away as if our negativity could reach out and touch them. Jack balled his hands a few metres away, watching everything, his face a mask of horror.

"If that's the case, then you can clear up this misunderstanding by coming with us."

"I don't have to go anywhere with you," I hissed. "I'm not whoever you think I am."

One of the men held up the image of Cem Kara beside my face. All four men looked between me and my father. I hid the shattering pain inside me because the photo turned into a mirror. A mirror image of me and the man who would kill me. The man who had so much blood and violence on his hands. A man who'd impregnated a nameless woman to create me.

Our black eyes were the same.

Our sharp cheekbones, straight noses, hard jawlines, and stern lips.

The only difference was our hair. His was darker and swept back with product. Mine was sun-bronzed and unruly.

"You look exactly like Cem Kara." The officer lowered the photo. "If the reason for that is a fluke of nature, then we apologise. But for now, we request you come with us."

"And if I refuse?"

"You'll be arrested."

"For what? For leaving the hospital early?" I bared my teeth. "Look, I just want to go home."

"We only want the same thing." The thin-lipped guy stepped closer. "Mr. Kara, we are under the impression that you are here illegally. Either you were kidnapped and smuggled into our country when you were a boy and none of this is your fault, or you knowingly broke our immigration laws by arriving without documentation. Either way, we need to talk."

One of the men whispered into his colleague's ear.

The thin-lipped guy nodded. "Look, if you have ID and can prove you are not Aslan Kara, we will apologise and bid you a good day." His eyes glinted. "But if you cannot provide us with ID, we are legally required to bring you in for questioning."

I struggled to breathe. I cursed my empty pockets. I hated that I'd never tried to purchase fake identification or at least stolen an Australian driver's license that I could pass off as my own.

The world fell out from beneath me.

Horror.

Fear.

Despair.

A shorter guy with buzzed black hair stepped forward. "So…do you? Have any ID to prove you are not the kidnapped son of Cem Kara?"

My morphine-muddled mind raced.

I quaked.

Every stitch, every crack, every fracture, it was all too much.

My grip on my temper threatened to unravel.

Bloodthirsty rage settled with its familiar red haze over my eyes.

I could fight.

I could run—

"I, eh…I lost my wallet in the car accident."

The thin-lipped guy's face lit up. "The car accident where a Peter Smithe drove into you? The accident where you sustained stitches to your left shoulder, cracked ribs, and possible hip fracture?"

"I—"

"It was Peter Smithe who advised law enforcement of your name. The name your girlfriend yelled." His eyes narrowed as he consulted something on his phone. "A Nerida Taylor, I believe?"

My world shrank to nothing.

Just this.

Just now.

Just this choice, this decision, this one fucking chance at protecting her.

"She means nothing. She was a one-night stand I met online—"

"What's going on here?" Jack's rough voice choked from behind me. He cleared his throat, doing his best to swallow some of the fear pulsing between us. "Can I ask why you gentlemen are delaying this man? A man who is clearly injured and just needs to go home and rest."

Fuck, Jack.

Damn you, Jack.

My bones snapped.

My heart shattered.

The four men narrowed their eyes at the one guy I never wanted to get in trouble for me. He'd done so much. He'd lose so much.

Jack threw me a look. I sucked in a breath. And I saw it all.

Saw his confession at harbouring me.

Saw his submission to whatever punishment would come for him.

And I couldn't do it.

I couldn't let him pay for my mistakes.

Neri would never forgive me.

I would never forgive me.

"Move along, sir. None of your business," one of the officers muttered.

"Ah, see, that's where you're wrong," Jack argued. "It is my business because—"

"Who the fuck are you?" I whirled on him with violence. My hip threatened to knock me out, and my voice wavered with grief I couldn't quite swallow. "Go away, old man! This is embarrassing enough without a complete stranger butting in where he doesn't belong."

Jack's eyes widened.

His mouth fell open.

I glowered at him as if I was one moment away from punching him.

The officers shifted, and one of them touched my elbow. "Let's go. We'll continue our questions elsewhere."

"No, you can't," Jack grunted. "You can't take him."

"I told you!" I growled, pointing my finger in his face. "Stay the fuck out of it. *Go away.*"

He trembled and shook his head.

Everything inside me gagged on despair.

I wanted him to fix this.

I'd give anything for him to find a way to take me home with him. Back to Nerida. Back to anonymity.

But I wouldn't let him pay for my mistakes.

I wouldn't let him suffer for the selfish decision I'd made to trespass on their lives.

I couldn't talk my way out of this. I had no ID. My injuries lined up with those used to confirm who I was. My own fucking father's face condemned me to my death.

My only options were to outright fight when I was barely strong enough to walk, or...say goodbye to a life I wanted more than anything and protect those who'd loved me for eight incredible years. Eight years that I wouldn't have had without them. Eight years where I'd loved blindly, lusted obsessively, and would always be so fucking grateful at finding my soulmate so young.

Neri.

What I wouldn't give to see her again.

To tell her how sorry I was.

To find a way to give her back her heart so I didn't take it with me when I died.

Neri...

Her name was a bullet to my chest, an axe to my neck.

"Aslan Kara, please step inside the vehicle," thin-lipped guy said. "Time to go."

Jack raised his hand. "Wait, you can't—"

"Enough!" I roared. "I told you to butt out. This doesn't concern you."

My eyes met his.

His filled with tears.

I couldn't look at him.

I'd break.

Balling my hands, I marched as steadily as I could toward the silver SUV.

The flash of handcuffs swung in one of the guy's hands, revealing how close they'd been to arresting me in full view of injured people and my father-in-law.

An icy whip wrapped around my wrists.

Terror shot down my spine.

No way could they imprison me.

No way could they trap me.

I'd lose it.

I'd snap.

Fuck, Neri...

I couldn't breathe at the thought of never seeing her again.

I...

I...

I can't fucking breathe!

My knees buckled mid-step.

Jack shot forward as if to catch me.

I swallowed my groan and righted myself, pushing him away. "Get a fucking clue, old man! *Go!* Get out of here."

Before they know you're the reason I survived here this long.

Before my father learns who you are.

Jack shook his head, his self-control breaking. Turning on the men, he snarled, "Can't you see he's hurt? He can't go anywhere. He needs to rest!"

"We'll take good care of him, sir."

"Leave him be!" Jack shouted, rousing the attention of other people. Some stopped to watch. My spine prickled with eyes. So many eyes. More eyes that'd seen me since I'd started hiding in plain sight.

"Sir, I suggest you don't involve yourself in affairs that have nothing to do with you," thin-lipped guy muttered.

Jack's mouth twisted to argue.

Horror shone in his eyes.

And my body chose that moment to break.

My heart blew through all the depression I'd suffered and all the terror I'd harboured.

It exploded with the worst pain I'd ever endured.

It shattered.

Pulverised.

Splintered.

It hurt worse than any broken bone.

It bled quicker than any severed artery.

I dropped to one knee.

I groaned as my hip throbbed.

Hands hitched under my arms as I was hauled almost kindly to my feet.

In a haze of pain, I was guided toward the SUV and helped inside.

Jack chased after us. "You can't take him. I won't let you—"

"Fuck off!" I snarled, wrapping my arm around my broken ribs, choking on tears I refused to shed. "Go away. I don't know you. Go harass someone else."

Don't let them know I love you.

Please don't—

Jack tripped. His face flushed white.

The thin-lipped man stepped into him, reading between the curses I threw Jack's way. "If you know this man, we have questions. Do you know where he's been staying here? Do you know who's been employing him? Any help you can provide in these matters—"

"He's nobody," I grunted, dripping with agony-induced sweat. "I've never seen him before." Groaning, I snapped, "I need another doctor. Either take me back into the hospital or—"

"We have our own physician. He'll take care of you and confirm if you're fit to fly."

"*Fly?* He can't fly anywhere—" Jack moaned, his eyes glittering with sadness. "Look, I'm just a concerned citizen, okay? I'm here to see my, eh, wife, but I can't stand by and watch you accost an injured man. It's not right."

"I suggest you go see your wife, sir, and leave the welfare of this overstayer to us."

"But—"

"No buts." Car doors opened and slammed as the men climbed into the SUV. Two sat beside me, one in the middle and another on his left, leaving me to stare at Jack through the window.

He shook his head.

222

He raised his hand.

I closed my eyes as I was driven horribly away from him.

Chapter Twenty-Eight

NERIDA

AGE: 20 YRS OLD

(Love in Swedish: Kärlek)

THE QUIET KNOCK ON THE FRONT DOOR ripped me from the couch where I'd been sitting beside Mum. Hope bloomed. Relief swelled. I practically skipped to the door.

My temper toward Dad faded now he was back.

I'd cursed his name for leaving me behind.

How could he?

How could he be so sneaky to wait until I'd been unable to ignore the urge to pee any longer and then driven off the moment I went to the bathroom? He knew I wanted to be there to pick Aslan up. He knew I *needed* to be there.

He'd practically had to carry me out of the damn hospital to get me home, let alone forbid me from returning.

He'd betrayed me.

Hurt me.

But everything was okay now.

Because he's back.

Aslan is home.

My heart squeezed. My lips twitched into a smile.

I ripped open the door. "Aslan—" The name of my forever after and soulmate died on my tongue as I blinked at only one man on the threshold.

All it took was for my eyes to meet my dad's.

A single second to sink into the sorrow pooling there and the regret scratched into his face.

And I knew.

No...

A vortex appeared beneath me, sucking me to the floor.

Guilt snatched me up.

Horror sucked me down.

I collapsed.

My heart stopped.

My ears rang as Dad kneeled before me. Mum charged from the couch. Their arms wrapped around me as I rocked.

Just rocked.

I rocked and pulverised.

No tears.

No screams.

Just silence.

Aching, breaking silence in my chest, my soul, my heart.

No...

He can't.

This can't be...

No.

I'm sorry.

So sorry.

My fault.

My fault.

My fault!

"I'm so sorry, Nerida." Dad's voice came from a long, dark tunnel. "I tried to stop them. They took him, but we'll get him back. I promise."

"How, Jack?" Mum cried. "How the hell do we get him back now he's in their hands?"

"I don't know, Anna," Dad choked. "I just know we have to try."

My eyes burned with vinegar.

My insides corroded with acid.

Aslan...

Shoving my parents away, I tripped to my feet and stumbled toward my bedroom.

The apartment mocked me.

The kitchen Aslan had installed.

The bathroom he'd renovated.

The lab he'd set up for me.

The bedroom where he'd loved me—

I bit my fist as a bulldozing sob ripped up my throat. I crashed against the wall. I slithered down it. I shook. I shivered. I stared at our bed where only yesterday Aslan had touched me, fucked me, and given me the best birthday I could've imagined.

My tattoo gleamed on my arm.

He's gone.

A keening noise escaped me.

Because of me.

A whimper crawled up my throat.

They've taken him.

He'll die...

Mum and Dad appeared on the threshold of my bedroom, hovering in the corridor as if unwilling to step into the sanctity of my sea-wedded marriage bed.

The dissociation when I'd watched Aslan being flung through the sky by a shitty red Mazda found me again, tugging me blessedly free.

I sank into it.

I didn't fight it.

I couldn't survive the grief and guilt whirlpooling around my legs.

I didn't have time to grieve when Aslan was still here. In Australia. Safe.

I'm going to keep him that way.

Bottling it up.

Swallowing it down.

I ignored my debilitating despair.

Launching to my feet, I snatched my phone out of my yoga leggings pocket. Tripping forward, I sat on our bed and prepared to go to war.

My fault...

"Neri...sweetie, a-are you okay?" Mum asked, drifting forward warily.

I ignored her and pressed the contact number for immigration.

Holding my phone to my ear, I looked up as it rang.

Dad frowned for a moment before understanding. "You're calling immigration?"

I nodded. "I'm going to call everyone I can. I'm going to ring every single person in charge until they free him. I'll visit the prime minister if I have to. Aslan isn't going anywhere." My voice sounded strange. So strange. Thick with unshed tears and hollow with heartbreak.

And when an operator finally came on, I sat stiff as a tree and rooted myself in belief that I could fix this.

I wouldn't stop.

I would *never* stop.

He's coming home.

To me.

By sea, moon, stars, and fate, this is not how we end.

This is not how he dies.

Not yet.

Not yet...

Chapter Twenty-Nine

NERIDA

AGE: 20 YRS OLD

(Love in Afrikaans: Liefde)

"WELL, PUT SOMEONE ON WHO CAN HELP then!" I shouted, pacing in my childhood bedroom, rubbing at my heart that'd forgotten how to beat properly without him.

Seven days.

Seven nights.

A hundred phone calls.

A thousand threats.

A million pleas.

And nothing.

Not one person could tell me where he was being held. Not one receptionist or officer could reveal sensitive information about an ongoing case.

I hadn't wanted to return to Port Douglas.

I'd fought when my parents had packed my bags and ushered me into their Jeep, all while I remained glued to my phone, ringing numbers like a madwoman, my desperation unravelling into something manic.

I couldn't remember the journey home or why they'd even brought me here. Something about them having to work. Something about me not being safe to leave on my own. Something about sticking together so we could bring Aslan home.

I didn't care about university.

I forgot all about my classes.

I was in a fugue.

A fugue of panic and regret where I couldn't sleep, couldn't eat, couldn't stop ringing agencies and government numbers over and over and *over* again, screaming Aslan's name, demanding to have him returned to me *because it's all my damn fault!*

My tattoo had healed enough to remove the Saniderm bandage.

My neck felt empty from my missing sea lion necklace.

Pinprick wounds dotted my palms from clutching Aslan's shell so tightly as my last link to him. But no matter how many times I whispered into the singing shadows of its conch, no matter how many times I begged, cajoled, or threatened, it didn't bring him back.

It didn't help me find him.

It was just a shell.

A useless, pointless shell just like I was a useless, pointless girl who couldn't get anyone to *talk to her*!

"You there, ma'am?"

"Yes," I snapped. "Put me onto someone who's dealing with the Aslan Avci case."

"Just like I told you yesterday and the day before that, there is no one by that name being processed."

"Aslan Kara then."

"Nor that name."

"You have to know something!"

"Don't get irate, ma'am. I'm only trying to help."

"But you're not. Not at all! I can't let him go, do you hear me? I won't. Get me someone who's in charge! It's an emergency. He can't be deported. I'll sponsor him for his visa. We're engaged. Just give me the paperwork, and he can become Australian by marriage!"

"Ma'am, you really need to talk to someone else. Try calling Department of Home Affairs."

"I did that. I've spoken to them twenty times."

"Then I can't help you."

"Wait—"

"Goodbye."

"*ARGH!*"

Furious tears burned.

Acid splashed in my insides.

Familiar burning, stinging, aching pains of loss and denial swamped me.

I couldn't survive it.

Couldn't withstand the rapidly building pressure.

Dialling the number for immigration that I'd grown to know by heart, I listened to the ringing.

While I was trying to find him, I couldn't break.

While I fought for Aslan, it wasn't over.

I would marry him tomorrow if it meant they'd leave him alone. I would hand over my childhood diaries of loving him for years. I would show them my tattoo for the commitment we'd made to one another.

They couldn't deny that he was wanted.

That he wasn't a valuable member of society because he was.

So, *so* valuable.

He's mine.

My everything.

I'll do anything!

"Hello, Australian Immigration, how can I help?"

"I need to speak to the case officer in charge of Aslan Avci, Aslan Kara's visa case. I'm his fiancée, Nerida Taylor."

Silence, followed by a huff. "Ms. Taylor, I told you a few hours ago, there is nothing we can do."

"Let me see him. I can get this all straightened out. We're engaged, doesn't that mean anything?"

"I suggest you wait a few days to hear from Aslan himself. Perhaps then you can—"

"He'll be dead in a few days!"

"Like I told you before, no one in our custody is in danger of dying. I'm sorry. Have a good day."

I choked on a howl as the line cut off.

Please.

Someone.

Anyone!

I'd stopped caring about implicating myself.

I gave up my name as if it were bait to trap the monster holding Aslan. If they wanted to know how he'd stayed in the country this long, then fine. If they wanted to arrest me for harbouring him, so be it.

In the dead of night when there was no one awake to call, I researched the trouble my parents would be in if I recounted every year Aslan had lived with us.

The Migration Act carried a maximum penalty of ten years for people smuggling and concealing a non-citizen. Ten years I would happily serve on their behalf if only Aslan was released. I'd serve every day for a hundred years if they gave him an Australian passport and permitted him to stay.

If they didn't send him back to Cem Kara.

If they didn't ship him to his death.

I'd never ask for anything else.

Never strive for anything more.

I'd happily rot in jail to protect my parents and my husband.

I didn't care what happened to me.

Just him.

Only him.

None of this matters without him!

Dad agreed. Mum agreed. They fought as fiercely for Aslan as I did. Dad disappeared for hours at a time as if physically hunting for him and visiting anyone with a smidgen of power who could help us.

He even told Wayne Gratt, the detective who'd taken my statement and Dad's friend, the truth about Aslan.

We were past caring what would happen to us.

Past fearing anything but the worst.

The worst being...

No.

Don't think it.

I bit my fist to contain the welling screams inside me.

I wouldn't let that happen.

I refused to lose him.

Not now, not ever.

Teeth marks and cuts covered the back of my hands from where I'd shoved my knuckles as far as I could inside my mouth to stop my sobs. Here, in my childhood bedroom with my parents down the hall, I couldn't let go. I couldn't free the wet chaos inside me. I couldn't howl at the moon or beg the sea to intervene.

I wanted a tsunami to crash over Australia and rinse Aslan free from wherever he was being held. I wanted a fire to chase his capturers out of whatever prison he was in. I wanted plagues and hurricanes. I wanted every natural disaster imaginable to come to my aid and find him.

Honey messaged me constantly, trying to help.

Billy rang government agencies on my behalf.

Dad hired an immigration lawyer who stayed at our house for two full days, hounding her contacts and demanding to speak to someone in charge of Aslan's case.

Mum did her best to contact someone in parliament.

Teddy spoke to as many news sites as possible.

Eddie tried to get our story on social media.

And I did my best to stay alive even though every part of me was dead.

He didn't have his phone so I couldn't track him. I had no way of contacting him or touching him, kissing him, *loving* him...

I'm sorry.

Fuck, I'm so sorry.

Eight years he'd been by my side.

Eight years I'd heard his voice and touched his body and whispered goodnight in the dark. Eight years I'd loved him, secretly and wantonly, and to have him suddenly *gone*...

He's not gone.

He can't be.

It's just...not possible.

Each time I hung up from a stranger who didn't care, loneliness pounced with deadly claws.

I'd leap into another phone call.

Another frustrating, worrisome, unsuccessful phone call.

I ran from facing the truth.

The truth that Aslan was out of my reach.

If I couldn't find him in time.

If I failed to bring him home.

Then we, him, this, *us*…was over.

And that just couldn't happen.

Love stories like ours didn't end at the beginning.

Romances like this were epic and everlasting, and if Aslan dared to die, and I was left all alone, then…*what was the point?*

What was the point of falling?

What was the purpose of love when it was sharper than any knife, crueller than any enemy, and as merciless as death itself?

If Aslan was taken from me, then…I was ash and dust.

I was nothing.

And just like nothing, I would cease to exist.

Because how could I exist without him?

How could I go on without him?

How could I find purpose in life when my very purpose had been stolen?

I can't.

I won't.

I'll find him…

Chapter Thirty

ASLAN

(Heart in Sanskrit: हृदयम्)

I WAS GIVEN A WINDOW SEAT.

Thoughtful, I supposed.

Or sadistic if they knew what awaited me down there.

I expected my heart to stop pumping as we descended into İstanbul. Dusk was falling, triggering streetlights and crushes of buildings to glitter with a welcoming honey glow. The Bosporus Strait sliced like a dark ribbon through the city, providing a natural boundary between Asia and Europe, connecting the Black Sea to the Sea of Marmara.

My eyes skipped over the view, remembering moments, recognising landmarks, drinking in the sprawling city as it soaked up the last spiels of sunset.

I'm...home.

The last time I'd seen this view, I'd sat next to Melike as I pointed out mosques, towers, and bazaars as we soared away from the only country we'd ever known. I'd travelled on a passport that wasn't in my real name, fearing for my parents' safety as we came out of hiding to flee, never knowing that it was my fault we were running in the first place.

My hands balled as the wing flaps activated, slowing our descent, lining up for the runway below. I glanced at Roger, my escort. The thin-lipped, blond-haired guy who'd accosted me outside the Townsville Hospital. I'd learned his name thanks to the many hours we'd shared in a tiny interview room as he tried to uncover my secrets. He'd been my last contact on Australian soil and had grown into a strange kind of acquaintance.

An acquaintance escorting me to my death.

Tearing my gaze off his slack jaw as he snoozed, I focused on my homeland again.

It'd been so long.

Too long.

Homesickness slammed into me. Memories of my family's house in İzmir crowded me. Flavours of my mother's cooking and the scents of the spice markets all swirled with the awful knowledge that I might be home, but this wasn't where I belonged.

Not anymore.

I belonged with Neri.

Back there.

Far, *far* away.

Twenty hours, two plane rides, and a nightmarish week of unendurable separation between us.

They didn't even let me call her to say goodbye.

That was the part I couldn't stomach.

It was an open wound.

A festering disease.

I didn't know how long I'd remain a free man once the plane landed, but I had no intention of dying without hearing her perfect voice one last time.

The moment I cleared customs and Roger completed his task at placing me firmly back into Turkey, I was running.

He might have escorted me out of Australia. I might have been given a temporary right to fly, guided through the transit lounge in Dubai like a criminal, and kept guarded as we waited for our connecting flight, but according to him, I was a free man the moment I stepped foot into İstanbul.

Therefore, I would run as a free man.

I would run on a healing hip and do my best to breathe around cracked ribs.

Perversely, I was grateful for the week I'd been held as it'd given my body time to heal. The pain was still there. Stitches still held my torn shoulder together. And my head still pounded from being split open, but…I wasn't as weak as I had been when Jedda had tried to help me escape. I wasn't as afraid as I'd been when I'd screamed at Jack to go away.

I had strength.

I had speed.

I'm ready.

"Damn, how long have I been out?" Roger smacked his lips and shifted in the uncomfortable aircraft seat. Cricking his neck, he yawned and leaned over me to look at the view. "Pretty place. Pity I didn't have any annual leave. Would've been keen for a weekend to explore."

I studied the growing buildings and tried to see my birthplace through a stranger's eyes. Ancient blended with modern. Tradition braided with metropolitan. Out of all the countries in the world, this one was the richest in artefacts, history, and culture. "A weekend would be pointless. You could spend a year here and still miss out on everything Turkey has to offer."

He huffed and stretched his arms above his head. "Guess I'll have to come back some time and have you be my tour guide then."

My shoulders stiffened. My eyes narrowed. "You know what I told you about Cem Kara. I'll be lucky to survive until dawn."

He dropped his arms. "You keep claiming he'll kill you, but…he's your father. Why would he use all his clout and power to find you? Why would he call every day checking on your welfare? Why would he pull strings to get you home as soon as possible, fight to waive all criminal charges against you, and then agree to personally be responsible for your arrival if he didn't care about you?"

Roger yawned again and scratched his five o'clock shadow. "Forgive me, Aslan, but I think you've been fed stories by the people who stole you and now those stories have morphed into unfounded nightmares—"

"You see the businessman online. You talk to the fake persona on the phone. But you don't know him. Not really. It's a front. A mask. A disguise he's spent decades perfecting."

"No one can be that meticulous or fake the level of joy at hearing you've been found." Roger whistled under his breath. "Just think if the driver hadn't confessed your name, you would've spent another decade lost in a country that isn't your own."

My cracked ribs felt as if they'd shattered.

Another decade with Neri.

Ten years of loving her, being with her…being free.

I tried to speak around the howling loss. "I refused to give my name for this very reason." I sighed and pinched the bridge of my nose.

This argument was getting old.

Frankly, I had no more patience or energy to try and make them see the truth.

What was the point?

I'd lost.

Cem had won.

My father had built himself a fan club within Australian immigration, and each time I tried to make them see the truth, I was looked at as if I was a stupid little boy who'd been brainwashed by the smugglers who'd stolen me.

I hated that they spoke the Avci name as if it were a curse word.

I cursed them for believing Kara wasn't a monster.

Gathering my weary strength, I said, "I'll say this one last time and perhaps you'll remember it when you try to find me to be your tour guide and learn that I died mere hours after you brought me here."

"That's not going to happen—"

"My father is excellent at using good publicity. You see him as a politician, but that's just a camouflage. He killed my adoptive uncle and aunt.

He tried to kill the parents who raised me. I've told you the truth so many times in that awful interview room, yet each time that bastard calls to see what plane I'm on and what time I touch down, you don't believe me."

"He's a powerful man. He spoke to the prime minister on your behalf, for goodness' sake! He even offered to hire expensive lawyers to protect the Taylors for harbouring you all this time."

He held up his hand, already seeing my twisted face and knowing how vehemently I'd defend them. "And before you go on again, you can't pretend that they don't know you. The Taylors lodged three visa applications for you in forty-eight hours. They're openly admitting to harbouring you, despite the risk of jail time. They even hired a visa consultant that is a right pain in our ass. And their daughter? The one you say is nothing to you—a cheap one-night stand—well, she's still calling a hundred times a day." He raised an eyebrow. "You weren't permitted phone calls, but if you could have, would you have retained this useless attempt at not knowing them or would you have spoken to her?"

Just like every time he mentioned Nerida, my insides turned into stone. "I told you, she's no one. I've never heard of her or her parents before in my life."

"Uh-huh. Sure."

The lawyer I'd been assigned (who hadn't helped my situation whatsoever), had said denial was the only way to protect Nerida, Jack, and Anna.

It was my only weapon.

Denial.

Denial.

Denial.

No, they didn't house me.

No, they didn't employ me.

No, I didn't love them.

No.

No.

No.

What could they do? Strap me to a lie detector?

Who knew…maybe they could?

But it was too late for that.

Jack and Anna had indeed thrown all caution to the wind and confessed to hiding me. Neri clogged immigration's phone lines, demanding my release, all while Cem prevented any charges being brought against the Taylors in the disguise of being so caring, so kind, so wonderful.

Fuck.

"Honestly, Aslan, I don't understand why you hate the bloke. He's looked after the people you obviously care for. He's paid for all your repatriation. He's gone out of his way to ensure your trip home goes as smoothly as possible. Why on earth would he do all that if he didn't want you back, safe and sound? Why would he protect the Taylors for housing you if he didn't feel completely indebted to them for looking after his son when he couldn't?"

I winced.

I'd physically thrown up the morning when I'd been dragged into the interview room and heard the sentence with my father's name and the Taylors mixed together.

He knows.

He probably already had their address, phone numbers, and a comprehensive spreadsheet on their habits and vulnerabilities.

He'd proven in one vicious swipe that no one was safe.

He'd also snared me in whatever cage he'd weaved because he'd proven he could snuff out the Taylors as easily as he'd protected them.

He's using them to control me.

It made my choice to run the hardest decision of my life because…if I ran, I put them at risk. But if I didn't, I would die.

Two choices that would ultimately destroy me.

My voice was not my own, full of glacial control as I fought for strength. "He's playing a game, don't you see? He's a master at manipulation and deception."

The fact that Cem Kara knew about Neri?

The pain in my body couldn't compete with the agony in my soul.

I needed to protect her.

I needed to change her name, run away with her, and hide her before it was too late.

But I can't because I'm being moved around like a fucking pawn.

I hadn't even landed in Turkey yet, and Cem had found a way to leash me. A way to show me that he owned me whether I wanted him to or not.

I'd seen the document myself.

Seen his signature on his statement that the Taylors were to be left alone for their involvement in my disappearance. I'd seen the obscene dollar amount he'd donated in thanks to the Australian government for keeping me safe. I'd choked on bile at his hand-written note painting an image of a heartbroken father whose dream had finally come true at finding me.

I snorted under my breath.

I'd been named after a lion, but him? He *was* one. He was the biggest, baddest fucking predator who treated everyone else like dumb little mice. Mice he liked to toy with, play with, and move around on a chessboard of his own making until he was ready to pounce.

Roger sighed again and glanced around the half-empty cabin before saying quietly, "Look, I did what you asked me to. I researched him. I did see a few rumours of him being involved with drug activity before he became more active in politics, but he seems like he's left whatever darkness he used to partake in behind. I think you need to give him a chance."

I caught his stare. I exhaled hard. And I turned away to stare out the window.

I didn't care anymore.

What was done was done.

I'd been denied a phone call to Neri.

I'd been shoved on the first available plane once their doctor had cleared me for travel.

I was here now.

Soaring above Turkey, flying toward a war that I would fight tooth and fucking nail to win. Cem might've manipulated officials, bureaucrats, and even the damn prime minister, but he wouldn't manipulate me.

How many webs did he thread around the world searching for me?

Maybe Emre had been right. Maybe we should've kept going to Antarctica.

Perhaps then we'd all be alive.

But I would never have met Neri.

I grunted at the hot strike of agony that always came when I thought about her.

If I hadn't met her, I would've lived a half-life, yet…in some awful screaming part of me, I wished I'd been able to stay strong that night in the Craypot and never kissed her.

She could be with someone else right now.

Someone with a boring name and a boring past.

My chest hurt.

My heart ached.

I could never go back to Australia. I'd been flagged as an overstayer and marked as banished. If I was caught trying to enter, I'd be arrested and imprisoned.

I was banned for life.

So where does that leave us if I somehow survive this?

Glancing back at Roger, who drank from his metal water bottle, I urged, "Let me fly with you back to Dubai. I'll make my own way from there. You would've done your duty in kicking me out of Australia. Why do you care where I go next?"

"I care because I take my job seriously." He sighed and smiled at a flight attendant who walked down the aisle, glancing at everyone's seatbelts as we began the final descent. Screwing the lid back on his water bottle, he said, "I've grown to like you over the past nine days, Aslan. You're not a bad bloke. I see how your childhood would've been confusing, being raised by the very people who kidnapped you—"

"Not this again. I told you. *They did not kidnap me.* They saved me."

"Nevertheless, they smuggled you into a country and then left you—"

"They died. It wasn't like they chose to abandon me."

"You're right. Sorry. Regardless of their relationship with you, I'm sure you loved them. You didn't know any different."

My shoulders slouched.

Talking to this man riddled me with frustration.

There were so many arguments.

So many things I wanted to yell.

But it wouldn't make a damn bit of difference.

My thumb ran over my tattoo.

Sharp tears came to my eyes. Neri's twentieth birthday might be my last memory of her. What I wouldn't give to go back to that tattoo parlour and run away with her. To never go to dinner. To stay in our apartment where it was safe. To never do something as stupid as thinking we could go out without disaster finding us.

The lines of black ink raised slightly with their final healing now I'd taken the clear bandage off. I traced the lion like it was brail, imprinting the siren's face into my soul.

I had a piece of Neri with me.

She had the mirroring mark.

That knowledge did its best to comfort me, but there was a splinter in my heart that I couldn't pull out.

My shell.

The shell she'd given me when she was fourteen was gone.

I'd lost it in the fight.

It was probably driven over by the car that hit me.

I didn't think losing such a simple thing would hurt me as much as it did, but I couldn't stop thinking about it. Couldn't stop missing it, lying awake in my cell, trapped in a security building somewhere in Brisbane.

I'd thought of it as my good luck charm, but now…that luck was empty.

The familiar darkness full of depression and unhappiness coiled around me. Grief did its best to squeeze me tight, scrambling my focus for what had to happen tonight.

I needed to hide and hide fast.

I needed to disappear and hope to God Cem didn't take out my disappearance on Neri.

Could I take that chance?

Could I be selfish enough to try?

The plane jerked and roared.

Tyres kissed land with a skip and a hop.

Its wings bowed and shivered, no longer needed in the sky.

I jerked out of my depressing thoughts as the engines snarled in reverse, slowing our race down the runway.

Roger didn't speak to me as we taxied to the gate.

He stayed quiet while he grabbed his backpack, raised an eyebrow, and waited for me to slip out of our row before following me into the busy terminal.

I didn't wear handcuffs, but I was shackled to him in so many ways.

He was the only thing keeping me safe now I was home, and my instincts leaped into overdrive.

Waiting in line at border control, I watched him gather all the paperwork on me, preparing to insert me back into Turkey.

I felt like a wayward child. Like a pet being hand delivered to its abusive owner.

"I need some money," I muttered as we shuffled forward, next in line.

"I have a care package to give you when we've left airside." He nodded at the immigration officer as we were beckoned forward.

My heart pounded as I went with him, my gaze darting around the cavernous hall, searching, fearing, waiting.

Would Cem grab me the moment I stepped out of the airport?

Would he wait until I was in the city?

How would he do it?

Does he even know I've landed?

Stupid question.

Of course, he knew.

He knew my flight number.

He probably had the whole airport surrounded.

I didn't watch as the border agent studied my temporary travel documents and stamped Roger's crisp, envy-inducing Australian passport. The sounds of my mother tongue flowed from three agents chatting in a booth down the line.

All around me, English threaded with Turkish, and a part of me that'd missed the rhythm and flow of my own tongue found a smidgen of happiness.

English was now the language I dreamed in, counted in, lived in. It'd become the tongue I cursed and conversed in, but Turkish would always be the language of my heart.

I suddenly wished I'd taught Neri more.

I wished I'd shared every part of myself with her so she could whisper into the darkness, and I might hear her, feel her, and continue loving her even so far away.

"Come on," Roger commanded as heavy stamps pounded on our documents, and we were cleared for entry. He nodded at the agent, scooped everything up, then guided me forward.

Each step, my hackles rose.

Pain from my injuries was muted beneath my fear.

Each distance we travelled, I grew tense and jumpy and more sensitive than I'd been in years. My skin buzzed. The hair on the back of my neck rose. My entire body hummed to a different frequency, just waiting to be shot.

Roger went to baggage reclaim. We stood silently side by side while he waited for a small silver suitcase to appear. Once he'd snagged it, he marched toward the final set of doors. The final frontier between me staying alive and dying.

I slammed on the brakes, pain in my hip and ribs flaring.

I shook my head.

My voice cracked as I breathed, "Give me some money. I need to buy a phone. Right now."

He studied me. Noticed the sweat on my upper lip and the jittery shakes of my hands. His stern face softened as he reached into his backpack and pulled out a manila folder. "Here."

Snatching it, I peered inside. The paperwork I'd been forced to sign in that awful interview room was there, acknowledging that I could never return to Australia. My statement that I didn't know Anna, Jack, or Nerida Taylor, and the scant information I'd given on my dead family, why we'd run, and why I couldn't be deported.

Not that it'd made a shit tonne of difference.

Grabbing the neat bundle of Turkish Lira beneath the papers, I swiftly counted money that I hadn't held in so long. It seemed foreign after the bright plastic bills of Australian currency.

"There's the equivalent of three hundred Aussie dollars there." Roger squeezed his nape. "Just enough to get you home and into the city. I'm sure your father will support you while you get back on your feet."

I didn't bother replying.

I was done trying to convince him of the man my father was.

Shoving the Lira into my jeans pocket—the jeans that I'd been provided with after a week in detention—I rubbed my sore ribs beneath my black t-shirt, cursed the discomfort in my hip, and looked at the last Australian man I'd ever see. "Are we done here?"

"No." He frowned. "I have to spend the night. There isn't another flight home until tomorrow. Tell you what, I'll pay the fare to get into the city. Save that cash for something else."

My mind raced.

I wanted to be alone so I could figure out how the fuck I could stay alive and protect Neri.

But…if I was with him, the chances of getting pounced on were less.

Unless Cem's waiting right outside in the arrival hall.

My lungs stuck together.

This might be my last chance.

"Let me buy a phone on the way out, and I'll catch a ride with you."

"Okay." Roger smiled. "I need some data to call home myself."

Silently, we headed toward the doors from baggage reclaim to Turkish soil. People waved and leaned over the barrier, looking for loved ones as they drifted out.

My heart leaped into my mouth as I scanned the many happy faces.

Please.

Don't be here.

I need more time.

I need to hear her...

I exhaled heavily as I didn't spot a man who looked like me.

No burly guards.

No hitmen who didn't belong.

My eyes skipped all over the place as Roger beelined for the phone kiosks and bought a local SIM for his own phone. Grabbing the cheapest phone I could, I paid, tossed out the box, and did my best not to run.

I stayed calm as Roger guided me out of the terminal and into the much colder air. My nose inhaled the unique welcoming scent of my homeland.

My soul careened around inside my body as Roger marched toward a taxi.

He threw his suitcase in the trunk.

We climbed in.

And we began the forty-five-minute journey into İstanbul.

Chapter Thirty-One

NERIDA

AGE: 20 YRS OLD

(Love in Sanskrit: सनेह*)*

SHRILL RINGING PIERCED MY EARDRUMS.

I shot upright, my eyes flying around Aslan's sala-bedroom, my memories blessedly quiet. His wind-swept, masculine scent surrounded me as I fumbled in the bed coverings, searching for my phone.

The heartache that I could never get free from woke up far too fast, crushing my chest with the knowledge that even though Aslan's scent surrounded me.

He didn't.

He's gone…

Tears gathered into a wet ball in the back of my throat.

Nine days since the accident and tonight was the first time I'd actually been able to fall asleep.

But only because I'd crawled into Aslan's bed.

I couldn't stay in my room.

Couldn't stay in the house where every nook and cranny was melancholy and heavy, mourning Aslan as if he was already dead.

My eyes stung at the brightness of my phone screen as I swiped 'answer call' and noticed it was two in the morning.

"Hello?"

A crackle.

A delay.

And then, the best fucking sound of all.

"Nerida? Oh, thank God. I'm so sorry for calling so early there. I'm sorry for waking you. I'm sorry I couldn't wait till a more reasonable hour but—" His voice cracked. *"Kahretsin, seni özledim."* (Fuck, I miss you).

"Aslan—" Sobs I'd fought for so many days clawed out of me with needles and pain.

I cried.

I cried so damn hard.

Tears rained, and I rocked in Aslan's bed. His bed where we'd hugged and touched and kissed. Where we'd whispered about our future and made so many promises to one another.

"Ah, Neri. Please…please don't cry—" His baritone wavered wetly, hinting I wasn't the only one breaking.

"Aslan…" I pressed my phone hard against my ear. "How…?" Sucking back sobs, I did my best to swallow my grief all while choking on never-ending guilt. "I'm so sorry I didn't listen. I'm so sorry I spoke to those creeps and then distracted you. This is all my fault—"

"Your fault?" His voice rose in surprise. "None of this is your fault, *canım*."

"But I—"

"It was them, Neri. Not you. Never you. You were only trying to protect me."

"And look what happened." I wiped my mouth and shook my head. Now was not the time. It didn't matter. Nothing else mattered apart from getting him home. "W-Where are you?"

I sat straighter.

I wouldn't waste a single moment to sorrow…not while he was here…linked to me through a tiny phone in such a monstrous world.

"Where are you, Aslan?" I gasped again. "I'll come. Right now. I'll come find you."

He took his time replying, almost as if he didn't want to. "I…I'm in Turkey."

Every part of me shut down.

I launched out of bed and shot into the garden. I needed air. I needed stars. I needed the damn moon to somehow bring him back to me. "How long? How long have you been there?"

"About ninety minutes."

My mind raced a million miles an hour.

I hadn't been able to stop him from being deported but I could do everything possible to keep him alive. "You need to get out of there."

"I know. I—"

"Where are you exactly?"

"I'm close to Taksim Square, on Istiklal Caddesi. The agent in charge of escorting me home is staying in a hotel here."

"You're with him right now?"

"No, we just parted ways. We caught a taxi together from the airport."

"So you're alone?"

He sighed. The faint clang of activity and hum of voices echoed down the line. "No. I'm surrounded by people. Locals. Tourists. Istiklal street is a hive of shops and eateries at night. I figured I was safer in a crowd."

I paced the garden, my eyes falling on the pool where Aslan had helped time my breath hold so often and where he'd sunk inside me when we were fooling around beneath my parents' noses.

"Can you get to a consulate or something?"

"And say what?" he asked, his tone tired and strained. "I'm Turkish looking for a way out of Turkey?" A low growl fell from him. "I-I have a plan, Neri, but...I need to tell you something before I do it. Okay?"

I froze. "What? What is it?"

"I know you called about me. That you lodged visas and—"

"They never let us speak to you." My hands balled with rage. "I called every minute, and they never showed an *ounce* of humanity."

"I know. But they're aware of who you are, despite me trying to deny your involvement in me overstaying."

"Then why haven't they come to question us? We haven't exactly been shy with the truth. We don't care about the repercussions as long as we can keep you alive."

"And I can't tell you how grateful I am, *aşkım*, but..." He sighed heavily. "You're not going to get in trouble."

I frowned and stared at the dark house where my parents slept. "How do you know that?"

"Because Cem Kara explicitly said you were not to be prosecuted for keeping me alive when he couldn't. He...he's made friends in high places. He's already got them on his side."

Ice frosted over my lungs. "What? How?"

"He knows who you are, Neri. He knows about Jack and Anna. He deliberately made an impressive donation on your behalf, so you won't suffer the consequences of taking me in. I've seen his statements and signature myself."

"But...why would he do that?"

"So you're left alone and at his mercy."

"I don't understand—"

"If you're prosecuted, he can't get to you. This way...you're his."

Sickness splashed on my tongue. "W-What are you saying?"

"I'm saying that he probably knows everything about you. He knows I know, and he's using you to send me a message."

My knees threatened to give out. "A message that he can kill us if you try to run again?"

Aslan cursed under his breath. "Exactly. He's trapped me, *canım*. I'm alone in my homeland, and I'm fucking petrified because I'm too far away to stop him from hurting you. He could do anything. His men could be on their way to hurt you right now and—"

"Don't worry about us. Just worry about yourself."

"I can't. Don't you see?" A rustling as if he moved away from a noisy part of the street. "I had plans of smuggling myself out again. I have no idea how. I don't have contacts. I don't know who to approach. I have no money, for fuck's sake, but...I was going to ask you to fly to London. To find a way to help me get to Europe. I was going to be selfish enough to see if you'd stay true to your promise and live with me in a different country." His voice lowered. "We could've hidden in Asia or vanished into America. As long as we were together, I didn't care where we lived."

Tears crackled in his voice as he snarled, "I would've gone anywhere with you, Neri. I was willing to fight—"

"Why are you speaking in past tense?" I marched toward the sliding door leading to the kitchen. I was going to pack. I was going to throw everything I needed into a suitcase in five seconds and then book a flight. "I'll leave right now. I'll wire you some money somehow. I'll call whoever I need to and find some guy with a boat to get you out of there—"

"You can't," he said quietly, morosely. "If I go missing, Cem will come after you."

I tripped on a raised nail of the deck, my hand slapping against the sliding door. "He wouldn't. He knows you're there, not here. Why would he—"

"He would hurt you to get to me. If he went to this much trouble to protect you, it wasn't out of the goodness of his heart but because you're his leash on me."

"A leash that you don't have to wear, Aslan. Don't worry about us. We're fine. We can take care of ourselves. Just worry about yourself and come home to me."

"He could take away your livelihood. Just because the government is appeased at the moment doesn't mean they won't still prosecute."

"Who cares!?" I snarled in the night. "Do you honestly think I care if I get a criminal record? Do you think Dad or Mum care? *We love you.* We would do anything for you. If it's a matter of dealing with the choices we made or keeping you alive, I can speak for everyone involved that we'll do absolutely *anything.*"

"And that makes me love you even more, but—"

"But nothing. Hide, Aslan. Go wherever you can to hide. Give me an hour, okay? Give me an hour to book a flight and—"

"You can't come here—"

"I know. I'll do what you said and fly to London. If I have to rent an entire yacht to come and collect you, I will. Just...stay hidden, and we can get through this, okay?"

Someone laughed in the background. "Hang on, I'll just get somewhere quieter."

"No. Don't." I froze with fresh fear. "Stay in the crowds."

He came back on the line. "If we're going to do this, Neri, I need you to clear it with Jack and Anna first. I refuse to die. I refuse to lose you. I'm selfish enough to say I'll fucking swim to Europe to keep you, but…Jack and Anna have to know the danger they're in. They should go away for a while. Go somewhere—" He grunted as if someone had bumped into him. "Fucking hell, it's a madhouse here tonight."

I pictured him surrounded by tourists in a brightly lit street. Of lanterns and quaint shops. Of music and enticing aromas. Such a blissful picture ruined by his homicidal father stalking him.

Sighing heavily, I stepped into the house. "I'll go wake Mum and Dad right now, and they can tell you exactly what I just did. We're in this together, Aslan. You're family. We'll do anything for you…okay?"

He exhaled. "*Seni çok seviyorum,* Nerida. You mean everything to me."

My heart hiccupped as I cut down the corridor. "I love you too, Aslan. More than life itself. I'm so, so sorry."

"Neri…" His tone turned harsh and almost violent. "I need you to know how grateful I am to you. For everything. I-I was born for you, and the past eight years of loving you have been the best eight years of my life."

Fear tiptoed through my chest. "Tell me in person. Tell me when we're together again."

"I love you, Nerida Avci. In this life and the next. In every life hereafter. If anything happens—"

"Nothing is going to happen." I paused outside my parents' bedroom, dressed in night shorts and a silver cami, my knuckles white as I clung to my phone. "You'll see. Everything will work out—"

"I'm yours, *canım.* I was yours before you even found me. I'll be yours long after I lose you. I need you to know that. I need you to know how much I adore you. How much you mean to me. How much you've *always* meant to me."

Tears pooled hotly down my cheeks. "*Seni çok seviyorum,* Aslan. For always. Forever. Now, stay where you are and—"

"Ah, fuck." His voice was just a puff of frigid air in my ear.

I went rigid, wishing I could see through the phone line. Wishing he'd called me on FaceTime. Wishing he was here and not thousands of kilometres away.

My instincts prickled.

That knowing little nudge turned into the sharpest blade, stabbing at my heart.

"Aslan…what is it? What happened?"

The whooshing of air and the snatches of people enjoying life faded in and out as if he cut through crowds in a rush. "Aslan?"

"I think…I think he's here."

I clung to my parents' doorknob. My pulse turned wild. "Can you see him?"

"No, but two men in black suits are following me."

I was sick.

Weak-kneed.

Deathly afraid.

"Can you get into a hotel? Go find the agent who dropped you off."

"I'd have to cut across the square," he growled. "It's too far."

"Then go into a restaurant, a store…something!"

His breathing picked up as he jogged. "Neri…remember your promise? Your promise that you'd never come here? Cem knows you exist, but as long as you stay in Australia, he hopefully won't come after you. He has no reason to. It's me he wants. If he gets me, then…just promise me you'll stay away. That you won't come looking for me. *Promise me.*"

I shivered.

I trembled.

I could barely hold my phone. "Why are you saying this now? What's happening?"

I need to know.

Need to see!

"Nerida…I need to hear you vow you won't come looking for me if something happens."

"Nothing is going to happen because you're going to be fine——"

"*Promise me*, Nerida," he snapped.

Tears fell faster as I quaked outside my parents' door. I wished I could teleport to wherever he was. I wished I was magic and could appear at his side and see whatever nightmare he saw.

To fight beside him.

Live beside him.

Die beside him.

My insides didn't just prickle, they *howled*.

Messages and energies, knowings and terrors.

I tasted it. Felt it. Breathed it.

Danger.

Peril.

Death.

"Aslan…run. Run as fast as you can."

"Neri——"

"Run and hide. I'm flying to England tonight, today, right fucking now. I'm flying there, and then I'm coming to get you on the sea. You only have to hide for a little while, Aslan. Just a little while and——"

"It's too late." The phone line went quiet as if he'd stopped running, his breathing echoing with tatters. "Fuck, Neri. *Fuck!*"

"Aslan. Speak to me. What's happening?" My knees bounced. My bones broke. "*Tell me!*"

An awful noise.

A cold laugh that wasn't his.

"I love you, Nerida. I'll always—"

A soft pop like a champagne cork.

A clatter of noise as if he'd dropped his phone.

My heart roared in my ears as I tumbled against the corridor wall. I pressed my phone excruciatingly hard against my ear. "Aslan? ASLAN?"

The scraping of fingers. The rustle of someone picking up what was dropped. My heart begged for hope. It sat up with false belief that Aslan had just bumped into someone and dropped his phone.

But in some deep, dark horrible place inside me, I knew.

I knew before *he* said anything.

I knew before I spoke to his father for the very first time.

"Is that Nerida Taylor? The third-year marine bio student who dwells at number eleven Helmet Street, Port Douglas?"

Everything shut down.

My heartbeat.

My fears.

My life.

"W-Who's this?"

A soft chuckle. A voice that sounded eerily like Aslan's. "If I'm to believe the reports on what my missing son has been up to, I suppose…I'm technically your father-in-law."

I backed up.

I crashed against the opposite wall. "W-Where's Aslan?"

"Oh, don't worry. He's home now. Back where he belongs."

A gusting in my chest.

A tearing in my soul.

"L-Let me talk to him."

"Oh, I'm very sorry," he purred. "But that won't be possible."

Tears nettled.

Horror settled.

"What did you do?"

Don't tell me.

Don't say it.

Don't—

He sighed sadly. "Well…he's not breathing at present."

It's not real.

This isn't real.

Wake up, Nee.

Wake up!

"Silence?" he drawled. "I must admit, I expected a scream."

"I don't believe you."

"Doesn't matter. What's done is done. I'm sure you always knew this wouldn't last."

"Please…" The world went stark white. I clung to sanity as my heart fissured down the middle. "Please let me speak to him."

"You will never speak to him again."

Even now.

Even with my intuition screaming and ears ringing, I didn't believe it. I couldn't.

It just isn't possible.

Surely, I'd feel different.

Feel his loss.

Feel an emptiness.

A howling, hollowing, cavernous vacuum.

"You're lying," I choked.

"I'm telling the truth," Cem Kara hissed. "My son was stolen from me. He died when he was just eight months old, and whoever this man is, dead at my feet, he has *finally* been dealt with."

I gasped.

I grunted.

I dropped to my knees. "You're lying. You're *lying*! He's alive. He's—"

"Gone." A long-suffering sigh followed by, "Pleasure talking to you, daughter. Do what my son suggested, and don't attempt to come here. You stay where you belong, and I'll stay where I belong." His tone softened. "My condolences. I know what it's like to lose him, and it's the worst pain imaginable. I'll tell you what, if the pain becomes too much to bear, call me. I'll keep this phone so you can reach me. After all, we are family now."

"Stop," I breathed. "Stop lying and—"

"He's gone. I pulled the trigger myself."

"He was in a crowd."

"He was in an alley, courtesy of my men shepherding him to where I wanted."

I cracked right down the middle.

A splitting. A ripping.

I can't breathe…

"Goodbye, Nerida Taylor."

The line went dead.

And for one terrible moment, I didn't feel anything.

Not one blessed thing.

But then, it gathered.

It churned.

It built and built and spun and spun, and when it collided, I broke.

He's…gone.

He's dead.
He's dead.
He's—
I fell to my hands and knees.
I opened my mouth.
And screamed.
I screamed.
And screamed.
I screamed as my parents fell out of their bedroom.
I screamed as they gathered me close.
I screamed as my insides tore to pieces and my heart bled dry and the world went dim.
My lower belly sliced with despair.
I screamed.
I roared.
I howled.
I screamed and screamed and screamed...until I fainted.

Chapter Thirty-Two

NERIDA

AGE: 20 YRS OLD

(Love in Javanese: Tresna)

POP.
Pop.
Pop.
That quiet puff that sounded like a champagne cork was the only thing I could hear on a loop inside my head. The bullet piercing Aslan. The weapon's noise as he died.
Pop.
Pop.
Pop.
Great heaving sobs cracked my ribs as I curled into a ball.
I didn't know where I was.
I didn't care.
I was gone.
No more.
Dead.
I couldn't handle the absolute crippling despair.
He's gone.
He killed him.
He's—
I screamed.
I kept screaming.
My throat oozed with blood.
My ears rang from horror.
My insides kept stabbing and slicing, killing me from the inside out.
I was glad.
I wanted to die.
I *needed* to die.

I had to chase him, follow him, find him.

This life was over.

But the next hadn't begun.

I can find him.

Before it's too late.

We could be together again.

Somewhere else.

Somewhere new.

With new faces and new fates. New lifetimes and new promises.

I'm coming, Aslan…wait for me.

"You have to do something!" my father's voice yelled over my shrill screams. "She hasn't stopped since we found her in the corridor like this."

Hands pressed me down.

The blur of doctors surrounded me.

A bright light in my eyes.

I screamed and thrashed.

I broke and crumpled, not caring my heart skittered out of control or adrenaline made me sick.

The sooner I died, the sooner I could find him.

I need to find him.

"ASLAN!" I punched the closest person holding me in this life. I kicked at another. I fell off the hospital bed where I'd been placed.

Feet pounded as reinforcements came running.

I was picked up.

Carried.

Shoved back down.

More hands imprisoned me.

"Please!" Mum's sobs cut through the ringing in my ears. "She's going to kill herself if she continues! Give her something. Anything!"

Pop.

Pop.

Pop.

The gunshot.

The firing.

The split-second ending that stole Aslan's life.

I screamed and howled.

I screeched and sobbed.

I couldn't contain my anguish.

There wasn't enough lifeforce inside me to withstand it.

I was dying.

Withering.

Haemorrhaging.

"Aslan!"

"She's going to have a heart attack if you don't do something!" Dad roared.

"Administer a sedative," someone commanded. "Now."

"But, Doctor, her blood work from Townsville University Hospital came back. It shows she's—"

Pop.

Pop.

Pop.

I hissed and struck at the people holding me down.

I needed to run.

To disappear into the sea and swim to Aslan.

He needs me!

He's on that wreckage.

Shipwrecked by a storm.

He's drowning…

"ASLAN!"

"Just give it to her," Dad bellowed. "I can't stand this. I can't handle seeing her like this. DO SOMETHING!"

"Do it." Hands pushed my shoulders against the bed.

My eyes flared as I studied the crush of doctors through my river of tears. "Nerida…listen to me. You need to stop, alright? Take a deep breath, and we won't have to sedate you."

I stilled for a moment.

I played possum until the pressure on my shoulders softened.

And then, I launched up.

I fought and won.

I fell off the bed again and tried to leap to my feet.

I'm coming…

The sea.

I need the sea.

I'll swim—

"Neri. Stop. Baby. Please, stop!" Mum landed beside me, all while hands wrenched me from the floor and shoved me back onto the bed.

I screamed harder. Louder.

I'd lost the ability of speech.

I forgot how to speak words.

I couldn't tell them how I burned inside.

How I stung and seared and shattered.

This pain wasn't describable.

It was utterly *indescribable* as it tore through me, snapping every bone, scribing its excruciating autograph onto my soul.

I would always wear its mark.

Always belong to the devil.

This was hell.

And I couldn't survive it.

I didn't *want* to survive it.

I was poisoned.

Infected.

Diseased.

I was dying.

My bones were rotten.

My blood just ash.

I had nothing left.

Nothing.

My screaming stopped.

My tripping heart seized.

I lay blinking on the bed, gasping for air that wouldn't come, blinded by lights, crushed beneath the weight of agony.

Down and down, it pushed me.

Tearing me apart.

Shoving me into the crust of the earth.

Gagging me, choking me.

My body rejected life.

My ribcage flew up as I clawed at my throat as devil's claws wrapped tight.

I can't breathe—

I don't want to breathe.

So why did I fight?

My heart split down the middle.

My skull cracked with pain.

I screamed.

My mother cried and my father yelled and the sharpest prick of a needle stabbed my arm.

The sigh of relief from those around me acted like a blanket as the icy, sickly drug blazed through the mania in my veins.

I went limp.

Lost.

Alone.

So, *so* alone.

He's…gone.

The pain was different now.

Heavy as a mountain.

Colder than an iceberg.

A landslide covered me, burying me beneath sludge and stone.

A tomb.

A cache.

A blissful, blotting ending.

I sighed into it.

I was swept away.

And the final thing I heard was a worried doctor's question. "Did you know? Did you know she's pregnant?"

Lights snuffed out.

Darkness bloomed.

I let go.

Chapter Thirty-Three

NERIDA

(*Love in Dutch:* Liefde)

TEARS DRIPPED SILENTLY DOWN MY CHEEKS. MY head pounded with a familiar headache. A headache that I'd often suffered ever since that horrendous night.

I trembled where I sat, sinking into the present moment and leaving the past behind. I stiffened as I noticed my fingers linked ever so tightly with Dylan's.

He sat braced beside me, his gaze full of pity, our palms sweaty where we gripped.

My chin tipped upward as I glanced at Margot. She didn't speak where she sat opposite me. Wetness tracked down her cheeks as she shook her head. Over and over again.

Wiping at her tears, she breathed, "He died? Truly? He's dead?"

I flinched and pulled my hand from Dylan's.

The conservatory with its pretty palms and lush greenery mocked me with vibrant life, all while I hovered in the death that I'd begged for so often when I was twenty.

I looked back now and pitied that girl so much. I was embarrassed by her and sad for her. I'd hated her and cursed her. But most of all, I was thankful that she'd survived. Against all her wishes to die. Despite all her despair and remorse and the insidious voices in her head to end it, she was strong enough to stay alive.

Without him.

I wished I could say that I found that inner strength because I wasn't a quitter. That I loved my life enough to brave the horrible emptiness and eternal loneliness, but…I couldn't.

I was still here.

I was still breathing…

Because of *her*.

My daughter.

"You were pregnant?" Dylan asked softly, ignoring Margot's question about Aslan's death. "Did you know before that night?"

Swallowing hard, I did my best to slip back into the dissociation of recounting my life. When I'd been enjoying the first flush of love and delicious ache of lust, I was more than happy to trade my decades and become a teenager once again.

But now we were no longer in a romance, we were in a tragedy, and I wanted to tell the rest of my story with that barrier in place of narrator not main character.

"No. I didn't have any idea," I said almost coldly. "When I fainted after Aslan was run over, they blamed my pregnancy. I remember feeling a strange kind of flutter in my lower belly that night. I remember the slicing pain as I screamed my heart out after hearing Cem shoot his only son, but it wasn't until a few days later, when I'd been discharged from the hospital and prescribed drugs to help my catatonic depression, that I fully understood what that meant."

"That you were carrying Aslan's child?" Dylan asked softly.

"I'd lost him, but a small piece of him remained. I hated that as much as I was grateful. Deep within me, life existed. Life created with my soulmate. I wasn't as alone as I thought, which meant…I couldn't be weak. I couldn't give in to the temptation to end it all. I had to live."

My hands shook as I swiped at my tears. "It was that gift alone that gave me the strength not to take those mind-fogging drugs. To endure the agony of loss. To do my best to eat when my parents brought me food and to shower when they guided me into the bathroom. I stopped living for me…but I survived for her."

"What's her name?" Margot whispered.

I winced. "Ayla."

"That's so pretty."

"It means moon's halo or moonlight in my husband's language. I named her for him." My heart pinched as I rubbed my chest. "I made sure she was fluent in Turkish. That she knew her father through my memories and many stories. He was dead. My heart was dead, but I kept him alive for her."

Dylan sighed. "That couldn't have been easy."

"It wasn't easy living with the fact that I'd let my impulsiveness make such a massive mistake. I suffocated on guilt for years afterward, taking the blame for that night."

"But it wasn't your fault, Nerida." Dylan scolded. "It sounds as if those guys were going to attack, no matter what you did."

"Perhaps." I shrugged. "Regardless, I shouldn't have stopped Aslan—"

"If you didn't, he would've probably killed that drunken idiot and added another body count to his tally. He could've been arrested for murder and deported as a criminal."

I narrowed my eyes. "Your black and white approach does not ease the regret I carried."

Dylan rolled his shoulders. "I apologise. I just want you to see that Aslan was right. It wasn't your fault."

I sucked in a breath, scrambling to change the subject. "Ayla...my daughter." I sat taller. "She saved my life when I didn't want it. She gave me something to live for."

"Forgive me for the indelicate question," Dylan said, allowing me to guide the conversation forward. "But...how did you fall pregnant in the first place? I thought you were on birth control?"

"I was. And I was diligent in taking it. However..." I managed the smallest of smiles. "I underestimated the venom of the *glaucus atlanticus.*"

"The sea slug?"

"The week after I was stung, I was pretty nauseous. I didn't want to alarm Aslan, so I hid the fact that I still threw up every now and again. He looked after me so well. He tended to me, doted on me, and made me feel loved in every way he could." I looked at the two reporters pointedly.

"You had sex. While you were sick." Margot shifted a little. "The pill's effectiveness would've been diminished."

"I was stupid. Love struck, stupid, and rather obsessed with Aslan's touch. And he...well, he didn't know we should properly take extra precautions. He trusted me to be in charge of that part of our relationship. I messed up." I sat taller. "But I look back now and can honestly say if I hadn't been stung by that blue dragon and accidentally gotten pregnant through sheer ignorance, I don't think I would be alive today. I think...I think I would've done something drastic, and it pains me to admit that."

"You truly are a surprising woman, Nerida," Dylan muttered. "You willingly tell us about Aslan butchering Ethan—"

"Oh my God!" Margot exclaimed, cutting Dylan off. "*That's* why you don't care if we print what Aslan did to him. It's because he's not here to pay for the crime." She flinched all over again. "Damn, that...that breaks my heart."

Dylan scowled at her. "As I was saying, you willingly share something as dark as potential murder, yet in the same tale are happy to discuss the allure of suicide."

"I am."

"Why?"

"Because people need to understand that those thoughts are normal. That level of despair can come for you out of the blue. I drowned. I admit that. I was happy to never come up for air again, but...I was given a reason to keep trying. A reason that made me accept that the life I'd adored and the man I'd cherished were gone, but...it didn't mean my life had to be over. I just had to be strong enough to accept the differences and make the choice."

"That's inspiring." He bit his bottom lip. "And surprisingly…helpful." He paused as if debating on whether to share. "I-I'm not new to grief myself. I lost my wife in childbirth with our second child ten years ago." He looked away. "I had the same feeling as you. The same tug to end it all. But…I couldn't do that to my son."

"I'm so sorry about your wife, Dylan."

"I appreciate that. Not a day goes by when I don't miss her."

I held his stare, sharing so much pain. So much pain that existed in the hearts of the lovers left behind. "Do you see why I wanted to be frank? Do you feel better, knowing you weren't alone in that cesspit of despair?"

He sat in my question for a moment before nodding. "I do. It helps to know that the emotions I had toward my son were normal. Part of me hated him for preventing me from chasing after my wife. But most of me loved him because he kept me alive. I struggled for years with those two warring parts of me."

"Exactly." I grabbed his hand and squeezed again. "I felt the same loathing. A loathing that makes me sound like a monster when I admit I cursed my own daughter. The entire nine months I carried her, I tangled with love and hate. I loved her for safekeeping a piece of Aslan's soul, but I hated her for keeping me in a world where he was gone. Those feelings only began to fade after she was born, and I did something rather idiotic."

"What did you do?" he asked.

"Soon. I'm working toward that part. I'm nothing but a woman of mistakes." I patted his knuckles and leaned back again. "Recounting my youth has the unfortunate side effect of revealing how much trouble I caused by not thinking. I let passions rule over common sense. I let pain guide me instead of logic. I do wish youth would come with wisdom instead of learning it the hard way."

Dylan glanced at Margot before looking back toward me. "I'm assuming…and I'm asking this for my benefit as well as Margot's, that your daughter is still alive and well?"

I nodded. "She is."

His shoulders slouched. "That's a relief. But also…rather perplexing."

"How so?"

"Well, you're extremely private about your personal life. I did some preliminary research on you before coming here today, and apart from a scant page on your company's website, there's no mention of your daughter."

I smiled and plucked at the blanket across my legs. "I was willing to share my science with the world, not my soul."

"Because you lost your soulmate?" Margot whispered.

I looked up with a small shake of my head. "Because it was no one's business. My daughter deserved a normal life. She deserved to be wild like I had been, rebellious and reckless, to make mistakes and be stubbornly passionate. If the world had known about her and what happened to her father, she would've had eyes on her, which would've brought boundaries and judgements. She wouldn't have learned to listen to her own intuitive nudges or become who she is today."

"And who is she?" Margot asked quietly.

"She's my shining star," I whispered. "She's involved with Lunamare. Alongside a large team overseen by Theodore and Edmund, of course."

"Wait…so that actually happened? Teddy and Eddie are your business partners?" Dylan asked with a quirked eyebrow. "Honey's brother and brother-in-law?"

"Business partners?" I shook my head. "No. They are so, *so* much more than just that." I sighed and rubbed my temples, willing my headache to fade. "I met them through Honey, but none of us could guess how close we would become. How much I'd fall in love with both of them."

My voice turned sad with the past. "Honey was the sister I never knew I needed. She's another soulmate without a doubt. She still is, even though we're old and grey. She and Billy have enjoyed the farm life they always dreamed of, and I'm godmother to their five children, but…without Teddy and Eddie, I don't think I would've survived. Even with Ayla."

"How so?" Margot murmured.

I straightened my spine, gathering courage to keep telling my tale. "Two weeks after Aslan was shot, my father travelled to Townsville to tell Griffen Yule what'd happened. Griffen's unofficial renovator and book-keeper was dead, and I was far too broken to resume my studies—"

"Hang on." Dylan held up his hand, his mind whip fast. "You're telling me that you've worn the title of a marine biologist turned utopia mastermind for decades, and yet…you never graduated?"

"Correct." I managed a small, sad chuckle. "I never went back to school. I was pregnant. My heart was in pieces. I wasn't in the right headspace or lifespace to resume."

"Wow." Dylan breathed. "That's—"

"A lie, I know." I shrugged. "But just because I don't have an official degree doesn't mean I'm not a marine biologist. I'm second generation. I've dedicated my life to the ocean."

"You were saying…?" Margot prompted, cutting Dylan's surprise off at the knees.

For a moment, I forgot. Old age made my mind a little dithery, but then I remembered and continued, "My father stayed down south for a few days, packing up our things. He donated our second-hand furniture and brought back boxes of clothes and mementos. He closed that chapter of our lives so I didn't have to, and when I padded down to the beach at three in the morning—which had become my habit to scream at the moon for taking Aslan from me—I stopped and just stared at those boxes stacked in the garage.

"I found myself opening a box and on the top was my sunset dress. The exact replica to the one I'd worn when I was raped. The one I'd been wearing when Aslan had been beaten and shoved into the street."

"Oh, no." Margot gasped. "That dress was cursed."

"It was."

"W-What did you do?"

"I did what any grieving young widow would do. I lost myself. I fell into fury for that dress. For that bad omen. That *cursed* piece of clothing. I took the box holding Aslan's work shorts and well-worn t-shirts, jumbled together with my pretty skirts and tops, and I placed them in a pile on his bed in the sala.

"The sala where I'd slept ever since Aslan had gone. The sala that used to hold so many happy dreams but now only swirled with nightmares. I bundled up the sunset dress. I poured my mother's favourite lychee liqueur over it, stole my father's lighter that he used for an occasional cigar, and…I set it all on fire."

"Oh my God." Margot reared back. "You set the sala on fire?"

"I destroyed it. Aslan had lived in the bottom of our garden for six years. He was family, yet he hadn't been permitted to live in our house—no matter how cramped that might have been. I think, in that moment, I hated my parents for that. I hated that he'd been designated a kennel like the family's pet outside. I had so many emotions coursing through me. Some evil, some tortured, some completely crazy. I believed if he'd just lived permanently in the guest room, he wouldn't have been found. He wouldn't have been hurt. He wouldn't have been killed.

"It was that insane logic that made me burn it to the ground, my dress included. The dress that caused the two worst events of my life.

"I watched the fire chew through our clothing. I stepped back as it ignited Aslan's bed. I tripped down the three steps as the walls caught fire. And I waded into the pool clutching Aslan's shell as the roof blazed.

"It only burned wildly for a few moments before my dad came running. The neighbours called the fire department, and it was put out not long after."

"Did the structure survive?" Dylan asked.

"Not really. Everything was black char and oily runoff. It took my poor father weeks to clean up the mess and a full skip hire to get the rubble to the dump. He turned the remaining platform into an outdoor sitting area with two lonely chairs and a wave sculpture my mother found at a local market. It was quaint, but no matter how many potted flowers my mother planted, it never quite shed off its shadows. Even in full sunlight, it had the otherworldly aura of a cemetery."

"Where did you sleep after you burned it down?" Margot hugged herself. "If you couldn't stomach to be in the house and you burned down the one place where you felt close to Aslan…where did you go?"

I caught her eyes and sighed. "Teddy and Eddie's."

"What do you mean?" Her forehead wrinkled. "You moved in with them?"

"I wasn't really given a choice." I shook my head, remembering the intervention. The panic in my mother's kind stare. The hesitant way my father touched me as if I'd break beneath his touch. They'd not only lost Aslan, but they also had to watch their daughter spiral. Their very pregnant daughter. Their daughter who'd turned into a living ghost, dwelling in this life and the afterlife, still unsure if she wanted to remain or go.

"Teddy never did anything by halves," I said. "When I told him the best place to anchor an underwater community was the Great Barrier Reef, he took that suggestion and ran with it. Eddie wanted to make a mark on this world and believed wholeheartedly in his new husband's crazy idea to try something impossible. While I'd been studying in Townsville, they'd found a run-down sprawling three-bedroom house only a few streets away from my parents. They'd scrimped and saved for the down payment and taken possession a few months before Aslan died.

"I hadn't even seen their place. They'd given us a video tour one night when we'd had one of our regular brainstorming, drinking sessions, but it was foreign to me. A fresh start where no memories of Aslan would haunt me and nothing could trigger me to break. When Dad called Honey to ask for her help with my mental state, she turned to Teddy. She and Billy were still in Sydney and too far away to be of immediate help, so…she asked her brother to save me."

"Save you how?"

"By taking me in."

"As a charity case?"

"As a protective measure for their business. You see…we'd already applied for a company name the year before. We'd been practically giddy as we FaceTimed and signed the documents that listed me and Aslan, Teddy and Eddie as equal shares in the Latin named creation Lunamare."

"You did say Aslan was the one who named it. How did that happen?" Dylan asked gently.

"Well, for one thing. Naming a company is hard. All the good ideas are taken and after a while, frustration kicked in. Once we'd exhausted everyone's suggestions, Aslan had kissed me and whispered, "'Why don't we name it after the forces that brought us together?'"

I smiled with heartache, recalling that wonderful evening. "I think by now you'll see there was a theme to our life." I spun my wedding ring, glancing at my lion and siren tattoo beneath my shawl. The ink was faded now, the lines no longer as crisp. I'd lost count of how many times I'd stroked that lion in the dark. How many times I'd sobbed into my arm and willed Aslan to feel me, to know I still loved him.

I didn't need my intuition to tell me that I would never find another like him. No one else was Aslan. I wanted no one else but him. I'd been forbidden from following him while I was still so young. I had his daughter to birth and his child to raise, but I knew in myself that I would wait. I would be a mother but never a lover. I would be a parent all while revoking the title of wife.

"The moon and the sea were the instruments of fate that brought us together. Latin was a big part of my world with biology and science. And one of the most poignant things Aslan ever said to me was: 'Without the moon and the sea, we would never have met.'"

"The luna and the mare," Margot whispered.

"Exactly." I nodded. "The moment we combined those words and typed them into the search box to see if anyone else had claimed it, we knew it was ours. The fact that it was free was perfect. The fact that six years later we started a charity under the name Cor Amare was also fitting. The theme had come full circle."

"Cor Amare?" Dylan asked. "I've heard of that. You clean up the oceans and donate millions per year to protect endangered sea life. Don't you also donate to underprivileged people? Schooling and housing, that sort of thing?"

"We do. In a way, I feel like that's our greatest achievement, not Lunamare."

"What does it mean?" Margot grabbed a calico lacy cushion and hugged it. "I don't know those Latin words."

I held her stare. "*Cor* is heart. *Amare* is love. My heart was torn, and my love was lost. It fit."

"Uh, that's so romantic," Margot breathed. "So you never…not once? Aslan was your last?"

"He was my last." I nodded. "I couldn't answer you before when you asked if he was my first, but I can tell you with every breath in my body that he was my last. My always. My forever."

"You were never tempted to find salvation in someone else's arms?" she asked.

"Never. Not once."

"So…you moved in with two men who lived in happily wedded bliss…while pregnant?" Dylan helped guide me back to the story. The story that made me bleed with misery.

"I did." Linking my fingers together, I sat straight and said, "My parents didn't want me to go. They feared I'd do something stupid if I was away from them, but I overheard what Teddy said to them as he pulled them aside. He told them, in no uncertain words, that I was dying from a broken heart. That in order to keep me alive, I had to be free of everything that might tear out the rest of that broken heart. He convinced them I could move into their spare bedroom indefinitely. There were no memories in their home. Nothing to trigger me or make me spiral. When my father told them that it wouldn't just be me for much longer, that they'd end up with a second house guest in a matter of months, Teddy truly became my knight in shining armour. He mentioned that he and Eddie had always wanted a child of their own. I'd seen their strict ten-year life plan. I knew they had goals of building a successful architect business, doing something ground-breaking that put their name on the map, and then adopting a child and becoming a true family.

"The idea that in a few months I'd deliver Aslan's baby didn't scare them. They vowed I could be as melancholy as I needed because they would be there. They would help me with every step. They would never evict me or my daughter and would do whatever they could to make my loss a little easier. They went so far beyond their assigned role as business partners that I collapsed again. My heart had skipped, and my vision had faulted, and by the time I was stable enough, my mother was nodding, and my father was agreeing, and it was settled.

"I moved into the spare bedroom of Mr. and Mr. Ross—Eddie happily took Teddy's surname—and for the months left of my pregnancy, they helped me forget. They coddled me, went to birthing classes with me, they hugged me when I broke and helped honour Aslan's memory by speaking of him often.

"I didn't feel wrong living with them. I didn't feel like I betrayed Aslan as his child was raised by two other men. In a way, Teddy and Eddie helped me keep Aslan alive for Ayla because when I couldn't speak around my despair, they were there, telling her stories of when they'd first met Aslan on FaceTime or the texts between the three of them while Aslan learned how to renovate and needed to ask a question that YouTube couldn't answer."

"So…they became Ayla's surrogate fathers?" Dylan asked, scribbling a few notes.

"They did more than that," I murmured, remembering those heartsick days when they went out of their way to make their house my home. They'd dragged me into town and forced me to pick a paint for my new room. They transformed the walls into a rich dark grey and decorated the space with a coral-inspired silver chandelier, ivory bedspread, driftwood side tables, gauzy white curtains, and cream shaggy rugs. "They became my salvation. They didn't treat me as if I'd shatter. They didn't watch me as if I was one switchblade away from ending it. They gave me space to mourn but also forced me to focus on work.

"They were willing to give me a home but only because we were partners. Partners with a dream, a destiny. The impossible hope of creating a world where disease, plagues, and natural disasters couldn't find us.

"I don't need to tell you how appealing that became after losing Aslan. I wanted to run and hide. I wanted to vanish beneath the waves and disappear into the salt. The impossible task of making Lunamare a reality consumed me, and I was grateful that we spent nightfall sketching our spheres, drawing meadows of seaweed to act as the waste purifier, and arguing over how best to recycle air.

"As I moved closer to my delivery date and my stomach ballooned, they happily, generously turned their third and final bedroom into a nursery. They didn't let me refuse. They nodded along as I blabbered that this was only temporary. That one day, I would be back on my feet. I would remember how to live. I would figure out a way to survive without Aslan.

"But when I stepped into that room for the first time, I'd dropped to my knees, hugged my bulging stomach, and sobbed. My pregnancy was a blur of tears and sorrow but kneeling in that nursery, I felt I could reach out and touch Aslan.

"They'd taken a photo of my tattoo, blown it up, and used the design to paint a fine line mural on the wall by the wooden crib. The lion watched over my baby while the curtains glittered with stars, the ceiling was painted with the waxing and waning phases of the moon, and the floor held rugs of blue layered over one another in different shades, mimicking waves upon the shore."

"It sounds as if they should've gone into interior design instead of architecture," Dylan said softly.

I nodded, remembering how that room sticky-taped my bleeding heart just enough that when I went into labour and was rushed to the hospital at four in the afternoon with two married men and my very anxious parents, I managed to feel something other than despair.

The pain had been astronomical.

I'd been in labour for thirty-three hours.

But when Ayla Avci came into the world, I'd smiled.

I'd smiled and wept and fallen madly in love with the daughter Aslan had given me.

And that night, when everyone had left the hospital and my daughter was sleeping in a bassinet beside me, I'd clutched Aslan's shell and whispered into its peach and cream spikes. "You have a daughter, *kocam* (my husband). A daughter with dark hair like you, dark eyes like you, and the same serious little mouth."

Tears had poured.

Grief had snapped.

Anguish pushed me deep.

And an awful little whisper appeared, hissing in my ear, revealing I was free now.

I was no longer carrying life.

That life was born.

That life was perfect.

Which meant I was free to do whatever I wanted with mine.

Those whispers never left me alone.

For four months, I did my best to ignore them.

I learned how to nurse, bathe, burp, and feed my newborn.

Ayla was passed from one embrace to another, chortling at her two uncles, blowing bubbles at her grandfather, and trying to smile at her grandmother.

Everyone was besotted with her.

So they didn't notice me.

Didn't notice me fading, faking, failing.

They didn't notice until I was on a plane, and it was too late.

Chapter Thirty-Four

NERIDA

AGE: 21 YRS OLD

(*Love in Lithuanian:* Meilė)

MY BREASTS THROBBED AS MY BODY SLOWLY stopped producing milk. Forty-eight hours since I'd seen my baby or nursed her. And it hurt. Emotionally, spiritually, physically.

I didn't know how I'd left her.

I didn't fully remember making the decision.

It was as if a higher power had corrupted my mind, invaded my choices, and when I'd woken up, I was in Turkey.

I winced as a sharp pain lanced through my left breast.

The bruising had started in the sky, and it was all I could do to ignore the instinctual urge to turn around and run back home to my child.

I needed her.

I probably needed her more than she needed me.

Regardless that I'd run away, I didn't fear for her well-being.

I knew Teddy and Eddie would take great care of her. Better care than even I was capable. She would want for nothing.

My phone rang for the millionth time since I'd stepped off the plane and turned it back on. A thousand missed calls from my parents. Hundreds from Teddy and Honey.

If only ghosts could call from the other-side. I'd happily answer if Aslan's name popped up on my screen. If some angelic number appeared and let me talk to him in the underworld.

Sighing heavily, I rubbed at the grit in my eyes from long distance travel and pressed accept. Raising the phone to my ear, I braced myself for the barrage of anger, questions, and blame.

I didn't speak.

I just waited.

Silence echoed down the line before the quietest question. "You're in

Turkey…aren't you?"

I'd grown so used to swallowing tears, my throat was raw from all the salt. My insides preserved like salted herring. But it didn't mean I'd learned how to stop it leaking out of my eyes. "I'm sitting in Istiklal street," I murmured. "I'm watching trams and people, inhaling sunshine and exotic scents, soaking in the birthplace of my dead husband."

Teddy sucked in a breath. "We got your note. Your parents are frantic."

"I just…I had to come. Even though I've broken my promise to him, I didn't have a choice."

"It's the anniversary of his death." Teddy sighed. "To be honest, I expected you to do something like this. You've been ever so quiet, Nee. I've been worried about you. Even Ayla couldn't bring you back these past few weeks."

I gave up trying to stop my tears and sat on the bench as people shopped and laughed. I could see why the guidebook on the plane said Taksim Square was the heart of modern Turkey—it buzzed with life, it hummed with happiness, everything was brightly lit and prettily decorated. Flowers spilled from shops and souvenirs glinted in the late afternoon sunshine.

I'd only been in Turkey for an hour, yet I could already feel a tug that I belonged. I belonged to a country I'd never visited all because I belonged to a man who was born here.

"I…I can't stop thinking he's still alive, Teddy," I whispered around my tears. "I should feel it…shouldn't I? Shouldn't I feel that void of him missing? Shouldn't I sense that he's gone? Why don't I feel that emptiness? Why do I feel as if he's still here?"

"I don't know, Nee. I suppose that's grief? You haven't exactly gone through the seven stages of healing yet. You've barely made it through the first one. You're still firmly in denial."

"I'd accept it if it felt like he was gone." I blinked as a happy child darted past with a tatty teddy-bear. "He said he heard me screaming for him when Ethan raped me, so why do I feel him screaming for me now? Why does my heart fall into palpitating episodes when I'm asleep, yanking me from my nightmares? Why do I sometimes feel as if he's watching me? Why do I hear him or smell him or—" I snapped my lips closed, choking on the secrets I hadn't told anyone.

I hadn't confessed that at three, four, five in the morning, when I was supposed to be deep in dreams, I would lie stiff and trembling in my bed, so sure, so absolutely, *certainly* sure that he was alive and calling out for me.

"I don't have those answers," Teddy said softly. "But…if going to Turkey will help you heal a little, then…I'm glad you went."

"I'm sorry I didn't tell you I bought a ticket. It was last minute. I didn't plan it. I just…I saw the date. I saw that somehow a year had passed and…I booked a plane, drove to the airport, and landed here before I truly realised what I was doing."

"I'll send Eddie to pick up your Jeep so you don't come back to exorbitant parking fees."

"Thank you," I said. "H-How's Ayla?"

"She's fine. Was a bit grizzly when she had a bottle shoved in her mouth instead of your boob, but…she's fine."

"I left as much breastmilk as I could." I hung my head. "Fuck, I'm a terrible person, aren't I? I made so many mistakes where Aslan was concerned. And now I'm doing the same thing with my daughter. I shouldn't have come here. He told me not to, so what am I doing? Breaking my final promise to him. Fuck—"

"Hey. It's alright. You have to do what you need to do. If you need to visit his homeland to say goodbye, then so be it. You're grieving, Nee. Don't be too hard on yourself."

Standing in a rush, the street swam from my lack of food, sleep, and hope. Ayla had kept me alive this far, but I hated to admit I was floundering. If I hadn't been lucky enough to be adopted by Teddy and Eddie and for them to be the best nursemaids, uncles, and big brothers to my baby daughter, I honestly would've perished months ago.

"I'll head back to the airport. I don't know what I'm doing here. I have no hotel booked. I didn't even bring a suitcase. I just…I needed to see the last thing he saw. I needed to see if there was blood on the street or some sign that his father lied to me."

"I get it. I truly do." The sound of Ayla's happy chortle came down the line, followed by Eddie's deep baritone as he played with her. Most likely on the little white playmat with the mobile full of whales and dolphins that my mother had bought for her.

A pang of vicious homesickness filled me. My breasts leaked, and I plucked at my lilac jumper, doing my best not to end up with wet patches. Hearing Ayla automatically made my body ready to feed her, and it made me feel a thousand times worse.

God, what am I doing?

I left my daughter for this.

I let selfishness take me away from her when there's nothing here but dashed hopes and death.

"I-I'm coming home."

"No. Wait. Look, you're there now. Why don't you reach out to some of his family—"

"They're all dead. Cem Kara made sure of that."

"Shit." Teddy's tone went instantly serious. "Do you…you don't think he knows you're in Turkey, right?"

Ice dripped down my spine, followed by the awful knowledge that I didn't care. I honestly didn't care if he knew. He could kill me for all it mattered. I would miss my daughter, but…she wouldn't miss me. She'd have Teddy and Eddie, and…*perhaps that's the best for everyone.*

Stop it.

Don't go there.

Not again.

You promised.

Death slinked through my mind, whispering like it had in those early days, taunting me with freedom from this everlasting pain. This never-ending *guilt.*

I shut it up, I blocked it out, but not before an evil little thought said…

Call him.

I froze.

An idea unfurled.

A terrible, *awful* idea.

"Teddy…I-I've got to go."

"Go? Go where? Do you want me to book you something online? Where are you staying tonight? You need to call your parents so they at least know you're alive."

"I'll call them after."

"After what?"

"After I do something I should've done months ago."

"But—"

"Look after my daughter. I owe you. I love you."

"Neri—"

I hung up on him.

With shaking hands, I scrolled through my contacts and hovered over the number that'd called me at two in the morning a year ago. The number that'd been Aslan's but was now his father's.

Cem's invitation squatted in the back of my mind, oozing with filth.

He said I could call him.

He said we were family.

My finger stabbed the button.

My phone started ringing.

Sitting heavily back on the bench, I focused inward on the strange kick in my heart that happened every now and again with the inherent belief that Aslan wasn't gone. He couldn't be because I still *felt* him. I still felt his soul knotted ever so tightly with mine, and I had to know.

The phone rang and rang.

It rang so long I feared he wouldn't pick up, but then…

A soft click.

A masculine sniff.

"Well, well, if it isn't my sweet daughter-in-law. This *is* a pleasant surprise. I hear you have your own daughter now, Nerida. I will admit, the temptation to visit my grandbaby has been strong."

A full-body shudder worked through me. Abhorrent hate. Repellent loathing for this son killer, this life stealer, this *monster*.

"I think you're lying," I hissed.

"Lying?" He chuckled softly. "About what, *kızım?*"

"I think Aslan is still alive. I want to talk to him. Let me see him. I'm in Turkey and—"

"You're in Turkey?" His accented drawl snapped into an aggressive bark. "That was sudden."

"I'm in the street where you shot him. Come get me. Show me where you buried him. Prove to me that you're telling the truth and—"

"I told you to stay where you belong, Nerida, and I would give you the same courtesy. Have I not stayed true to you? Have you been implicated for harbouring my son? Have you been questioned or detained?"

"You know we haven't."

"Then you're welcome. I have no war with you or your family. But…you are not welcome here, and I don't take kindly to people surprising me."

"Give him back to me."

"He's a pile of ash."

My heart ripped down the middle. "*Liar.*"

"I would give you his remains, *kızım*, but—"

"Stop calling me your daughter. I'm not. You're not Aslan's father. If you were, you would never have been able to hurt him."

"Aslan Avci was not my son. Aslan Kara was. And he died when he was just a babe."

"And you murdered those who tried to give him a better life."

"A better life?" he snarled. "I was going to give him the world. He was *my* world. I only did what any parent would do." His tone deepened. "Tell me, *kızım*, if someone stole Ayla, what would you do? Would you hunt for her? Would you search for her? Would you slaughter those keeping her from you? How far would you go to protect your own flesh and blood?"

Fury blazed through me. The urge for bloodshed at the very mention of someone hurting Ayla burned like lightning in my veins. "I would do whatever it took to keep her safe—"

"Ah, so you *do* understand. You admit that you see why I went after the Avcis? I'm not a bad person, Nerida. I was merely a heartbroken father, desperate to find his only son."

"Don't twist this. You didn't have to kill them."

"But I did. They stole more than just my boy from me; they stole my heir. They stole any chance at trust. I live a lonely existence. My generals obey me. My politicians bow to me. But I can't trust any of them to rule in my stead. Aslan was my one chance at being happy. My one chance at retiring, knowing everything I've built was safe in his control. And the Avcis stole that from me."

"You speak of Aslan as if you still love him."

"I do. Very deeply."

"Then how could you kill him in cold blood?"

"Oh, it wasn't in cold blood, *kızım*. It was very much planned and premeditated. I told you. That man was not my son."

"He was more your son than anyone. If you knew what he—" I cut myself off.

Don't.

Think, Neri.

Think before you act for once in your miserable life.

Cem paused for a moment, the silence turning sharp with questions.

"Is there something you want to tell me?" he asked quietly. "You do hold an enviable place in my son's past, after all. Out of anyone, living or dead, you knew him the best." He sucked in a breath. "So…tell me. Prove to me why I made a mistake killing the imposter who was my flesh and blood. Go on."

I glowered at the happy families all around me, and my heart bled all over the pretty street for what I'd lost. I tasted the truth, rolling it on my tongue, before deciding…*fuck it.*

What could happen?

Aslan was dead.

He'd told my father what he'd done to Ethan.

I was merely repaying the favour by telling his.

"Aslan Avci was good and kind, sweet and hardworking. He loved math and said that numbers felt differently—"

"He did?" Cem interrupted with a gasp. "He saw in colour?"

I scowled. "He was secretive about it but only because I'm guessing whatever gift he'd been given came from you. A gift he wanted nothing to do with."

He snorted but didn't retaliate. "There's a genetic trait in our family. My father had it. I have it. Seems my son had it." He paused, then said, "It will be interesting to see if Ayla has inherited the Kara synesthesia genes. Keep an eye on her, *kızım*. She could be far more special than you know."

"Hearing my daughter's name on your tongue is repellent."

"Why? Because you're beginning to understand me? Because you would do the same thing I did if someone dared steal your child?"

"*Enough.*" Running a hand through my hair, I bent forward. "I'm *nothing* like you."

"As you wish. But please…finish what you were going to say about why Aslan was more my son than any other. The boy you've mentioned, who loved math and avoided conflict, sounds like an Avci, not a Kara."

"Will you let him go if I tell you?"

"He's dead, *kızım*. I am sorry you cannot believe that."

Anguish cracked through my spine; I clung to the only emotion I could.

Anger.

Hate.

Bone-deep loathing that this man still existed.

I wanted to hurt him like I hurt.

I wanted him to grieve like I grieved.

I wanted him to admit that Aslan didn't deserve to die.

"He was your son, Cem Kara. He might have the morals of the people who raised him, but deep inside, he was yours."

His voice turned sharp. "Tell me."

"I was raped when I was seventeen. Aslan was the one to find me. I asked him if he'd kill for me…he agreed." My hand tightened around my phone. "He hacked off two of my rapist's fingers. He shot him in the left calf with a harpoon. He would've cut off his cock and scooped out his eyes if I hadn't stopped him. Even in that haze of fury, he listened to me. Protected me. But…he didn't obey me when I told him not to kill him."

"My son killed someone?"

"Does that hurt you, knowing that? Knowing he was more like you than you realised? That you murdered your son before you even got to know him?"

Silence.

More silence.

Finally, Cem cleared his throat. "I am sorry you endured rape, and I am glad my son did his best to make it right. I bid you safe travels, Nerida. I will permit you to remain in my country for seventy-two hours. Eat our food. Explore our city. But then go home to your daughter. Or…I will escort you back myself. I look forward to your call next year, *kızım*."

He hung up.

My arm fell into my lap.

I began to shake.

To quake.

God…w-what have I done?

What on earth possessed me to say such things?

Why confess what Aslan had done when it didn't make a shred of fucking difference?

It didn't reincarnate him.

It didn't summon him from the grave.

I…I know why.

My trembling hands curled around my phone as my teeth clenched.

I did it to rip out Cem's cold, dead heart.

To stab a blade of doubt that his son and heir was still his, regardless that Aslan fought against his true nature most of the time.

Violence flowed in his veins.

Ferocity and viciousness were as much a part of Aslan as protectiveness and affection.

He was a lion, after all.

And lions could love their pride all while shredding their enemies into pieces.

I hope Cem is cursing himself.

I hope he's hurting.

I hope he gets run over by a bus and fucking dies.

Chapter Thirty-Five
NER¹DA

AGE: 21 YRS OLD

(Love in Nepali: Māyā)

One year, one month…

I ONLY STAYED IN TURKEY FOR FORTY-EIGHT hours. Instead of visiting the tourist attractions, I went to the local library and read as many historical newspapers as I could about Cem Kara. I stalked the streets searching for someone who could prove that the crime lord that Aslan had been unlucky enough to be born to had a weakness I could exploit.

I even hunted down the local police station. To ask questions and point fingers.

I intended to take my improving Turkish and demand to know about the Kara empire. I needed to understand how Cem trafficked girls, ran drugs, laundered money, all while brainwashing the public into believing he was fighting for their rights by trying to gain greater power in parliament.

He had one foot in the dark and one foot in the light, and no matter where I turned, the despicable deeds he did were just rumours and gossip, yet the humanitarian work and donations of his time and money garnered headlines.

On the second day of snooping, a man in a black suit appeared outside my hotel.

A man who stepped in front of me.

A man who didn't touch me but made it abundantly clear that I had no option but to slink inside the limousine purring at the curb.

I got in.

I'd long forgotten how to listen to self-preservation.

If Cem wanted to kill me, fine.

If he wanted to bring me to dinner, so be it.

If he wanted to prove to me that Aslan was alive and show me that I wasn't going absolutely crazy, then I would get on my knees and thank him.

However, none of those things happened.

Cem Kara stayed true to his word and escorted me to the exit of his homeland. He hadn't even lasted three days before pushing me out. As I stepped unwillingly into the airport, the driver passed me a leather case with a first-class ticket back home, a care package with a face mask and toothbrush, and…a grainy, age-stained photo of a gorgeous plump baby dressed in a lion-covered onesie.

I stumbled.

I choked on tears.

I didn't know why Cem had given it to me.

Was it meant to be an apology or some mind game?

Was he pure evil or trying to repair his wrongs?

He petrified me because the level of calculation and commitment to doing what he believed was right left no room for emotion.

He wasn't just a predator.

He was a hunter.

A hunter who liked to torment his prey with hope instead of misery.

I didn't remember the flight home.

I didn't remember how I stumbled back into Teddy and Eddie's house at midnight, all while clutching that photo of baby Aslan as if it would somehow bring him back to me.

I think I scared them as they guided me, unspeaking and unblinking to my room and put me to bed. I scared myself because all I could see, all I could think about was Aslan.

Aslan.

Aslan.

He'd been an adorable child.

His mouth reminded me of Ayla's, and his dark eyes, looking so seriously into the camera, were direct replicas of his daughter's.

The next day, Eddie knocked quietly on my door and brought my baby to me.

The moment I saw her, I didn't notice the tall, slim Australian man with wavy light-brown hair and intelligent hazel eyes. I didn't feel his hug as he sat on my bed, gathered me close, and passed Ayla into my arms…

I only saw her.

Felt *her.*

I dropped my head into her clean, powder-scented curls and cried.

I knew I couldn't keep doing this.

I couldn't keep sobbing into her perfect soft skin.

I couldn't keep breaking all over her.

But in that moment, cradled by Eddie and curled around my child, I gave myself space to let go.

At some point, Teddy joined us. His blond hair so similar to his sister's, his green eyes far too vibrant and astute, his lips plump and quick to smile. I sat between the two husbands, and they pressed matching kisses against my temples.

And despite everything.

Despite my hollowness.

My hurting.

My haunting, harrowing pain, I managed to lift my head, kiss both men on their whisker-covered cheeks, and have enough strength to face yet another month without him.

One year, two months...

I framed Aslan's baby photo and placed it on my bedside table, next to a picture my parents had taken of us one evening after we'd told them we were together. I sat on Aslan's lap at the glass table outside. Our plates held remnants of dinner, and the setting sun cast the garden in a ruby, golden glow. I hadn't even known they'd taken the picture. My eyes were locked with Aslan's. His lips slightly parted, his gorgeous face full of love as he studied me. The moment captured our visceral affection. Raw and blatant connection.

It broke my heart each morning to wake up to our lost love, but...it also forced me to be brave.

I'd gone to Turkey against his wishes.

I was still alive despite talking to Cem twice.

I had the horrible feeling that my father-in-law enjoyed keeping me that way, ready to toy with at any moment.

I'd spent a year grieving.

I hadn't moved past denial. I doubted I ever would because to accept would be to say goodbye, and that was an impossibility.

I had absolutely no idea *how* to heal.

So...I stopped trying.

I accepted that the hurricane that blew my ribcage apart and the tsunamis that drowned my heart were a part of me now and forever. I threw myself into being the best mother, daughter, and business partner I could be.

Mum and Dad came round for dinner twice a week.

They fussed over Ayla, and Dad offered his help to see if anchoring a biosphere on the reef where we'd been planting lab-grown coral for years could withstand currents, storms, and tectonic plate movement.

Life stubbornly dragged us all forward, and I often caught Mum looking at me with worry. Her eyes would well with tears whenever she looked at Ayla playing with her colourful blocks, and she'd hug me with arms that recognised my pain and offered a safe harbour if I needed to crash.

I knew they missed Aslan just as much as I did.

Pieces were missing from all of us, yet we did our best to borrow those pieces from each other.

We became close.

Very close.

And when Teddy finally announced he and Eddie might finally have a design that incorporated all the necessary technical requirements to hypothetically work, I stepped into my role of fundraising.

I threw myself into work with single-minded determination, filling my days with far too many things. The only problem was, I hadn't figured out how to crowd my nights, and that was where Aslan still found me.

One year, four months…

"My heart doesn't beat right when we're not together, aşkım."

I arched beneath him and kissed his perfect lips. "That's because we don't have separate hearts anymore. We only have one."

His body thrust into mine, penetrating and invading, reminding me I was his, all while giving everything he was to me. "I like the thought of that." He licked my bottom lip. "We share our bodies, so why shouldn't we share our hearts too?"

"Why indeed." I gripped his ass as he rocked deeper inside me. "You've taken everything else anyway."

"And I won't stop." His eyes tightened as we chased spindling pleasure. "Know why?"

My head tipped back, loving the way he collided with me. "Because you can't stop until I'm yours?"

"Oh, you're mine, Neri. You were mine the moment I first saw you. I won't stop because—" His eyes suddenly flared. His body jerked. Shadows misted from all corners of the room, crowding him, whipping around his throat, lashing like black ropes over his chest.

The darkness wrenched him back, withdrawing his body from mine, and throwing him to the ground.

"Aslan!" I scrambled off the bed, dropping to the floor after him. "Wait—"

"Neri—" His eyes met mine as the darkness thickened.

It clotted and hissed, then snatched him into nothing—

I woke with a gasp like I always did.

I rubbed at the bruises on my knees from falling out of bed that'd become a bad habit.

My mouth was sour from dream screaming.

My body wet from dream needing.

The house remained quiet and comforting around me, but I couldn't be there.

Like most nights, I grabbed my white dressing gown, slipped into it, and padded out of my room. I checked on Ayla, sleeping with her little fists above her head, her face so serious even while slumbering. With a kiss to her chubby cheek, I drifted past Teddy and Eddie's bedroom, and cut through the designer lounge where Teddy had somehow turned second-hand eclectic furniture into a boho chic fit for a beachside magazine.

The sliding doors into the overgrown garden made no noise as I disappeared outside and followed my well-trodden path through the side gate, over the front lawn, and down the street to the beach.

Draping my dressing gown on the branches of a twisted banyan, I ripped off Aslan's t-shirt that I slept in, and moved naked in the clouded moonlight to the sea.

No one knew I took these two a.m. swims.

No one needed to know.

This was the only cure I'd found for my chronic grief-stricken disease.

I'd grown reckless swimming in the ocean at a time when creatures came out to feed. I felt no fear as I splashed while monsters cruised below. In a way, I was offering myself up to fate. If it answered my call and took me one day, then I would know Aslan was indeed dead, and it was time I returned to him. But each night, as I cut through the black-silver water, pushed myself until my lungs burned, and kicked legs made of lead, I somehow survived.

Nothing came for me.

Nothing stopped my nightmares.

And by dawn, I was rinsed clean enough to face another day without my heart.

One year, six months…

"*Seni seviyorum*, Ayla." I blew bubbles on my daughter's neck as she flounced around in the bathtub. "Do you know what that means? It means I love you. Daddy would say that to you if he were here. He'd also say *sen küçük bir balıksın, tıpkı annen gibi*, which means you're a little fish…just like me."

She squealed and splashed, her busy little fists snatching up a wind-up clownfish as it flapped around in the bathwater.

"Another language lesson?" Teddy stuck his head into the steamy silver-tiled bathroom, depositing a fresh towel on the lid of the toilet. "She said her first word yet?"

"Nope."

"Do you want it to be Turkish or English?"

"Either." I shrugged. "She's going to be bilingual, so whichever comes first is fine."

"You're turning me bilingual." Teddy grinned. "This entire household will switch between two languages as if we're natives."

"That's my hope." I gave him a smile that I hoped hid all my heartbreak. "I want her to know him...even if he's not here."

"Ah, Nee." Crossing his arms, Teddy leaned against the doorframe. "She knows. And he knows. Wherever he is, he's watching both of you."

I sniffed and changed the subject. I'd become a master at that now. "Go on. Lesson time for you. Say something."

He frowned in concentration, finally stumbling over vowels and accents. "*Biraz türkçe konuşabiliyorum.*" (I can speak Turkish a little bit).

I now understood how difficult it would've been for Aslan to hear me butchering his tongue. I wasn't fluent yet, but my ear had matured enough to know when the pronunciation was right or wrong. "Hey, that's really good."

"I have a good teacher. Between you and Anna with her apps, I'll be a pro."

"Talking about me in Turkish again?" Eddie appeared, smacking a kiss on his husband's cheek. "I've been learning too. See... *ailemi seviyorum.*" (I love my family).

My heart stopped.

Anger feathered through me for a split second.

This family was missing a significant part.

Teddy flicked me a glance, hearing my quick inhale. Cocking his head and pursing his lips in apology, he wrapped his arm around Eddie and announced, "I have good news for you both. That Kickstarter you started last month, Neri? It's already hit the target. We have enough to start building a prototype."

"Oh wow, really?" Eddie blinked before shooting me a glance. "You know I mean I love our family, including the ghost that haunts us, right, Nee?"

"I know." I ran my fingers through Ayla's damp dark hair. "Sorry...I thought I'd stop being this...raw."

"You can be as raw as you want for as long as you want." Eddie blew me a kiss. "But right now, I need to know more about this prototype. Were my sketches approved by the local council as a dwelling?"

Teddy frowned. "Well, seeing as there's no such thing as a council for undersea living, I'm guessing the further along we get with Lunamare, the more red tape we're going to have to bulldoze through, but for now, we've sourced glass thick enough to withstand pressure up to twenty metres. We've found marine-grade steel that can last a hundred years without losing its structural integrity and have almost figured out the sealing complications. Our spheres will look more like Frankenstein decagons, but it will do. We need to get something into the water so we can start figuring out filtration and air flow."

The two men looked at me as I grabbed the towel, wrapped it around my daughter, and hoisted her from the tub. "You ready to hustle up some more money, Nee?" Teddy asked.

I frowned. "I thought you just said—"

"I said we had enough for the preliminary builds, but we need somewhere to test."

"I figured we'd rent the local pool. My parents' one isn't deep enough."

"I don't want to risk people seeing what we're doing, even if it's the local minnow swimming school. I want to test at any time of the day."

"What are you saying?"

"I'm saying I want to build a pool. In our back garden. And not just any pool but one with at least a five-metre bottom."

"You're crazy. No one will approve that." I laughed as I dried Ayla, kissing her cute little nose as she pressed her damp hands against my cheeks. "*Seni seviyorum,*" I murmured, determined to scribe those words on her tiny, perfect heart.

"No laughing, woman. Make it happen." Teddy winked, grabbed Eddie's hand, and dragged him down the corridor. His voice trailed back. "Come join us after you've put your little moonbeam to bed. It's time we got this show on the road!"

One year, eleven months...

"Bloody hell, it's so deep it's giving me vertigo." Honey clung to my arm as we stood at the edge of the almost completed swimming pool. We'd gotten planning permission to add a pool into Eddie and Teddy's back garden, but...we hadn't been exactly truthful on how deep it was.

We kept a temporary fence around it at all times while it was being dug, doing our best to prevent nosy neighbours from tattling on us. Once there was water inside, it wouldn't be as obvious, but right now, it looked like an asteroid had drilled its way into the ground.

"It's been a daily battle to keep an eye on Ayla so she doesn't fall in," I said. "It literally keeps me up at night."

Which I'm grateful for as I can't have panic attacks about Aslan still alive, somewhere, out there...stolen from me.

Honey blanched. "Oh God, I can imagine. Especially now she's walking."

"She's into everything." I smiled and looked at my rascally daughter currently being bounced in Billy's arms a few metres away with my parents. For such a gruff burly guy, Billy was one of the gentlest souls I knew and the best husband to Honey. We'd all married young, but...we'd all known we were meant to be. "Did Teddy tell you that her first word was 'kitty?'"

"Kitty?"

"Yeah, she pointed at the lion mural in her room and went *rarrww* then, clear as day, announced it was a kitty."

"Wow, that's so cool."

"Don't tell your brother, but I've been secretly whispering that her dad was a giant kitty into her ear at night. I wanted her first word to be Aslan, but..." I shrugged.

She sighed sadly. "How are you doing? With all of this?"

"It's been almost two years."

"Two years is nothing with how deeply you guys loved one another."

Honey was my best friend. We talked every day. We shared everything. I trusted her more than I ever trusted Zara, and I loved her with all that was left of my brutalised, broken heart, but...I didn't have the strength to share my agony.

I doubted I ever would.

After my parents found me screaming in their corridor after Aslan was killed on the phone to me, I never wanted to reach that level of despair again.

I'd barely crawled my way out the first time, but that chasm was always there. An abyss inside me just waiting to drag me back. To pull me down into a screaming void that I could never escape from.

Ignoring her question, I leaned into her and squeezed her arm looped around mine. "I'm really glad you came to visit."

She gave me a sad smile and a quick kiss on my cheek. "Me too. Annoying that we have to sleep in a tent in my brother's back garden—seeing as all his rooms are full—but I love this for you. I love that you guys made a life together. It might not be the life you wanted or the life anyone foresaw, but...I feel as if I truly do have a sister now, living with my two brothers."

"Do you mind?" I asked quietly. "That I live with them, and you live in Sydney?"

"Mind? Why on earth would I mind? You know I'm joking about the tent, right? It's super hot, so it will be fun. To be honest, I'm rather looking forward to having some outdoor sex with my man." She snickered. "I promise we won't be too loud."

I laughed to hide the painful pinch in my heart. I sometimes heard Teddy and Eddie making love through the thin walls. My heart would quicken, and my body would melt, and I'd lie in a different kind of nightmare to the ones that usually woke me up.

I missed having sex.

I missed having sex with Aslan.

I was almost twenty-two, yet the thought of ever being touched by another man turned me as celibate as a nun.

My desire to continue playing the happy widow faded, and I extracted my arm from Honey's. "I'm going to get dinner started."

Her face fell. "Do you want any help?"

I shook my head and kissed her cheek. "Nah, some alone time would be good. Keep an eye on my little moonbeam, would you?"

"Of course." Honey grabbed my hand as I stepped away. "Nee?"

I raised an eyebrow, flinching a little as my heart chose that moment to skip erratically, almost as if someone had plugged me in and sent a surge of electricity through my veins, defibrillating me for no reason whatsoever. "Yeah?"

"I'm so proud of you. So proud of the prototype you guys have built and the endless hours you're putting in to make this dream come true, but...I have to ask." Stepping into me, she lowered her voice. "If you find a way to live beneath the ocean...are you ever coming back to shore? Are you running away, Nerida?"

I gave her the respect of thinking about her question.

But I couldn't give her my truthful answer.

Smiling, I shook my head and gave a convincing lie, "Of course not. I'm exactly where I want to be."

She let me go and headed toward Billy and Ayla, stealing my daughter off her huge husband and beaming at her.

Ayla might've been born to a lion and a siren. She might come floating with me in the ocean and spend most of her days playing in her paddling pool or blowing bubbles in her bath, but she wasn't a creature of the sea like me.

She wasn't gifted her soulmate by the waves.

She wasn't afraid of what could be taken away.

She didn't have anything to run away from, so until she was an adult in her own right, I wouldn't be running anywhere.

But the day she no longer needed me...I was slipping beneath the surface and never coming up again.

Two years...

I called him at two in the morning.

The same time he'd shot Aslan two years ago.

I stood on the starlit beach, gripping the shell Aslan had lost the night

283

everything went so dreadfully wrong. The night of my birthday. A night that'd become horribly entwined with my life getting older and Aslan's coming to an end.

I listened to the waves hissing on the shore.

I waited…

"*Tekrar merhaba, kızım.*" (Hello again, daughter).

A ripple of pure hatred shot down my spine as Cem's voice filled my ear. His voice sounded so similar to Aslan's. His deep rich tone echoed in my mind even now. My husband's face forever tainted because it was the mirror image of his murderer.

"*Bana hayatta olduğunu söyle,*" I hissed. (Tell me he's alive).

"You speak Turkish now?"

"I've been dedicating myself to becoming fluent."

"*Etkilendim.*" (I'm impressed).

"Tell me. Tell me you lied."

He chuckled. "Another year and you're still in denial. I don't think this blind faith in his existence is healthy, *kızım.*"

"Stop calling me that."

"Stop calling me on the anniversary of your loss."

"Give me back what you stole, and I won't have to call again."

He laughed out loud. "I see why my son fell in love with you. You have claws. I like it."

Tears rolled down my cheeks despite the loathing searing in my blood. Sorrow tangled with my hate, and I slipped just enough to beg, "*Lütfen. Lütfen bana gerçeği söyle.*" (Please. Please, tell me the truth).

"The truth is he died two years ago." A rustling sounded as his voice darkened. "I watch you, Nerida. I watch you raising my granddaughter. I watch you playing with dreams and wishes. I suggest you stop. I suggest you accept that he is gone. I would hate for Ayla to lose her mother as well as her father."

My chest fissured. "W-What do you mean by that?"

"I mean, you're killing yourself, *canım.*"

My knees gave out, dropping me to the sand.

That word.

That single word that Aslan had whispered to me a thousand times.

A word that meant everything yet somehow nothing.

A word that took my breath away.

The crescent moon watched over me sadly as tears poured silently down my cheeks. "I know he's alive."

"You are mistaken."

"I know he's still here because we share the same heart. That heart is still beating, even if it's broken. I would feel it if he was gone. I *know* I would."

"You need to stop this nonsense. Aslan Avci is dead. It's time you accepted that."

He hung up.

I bowed in the sand.

And I cried.

Chapter Thirty-Six

NERIDA

AGE: 23 YRS OLD

(*Love in Māori:* Aroha)

Three years...

I STOOD ON THE DECK OF *THE FLUKE*, staring at the mid-afternoon sun. The weather was hot, bright, blue, and beautiful, yet today, the sublime perfection of the ocean didn't affect me.

The glittering sunlight couldn't pierce my lonely heart.

The swooping seagulls couldn't turn my sorrow into a smile.

Three years.

My constant headache pounded, my ceaseless guilt suffocated, refusing to believe it.

Three years...

Nine days ago, I'd turned another year older.

And today was the anniversary of Aslan's death.

Despite my heavy cloak of misery, the year had passed quickly. Teddy and Eddie had enlisted the help of a local builder to construct the plans they'd drawn. I continued fundraising and even managed to get a few newspapers to take notice of us. We also received a moderately sized donation from the Sydney Aquarium to fund our progress, with the proviso that the day we created a liveable environment, they would have access to the first sphere for their own uses.

Their request had given me the idea to sell future leases. For a few thousand dollars, those who could afford it could rent a biosphere and have their names noted on the founding investors, all while Lunamare was nothing more than an impossible dream.

Unfortunately, testing on the strange-looking decagon had not gone well. After months of tweaking, welding, and amending, the structure never remained watertight in our pool for long.

Eddie was the more rational minded out of me and Teddy, and he grounded us with reminders that we were trying to do something no one else had ever done before. Sure, there were pods around the world that marine biologists, engineers, and saturation divers lived in while doing infrastructure work and deep-sea welding. Sure, there were rigs and outposts with moon pools and submarines, all built to withstand the immense weight of the ocean.

But…they were for short-term use—to visit and then leave. Not a forever home with sunlight, a permanent letter box, and whales as your next-door neighbours.

Regardless that I needed this to happen quickly. Regardless that I clung to the one-day hope of vanishing into a different world, the process couldn't be rushed.

As more failures happened and more frustration set in, we constantly pushed each other to come up with better ideas. Working took over my life, giving me somewhere to hide from my grief.

If I wasn't caring for Ayla, I was caring for Lunamare, and on the nights I couldn't sleep, and the yearly storms rolled in thanks to a vicious rainy season, I sat watching every underwater movie I could.

The Abyss and my childhood love of *Ocean Girl* were among my favourites. I'd scribble notes in the dark—nonsense notes, hopeful notes— and suggested we were going about this all wrong.

We were trying to build a house.

A house with foundations and front doors.

A house that would work on land but not in the water.

We were wasting our time because what we should be building was something the ocean would create itself. A bubble perhaps. A blob or piece of froth, something that could flow in the current rather than fight it.

Every waking moment, I felt endlessly guilty and dreadfully helpless.

I'd searched for him.

I'd hunted and scrutinised, not willing to take Cem's word that Aslan was dead.

What sort of wife would I be if I accepted one man's assurance that my soulmate was gone? *Especially* when my heart said otherwise.

But I could only make so many phone calls. Only utter so many threats for the truth before I was labelled crazy and grief-stricken.

No one took me seriously.

No newspapers mentioned Aslan's name.

No local blogs or radio stations discussed Cem or his son.

I tracked every article that mentioned Kara…and nothing.

To the world, Aslan was dead.

But to me?

He was very much alive.

Within me.

Haunting me, hurting me.

It was a daily battle to stay in Australia and not run back to Turkey. Not to tear that country apart; to look under every rock and peer into every shadow.

What if he was out there?

What if he was waiting for me to find him, and instead, I was here?

Snuggled into his daughter, using her soft, comforting shape as my safety net so I didn't break apart and dissolve in a river of despair?

Shaking myself back to the present, I glowered at the ocean.

I'd wanted to keep working today. I had a podcast interview with a local university to build awareness of our company, but Teddy and Eddie had dragged me from the house for *this*.

This nightmare.

We'd met my parents at the dock and before I knew it, Ayla was sitting on my father's knee as he skippered us out to sea and my mother hovered close by as I clung to the railing, letting the breeze blow my mind free from thoughts of Aslan hurting Ethan on this boat. Aslan making love to me on this boat. Aslan making me laugh and cry and beg and *live* on this boat.

My lips tingled from the memory of his CPR. My cheeks pinked at the blowjob I'd given him below. My core clenched at the way he'd come inside me with our eyes locked and bodies still, sending us straight into the most spiritual connection of my life.

So many moments, so many secrets.

Today, I'd been forced to participate in this awful, terrible excursion, but tonight...when everyone else was asleep and two a.m. rolled around, I would sneak down to the beach and make my yearly phone call.

I'd indulge in my sickening addiction.

Speaking to Aslan's father wasn't healthy.

I knew that.

But...I couldn't help myself.

I couldn't stop myself from hoping that if I called Cem often enough, reminding him of the night he'd stolen my soulmate, that he'd one day confess his sins and admit Aslan had been alive this entire time.

He'll give him back to me.

I could prove to everyone that I'd been right to never give up hope. To never stop fighting, believing, *knowing* that Aslan was alive.

I wasn't going crazy.

I was sensing things even science told me I shouldn't feel.

"Ready, little fish?" Dad asked gently, pulling me from my thoughts and dropping me back into the sea where *The Fluke* rode gentle swells. We'd been anchored here for half an hour. Low Isles gleamed in the distance with its lighthouse, sand, and palm trees.

I took Aslan's virginity on that beach.

We'd gotten married in the shallows.

The sky had rained with colours, giving us the best wedding gift.

My heart spasmed.

Tears stung.

Now, tourist boats dotted around the reef, children ran riot on the beach, and my mother opened the packages she'd mysteriously stowed, laying gorgeous flower wreaths on the table where Aslan had worked with his laptop, helping my parents make sense of their data.

I almost jumped overboard.

I almost scooped up my daughter and dived into the sea, needing to be as far away as possible.

"Neri…you okay?" Dad asked.

"Not really." I patted his hand as he squeezed my forearm, his fingers wrapping around my lion tattoo. "But I'll do it if that's what you want."

I'm not ready to say goodbye.

I'll never be ready.

"I think it's important." His dark-blue eyes glimmered with sadness. "I think it's time you let him go, my love. I'm…I'm worried about you."

I smiled and reached up to kiss his weathered cheek. "I'm fine, Dad."

"You're surviving. There's a big difference." He cast a look at Ayla who held Eddie's hand after stealing a frangipani from one of the wreaths. Her shoulder length sable hair had bronzed like Aslan's used to. Her dark brown eyes soaked up the sun. And her lips smiled with a seriousness that looked a little stern on such a happy toddler.

"She looks so much like him," Dad murmured. "It hurts me sometimes at how similar they are. I can't imagine what it must do to you."

"It actually helps," I said quietly, staring at my darling daughter. "She's a part of him. His blood flows in her veins. Her heart shares his beat, just like mine."

"I'm so sorry he's gone, Nerida. I wish I could bring him back for you. But I don't have that power. No one does. You need to accept he's gone, little fish. You need to accept that he's never coming back and do your best to start healing."

I knew my dad's suggestion came from concern, but…it irked me.

It hurt me that my entire family walked on eggshells around me because they feared I'd start screaming like I had that day.

I'd stopped insisting that I felt him.

I stopped trying to explain that an unexplainable part of me screeched and clawed, desperately sure he was still alive.

That certainty was violent.

Messed up.

Agonising.

I hid a lot of how I truly felt.

My denial of his passing wasn't socially acceptable.

They wanted to move on…yet I would always cling to the past.

The gunshot I heard on the phone might not have been real.

The confession from Aslan's murderer might be a lie.

Aslan still existed because…my heart said so.

But my heart might be the biggest liar of all.

Maybe this was how all death felt?

Maybe my refusal to believe was normal?

Maybe this blind hope was normal?

Maybe this inconsolable depression was exactly *normal,* and I was as deluded as people whispered.

He…

He's dead.

I tried the truth on for size.

Every molecule in my body boycotted it.

I wanted to retch. To shake. To cry.

No.

He's not.

He can't be.

I hunched.

Those words.

That vicious conviction.

He can't be.

And there was my answer.

He can't be dead.

Because if he is…

My soul *would* tear itself down the middle. I would slip into the screaming abyss. I would perish because I couldn't live without my other half.

While I denied it, I could keep breathing.

But if I accepted it?

If I believed in this funeral and said goodbye…

I'll die.

Ayla giggled as Mum scooped her up and pointed toward the dorsal fins of curious dolphins who'd most likely heard our engine and come to say hi. I didn't care if it was Sapphire and her pod. Right now, I barely cared about anything.

The sun shone on my daughter's hair. Her laughter wrapped around my heart. And I clung to this moment, desperately trying *to* care.

Right here.

Right now.

If I could anchor myself in this world, if I believed Aslan was out there *somewhere,* then I could stay alive for the sake of my child.

I could go through this tragedy called life until the day when I couldn't keep hoping anymore.

Shaking away my misty, macabre thoughts, I focused on my dad. His navy eyes met mine, his salt-and-pepper hair fluttering in the warm breeze. He looked at me so worriedly, so sadly, my stomach flipped.

Before I could speak, he bent and whispered, "I feel so bloody guilty that we didn't try harder to get him back. It's been awful these past few years without him. His loss is felt every time I look at where his sala used to be. I should've done more. For both of you. I should've—"

"Dad." I grabbed his hand. "It's okay."

"I'm so sorry. So sorry we couldn't stop him from being deported."

My lungs closed, but I did my best to console him, even though no one could console me. "We tried. Cem Kara has far more power than anyone imagined."

His jaw worked. "Just knowing you went to Turkey makes my blood turn cold. He could've taken you too."

"I plan on going back again one day. Once Ayla's older, I'll show her where she came from. I want her to know she has two countries to call home."

"But...but what if he takes her?" Dad choked. "You *can't*, Neri—"

"He could take her from here." I stiffened against the ice frosting my spine. "He could take any of us. But he hasn't."

"Which leads to a horrifying question of *why*?"

I had no answers for that. It kept me up at night too. But...in some strange way, I understood Cem a little. He'd killed to get his son back, even if he'd shot him. He knew what it was like to lose a child. I didn't think he'd inflict that pain on me...as crazy as that sounded.

Ayla was his granddaughter.

His blood.

His *last* blood.

"Should we do this?" I said, changing the subject.

"Are you truly ready?" Dad asked gently.

No.

Never.

"If it's what you guys need to do, I'm okay with that."

But I'm not saying goodbye.

Mum overheard me and drifted forward in a black sundress. She passed me a heavy wreath, the leaves slightly damp and the flowers heavily perfumed. "You go first, sweetheart."

A shuffle of movement as Eddie and Teddy collected their own wreath, and Mum and Dad claimed the last two. A tiny one remained on the table and tears leapt to my eyes as I scooped it up, stroked the silky petals, and passed it to Ayla.

"Pretty." She smiled, her eyes so dark and perfect.

"Not as pretty as you," I whispered, ducking down and kissing her forehead. "Do you want to throw the flowers into the sea with me to say goodbye to Daddy?"

"No." Her nose wrinkled. "Keep. I want to keep."

My heart squeezed, wondering if she felt the same thing I did.

For me to believe in a fairy-tale was fine. If I needed to exist in a storybook where I wasn't alone, all to somehow cope in my lonely life, then that was my burden to bear.

Not hers.

She was just a child.

A child with two surrogate fathers who did their best to hide the failings of her mother.

"You can keep it, sweetie." Dad chuckled.

I nodded and stepped back. "How about we dry that one and hang it on your bedroom wall, next to your lion mural?"

"Yes!" She bounced up and down, staying at my side as I padded barefoot in my cream shorts and white t-shirt. I stopped at the side of *The Fluke*.

My family lined up beside me, their wreaths hanging in their hands.

What was a widow supposed to say at a funeral?

How were you supposed to put into words the pain, the loss, the longing?

Someone else should say goodbye because I would *never* utter those words.

It took me a while to figure out what to say, but in the end, I murmured, "This is just a pause. A pause in the story of our life. One day, I will find you. Someday, I will be yours again. Until that day...*seni çok seviyorum*, Aslan." (I love you so much).

Dad pressed close as I dropped my wreath into the water.

It plopped onto the blue-crystal surface, swaying in the current, enticing fish from below to nibble at the pretty petals.

I didn't hear the eulogies my parents gave.

I ignored all their epitaphs.

Not because it hurt to listen but because my heart was elsewhere...across the sea, flying over exotic lands, slipping safely into a Turkish boy's pocket...wherever he might be.

"Nerida, can...can we talk to you?" Teddy asked quietly from where he and Eddie sat opposite me at the battered dining room table where we'd spent untold hours bickering, brainstorming, and sketching for Lunamare. If we were working for a wage, the amount of hours we'd put into this company would've bankrupted us before we even finished our first prototype.

Putting down my pen from adding to my to-do list for tomorrow that included more promo and a meeting with the manager of a local deep-sea diving operation that had their own submarine, I nodded. "Sure? What's up?" Grabbing my lemon and ginger tea that I'd taken to drinking before bed, I looked between the two men.

My chest tightened with love for them. At the way they held hands on the couch when we had movie nights. The way they swatted each other's butts with the tea towel when they cooked side by side. The way Eddie would do the laundry and Teddy would load the dishwasher, shouldering equal domestic duties because they were a team.

I did my best to share the workload. I cooked a few nights a week. I even mowed the lawn a few times. I often stayed home with Ayla so they could go for a romantic meal out in Port Douglas. Despite their inclusion of me and Ayla in their life, we were still the third wheels. Still outsiders in their love.

"We, eh…we had something drawn up." Eddie flicked a worried look at Teddy before slipping a piece of paper toward me, pushing aside the schematics of our latest render. "If we're completely out of bounds, tell us. There will be no hard feelings whatsoever. You know we told you, you are welcome to live with us forever. We're in business together, and I fully believe that we will spend the rest of our lives making our dreams come true…*together*. We love Ayla as if she was our own. We love you as if you were our sister. We are fully aware that she belongs to Aslan and that we could never replace him, but…"

"But?" I glanced at the paperwork.

The *adoption* paperwork.

My head snapped up. "Wait, you want to *adopt* her?"

"We want to give you peace of mind that if you ever decide to go…looking for him, or if anything happens to you, that your little moonbeam will be safe. She has us for life, that's an absolute given. But we wanted to give you the chance to make it official if you feel any way as if…you're not truly our family." Teddy reached across the table and took my hand. "I see the way you sometimes look at us, Nee. I see the loss in your eyes, and I hate that we have each other and you have a broken heart, but…you *are* one of us. Eddie and I might be married, but there are three of us in this relationship. I need you to know that. You are not a third wheel. And neither is Aslan's daughter."

Tears stung, then welled.

The fact that I'd just been thinking that we were outsiders sent goosebumps down my spine.

"We know his name is on her birth certificate. We know you changed yours to Avci last year. We aren't trying to replace him, Nee. We're just...we just wanted to give you peace of mind that she has us forever. Just like you do."

I stood and went around the table. Teddy shoved his chair back, and I sat on his lap. My knees touched Eddie's as he turned to face us, and I sat enveloped by two of the best men alive.

I studied both of them.

I set aside my own need to keep Ayla fatherless because no one else would ever compare.

I tried to see what would be best for her.

Honey and Billy were her godparents. Mum and Dad would raise her in a heartbeat if anything ever happened to me. But Teddy and Eddie...they were different.

They saw more than anyone else because they saw me every day.

They know...

Brushing my hair back, Teddy whispered so not even the evening shadows could hear, "We see you sneaking out at three in the morning, Nee. We know you go swimming. We know you're searching for meaning. And we know that one day, you might not be able to stop yourself from getting on a plane and returning to Turkey. The adoption papers are our vow to you. Our vow that you can do what you need to do and *always* know that Ayla is safe. You can be free to find your own happiness."

Eddie cupped my cheek, his hazel eyes far too intense. "If there comes a day when existing isn't enough, at least you know she's taken care of."

I nodded and wiped away my tears. "Thank you. Both of you. You know she's yours and I would never take her away from you. You will be a part of her life until she's married and becomes a mother to her own children, but...I also hope you can understand why I can't sign."

Teddy gave me a smile.

Eddie smirked. "We knew that would be your answer but wanted to offer anyway."

"I'm grateful. Truly. Ayla is so lucky to have you. *I'm* so lucky to have you. But for now...she belongs to Aslan."

Perhaps one day, I would sign those papers.

Maybe one day, I would turn my back on this life and become terribly selfish.

But for now, Ayla belonged to a ghost.

And while she only had one official parent, it kept me firmly rooted in reality. I would never jeopardise her future or her life. I would never run away or put my needs first.

If she had two legal fathers...the temptation to be selfish might break me.

I might hunt Cem Kara.

I might let loose all those monsters in my soul. Those bloodthirsty, savage beasts ready to claw, tear, and destroy.

I might do whatever it took to learn, once and for all, if I was delusional...

Four years...

"Everything looks perfectly normal, Ms. Avci." The cardiologist looked up from studying my ECG and echocardiogram.

I still flinched when addressed with Aslan's last name. I couldn't take it through marriage, so I'd changed it the only other way I could.

By choice.

"I can't see why you would be suffering intermittent palpitations. Your bloods are fine. You're fit, healthy, and young." His bushy white eyebrows knitted together. His tanned skin at odds with the health warnings to 'slip, slop, slap'. "You say you have no idea what triggers them? No particular foods or stresses?"

I folded my hands in my lap, fighting off impatience, all while burning up inside for answers.

I'd hoped.

I'd truly hoped that there'd be some magical diagnosis that my strangely skipping heart at three in the morning wasn't because of biology but spirituality.

Because of *him*.

I had no history of heart issues.

My lineage of family were all healthy and still mostly alive—minus my dad's parents who died in a car accident. My mum's parents lived in Bali after retiring there twenty years ago, and my mother's brother regularly ran in charity marathons down in Brisbane.

Yet me?

I'd somehow been afflicted by a condition no one could label or cure.

"I've been keeping a heart diary, like you told me last time we met. I can't pinpoint anything that has a theme. Some months I get them often and some none at all."

"How about lately?"

"They're not as frequent, I will admit."

And how could I say that that scared me? If I did feel them from Aslan, what did it mean that they were few and far between these days?

Was he better?

Was he dead?

It means you've lost your bloody mind, Nerida, that's what!

When are you going to stop doing this?

When are you going to finally accept that he's gone?

He's dead.

He's been dead for four fucking years!

You're deluding yourself.

You're looking for truths when the only one is…you're delusional!

Anger blazed through me. Self-hatred. Frustration.

I was so *sick* of feeling like this.

Of wallowing in denial and clinging to the blind belief that Aslan would appear one day on our front lawn. I could picture it so clearly. I could feel him so intensely. I could touch him in my nightmares and hear him in my daydreams.

He was everywhere.

All around me.

Inside me.

Still.

I saw him at the supermarket.

I heard him on the docks.

I caught glimpses of him when I gave interviews, and swore I saw him driving away from Bunnings the last time I went to buy more marine-grade bolts for our latest prototype.

It stabbed me in the chest each and every time.

It made me choke on tears.

It made me hear that awful *pop, pop, pop* all over again.

I just needed it to stop.

I needed to move on.

I needed to be healed.

I was finally ready to say *enough*!

Ayla was three now. She'd grown into a gorgeous little girl who bewitched me body and soul. She whispered to Aslan in the shells she gathered from the beach, doing what I taught her with the shell Aslan had lost. She cried over dead jellyfish washed up on the sand and squealed in absolute glee when I started taking her swimming with Sapphire and her pod.

She completed me.

She *was* me.

I was whole when I was with her.

Yet when I wasn't with her, Aslan would come for me. He'd crowd my thoughts and suffocate me with everything that I'd lost and everything I stubbornly held on to.

It's not healthy.

It's killing me.

I can't—

"Ms. Avci...Nerida?" The doctor leaned forward and patted my knee. "Is everything alright?"

I blinked.

My painful fury siphoned away, vanishing into a dirty drain by my feet, gurgling and swirling, ready to crash back over me the moment I was on my own. "Is there...I mean...I've read online about scientific evidence of a sixth sense between twins. They can sometimes detect when another is hurt, even pinpointing the location of pain. Some are said to be mildly telepathic."

He frowned. "You're saying you have a twin?"

"No. I'm an only child."

"Then why are you asking about the twin phenomenon?" He cocked his head and reached for a pen, fiddling with it.

My courage fled, and I almost told him to forget it, but with a quick blurt, I said, "Is it possible for someone to share that same phenomenon with a loved one? Someone not related but someone they were extremely close to?"

He leaned back in his chair. "You're suggesting that your palpitations are caused by second-hand awareness? That you can *feel* someone you love having heart irregularities?"

When he said it like that?

In that slightly surprised, slightly scornful tone?

It made me fold in on myself and sigh. "No. I'm just...tired, I guess."

"Poor quality sleep can definitely contribute to A-fib." Clicking his pen, he reached for his prescription pad. "How about I give you a short dose of sleeping tablets and see if that—"

"I'm fine. I don't need sleeping pills."

Sounds like you need a psychiatrist.

Perhaps, I should call the therapist who'd helped me after what Ethan had done.

Either way, I needed help.

I accepted that.

I couldn't keep lying to myself and everyone else.

I couldn't keep believing I felt twitchy and wrong just because Aslan was still alive and calling for me.

This has gone on long enough.

You know that.

Four years and nothing.

Not one sign he was still alive

Not one news article that Cem Kara had found his missing heir.

No one knew I was here at this appointment.

No one knew my heart played a pounding tune on my ribs or its random flutters made me breathless.

No one knew because I didn't tell anyone.

As far as they were aware, I was fine.

Better than fine.

I'd convinced everyone I was like them.

Moving on.

And in reality, I was sinking.

Deeper and deeper.

Quicker and quicker.

Into madness.

Standing quickly, I balled my hands. "Thank you for taking the time to go over my results, Dr. Hammond."

He stood too, placing my file on his desk. "If you're truly worried, we could perhaps put you on a course of beta blockers. They regulate your system and can even help with anxiety—"

"I'm not anxious."

He studied me as if he didn't believe me.

"I-I've got to go." Marching to the door, I wrenched it open and practically ran to my car.

Tonight was four years since Aslan was shot.

I had a phone call to make.

"Çok tutarlısın, kızım." (You are consistent, daughter).

I sat on the sand, my eyes locked on the stars above, my ears full of the softly snoozing waves.

"Without fail at seven p.m., you call me," Cem added.

"It's two in the morning here. The same time you murdered him."

"Ah, was that the time?" He chuckled. "All I remember was I was hungry and needed to go home to eat."

"You repulse me."

"You said that last year. No new insults to share?"

"Give me your address. I want to come visit."

"Why? So you can rifle through my house and try to find him?"

"So I can prove that he's still alive."

He sighed heavily. "This has got to stop, *kızım*. I'm afraid for you. Your mind is broken as well as your heart."

"My mind is fine."

"But your heart is not." He clucked his tongue. "I know about the specialist appointment you had today. Are you going to leave Ayla an orphan? How about I take her? She could be my heir. I rather like the thought of a girl taking over my empire. It would go against many traditions and delight me no end."

Molten fury poured through me. "You will never get within ten metres of my daughter."

"We'll see."

I hated that cryptic reply.

I stewed with one of my own.

Before I had a suitable slur or slander, he murmured, "Allow me to put you out of your misery, Nerida. Aslan Avci is dead. You have my absolute word. He is dead. I made damn sure of that."

Snow settled over my heart. Soft and silent, gentle and hushed. I didn't know why, but those words did something to me. They nudged my foggy intuition. They itched and nibbled at something unexplainable.

The conversation paused for a long time.

Almost long enough to hang up.

But then a question spilled free, straight from my soul. "And what of Aslan Kara? Is he dead too?"

"*Beni bir kez daha şaşırttın.*" (Once again, you've surprised me). His voice deepened with a strange hitch of...pride? "You continue to reveal why my son fell for you. You were worthy of him, I see that now."

"You're saying he's alive?"

"I'm saying we're both in love with a ghost." He sucked in a breath. "If you need evidence, perhaps I'll send you his bones for your birthday."

My stomach sloshed with nausea, but I hyper-focused on his last sentence. "I thought you said he was ash."

The line crackled.

My skin prickled.

Finally, the softest chuckle. "I did, didn't I?"

He cut off the call.

He left me alone with the stars, the sand, and a million useless shells that couldn't bring Aslan home to me.

Chapter Thirty-Seven

NERIDA

(*Love in Galician:* Amor)

"BY THE TIME FIVE YEARS ROLLED AROUND, I'd spun my ring a million times, stroked my tattoo a thousand times, and begged the moon and sea to return what was rightfully mine."

"God, I don't even know how you coped," Margot whispered. "My heart is bruised just listening to your story, let alone living it."

I licked at a salty droplet as it rolled down my cheek. My head throbbed, and my eyes stung with sadness. I'd wanted to stop reciting my tale, but I couldn't. Just a little more and then I could say the magical words *The End*, thank these lovely reporters for listening, then usher them out of my house so I could go and spend time with my ghost.

Five decades had passed since that horrific time of anguish, yet the blades of grief still cut far too sharply. I'd learned the lesson of loss far too well, and it'd scarred me forever. It'd cut me so often, so deeply, its lacerations riddled my soul, calcified my arteries, and patched up the disfigured parts of me. I had somehow survived in a world looking whole, all while being eternally wounded.

I would never wish that level of agony or helplessness on anyone.

I never wanted to feel such misery again.

Yet I'd endured it while confessing my tragedy. I'd done it so people could one day read about a scientist who followed her spirit. About a marine biologist without a degree. About a successful businesswoman who was nothing more than a heartbroken wife.

"Did you want to stop, Nerida?" Dylan asked gently. "It's one o' clock in the morning. Surely you'd like to—"

"If you're okay to stay, I'm okay to keep talking."

"Of course." He frowned. "But I wouldn't be doing my job if I didn't suggest perhaps a break? Some tea? Some painkillers for your headache?"

I smiled. "Your kind concern is appreciated, but I'm alright." Sitting straighter, I glanced at Margot who flipped to a new page in her notepad.

Her tired-glassy eyes met mine. "I'm so glad you had Ayla to get you through. I'm so glad you had such a deep relationship with your business partners. It sounds as if without their support it would've been hard—"

"It would've been impossible. I wouldn't have made it." I smiled softly. "And I told you, Teddy and Eddie are more than just my business partners. I might have been the inspiration and was lucky enough to come up with the finished design and even envisioned most of the operating systems, but without their tenacity, skill, and stubborn belief that we could achieve our dream, Lunamare wouldn't have had a happy ending. They are the lifeblood of this impossible creation."

"Would it be possible to see the biospheres?" Margot asked, twirling the ends of her hair as if needing to keep her hands busy. "Would that be okay?"

I nodded. "Of course. You're welcome to spend the night on Luna Reef if you wish. We have two spheres dedicated to showing potential residents how the homes work. Everyone who stays immediately wants to become a hybrid human."

"Hybrid human?" Margot asked.

"Yes." I forced a smile. "The longer you live in the sea, the less inclined you are to choose land. It's a side effect, unfortunately, of living in such a magical water world. Everything seems better down there. Healthier. Happier. Our community is supportive and inclusive, ensuring we live in harmony rather than bickering."

Dylan smirked. "Some might say it sounds like a cult."

I shrugged with faint surprise. "You know...I never thought of that. But I suppose there could be rumours that we're up to something nefarious. After all, we all share the same morals of hard work and stay mostly quiet about our successes with reversing certain medical conditions."

"Wait, what? You haven't mentioned that before—"

I held up my hand. "A story for another time, I'm afraid. This interview is already long enough to create a book. Two books. A trilogy even. If you'd like to know more about our advances in healthcare and what methodology we employ, you'd be best to speak to our head physician, Ayla."

"Wait..." Margot's eyebrows shot into her hair. "Your daughter is the head doctor?"

I smiled with pride. "She is."

"Wow." Dylan shook his head with awe. "You're nothing if not a woman full of surprises. And a lineage of intelligent progressives. In fact...that would be a great angle for the article. You're right that we have enough content to make this far longer than just a puff piece. I'll run it by my boss to see if we could do a feature or even a series of podcasts and blogs. I'd love to talk to Ayla about her medical background and growing up half Australian and half Turkish." Dylan's eyes swam with ideas. "We could include photos and testimonies and—"

"If you don't mind, Dylan, I'd like to get back to the story." I interrupted him. "Like you said, it's late, and I have something I need to do."

"Of course. Sorry." Dylan scratched his bearded jaw. "We'll call your company next week and set up a tour."

"Just tell them Nerida cleared your access, and you'll be shown the maintenance side of things as well. I could even arrange meetings for you with Theodore and Edmund. They don't work every day anymore—none of us are getting any younger—but I'm sure they'd be happy to go over the technical aspects with you and introduce you to their team."

"That would be great, thanks." Dylan settled back against the mismatched cushions. "Now…you were saying?"

Taking a sip of lemon water that Tiffany had brought a little while ago, I sucked in a breath and said, "For five years, I stubbornly clung to the idea that Aslan wasn't dead. I researched everything I could on soul links and the often-ridiculed notion of spiritual connection. As each month passed and I waited for a sign that Aslan was truly gone, Ayla kept growing. She evolved from an adorable toddler into a wonderful little girl. A girl with my feisty streak that used to drive my father up the wall. She kept me on my toes, she leaped into our deep swimming pool the moment she'd wake up, and was obsessed with Turkish food. Teddy, Eddie, and I did our best to teach her about a culture she'd inherited yet never visited and regularly took Turkish cooking lessons, courtesy of YouTube.

"She was so bright and inquisitive and showed an aptitude for medicine early on. She was always trying to patch up her uncles' cuts and scrapes as they fiddled with the latest prototype. She knew all the words for bandages, painkillers, tonics, and creams. In fact, I knew she'd become a doctor the same week I realised she shared the genetic trait that made Aslan see numbers in colour."

"She has synesthesia too?" Margot asked.

"She does. She was obsessed with puzzles when she was younger. Didn't matter if she had no idea how they went together. She would rather play with a Rubik's Cube or number blocks over a doll or cuddly toy.

"One day, after preschool, she mentioned the teacher had told her off for saying that the colour pink was called six. She'd been a little stubborn, and the teacher had been a little demeaning, and in the end, Ayla had burst into tears because to her pink *was* six, orange was three, tens were grey, and the rainbow held numbers in every spectrum.

"I'd been tempted to call Cem that night and tell him that the Kara family trait was alive and well, but I'd never called him outside the anniversary of him killing Aslan before, and I didn't want to slip onto an even slipperier slope of madness. Instead, I threw myself into researching synesthesia. I learned how intelligent my child was. How much she'd inherited from Aslan. How much she could contribute to the world. And just how special she was…just like Cem had said she would be."

I sucked in a breath. The fire that'd burned my life down was slowly dying and leaving nothing but ash in its wake. Ash that I'd risen from. "That night, I walked on my silent, empty beach and finally heard a little whisper deep inside me that it was time.

"It was time to let go.

"It was okay to let go. To admit that he was gone. To say he was dead. For so long, I couldn't even *think* those words. Couldn't visualise him as a corpse. Couldn't bear to imagine that he'd been nothing more than ether for five long years.

"I walked beneath the moon for hours, splashing through the sea, and I slowly, painfully, unwillingly said…*okay*.

"Okay, he's gone.

"Okay, I'm alone.

"Okay, I'll never see him again because as special as Aslan had been, he couldn't stay. Not after he'd given me his equally special daughter. They were too unique, too wonderful, too bright and blazing like a shooting star to stay on earth for long.

"I would never be able to live the life I wanted with him by my side.

"I would never know blistering happiness.

"I would never fall asleep with someone beside me.

"I would never love another or be touched by another, and…that was okay too.

"I was…okay with saying goodbye. It'd taken five long years to reach that level of acceptance. It was the greatest struggle of my life, a constant battle to stay in reality and not slip deeper into insanity. But…in the dark on that beach, I finally took that first unwilling step out of grief, shedding denial and slipping into anger, bargaining, depression, guilt, hope, and acceptance.

"I doubted I'd ever *truly* accept, but I *accepted* that fact. I was okay with always living a half-life, just as long as I did the best I could while I lived it. I stopped feeling guilty for laughing with Ayla and I gave myself permission to find pockets of happiness here and there.

"I hoped by finally letting go, I would've found closure. Instead…it brought the worst pain I'd ever endured. Accepting his death felt as if it'd just happened all over again.

"I broke. I shattered. I kneeled in the shallow sea and sobbed beneath the clouded moon. I slipped into that screaming abyss and lost every piece of me.

"I felt all the pain, all the loss. I was torn open, split wide, and ever so empty. So, so empty because I finally accepted that my heart flutters were just my relentless pumping organ trying to remember how to beat without him. It wasn't some link between him and me. Not some peculiar, mystifying connection between soulmates. It was just me. Just me and my broken body fighting to function without his."

"Oh, Nerida." Margot came to my side and kneeled at my feet. She took my hand in hers, tears rolling down her cheeks. "I'm so sorry. So, so sorry for your loss."

I blinked and noticed my own sodden cheeks. I studied this sweet, young woman who wore her tender, untouched heart on her sleeve, and the first twinges of a grateful smile tugged my lips.

I curled my fingers around hers.

I squeezed her hard. "It's okay. Don't cry for me. Like I told you before I recounted Ethan's rape, see me as I am now: as an old woman who has loved. A successful visionary who turned the impossible into possible."

"Oh, I do. I definitely do. I just…" She sniffed and shrugged. "I can't help wishing your story had a happy ever after in romance as well as in business."

I leaned forward. My pulse tripping quicker. "Who said it doesn't?"

She scowled. "Well…you did." She reared back, her gaze diving into mine. "You mean you met someone else, after all? You remarried?"

I looked down at my wedding ring that'd turned thin from years of spinning. The inscription was faded. The diamond chipped in one corner. But nestled beside it was another gold band. A second troth. A second wedding.

"I remarried, yes."

"*What?*" Margot shot upward and stumbled to her chair. Betrayal covered her pretty face as if I'd personally cheated on Aslan. "But you said—"

"I said Aslan Avci was dead."

"So how could you—?"

"I could because everything that I accepted that night on the beach was a lie."

"I-I don't understand." Her nose wrinkled.

"That night, I believed my heart issues came from my own inability to move on. But three months later, I had scientific proof that soulmates *do* exist."

"Wait…I don't follow." Dylan scowled. "What proof?"

I held his incredulous stare. "I've been written about in medical journals and studied by sceptical physicians. I've been poked and prodded and questioned by all manner of professionals, but in the end…their evidence was conclusive." I smiled, my chest growing warm. "Thanks to my heart diaries. Thanks to my diligently nervous notetaking, time stamping, and durations of palpitating episodes, I had concrete proof of the moments I was afflicted with A-fib. All those pains, all those flutters, all of those fears vindicated because…it proved that I wasn't suffering a unique event…I was sensing another's."

Dylan and Margot shared a look.

They glanced at me as if I'd lost my mind. Questions filled their faces that perhaps I'd been a few screws loose all along and this entire interview had been an utter waste of their time.

A complete fabrication.

Nothing more than ramblings from a madwoman.

But nothing could be further from the truth.

This was real.

I was *real.*

I hadn't just found a way for humans to dwell under the sea like my childhood dreams, but I'd also irrefutably proven that love could transcend time, distance, and common sense. There were no instruments in our modern world to test the power of true love. No exams or machines capable of learning how strong that love could be.

The *cor* was still a mystery.

Our *amare* still nothing more than fantasy.

Until me.

Until my diary of dates and times…a diary that correlated to every day and time of someone else's pain.

"The night I said goodbye was the night the world shifted, the universe answered, and all the wishes that I'd given up on, all the hopes that I'd had to slay all rose up, knitted together, and somehow brought me my heart's desire."

"Nerida, I think we should stop," Margot whispered.

"I agree." Dylan nodded sternly. "I think we're all overtired and—"

I laughed out loud.

I gave into the bright white light glowing inside me. "Aslan Avci was dead. Cem Kara told the truth about that. I never saw that eager-eyed, math-loving boy again."

"Then why are you smiling? A-Are you quite well?" Dylan scowled.

My shoulders drew back, my heart grew wings, and I confessed the words I'd been hoarding since we began this tale. "Over five long years. Sixty-three awful months. Almost two thousand days, my darling Aslan suffered. And I felt him. Through all of it. I heard him summoning me. I endured his torture. I let others tell me I was mad. I believed it most days. But then…one night…he returned to me. I never saw Aslan Avci again, but Aslan Kara appeared on my front lawn, just like I'd foreseen. Broken and in pieces, dangerous and crucified…but *alive.*

"Alive.

"Breathing.

"And *mine.*"

Chapter Thirty-Eight

ASLAN

(*Heart in Greek:* Καρδιά)

Present...

I STOOD BESIDE MY FATHER, ACCEPTING praise and welcome just like I'd been taught. I had no thoughts. No feelings. Those had long since died inside me. I only lived to obey. Only lived to be what I was *told* to be. To serve my legacy and take my rightful place as his heir.

Glancing around the stunning smoking room with its hexagon-shaped floors, pastel-plastered walls, intricately painted ceilings of the cosmos, and gold-gilded fireplace, I braced my shoulders and tried to be like him.

Like my mentor, saviour, and kin.

Our black suits were the same.

Our tall height almost identical.

Our faces cut from the same dark marble, our hair sleek and styled. He wore age, while I wore youth. He wore experience, while I wore scars. He wore dangerous power, all while I wore every night he'd held me sobbing at his feet.

The things he'd done. The bones he'd broken. The screams he'd wrung.

Sweat beaded on my spine, proving that for all my conditioning, I was still afraid. All my years of persecution, he hadn't quite robbed me of my primal instincts to fear.

I feared.

Fuck, I reeked of it.

Yet I kept my shoulders back and chin tipped up.

I caped myself in arrogance so I might finally be free.

Cem laughed with a man he shook hands with. Soft ribbons of smoke curled from those indulging in *nargile.* Low timbres of conversation flowed around the room, swirling around the clustered men, singling out a few as they shot looks my way and wondered.

Wondered where I'd been for almost three decades.

Wondered if I was truly Cem's son.

Not that there was any denying it.

I was my father's heir. You only had to see us in the same room together to be sure of that. I could be his younger twin. A clone he'd commissioned and designed. A son that'd returned to him with so many flaws. Flaws that he'd spent years eradicating.

Scents of hash and tobacco made the air heavy and misty as the small congregation of my father's most trusted generals all watched me warily. They'd heard about me no doubt. One or two I remembered from their part in breaking me into the man I was today.

The past five years had been…

I balled my hands and struggled to find a word.

An English word. A Turkish word.

What word could describe what I'd endured?

In the end, I gave up because there was no such description.

I'd survived, barely.

I was alive, mostly.

Yet I wasn't me.

My soul had died, and in its place I was empty.

The tricks he'd played. The tests he'd given. The torture he'd wielded.

I'd endured as much as I could.

I'd endured until I broke.

Now, my empty mind was pliable.

I was exactly what he needed me to be.

A man with a bushy black moustache and equally bushy black eyebrows came to stand before me where Cem and I waited on a small dais in the southern alcove of the smoking room. Royal-blue velvet curtains draped on either side of us, muting the light coming in from the moody stained glass window.

Bowing at my father, the man shifted closer to me. His shiny shoes nudged against the carpet-draped podium.

His dark, cruel eyes met mine.

His thin, malicious lips tipped up.

And with a suave bit of showmanship, he reached for my hand that wasn't clutching my cane and brought my knuckles to his lips.

I was empty.

Hollow.

Forsaken and devoid of any other emotions than the ones Cem had programmed into me.

"It is an honour, *efendim*, to finally kiss the hand of the pure-blooded son of my *patron*. My knife is yours, my death is yours, my loyalty is yours until the end."

The familiar dialect of my native language swirled inside my head.

I hadn't heard English in so very long.

Efendim echoed over and over. The Turkish word for my lord or master.

I was no longer a refugee.

I was a lord.

And my father was the boss. The *patron* of these cutthroat dealers and traffickers, killers and criminals. But also in the room were members of parliament. Two men who'd risen up the ranks thanks to Cem lobbying their parties and buying their souls in the process.

Cem watched us closely.

Watched his generals pay homage to the man who would lead them if he died.

He watched *me*.

My skin prickled, and more fear percolated in my belly.

I wouldn't give him any reason to put me back down there. To turn on that machine again. To give me another lesson I might not survive.

"I accept your knife, your death, and your loyalty," I said firmly. "We are bonded until the grave."

My mouth worked.

My tongue formed Turkish words.

And another general came to swear his allegiance.

I accepted his pledge. I gave one of my own.

I repeated the ceremony until the twelve men in the room had all given me their lives and loyalty, and Cem nodded silently in approval.

Only once everyone had lined up below our dais did Cem come toward me, place his hand over mine on my cane, and say to his generals, "My son, my lion. I call to each of you to teach Aslan how my empire runs. His education will begin in earnest with every operation from the lowest of drug runs to the most expensive female trade. He will learn the languages of politics, he will become fluent in the darkness where we hide our other wares, and through your guidance, you will inherit a worthy leader for when I am gone."

Cem faced me, smiled, and kissed my freshly shaven cheek.

He'd told me about this part.

He'd schooled me on what was expected between the current boss and the newly crowned master.

I held out my left hand.

Taking a delicate jewelled knife from his breast suit pocket, Cem sliced my palm from thumb to pinkie.

Blood welled.

Dark and ruby.

But I didn't flinch.

I barely even felt the pain.

It was nothing to what I'd learned to endure.

Without a word, Cem handed the pretty dagger to me. Shifting as best I could and resting my lionhead carved cane against my thigh, I took his offered hand and cut him with the exact same slice.

His nostrils flared.

He sucked in a breath.

He showed a greater reaction than I did, and the men watching us noticed.

Some frowned a little. Others looked at me with greater appreciation. And I held their curious stares as I clamped my bleeding hand to that of my father's. Our blood beaded and dripped onto the carpet below, squeezed out by the savage grip we used.

"By blood we rule, by blood we die, by blood we stay loyal and true." Our voices blended.

And just like that...I officially became Aslan Kara.

"You look tired, my son." Cem came to my side where I'd invoked the shadows to hide me. Smoke continued curling, and the conversation kept flowing. We'd all moved into the cavernous dining hall where the heavy beams, rich artwork of mythical beasts and beauties watched us eat off fine china and crystal.

I'd eaten but not much.

I'd drunk but not enough.

My hand throbbed beneath its fresh bandage, and the matching one on my father's palm bound us even tighter together.

I didn't know what was expected of me or where I was supposed to go. I knew where I'd come from, but...he'd promised I wouldn't have to return. Then again, he'd said that before and I'd just spent two weeks having a 'refresher'.

I'd passed his final test.

I'd accepted my place and forsook a past that belonged to the dead version of me.

"I would be grateful for a rest." I nodded respectfully. "If you let me know where my new room is, I'll gladly—"

"Oh no, you might have graduated to being named as my official heir, Aslan, but you will never be left to walk around unguarded " His face softened a little. "Not because I don't trust you, of course, but to protect you while your power is still new. There will be those looking to test you. And until you have earned their loyalty through your own merit and not just an oath, I want you protected at all times."

"I understand." I smiled. "I appreciate you thinking of my safety."

His gaze flickered to my left leg and the way I fisted my cane.

Was there guilt in his eyes?

Perhaps a tiny shred of shame?

But then he blinked, and it was gone, replaced with pride and blinding love. He loved me while hurting me. And now he loved me while crowning me. I didn't trust that love, but it was the only thing I'd been able to cling to while drowning in absolute agony.

"You did well today. Faultless, in fact. Continue behaving this impeccably and we will never have to go below again. How does that sound?"

My thighs turned to stone to prevent trembling. "I would appreciate that."

The searing, slicing pain—

My heart dying thanks to excruciating electrocution—

Sweat drenched my back as I shoved the flashbacks where they belonged.

Into my past.

Where dead things rotted.

I was dead.

I was reborn.

I'm his.

"Good." He slapped me on the back and snapped his fingers at two of his black-suited militia that guarded every room in this colossal mansion. "Escort my son back to his chambers. You know which one is his."

"Yes, *patron*." Both men bowed, snapped to attention, then waited until I moved away from my shadows to march in front of them.

March.

Ha!

It didn't matter if I thought of that word in Turkish or English, it was still a mockery to the way I moved.

Hobbled was more apt.

Staggered could also work.

I would never march again.

"*Iyi geceler*, Aslan."

I looked back at my father. "Goodnight to you too, *baba*."

A few generals stood from their seats at the table as I moved past. Some tipped their wine goblets in my direction. Not one of them mentioned the way I moved or whispered behind my back.

Not until I was out of ear range at least.

The moment I was out of the dining room and standing in the echoey foyer with its metallic-mosaic tiles, crystal-dripping chandelier, and dark-oak doors leading off to other rooms, I paused and turned to my two guards.

I knew they would lay down their lives to protect mine if we were attacked.

But they wouldn't hesitate to take mine if I tried to escape.

I knew first hand.

I still wore that scar.

I won't make that mistake again.

"Which way?" I asked in Turkish. Faint remnants of English crashed inside my brain. I'd been fluent once, but now I struggled to remember certain words. I struggled to remember a lot about that place, those people, that time…

"Follow." The shorter of the guards strode ahead, leading me down the long intricately tiled corridor to the sweeping staircase in the heart of the mansion. Forest green, navy blue, and vibrant gold all swirled together, flowing down the marble steps with carpet thick enough to sleep on.

The two guards began their ascension. Their holstered pistols appeared at their lower backs as their blazers swung.

I slammed to a stop. My hand fisted the polished banister; my other sweated around my cane.

Kahretsin.

"*Efendim?*" The guards paused and looked back at me. "Did you forget something?"

I clenched my jaw.

I shook my head.

I climbed the first step.

It hurt.

Fuck, it hurt.

It pinched and stabbed, bruised and ached. No matter how much weight I put on my cane, I couldn't get away from the pain. No matter how much I tried to walk like a lord, I almost crawled up those stairs like a fucking beggar.

Tears shot to my eyes as I locked down my agony and stepped to the next and the next.

My journey up those stairs was depressingly slow. My damaged heart pounded and fluttered by the time I reached the decadent landing. Only two weeks I'd been in the caves, but the strength I'd gathered was once again destroyed.

My cane tip sank into the thick carpet. The carved sideboard held a vase of flowers wider than two men.

The fragrance teased my nose as we drifted past.

Sweet and subtle, like honeysuckle—

No.

Like frangipani.

The moment my mind ripped that word from the tomb where I'd shoved all my memories, I stumbled.

I didn't have the strength or the balance to stop my fall.

I landed on my knees.

I grunted with pain.

My mind swam as the two guards came back and unceremoniously picked me up. One on each side, they helped me down the stretch of corridor.

Expensive landscapes and impressive renders blurred as I clung to coherency. I lost track of how many doors we passed before they finally stopped, turned the ornate handle of the one we stood before, and pushed it open.

Without a word, they helped walk me inside, only stopping once they'd placed me on the plush purple couch under the high bay window.

Backing away with a bow, they kept their eyes on the carpet. "Can we do anything else for you, *efendim*?"

I had no doubt they'd tell the rest of the hired help how useless I was. How fragile and pitiful and broken.

But that was my father's problem, not mine.

I'd begged for death enough times to think the devil himself had forgotten me. No matter how close I came to dying or how often my heart stopped, I never managed to *stay* dead.

I'd be grateful to anyone who succeeded.

But my father would be distraught.

Five years of hard work.

Five years of reconditioning.

All for nothing if one of his guards whispered to one of his enemies that his broken son would be easy pickings.

Sitting upright, I placed my hands on my thighs. "That's all. You're dismissed."

"We'll be outside your door if you need anything." As one, they turned on their heel and stalked out of the suite. The click of the only exit closing sent a frisson of fear through me, but I shut it down immediately.

It didn't matter that I was closed in.

I'd been imprisoned in a cage for five years.

At least this new one was so much better.

I'd lived in decadence on the days that I obeyed. But this new suite was given now I was a lord.

A suite I already hated.

Gritting my teeth, I struggled to stand, grabbed my cane, and shuffled forward to investigate. The gold, green, and blue carpet flowed through every room, lapping at the legs of gilded tables and fancy furniture. A table full of colourful glass bottles glittered in the late afternoon sunlight, and the closed double doors depicted a battle scene.

I hoped this led to the bedroom.

I wanted to sleep.

To forget.

To hide.

Running my fingers over the carvings, I pitied the poor people skewered on the ends of spears and swords. Horses jumped over corpses, and flags flew in the distance with the crescent moon and single star of my country.

Bracing myself, I pushed the doors apart and gasped at the splendour before me. The wall to my left was entirely made of an antiquated mirror. Tarnished in the corners and speckled throughout, the murky image refracted the room so it seemed there were two beds, two balconies, two potted palm trees.

The bed could house ten people. The pillows piled high with lace, jewels, and silk. A bronze chaise waited at the foot of the bed while lamps made of blown glass with smoky brown swirls stood sentry at the head on either side.

No bedframe, just rivers of silver blankets and perfectly pressed sheets.

I'd never seen anything so inviting.

My body threatened to drop to the floor before I could experience the relief of falling face first into its cloud-like welcome.

I could sleep for decades.

I could sleep until I died…

Something moved amongst the mountains of pillows.

Something dressed in the same glittery silver as the coverings.

Slowly, a girl sat up.

A stunning girl with dark-brown hair styled in floaty waves over her slim shoulders. Her cheekbones were high and her eyelashes so thick they moved like fans over her intense dark eyes.

I froze.

Without a word, she slithered off my bed. The scarves she wore flowed around her like water. They barely covered her breasts and swayed seductively around her legs as she padded barefoot toward me.

I fisted my cane.

I schooled myself not to move.

As she walked past the mirrored wall, I caught sight of myself.

I didn't recognise the man staring back.

When I'd been bathed, pampered, and dressed in my suit this morning, I hadn't been given a mirror. I'd been shaved by my father's personal groomer and dressed by his personal tailor.

I stared into the haunted eyes of a stranger.

The girl reached me.

She was a lot shorter than me. Shorter than someone I used to know in my past. A girl I'd loved. A girl I—

My eyes snapped shut as I scrubbed all memories of her away.

He hurt me the worst whenever I thought of her.

She was pain.

So, so much *pain*.

The huge scar on my left forearm was the only remnant I had that I'd once felt something for her and inked myself with something to remember her by.

Fluttering her ridiculously thick lashes, the girl undid the buttons of my blazer and inserted her bold hands inside. Her touch was cool as she ran her fingers up my chest and over my shoulders, pushing the jacket away.

I didn't move.

I never moved when someone touched me.

I'd learned that lesson well.

I stood as still as a statue as she tugged the jacket off my wrists, stole my cane just long enough to remove the blazer entirely, then pressed the carved lion's head back into my palm.

Fisting it, I struggled to breathe as she repeated the process with my black shirt.

She took her time with the buttons.

She undid them torturously slowly.

I twitched and waited, trained to expect far worse.

When she had me standing bare chested before her, her eyes tightened as she looked upon all my scars.

I kept my gaze far away from the mirror.

I couldn't look.

Couldn't see.

I wanted her to stop.

I wanted to be left alone.

But I had no say. I never had any say in the torture I'd been given.

And this was just another level of torture, wrapped up in beauty, delivered with softness, all while I waited for the agony I knew would come.

In a cloud of floral perfume, she swayed forward, pressed a kiss to one of the many scars on my chest, then her hands went to my waistband. She unbuttoned and unzipped me; she sucked in a breath as my slacks fell to the floor.

Cool air licked around my legs. My skin prickled, my hair stood on end, and the agonising phantom pain that was far worse than any session in the machine ripped my eyes to the mirror.

I couldn't help it.

I couldn't stop myself.

The moment my gaze landed on my disfigured form, I lost the numbness he'd drowned me in.

A surge of absolute *fury*.

A crest of murderous rage.

I remembered.

Fuck, I remember—

"Get out," I breathed coldly, deadly.

The girl backed away, her delicate hands folded in her scarves. "But I'm your present, *efendim*. I am yours to do with as you wish."

I couldn't look away from the ruination of my body.

"Go," I hissed.

"But—"

"Go! *Get out.* Fucking LEAVE!" I roared, emotions surging, passions colliding.

She ran.

She bolted to the door and vanished, all while I tripped forward, falling to my knees as my pants wrapped around my ankles.

Fierce tears shot to my eyes as I fought with the material. Shifting onto my ass, I kicked off my only shoe, shoved the trousers off, then froze solid as I dropped my hands to my left leg.

To the mottled and ugly flesh that ended in a mottled and ugly stump.

To the prosthetic that cupped the missing limb just below my knee cap.

The prosthetic didn't fit right, didn't move right. It turned me into a cripple.

Vicious, vicious anger poured through me as I unbuckled the fake limb, ripped off the padding, and threw both as hard as I could into the murky mirror.

The wooden limb crashed against the mirrored wall.

The image of me shattered.

Glass rained in a thousand shards.

And all my conditioning flexed, crinkled, and tore.

A tear in the numbness.

A hole in the torment.

And for one blessed moment, I remembered.

Her.

Then.

Everything.

Neri…

I choked as my heart palpitated and forgot how to beat.

Neri…

I grunted as it continued flopping and floundering in my chest, its beat broken from what he'd done to me.

NERI!

My eyes rolled back

My mind shut down.

I passed out cold on the carpet.

Chapter Thirty-Nine

ASLAN

(Heart in Finnish: <u>Sydän</u>*)*

Five years earlier...

If I WOULD'VE KNOWN COMING BACK TO life would've hurt so much, I wouldn't have bothered. If I would've been told that opening my eyes would condemn me to a fate worse than death...I would've happily passed away and been free.

Regardless that I harboured true fear at leaving Neri a widow. Despite my horror at being the one person alive who would hurt her the worst with my death, I was weak enough to admit I would've chosen to die that day.

Because all the following days were worse than fucking hell.

It started with a dim ache in my lower left leg that built and built until fire replaced my blood. In the short moments between oblivion and awareness, my body switched from blissfully heavy with sleep to burning alive with motherfucking *pain.*

So much pain.

Everywhere.

All at once.

I was hot, then cold.

Sweating, then shivering.

My muscles twitched. My heart couldn't stick to a proper beat, too fast, too slow, skipping and pounding, *pounding* in my ice-fire chest.

I groaned.

I screamed.

The pain only got worse. Tearing me inside out. Eating me. A thousand teeth were eating me. Chewing their way through my searing veins and gnawing at my frost-frozen bones.

I bowed in bed with a sudden jolt of misery, only to fall backward and gasp for breath.

I was drowning.

Drowning on air.

Choking on oxygen while my heart forgot how to pump.

"Fucking hell, what's wrong with him?" a man snapped in Turkish. My brain was confused hearing my mother tongue.

"I thought you said he'd wake up after a few hours and be no worse for wear," the same man snarled. "He's getting worse. He's turning grey, for fuck's sake. His breathing is slowing."

"Perhaps he's allergic—"

"Are you trying to blame your incompetence on my *son*?"

"No, *efendim*. Of course not."

"You got the dosage wrong." A loud crash as if someone had thrown something. "Get my doctor up here. Right now. He's dying!"

"Yes. Of course. Right away, *efendim*." A door banged, leaving silence interrupted by the heavy breathing of someone beside me.

His hand wrapped around mine. His head landed on my shoulder. He sucked in a wet breath that sounded suspiciously like a sob. "Please, Aslan. Hold on. It wasn't supposed to be like this. If I wanted you to die, I would've used a bullet, not a tranquilliser. Hold on. It will be okay. I promise. Just hold on for me. You're finally home. You can't leave me again."

The pain pushed me deep.

I faded.

Time skipped.

I woke to different hands touching my burning body, the pain somehow even worse. I was no longer being eaten alive; I'd been eaten. Every organ was exposed. My skin was flayed. My blood pooled all over the floor.

Please.

Fuck, please....make it stop!

"He's suffering a reaction to xylazine. See how his skin is turning black around the puncture wound? It's necrosis. His tissue is dying."

"Stop it then!" a man roared. "*Do* something."

"It's not easy to fix. How long did you say he's been like this?"

"Ten hours."

"Ten—?" The man cursed. "You should've called me immediately, *efendim*."

"He was tranquilised. He was resting fine. The sedative worked perfectly until he started rousing."

"But now it's killing him."

"I command you to keep him alive!"

A long pause before the doctor said, "I will remove some of the damaged tissue. I cannot promise it will stop the spread. It depends how much damage has already been done. He will need antibiotics internally and externally. When was his last tetanus injection?"

"How the fuck am I supposed to know? He was stolen from me when he was eight months old!"

A flurry of movement followed by a prick in my arm. "There. I've given him tetanus so that's one less thing to worry about. I've also administered tolazoline. It's not approved for use in humans but acts as a reversal agent to xylazine poisoning in ruminants. Hopefully it helps…. For now, please leave the room and let me work."

"I'm not going anywhere."

"Fine. Then shut up and stay out of my way."

A roar that sounded like a bear. "I will tolerate you speaking to me like that if you succeed in stabilising my son, Çetin. But if you do not…you and I are having words."

"Yes, *efendim*. I apologise. I'm only concerned. I despise the use of xylazine and have seen far too many deaths. Y-You don't deal in this substance, do you, Kara?"

Another pause.

"I would never sell drugs that kill. If I'd been aware the dart was this dangerous, I would've found another way to subdue him. Do you honestly think I would put my own flesh and blood through this?"

"No. I believe this was an honest mistake."

"Then fix it…please."

"I'll do my best, *efendim*."

The darkness opened wide.

The fire turned black.

It swallowed me whole.

My eyes opened.

Light stabbed me right in the skull.

I winced and closed my eyes again, hissing as I slowly sank back into my body and stopped floating in some place I couldn't remember. My ribs and hip ached from the car accident, and the stitches in my shoulder caught on the sheets behind me. All the bruises from the men beating me up that night did their best to make me suffer, but those pains were nothing to the aftershocks of flames that'd scorched my entire body.

A shuffle of clothes before someone rested their hand on my shoulder and leaned over me. A mask was removed from my mouth and nose, taking away the faint breeze of air.

I froze as my eyes locked on Cem Kara.

I tried to speak, but my throat was too dry.

I went to push him away, yet only succeeded in raising my hands a little.

Hands that were slightly grey while my left one was stabbed with an IV. My lion and siren tattoo glinted in the sunlight beaming through the open windows. The ink was overly perfect, freshly done with crisp, sharp lines.

My chest tightened; my cracked ribs pinched.

Neri's birthday.

A night that'd started off so well but then turned to absolute shit.

Is she okay?

Fuck, she'll be so worried—

"If you're concerned about your complexion, rest assured you're looking a thousand times better than before. The intravenous antibiotics have combated your infection. You're on the mend," Cem breathed as if truly relieved. "It was touch-and-go for a while, but you're a fighter." He smiled. "Like me."

My skin crawled from him touching me, and despite my weakness, dizziness, and pain, I did my best to sit up. I wanted to run. I needed to get back on a plane and return to Neri.

You can't.

You're forbidden from going back there.

Nausea splashed on my tongue, and fresh pain centred in my chest.

Fuck, Neri, I'm so sorry—

"Easy. It's okay. You're safe." Cem shook his head, patting my shoulder as if he truly cared. "Don't fight the process of waking up. You've been unconscious for six days. It's natural to be weak."

Six days?

Six

DAYS?

How?

Fuck.

Neri.

The phone call.

The shot to my leg.

Then nothing…

My eyes flew wide as I locked on my biological father. He'd aged from some of the images I'd found on Google. His hair silvered at his temples and was mussed as if he'd been running his hands through it. The lines around his eyes seemed deeper, and the creases around his mouth hinted at all the rage and violence he held back, camouflaged with a smile.

"W-Where…" I licked my lips and swallowed. "Where am I?"

"Home." He squeezed my shoulder. "You're home, Aslan. You're finally home."

I frowned, flinching with an awful headache. "This isn't my home."

"It is. You'll learn to understand that soon enough." Dropping his hand, he leaned back in the chair he'd pulled close to the bed where I lay. A quick glance told me all I needed to know. I was no longer in Australia. If the richly decorated room with its heavy mustard drapes, glass side tables, carved doors, and leather couches didn't alert me, the sunlight did.

It was different from the Australian sun. Not as yellow. Not as bright.

"What happened?" I asked, vaguely remembering the argument with the doctor about a drug I'd never heard of.

Cem busied himself with helping me sit up a little and fluffing another pillow behind me. His presence made my skin crawl. But my weakness meant I had no choice but to endure it.

Only once I nodded that I was comfortable did he sit back down and say, "I followed you from the airport. I figured allowing you to travel into the city worked to my benefit. I didn't want to cause a scene, you understand. But now, I wished I'd just approached you the moment you stepped out of the terminal. If I had, you would've just gotten into my car, and we could've had a wonderful family dinner catching up. I wasn't aware you were injured so badly from the car accident. You wouldn't have been able to put up much of a fuss in your current state."

He shook his head with a wince. "I owe you a huge apology, Aslan. I let hate taint my actions and figured you'd view me as a monster. That you'd try to run from me. When my men herded you toward that alley, I should've just *talked* to you. You're a grown man, not a brainwashed child. I'm sure we could've had a reasonable discussion, and all of this would've been avoided, but...I didn't. And for that, I will bear the weight of guilt for the rest of my life."

I hissed between my teeth as my lower left leg twinged. A burning little twinge. "You shot me in the leg."

"I did. With an animal tranquiliser dart that I was assured had been amended to be a safe dosage for a human."

"But it wasn't?"

"No. Unfortunately, you received a high dose of xylazine. The side effects of which are..." He gritted his teeth and swallowed a growl.

"Are?" I asked, unable to believe we were having a normal conversation about a very un-normal subject.

He'd hunted me.

He'd *shot* me.

He'd hurt me and now I didn't know if I would survive or...not.

Six days!

I needed to get back to Neri.

I needed to talk to her.

She'll be frantic.

But for now...I had to tread carefully.

I'd been terrified of this man ever since my adoptive father had told me why we'd run and why I could never return to Turkey. I'd made Neri vow to me she would stay the hell away from him. His very existence had threatened mine even across thousands of kilometres.

To be in his presence?

To be talking to him?

It hurt my already hurting head; I couldn't get a grip on this new reality.

Will he let me go?

Perhaps, I had him all wrong, and he merely wanted to meet me.

Maybe now he had, he'd help me return to Australia *legally*. He could put all his money to use and figure out a way to revoke my lifetime ban from ever flying back there.

Don't be fucking stupid.

This man is a murderer.

A drug dealer and a trafficker.

Cem wiped his mouth with his hand and finally said, "The doctor removed a fair bit of flesh that had died. Your leg will require rehab, and you must be smart about continuing the course of antibiotics. If you don't..." His shoulders stiffened. "Well, we won't get ahead of ourselves. For now, you are here." His watery eyes met mine, and he sighed with a horrifying kind of contentment. "You're here. My son is *here*. Finally."

He reached for my hand, squeezing me hard.

My skin didn't just crawl, it rotted.

I *despised* him touching me.

I hated that he genuinely cared.

I hated that my world was upside down, back to front, and the smog in my head prevented me from figuring out how the hell to get the fuck away from him.

He's the reason Melike and my family are dead.

He's the reason—

"You have no idea how much I've longed for this moment," Cem murmured. "How many years I've spent searching for you. How many governments I've bribed, and airport alerts I've put out. When Emre Avci returned to İstanbul to fly away with you, I was so, so close to claiming you then. I was only fifteen minutes behind. I flew to Asia after you. I flew to Indonesia, always just a little too late. And then...you vanished."

A tear rolled down his weathered cheek as I forcibly extracted my hand from his and wiped it on the sheet as if his touch contaminated me.

He nodded sadly but continued, "You vanished into thin air, but I never stopped trying. Never stopped reminding the police of who you were and hounding international law enforcement to tell me if you appeared. I was beginning to lose hope, but then I received a phone call at four in the morning that an Aslan Avci was in a hospital in Northern Queensland." His lips twisted. "I hated that you were going by that name. That you took that traitorous name, but..." He sighed with a beaming grin. "You were alive. You were *alive,* and I got on my knees and prayed in gratitude. To know you were still breathing. Still mine." He sighed heavily and kissed his fingers before raising them to the sky. "And now…you're here."

I bared my teeth. "You're the reason I was deported."

"Well, not entirely." He scowled. "You were an illegal overstayer, Aslan. Your fate was already written. I merely…rushed the process along, cut through the criminal charges, and got you here as safely and as quickly as I could."

"And what of the Taylors? Why are you helping them? Do you plan on hurting them through me?"

"Hurting them?" His eyebrows shot up. "I would never dream of it. Unlike Emre and Jale, the Taylors kept you alive for me to find. You exist because of them. I would never hurt them." His eyes flickered with evil before he looked away.

"Say it," I growled. "Say what you're hiding."

"How do you know I'm—"

"You're using them to keep me in line. You won't hurt them unless I give you a reason to."

He reared back, his face full of offended surprise. "How could you think such things?"

"I know who you are."

"No, you know what that baby-stealing bastard told you."

"I've read the fake news on you. I see you hiding behind your lies."

"The news is all bullshit, good or bad. You know this."

"There is truth—"

"Fine." He stood up, his temper appearing in a flash. "You want truth between us? You want to talk of boundaries and expectations when all I want to do is love you? *Fine.*" His arms crossed; Turkish words flowed thick and fast. "The Taylors are safe. That girl who loves you is safe. You have my absolute vow that I won't touch them. They will never pay for harbouring you. They will never be punished for keeping my only child alive. But you are right…if you think you can return to them, then…we will have a serious problem. You are here to take your rightful place as my heir. She was your first love, I get that. I loved a slave girl before I met your mother—"

"M-My mother?"

He smiled slyly. "You know so much about me, yet you know nothing about your mother, am I right?"

"Is she here? Is she alive?"

"She died two weeks after giving birth to you. You were the last gift she gave me. It made you even more special."

I didn't know why my heart panged for a woman I'd never met. "How?"

"Sepsis." His face fell, and he dropped back into the chair beside me. "That's why I'm so sorry for sedating you, Aslan. The doctor said you run the risk of dying the way she did…if we don't get your system stabilised."

My ears rang.

My mind tripped with words, threading Turkish with English. It'd been so long since I'd held a fluent conversation that I found it far too easy to be swept up in it, dragged along with the beauty of a tongue I was born to, all while it carried me further away from the language I shared with Neri.

"Neri…" I choked. "I need to call her. To tell her I'm—"

"I told her you were dead."

"*What?*"

"It's for the best."

"Y-You can't. *Fuck.*" I shot upright, ignoring the spinning room and burning bones. "You can't let her believe that. It's a lie. She'll be—"

"Heartbroken? Yes, she most likely will be. I know the ache of heartbreak, Aslan. Your mother, Defne, will always haunt me, but…it's for the best. You will eventually move on and find a woman worthy of your future rank. And the pretty Australian girl you had a fling with will be nothing more than—"

"She's my *wife*," I hissed. "I will *never* marry anyone else."

His eyebrows rose. "Your wife? Her last name is still Taylor. You were illegal. How—"

"It's done. We're bound in every way that counts. Let me call her. Right fucking now. You can't let her keep thinking I'm dead." Sourness splashed on my tongue as my temperature rose and weakness crawled through my limbs. "Fuck, she thinks I've been dead for six days. She'll be…she'll be distraught."

"She will heal."

"But I won't! Let me go. I don't want to be here. I don't want to be your heir. I'm not your son! You killed my uncle and aunt. You are the reason my parents, sister, and cousin are dead—"

"Careful, Aslan. Those people were not your family. *I* am."

"You will *never* be my family."

The room chilled as Cem turned to stone beside me. "You are correct about that. For now. You carry my blood, yet you are corrupted by others. I'd hoped…" He sighed and shook his head. "I'd hoped not to have to discuss this so soon, but…you give me no choice—"

"Just let me tell Nerida I'm okay, alright? I'll stay here while I heal, and then—"

"You'll leave me again?" He shook his head. "No, that's not possible."

"If you truly care for me like a father, you would want me to make my own life."

"The life I offer you is incomparable."

"I don't want it. I could never do what you do and hurt those you hurt."

"That's because you're weak." He sniffed as his eyes welled with fresh tears. Crocodile tears. Tears from a murderer. "It's up to me to make you strong again."

My heart skipped a few beats as the tug of fog and spinning dizziness threatened to pull me under. I wasn't in any condition to fight or even argue. I accepted that, for now, I was stuck here. And while being stuck in a bed with drugs flowing in my veins to keep me alive, I had no choice but to play nice, but...I also couldn't lie.

I couldn't say I'd be something I could never be...life or no life.

Taking a deep breath, I whispered, "Can't you choose another heir? Someone you know? Someone who is already what you want?"

"There is no such person."

I frowned. "But...I thought you wanted to kill me. My father—"

"*I* am your father," he snarled. "Emre was a thief."

"He will *always* be my father. You are nothing more than a murderer."

Cem's entire demeanour turned black. "I figured you'd have concerns, Aslan, but I didn't think you'd be suicidal with them."

My hands balled. "I've run from you my entire life. I've spent the last decade believing you were hunting to kill me." My head pounded as I growled, "I don't understand why you haven't. I'm a threat to your empire, aren't I? I'm the only one who can claim what you've created—"

"You are." His chest puffed up with pride. "I could've chosen another. I could've adopted or pretended that I'd sired a second son, but...no one could compare to you."

"You don't even *know* me."

"True. But...I have been learning. I've been investigating everything you've been up to for the past twenty-four years, and I like what I read. You are loyal and loving, protective and proud. You are right that I did toy with the idea of ending you more than once. After all, you have spent far too many years being brainwashed by that fucking thief Avci, but...I wanted the chance to get to know you. And...if you get to know me, perhaps you will see we are more alike than you think."

My heart thundered.

I already knew I was too like him, and I'd never even met him. The colours in my brain, the violence in my soul.

I could blame Neri for that.

The moment I mutilated Ethan for her, then sank inside her wet warmth, I couldn't restrain myself anymore.

She activated a switch in me. A switch that commanded I raze the world for her. A switch I couldn't turn off.

"I will never be your heir."

"Then we are at an impasse because now that I know what it would feel like to have you die...I will never kill you." He reached for my hand again, but I ripped it out of his grasp. The motion cost me, and I gasped for air.

Lowering his arm, he tipped his chin down. "You stayed alive for me,

Aslan. You were so close to death. One breath between fading or staying. I accepted that if you died, then my choice had been made. I would accept that you had to die to protect everything I've worked so hard to build—"

"You traffic people and ruin families. Your life's work is nothing to be proud of."

He paused before nodding. "I agree that some of my business dealings are…underhanded…but I also do good. I am on the board of many charities and donate—"

"As a front. A cover-up for who you truly are."

His nostrils flared as his eyebrows came down. "I am prepared to give you leeway, Aslan, but don't judge me before you know me. Don't be short-sighted. Despite common sense saying I should kill you, I am willing…no, I am *desperate* to have you return to me. I've missed you every day since you were stolen. I've hurt people, I will not deny that. I have no qualms about using force for my own end, but I don't want to have to use that force on you. I don't want to fight."

"Then you should never have come after me. Just leave me be. If you can't kill me, then great. I-I owe you my thanks. I will sign any document you need proving I don't want your business. I vow I will never attempt to take it. We can just go our separate ways and—"

"I am not a patient man. In my fantasies, you slip into my world as easily as if you were never taken, but I am aware you will need time. I am willing to give you time. In fact, while you fought to survive, I made a vow that if you lived, I would do whatever it took to prove I am your flesh and blood. I don't want to kill you. I don't think I ever did. I merely want to love you and give you more power, more wealth, more opportunity than you could ever claim living in a shed in some scientist's garden."

"Leave them out of it," I hissed. "They loved me. They never did anything to hurt me."

"Are you so sure about that?" Cem raised a manicured eyebrow. "I read an interesting police report from a few years ago. A domestic violence account where Jack Taylor beat you—"

"He thought I'd raped his daughter."

Just how fucking deep does his reach go?

"Now what would give him that idea?" His dark eyes twinkled. "Did you force yourself upon her?" He held up his hands before I could reply, chuckling. "No judgement from me, of course. However, if you did, I find it surprising how shattered she was when I told her you were dead."

My heart fisted. Thorns wrapped around it and punctured the useless organ. "You have to let me talk to her."

He smiled sadly. "That is the one thing I cannot give you."

"You can't let her suffer thinking I'm gone. You can't be that cruel—"

"*Cruel?*" His narrowed eyes blazed with black fire. "I suffered over

325

twenty years thinking you were dead. I spent the first five years mourning you with a despair that almost broke me. You were *taken from me*, Aslan. My baby son. My only son. I know how excruciating loss can be, so don't you dare speak to me of cruelty."

I breathed hard, doing my best to figure out how to handle him and protect Neri at the same time. Whatever painkillers and antibiotics flowed in my blood scrambled my thoughts and made my skin glisten with sweat. "Look…I told you I'll stay while I heal. We can even remain in touch if that is what you wish, but…I can't let her think I'm dead. I won't let you—"

"Nerida Taylor is a part of your past." He stiffened. "I suggest you let her go just like she will learn to let go of you. You will never see her again." Looming over me, his tone turned thick and terrifying. "I've dedicated my entire life to finding you, Aslan. And now that I have, you *will* rule in my stead. You will learn that this is your rightful place. I will do whatever it takes to turn you into the man you would've been. And once you have accepted your place and proven you are my trueborn heir, you will inherit all that I have built. And you will do it gladly."

I held his stare even as pain tugged me down. "You can't make someone do something they don't want to do."

He nodded, clasped his hands, and stood. Looking down at me, he said softly, "You are my son, so I will treat you as such. I am obligated to love you and treat you with respect because you are my flesh and blood. But…you are also a stranger. We are strangers to one another, which makes us enemies."

His face distorted with the darkness that he hid so well. Darkness I sensed because it sang to the darkness inside me. I might have lived across the world to him. I might've been raised by good, kind people and fallen in love with a sweet, wonderful Australian girl, but I couldn't escape this man or ignore the potency of his blood.

"You get one chance, Aslan. One chance to prove to me that you are still mine, or…I will *make* you mine."

I stiffened. "I will never be yours."

He sighed. "Please don't make me show you how easily a person can be broken." Touching my cheek, he studied my face as if imprinting me. "We are more alike than you want to admit. The sooner you accept that, the sooner you can be happy."

Shoving his hand away, I held his eyes so the room didn't turn upside down. "We are *nothing* alike."

He chuckled sadly. "And I suppose it's up to me to show you how wrong you are. I'll tell you what. Once you are strong enough, I will request a paternity test. How about that? If you're so sure you are not my son, then let us have blood speak the truth. But…if the results show what we already know, then you are mine, Aslan."

His hand suddenly pressed against my throat, shoving my pounding skull into the pillows. His touch pinned me with dominance, but he didn't choke me. He merely held me in his paws and growled, "I love you, Aslan. As the stranger you are and the son you will become. I only do what I must to protect my empire so I can one day give it to you. And I know you won't believe me, but remember that each time I hurt you, it hurts me ten times worse."

Letting me go, he looked at the floor as if unable to hold my stare. "You have four days to decide. Four days of convalescing before you are moved to your new quarters and we will begin your education."

His gaze snapped to mine. "Rest well, my son. You will need all the strength you can muster."

Chapter Forty

ASLAN

(*Heart in Javanese:* Ati)

"WAKE UP. WAKE UP, ASLAN. TIME TO see your new home."

I cringed from the annoying tapping on my cheek, cursing the pain that encroached on my body the more sleep ebbed away from me. I wanted to dive back into the dreamless state. It was better there. Painless there.

"*Efendim*, I really must insist. I gave him the light sedative as you requested. I obeyed your guards and your desire to move him down here. But...this will not do. He needs sunlight for health. He needs rest. He's not ready—"

"That's my decision to make, not yours."

My eyes opened just in time to see Cem whirling on an older guy. A guy with a stooped back and bowed legs, his dark eyes intelligent but also kind. Far, far too kind to be mixed up in this den of beasts.

"It's been three weeks," Cem hissed. "His stitches have dissolved. The X-ray you took showed significant improvement to his ribs and hip. His fever is mostly gone, and the antibiotics have kept him alive. I wanted to begin his training weeks ago, yet I obeyed your suggestions. But now, I'm done waiting—"

"He's not ready, *efendim*." The doctor rolled his shoulders into an even deeper hunch. "Injuries like this take time. His system has a lot to overcome. Outwardly, he might be on the mend, but inwardly...he still has much to—"

"Enough." Cem crossed his arms over his immaculate graphite suit. "He is my son. He carries the Kara bloodline, which makes him strong. He is strong enough. But...if you are this insistent, tell me one reason why he can't endure a simple lesson? Tell me and I'll have him sent back to that sick room he's been going mad in."

Cem shot me a look, his eyebrows raising when he noticed I was awake. With a quick nod, he looked away again, glaring at the doctor. "He's doing himself more harm up there than he will be able to down here. He attempted to escape last week. He tried to knock out a guard a few days after that. If he's well enough to fight, he is well enough for this."

"That is instinct, *efendim*, not proof he is healed. His body is still weak. His leg is still—"

"Badly mangled and will always have half his calf missing, but you did your job. He's alive. I called you here to assess and clear him for his lessons, not to argue with me."

The doctor flashed me a look where I'd been laid on a bed carved from rock. Thick furs insulated me above and below along with a pile of woollen blankets stacked on the floor beside the three-legged stool serving as a bedside table. But the missing softness of a mattress wasn't the only sign I was no longer in that awful room with its locked doors, barred windows, and mocking courtyards below.

Cem was right that I'd tried to escape on a leg that had no strength. I'd fought back tears full of horror as I'd unwrapped the bandage around my calf one night, coming face-to-face with what they'd done to me.

Half my muscle was missing. Streaks of darkness still marbled its way through my remaining flesh, hinting the infection had been bad.

I hadn't been thinking.

I'd just wanted to *run*.

I missed Neri with all my heart and miserable fucking soul.

I let anger give me energy, and it'd only taken an hour to jimmy the lock with a safety pin and metal nail file I found in the bathroom and open the door. I limped through the dark. I'd hope I would be free to disappear into the night. However, I only made it half-way down the corridor before I'd been knocked to my knees by a diligent guard and then carried like a dead deer back to bed. I'd tried to knock out the next guard who delivered my breakfast, desperate to steal a phone so I could call Neri.

But my strike hadn't been strong enough. The guard had struck me back.

I'd spent the next few days nursing a black eye.

Cem Kara never came to see me again.

He said he would give me four days, but those four days had turned into weeks as my system remained stubbornly sick.

I wasn't healed yet, but…it seemed my father had run out of patience.

I sat up in the thick musty-smelling furs. I blinked at the new room I'd been given. Not that it could be called a room. More like a cave. Or a catacomb. Memories of travelling with my parents when I was little—before Melike had been born—came to mind

We'd travelled to Cappadocia and spent hours exploring the caverns, caves, and underground pathways of Derinkuyu, the supposed oldest city in Turkey. I remembered the trip so clearly because I'd run off and gotten lost in the narrow, cold, and crowded corridors.

Turkey had hundreds of underground cities. Derinkuyu was spread over almost five-hundred kilometres, but there were over two hundred similar places. Most of them with one, two, and three layers of habitation beneath the earth, creating a metropolis hidden in the ground.

Is that where he's brought me?

Are we even in İstanbul anymore?

I glared at the little niches cut into the wall. Electric lights flickered, blending modern with ancient. The floor was uneven with chisel marks and a rudimentary table and chairs sat in the centre. A low archway led to an identical cave beyond with a toilet in one corner, a wash bucket, a drain in the middle of the floor, and a towering cabinet pressed up against the back wall. A large bronze padlock hung off its metal rings, keeping the lattice doors closed.

What the hell is in there?

Where the fuck are we?

My heart picked up its pace.

At least that part of me had healed enough that it didn't skip and trip so often.

I was driven by panic to tell Neri I was okay.

Haunted by dread that if I didn't run soon, I might never be able to.

My body blazed, my bones ached, and the very idea of fighting my way out of this place was fucking laughable.

I was useless.

Helpless.

Trapped.

The doctor's eyes landed on me from across the small cave. He winced as if apologising for what would happen, then bowed at Cem. "If the lessons are short, he should be okay." He tripped over his words. "But…only short, mind you. His system cannot handle much before a secondary infection could spread—"

"I will keep them short." Cem nodded and held out his hand. "Now, do you have the paternity results?"

"Oh, yes, of course." Fumbling in his black satchel hanging off his hunched shoulder, the doctor passed Cem an envelope.

Ripping it open, Cem's gaze scanned the page before he grinned. "That's all for now, Çetin. You will be summoned if required."

"As you wish, *efendim*."

"You two stay," Cem commanded, narrowing his eyes at the guards standing by the only exit—a barred metal door that looked suspiciously like the bars of a prison cell.

Not saying goodbye to the doctor, Cem marched toward me on the fur-lined bed before tossing the paperwork on my lap. I caught it before it fluttered to the ground and skimmed the Turkish text.

A lot of numbers in neat columns. A lot of duplicate digits and scientific speak before the conclusion that I already knew but choked on anyway: *The man tested is the biological father of the child. The probability of paternity in this case is 99.99%.*

Well, fuck.

Cem chuckled. "It's a day of good news. Now that you have evidence that we are, in fact, related, are you willing to see where you came from? To accept that you carry a part of me inside you and are destined to become a man so much greater than what you were prepared to settle for?"

I scrunched up the results and tossed them on the floor. I didn't even know when he'd taken a sample of DNA from me.

It creeped me out.

Was nothing my own anymore?

"Why was the doctor concerned about lessons?" Ice flowed down my spine. "They're not just normal sessions where you talk to me and I listen, are they?"

With an almost sad look, Cem sat beside me and clamped his hand on my left thigh. I jerked away and stood up, only to fall back down again thanks to the missing muscle in my calf and the sickly weakness in my body, even now.

"Don't strain yourself," he whispered as I panted hard on the furs, my vision fading in and out. "And yes, you're right. We'll start easy today, but…there will be some days that will be hard if you don't show aptitude."

"What are you going to do to me?" I kept my chin high even as every bone in my body seized.

"I'm going to…for loss of a better word…reprogram you."

"*Reprogram* me?" My lips pulled back off my teeth. "What the fuck does that mean?"

"It means that by the end of our training, you will remember who you truly are. You will forsake what you think you love. You will want different things. *Remember* different things. I will paint the life you would've had if you'd remained mine, and you will understand I do this out of love and care." He smiled sadly. "We will no longer be strangers but will be exactly what we are: father and son."

I stood again, swaying a little but able to stay upright. "Let me out. Right now." My eyes flew around the space. "Where the hell are we anyway?"

He stood and clasped his hands together as if he was a real estate agent showing me a fancy investment. His charcoal suit, dark-grey shirt, and silver tie were a direct contrast to the exposed earth and gritty dust surrounding us. "We are beneath my home in İstanbul. I have many homes strategically placed around Turkey, but this one is my favourite."

His eyes lit up with fond memories. "I had it built before you were even conceived. While digging the foundations, the workmen found this." He spun on his heel, opening his arms as if he presented me with a mountain of gold. "A pocket of undiscovered catacombs. A perfect piece of my ancestor's past." He snorted. "It was also my first encounter dealing with a government official who wanted to halt building, thanks to my foreman tattling. They tried to revoke the dwelling permit—it was now a place of historical importance, not a piece of rural landscape—but…I didn't give in without a fight, and my money turned their no into a yes, and these caves were never noted on the title."

He lowered his arms. "They've come in handy over the years."

The ice was back, along with sleet and suffocating snow. "Handy for what?"

He sighed and lowered his chin. "You're intelligent, Aslan. I'm sure you can figure it out."

"Torture."

"I don't like using that word. I prefer…methods of persuasion."

I struggled to swallow. "That's what you're going to do? *Persuade* me?"

He flinched. "Like I told you, this will hurt me more than it will hurt you—"

"I doubt that."

He marched into me.

I almost fell back down again from his sudden stalk, but he clamped both hands on my shoulders and steadied me.

If I trusted I could remain standing, I would shove him away, but sourness splashed on my tongue, and grey spots danced before my eyes. "Let me go."

"If I did, you'd fall, and it's my job to give strength to my only son." His gaze fell to my mouth before flicking back to my eyes. "It is my duty and my sacrifice to give you back your strength, Aslan. The strength that was stolen from you by that bastard Avci."

Grabbing his wrists, I tore his hands off my shoulders. I stumbled but stayed upright. "You speak of the Avcis as thieves and criminals, all while talking of torturing your only child."

"Not torture." He winced. "Persuasion."

"No matter what you do to me, I won't suddenly fall in love with you or agree to be your lapdog. You might as well kill me because it's going to be a waste of both our fucking time."

He sighed heavily. "Unfortunately, my methods are rather tried and true at this point. They are fool proof. The only question is how long it will take…not if I'll succeed."

He stepped back, giving me room to breathe. "I'll tell you what. I'll give you one final chance before we begin. Once we start, there will be no more chances until the end. But…just this once, because I love you with all my heart, I will give you the opportunity to surprise me."

His lips tilted into a sad smile. "I would really love you to surprise me, Aslan. Prove to me you *are* me. That you are worthy of my empire. That you house the heart of a beast and have become the savage lion I named you after. Do that and we will go back upstairs. We will share a drink, good food, and I will summon my generals to swear allegiance to you. Do that and all of this is over."

My mind swam with images of Neri.

My heart shattered into pieces that she'd endured a month of believing I was dead. Was she okay? Had Jack and Anna gone to Townsville to collect her? Was she forcing herself to survive and go to uni, or had she been as broken as me and utterly unable to think around the aching, suffocating hole inside?

What about Griffen and our apartment?

What about Billy and Honey, Teddy and Eddie?

What about Lunamare and the freshly stamped company registration that we'd all signed one slightly drunken night via Zoom?

My chest folded in on itself, snapping my healing ribs and using them as pitchforks to stab my heart.

Fucking hell.

I *needed* her.

I needed her to function, to heal, to survive.

If I never saw her again, I didn't want this life. I didn't want to fight because there was nothing to fight for if I didn't have her.

"I'm taking your long pause to be that you're thinking about my offer?" Cem asked softly.

The guards didn't move from their position by the exit. Their eyes never looked away from me, seeing too much, watching the unravelling of my hopes, dreams, and soul.

Swallowing hard, I asked, "W-What would I have to do to prove myself?"

What do I have to do to earn your loyalty so I can turn around and kill you?

Cem studied me for a moment as if he could hear my internal hate. Finally, he scratched his jaw and held out his hand. A guard stepped forward without a word and withdrew the pistol from behind his back. Placing it into his boss's hand, he backed up and stood by the wall.

Presenting the gun to me on his outstretched palm, Cem said, "Three things. You could prove you are my heir with just three little things."

I didn't take the weapon.

I didn't speak.

Cem fisted the gun and wrapped his finger around the trigger. Aiming it at my chest, he muttered, "Kill a traitor, rape a slave, and transact a business deal with female flesh. Do that and your lessons have already been learned without any tutoring required."

My mouth went dry.

My left leg burned.

Balling my hands, I choked, "You want me to kill, rape, and traffic?"

"I do."

"The fact that you think that's possible shows how insane you truly are."

"You *will* do those things, Aslan, mark my words."

"Not while I'm alive."

"There are different levels of being alive, my son," he said quietly. "Don't make me prove that to you."

"I will never sell another. I will never kill another. And I will certainly never rape someone."

"When the day comes that you do, I won't say I told you so but will merely welcome you with open arms."

I snarled like a caged animal. Which I was. And caged animals ended up doing stupid things. I wished I was stronger. I wished I stood a chance at taking on three men, guns, and untold guards above us.

I wished I could shoot my way out and fly home to Neri.

Home.

Even if I managed to escape, even if I managed to find Neri in a different country and we vanished under different names, could I do that to her?

Could I be that selfish?

Could I ever look at her again if I do the things Cem says I'll do?

I froze.

Fuck.

If Cem somehow broke me enough to become him, I would never be able to look Neri in the eyes again.

I would be as bad as Ethan.

I would be *worse.*

"Choose, Aslan." Cem waved the gun, the muzzle still pointed at my heart. "All it takes is a single nod."

The pitchforks in my chest turned into spears and stabbed me in the lungs.

Fire seared through my blood as I fought for a way out.

I could barely walk.

Barely see.

I was weak and mildly feverish, and the adrenaline flowing in my system was enough to wipe out all the energy I'd been able to claw back.

Even if I made smart choices or stupid decisions, this wouldn't end well for me.

Sorrow crashed coldly as I gathered my embarrassing strength, crossed my arms, and glowered at the gun. "I will never do what you want me to do. I will never be *you.* No matter what you do to me. No matter how badly you torture me. I will *never* be your son."

Cem sighed. "I won't deny that doesn't hurt, but…I understand."

"Are you going to shoot me now?"

Instantly, he lowered the pistol. "I will never shoot you again." His gaze went to my left calf. "I'm sorry I shot you in the first place. I just…I hope the infection has been stopped and you'll regain your strength in time." A thought crossed his face, making him stand taller. "I'll commission a cane to be carved for you, how about that? A lion's head with a flowing mane. You can use it while you learn to walk again."

"I'll stick it up your ass."

His shoulders sank. "Unfortunately, at this moment in time, I believe you would." Holding the gun out to the side, he waited as the guard came forward and claimed it. Slipping it beneath his blazer, the guard turned to go, but my father said, ever so quietly, horribly coldly, "Bring in the chair and unlock the machine."

"Yes, *patron*."

As one, the two guards left.

My breath caught as a loud noise and squeaky wheels sounded. It echoed in the chambers of the caves, loud with earthen acoustics.

I wanted to ask what would happen but…what was the fucking point?

I'd pushed him to do this.

I'd thrown his choices in his face.

My heart clawed into my throat as a heavy wooden chair with sturdy platforms for arms and feet was tipped backward and wheeled into the cave. The guards didn't stop until they cut beneath the arch and placed the medieval-looking chair above the drain in the floor of the other catacomb. Leather straps dangled off the armrests, back, and legs. Buckles glinted in the electrical sconces.

Once the chair was positioned, one of the guards pulled out a key and unlocked the lattice-doored cabinet.

The doors swung wide.

I tripped backward.

My missing calf muscle sliced with agony as I landed heavily on the fur-lined bed.

Fuck.

FUCK.

Cem shifted toward me, placing his hand on my shoulder.

I was too fucking terrified to shake him off.

I couldn't tear my eyes away from the huge machine with dials, switches, and a giant voltage wheel with a colour swatch above fading from green to red.

"Like I said, Aslan, my methods are tried and true. I will never push you beyond your tolerances. I will never actively try to deliver more pain than you can handle, but…you *will* feel pain. It will be delivered via electrodes on your body—sometimes your temples, sometimes your genitals, sometimes the soles of your feet. Other times, the electrodes won't be used at all."

He snapped his fingers, and a guard came running with a long wand with two metal spikes. Fisting it, Cem waved it around as if he could conjure magic. "This is called a picana. It's used when I wish to target a localised area and deliver… intense responses."

Sweat beaded down my spine.

My heart chugged and choked.

No wonder the doctor had fought for me.

No wonder he tried to bargain for more time.

Even the healthiest of people wouldn't survive this.

No one could survive electrocution.

The other guard came to join the one standing beside Cem after delivering the nasty torture wand.

With barely a nod, Cem stepped back and muttered, "Strap him into the chair."

A rush of violence shot down my limbs.

I soared upright.

I swung.

I managed to land three punches before my body forsook me, my vision betrayed me, and the last thing I remembered was the guards dragging me between them and the nasty bite of leather as I was fastened in.

Chapter Forty-One

ASLAN

(Heart in Dutch: Hart)

Two months...

"A NEW DAY. A NEW LESSON. STRAP him in." My father's command cut through my half-dead state. I didn't have the chance to wake up properly before strong arms hoisted me out of the fur-lined bed and dragged me back to the chair.

Every part of me begged for it to end.

I had no fight left.

No hope.

I had no idea how much time had passed, only that each lesson was worse than the last. To begin with, they'd been short. A few questions, a few zaps. It hadn't even hurt that much. The voltage had stayed firmly in the green, and I'd ridden through the teeth-snapping, blood-stinging, involuntary spasms without too much hardship.

Each time Cem touched me with the picana or stuck electrodes to my head or feet, he'd cup my cheeks and apologise.

His despair was genuine.

His dedication to my lessons steadfast.

He both loved me and hated me, and that recipe drove me straight into hell.

Blinking back the blur of bad sleep and the heavy wash of sickness that seemed to be getting worse, I smacked my lips and forced myself to focus.

Each morning a guard came into my room, forced a bunch of pills into my mouth that I assumed were antibiotics, then stood over me while I ate.

The food I was given rivalled any expensive restaurant.

Hearty *keşkek* and delicious *şiş köfte*.

So many meals that I hadn't had in so long and I wished I could enjoy them.

The aromas made my stomach snarl with delicious expectation, but every morsel tasted like dirt.

I lived in dirt.

I breathed in dirt.

And when the guard was satisfied I'd eaten every bit, my body rebelled and purged it. I'd barely reach the toilet in the second cave before hurling up the rich food. Food my body desperately needed to keep down.

It wasn't by choice.

I wanted to get stronger, not weaker.

I hated that my ribs were beginning to show and the hole in my calf seemed bigger every day. The black trackpants and sweatshirt I'd been given hid the worst of my condition, but beneath it…I was wasting away.

I didn't know why.

I cursed the worsening coherency of my mind.

If I could just get my body healed, then I could finally think straight and not lose myself to fantasies.

I lived in dream worlds.

I babbled to Neri.

I saw pretty-jewelled fish swimming in my catacomb.

I felt the heat of the Australian sun and swore I felt the undulation of the Coral Sea beneath my bed.

If I could stop the hallucinations, then I could finally think straight.

I would be able to figure out how to grab a gun and shoot my way out. Neri.

I can go home to Neri…

My head tipped forward as Cem buckled in my right arm. He'd already strapped in my tattooed arm, but he still wore his usual scowl of disapproval while glowering at it.

Did he hate all tattoos or just that one?

Did he know Neri had the same?

Did he hate that I'd willingly marked myself as belonging to her all while forbidding him the same right of owning me?

"Roll up his pant legs. I think we'll do his ankles today," Cem muttered as if he was discussing the weather and not where to torture me.

At least he hadn't carried through with his threat to electrocute my balls. Not yet, at least.

I moaned as the guard's hands roughly jerked up my trackpants. I hissed as air swirled around my blazing calf and another crest of lightheadedness made the cave fade for a moment.

"Eh, *patron?*"

"What is it?" Cem barked, fiddling with the dials on the machine.

"You might want to take a look at this."

With a soft curse, Cem came toward me, glanced down at my left leg, then blanched. Dropping to his haunches, he grabbed my ankle and pressed his thumb into the wasted, missing muscle.

I groaned in misery.

I flushed with nausea.

"How long has your leg been like this?" His head snapped up, his eyes sharp on mine. "Aslan? How long?!"

Too sharp.

The only sharp thing when everything else was fuzzy.

And soft.

Fuzzy and soft and—

"Aslan." Cem's hands landed on my cheeks. "Why didn't you fucking tell me!?"

I licked my paper-dry lips. "I-I don't know what you want me to tell you."

This was how he started his lessons.

First, he'd make me admit something true.

Was I in Turkey?

Yes.

Was I Aslan Kara?

Unfortunately.

Was I in love with Neri Taylor?

Undoubtedly.

I replied in my head but never out loud, and he'd shock me each time I refused. He'd only stop once I was forced to confess what he already knew.

Once I did…that was when the true fun began.

Flinching, already feeling the shocking heat and horrendous twitching from electricity, tears stupidly came to my eyes. "You haven't asked any questions. I don't know—"

"You're sick, you stupid boy!" he roared. Launching upright, he snarled at the guards, "Unstrap him, carry him upstairs. Get Çetin here. Right now."

"Of course, *patron.*"

I was only vaguely aware as the buckles were undone and the leather let me go.

The heat in my blood and the aching, breaking pain that'd steadily been getting worse chose that moment to crash.

It crashed and drowned and with a soft sigh…I gave in.

"I told you to hold off until his body could withstand it," a male voice said coldly. "I also told you he couldn't stay on antibiotics for the rest of his life. They were bound to stop working. I'm surprised they lasted this long."

"Well, what the fuck are you going to do about it?" Cem growled. "The black has spread. It's on his shin."

"It's worse than that I'm afraid. The X-rays show the bone is compromised. The tissue is no longer just dying, so is the bone beneath."

"Fuck," Cem gasped.

My eyes fought to crawl open.

I blinked at the sunshine pouring into the room.

Sterile and white with concrete floors, hard beds, and a wall of light holding X-rays of my damaged leg.

The images danced and blurred as my body fought to stay awake all while being ripped into sleep by a heavy undertow.

Something was wrong with the image.

My skeleton glowed white yet around the area where the doctor had carved out my calf muscle as if it was a ham steak for dinner, the bone was now gritty and grey. Black spots dotted up and down my leg, creeping ever closer to my kneecap.

Fuck, what does that mean?

The world spun, and I closed my eyes again, doing my best to stay aware even if I couldn't focus.

"It means we have to take drastic action. Immediately."

"Define drastic action," Cem commanded.

"We must do what I advised in the beginning. The xylazine has destroyed any and all healthy cells. They are dead and the longer they are attached to his body, the more the necrosis will spread. He's survived this long thanks to the antibiotics, but now he's on a very dangerous trajectory."

"How dangerous?"

"He will die."

My eyes flashed up. "W-Wait…what?"

Cem shot me a look, his forehead furrowed and agony blazing in his gaze. "Aslan. Hey. How are you feeling?"

I cringed away from him as he came to my side and rested a fatherly hand on my very damp forehead. The gesture was so kind, so worried that my sickly heart kicked with confusion.

This man was my enemy.

He *hurt* me.

He made me scream.

Yet…he looked at me with endless love in his gaze and tears of regret welling on his lower lashes. "Aslan…why didn't you tell me you were getting worse?"

His question made sense, but I couldn't form a sensical answer.

I'd felt like death ever since I'd arrived here.

I'd forgotten what it felt like to be normal. To have an appetite and power. I had no sex drive, even if I was lucky enough to have dreams of being inside Neri. I couldn't remember a time when I didn't exist without palpitations. I was cold all the time and suffered nausea like it was my new baseline.

Hadn't I always felt this badly?

It hadn't gotten worse.

I'd just gotten weaker.

"It's okay," Cem soothed. "I know you're not in a state to talk. I'm sorry I've been away for a few days. If I'd come to see you sooner, I—"

"You couldn't have avoided what has to happen," the doctor said softly. "You know what we must do. The question is do you trust me to do it here or would you prefer moving him to the hospital?"

"No hospitals," Cem snapped. "You have a full operating studio here that is far better than anything anywhere else. *My* only question is…are you sure there's no other way?"

"None. He's dead if you don't authorise this."

A long pause where hot sticky sleep crept over me again. Finally, Cem exhaled hard and said, "Fine. Summon your best team and ensure they all sign the necessary paperwork. You have my blessing to use whatever resources you need."

"Thank you." The doctor sounded relieved; I opened my eyes again.

The fever cut through me like a sizzling knife, and my leg ached like a motherfucker. That was the source of all my discomfort. If only it would stop aching and burning, I was sure I'd be okay.

"I…I need some painkillers," I muttered, my voice barely louder than breath.

"I know." Cem ran his fingers through my sick-sweaty hair. "I know. And you'll have them." Snapping his fingers, Cem ordered, "Dope him up. Knock him out. I don't want him to suffer a moment longer than necessary."

"As you wish, *efendim.*"

A rustle of clothing and a sharp prick in my arm. "Sleep now, Aslan. When you wake…everything will be better."

I willingly chased the thick happy clouds.

I waited to be sucked down deep.

But then I heard words not meant for me, and my heart screeched to a stop.

"I'll amputate below the knee. The joint doesn't look compromised. At least with the joint intact, he'll find it easier to adapt with a prosthetic."

What?

No.

No.

Fuck.

NO!

"Do what you must. Save my son."
Wait.
Don't.
Don't cut—
I screamed.
Sleep pounced.
I passed out.

Chapter Forty-Two

ASLAN

(*Heart in Lithuanian:* Širdis)

Six months...

"HOW DOES THAT FEEL?" THE YOUNG doctor with black hair, brown eyes, and empathetic smile asked. Our fourth session together and he damn well knew how it felt.

Foreign.

Wrong.

Not a part of me.

"It's fine," I muttered, refusing to look at my leg.

At the stump below my knee.

I didn't care it'd been four months since I'd gone to sleep screaming and woken up screaming. The first thing I'd done as the anaesthetic wore off was jack-knife up and grab at my left calf...only...there had been no calf.

No foot.

No shin or ankle or toes.

Just nothingness.

I couldn't comprehend the missingness...the *wrongness*.

My body still felt as if it had two feet, ten toes, and was equally balanced like nature had designed. I even felt myself grabbing that missing leg. Felt my fingers on non-existent flesh. Felt a scratch that couldn't be scratched and an ache that couldn't be soothed. The phantom awareness fed me what my neurons believed still existed all while there was *nothing*.

Just bandages and pain and a stump where I'd once been whole.

I would never run again. Swim again. Be *me* again.

I was dead.

Neri believed it.

And now...so did I.

It was too much.

Missing Neri.

Missing myself.

Missing the future we could've had and knowing the future I would have to endure.

I snapped.

I sank.

I sank into the depression I'd never been fully free from.

I stopped fighting the black fog and sticky misery.

And I didn't get back up.

The doctors kept me sedated.

Time passed without my knowledge.

My body healed.

The bandages were changed.

And by the time another month rolled around, I was slowly weaned off whatever drugs they'd pumped into my system, and the nightmares began.

Nightmares of Neri being strapped into that agonising chair.

Neri being sold as a slave.

Neri being raped by me all while my father held a gun to my head to do it.

I stopped sleeping.

I couldn't bear to close my eyes.

I would rather suffer in a world where I'd been butchered than endure a dreamworld where Neri screamed.

The insomnia worsened my state of mind.

The inability to move on my own without a walking frame or wheelchair shattered my self-worth.

I was nothing.

Fuck, if Neri could see me like this?

It would kill her.

I was glad.

Glad she thought I was dead.

At least she remembered me strong and healthy and not this wasted, shattered man I'd become.

The only light in the sea of darkness was I hadn't been taken back to the catacombs. I was given the room where I'd healed in before. The king bed was lowered so I could swing my right leg to the floor and push upward without falling. The bathroom was modified, and the shower widened so I could wheel my frame beneath the water and not run the risk of slipping.

All razors, nail files, knives, and pointy instruments were removed from my vicinity.

Cem never asked if I was suicidal, but I supposed he sensed it. It didn't take a genius to see the emptiness inside me or the corroding hatred in my eyes.

He visited me often. He showed me reports on his businesses. He educated me like a normal teacher would his student and told me things I would never be permitted to tell another.

Every lesson trapped me tighter into his world, ensuring I could never leave.

Not alive anyway.

His rich, deep voice was eerily calming as he explained how tourist women were targeted around Europe and the Middle East. They were taken when an opportunity exposed itself, then each woman was shipped to one of Cem's holding facilities. There, they were tagged like livestock, assessed for quality, and sold to specific buyers.

I tuned out when he spoke of those trades.

I blurred my eyes when he pushed photos beneath my nose of successful sales and repeat customers.

He held nothing back.

I knew he had twelve estates in Turkey, two in England, one in Germany, and a top-secret bolthole in Sicily. He visited me late one night when I stared at the TV, willing the nonsense on the screen to erase the madness in my head, and showed me pictures of his homes.

He promised we would go one day.

He would take me to each of them, and I could choose one for myself.

I let white noise fill my ears.

I closed my eyes and sank into the deep.

I shut down—

"*Efendim?*"

I flinched at the young doctor calling me his master.

"Do you wish to stand? This is just a prototype. Eventually, a high-tech one with a foot matching your natural one will be cast. This is just so you can learn how to walk again. Your father has given strict instructions that you are to get strong as quickly as possible."

I didn't care.

I'd lost all will to survive.

"Come on." The young doctor grinned. "It's been months since your surgery. Your body is ready to wear one of these."

I growled under my breath.

Just because my physical body had healed didn't mean my mind wasn't still in fucking pieces.

This doctor was pissing me off.

Where was Cem's personal physician? The one who'd hacked off my leg? I hadn't seen him in a while. Perhaps Cem had fired him for taking my leg and every shred of my self-worth.

I was worthless to him now. How could you train up a son when he would rather be dead?

"Get up," the doctor urged, placing the despised walking frame in front of me. "We need to start your rehab."

I stood but only because he hauled me upright. I swayed, and my teeth crunched together at the godawful pressure from the prosthetic wedging far too tightly against my stump. No amount of gel pads and cushioning could soothe the grinding ache.

The leather straps on my quad dug into my flesh, and the contraption around my knee bit like tiny beasts.

"That's it. Try putting your full weight into the limb. Trust it. It can hold you, I promise."

Clenching my jaw even tighter, I did the opposite. I let my right leg take my full weight, my nostrils flaring at the claustrophobia clawing to rip the offending fake leg off and hurl it through the window.

Get it off.

Get it the fuck off!

Sweat ran down my back, and I was moments away from snapping when Cem strode through my bedroom door, nodding at the four guards stationed there. "Aslan!" He clapped his hands as if this was a happy day and I was the prodigal son. "You look better." His eyes went to the wooden limb socketed at the bottom of my stump. "Ah, you're up and walking. Even better news!"

Phantom pain shot through my confused nervous system, and I swore I had a cramp in the arch of my missing foot. My big toe itched. My calf muscle twitched.

All things that couldn't possibly exist because that part of my body was now most likely fed to Cem's Rottweilers that patrolled outside my barred and locked window.

I shuddered as black loathing rolled through me.

If I could, I'd slaughter my father and then myself.

Anything to be free from this powerlessness.

"Leave us," Cem barked.

Immediately, the doctor bowed, squeezed my arm, then left.

Cem stopped before me, snapping his fingers and smiling as a young woman with dark-brown hair pinned in a bun on the top of her head came scurrying into the room.

She kept her eyes far from mine, her bare arms straining to carry a heavy white box. The dress she wore could better be described as a potato sack, skimming her ankles with faded cream fabric.

"Put it on the bed," Cem commanded. His Turkish order seemed both threatening and fatherly as the girl did as he asked, then darted back out the door.

I had no idea who she was and didn't care. She was probably a slave Cem kept for himself.

Sitting down beside me, Cem waited until I gave up the pretence of wanting to learn how to walk on a piece of wood and patted my shoulder. He never looked away as I sat heavily, kicked away the walking frame, then fumbled with the buckles.

The minute they were undone, I yanked off the fake leg, threw it to the ground, then gingerly unwrapped the thick padding.

No matter how many times I saw myself naked in the mirror. No matter how many nights I sat in the dark and studied my huge scar, it never got easier. As far as amputations went, I supposed it'd been done well. I'd had no infection or adverse reactions. My body had healed enough that I was no longer feverish and could keep food down.

But each time I ran my fingers over what was left of my leg, I shuddered with abhorrent disgust. It repulsed me. I felt half-human. It made me sick to my bones because it signified how far I'd fallen and how destroyed I was because I could never climb back up.

Cem cleared his throat, his eyes on my stump. "I don't know how many times I can apologise, but I know it will never be enough. This was not how I wanted our reunion to go."

I ignored him and shoved my trackpants over my stump. With a practiced move, I tied the empty part of the leg into a knot so it didn't dangle, then wedged my face into my hands and dug my elbows into my knees.

I cursed that I both hated his visits and enjoyed them.

When Cem was here, my hate had something to latch onto.

When he was gone, that hate latched onto me.

It was fucking exhausting.

"Look, Aslan…" He reached to squeeze my shoulder.

I shrugged him off with a growl. "*Don't.*"

Dropping his hand, he muttered, "I know the past few months have been hard on you. I know you're not sleeping, and I understand why you're choosing to fade from this life instead of learning to accept it. But I need you to make an effort."

Effort?

Would killing him be defined as making an effort?

"You need something to take your mind off recent events. Obviously, I don't know what you used to do for fun or what your hobbies have been, but…if you're anything like me, I'm guessing this might spark some interest." Rummaging in the box, he pulled out a stack of workbooks and tossed them into my lap. "If you *are* like me, numbers are your outlet. Ironically, it was through my love of numbers that I lost you. I hired Burak Avci because I liked how his brain worked with sums. His accountancy firm was second to none, and I appreciated that his brother was a math professor."

"Emre was more than just a math professor," I hissed. "He was a man ten times your worth."

Cem ignored me. "Until Burak stole you from me and gave you to

Emre, I was friendly with him. He didn't have synesthesia, but he did have talent. Did you know only four percent of the population has synesthesia?" He studied me closely. "It's a genetic trait where the most common type is grapheme colour."

Fuck.

I dug my thumbs into my eyes.

He does have it.

"Do you see numbers in colours too, Aslan?" he asked softly. "Sometimes I can even taste them or a particular sum will smell sweet and sharp."

He can taste a number?

I'd never had that.

Figures felt like ivory and silk in my mind and glowed with pigment, but I'd never *smelled* an equation before.

Gritting my teeth, I ignored his questions like I always did.

"If you do…then numbers can become a bit of an escapism. I can't remember how many times I zoned out when doing puzzles and math quizzes when I was a boy. I preferred them over TV or sports or even girls to a certain extent." He chuckled. "In this box are samples of accounts from my companies over the past few years. I never did hire another accountant after Burak stole you. In fact, I fired a lot of my workforce because I lost trust in those I believed I could count on. I run my own books now. It takes me hours a day. And if I'm honest, I'm running behind and need help."

Pausing, he cleared his throat. "I will make you a promise. For now, I don't expect anything from you but to heal. Physically and mentally. You have my word that you will not be 'persuaded' again until you have gained back your strength. There's absolutely no point in me training you in this current state. You'll just shut down further, and I refuse to lose you again. You have my permission to do whatever you want…within this room, of course. If you want to run my books, then I will bring you every ledger and trade. If you want to know more, I will gladly tell you. This is my compromise, Aslan. I hope you will be willing to meet me halfway."

Grabbing more books from the box, he placed them gently beside me. I didn't look up.

This was eerily similar to Griffen Yule offering me a job looking after his rentals. Only difference was Griffen's business was legal…and this was most definitely not.

"These are the latest accounts I haven't had time to tally. Follow how I've done it in the other books. Learn my system or make up your own. I trust you." He sighed heavily. "Fuck, how long I've waited to be able to say that." His hand landed on my shoulder and squeezed. "I trust you, Son."

I went to shrug him off again, but he dropped his hand before I could revoke him. "You *are* my son, Aslan. You might not be whole at the moment—in body and mind—but you will be. Run my books, heal yourself, and then we shall see where we go to from here."

Standing, he loomed over me for a moment before adding, "*Seni seviyorum, oğlum.*" (I love you, Son).

He left me.

He left his books on my bed.

And despite myself, the allure to open them overwhelmed me.

With shaky desperation like an addict needing a fix, I grabbed a freshly sharpened pencil from the case full of rulers, erasers, pens, and notepads, then sank into the orderly world where fractions became whole and divisions always yielded a perfect number. Colours exploded in my head, casting light on the darkness inside me, giving me a much-needed reminder of brightness.

That night, I finally found salvation.

I'd used sudoku in Australia to run from the shadowy sickness of my grief.

And without noticing, I did it here.

I used the income and expenses of a crime lord to forget.

I lost myself all over again but this time…

I remembered who I was.

What I was.

And who I belonged to.

Neri.

I belonged to Neri.

As long as I remembered that…I wouldn't be entirely lost.

As long as I remembered her, I stood a chance…

Chapter Forty-Three

ASLAN

(*Heart in Nepali:* Muṭu)

One year...

"YOU'VE BEEN LYING TO ME!" CEM growled as the door swung open, and he stalked into my room.

I paused mid push-up, sweat dripping off me, my shoulders and biceps burning, my stomach flexing to keep me balanced in a one-legged plank.

"Get the fuck up." Cem planted himself in front of me. "Now."

I pushed upright. Thanks to my much-improved core strength, I easily sprang to my foot, balancing on one leg, refusing to use that fucking walking frame or dust-covered wheelchair.

I wasn't dead yet.

I refused to fucking die.

By his hand or mine.

The only one who could hate me was me.

The only one who could be repulsed by my body was me.

And if I chose to do the opposite?

If I chose to accept my limitations and work with them, then wasn't that a better use of my time?

I was caged in like a beast. I hadn't been out of this room in ten months. The only outlet I had was food, exercise, and Cem's accounts.

I succumbed to the nightmares about Neri because I needed sleep for mental health.

I avoided the urge to think about her during the day because I needed to focus on how to return to her.

I refused to be a hypocrite for the rest of my life.

If Neri could heal from rape, then...I could heal from this.

So what if I'd been violated?

So what if I was a prisoner, and a piece of me was missing?

I repressed what I couldn't face and strived to fix what I could. My mind created more and more compartments. More walls and locks where I could and could not go. This was just another thing I would deal with once I was free to do so.

I'd made the most of my incarceration.

I was breaking out next week.

I'd overheard the guards talking about a big shipment arriving—a shipment of what, I didn't have a fucking clue—but Cem would be away, which meant he'd take most of his guards with him, and those left behind were so used to me being a meek, one-legged prisoner that they wouldn't see me coming.

My hands curled as I shot a look at my bed. Beneath the mattress, I'd hidden six butter knives that I'd painstakingly sharpened with the scissors from the accounting box and toothpaste for grit. I only stole a knife when a particular guard was on duty—a non-observant one.

My plan was to stab as many men as I could, as quickly as I could, then steal a gun or two.

In a few days, I was leaving and never coming back.

My blood burned with hope at calling Neri—telling her how much I fucking loved her, then jumping on a boat and vanishing somewhere safe.

Throwing me the face towel I used to wipe off my sweat while I trained, Cem wrinkled his nose. "You need a shower."

I grinned. "Am I offending you, *baba*?"

His eyes narrowed. "I'm glad you're back to your old snarky self, Aslan, but I wouldn't push me too far." He glanced at the many workbooks I'd been given. His current ledgers and illegal activities teetered in different piles, some tabulated and balanced while others waited to be opened. Resting on the ornate desk beneath the window, an ancient laptop slept, its silver casing decorated with sticky notes from previous accounts.

Cem gave it to me the day I agreed to run his books.

The first thing I'd done was try to message Neri via the internet, only to find the WI-FI chip had been removed. It was as useless as a paperweight. The only thing it could do was type up Cem's handwritten archaic notes, turning them into neat and brightly-coloured spreadsheets.

It was the one aspect of his business I wasn't appalled by.

Numbers weren't people.

Figures weren't slaves.

I could pretend I was working for Griffon Yule again. Thanks to numbers, I was more centred and calmer than I'd been in a while.

"Why are you here?" I curled my upper lip, swiping at my sweat. I could balance on one leg as easily as I used to stand on two. It'd taken time. Those phantom twinges still happened as my missing toes tried to dig into the carpet, and I swore I felt the same breeze curling around my right leg. On the days when the black smog of depression tried to suck me under, I'd glower at the wheelchair in the corner and want to give in.

But then I'd renew my efforts and double down on my determination to get free. I'd do whatever it fucking took to get out of here.

"Why don't you use the walking frame?" Cem asked. "Or better yet, try that prosthetic."

Tossing down the towel, I shrugged back into my white t-shirt. "I don't want to rely on anything that can be taken away from me."

He scoffed. "No one would take away your leg."

I caught his eyes. "You already did that."

"You know what I mean."

"Yes, I know exactly what you mean. You want me reliant on something. A fake leg, a walking frame, a cane—"

"I haven't given you your cane yet. I told you I would when you did something to deserve it."

"Ha." I waved at all the boxes of his accounts. "I've been working up here like a troll in a cave counting gold for months. What more do you want me to do?"

"Do those three things I asked you a year ago, and you can join me outside. No more chair. No more future persuasion."

A chill ghosted down my spine at the mention of the chair. I'd lived in fear of being strapped back into it, but so far…he'd been true to his word.

I bared my teeth. "Like I told you then, I am *never* going to kill, rape, or traffic."

He snorted. "One day, Aslan. One day." Darkness filled his already lethally black stare. "Anyway, I didn't come here to chitchat."

"Why did you then? How about you just fuck off, and I'll go take that shower?" I hopped toward the walk-in wardrobe where my prison uniform awaited. Black track pants, black sweatshirts, and white t-shirts all lined up in a row.

Cem followed me. "You might want to hold onto the wall."

I glowered at him. "Why?" Fisting a fresh t-shirt and trackpants, I hopped and turned to face him. "You planning on finally killing me?"

A cold, sly smile crossed his face. "No, I merely want to tell you who I spoke to today, and I feel the blow might be a little upsetting." Lifting his hand, he pretended to inspect his fingernails. "Did you know it's been a year since you returned to me?"

"A year since you shot me, then left me in feverish amputee hell, you mean?"

"Semantics." He lowered his hand. "What if I was to tell you if you came with me right now, if you killed one of my enemies, fucked a slave, then oversaw the shipment of eight shipping containers of cocaine arriving next week, that you could have everything you ever wanted?"

Leaning my shoulder against the shelving, I crossed my arms. "I seriously doubt you know what I want—"

"You want Nerida. You want to live together in a country where you can legally get married. You want a family with her. A home where you can always be safe."

I froze.

I wobbled a little and balled my hands in my fresh clothes. "I never want her name on your tongue again."

His face hardened. "You lied to me, Aslan."

"What? How—"

"I've been asking you for months if you see numbers in colour. You took to running my books without any wars whatsoever. Even I'm blown away at the intelligence you possess. I've asked you numerous times if you inherited my trait, yet each time you sneer and say you would never accept any gift that came from me. Genetic or otherwise."

"So?"

"So…I happen to know you *do* see in colour. That you were secretive about it back then, and you're secretive about it now."

My heart slowed to a dangerous beat. "Who-who told you that?"

"I also know that you've killed someone."

"No, I—"

"You shot him in the calf with a harpoon—ironically in the same spot as I shot you with the tranquiliser. Unlike me, who has fought to make amends ever since, you cut off two of this man's fingers, were about to cut off his cock, then threw him overboard."

A blizzard filled my chest. All the strength I'd cultivated and power in my body vanished. My right leg threatened to give out; my voice resembled a churning storm. "Y-You spoke to her." Pure fury fired through me. "You spoke to Nerida? What. The. *Fuck?*"

Launching myself at him, I managed to hop the short distance and swing a fist.

It landed against his cheekbone, but I didn't have the power.

He grunted and retaliated.

He struck me in the jaw, sending me swaying to the side.

If I had two legs, I would've absorbed the blow.

But with only one, I fell.

My balance forgot.

My body believed it had two feet

That awful fucking phantom feeling convinced me that if I just put my left leg out, I'd be stabilised and could throw another strike.

I cried out as I landed on the end of my stump.

Blinding pain shot through my remaining bones, and pain-sweat flashed over my skin.

"I told you you should've held onto the wall." Cem stood over me and snapped his fingers. Two guards came running. They crowded into the walk-in wardrobe, towering over me on the floor.

Ducking to his haunches, Cem lost any signs of being my shame-filled father and instead turned into my torturer. "This is my fault. I see that now. I wanted to give you time to heal, and you've done that. You are strong. You are healthy. But your temper is corrosive, and your hate for me will only lead you down a path where I cannot save you." Clucking his tongue, he added, "And yes, you're right. I did speak to Nerida. We had a lovely chat. She's here, actually—"

"*What?*" I looked up, riding through the waves of agony. "She's in Turkey?"

What was she *thinking?*

She disobeyed me.

She broke her promise!

White-hot panic whipped through me at the thought of Cem selling her, using her, hurting her.

Of course, she came.

Of course, she wouldn't let me go that easily.

She was impulsive and reckless and passionate and—

Fuck!

"Don't touch her, you bastard. I-I'll do whatever you want. Just leave her the fuck alone—"

"I've given her a few days to mourn you in our homeland, and then she's aware she has to leave." Cem sighed. "I won't hurt her. I have no animosity toward her. She's technically my daughter-in-law, after all, and I'm loyal to my family. Unlike some. She loves you enough to refuse to believe you're dead—"

"She knows," I breathed, a certain kind of unexplainable understanding slamming into my chest.

She knew.

She knew because we shared the same heart. We'd vowed to be one and she could feel, as well as I could feel her, that she was out there…somewhere…alone and in pain but *alive.* I had no doubt that if she died, I would feel it. I would know the moment she took her last breath because it would be the end of mine.

I'd heard her screaming for me when Ethan hurt her.

She heard me screaming for her now.

Neri.

I'm here.

I'm yours.

I'm going to find a way to get back to you…I promise.

"Please." I swallowed back my rage. "Don't let her think she's going mad. Tell her. If you love me at all, you'll tell her I'm alive and—"

"How will she know you're not gone?" Cem asked suspiciously.

My eyes burned with motherfucking tears.

I didn't want to tell this bastard anything about her.

I wanted her to be completely unknown to him.

But…if it made him pull her out of the awful pit of misery? If he helped me give her salvation?

"She…she's always been in-tune. She knew when her childhood friend died from a dog attack. She…senses things."

He watched me closely. "A talented boy falls in love with a talented girl, it seems."

"Just let me talk to her. Let me tell her I'm alive, and—"

"The day you truly become my son, Aslan Kara, is the day I will willingly let you call her. If you still love her after you take your rightful place by my side, you have my blessing to bring her to you. You can rule my empire together. I am not such a cold-hearted man to deny two people who love each other—"

"Yet you'll happily let her endure a year believing I'm dead?"

He shrugged. "Call it character building."

"Fuck you," I snarled. "Fuck. *You.*"

He curled his upper lip. "Think of it this way, if she finds another while you learn who you truly are, then she was never meant to be yours. She was lying, and I'd rather you wait to see if she is loyal than be blindsided when she betrays you."

"She would *never* betray me."

"I guess you'll know soon enough, won't you?"

"I hate you," I hissed.

"And she thinks you are dead." He shrugged almost sadly. "And really, that isn't a lie. Aslan Avci is dead. The boy she hid with her parents' help did die. I think he died the day you murdered her rapist."

I flinched.

I choked on tears.

I'd protected her through bloodshed, and it fucking killed me that I couldn't do it now. I would kill my own flesh and blood for a single phone call to tell her I was okay. That I would see her again. Love her again.

That awful depression was back.

It sat heavily on my chest, crushing me into the carpet.

You're weak.

You're not worthy.

Let her go.

Why would she take you back when you're in pieces?

Shaking my head, I warred against those miserable lies.

I'm strong.
I'm worthy.
I'm going back to her…somehow.

My heart skipped an annoying beat, not knowing if it should listen to sorrow or to hope.

So what if I was missing half my left leg?

That didn't define me.

So what if I'd been going stir-fucking-crazy in this room?

I was still functioning.

I was still alive.

I was *adapting.*

She won't be adapting.

She'll be fucking breaking.

My hands balled.

He'll pay for this.

Fucking hell, he'll pay.

What I did to Ethan would be *nothing* compared to what I did to him. For the agony he let Neri endure. For the separation he'd forced us to suffer.

As if sensing my unravelling violence, Cem stood upright and glanced at the guards. "Pick him up."

Instantly, hands wrapped under my arms and hauled me to my foot.

I tried to shove them off me, but they held fast, making me growl like an animal. An animal that would resort to biting and going feral if it meant I could get out of here.

She's here.

In Turkey.

If I could just get to her.

If I could use my knives and escape—

"There will be no escape, Aslan," Cem muttered, reading the burning emotions in my eyes. "In fact, I see that my procrastination in resuming your education was because I was so hopeful. I cannot tell you the happiness I felt hearing you'd killed someone. You avenged your lover. You spilled his blood and mutilated his body, all in the name of loyalty and love."

Stepping into me, his eyes held mine. "You think you'll never stoop to hurting another again, but I'm telling you now, you will. You have that fire within you. You have that fury. Every person has good and bad, light and dark, and I hate to tell you, Son, but we—you and me—embody more darkness than light. You are my *son*, Aslan. Knowing you've taken a life just makes you all the more special to me. I need you as my heir, not my accountant. And it's finally time to make that a reality."

Marching out of the walk-in wardrobe, he barked, "Bring him. We're going to the catacombs."

"What? *No.*" I fought. I kicked my good leg against the door frame as I was dragged out. "I don't want to go back down there."

Two more guards appeared.

Without speaking, they grabbed my full leg and half leg and whipped them out from underneath me.

"Get the fuck off me!"

I went rogue.

I thrashed and squirmed.

I kicked and punched.

But nothing helped.

The four men didn't drop me or let me go.

"Don't tire yourself out, Aslan," Cem muttered. "We have a big day ahead of us. Today is the day we begin your training for real. No more short lessons. No more half-strengths. Today is the day I break you, so I can mould you into who you truly are."

Chapter Forty-Four

ASLAN

(*Heart in Māori:* Ngakau)

Two years...

"AGAIN," CEM COMMANDED.

I didn't have time to tense before the familiar zapping surge of electricity tore through my muscles.

My teeth clamped down on the rubber bit shoved in my mouth.

My hands spasmed.

My bones smoked.

I can't breathe.

I can't—

The sizzling, snapping pain suddenly stopped, and my entire body went from seized to floppy. Gentle hands landed on my sweaty cheeks. The rubber bit was removed from between my teeth. My father's face appeared in my still jerky vision. "You are my son. You are strong and smart and ready to take your place at my side. Who are you, Aslan?"

His words weaved around my electrocuted brain. The mind-washing was familiar. Implanted thoughts that didn't belong slowly wriggled their way into my psyche.

I'd lost track of time.

My skin was pale from lack of sunlight.

The strength I'd cultivated from exercise had long since wasted away.

Some days, I had enough power in my arms to feed myself, but most days, after a particularly gruelling persuasion session, I could barely swallow.

Those days were the ones when my father was the kindest.

He'd unstrap me himself. He'd bathe me himself. He'd tuck me into bed and hold up a cup of the sweetest tea to my lips. He'd whisper how wonderful life would be once I woke up to who I truly was. He'd push back my overgrown, tangled hair and murmur just how proud he was of me. Just how far I'd come. And how much further I had to go.

Thanks to the sugar in the tea and the kindness of his touch, those nights I actually slipped into dreams instead of nightmares. I dreamed of standing tall and proud on two legs, not one. I swelled with gratefulness at the fortunes in my bank accounts and the many employees at my beck and call.

I forgot that my empire was built on the blood and bones of others.

That the kingdom I was to inherit was rotten at its core.

I relished in the screams of others because it meant I was no longer the one doing the screaming.

And by morning, I'd shiver and huddle into a ball as insidious thoughts swirled inside my fractured mind.

I am his son.

I am his rightful heir.

I am strong and ruthless and bow to no one.

I'd raise my head, desperate to see Cem striding into my cell, needing his approval, ready to get on my knees and tell him the epiphany I'd had that I belonged to him and I was finally ready, but then my eyes would land on my tattoo, and I'd remember.

A snap.

A slice.

A vision of Neri sparkling in the sea and the delicious taste of her adoring lips.

I'd stroke the inked lion—the symbol of who I used to be—and kiss the siren who used to be mine. In an instant, my heart would kick back into life, refusal would suffocate all the brainwashing and prior convincing, and I'd cling to the truth.

The lies Cem kept feeding me didn't stand a chance.

As long as I had my tattoo and my love for Neri, he couldn't break me enough to change me.

I knew who I was.

I'm hers.

I would never forget her. Never forsake my morals or the people who had raised me.

I am good.

I am loved.

I am better than this.

At least Cem didn't know my dirty secret.

I overheard him muttering to his doctor the other day when I was assessed after a particularly long session. "He should've broken and become malleable by now. What's going on?"

"I cannot say, *efendim*. Perhaps he is mentally stronger than you think?"

"Perhaps," Cem whispered. "He is my son, after all. But... I wonder if it's something else. Some trick he's employing to erase the suggestions I'm giving him? Why else has he not improved after a year of this?"

A year?

I'd suffocated at the thought.

A full year I'd existed in these caves, howled at their walls, and pissed blood from electricity frying my veins from the inside out.

Two years since I've seen Neri.

My heart no longer resembled a normal beat. Even when I was left alone to rest beneath my furs and blankets, it remained confused and skippy. The trips and hiccups made me woozy and breathless. And some days, I was actually grateful to be strapped into the chair and hooked up to the machine because it would sync my heart back into something resembling a regular thrum.

That first shot of stinging current killed me but also reincarnated me.

Once the machine was turned off, I'd suck in a thankful breath, my chest no longer pounding like untuned drums.

But it would only last a few minutes before another crack would whip through me, and my rhythm would screech and scramble with another shock. Another bolt. Another attempt to *improve* me.

"Aslan?" Cem put his fingers beneath my chin and tipped my head back. My skull cracked against the chair that I'd spent an untold number of hours in. "Did you hear me? You are my son. You are strong and smart and ready to take your place at my side. Do you agree?"

I could feel it.

The tug.

That awful, endless tug to give in.

To repeat what he said.

To believe what he said.

To *be* what he said.

But my eyes sought salvation and landed on my tattoo.

The sconces around the cave glittered on the black lines in my flesh and I focused all my will, all my soul onto the dreamy face of the siren as she cuddled into the mane of my lion.

She trusted me.

She loved me.

I'm hers, not his.

She's my master, not him.

She is my home, not this.

My spine slowly straightened, and I looked him in the eyes. The straps against my wrists held me in place, and the quad buckles kept me from shifting, but I didn't need to run.

I'd finally learned that there would be no running. Not because I only had one leg but because Cem would never let me go.

Not now.

Not after.

I would die down here, but I would die as Aslan Avci, not Aslan Kara.

"I am not your son," I grunted. "And I will *never* rule in your stead."

He hissed and jerked backward. "Again," he snarled at the guard operating the machine.

I went to inhale—

Too late.

A sizzling arc of execution sliced through my organs, bones, and brain. I turned rigid. I bit my tongue. I jerked and seized, but I didn't care anymore.

There was no preparing for this type of persuasion.

No enduring it or accepting it.

Each shock was as agonising and as blistering as the first.

It felt as if a thousand men punched me all at once. As if rats clawed at my flesh and ants burrowed in my blood. And by the time the current ceased turning my body into a pyre, I had nothing left.

I was just a pile of body parts, gasping and twitching on the chair.

"How many fingers am I holding up?" Cem asked softly, shoving his hand beneath my face. "How many?"

I blinked back the haze and willed my tongue to work.

This was another one of his games. He said he borrowed the brainwashing tactics from the book *1984*. He sounded rather enamoured by that tale and the ministry that managed to convince people of impossible facts and outlandish laws.

"Three," I gasped, still twitching a little as residual sparks erupted in my veins.

He tutted and curled away the three fingers he'd been holding up. "Again."

I groaned as another shock slammed into me.

On and on.

Hotter and hotter.

Broiling and defibrillating, flaming me alive.

I slumped as the current stopped.

I couldn't hold my head up anymore. My bones were noodles. My muscles nothing more than tenderised meat.

My father waited for the electricity to fully leave my system before cupping my chin and raising my eyes to his. "How many fingers am I holding up, Aslan?"

He held up all five.

I blinked and fought the urge to sob.

What the fuck does he want me to say?

I tell him the right number, and he doesn't accept it.

"Five," I moaned.

Shaking his head, utmost disappointment clouded his dark stare.

He let me go.

I was able to keep my eyes on him, barely.

Clasping his hands together, he murmured, "I spoke to Neri again last week."

My scrambled heart hopscotched. I licked my lips. I had questions, so many questions, but I didn't have the strength to ask any of them.

Is she okay?

Does she still think of me?

Has she moved on?

Cem gave me a sad smile. "She's killing herself."

What?

"She can't accept that you're gone, and it's making her mad."

Neri…

Fuck, I'm so sorry.

"She's learning Turkish." He smiled. "She almost sounded native on the phone."

I'm so proud of you.

I wish I were there to listen.

To talk to you.

To kiss you.

Love you—

"I told her that you're nothing but ash and to forget about you."

I hate you.

I'll kill you.

One day, I'll—

"Oh, and by the way, the answer isn't five. One day, you'll learn what I'm truly asking." He stiffened and commanded, "Again."

Electricity swamped my thoughts.

I forgot my name, Neri's name…everything.

Two years, two months…

"Promise me you won't forget me." Neri pressed her mouth to mine, forcing her tears and fears into my mouth.

I shook my head and crushed her in my arms. "Never. It's an impossibility. I'll forget myself before I forget you."

She crawled onto my lap and snuggled into my arms like the siren did into the mane of my tattoo. I wrapped myself around her. I rocked her close, all while my eyes stayed locked on the door before us.

Any second now, they were coming.

To take her away.

To sell her.

Because of me.

Because of who I was.

Because of the excellent trade I'd negotiated.

I'd gotten a high figure for her.

A fabulous number for her sale.

The income I'd earned from selling her would look so pretty in my records and would fit so nicely into my overflowing bank accounts.

"Aslan...please don't do this." She rained kisses along my throat. "You don't want to do this."

I pressed my cheek against her frangipani-smelling hair. "You're right. I don't want to sell you, but it's already done. I have to, don't you see? I have to because this is business, and you are merely a transaction. You now belong to someone else because it makes my father happy, and I am my father's son."

"You're not his son. You're nothing like him."

I pulled away and looked into her tear-wet eyes. An awful confession poured out of me. "But I am, Nerida. I am him. I am a Kara."

"No, you're mine. You're a Taylor. Take my name if Aslan Avci is dead. Take my parents' name. Take me, Aslan. Take me and run. We need to run." Her tears turned to sobs. "We need to run. Before it's too late. Run, Aslan. Run, run, RUN!"

I gasped as the nightmare broke.

My broken heart did its best to beat with scrambled impulses as I pushed my weary body upright. The furs around me were warm, but the rock beneath me was mercilessly hard. My missing leg still felt the heat and weight of whatever dead animal kept me covered, and I did what I always did when my dreams bled into the doctrine my father was pushing.

I'm not like him.

I'm not.

I would never hurt her.

I would never sell her.

I was almost sick at the thought.

Grabbing my left arm, I ran my thumb over the inked siren. I bowed over it. I prayed to it. I begged it to help me. To keep me sane. Stay human. Stay hers.

I'm yours, Neri.

Until my last breath, I am yours.

I'm still here.

I still love you.

But I hope you're moving on.

I hope the pain is fading.

I hope you believe I'm gone because the thought of you in this much agony is too much to fucking bear.

A single tear ran down my cheek as I pressed a kiss to the siren. The screech of the cell door opening wrenched my head up.

My father strode in, dressed in his typical black suit, polished shoes, and swept-back hair. Deeper grey glimmered at his temples, and a few more lines etched around his eyes, but apart from those signs of ageing, he looked formidable and in no mood to retire—heir or no heir.

Dropping my arm, I swiped at the weak wetness on my cheek and struggled out of bed.

A few accountancy records were stacked by the wooden table. He'd given them to me as a reward for behaving in our last session. I had no idea what I'd done to deserve the gift of numbers, but I'd poured through them. I'd found a few mistakes in his math. I'd relished in the scratch of my pencil and the orderly formation of figures inside my tangled mind.

Cem stopped before me. His gaze swept over my soiled t-shirt and black sweatpants before landing on my tattoo. An awful glint of something appeared, then disappeared in his stare. Slowly, he met my eyes and lowered his chin. "Did you sleep well, Aslan?"

I balled my hands and stood dead straight, my stump hovering above the ground as my right leg kept me balanced. "I did."

"I did. Thank you, *baba*," he corrected me. Tilting his head, he waited with narrowed eyes.

Gritting my teeth, I muttered, "I did. Thank you, *baba*."

He grinned as if I was perfect in every way. "You've had a few days off. I figured some time away from the machine might do you good. Do you wish to begin, or are you ready to take your rightful place beside me?"

Once again, his gaze snapped to my tattoo before locking back on mine. I didn't move.

He asked this each time he came for me.

He made the torture *my* choice.

All it would take was my allegiance.

My admittance that I'd kill, rape, and trade in his name.

That I was a Kara.

That I was *remade.*

And each time, I couldn't do it.

I couldn't scrub Neri's face from my mind or the horror I felt each time I dreamed of selling her all because that was what my father wanted.

I was a spineless coward in my dreams.

But here, in this life that was slowly being snuffed out with each electrocution, I would stay loyal until the end.

"I believe I need more persuading, *baba*," I murmured.

His eyes flared. His lips twisted. He snapped his fingers, and two guards came for me. "So be it."

Two years, six months...

"What do you say, Aslan?"

I bowed my head and clutched at the wall as the guards deposited me on the threshold of the conservatory. Sunlight streamed through the glass walls and ceiling. I'd never seen so much light.

It hurt.

It seared.

It was another form of electricity, assaulting my cave-adapted eyes instead of zapping through my bones.

"Thank you." I licked my cracked lips. "For letting me see the day."

Cem marched toward me and held out his hand. "Come. I figured a nice luncheon was in order, don't you? You need some sun. Doctor's orders."

Ignoring his offer for support, I hopped away from the doorway and headed toward the wrought-iron table and chairs in the middle of the marble patio. Palm trees and ferns crowded the space, making the air dense and damp, rich and humid. A fountain babbled somewhere, and the chirp of birds granted an innocent tropicalness I didn't trust.

My balance was a little off, and I swayed forward, catching one of the chairs before I fell. Another few months had blended into time I would never get back, and my body was sick again.

I was cold all the time. I could barely think around the incessant pressure of despair.

So many days I willed myself to just give in, to get it over with.

But then evenings would come, and nightmares would haunt, and I'd wake with renewed purpose with another vow to my tattoo. My ink represented everything stolen from me and everything I would one day earn back.

I'd grow strong again.

Stubborn again.

And by the time Cem came for me, the entire vicious circle would begin again.

And again.

And *again*.

My back prickled as I sat down. Cem came to join me.

I didn't like things out of the ordinary.

And this was definitely out of the ordinary.

I didn't like surprises.

Because the payment for them was more than I could pay.

"Tea?" Cem asked, pouring some into a fine china cup before I could say yes. Four young women in matching cream dresses scurried forward, laying the table with huge platters of *babagannuş*, fresh bread, *şakşuka, yaprak sarması*, and too many other dishes to count.

My stomach rumbled even though I'd learned the hard way that a full belly when being electrocuted equalled projectile vomiting.

"Here. You must eat." Cem piled my plate with a little of everything. Each dish glistened with oils and spices, but I couldn't smell anything. I wondered if the sessions on the chair had fried a few circuits in my senses.

My heart tripped over itself a few times before latching onto a steady beat.

I didn't reach for my fork.

I didn't give him the satisfaction of keeping me alive all while he killed me.

Placing a forkful of delicious-looking food on his tongue, he chewed while watching me.

His eyes never looked away, his face unreadable. Ever so slowly, his left hand came up and placed something slim and violent on the table.

I froze.

My nostrils flared.

Cem swallowed and waved the wand he'd used on the soles of my feet, my cheeks, my temples, and even my balls when he felt particularly diligent in his training.

"Eat something, Aslan, or I'll have to use the picana."

That awful rod. That despicable stick of torture.

It didn't matter that the electrical current wasn't as hot as the machine. It still hurt, still made me twitch like his puppet, and still made me drop to the floor if I wasn't strapped down.

My hand trembled as I scooped up something and shoved the fork into my mouth.

The moment I chewed, Cem lurched forward and pressed the two prongs of the picana against my chest.

I grunted as a searing bolt tore through me.

My fork clattered to the metal table, splashing *babagannuş* everywhere.

I tipped sidewards.

I went to fall.

But he pulled back, the current stopped, and I managed to hold myself upright.

Gasping, I choked on my mouthful.

Cem carried on eating as if nothing had happened. "Is the food to your liking?"

"Yes, *baba*." I swiped my mouth where uneaten food dribbled out of my lips. I fought my shakes, but they only grew worse because I didn't understand.

I didn't know why some days he shocked me and others he didn't. I didn't know why some days the answers I gave to his endless questions were right, and some days they pissed him off so much he turned up the machine far too high.

If I knew what I was supposed to do, I would do it.

No, you wouldn't.

You'd take the punishment to stay true to Neri.

I stilled.

Perhaps that was the problem.

Maybe he knew that.

I stiffened as my gaze fell on my tattoo.

If he ever learns that's how I'm avoiding his mind games…

My head wrenched up. I swallowed hard as a slow smile tipped Cem's lips. With eerie calmness, he reached across the table and pressed the prongs of the picana against my ink.

"I think you just gave away your little trick, Aslan."

I didn't move my arm away.

I wouldn't give him that satisfaction.

Instead, I sat taller, shoved another forkful of food into my mouth, and dared him, just fucking dared him to shock me.

With a low chuckle, he sat back.

He toasted me with his tea.

And I feared what the fuck he would do next.

Two years, nine months…

"I'd hoped, Aslan. I'd truly, truly hoped."

Cem threw a bucket of icy water over me where I'd passed out in the chair. I came to, spluttering and choking, already fearing the extra sizzle of electricity now I was wet.

I had so many scars over my body—not from blades or daggers but from electrode burns. Water made them sear ten times worse. Some wounds had become infected, leaving me with lesions and scabs that made me look like something only written about in horror stories.

To make matters worse, the oversensitivity I'd been born with—that'd granted such pleasure and intensity when I'd made love to Neri—was now my enemy. My skin didn't just zing with electricity, it blistered. The phantom pain of my amputated leg made me sob in the dark as I tried to rub away the bone-deep ache or scratch the incessant itch on my missing ankle.

No matter how hard I clung to sanity and grasped at every memory of Neri, each day I was losing.

Little by little, quicker and quicker.

The walls were closing in.

The chains in my mind were buckling.

I don't know how much more I can take.

Ducking to his haunches, Cem rested his hands on my bare thighs.

I'd been stripped naked for today's persuasion.

He'd used the picana between my legs.

I'd sunk into oblivion when my body had decided it couldn't withstand the torture anymore.

Tutting under his breath, he repeated softly, "I truly hoped that it wouldn't come to this." His fingers dug into my kneecaps. "You're so close. So close to being mine but you keep clinging to the past. To who you used to be. To *her*." His gaze fell on my inked arm. "And I know how you're doing it."

Standing, he drove his finger into the sallow flesh of my forearm, right in the eye of the lion. "You look at this. Each time you slip and start to fall, you look at this as if it's your saviour."

The two guards who always accompanied him down here shifted on the spot. They never said a word during our sessions. Most of the time I never saw their faces, but I flinched as one coughed under his breath and the other made a low groan, almost as if even they weren't ready for whatever Cem was about to do.

I trembled as my skipping heart raced.

I kept my gaze firmly away from my inked siren.

I had no energy to talk.

Whatever he wanted to do, I had no say in it.

I could fight or scream, and it wouldn't make a damn bit of difference.

The only power I had down here was *in*difference. Apathy. The cold detachment of shutting down.

Footsteps drummed around the echoey caves just before Cem's personal doctor marched into the catacomb I called prison. My heart flickered with hate, and a morbid thought popped into my head as my gaze fell on his black bag. Perhaps my leg was in there. Maybe he'd preserved it and returned to sew it back on.

The doctor slowed to a stop as he examined me in the chair.

No one undid the buckles around my wrists, waist, throat, or thighs, and I sat like a good broken toy, not caring about anything.

"He's sick again, *efendim*." He wrinkled his nose. "Look at his complexion. His eyes."

"He has no fever," Cem argued.

"He's not getting the vital vitamins being locked down here for years on end. He needs sunlight. He needs fresh air. He needs—"

"I give him the best food from my chef. He knows that he has a king-sized bed and luxury apartment awaiting him the moment he accepts that we are family. He could make this all stop tomorrow."

"He is stubborn…like his father." Dropping his bag, the doctor opened it and rummaged inside. "If he's determined to stay down here, make him take one of these every day." The rattle of a bottle landed in Cem's outstretched hand.

"What is it?"

"High strength vitamin D for immunity and bones. He'll also need K2. And possibly some quercetin. Along with another round of antibiotics…for after today's exercise. Just in case."

"Fine. You know I want him alive and in good health, so prescribe whatever he needs. But…" His voice changed from typical frustration to fucking chirpy with hope. "I have reason to believe he won't be staying down here for much longer after today."

"Oh?" The doctor quirked his eyebrow.

My ruined heart did its best to find a regular rhythm all while begging to stop altogether.

Whatever Cem had planned, I wanted no part of it.

My fists curled, and despite myself, I tugged against the binds. I'd fought against them so much that the flesh around my wrists had turned calloused from ligature scars.

"Thirty more minutes, Aslan," Cem murmured. "Then you have my word that you'll be released."

My eyes met his. Black to black.

In a spur of whatever emotion he felt for me, he bent over and pressed a kiss to my sweaty forehead. "I love you. You'll trust that soon enough. You'll reciprocate that…sooner rather than later."

Pulling away, he nodded at the doctor. "Proceed, Çetin."

"Are you sure?" Çetin's voice sounded reluctant. "I've never denied you anything, but this seems particularly—"

"Necessary," Cem snarled. "Do it."

"As you wish." The doctor sighed, braced his shoulders, and commanded, "Guards. A table, please."

Instantly, the two guards leapt into action and dragged the single wooden table to the edge of the medieval chair where I was strapped. Without another word, the doctor unloaded a few things from his bag: gauze, bandages, packaged sterilised scalpels, alcohol, and finally, a syringe full of liquid.

His eyes met mine with an apologetic wince. "This won't hurt as I will administer a local anaesthetic—as per your father's request, but I suggest you look away."

"No, he is to watch," Cem said coldly. "I don't want him in pain. This isn't about pain. This is about removing the past. It's about proving he is more than he thinks he is, and no number of tricks or time can save him."

I couldn't catch a proper breath.

Fuck...no.

He can't be serious.

He wouldn't cut me again.

Would he?

Looking at me, he added, "Your past ends right now, Aslan. That dreadful tattoo will be removed, and with it, any ideas you can ever return to that life. Your future is bright, and it is *here*, not there. You are so close to embracing it. I'm not going to waste any more sessions on you. Not when you are ready, and I need you by my side."

Slicing fear cut through me. "What the hell are you going to do?"

"Çetin. Please tell my heir what is about to happen."

"Of course, *efendim*." The doctor bowed his head and ran a soaked pad all over my arm, wiping my tattoo thoroughly. The sharp whiff of disinfectant shot up my nose, hinting that if my neurons were seared from the thousands of shocks over the past few years, my sense of smell had returned at the worst possible time.

"I will numb the area and then surgically remove the epidermis and dermis layers of your skin. Depending on the size of the removal, I will either apply a skin graft or sew up the ends of the wound. You will have a decent scar after the surgery, but your forearm will no longer bear any ink. You will suffer no ill effects. I give you my word on that as a physician."

I went deathly cold, glowering at my torturer. "Cem...don't."

"I am your father." Cem crossed his arms. "Address me as such."

"*Baba*, please." I shivered and struggled in the chair, speaking a string of Turkish. "Don't. Don't cut me again. I don't want you to take another part of me. *Please*."

I hated that I went straight to begging.

No cursing.

No commanding.

Just straight-up whimpering because if he took my tattoo...if he took Neri from me. Took *myself* from me.

I had nothing left.

I'd be lost.

Lost and broken and...

Fuck.

He'll win.

I wouldn't be able to withstand him.

I-I'll become his.

"*Baba*, don't do this. Take me upstairs. We'll talk. I'll listen for once. I promise I'll—*fuck.*" I hissed in pain as the sharp stab of a needle pierced my arm.

I thrashed in the chair, but it made no difference. The leather straps had never yielded before, and they didn't yield now.

I was trapped.

Tied down.

Completely at their fucking mercy.

My pulse skyrocketed as the doctor stabbed me repeatedly, following the edge of my tattoo, administering the numbing drug until my entire arm felt spongy and sluggish and soft.

"No. Fuck. Don't. I don't want you to do this. Don't cut me again. *Please.*"

"I don't want to do it either," Cem whispered. "I considered laser or other ways of removal, but they all take time. And we don't have time anymore. This is the quickest way to free you. Believe me, causing you pain is the last thing I want to do. I love you, Aslan. With all my heart. I'm only doing this for your protection and future happiness."

"Fuck you." My temper snapped, hot and brutal, as the doctor ripped open a scalpel and placed it inside a metal tray beside a stack of gauze and something that looked suspiciously like skin floating in a vial. "I'll never forgive you for this. No matter how much you break me. No matter how much you think you've won, one day...I will remember. I will fight back. I will hunt you, hurt you, and then I will motherfucking *kill* you."

Terror tore through me, and I let loose another torrent of filth. "I will rip you apart, Cem Kara. I will dismantle your empire. I will slaughter your men. I will piss on your bones and dance on your grave. I will fucking *end* you."

"I appreciate your fury, Aslan. You are living up to your name quite well, but...you will never hurt me." He sighed heavily. "Want to know why?" His eyes flashed. "Because I have never failed at this. Not once. And I will not fail my only son. This is the beginning of us, Aslan. This is the beginning of everything."

Nodding at the doctor, he ordered, "Do it."

Memories of passing out just before they hacked off my leg ploughed into me.

The *helplessness.*

The tragic awful powerlessness.

That was the worst part.

Knowing my body wasn't mine.

My mind wasn't mine.

My life was theirs, and they could do whatever they damn well wanted.

"Fuck you!" I screamed as the knife traced the outline of my lion's mane, tugging and pulling but painless. "Fuck all of you!"

No one replied.

My blood plopped onto the floor.

I kept on screaming as my siren was slowly peeled off me.

Three years...

"I spoke to Nerida tonight. It seems she's formed a habit of calling me each year on the anniversary of your death." Cem chuckled as he finished buckling the leather around my left arm.

My eyes locked on the ugly scar where my tattoo used to be.

I supposed I should be grateful that I'd gotten so sick after the surgery. For a simple 'routine' slice and dice, my system went into shock.

My lack of health folded in on itself and I spent the past few months in a fugue of antibiotics, painkillers, dreams, nightmares, and misery. The fever had wracked me to the point of becoming skeletal again, and I had nothing left.

Nothing.

My memories of Neri were tainted with blood.

My recollections of happiness and being in love were completely swamped by grief.

I was heavy inside. Endlessly fucking heavy and full of sadness I couldn't swim out of.

I was down on the ocean floor.

Smothered by salt, gagging on brine.

My ears rang as the guards finished securing my thighs to the chair.

My first day back and my heart didn't kick, didn't flinch, didn't climb above the erratic beat it now called normal.

I had nothing left to give.

I'm done.

Patting my cheek, Cem said quietly, "She still believes you're alive."

I'm not alive.

I'm dead.

The breath in my lungs is rancid.

The thoughts in my head are rotten.

Forget me, Neri.

There's nothing left anymore.

I didn't respond, and Cem clucked his tongue. "I thought you'd be a bit more lively after a few months of lying around all day. You're healed. The doctor gave you a clean bill of health." He ran his fingertips over my newly healed bright-red scar. "Even your arm is neat and tidy. You'd never even know anything used to exist there."

The smallest urge to shout back. To scream in his face. To spit on his shoes.

But then the urge was gone, sinking into the oily, festering pit inside me.

Ducking to his haunches, Cem looked up at me.

I stared blankly into him, not focusing, not caring.

"Aslan…" He winced and cupped my cheek. "Rally round, son. It's okay. You're doing so well. One more day and that's it. I promise. One more day and then you and I will leave this place forever. You will never have to come back down here. I'll take you to the *hammam* (Turkish baths) where you'll be pampered and massaged for hours. I'll order all your favourite foods. I'll dress you in all the finest clothes. You will be free, Aslan."

I looked away.

I had nothing to say.

Silence thickened.

Slowly, Cem stood and nodded at the guard operating the machine.

I didn't move as the electrodes were hooked up to my shoulder sockets—one of the few places that didn't have scars from previous shocks.

Stepping away so he wouldn't run the risk of being electrocuted by touching me, Cem ordered, "Moderate power. Five seconds."

BANG.

I groaned.

My back snapped in half as power as hot as the sun and sharp as daggers bolted through me.

One.

Two.

Three.

Four.

Five.

Numbers.

They were the only thing I had left now.

Counting the seconds while I sizzled alive.

One.

Two.

Three wishes that I could just die and be done with this.

I involuntarily gasped and fought to survive as the power cut off, leaving my organs smoking, my blood popping, and my bones ready to glow in the dark.

This kind of persuasion wasn't new

I'd endured this over and over for years.

Yet…right there, in that moment with no tattoo to cling to and everything stripped from me in the form of skin ribbons, chopped legs, and hot fevers, I reached my threshold.

I'd been whittled from whole into nothing.

I'd been cut and shocked. Tortured and brainwashed.

And my body and mind finally said...no more.

No more!

I cracked.

All those spiderweb fractures.

All those fissures that'd been working their way through me finally eroded my sanity.

With an earthquake that tore my soul in two...I started to cry.

Silently, stiffly, tears rained down my cheeks. I didn't have the strength to do anything else.

I couldn't blink, couldn't sniff, couldn't cope.

I just wanted to die.

Please, please let me die.

Cem's hands landed on my cheeks and tipped my heavy head back.

His face danced and puddled in my tears.

He looked like a painting. A watercolour. A bleeding canvas where all my hopes had been drawn over, scrubbed out, and now I was empty.

Ever so slowly, he held up one hand.

Two fingers stuck up as he curled the rest into a fist.

With a tenderness that made my shattered heart splutter, he whispered, "How many fingers am I holding up, Aslan?"

And I knew.

I finally understood.

I sighed as blistering, comforting warmth coiled through me.

I get it now.

What a relief.

What a gift to sink into understanding that it wasn't the answer that mattered but my surrender.

My surrender to him.

To this.

To everything he wanted me to be.

Licking at my tears, I sucked in a breath and whispered with every broken piece of me, "How many do you want it to be, *baba?*"

My torturer, abuser, mutilator, and capturer suddenly choked on a sob. His forehead crashed against mine and tears ran down his face. "Finally, Aslan." He kissed me, smothering me in affection. "*Finally.*"

Leaning back, he stroked my cheekbones with his thumbs as he asked, "Who are you?"

I sank deeper into the surrender where it was soft and suffocating, enveloping and numbing.

Just like the scalpel had been nullified by anaesthetic, my breaking was hidden by my abdication of everything that I knew and loved and ever was.

I'm nothing.

And it was liberating.

"I'm whatever you want me to be."

"Where are you?"

"I'm exactly where I'm supposed to be."

"Who is Nerida Taylor?"

"Who would you like her to be, *baba*?"

"Are you in love with Nerida Taylor?"

"Do you want me to be in love with her?"

"Good boy." He kissed my cheeks. "Good boy. I'm so proud of you."

I didn't react.

There was no need.

I was gone.

I was reprogrammed.

Fixed.

Free.

Standing, Cem said, "Tonight, on the phone to Neri, I gave her my absolute word that Aslan Avci was dead. I told her I'd made damn sure of it. Was I right to tell her that?"

Slowly, as if someone else pulled my strings and made me move, I answered, "Aslan Avci is dead."

"And who are you?" He crossed his arms, his eyes searching mine as if still believing a part of me would fight.

"I am yours."

He groaned as if I couldn't have given him a better gift.

"Unstrap him," he snapped.

The guards shot forward, unbuckling the leather and releasing me.

All it had taken was one last electrocution.

And it was done.

Giving me a smile, Cem headed toward the open exit. Disappearing for a moment, he came back in with a long, polished stick. Holding it horizontally in two hands, he presented it to me like a sword to a knight. "This is for you. Today, you deserve it. I'm so happy to finally have you back, Aslan. After almost three decades of searching and hoping, you are finally back where you belong."

Using the arm rests of the awful chair, I stood and braced my lean belly to balance on one leg. My black track pants hung off narrow hips, tied in a knot below my left knee. My strength had vanished thanks to the darkness and fevers. I would have to build a better core so I could compensate for the lack of a second foot, but I was steady enough as I reached out and took the cane my father offered.

I didn't speak as I ran my fingers over the dark polished wood before studying the complex carving of a lion roaring and its flowing mane offering the perfect grip for my palm.

"It's beautiful."

"Like you," Cem whispered. "My beautiful boy."

Slowly, I pressed the metal end against the stone floor of the cave and braced against it.

I hopped forward, relying on the cane more than I normally would after the months of illness.

The new scar on my arm twinged as I balled my hand. The pulled-together flesh tight where once there was a tattoo.

That ink was gone now.

Just like the man who loved a siren was gone.

I was empty.

Silent.

Nothing.

"Shall we go home?" Cem asked with tears in his eyes.

I nodded. "Thank you for the gift, *baba*."

He embraced me and kissed my cheek. "Thank you for remembering who you are. I know you'll feel a little strange and empty right now. You'll be hungry for new thoughts and longing for truths that you can trust, but all I ask is patience. Those answers will come. You are a clean slate, Aslan. You will learn who you were meant to be with time, and it will be my honour to teach you."

Looping his arm around my waist, he pulled me forward. "Now, lean on me. I know you haven't been well and you're weak. Allow me to take care of you."

I didn't say a word.

I merely let him support me as the click of my new cane echoed, and the shuffle of my hop ricocheted around the cave that was no longer my cell.

I let him guide me from the catacombs, turned my back on my pain, and left a trail of submission behind me.

I was his perfectly disciplined pet.

I was his mind-blank son, and finally…I was home.

Chapter Forty-Five

ASLAN

(Heart in Galician: Corazón*)*

Present...

BLOOD, BRAINS, AND CHIPS OF BONE went flying.

The gun kicked hard in my hand, the sharp scent of gunpowder clouding around me.

The thud of his corpse as he fell.

The shatter of his skull as he died.

Who was he?

I didn't care.

What had he done to deserve this?

It didn't matter.

My father had told me to shoot him...so I did.

"You did well, Aslan." Cem grinned, holding out his hand. "Now, give me back the gun."

Instantly, I spun the handle and passed it to him. Ten guards surrounded us, keeping Cem and me safe from any enemies. The dark warehouse had minimal lighting on, pretending to be a disused factory instead of the sorting and packing headquarters where shipments of pure cocaine came in to be weighed, bagged, then given to mules to carry worldwide or sold to local gangs to distribute.

Ever since my breaking two years ago, I'd been slowly shown behind the curtains of Cem's operations. For most of my fourth year with him, Cem treated me like the lord he said I was. He flew me overseas in his private plane and smuggled me past border officials thanks to obscene wealth and power. He did what he promised, taking me to his estates and boltholes, revealing every mansion and palace.

He kept me hidden because he said he wasn't ready to tell the world who I was, even though he'd made it very well known to his generals. He said he wanted to keep me for himself before letting me loose as his heir.

But I guessed there was another reason.

I suspected that year was a test. A test to see if I meant what I said and wasn't faking what I did.

Each night we spent together in some library in some expensive home, drinking expensive liquor and discussing his expensive tastes, I felt him watching me, studying me, trying to see if there was a part of me that wasn't shattered.

A part ready to rebel.

But I didn't care.

There was nothing to watch, nothing to study.

If he wanted me to smile, I smiled.

If he wanted me to kill, I killed.

I'd sunk willingly into surrender and had done what my body forced me to do.

I healed.

I grew strong on the outside, but on the inside, I was riddled with weakness and wrongness. I had nothing left. No fight. No free will.

I was his perfect plaything, and as long as I remained in that listless numbness, I was safe. As long as I forgot the siren of my past and ignored the dreams of moonlight on turquoise sea…I wasn't hurt, wasn't tortured, wasn't chopped into pieces or flayed alive.

I would rather be adrift with none of my own convictions than be strapped into the chair again, so I let his warped education convert me. I forfeited who I'd been for the new man he'd made me.

That fourth year was a blur of disillusion and merciful disinterest. Just because I no longer existed unless he told me how to exist didn't mean I'd suddenly been implanted with his wants and desires.

His empire was his.

I would run it if he wished, but I didn't care why or for how long.

How could I?

How could I care for anything when I was impervious to everything?

"That's what happens to traitors," Cem snarled, yanking me back to the murder I just committed at his command. He shoved his pistol back into the holster beneath his immaculate suit. "Steal from me and it's not a matter of *if* you'll get caught but *when*."

The thirty or so workers in the coke factory kneeled in their underwear. Men and women.

They all trembled and bowed with their foreheads kissing the concrete floor. In the back of the warehouse, where the windows had been blackened and the walls reinforced, bright lights shone on massive trays full of white powder. Workers wore masks to prevent inhaling the potent dust, and crates of little plastic baggies to be filled and sold were delivered daily to keep up demand.

I knew the weekly cost of those baggies.

I kept tallies on the many overheads and expenses of running so many different enterprises in this empire. The drug trade was the most lucrative after the payoffs to politicians and police, lobbying for lesser laws, and the 'donations' Cem gave to shopkeepers to ply our product over anyone else.

"Get back to work," Cem snarled. Spinning on his heel, he marched forward, always so bold, always too quick.

I struggled to keep up, limping beside him, the click of my cane loud in the echoey warehouse.

By the time we reached the exit, Cem had slowed his pace and visible annoyance pinched his eyebrows. "I don't know why you don't let me get a proper leg made for you. Money is no object, Aslan. You could have the finest titanium or carbon steel. Fuck, you could probably have a robot limb fashioned that could make you fly if you wanted. Why do you insist on hobbling around on a piece of unfitted wood that was only ever meant to be temporary?"

Because the pain keeps me subservient.

Because the cane reminds me of what I had to give up to be accepted.

Because without the constant discomfort and hobble, I might start to remember that I'm not a cripple and I'm not your pet and that would not be good...for either of us.

Cem believed that the moment I'd snapped and surrendered to him, I was 'cured'.

Unfortunately, that submission had only lasted for nineteen months and had been slowly fading ever since.

When he'd locked me in the cave again for my two-weeklong reminder, just before officially naming me his successor, I'd come face-to-face with how many lies resided inside me.

He'd electrocuted me, like before.

I'd endured, like I always did.

I submitted, like I'd been trained.

But a fractured part of me, a carefully hidden and hating part, tasted the first flavour of mutiny.

I didn't like it.

I fought against the whispers slowly returning to my mind.

The daydreams of a girl I wasn't supposed to remember.

The longing for a home that was forbidden.

I wouldn't jeopardise my existence by letting myself wake up from this sleep he'd trapped me in, but... I also didn't know if I could stop it.

Only pain could do that.

The pain of my missing limb.

The pain of the buckles around my thigh and the clunky carved foot that was shoved inside a polished shoe Cem had insisted was used to hide the fact that his son and heir was damaged.

Damaged by him.

Hacked into pieces by *him*.

I knew he disliked that I wasn't whole.

That I was disabled, for use of a better word.

But it hadn't stopped him from publicly announcing me as his next in line.

I wore the scar on my palm to prove it.

He'd given me power.

But with that power came retribution, and if I ever stepped out of the fog of obedience, a bullet would fly into my brain as quickly as the one I'd sent into the stranger I'd just dispatched.

His guards were loyal.

His guards were fucking everywhere.

"I'm fine, *baba*," I muttered as I followed him outside. Glancing at the full moon above, we were ushered into a black SUV. Guards climbed into the three SUVs in front and behind us before we pulled out in a snaking convoy.

My fist curled around my cane as I stabbed it between my legs. The roaring lion glowered at me in the gloomy car interior. "Are we going home?"

Cem shot me a look where we sat side by side in the backseat. He typed something on his phone; I tore my eyes away from the glowing screen.

I'd been given everything I could ever want.

I knew the pins and passwords to Cem's every account.

He'd taken me to his bank manager and had my name listed on every document required for access and transfers, and he'd even amended his will so I, and only I, inherited his almost billion-dollar empire.

He gave me his trust by giving me his business.

Yet he never gave me access to a laptop, phone, or tablet.

For a long time, I hadn't cared. My brain was mush, and I'd existed in an in-between place of submission and servitude.

But now...those little whispers hissed to snatch his phone.

To call a siren.

To message my soulmate—

"No. We have another errand to run tonight. We're visiting the *Peri Ev*."

My insides turned to ice. I hardly ever translated Turkish to English in my head anymore, but that name, it fucking horrified me. *Peri Ev*. Fairy House.

"Has there been a new arrival?" I asked coldly.

Cem finished typing and put his phone into his breast suit pocket. "Yes. Six new girls. Four are accepting. Two are not. They're causing problems."

"What sort of problems?"

"Breaking in problems." He shot me a look. "That's where you come in."

"Me?" A shiver ran down my spine. "What do you expect me to do about it?"

"Teach them a lesson. Show them that no is not an option. We cannot sell merchandise that doesn't behave, Aslan. You know this."

"You want me to fuck one of them?"

His eyes narrowed. "Is that going to be a problem?"

I held his stare and ignored his question. "Did you mean what you said? That the day I became your son, you'd let me pick my own woman?"

He stilled beside me, his nostrils flaring. "Are you finally ready to take a wife and make your own heir, or is a piece of you still clinging to your Australian fling?"

My teeth gritted. He knew she was more than just a fling. And he also knew that Neri was the trick I'd used to avoid his mind control for so long.

But I daren't speak her name.

I barely even had the courage to *think* it.

But I also couldn't tell him that the chances of me having an heir with anyone was slim to none. I could never sire a child with someone who wasn't *her* because my body was incapable.

I looked out the window at the pretty streets and imposing buildings.

I didn't reply.

"This is Tulip," a big-breasted woman with black hair down to her ass and a slim cigarette dangling on her bottom lip said. Puffing on her smoke, she cocked her head at the naked girl bowing at my feet. "She's refusing to use the arts she has been taught, which means she cannot be sold. She claims all the men I've brought her don't deserve her pussy or her mouth." The madame grinned with yellowed teeth. "But she cannot say that now."

Striding forward in her chunky combat boots and floaty purple dress—a direct contradiction of fashion—the heavy-set woman kicked the naked girl and spat on her bare thighs. "See, Tulip? See that I do care? You said no man deserves to touch you. Well, I have brought you a lion."

Turning to bow at me, the madame blew out a ring of blue smoke. "Thank you for coming, Aslan Kara. We have heard much about our *patron*'s heir. It is a pleasure to serve you. I just wish I could offer you a girl better trained, but…" Her dark eyes flicked to Cem. "Your father insisted that you are skilled at pleasure and can help break in this new fairy. We have a trade lined up with a most honourable client, but…until she is correctly trained…well." She chuckled with a shrug. "She will have to have her wings clipped here, so she knows her place and doesn't dishonour our reputation for the highest quality girls."

In another life, I would've been appalled.

If I hadn't had my humanity electrocuted out of me, I would've questioned why a woman was happy to trade in her own sex. How could she distance herself from offering up a girl to rape when it could so easily happen to her?

But I didn't care.

All I cared about was going home, locking myself in my room, and ripping off this splintering excuse of a leg.

"I'm not interested," I muttered.

My father sniffed beside me. "You will do your part, Aslan. As we discussed." Grinning at the madame, he added, "Now, Elif, please show me the rest of your fairies. I heard a prominent American businessman is paying us a visit next week. He's requested a private viewing of at least three girls that could fit into his uses back home."

"Of course." Elif bowed. "This way." Stomping to the door, her purple dress swirled and twinkled.

"I'll leave four guards outside, Aslan." Cem clapped a hand on my shoulder. "To protect you."

"Thank you, *baba*." I nodded. "Very kind of you to keep me safe."

"Always." He squeezed me affectionately, then let me go.

The snick of the closing door sent prickles down my back. The silence in the small but decadent room thickened as my gaze fell on the naked girl, and hers rose to me towering over her. Blonde hair, blue eyes—

Crystal-blue eyes. Sea-glass eyes. Sky-blue eyes.

Neri's eyes.

I swayed a little; I clutched my cane.

The girl noticed, her stare narrowing on my walking stick. "So you're the one who's going to rape me first?"

The twang of English.

The foreignness of a language that I used to speak so fluently but now sounded so wrong.

It didn't belong in this country.

She didn't belong in this country.

Every awful nightmare I'd had of actually letting Cem bring Neri here to rule beside me popped like dirty bubbles.

I could never.

I would never.

Fuck, I could *never* do that to her.

This was what I was.

A peddler of skin, a plyer of drugs, a murderer of innocent men.

"You fucking asshole." She shot to her feet and balled her hands. "You probably can't even understand me. You're nothing more than a savage. Well, do your fucking worst. I'm done fearing you pricks. Karma will get you one day. One day, you'll be sold into slavery. One day, you'll be so fucking hurt you'll wish you were dead. And when that day happens, I'll be there. I'll be a ghost watching you suffer, all because of what you did to me."

My ears rang as my mind slowly remembered the nuances of English and the syntax of righteous hate.

I'd forgotten how that tasted.

How fury burned the tongue.

How rage ached the teeth.

How anger blistered in your bones and sliced dangerously through your blood.

The tiniest shroud of my conditioning fell away, all because of this hot-tempered American girl. This feisty, angry girl who would most likely be sold and screaming by tomorrow. She'd last a week, a month, a year before she was tossed away like a broken toy, replaceable and forgettable.

My knuckles whitened around my cane.

Fuck.

She bared her teeth and marched toward me.

I couldn't move back.

I'd never quite mastered that on this fucking leg.

I stood my ground as she slapped my cheek and hissed, "I hope you die. I hope you fucking—"

I backhanded her.

One moment, she was standing. The next, she groaned on the floor.

Ice settled over me.

I hadn't meant to strike her.

I hadn't commanded my arm to do such a thing.

Yet…it'd happened.

Because I'm my father's son.

She was disrespectful. Rude. And didn't know a damn thing about me.

I'd already been tortured. I'd been raped of thoughts, hopes, and sanity. I was a ghost of the man I'd been and…

None of that is her fault.

Pinching the bridge of my nose, I sucked in a shaky breath. Out of the corner of my eye, I caught my reflection in the huge gilded mirror angled to catch every activity that might happen on the bed. The reflection shimmered strangely, oddly contorted.

Another bolt of ice tumbled down my spine.

We're being watched.

The mirror was two-way.

I didn't know how I knew, but it was so fucking obvious.

Cem hadn't gone to see other fairies. He'd gone behind that mirror to see if I obeyed.

My chest suffocated with jumbling emotions, but the one that won the quickest was black-dripping mirth.

I chuckled under my breath.

I couldn't control my sick laughter.

I'd been thrown in here as the lion ready to devour the mouse.

I'd thought I was better than that.

I'd *hoped* I was better than that, even after five years of brainwashing.

Turns out…I'm not.

I'm as bad as him. As awful and sick and monstrous.

Cem will be so proud.

Dropping my hand, I limped forward, my cane sinking into the carpet.

The girl scurried away from me, scrambling over the embroidered cushions on the floor. She was pretty in a wholesome way. Full chest, rounded stomach, waxed pussy. She had a tattoo of a sunburst on her right hip and her light hair hung dead straight to her chin.

She looked so pale scurrying over the emerald and ruby rug. So afraid as she bumped against the bed where four carved posts soared to the black ceiling with swathes of gold velvet draped down the sides.

If Cem wanted a show, I'd give him a show.

Sitting heavily on the bed, I kicked out my fake leg, tossed my cane behind me, and snarled at the girl on the ground. "Kneel between my thighs," I growled in English.

The words had a magic.

A wonderous kind of power that gave me what my tattoo had done.

They were a link.

A direct tether to a past I couldn't forget and the shreds of my old self bled through.

I might be Aslan Kara.

The son of a Turkish crime lord and successor to all his fortunes.

But…I was also an orphan, refugee, and husband.

Fuck…I'm a husband.

To Neri.

Just saying her name sent another frisson of freedom down my spine.

I sucked in a breath.

Hope barrelled through me.

If I could think of her name without flinching…perhaps…perhaps—

Cem will know.

He'll put you back down there.

He'll strap you to the chair.

He'll turn on the machine.

Cold sweat broke out over my forehead, and I bent down, snatched the girl's hair, and dragged her unwillingly between my legs. Snapping my thighs together, I held her there even as she struggled. With swift fingers, I unbuckled my belt, popped my button, and tore down my zipper. My tailored suit was made of the finest material and the slacks splayed open in invitation. Spreading my blazer and untucking my black shirt, I didn't bother shoving down my boxer-briefs.

"Fuck you!" the girl screeched, trying to bite me as I hauled her closer.

Burying my face into her neck, I hissed into her ear, "I am not like the others. I won't hurt you, and I'm sorry that I just did. But if we're both going to survive tonight, you need to pretend."

She stilled and sucked in a breath, listening.

"Pretend to suck me off."

She wrenched back. "I'm not putting my mouth on any part of you—"

"Quiet," I snarled, shooting a look at the mirror. "We're being watched. Behave and pretend, and I'll do what I can to get you out of here."

Her hands landed on my bunched quads. "Why should I believe you?" she whispered. "You're just like them. You *are* one of them."

"I'm not."

"Prove it."

"I'm trying."

"Get me out of here."

"Pretend to suck me, and I'll do my best."

She fought me until I let her go just enough to look me in the eyes. She stared at me for the longest moment. She dove into the wreckage of my soul. "Help me," she breathed. "Please…"

I didn't reply.

I didn't want to lie that I might not be able to.

I sucked in a breath as her hands slid up my thighs and went to the waistband of my boxer-briefs.

My hands landed automatically on her shoulders to stop her.

I didn't want her touching me, regardless of what I just said.

She could be a real fairy with pixie dust and love potions, and I wouldn't be able to get hard. I wouldn't be able to come.

I was as flaccid as I'd ever been.

But how much could the people behind the mirror see?

Would they be able to see my nakedness or know that this was a sham?

Glancing around the room as subtly as I could, I searched for other mirrors.

My heart sank as I glanced into the canopy of the four poster.

Not a mirror.

Cameras.

Red-blinking, recording cameras angled right at my fucking crotch.

Shit.

My stomach roiled.

My heart pounded.

My hands fell off the girl's shoulders as I surrendered yet again to another version of torture.

She looked up from my lap, her gaze burning with fear, her eyebrows pinched together. "So I just pretend…?"

"I-I—" My voice cracked. I swallowed hard. "I don't think that will be enough."

Hate hardened her face. "If you're playing me, I'll fucking—"

"*Quiet*," I seethed. "Just…free me and angle over my cock. Don't do anything more."

She cursed under her breath.

I waited for her to fight me.

My brain whirred with a new plan to prevent us from being hurt tonight, but she finally obeyed and shifted higher on her knees.

With my heart in my throat and my eyes locked on the mirror, I pasted an expression that I hoped resembled lust and greed as the girl exposed me.

Flicking me a glance, she reached for me.

I flinched as her hands curled around a part of my body that hadn't been touched without pain in so many years.

It sickened me.

Repulsed me.

"Just…act like you're sucking," I hissed, doing my best not to enunciate English words in-case Cem could read my lips in the mirror. "I don't want you to actually—"

I groaned as her mouth encircled my tip.

Hot and wet.

Sick and twisted.

I froze in horror.

Maybe I would get hard.

Maybe the electrocutions had fried that part of me.

Perhaps my steadfast, soul-bound loyalty to Neri had broken in the years I'd been abused.

I didn't want to know.

I wouldn't fucking survive if my body betrayed me as well as my mind.

But I couldn't stop her.

Couldn't throw her across the room or smash in the mirror.

Cem still believed I was fully under his control.

I wouldn't let him believe otherwise. Not yet. Not until I had a chance at finally getting free.

I couldn't breathe as the girl's head bobbed up and down. Whoever was watching would have a perfect view of her bare ass as her mouth pumped between my spread legs.

It would look convincing.

It *felt* convincing.

I gritted my teeth as the violation of her mouth proved that sometimes an act of love could be done out of desperation. Both of us were trapped. Both of us hated the other.

A few minutes ticked past while she worked on me.

The horror that I might respond slowly faded as I shrivelled inside.

The longer she sucked me, the more I shut down until I didn't feel her. Didn't feel her mouth or touch or much of anything.

I was numb.

Just like I'd been for almost two years.

And I liked it.

It let my mind skip to other scenarios.

I wouldn't be able to fuck her.

With the cameras angled all around us, the footage would show I faked it. There was no way I could have sex with this girl without it being completely fucking obvious that I was soft.

Cem was shot in the groin.

The thought exploded in my head. The memory of Emre telling me the story of Cem's unfortunate shooting roared in my ears.

Is it true?

If it is…

I moved before I even knew what I was doing.

Wrenching the girl off my lap, I shoved her back and threw one of the cashmere blankets from the bed at her. "Here."

She licked her lips and grabbed the blanket. Her face shot white. "W-What are you going to do? I-I did what you said. I even went so far to actually *do* it. Despite every bone in my body saying it was wrong." Tears shot to her eyes. "I did what you said! Now you have to help me. Keep your side of the bargain and—"

"Enough." Soaring to my feet, I grabbed my cane and limped with my pants undone and my soft cock out all the way to the mirror. I showed my shame. I let the world see my defection.

Because I wasn't the only one with this problem.

My impotence came from true love.

My father's came from a bullet.

I'd never seen him with a woman.

Never heard him fucking or smelling of perfume or lust when he came to hurt me.

It was a gamble, but one that I was bold enough to play.

"You want me to fuck her, *baba*?" I growled into the mirror. "Well, I can't. I can't get it up. I'm broken…just like you." I grabbed myself and jerked. "My cock doesn't work. I can't sire a child. I can't fucking get hard or—"

The door to the room slammed open.

Cem stumbled inside. His usually handsome face was drawn and eyes wide with horror. Charging toward me, he wrapped me in the tightest embrace, all while my hand remained locked around my useless cock.

Useless, unless Neri was near.

But he didn't need to know that.

He would never know I couldn't keep my hands off her. That I could come just from being inside her. That we'd have sex twice, three times a day, and each time she made my world ignite. Being with her was spiritual as well as sexual. Being with her was where I came alive.

As far as he was concerned, I was a pointless virgin who shared the same affliction as his mutilated father.

"You know about me?" He pulled back. He didn't spare the girl a single glance, his entire attention on me. "You know? How?"

I nodded as I stepped out of his embrace and tucked myself away. Zipping up my slacks and buckling my belt, I said, "Emre told me. It was why you were so set on finding me. You couldn't have another child. You were shot—"

"Right in my dick. I almost bled out." He flinched. "When I woke up, I was a completely different man to the one I'd been when I heard the gun go off."

"I'm sorry."

"I lost both my testicles and half my cock."

"I'm—"

"I haven't been able to find pleasure in almost three decades."

"I—"

"To hear that you live that same nightmare?" He shook his head. "Fuck, it kills me, Aslan."

I pointed at the girl. "It wasn't her fault. As a present to me, release her. Let her go. She tried. She was willing and obedient. She deserves to be allowed to go home."

Cem threw an unreadable look at the girl. Finally, he nodded. "Fine, yes, I'll let her go." Wrapping his arm around my shoulders, he guided me toward the door. "Let's go home. I'm sorry about this. I-It won't happen again."

I limped beside him, my cane swinging.

We exited into the plush corridor.

Cem nodded at an evil-eyed guard on the way past.

The guard tipped his head at the silent command.

My heart lurched.

No.

Don't—

Before I could stop him, the guard marched in, withdrew his gun, and shot the blonde girl in the head.

"You said you'd release her!" I roared, limp-pacing the immaculate study where Cem had commanded I join him for a late nightcap before bed.

"You haven't raised your voice in years, Aslan. Why on earth are you this irate about a nameless slave girl?"

"Because I gave her my word."

"Your word that you would help her."

"Yes!"

"You did help her. She's free now."

"She's dead!"

"Some might say that was a better existence than being traded to a new master."

"You're the one doing the fucking trading!" I shouted. "Shut down that part of your company. Shut down the Fairy House. Fire that awful Madame Elif. Stop hurting people, Cem!"

He went deathly still. "I am your father, Aslan. I thought you understood this."

"Fine!" I whacked my cane against the fireplace, chipping off a piece of marble from a delicate flower wrapped around a motif of swans and river reeds. "Please, *baba*. I will do whatever you ask of me. I will run your empire just the way you want it. You have my word I will dedicate my life to your business, just like you want me to. But I will *not* run a trafficking ring. No amount of 'persuasion' will change my mind. No amount of girls or—"

"You lied to me, Aslan. You lied to my face. Again. Don't you think that's why I got you out of there so fast?" He stood from where he sat in a wingback by the bookcases, nursing his tumbler of liquor. Striding toward me, his face slipped into pure malice. "You're not the only one who can put on a performance. Do you think I bought your little sob story? Do you honestly think I would've let that girl live after you made her believe the boss and his heir are eunuchs? Do you truly think I give a rat's ass about her life when *you're* the one putting both of us at risk?"

"Me?" I bared my teeth. "How?"

"You will give me a grandchild, Aslan. I've worked too hard for too long to let what I've built only last your generation. This wealth will be passed down through our lineage. You will have more than one heir, so if one goes missing, you don't have the same misfortune as I did at hunting them down. In fact, you will give me many. And sooner rather than later. I'd hoped you would choose a nice Turkish girl. I'm traditional and want you to be married with a woman on your arm who will support and adore you. But...I was also happy with you spreading your seed to any girl you wished. You could've had a harem for all I cared. I don't care where my grandchildren come from as long as they are yours."

"Aren't you listening?" I snapped. "I can't sire any children because I can't get it up!"

Stopping close, too close, he sipped on his *rakı*. The white cloudy liquid made from grapes and aniseed tainted his breath as he snarled, "Five years I've spoken to Nerida Taylor. Five years I've known something that you do not."

Familiar horror oozed through me hearing Neri's name on his tongue. "Don't talk about her. She's in the past. You said you'd leave her alone—"

"You're going to marry her."

"What? How?" My knees almost gave out. I clung to my cane. "She thinks I'm dead. Remember?"

"Tomorrow, I'm going to arrange men to go and collect her."

"Fuck no, you're not." I tripped away from him, my limping worse as my balance grew scrambled. "Leave her the fuck alone. We had a deal."

"A deal that I'm beginning to think is also a lie."

"I don't want her anywhere near this place or you," I seethed. "Forget you even know she exists."

"Just how long have you been chewing on your true thoughts, Aslan? I thought we'd erased all those feelings. You have no more tattoo to cling to. Nothing left to need. I've given you everything you could ever dream of and this is how you repay me?"

"If you go after Neri, I'll kill you myself."

"And there it is." He toasted me and swallowed the last mouthful of *rakı*. "The truth. Finally."

"Truth? What truth?"

"Listen to me, Son, and listen to me well. I *will* bring Neri here. You can keep her just like you've always wanted. I'll arrange a nice wedding for you both, and you can decide how much she will learn of our family enterprise. You can keep her in the dark and on her back or you can have her rule beside you, it makes no matter to me." He stalked toward me, backing me into the wall. "And in return, you will fuck your new bride until you knock her up like you've done once before. You will get her pregnant again. You will pop out another child and another and another. As long as you obey me, Aslan, the mother of your children will not be harmed. But betray me again, try to lie to me again, and I will slit her throat from ear to ear. If you even *think* about going behind my back, I'll have Çetin flay her alive. Do. You. Hear. Me?"

My ears rang. "I-I—" I swallowed hard. "What do you mean...get her pregnant *again*?"

He patted my cheek, chuckling. "Smile, Aslan. You're going to get what you miss most of all. I'm giving you what you need. And I'm not even going to strap you into the chair again, even though I suspect you greatly need another session. I won't hurt you again because I see now that Neri is the key to your obedience above everything else. Pity I realised that too late. But at least your little stunt tonight proved that once she is here, you will behave yourself. I know you will. Because you value her life over yours."

I couldn't keep up. I felt electrocuted by his words, just as excruciating as the machine. "I-It wasn't a stunt. I truly can't fuck anyone—"

"Only Neri."

"Even her. I never touched her. I can't—"

"Are you not listening, Aslan? You can't lie your way out of this. You can't try to convince me that you're a sad little virgin who's always had a cock that doesn't work. You can't hide the truth."

"What truth?"

"The truth that you and Neri had sex."

"You can't possibly know that unless you had cameras in our fucking bedroom—"

"I have evidence." He grinned. "Want to see?" Putting his empty glass down, he went to the bookcase, tilted a particular leather-bound volume, and revealed a safe tucked in the shelves. Inputting the code, he opened it, yanked out a photo, and marched back toward me.

I stood by the cold fireplace.

I couldn't fucking move.

He grabbed my hand that wasn't wrapped around my cane and shoved the photo into it.

"Here."

I raised the picture.

And every smothering imprisonment, every painful shock, every slice, dice, cut, and flay disintegrated.

The conditioning he'd wrapped me in.

The reprogramming he'd forced into my brain.

It broke, smoked, burned to the ground, and I *remembered*.

Everything.

I felt.

Everything.

I choked.

On everything.

Tears shot to my eyes as I drank in a picture of Neri. She stood on *The Fluke*. Her face was drawn, her eyes full of sorrow. In her arms, she held a heavy wreath made of pretty flowers. They were moored off Low Isles. The island where we'd married beneath the moon and consummated our vows beneath the stars.

He's been spying on her.

All this time.

"Do you see the similarities, Aslan?" Cem said softly. "My men zoomed in as much as they could, but it's enough to see the truth."

My wet gaze tore from the love of my life and locked on the little girl tucked in Jack's arms beside Neri. A little girl with chocolate hair, blended skin, and such a serious little mouth.

Mine.

The truth slammed into my chest, making me woozy.

Mine.

I knew that in every cell, every atom, every nucleus, and breath.

I couldn't look away from her.

My heart wouldn't stop pounding.

"You have a daughter, Aslan," Cem whispered, slotting into my side. "I joked to Neri on the phone recently that perhaps I would make your daughter my heir, seeing as Neri still believes you're dead." He tapped the photo. "In fact, this was taken a couple of years ago. They held a funeral out to sea for you. The flowers floated long after they'd gone, all while fish nibbled at them from below. But your daughter never threw her wreath. She gripped it tightly and took it home with her."

He pried the photo out of my seized hand. "You'll get to meet her soon enough. I'll ensure my men bring both girls to you. Won't that be nice? Your girlfriend and your daughter. We'll have a family reunion, just the four of us." His voice filled with undiluted joy. "I will finally get the chance to have a child running around."

He's a psychopath.

He truly believed we could be happy after all of this.

That I would let him trap them just like he'd trapped me.

I'll kill him.

Tonight.

Before he kidnapped Neri and my...my daughter.

Fuck.

My chest spasmed, and my hand slipped on my cane. "W-What's her name?"

Cem finished locking the photo away before turning to me and grinning. "Nerida named her Ayla. I must admit, I like that she chose a Turkish name. She will make a good partner for you. I see that now."

I blocked him out.

My ears buzzed. My head swam.

Ayla.

Neri called her after the moon. The moonlight and moon halo that'd guided us together. The one thing that was so sacred to us.

Fuck.

I couldn't love her any more if I tried.

I missed her *so fucking much.*

She had a child without me.

She had to raise our daughter alone, all while she thought I was dead.

The guilt.

The regret.

The failing.

I couldn't.

I can't—

Pain roared through me.

Loss.

Grief.

Misery.

Sorrow.

It all centred in my chest.

It crushed my damaged heart.

And for the first time since the chair, the scattered beats that'd never truly healed from the thousand electric shocks forgot how to keep me alive.

A wrenching agony.

A terrifying nothingness.

I clutched my chest.

I dropped to my knees.

My heart pittered, pattered…

…and stopped.

Chapter Forty-Six

ASLAN

(Heart in German: Herz*)*

"ASLAN. WAKE UP. RIGHT THE FUCK NOW."

My eyelids rose unwillingly.

I groaned as a rush of nausea grabbed me around the throat. I went to lurch to the side of my bed and retch, but hands grabbed me, yanking me to the other side, not leaving me the hell alone.

"Stop. What the—" I smacked my lips, tasting sourness and sickness.

What happened?

Last thing I remembered was the god-awful pain as my heart gave up, followed by...nothing.

"You need to get up. Right now," Cem hissed in my face. He hadn't turned on a lamp, and my room was cast in darkness. I had no idea what time it was or how I'd gotten here. The only illumination came from the security spotlights ringing his immaculate gardens below.

My hearing chose that moment to work, and I winced at the sound of his Rottweilers going berserk. Their barking sounded feral. Loud and incessant. "Can you tell your bloody demon dogs to shut the fuck up?" I rubbed my temples where a headache pounded. "Some of us are trying to sleep—"

"Wake up!" Cem slapped me.

I reared back, blinking.

Memories slammed into me.

The photo.

Ayla.

He's going to take her and Neri.

Rage thundered through me, and I launched myself at him.

I have to kill him.

"I won't let you take them!"

"Stop this!" Backhanding me, Cem shot off my bed and ran into my walk-in wardrobe. "We're under attack. We'll discuss everything later. Right now, we need to run."

"Attack? Who's attacking?"

He didn't reply, throwing a pair of trackpants and a black hoodie at me. "Get dressed. Quickly." Tossing me my cane, he barked, "You don't have time to strap on that pointless leg. I'll help you."

His urgency bled through the night, and the parts of me still conditioned enough to obey rushed to slip the pants on and shrug into the hoodie. My core helped me balance easily on one leg as I fisted my cane and hopped toward him.

Without a word, Cem looped his arm around my waist.

My skin crawled. "Don't touch me."

"Now is not the time to hold grudges—"

"Don't fucking *touch me*." I shoved him away. "I don't need you carrying me like an invalid."

"We need to run."

"I can run."

"You're hopping on one leg!"

"Thanks to you!"

"We don't have time for this." Grabbing me around the cheeks, he planted a kiss on my forehead. "Despite everything, Aslan, I love you. I need you to know that. We'll talk about Neri and Ayla. I swear to you, I won't harm them. Please don't fight me tonight. Okay? Just trust that I'm doing everything I can to keep you safe."

Safe?

Like you kept your promise to that girl and shot her?

The sheen of terror in his eyes was so unfamiliar, so foreign that I softened just a little. "What's happening?"

"We're being raided. We need to get to the catacombs. There's a way out down there. I have men standing by to fly us away when we reach the edge of my estate."

"Fine." I clutched my lion cane. "I'll be right behind you."

"Don't lag. If you can't keep up, tell me and I'll help." His eyes narrowed. "Don't be an idiot, Aslan. You fall behind, they'll slaughter you where you stand."

My heart kicked.

I gasped, remembering something else.

"Wait...my heart...it gave out."

"It was a panic attack. Nothing more," Cem muttered, moving toward the exit. "I had Çetin check you over."

"It didn't feel like a normal panic attack."

He stuck his head out the door, checking left and right. Looking back at me, he asked quietly, "How would you know? Have you had panic attacks before?"

I smirked meanly. "Thanks to you, I've had many. In fact, all my issues are thanks to you."

He sighed. "We'll talk. Once we're safe. You have my word, we'll talk."

"Fine."

"Ready?"

I hopped closer to him, bracing my stomach and preparing to run with only one leg. Was that even possible? "Yes."

"Follow me. If we get separated, get to the caves as quickly as you can. Keep going past the one you were kept in. There's a door at the very end." With another look left and right, he charged down the corridor toward the sweeping staircase.

I chased after him the best I could.

In different parts of the mansion, men shouted, shots rang out, and anarchy echoed.

I wanted to ask who was raiding us.

Who would be that stupid?

But Cem didn't slow. He reached the stairs and bolted down them.

Gripping my cane with one hand and running my other down the banister, I hopped as fast and as steadily as I could all the way to the bottom.

Cem glanced back, his eyes wide with worry as a gunshot rang out far too close.

Was it another gang?

The police?

He led me toward the back of the house where the locked door waited to slip down to the ancient labyrinths below, but shadows appeared up ahead.

Five men all dressed in black.

"Freeze!" one of them yelled. "Stay right there."

Cem let loose a stream of Turkish curses before snatching my arm and dragging me into the closest room. Slamming the door closed, he looked for something to wedge beneath the handle, but the only thing in the vast space was a massive stone table holding the biggest vase of flowers I'd ever seen.

I'd been in here once before, and it was pointless. I didn't know what it was used for. Just another example of too much wealth. Too much space to be given an actual purpose.

"Fuck," Cem hissed. Dragging me to the back of the room, the bay window revealed more shadowy men slinking over the manicured box hedges outside.

Without a word, he shoved me against the wall.

Spinning to face the unlocked door, he yanked two guns from the holster hastily strapped over his black nightshirt.

He'd been asleep.

He'd been in bed.

Where were his guards?

"Where is everyone?" I whispered.

"At war," he panted. His eyes met mine, and in a split-second decision that changed both our lives, he passed me one of his guns.

I froze.

My fingers curled around the weight of it.

The mother-of-pearl handle sat like a glacier in my palm. The healing scar from the blood bind I'd sworn as his heir itched and every single despicable moment of the past five years rose and crashed over me.

I gasped as every pain, every cut, every agony crested, broke, and then washed away.

Leaving me empty like the day he'd broken me.

Pure of mind, escaped from expectation...

Free.

I sucked in the quietest, coldest breath.

I shivered.

Cem didn't notice, his attention locked on the door. "Shoot anyone who appears. We can kill them if we work together."

Kill?

Yes, he was good at that.

He'd almost killed me.

He *had* killed me as far as Neri was concerned.

And now, he's going after her.

After my daughter.

He'll brainwash them like he did me.

He'll torture them.

Hurt them.

Make them doubt their own thoughts and hearts.

He's your father.

Flesh and blood.

Don't...

If only he'd had empathy.

If only he'd proven he was a good person beneath the psychotic desire for control. But the small glimpses of kindness he'd shown me didn't equalise the sheer monstrosity in his soul.

He'd shot that girl as if she was nothing, all while pretending to care about my impotence. He knew all along I had a daughter. He tracked Neri, not because she was the mother to his grandchild, but because she was a pawn that could be used against me.

He didn't love me.

He *manipulated* me.

He's a master.

A master at this game.

A true psychopath, narcissist, and bastard.

He doesn't care.

About anyone.

My thumb flicked off the safety. My finger feathered over the trigger.

Boots came to a stop outside the door.

I have to keep her safe. Keep my wife, daughter, and family safe.

He was *not* my family.

He was my enemy, masquerading as kin.

Everything paused.

Everything stilled.

Almost in slow motion, men dressed in black with their faces covered and weapons raised, poured into the useless room.

Cem fired and went to push me sideways, but I hopped out of his reach. I dropped my cane. I brought the gun up with both hands. And I locked eyes with my biological father.

I looked into the nightmare that would always exist in my blood thanks to him.

I accepted the darkness that I would never be free from.

And for the longest second, Cem froze.

"I'm sorry," I whispered. "But I can't let you hurt them."

His eyes met mine with confusion and annoyance only to bleed into blinding shock. "Aslan, don't—"

I pulled the trigger.

He never got to finish what he would have said.

I was spared from yet another twisted sermon where he made me doubt everything.

The bullet barrelled right between his eyes.

A perfect hit.

A painless kill.

His gaze shot blank.

His legs gave out.

He collapsed at my feet.

Another wave crashed over me.

This one full of fears, questions, and crumbling conditioning.

I killed him.

Fuck, I killed him . . .

Men pounced on me from the shadows.

Four men grabbed four of my limbs, body slamming me into the ground.

A pistol wedged against my temple as my hands were wrenched behind my back and cold metal was snapped around my wrists.

"You're under arrest. Do not fucking move, Aslan Kara. Do not move or you'll die tonight, just like you killed your father."

Chapter Forty-Seven

ASLAN

(*Heart in Hungarian:* Szív)

Three months later...

I WAS DEAD AND DREAMING...THAT HAD to be the only explanation.

With shaking fingers, I pinched my left arm.

The arm that used to be inked but now just bore a scar.

I hissed beneath my breath as my fingernails dug into my grey long-sleeve shirt and pinched the flesh beneath.

Nope.

Not dreaming.

Not dead, either.

I was here.

In a place I feared I would never be permitted to step foot in again.

My heart skipped a few beats before settling on normal as I fought the sting of caustic tears. The weathered house with its newly replaced roof, sun-bleached fence, single palm tree, and familiar beaten-up Jeep Wrangler in the driveway seemed like something out of my many, many delusions while strapped to that awful chair.

I'd come to this very spot.

In my mind, I'd returned to Port Douglas and clung to memories of this street, this town, this home.

And now...I'm back.

Really, truly...back.

I couldn't breathe.

Couldn't dare to fucking hope.

This is real.

I kept my promise.

I came back to her.

If the Jeep was in the driveway, that meant Jack and Anna were home.

Is Neri?

My heart hammered against my ribs.

For three months, I'd wanted to call her.

For three months, I'd been controlled by a different kind of master to the one I'd shot and killed. I'd spent a month in prison. I'd been kept solitary and trapped, and by the time I was dragged into some office to speak to some guy, I was half feral with rage.

I wouldn't go through the pain again.

I wouldn't let someone else carve pieces off me and whittle me into nothing.

They could kill me for all I cared.

I'd protected Neri and my daughter.

I'd ended Cem so all the girls at the Fairy House and the workers in the warehouse were free.

I didn't care what they did to me as long as the pain was over.

But then, my life got…strange.

And now, I was back in a country that I'd spent eight years hiding in illegally.

My hand trailed to my pocket where my newly minted Turkish passport with its preliminary Australian residency visa gave me access, not just to visit but to *stay*.

I shuddered as disbelief tried its best to tell me my mind had snapped, and I was back in Turkey, dying in those catacombs, broken beyond belief. It took everything I had to trust that I wasn't deranged, that this was *real* as I stepped off the sidewalk where the taxi had dropped me off from the airport.

I had no bags.

No belongings of any kind.

I was just a man dressed in a grey shirt and black slacks, sweating beneath the Australian twilight sun but refusing to roll up his sleeves or trade trousers for shorts because of scars, amputations, and tragedy.

I was hiding.

Not quite ready to show what I'd been through but so fucking ready to live again.

At least, I now walked like anyone else.

I didn't limp or hop across the street to Jack and Anna's house. I marched like a man and the click of my cane was the only sign that I had a secret beneath my clothes. Soon, I wouldn't even need my cane anymore. In fact, I barely relied on it now, just like the doctors had said I would. Instead of the agonising, ill-fitted wooden leg that I'd refused to let Cem replace, this one fit like a tightly laced boot. A boot that felt almost normal even after just a few weeks.

My new transtibial prosthesis had a carbon pylon and foot, shock absorbers, silicone liners, and top-of-the-line technology. I'd run on a treadmill at the doctor's request. I'd scaled an obstacle course at my physiotherapist's encouragement. I'd jumped and lunged and was slowly building up faith in myself and the prosthetic. The only thing I hadn't done was swim.

My heart kicked again at the thought of returning to the Great Barrier Reef.

Of watching Neri dive again, hold her breath like a mermaid again, of *kissing* her again.

For the first time in forever, my body stirred.

My belly tightened.

But then terror dampened my urges.

Five years is a long time...she might have moved on.

My chest squeezed; I marched a little faster.

I paused by their front gate.

Memories of sitting with her in Jack's Jeep after I'd kissed her at the Craypot swarmed me. I'd known the moment she found me in the sea that I was hers. I would be hers until my dying day. But...if the loss of losing me— of spending the past five years thinking I was dead was enough to force her to find comfort with another, then...I would accept that.

I would let her be happy.

Because that was my entire purpose.

To make her happy.

My hands landed on the gate, but I didn't push it open. The thought of knocking on the front door seemed too formal, too...cold.

I needed to see my old home.

I needed to step into the garden where I'd lived and fallen in love. I needed to smell the chlorine that clung to everything and feel the stagnant heat before I could trust this was real.

Biting my bottom lip, I skirted the front garden, bypassed the Jeep, and cut down the side of the house. The glitter of the pool blinded me as I stepped into the space where I'd spent so many dinners, so many nights, so many moments.

The vegetable garden Neri had kept thriving along the fence was gone, replaced with pretty flowers and grasses. The boulders around the pool were dusty with unuse, and the sala—

I froze and clutched my cane.

The sala that Jack had so kindly turned into a bedroom for me was...gone.

I frowned as I studied the little patio area complete with a wave sculpture and table and chairs. No signs of the original sala or the room where I'd slept.

What happened?

Did they tear it down because of me?

Stepping onto the back deck where a few planks needed replacing, I glanced through the sliding doors to the kitchen beyond.

The smash of a pan and the yelp of surprise was the only warning I had before Anna tripped through the doors and stood gaping at me.

Jack stumbled after her, his white t-shirt and cargo shorts covered in red sauce from whatever he'd been cooking for dinner.

No one spoke.

I didn't think words were possible.

My heart skipped and squeezed as I drank in my surrogate parents. Parents who'd protected me, encouraged me, doubted me, hurt me, and ultimately given me a life I wouldn't have had with their daughter who was always meant to be mine.

Anna had more silver glittering through her sun-lightened hair, and Jack had deeper crow's feet spearing around his eyes. His belly had spread a little, and Anna's lips looked pinched as if the past few years had given her more reasons to cry instead of laugh.

But beneath the mark of age and time, they were still the two marine biologists who'd risked imprisonment and fines for me.

That affected me.

That knowledge slammed into my chest because my own father had used me, yet these people had loved me.

I forgave Jack for ever doubting me.

I swore fresh loyalty to Anna.

And I couldn't stop my quaking, shaking, absolute shattering relief at *finally* being home.

"Hello," I said quietly, trading the five years of Turkish for English that was slightly rusty on my tongue.

Anna let out a moan.

Jack slapped his hands over his mouth.

Tears shot to both their eyes.

"I-Is this real?" Anna gasped. Stumbling forward, she reached for my freshly shaven cheek and ripped her fingers back at the barest touch, almost as if she thought she'd touched a ghost. "H-How is this real?"

I held out my hand and didn't miss that her gaze flickered to my cane before darting back to mine. "I'm real."

"But…I don't understand." Droplets ran down her cheeks. "How? We…we thought you were dead."

"I technically was for a very long time. But I'm back now." I bowed my head. "I'm sorry it took me so long to return."

"How?" Jack dropped his hands, wringing his fingers. "I thought you were banished from ever stepping foot in Australia again?"

"Things are different now," I said, swallowing secrets and giving only bare essentials. I would tell them my story, but for now…I only wanted one thing.

Is she here?

"I'm legal. I flew here, just like everyone else." They didn't need to know I'd flown first class or had an escort or been personally welcomed by the chief of federal police.

That would come later.

Once I'd settled into who I was. Once I accepted the deal that I'd struck.

Jack didn't speak for the longest moment.

His tears welled and flowed, and then, with a guttural groan, he threw himself at me.

He tackled me and embraced me, and if I'd been wearing the other leg, I would've tumbled beneath his onslaught. It took every strength in my core to stay upright. It took faith in my new prosthetic to keep me balanced. I rocked backward on my two heels—one flesh and bone and the other carbon and steel—and hugged him back.

He buried his face into my neck and sobbed.

Fucking sobbed.

Anna broke into wet wails and threw herself at me too.

I clung to both of them.

My own eyes grew wet as I kissed Anna's hair as she hugged me so damn hard.

I lost track of time as they squeezed me.

I did my best to hide my impatience that the one person I was desperate to see hadn't come out to join us.

The longer the embrace went on, the more my heart skipped, and it took all my self-control to hold my desperation at bay and extract myself kindly and slowly.

"Where's Nerida?" I asked, my eyes searching the shadowy kitchen.

Jack stepped back, mopping up his tears with the back of his hands. Anna pulled a tissue from her shorts pocket and blew her nose.

They both shared a look.

A look I didn't like.

"She's not here…is she?" My voice slipped into despair. My heart threatened to stop beating altogether. "She…she found someone else?" The question was barely audible.

Of course, she did.

It's been five years, you idiot!

Five years.

Of course, she wouldn't live at home anymore.

Of course, she wouldn't wait for a dead man.

My back prickled.

Grief smothered.

Stepping backward, I clutched my cane. "I-It's okay. Eh, don't tell her I'm back, alright? In fact, I'll go. I don't want to upset her. If she's found happiness, then I don't want to do anything to destroy that."

Anna sniffed and grabbed my hand. "We'll take you to her."

"No, not if she's—"

"She'll want to see you, Aslan. Believe me." Jack leaned into the sliding doors and grabbed his car keys from the kitchen bench. "She doesn't live far from here. We'll go right now."

"But I don't want to hurt her."

"You won't." Anna shook her head. "We wouldn't say that if it wasn't true."

"So…she's not with anyone?"

Anna shared another look with Jack.

A look that tore out my heart.

"She *is* with someone," I choked. "Fuck, I can't see her then. I-I wouldn't survive. I just…" I did my best to extract my hand from Anna's. "I-I was told she had a daughter. I stupidly assumed that daughter was mine."

Fuck.

Cem had been playing me *again*.

Even in a grave, he still found ways to torture me.

Neri had had a child, but it wasn't mine.

That intrinsic knowledge I'd had the moment I set eyes on Ayla's photo had been wrong.

Fucking hell.

Neri had made a life with a man who'd helped heal her.

Someone alive after the funeral she'd held in my name.

She'd put me to rest.

She'd said goodbye.

She'd moved on.

What the fuck am I doing here?

"I-I have to go." I ripped my hand from Anna's.

"Her name is Ayla," Anna rushed. "And she's yours, Aslan."

My heart threatened to snap.

"How did you know she had a daughter?" Jack asked quietly.

I didn't have the capacity to answer him. "Ayla is mine?"

"She is." Anna nodded with a smile. "She's bilingual and wonderful and looks exactly like you."

My knees threatened to give out. I wanted to ask so many things. I wanted to know her, touch her, to catch up on all the years I'd missed.

But just because Ayla was mine didn't mean Neri was raising her on her own. She could've given my daughter a new father—a father who'd stepped in when I couldn't and supported Neri in parenthood.

My head turned woozy.

I couldn't stop shaking. "Just tell me she's happy and that's enough."

"You can see for yourself," Jack said.

Nonsense questions tumbled out of my mouth, driven by fear. "Did she move back here after she finished studying in Townsville? Did she meet someone in the same field? Does she still swim every day? Did she make her dream come true with Lunamare? I-Is she okay?" I shut myself up, breathing hard.

Jack closed the sliding doors but didn't bother to lock up. "She didn't finish her degree." He gave me a watery smile. "The loss of you prevented her from being able to. And, well…she was pregnant."

My chest spasmed. I pinched the bridge of my nose. "I'm so sorry."

"You're back now." He smiled and patted my shoulder. "How? I have no idea. And I want to hear the full story. I have so many questions. So many, many questions. But…before you tell us everything, you need to see her before you have a heart attack."

I winced at how true his words were.

I felt like I couldn't breathe without her.

Like my heart was one beat away from stopping for good if it couldn't have her.

Being here?

In this country? This garden? This place? It haunted me with memories of her. It drove me mad with want and need, and I honestly wouldn't survive if she'd replaced me.

I'd break in ways Cem had never been able to break me.

I'd waste away all while being so fucking grateful she had someone else to love.

Someone who looked after her when I couldn't.

I was in his debt, whoever he was.

I would walk away, all to protect her from more heartache.

My head was a mess.

My body a trembling fool.

"Please…I—" I swallowed hard. "Tell me what you're not telling me. Is she with someone?"

Anna took my hand as she stepped off the deck and waited for me to join her on the grass. I gauged the distance to step down and did it as smoothly as I could, relying more on my cane for balance so I didn't put weight into her grip.

She waited until we were halfway around the pool before replying. "Do you honestly think she could be with anyone else, Aslan?" Fresh tears rolled down her cheeks as she led me toward the driveway. "She refused to believe you were dead for years. She vowed she felt you, even when all of us said she was mad. She never stopped believing you were alive." Her voice caught. "We all feared for her state of mind. We asked her to get help. We did everything we could to support her, but…she never accepted you were gone. And now…now I feel absolutely *awful* because I didn't believe her. I didn't trust my own daughter. I didn't believe in the connection you two share."

She shook her head as we stopped beside the Jeep. "I-I don't have the words for how I feel seeing you again. I've missed you *so much*. We all have. But Neri…" She pulled her hand from mine with a wince. "She broke losing you, Aslan, and I honestly don't think I can watch when she realises you're not gone…just like she said. I won't be able to stand it. I can barely stand it now. I hate myself for the number of times I begged her to let you go. I was so worried about her. I didn't believe her. God, I didn't—"

"Hey, love. It's okay," Jack murmured, wrapping his arm around Anna. "We both didn't. We thought we were doing the right thing." His eyes met mine. "We should've trusted her."

My ears rang.

Hot tears threatened to spill. "S-She heard me calling her…"

My heart scrambled with joy.

She heard me…

She felt me.

Fuck, she felt me.

How much did she feel?

"She heard you, mate. Loud and fucking clear." Jack cleared his throat, unwound his arm from around Anna, then opened the Jeep's door. "But Anna's right. We can't be there when she sees you. I feel like I've let her down so badly. Five years of wishing she could move on. Five years of fearing she'd eventually drive herself insane or worse…all to learn she was right."

He wiped away a falling tear. "I doubted my own daughter. I failed her in so many ways. Just like I failed you. Fuck. This is insane. Seeing you again. Touching you." He struggled to smile. "Like Anna said, I don't have the words. All I can say is…we can't go with you. We can't watch Neri break again. But we'll be here, Aslan. We'll be here for when you're ready to tell us what happened."

Striding to me, he grabbed my hand and pressed the keys into them. "Go to her. She's number twelve on Baler. Go. She heard you, mate. Fuck, she heard you every damn day you were gone. Just like you heard her all those years ago."

He sniffed and bowed his head. "You once told me you killed for her. That you turned into the devil himself to protect my only daughter. Whatever you've suffered, Aslan. Wherever you've been and whatever nightmares you've endured, I need you to know that I will *never* doubt you again, never question you, never hold you back. You and her?" He shrugged helplessly. "I've never known anything as strong as the love you guys share. It's survived years of distance. Months of heartache. It's *real* and I'm in awe of both of you."

He stepped away and hugged Anna again. "Now, get over there. Meet your daughter. And try not to kill *our* daughter by coming back to life."

Chapter Forty-Eight

NERIDA

AGE: 25 YRS OLD

(Love in German: Liebe)

"I'M GOING TO GET YOU," TEDDY ROARED as he chased after Ayla.

"No, no!" she squealed and took off as fast as her almost five-year-old little legs could carry her, bolting through the side gate to the overgrown front garden. Eddie took off after them, growling like a moron.

Ayla's scream echoed with fun, joy, and excitement.

Just because Teddy had transformed this three-bedroom home into a boho chic dreamhouse and the back garden now had a five-metre-deep swimming pool, glass fence, and sparkly pavers didn't mean any of us were good at staying on top of swiftly growing tropical vines, weeds, and flowers at the front. Our poor letter box was being strangled again by some invasive plant.

"Eddie, it's your turn to weed whack!" I shouted after the two husbands, following my daughter's wet footprints from where she'd launched out of the pool and sprinted around the garden in an attempt to fly.

She was so sure she could fly after I'd shown her videos of exocoetidae, also known as flying fish, on YouTube. I was determined that just because I'd never returned to school didn't mean she wouldn't be a marine biologist if she wished to be.

She might look like Aslan and share his serious scowls, but she was me in every other way. I could barely keep her out of the water. I should've called her after the sea instead of the moon because she was adamant she was part fish and had stuck a painting on the fridge of a bubble pod last week, claiming it was her new room in Lunamare—if we ever built it.

Over five years and nothing to show for it.

We had a prototype we believed could work.

We'd solved the lack of sunlight issue, the foundation and anchoring issue, and tried to foresee as many complications with storms, sea-levels rising, and did our best to integrate with the environment rather than disturb it.

But…that was as far as we'd got.

Fundraising could only raise so much.

We'd exhausted all our own funds.

If we didn't get a decent cash flow soon, all three of us would have to find other employment. And that killed me because…I'd already had to say goodbye to one dream. I'd lost the most important person in my life. I didn't think I'd survive losing the vague but hopeful belief that one day I could live beneath the waves and find a smidgen of healing for my broken heart.

Enough, remember?

You promised you wouldn't do this anymore.

Sighing and pushing away my sadness, I broke into a jog to chase after my wayward daughter. My heart twinged just a little, toying with me. The strange palpitations had faded recently, and I hadn't taken up the cardiologist on his offer of a follow-up appointment.

I fully believed the skips were caused by my inability to let go, and I hoped, with time, they would eventually stop taunting me.

Ever since I'd kneeled on the beach three months ago and finally said goodbye to Aslan, I'd done my best to move on.

I knew I would never find another love.

I had absolutely zero interest in entering the dating scene and had to have a strongly worded conversation with Teddy and Eddie one night when they tried to set me up with one of their straight friends.

I was done with that part of my life.

I would never be touched again, kissed again and…*that's okay.* I'd slept with Aslan enough to have a decent rolodex of memories to use if the urge to climax appeared at two in the morning. Then again, my body was exactly like my heart and no longer had any interest in being touched. Apart from platonic hugs from Teddy and Eddie, and the special squishes from Ayla, I didn't really touch anyone.

"RAWWWWR!"

I rolled my eyes at Teddy's impersonation of whatever beast he was supposed to be tonight. He was particularly good at winding her up just before bedtime.

But…I couldn't stop their fun.

Who cared if Ayla's bedtime was all over the place? Who cared if she swam at six, seven, or eight p.m.? Who cared if she was on the beach when other five-year-olds were tucked up in bed and dreaming? She was wild, and I loved it. *It's the only way to live in the moment. And the moment is all she has.*

I laughed and ignored the wince in my heart as Teddy scooped her up and tossed her to Eddie. Ayla's little limbs went flailing, giggling as the two men tossed her around like a rugby ball.

I'd had a panic attack when they first threw her around as a baby, but she loved it above everything else. She begged for more the moment they finished, and I'd grown used to seeing her flying through the lounge and hucked into the kitchen, caught by strong, careful arms and showered with affectionate kisses.

I trusted them.

She trusted them.

We all trusted each other.

Life's okay.

I'll survive.

I'm so, so lucky for everything I have, despite losing him.

Crossing my arms, I slowed my jog and fought a shiver that appeared from nowhere. We were all dressed in swimming togs from being in the pool. All of us mostly naked and dripping wet.

My happy yellow bikini with bumble bees on the straps and strings was new—a treat to myself to try to find my smile. Ayla wore a matching yellow and bee leotard, and the husbands shared similar sandy boardshorts just like they shared most of their wardrobe. Being the same height and size came in handy when their tastes swung in the same direction of moody browns and atmospheric greys.

None of them looked cold, yet I couldn't stop the sudden trembling originating in my bones.

Rubbing my arms, I indulged the tossing of my daughter for another few moments before I became the voice of reason. "Okay, okay, that's enough. You'll make her throw up in a minute."

"More. More!" Ayla shouted.

Eddie caught her, twisted her upside down, and blew raspberries on her round belly.

"Ahhh!" She squirmed and giggled.

My heart swelled, pinching with pain that was as common as breathing but suddenly seemed extra sharp.

The rumble of my parents' old Jeep Wrangler sounded in the distance.

I held up my hand against the final red and gold spears of the setting sun, trying to peer down the road. It wasn't unusual for them to pop round at this time. Either to kiss Ayla goodnight or to share a quick drink with the boys and me.

Keeping one eye on the street where the Jeep's engine grew louder and one eye on my daughter currently being kissed to death, I smiled as the last light of the sun bounced off the Jeep's windscreen as it appeared.

I waved.

I couldn't see inside the Wrangler, but I didn't care if it was Mum or Dad or both. They were always welcome.

Clapping my hands, I grinned at the two men currently playing tug of war with my daughter. Eddie had her legs, and Teddy had her around the chest.

"Who loves me the mostest?" Ayla yelled, freaking beside herself with laughter.

"Me!" Eddie chuckled.

"Nope. I do!" Teddy blew his husband a wink. "Me!"

"Yay!" Ayla beamed.

God, she'll never go to sleep after this nonsense.

I rolled my eyes and laughed. "Alright, let's all calm down so Mummy doesn't have to be up all night with a hyperactive bouncing jellybean. Grandma and Grandpa are here to say night-night."

"Double yay!" Ayla struggled in their arms. "Down. Down. I wanna say hi to Nana and Pop Pop."

Laughing, Teddy placed her carefully onto her feet on the overgrown grass.

"Be careful," Eddie said affectionately as she tore off toward the Jeep. "Look both ways before you cross the street, moonbeam!"

The Jeep parked on the opposite side of the road.

The sun threw one last glowing light off the windows, blinding me.

I waited for the door to open.

For Ayla to skip into my parents' arms.

But then…something happened.

Something I couldn't explain.

Something science couldn't explain.

Maths or logic or common sense could *never* explain.

My heart wrenched in my chest as if it came clean away from arteries and veins.

My bones warmed.

My blood fizzed.

And…I knew.

I *knew.*

I knew before my knees gave out.

I knew before the car door opened.

I knew before Ayla skidded to a stop and said, "Wait, you're not Nana and Pop Pop."

My eyes met the coal-dark stare of someone I never thought I'd see again.

I choked on a sob.

Slammed to the ground.

And broke.

Chapter Forty-Nine

ASLAN

(Heart in Russian: Сердце)

EVERYTHING HAPPENED IN SLOW MOTION.

I was underwater or watching an old-school movie.

It didn't feel real.

This surreal, incredible, *impossible* moment fucking terrified me because…what if this *wasn't* real. What if this was a dream, and I was about to wake up?

I'd find myself back in the cave, strapped to the chair, with another bolt of electricity tearing up my insides.

Another delusion slowly killing me.

I wouldn't survive it.

Please, please be real.

My vision danced with sun flares and tears. My mind utterly unable to absorb the scene before me.

Neri.

Fuck.

Neri.

I forgot my cane and tripped out of the Jeep.

I left the engine running and the door open as a tiny girl on swift feet slammed to a stop before me. It took all my effort to tear my gaze from my soulmate's and look at my daughter.

In another moment, in another life, meeting the person I'd helped create would take precedence. I wouldn't be able to stop myself from scooping her up, inhaling her deep, and pledging everything I was to her.

But…in this life…the one that I didn't trust was real—the one that might be stolen and proven to be false—made me awfully selfish.

I only had eyes for her mother.

I couldn't breathe until I'd touched her and knew, once and for all…I was home.

My knees shook as I studied the little girl, dripping wet and clad in a bright-yellow swimming costume. She reminded me of Neri when she was younger. Always dressed in lycra and trailing droplets of water.

"Who are you?" She poked me in the thigh. "Where's Nana and Pop Pop?"

I swallowed hard and struggled to speak. "I…I'm—"

The two shirtless men who'd been playing with her darted across the sleepy street and scooped Ayla into their arms.

Part of me was jealous.

The other part possessive.

But in the distance, kneeling on an overgrown lawn, her eyes never wavering from me, Neri kept me trapped.

I felt her calling me even though she didn't speak.

I felt her heart summoning mine even though she didn't move.

I didn't have the capacity to feel anything else.

Just longing.

Soul-deep, raw, fervent *longing*.

"Aslan."

My name spoken by the guy holding Ayla wrenched my head up.

I blinked. I recognised him from long ago video-call sessions and late-night brainstorming. "Teddy?"

He nodded. "Hey, mate. Long time no see." Holding out his hand, he waited for me to place mine into his, then shook me hard. Glancing at the man beside him, I swallowed hard. "Edmund."

"Hi, Aslan."

Ayla reached for my cheek. Her small, clammy hand stung me like the bees on her costume. "That's my Daddy's name. Are you a lion too?"

A groan worked up my throat. A noise of desperation, disbelief, and despair.

She knew about me.

Neri told her about me.

Her little nose wrinkled as she cocked her head. "*Sen kimsin?*"

I swayed backward against the Jeep.

Fuck, she speaks Turkish too.

Neri had kept my culture alive. She'd given pieces of me to my daughter while I'd been nothing more than a ghost.

My ruined heart couldn't take this.

My pulse shot sky high, unable to cope.

"W-Who am I?" I repeated her question in English, my voice wet and scratchy. "I…" My gaze shot past hers and returned to Neri's. Always to Neri. Forever to the matching, missing piece of my soul. "I—"

I choked.

I stumbled.

I couldn't.

Neri plastered both hands over her mouth, holding back her sobs, but it didn't stop her entire body from shuddering. Her left arm held the same ink that'd been flayed off me and my mind tripped with horrors of before, then, and now.

I forgot what my daughter asked, and only one word shot to mind. A word I'd always associate with the love I had for my moon-given wife. "*Canim*..."

Burying her face into her lap, Neri cried brutally hard.

Teddy and Eddie glanced at her. An unspoken look passed between them. Without a word, they whispered something into Ayla's ear, reached past me to turn off the Jeep and lock the door, then turned and walked barefoot across the road. Teddy ran his fingers over Neri's damp hair and Eddie pressed a kiss to her forehead before both men padded down the side of the house and disappeared with Ayla.

I stood there for a millennia after they'd left.

The street was quiet and empty.

The sunset well and truly smothered by dusk.

Neri didn't move from her ball on the grass, and I didn't have the strength to walk to her.

We stared at each other.

Eyes devouring.

Hearts pounding.

Both of us afraid.

So fucking afraid this wasn't real.

But then...she started to crawl toward me. On hands and knees as if she didn't have the power to walk.

It broke my terrified trance.

I forgot I needed my cane for support.

I forgot who I was and what I'd suffered.

I ran.

I ran like I'd been able to run in the past, accepting the prosthetic as a part of me as I bolted across the road, leapt the curb, then slammed to my knees before her.

I felt no physical pain.

Only emotional.

Spiritual.

A ripping and slicing, a tearing and bleeding.

The grass was real.

The twilight was real.

She

is

real.

Neri crawled into me with the softest whimper.

And the moment we touched, everything gathered, poised, and *ignited*.
Our skin fired.
Our blood sang.
Our bones merged into one.
My arms snapped around her.
Never again.
Never fucking again would I let her go.

With an aching sob, she burrowed herself into me, not content with how tightly I embraced her, needing more, taking everything. Curling into my lap, her arms wrapped around my shoulders as she tucked her tear-wet face against my neck.

I gasped and shuddered.
I'd never felt anything so good.
So perfect.
So *right*.

My embrace turned violent. My desperation vicious as I crushed her to me, savage and punishing, feral and fearful.

She hugged me back, trembling with need, punishing both of us, hurting us in so many frantic ways.

"Tell me this is real. Tell me I'm not crazy," she moaned, pressing a kiss to my throat.

I tried to answer her.
I tried to speak around the river in my soul.
But...for the first time in my life, I lost complete control.
She did to me what that damned electric chair had never achieved.
She broke me.
Spectacularly, totally.
The walls in my mind tumbled.
The chains and locks—hiding all my compartments and neatly stacked boxes of torture, grief, and secrets—snapped and shattered.
No more lying.
No more pretending or coping or hoping to be better while unable to face the past.
I had no protection.
I couldn't hide.
And in that moment of breaking, I gave in.
I sank into the rubble left inside me.
I accepted everything that Cem had done.
I surrendered to myself.
To life.
To her.
And...I sobbed.
I gathered Neri against me, tucking her into my arms and heart, and

cried my fucking eyes out.

We rocked together.

Grieved together.

We let five years of misery wake around us and a lifetime of denial to finally wash free.

And that was how we stayed for days, weeks, years.

It felt as if the world kept spinning, but we were in our own universe. Singular and apart, found and finally free.

I didn't know how much time passed, but eventually, our tears dried up and our arms ached with cramps. Night had fallen, cicadas chirped, and waves crashed upon the sand down the road.

Streetlights had clicked on as we slowly untangled ourselves and pulled away just enough to look into each other's eyes.

We froze.

I couldn't explain the peace inside me. The humbling, honouring union that…everything would be okay now.

I had no more ghosts haunting me, no more fears or failures.

I'd let them all go.

I was empty and blissful and absolutely enraptured by this moment and all the moments we would make together.

We didn't speak as our gazes locked and our hearts did all the talking.

I cupped her cheek and ran my thumb over the streaks of salt on her skin. She leaned into my palm with a hitched breath, and it was as natural as coming back to life as I slid my fingers around her nape and tugged her forward.

Our noses touched first, nudging with the softest hello. Our breath touched next, mingling with our linked lifeforce. And when our lips touched for that first time in over five years, we didn't rush. Didn't deepen. We shivered and groaned, sinking into the taste of love and knowing that this was it for us.

We kissed.

Through death and time, separation and sadness.

We'd survived only to come back to the one place that made sense.

She and I.

Together.

Nothing would come between us.

Nothing else existed but this.

Always.

Just this.

Her eyelashes fluttered closed as I pressed my mouth harder against hers.

Her tongue feathered out and licked mine hesitantly.

I opened for her.

I welcomed her.

I shuddered as we licked and remembered, exploring one another and recognising what we'd lost.

We spent another decade kissing on her front lawn. Unhurried, uncaring, totally consumed by the dance and dark heat of tongues, lips, and lust.

Lust.

I'd forgotten what it felt like.

I'd shoved it out of my mind and forbidden my body to remember.

But it remembered now.

The longer we kissed, the harder I got. The more her fingers tugged on my hair, the more I clung to control so I didn't push her onto her back and take her right there, in front of her neighbours and their nosy cats.

With a sharp moan as if it hurt to pull away, Neri planted her hands on my shoulders and pushed back. Her lips were swollen and a delicious shade of red, making blood roar through my veins and my body snarl for more.

Climbing off my lap, she stood with a woozy sway. With a smile that captured the rest of my sorry soul, she bent down and offered me her hand. "Let's go inside."

For a moment, I panicked.

I'd never tried standing from kneeling before.

Would she know I was different?

I would tell her eventually.

She would see for herself that the man who'd left her wasn't the same man who'd returned but…for now, I wanted her to see me as whole, just for a little longer.

Gritting my teeth, I accepted her hand and manoeuvred myself enough that my whole leg took most of the heavy lifting. My other swung neatly into position and the prosthetic barely moved thanks to the snug fit and tight strapping.

It didn't ache or distract me, and I walked forward with her by my side.

We walked hand in hand down the side of the house where she now lived, past a deep-looking pool, over glittery pavers, and through a sliding door into an open-plan living, dining, and kitchen. Driftwood coffee tables, linen couches, and woven rugs gave it a beach-homey vibe.

Side lamps had been turned on, casting everything in a warm glow, but there was no sign of the guys or Ayla. Even traces of wet footprints had dried thanks to the age Neri and I had sunk into one another outside.

"You live here?" I asked quietly as Neri tugged me through the space.

My slight limp went unnoticed in the gloom as she nodded and caught my eyes. "Yes. For almost the entire time you were gone. I couldn't…" Her voice caught, and she swallowed with a quick smile. "I couldn't stay in our apartment in Townsville, especially not after I found out I was pregnant. And then I couldn't stay in my old room at Mum and Dad's. I-I don't know if you saw the sala, but—"

"It's gone."

She flinched. "I burned it."

"You did?"

"I didn't know how to deal with the loss inside me. I was angry and sad, twisted and grieving, guilty and petrified. It was best for everyone that I move somewhere with no memories of you." She stopped suddenly and wedged a fist into her belly. Her curves beneath her swimming costume threatened to undo me. "This is so surreal. I keep having to pinch myself that this is real. That you're truly here. That I've not snapped like everyone said I would, and I'm not rocking in some insane asylum talking to myself."

My chest squeezed.

Tugging her hand, I pulled her into me and wrapped my arms around her. "I'm here. This is real. I have the same problem. I keep thinking I'm going to wake up and—" I cut myself off. She didn't need to know about the catacombs or the chair. Not yet at least. She'd see for herself the minute she removed my clothes, but in this fragile moment, I wanted to be strong for her. "I'm so sorry I wasn't there for you while you were pregnant." I winced. "How…I mean…you were always so careful with birth control. I don't understand how it failed."

"The blue dragon." She laughed under her breath. "I can laugh about it now because I have—*we* have—the most incredible, wonderful daughter, but I definitely underestimated the venom of that nasty little nudibranch. I was sicker than I let on, and I guess my pill failed."

"Fuck, Neri. I'm so sorry. I shouldn't have given in to you while you were ill."

"Don't be." She stood on her tiptoes to kiss me. "You gave me Ayla." A darkness etched her face as she admitted. "I-I don't know if I would be standing here if I didn't have her. And that eats me up inside because…I would never have felt this again." She rested her fingertips over my chest. "Felt *you* again. Felt this overwhelming sense of rightness and home."

I dipped my chin and kissed her deeper.

We lost track of time as we stood in the middle of the home she shared with two men and kissed away the past. Her tongue touched mine, and I licked her back. Her lips opened wider; I followed. Our breathing slowly picked up, and the lust from before returned.

Sighing heavily, she sank back down to her heels and blinked up at me. Dreamy and teary but luminous with love.

Love that'd lasted five years of distance and despair.

"*Seni seviyorum*, Ne‡ida."

"I love you, Aslan. So damn much." Looking at her hand on my chest, she didn't speak for a moment before murmuring, "I know we need to talk. I know there are things you need to tell me and me to tell you, but…I'm not ready. A part of me already knows what you're going to say…somehow. I know that it will hurt to hear. I know I'll probably spend the rest of my life horrified at what you've endured to return to me, but…I just need to exist in this for a little longer." Her fingers dug deeper over my heart. "I need to trust this first. Trust us. Trust that no matter what happened, it doesn't matter because we're still here, still together. Everything else is over now…it's in the past. You're back where you belong."

Her eyes widened as fear swam thick. "Wait…*how* are you here? Are you safe? How did you come back? I thought you were banished from ever stepping foot in Australia again."

I clasped my hand over hers, pressing her palm to my chest. "I'm legally allowed to be here and to stay."

"How?"

I kissed her nose. "I'll tell you, but it's not a simple answer. And…I feel the same way. There are things I need to tell you and things I need to ask. But…none of it truly matters because it's done, it's gone, and for the first time in my life, I can honestly say…I'm okay. I'm truly, incredibly okay, and that's all because of you."

Ducking at my knees, partially aware of the strangeness of my bracing prosthetic and the ease at which I'd grown used to it, I kissed her again. It was too easy to love her. Too easy to want her. Far, far too hard to pull away and whisper, "I-I need you to know, I'm not expecting anything tonight. I understand if you need time, *canim*. I'm happy to do whatever you want as long as I get to do it with you."

She smiled softly beneath my lips. "Here I was afraid that dragging you into my room was too soon. That you'd think I only wanted you for your body."

I chuckled and hid my slight flinch. "My body—what's left of it—is yours. It always has been. Always will be."

Her eyes tightened with questions. I waited for her to ask, but she swallowed them down and turned on her heel.

Taking my hand, she tugged me toward the corridor. The wide space was lit by a strip of lighting along the skirting board, revealing doors equally spaced. "That's Ayla's room. Family bathroom. Eddie and Teddy's room. And this…" She pulled me over the threshold of a grey-walled, beachy space. Coral chandelier, shaggy cream carpets, and the scent of salt and wind as if she'd washed her white sheets in the sea. "This is mine."

I drank in her room.

I imagined her here, thinking of me while I thought of her.

But then, I froze.

I tripped to the side of her bed and snatched up a photo.

A photo of me in a lion onesie when I was a baby. I'd seen the same one on Cem's desk. Spinning around, I demanded, "How do you have this?"

Fucking hell, he'd been playing games with her too.

What a bastard.

What a lowlife fucking bastard.

If he wasn't dead, I'd kill him all over again.

For a few weeks, while I'd waited in prison to find out what sins I'd be charged with after my arrest the night I'd shot him, I'd actually felt guilty. My fractured mind tried to lay the blame squarely at my feet. That I'd misread his intentions. That he truly did love me. That he wasn't toxic or manipulative or dangerous.

But now, I saw the truth.

The *only* truth.

He was the worst creature alive because he could use truth and twist it into lies. He could use love and make it hurt worse than any weapon.

He deserved to die.

She hunched and rubbed her arms. "I spoke to him. Every year."

"I know. He told me."

She reared back. "He did?" Anger lit her crystal-blue eyes. "That asshole told me every year that you were dead. I screamed at him that I didn't believe it. I *never* believed it. My heart knew. My heart knew all along that you weren't gone." She rubbed at her chest. "It acted so strange, Aslan. I even went to a doctor to be checked out because I'd wake up with palpitations and suffer at such random times. But the cardiologist assured me I was fine, so I just assumed it was symptoms of a broken heart."

I lowered the photograph, trembling. "Y-You felt that?" My eyes suddenly locked on the other item on her bedside. A tiny keepsake from the deep that'd been my good luck charm before I lost it.

Snatching the spiny, peach-and-cream shell, tears clawed up my throat.

She kept it.

She—

"I spoke to you every night," she whispered wetly. Coming toward me, she rested her hand over mine as I clutched the gift she'd given me all those years ago. "Every night I felt my heart skip and double-beat, I begged you to feel me. Each time my chest pounded with an irregular rhythm, I rubbed that damn shell, begging to know if you were alright."

"Fuck, *canım*." I raised her hand and kissed her knuckles.

I should be used to her by now. It shouldn't shock me that her heart had scrambled like mine. That the fraught pain and terror I'd endured had transmitted through whatever connection we shared

This incredible, sensitive girl.

My all-knowing, intuitive soulmate.

She stood there in her yellow bikini, with all her beauty on display, and I fell to the bottom of my affection.

I'd never loved her more.

"I heard you, Neri," I breathed. "I just wish…I wish you hadn't heard me too."

She stilled. "What…what did he do to you?"

I shrugged sadly. "You felt it. Your heart felt everything."

"You're saying…" Her eyes widened. "You're saying you had the same palpitations? The same discomfort?"

"I'm saying—"

"Wait." She pushed me out of the way and opened her bedside drawer. "I noted the time and duration of each episode." Ripping out a spiral-ringed notebook, she trembled. "What if they match? What if—"

"Neri." I pressed my hand over the book before she could open it.

I had no doubt that if we were to take the times of her palpitations and convert them to Turkey's time zone, they would line up directly with the moments I was strapped in the chair.

How that was possible, I didn't understand.

How that was explainable, I might never know.

She was rare and unique and so fucking special that my knees gave out, slamming me onto her bed.

She gasped. "Aslan…are you okay?"

I laughed under my breath.

A long time ago, that word had been one of the most painful of my short sixteen years of existence. A four-letter, foreign word that didn't bring back my parents or sister or cousin. It had lost its painfulness, but it still had the power to ask the toughest questions, demanding a simple answer when there was no simple answer to give.

"I'm okay." I nodded. Wiping my mouth, I placed the photo and shell back on her nightstand. Slowly, I took the notebook out of her hands and put it back in the drawer.

I'm more than okay…

Something inside me was breaking apart, unfurling, and dissolving.

I might've fallen to the depths of my love for her, but I'd never felt lighter, less encumbered, or free.

She stepped into me. "Then what is it?"

"Those skips you felt." I looked down and took her hands. "You *were* feeling me."

"I was?"

I swallowed hard. I didn't want to do this so soon, but…if we were going to be together, she'd see anyway. "I was hurt. Often. He used electricity to make me submit. The current ruined my heartbeat, sometimes for days at a time."

"God…" Her fingers went stiff in mine. "H-How could he do that to you?"

"Because he believed he had authority over my mind and feelings. You'll see the scars soon enough…and when you do, I want you to remember that I'm here now. You felt me at my worst. You were there with me when I was so sure I would die. I *felt* you, Neri. Just like you felt me. I'm so sorry you endured what I went through. That you know what it feels like for your heart to forget how to pump. If I could love you anymore for that, I would, but I've already fallen with every part of me, and I know without a shadow of a doubt you kept me alive. *You* kept my heart beating. I fought for you, stayed alive for you, and I'm so fucking grateful you waited."

"Aslan…" A sob crawled up her throat. "God, Aslan…I'm so sorry. So sorry you suffered because of me. I was so stupid. So endlessly, so *recklessly* stupid. If only I'd listened to you. I've hated myself ever since that night. I can't stop the guilt. If only I stayed quiet, those bastards would've kept walking and—"

"Neri." I squeezed her hands. "Neri, listen to me."

She swayed and blinked, chewing on her bottom lip.

"I told you on the phone, and I'll tell you again, none of this was your fault. I'm grateful it happened, don't you see?"

"But—"

"I love you, Nerida. I came back to you." I raised her hands to my mouth and kissed her knuckles again. "I would've been caught eventually. Another day, another street corner…at some point, my time would've been up, and now…I'm free of all of it. I'm finally fucking free, and I'm not afraid anymore. How could I be afraid of the past when it's returned me to you? How can I be afraid of the future when I know that we're linked in ways that supersede everything? Nothing can hurt me again. Nothing can scare me. Nothing can take away this…this *bliss* inside me. I never thought it would be this easy. Never thought I'd feel this centred, this calm, this…*whole,* not after what he did. Not after five years of—"

I choked on so much, needing her to understand. "I'm finally free to love you with no fear. Knowing I have you, Neri? Knowing we are meant to be is the best kind of surrender there is. I surrender to you. And only to you. I give you everything that I am and…"

Pulling her into the V of my spread thighs, I untangled my fingers from hers and cupped her gorgeous face. "I need you, *canim.* I need you so fucking much. I've missed you every day for five years. I've dreamed of you, wished for you, begged for you. Be with me? Prove to me that you're still mine because every inch of me is still yours."

Tears ran down her cheeks, trickling over my fingers as she bent and kissed me. "I don't deserve you, Aslan. But I vow I will never stop loving you with everything that I am."

I groaned as her tongue speared into my mouth, sending us straight to hell.

Our kiss became a whirlpool of teeth and lips. My stomach clenched. My body hardened. The tingling heat between my legs felt so fucking good. It'd been so long.

So long since I'd wanted to feel this.

To sink into this vulnerability where I felt *everything*.

With her lips on mine, her hands went to the wide straps with bumble bees buzzing around her neck. Undoing the knot at her nape and the one in the middle of her back, she never stopped kissing me as the bikini top fell away.

I wanted to see.

To touch.

But her tongue stroked mine, dragging a groan from me as she shimmied out of the bottoms and stood before me bare.

Standing straight, she ended our kiss and tensed. She dropped her eyes as if afraid of my attention on her. I couldn't speak as I drank in her beauty: the slightly fuller breasts, gently rounded stomach from carrying Ayla, and the curvy hips I'd always loved.

She was older. Wiser. And oh, so fucking beautiful.

She flinched as I ran my fingers over the silvery stretch marks on her lower belly.

"I-I'm different to who you remember," she breathed.

"No." I shook my head and cupped her hipbones, tracing my thumbs over her soft skin. "You're perfect. You were perfect then. You're perfect now. You'll be perfect when you're old and grey and cranky."

She smiled. "Cranky, huh?"

"I can definitely see you getting stroppy with people."

"Oh, I'm rather good at that already." She ducked and kissed me. "Your daughter has made sure that I've paid for every stress I gave my parents when I was her age. She's a little tornado."

I sucked in a breath at the sudden flare of loss. "I've missed out on so much."

"You have." She ran her fingers through my longish hair. "But I promise I'll tell you every little detail. I remembered for you. I spoke to you every night before I went to sleep and whispered about her antics. I've taken copious amounts of photos so you can see her in every stage of growth. Her caterpillar stage, toddler stage, baby butterfly stage."

"I wasn't aware I gave you an insect for a child." I chuckled.

"It's the best way to describe her. She has wings now, and she's unstoppable." Her eyes dropped to my shirt and her fingers trembled a little as they landed on the button closest to my throat. "May I?"

I swallowed hard. And nodded.

With dexterous fingers, she unbuttoned my grey shirt, one at a time, parting the fabric and revealing all the moments I'd endured.

Neri might have captured Ayla's evolution with a camera, but my skin had captured mine with scars. Electrode burns. Tiny pockmarks from the picana. And the large angry line across my forearm.

She cried quietly as she pushed my shirt off my shoulders.

I had nothing to say as she traced my injuries and history. Pulling my shirt over my hands, she moaned under her breath as she noticed where my tattoo used to be.

She froze.

Her gaze shot to her own inked lion and siren before she dropped to her knees between my spread legs and pressed the most worshipping kiss on my scar.

I placed my right hand on her head and bowed over her.

Tears rolled from my own eyes as she came to terms with everything she saw.

I didn't know if she'd have the strength to ask, but on a tattered breath, she whispered, "Why? Why take it from you?"

"Because he knew I used the memory of us to fight his control. Each time he'd 'persuade' me, I'd cling to my tattoo and return to you. I lasted almost three years before he understood my trick."

Her fingernails dug into my arm. Her head shot up as her eyes blazed blue fire. "I'll kill him. I'm going to fly to Turkey and *kill him*."

I smiled softly. "You're too late."

Her eyebrows rose. "You?"

I nodded. "He was coming after you and Ayla. I couldn't let that happen."

Her eyes swirled with shadows. "I'm so sorry, Aslan. For all of it." Her face twisted with despair. "I know you say it wasn't my fault but…I'm the reason he hurt you. I'm the reason—"

"Hey." I pulled her up and stood with her. I didn't let her look away as I captured her chin and stared into her. "You were *not* the reason. Cem was. My illegal status was. You need to trust me when I say I couldn't keep living the way I was when everything I wanted could be so easily taken away."

My heart lurched at that truth, that constant worry.

It'd been so draining, so imprisoning.

"This is the last time you're allowed to feel guilty, do you hear me? If you need my forgiveness, you have it. But you also have my thanks. I've survived the worst that could possibly happen. That constant fear, that insistent need to hide and pretend are all gone. I can be *me*, Neri. I can claim you. Forever."

My voice turned soft. "I could never have married you, *aşkım*. Never have bought a home with you. Never been safe to live a normal life without fear of being hurt or deported. I think…I think that's why I struggled to move on from the past. Why I couldn't shed that depression. Why I never let myself be truly happy because everything felt so fragile and temporary. I wanted you so fucking much, but I couldn't truly keep you, and that made me angry because I was helpless."

She swayed in my hold. "But you were taken. You were hurt."

"I was." I kissed her softly. "But…it's over now. I'm back. And I'm not going anywhere."

"I'm in awe of you, Aslan…but I don't understand how you're here after you were deported."

"I'll tell you. After. I'll tell you everything once I've been inside you, made love to you, and proven to both of us this isn't a dream we'll wake up from. This is *us*. And…" I smiled against her mouth. "Considering you're still wearing the engagement ring I gave you, I think it's only fair we finally set a date for our wedding."

She gasped. "Are you serious?"

"More serious than anything in my life. I want to marry you with all my fucking heart. I want us to share the same name. I want Ayla to share my name. I want…" I paused with a frown. "Hang on. What *is* her last name?"

"Avci," she said quietly. "I…I legally changed mine. Everyone thought I was crazy, but a few years ago, when I was at my darkest, I filled in the paperwork and became yours, even if I belonged to a ghost."

"Fucking hell." I crushed her in my arms. I kissed her explicitly hard. "I love you, Nerida. So much."

She kissed me back, panting by the time we pulled away. "So you see, we don't technically have to get married—not that I don't want to, of course. I do. With all my soul. But…we already share the same name. Everyone already knows I belong to you."

I squeezed my nape. "Ah, well, that's not technically true."

"What?" She wrinkled her nose. "What do you mean?"

"Avci is no longer the name I'm known by."

"You took his name?" Her face darkened. "After everything he did to you? Why the hell would you do that?"

"I didn't have a choice."

"What? Why?"

Pulling my new passport out of my pocket, I flicked open the photo page.

She snatched it and hissed, "Aslan Kara."

"It was an unnegotiable requirement."

"A requirement for what?"

"Of coming back to you."

Sighing heavily, she tossed my passport onto her bedside table, hitting the photo of me as a baby. "I'm so confused."

"I know."

"I need to know, Aslan. I need to understand."

"And I'll tell you everything. I won't leave out a single moment."

Her eyes locked on mine.

I waited to see if she would demand to know everything now or…later.

Finally, she swallowed, rolled her bare shoulders, and said, "I have so many questions. I need to learn who you are now, but…I know enough that you're still mine. Still *him*. Still the shipwrecked boy I fell madly in love with." Her eyes flamed blue. "After."

"After," I breathed.

With a soft moan, she leaped on me.

Chapter Fifty

NERIDA

AGE: 25 YRS OLD

(Love in Chinese: Ài)

HE STUMBLED AND FELL BACKWARD ON THE bed.

I'd expected him to catch me. He always caught me.

He was still the same delicious man I'd known and loved all my life. His body might be covered in silver rounded scars, but he rippled with power. His biceps bulged, his forearms ropey with veins and strength, and his stomach etched with muscles even larger than when I'd last seen him flying through the air, thanks to that awful Uber driver.

Yet his balance seemed a little off.

His mouth came down on mine, distracting me entirely as he flipped me onto my back and shoved me higher up the bed. The dynamics of him shirtless and me fully naked sent my pulse skyrocketing.

I didn't know if Teddy and Eddie had taken Ayla to my parents for the night or if they were in their rooms, quiet as mice, giving us privacy.

Either way, I needed to be silent.

But with every touch, my breath caught and my lungs burned and the urge to cry and scream and launch into rapturous happiness only to huddle in a corner in panic had me locking my teeth together.

This is real.

He's here.

Please, please *don't be imagining this.*

Too many times I'd woken from a similar dream only to slam into reality, leaving me wet and unsatisfied, heartbroken and miserable.

He's alive.

He's here.

Slightly damaged and quietly secretive but *alive.*

I kissed him harder, pouring every part of me into him. I wanted him to taste how much I'd missed him. To feel my blind loyalty, shaky guilt, and absolute mad belief that he would return.

He'd once told me he would come back if he was able.

He'd demanded I promise I'd never go to Turkey after him.

I'd broken my vow, but he'd kept his.

He's here.

I couldn't stop thinking it. A mantra to keep me spiralling and dissolving into body-shaking sobs.

You're here.

You're here.

You're really, truly here.

I threw my arms around him and kissed him like the siren he called me.

I caught his bottom lip in my teeth.

I sucked on his tongue.

He attacked me back with an edge of violence I knew and loved.

His touch teased with pleasure and pain.

His kisses sharp and punishing. His breath haggard and harsh.

I tried to roll over him. To sit on top of him and sink down his length.

But he kept me pinned.

His hips between mine.

His hands in my hair.

His mouth stealing every indecent, erotic, sinful thought in my body. He kissed me the way I needed to be kissed. The only way we could kiss.

With accusation and apology.

With promises and penance.

I knew him.

Every part of him.

Yet he was different too.

A familiar friend and lover returned with secrets and a cursed last name.

He sucked on my bottom lip, scattering my thoughts as he drove his trouser-clad hardness against the throbbing in my core.

The need between us went from blazing to out of control.

Panting hard, he trailed his lips from mine to my jaw and down my throat. "Fuck, I missed you." His teeth scraped along my collarbone as he ducked down my body and took my left nipple in his mouth. He sucked me, licked me, worshipped me.

My back arched.

My hands landed in his gorgeous thick hair, tugging on the dark-sable strands. No sign of bronze from the salt and sun. He was darker. Inside and out. His eyes weren't haunted anymore, but they held things he hadn't shared. He still carried shadows, but there was also a glow—a strange sort of light that lit up those shadows. A glow that grew brighter the longer he kissed me and switched to my other breast, kneading me with greedy hands, making me whimper beneath him.

"Aslan." I moaned, trying to pull his mouth back to mine. "I need. God, I need—"

"I know." He shifted over me, sinking between my splayed legs, rocking his delicious erection against my wetness. His trousers were still in the way. They were the worst barrier imaginable. "I wanted to make this last, but…I don't think I can."

"Me either," I panted. "I just…I need you. Right now. I need to trust this is real before I wake up screaming."

His eyes locked on mine.

Shifting to his left elbow—the same arm that was now naked of our ink—his other hand went to his belt. He winced as he tried to undo it one-handed.

"Here." I dove my hands between us. "Let me."

Bracing himself over me, his fingers feathered through my hair as he arched his hips and bit his bottom lip as I undid, unzipped, and without any hesitation, pushed his slacks and boxer-briefs down his thighs.

I waited for him to roll off me and kick them away. To toe off his shoes and return to me fully naked.

But he didn't.

Instead, a darker shadow swirled in his eyes. A slight pucker between his brows. Another secret he wasn't ready to share.

I never looked away from him as my fingers curled around his hot, hard length. He filled my palm with impressive girth. I'd imagined touching him like this so many times but to finally be able to do it?

To have him in my hold?

To have him quaking the longer I touched him?

I shivered.

I *needed.*

He groaned.

My hand remembered him.

Every ridge and shape. All his heat and size.

An eternity could pass, and I would never forget how he felt. How perfect and velvety and big.

He hissed as I stroked him, up and down, slowly pressing my thumb against his crown and smearing the slickness I found there.

"Fuck, Neri." He growled, his hips pumping into my hand. "Have you forgotten how sensitive you make me, *canım?* It's been too long. Far too fucking long, and I—"

"You want me?"

"I'm *aching* for you, *aşkım.*"

"Then take me." I squeezed him hard.

He bucked in my hold. A guttural groan echoed in his scarred chest. "Keep doing that and I'll come before I'm even inside you."

A confession spilled out of me. "I'm slightly afraid."

His eyes flared, and he cradled me close. "Afraid? Of me?"

"Of this," I rushed. "I'm afraid of how much I want this. How much I need you to be real. Every part of me desperately wants this to be true, but what if it isn't?" Tears stung as they pooled and rolled down my cheeks. "What if I'm about to wake up like I always do, and I'm in bed, alone, like so many other nights?" I stroked him again, memorising his shape, his heat. "I don't think I could stand it, Aslan. I barely survived losing you once. But to have you back, only to risk losing you again…" I couldn't finish.

"Ah, Neri." He kissed me softly. "I'm right here. I'm never going anywhere. You have my word."

"But how can you say that? How can you know?"

"Because I know what it's like to lose you and I'll never let that happen again. *Ever.*"

"Promise?"

"*Söz veriyorum.*" (I promise).

The air crackled around us as we lost ourselves in each other.

I couldn't look away as he reached between us, removed my hand from around his erection, then shifted between my legs.

No words.

No whispers.

Only the softest moan as he guided his cock to my entrance and notched himself within me.

That precipice.

That sharp, wonderful mountain.

We teetered on the edge of it.

Then fell off together as he pushed. Slowly. Relentlessly. Spreading me with his size, penetrating my body that hadn't been touched in such a long time.

I arched beneath him, submitting and begging.

My nails landed in his lower back as he dipped his head and kissed me. He kissed me to distraction. He kissed me while making me his. He kissed me with every inch of his length, and when he finally sank deep, deep inside me, like a key forged for its matching lock, he pressed the softest kiss to my nose, and began to fuck me.

My teeth clamped on my bottom lip to hold back my moans.

He buried his face in my neck and bit my throat to silence his roar.

Our pace started languid and slow, a rock of love and affection, but it wasn't enough. It had never been enough for us. We needed that savage edge of cruelty. That brutal line of hard.

My bed creaked as he lost himself to me.

His fingers tangled in my hair as he pumped between my legs, driving his lower belly against my clit, hitting that humming spot inside me.

My legs spread wider, giving him everything.

Each thrust shattered the pain and loneliness of the past five years.

Each time he groaned and sank as deep as he could, he proved to me this *wasn't* a dream.

This was unbelievably real, and I couldn't stop myself.

I gave in to bliss.

I rode that wave of rapture.

I grabbed his ass and jerked him into me, and he read my mind as he turned into the predator he was named for.

His thrusts became sharp and stabbing punishments.

His breath caught, and his harsh kiss bit me with teeth.

"Come for me," he groaned. "Come around me. Come, Neri. Please fucking come because I—" He choked and shuddered. His back rippled and eyes flared.

I witnessed the moment he lost control as his eyes blazed black and his mouth fell wide. A feral snarl escaped as he gave up trying to stop his release and threw himself headfirst into it.

He drove into me as if he hated me. As if he wanted to eradicate all the hurt between us, all the loss.

And that was it.

The first splash of his orgasm. The final link of our physical forms unravelled the coil of tightness inside me.

It unspooled, caught fire, and ricocheted outward in waves of blinding pleasure.

On and on, over and over.

My body fisted around him; he growled in pain.

We didn't stop straining against each other, bruising each other, clawing at each other. My release wrung me dry, and by the time the magic in my blood faded and I opened my eyes, Aslan filled my entire world.

God, he's beautiful.

And here.

Alive.

Dark hair, dark eyes, dark soul…but a glowing heart.

A heart that had been hurt and tortured.

A heart that carried as many cuts and wounds as mine.

I'd felt him.

I'd heard him.

But now…he was home.

"Are you hungry?" I whispered, checking my phone on my bedside table.

One a.m.

I skimmed the text from Teddy that'd come in a few hours ago.

Teddy: *I don't know how this has happened or how he's here, but I now officially believe in miracles. I always knew you were special. I've often joked you're psychic, but…it's true. I know that without a shadow of a doubt. You never let go of him, and he never let go of you. Enjoy your miracle, Nee. Don't worry about Ayla. Eddie and I have her covered. She won't shut up about the man with her daddy's name, so be prepared for that whirlwind when you finally step out of your bedroom.*

I smiled and switched off the screen.

"What's amusing?" Aslan asked, welcoming me back into his protective embrace. We hadn't left my bed. I couldn't stop touching him, kissing him, doing my best to ignore the silly fear that the moment I stepped foot out of my room, this would all pop and disappear.

Snuggling deeper into his arms, I smelled sex on his skin and shivered for a fourth round. Three times he'd taken me in mind-blowing missionary. He'd never withdrawn from our first release—just like many times in our past—and our second love-making had been slow and fierce, borderline torturous as we rocked and ground against each other, doing our best to become one.

We'd dozed a little after that, and I'd woken as he reached for me, sliding me beneath him and kissing me deep to keep me silent as he pushed inside me, then drilled me hard and fast into my bed.

I'd never been in such a sated, post-sex glow, but…something niggled me. A tiny worry because he still hadn't taken his trousers off. He hadn't tried to take me in another position.

Why?

What did Cem do to him?

And am I strong enough to find out?

I caught his stunning stare, doing my best to swallow my concerns. "Teddy says Ayla has many questions about you, and we should be prepared."

He smiled softly. "I never imagined I'd be a father or that it would hit me right in the chest. I don't even know her, but I love her." He nuzzled into my neck. "*Onu seviyorum, ama… seni daha çok seviyorum. Eminim bunu itiraf etmem beni bir canavar yapar ama hiç kimse sana olan sevgimin yanına bile yaklaşamaz.*" (I love her, but…I love you more. I'm sure this makes me a monster to admit, but no one will ever come close to how much I adore you).

Pulling away a little, he quirked his eyebrow, waiting to see if I would ask for a translation. But…five years was a long time. Five years and so many lonely nights. I'd taken an online language course—when I wasn't obsessing over how to build Lunamare—and although my accent needed work and sometimes I got my verbs wrong, I was technically fluent in my husband's tongue.

Running my fingers through his hair, I murmured, *"Bunun seni bir canavar yapıp yapmaması umrumda değil çünkü ben de öyleyim. Kızımızı tüm kalbimle seviyorum. Ama seni tüm ruhumla seviyorum."* (I don't care if that makes you a monster because I'm one too. I love our daughter with all my heart. But I love you with all my soul).

He froze.

"You learned." Love lit up his dark stare until a ring of molten affection glowed.

"I learned for me. And for Ayla. I needed her to love you as much as I do. To know she came from the best man in the world and a country full of magic."

"Fucking hell." His voice caught thickly. "What did I do to deserve you, Neri?"

"You survived," I whispered. "You survived when you were sixteen, and you survived now, despite my mistakes."

He cupped my cheek with a trembling hand where we lay facing each other in bed. "Promise me, *canım*. Promise me we'll never spend another night apart. Not a single day without each other."

The deadly seriousness of his face and the familiar sternness of his delectable mouth made my blood thicken. Laying my hand on his chest, my fingertips buzzed with the thudding of his heart. "I promise. Forever and always."

The moment stretched until it cut me with poignancy. Too sharp. Too vivid. Far too vicious with unsaid things. My gaze dropped to his unzipped trousers. He'd removed his belt and pulled his boxer-briefs back up, but the fact he still wore them finally wore me down. "Why won't you get completely undressed? W-Why did you only take me in missionary when…we have a habit of using the walls, the floor, and everything in between?"

He smiled as if remembering our fast and furious antics, but then his face fell, and he sighed heavily. "You asked me before if I was hungry."

I frowned at him changing the subject, but before I could reply, he added, "I'm not hungry, *hayatım*, but I am craving a shower." He lowered his jaw and didn't look into my eyes. "Would you…do you want to bathe with me?"

My heart clenched at the sudden wariness in him. The coiling uncertainty working through his body. Why was he uncertain? If I didn't know any better, I'd think he was suddenly shy.

Urgency filled me to take away whatever worries he had, and I slipped from my bed. Slinking into my white robe hanging on the back of my door, I held out my hand. "Let's shower."

Without a word, he shifted to the side of the bed, swung his legs to the ground, then paused. His chest strained as he sucked in a breath, highlighting all those awful silver scars.

My hands balled as pure hate wracked through me.

If Cem was still alive, he wouldn't be for too much longer.

I'd hire every mercenary available to eradicate him. I'd summon all the monsters in my soul and tear him apart. I'd happily go to jail for making him pay.

I didn't care Cem was the reason my parents and I had never been prosecuted for harbouring an illegal immigrant. I didn't care that he'd protected us in his own twisted way.

He'd hurt my soulmate.

And that was punishable by death.

"*All it takes is a good reason and a bad day*," Wayne Gratt's quote from that show with Stanley Tucci echoed in my mind.

He was wrong.

Today was a great day.

Yet I was fully prepared to make a murderous decision to kill my father-in-law.

Aslan's knuckles whitened as he gripped the mattress. He glowered at the floor, whispering, "I know it's stupid. I know you love me far deeper than physical appearance, yet…" He shook his head with a scoff. "I can't help feeling as if I should…apologise."

"Apologise?" My eyebrows shot up. "For what?"

He shrugged sadly. "For who I am now." His lips twisted into a snarl. "But…that's wrong because I *know* it won't matter, and if I'm honest, I've already come to terms with it myself. It took me a long time, I admit. I didn't know if I'd ever be able to fully accept but…a few weeks ago, I learned that I'm still me. Even if pieces are missing."

Ice trickled down my spine. "Aslan…you're scaring me."

His head ripped up. With a soft grunt, he zipped up his slacks, pushed off the bed, then strode toward me a little stiffly. "That isn't my intention, *aşkım*. Forgive me. I was merely thinking out loud." He smiled and bent to kiss me. "Honestly, I'm okay. I'm surprisingly okay. Fucking great, actually."

I accepted his kiss, but it didn't calm my skipping heart.

"Come on." He took my hand. "Let's get clean, then we can sleep." Unlocking my door and leading me down the corridor, he glanced at me for confirmation. "Which door was it again?"

"This one." Padding quietly down the carpeted hallway, I opened the family bathroom and waited until Aslan was inside before turning on the light and locking it.

He stood in the largish space, turning on the spot as he took in the huge slab of wood with two glass bowls and black taps that acted as our vanity, the mirror in the shape of three rolling waves, the bathtub where Ayla splashed and giggled every night, and the double-man shower that Teddy had been adamant he wanted because why shower alone when you could shower together?

I'd been secretly jealous of him and Eddie's long steamy interludes in here while I played outside with Ayla, but now…I got to enjoy the huge rain head with my lover and marvel at the glittery mosaic tiles as he slipped into me from behind.

My hands shook a little as I slipped out of my robe, gathered a fresh towel for Aslan from the rolled-up stack in the rattan shelving by the door, and placed it on the rail beside mine.

His eyes never left my naked skin. The way he studied me made my nipples pebble and all those butterflies from my youth flutter and fly, proving that I must've swallowed an entire galaxy of them because they'd never died.

"You're so fucking beautiful," he murmured as his right hand went to his cock and stroked the hard outline in his trousers. "Five years without you, and now I can't get enough."

I stepped toward him.

I curled my hand around his on his erection. "Get naked then, so you can have me again."

He swallowed loudly. "Only you, Neri. Only you have this power over me. And I'm so fucking grateful."

I went to drop to my knees and pull his pants off, but he stopped me with a quick catch of my chin. "Wait." Shaking his head slightly, he sighed and stepped away. "There's something I need to show you first."

Holding my stare, he hooked his thumbs into his boxers and trousers, then pushed them down with a sharp inhale.

They tumbled to his feet.

For a moment, I thought he wore a knee brace. Something runners wore to protect their joints.

But then I saw metal where flesh ought to be.

I went rigid.

I didn't move as he held onto the towel rail and kicked away his trousers. Balancing on his right leg, he unthreaded the laces of his dress shoe then kicked it off.

The foot that appeared gleamed a silver-black with a mechanical ankle that moved like a real joint. Holding his breath, he slowly shifted his weight onto the prosthetic and tore off his shoe and sock on his right.

His bare toes curled into the bathmat, so at odds to the metal ones next to them.

He didn't speak.

Neither did I.

I couldn't take my eyes off it. Off him. Off what he'd had to endure.

I didn't cry.

I didn't fall.

I merely tripped deeper into love with him.

Endless love, unconditional, unequivocal, *unlimited* love.

He thought I wouldn't find him attractive? That I would feel him lacking? That I would judge him for this? Ask him to *apologise* for this? *God.*

I shook my head, struggling to catch my breath.

I was in *awe* of him.

Absolute fucking awe.

He'd returned to me missing pieces of his body, yet somehow, his soul had healed. The fractures in his spirit from losing his family and having to hide for so long were neatly knitted and whole.

He wasn't the same man who'd been deported.

He was more.

So, *so* much more.

He'd not only accepted the change in his appearance and ableness but had done it with grace and confidence that I found inspiring and stirring and downright erotic.

Stepping into him, I stood on my tiptoes, plastered my nakedness to his, and kissed him.

His head tipped down, his powerful arms encircled me, and with the strength I knew and loved, he picked me up and carried me into the shower.

He didn't trip or stumble. He barely even moved with a limp, and when he put me down, spun the tap to rain us in hot water, I pulled away from his kiss and breathed, "You were beautiful to me before, but now? There are no words, Aslan. No words for how I feel about you. I'm home when I'm with you, and I know in the depth of my being that I'm not meant to exist without you."

"I feel the same way," he whispered. Tears glimmered in his eyes, mingling with the sparkling water. "Thank you. For accepting me as I am."

"No." I shook my head. "Thank *you*. Thank you for finding me again. For forgiving me. For loving me as much as I love you. In all shapes and sizes."

"Always." He kissed me. "Forever."

I kissed him.

Steam rose around us.

Pulling away, he grabbed my favourite frangipani shampoo and spun me to wash my hair.

With his strong hands on my head, he finally told me everything.

Chapter Fifty-One

ASLAN

(*Heart in Chinese:* Xīn)

"YOU PROBABLY HEARD HIM SHOOT ME WHEN we were on the phone together. I thought it was a bullet as the pain ripped through me, but then...sleep crushed me so damn fast, I didn't have time to tell you goodbye. That haunted me for so long. That I'd left you so suddenly, without a single farewell.

"I woke up in his compound, sick and feverish, suffering from a reaction to the tranquiliser. For weeks, I was in and out of consciousness, and when I was finally strong enough to stay awake, I understood how close I came to death.

"Unfortunately, that was the start of a long list of illnesses. I grew strong, only for him to strap me to the chair and begin my 'reconditioning'. My system wasn't ready for such abuse, and I slipped again. As I passed out, I heard his doctor talking about amputation, and I'd never been so fucking scared in all my life."

I trailed my fingers down her back, spreading suds and scent. "By the time I woke up, I was missing a piece of myself, and I confess it sent me into a pit of self-loathing. He let me heal for a few months, but mentally, I was getting worse. He gave me his ledgers and accounts to pull me out of the darkness, and...despite myself, the allure of numbers worked.

"I dragged myself back into hope and did what I could to make my body strong again. I had no intention of dying there without seeing you again and didn't care what I had to become to make that happen."

My heart skipped and I dropped my voice until it was barely audible above the shower. "I won't bore you with the years of torture—you felt it all anyway. The electricity broke me, but only after he took my tattoo. It took him three years, but when I finally surrendered, I had nothing left.

"That fourth year, I behaved the way I was supposed to. I didn't think of running, because how could I? I hobbled around on a poorly fitted prosthetic and refused his offer for a better one because I knew I wouldn't be able to stop myself if I felt strong enough to run.

"But by year five, even that pain wasn't enough to keep me obedient. I dreamed of you constantly. I burned for you, missed you, and when I refused to sleep with a slave and admitted I would never be able to take a wife who wasn't you, he turned his threats to snatching you and Ayla.

"That was the night we were raided by the police. The girl he'd commanded I sleep with—the girl I refused, and he shot in the head—was an undercover agent for an international sting on his empire. She was only meant to watch, but she was caught and sucked into the operation. Instead of letting fear stop her mission, she did what she could to bring him down, regardless of the risk. Cem's been wanted for decades. Law enforcement have tried to nail him on so many charges, but they never quite stuck. They were never able to catch him in the act, but unfortunately for him, the day he ordered one of his guards to shoot that poor American girl, the transmitting device she'd smuggled inside herself and hooked up to the camera feed in his Fairy House recorded valuable evidence of his crime.

"They had him on record for murder. And so…they came for him.

"When the police raided in the middle of the night, Cem tried to get me out. For all his shortcomings as a father and all his monstrosity as a person, he did love me. Or at least, he thought he did. Maybe he didn't know the meaning of love, but…he made the biggest mistake of his life thinking I could ever love him back. He gave me a gun. A gun to use against our enemy."

I swallowed hard. "I shot him. Point blank. Just before I was swarmed by police and arrested."

Neri stiffened beneath my hands, but she didn't say a word.

I kept speaking and stroking her wonderful curves. "For four weeks, I rotted in a solitary cell. They took my leg, my cane, my hope. No one told me what was going on, and no one came to help. By the time I was pulled out of prison and dragged to meet the chief of the international operation, I was half delirious.

"I just wanted to leave. I just wanted you. And if that meant dying so I could wait for you on the other side, then so be it. I wanted everything to be over so I didn't have to keep missing you every fucking moment of every damn day. But then…things got strange."

"Strange?" she whispered, turning around and shivering as I ran my soapy hands over her full breasts.

I didn't look up, hypnotised by her body as I said, "The men who arrested me that night told their chief I'd been the one to pull the trigger and kill Cem Kara. They knew who I was. They knew I was his biological son, and also knew—through one of their many snitches—that only a week before, Cem had pledged me into the family business and made each of his generals swear me their allegiance. With him dead, I was the next ruler. I had all his power and commanded his men's loyalties. With one bullet, I became their greatest asset because I'd killed my own father. I'd betrayed him for the same reasons they were trying to shut him down. And that…well, that made me valuable."

"Oh my god," Neri gasped.

"I expected them to throw me in chains or kill me, but…they offered me a deal." Guiding her beneath the raining showerhead, I rinsed her hair before saying quietly, "The chief locked the door, unhooked his phone, and pulled out a top-secret file. I was in that room with him for six hours, and when I walked out…I was a free man."

"I-I don't understand."

"Only he, one other agent in the AFP, and I know. I was sworn to secrecy, but I could never keep a lie from you, so…I'm telling you this on the proviso that no one else can find out. No one. Do you hear me? Not a damn soul. We come up with a story for everyone else."

I waited for her to catch my eyes and nod. The intensity of her blue gaze fisted my heart.

I sighed as I accepted her promise, then murmured, "His terms were simple: inherit everything. Every penny. Every wrong and terribly bad thing. They promised not to confiscate Cem's wealth, if I legally accepted the name Aslan Kara, assumed my rightful place thanks to my birth right and succession, and become the next ruler of my father's empire."

My lips curled back. "Not to *become* him, but to prevent another from rising up to replace him. They wanted access to the largest crime family in Turkey. They wanted to quash uprising gangs and learn where every girl Cem had sold had ended up and with whom. They wanted to know who supplied his drugs and who bought the most. They wanted to know how trades were made, secrets were kept, laws were amended, and how many politicians—not just in Turkey, but worldwide—were on his payroll.

"When I marched back into my father's mansion on a newly fashioned leg and a world of secrets inside me, I honestly feared I'd be shot by the very same guards that'd hurt me in the past. I stalked past men who'd helped Cem torture me. I outright ignored a guard that'd knocked me out for trying to escape and did my best not to punch the one who'd pushed me to my knees each time Cem wasn't watching all because he could.

"I summoned Cem's generals—*my* generals—to a meeting in the smoking room. The same room where I'd sworn a blood bond to my father, and he'd named me his heir. They came but not willingly. They sulked and scowled, expecting me to rip apart my father's empire, so you can imagine their surprise when I told them that the only part of his business that I was shutting down was the Fairy House. All the girls were handed over to the people I now work for to be debriefed and sent home so they didn't compromise my position as their double agent.

"Overnight, the trafficking side of Cem's kingdom was dismantled and the girls safe. That gave me some peace of mind but not a lot. I-I've done things I'm not happy about, Neri. I've hurt people because Cem told me to. I've killed—"

I cut myself off, breathing hard. Focusing on the better parts of my story, I said, "The drugs and money laundering, the many assets and homes around the world are now mine to run as I see fit. Not because the police are corrupt and want in on such a world but because they're using me to flush out the men and women using such things."

I shrugged. "It's not forever. I don't have to play the part of a crime lord for the rest of my life. Eventually, they'll have me shut it down, but I do have to do it until they are satisfied they've cleaned up as much as they can. Which means...I-I have to go back to Turkey soon."

She gasped and went to argue, but I placed my finger over her lips and whispered, "Just to visit. I live here now. I have the visa to prove it. My visits to Turkey won't be long, but I do need to be seen. My country isn't evil, *canım*. Not like him. Turkish people are mostly good and gracious and will give the shirt off their backs to strangers. My father tried to taint that. He smeared my culture and my home with his greed. I suppose every city has good and bad. Every country has a balance of evil and goodness, but I feel as if it's my duty to clean up the mess my father made. To restore my heritage the best way I can. To be loyal to my origins, all while ensuring my generals do what I've commanded them to do."

"So that's how you were able to come back to Australia?" she asked quietly. "By working with law enforcement?"

I shrugged. "It was my only condition. They've asked me to sully my name and do things I'm definitely not comfortable doing. I would prefer to shut everything down, not become its figurehead. In return, I asked for you. I demanded a passport, visa, and the promise that while I'm in Australia, I will be left alone. In return, I will keep my side of the bargain and continue feeding them information of deals and shipments. I'll do whatever it takes to repent for what my father did."

"That's why you accepted the last name Kara." She bit her bottom lip, stroking her hands over my bare chest, making me tremble. "That's why you accepted your inheritance."

I nodded. "Cem killed Aslan Avci. That part's not a lie. The moment he took my leg, my tattoo, and my sanity, I lost that part of myself, and I...I became stronger for it. As much as I don't want to admit that I'm like him, there's an undeniable part that is. I'm not always a good person. I'm happy to do bad things if it protects those I love. The only difference between Aslan Kara and Aslan Avci is...I'm no longer afraid of that darkness inside me. I don't need to run from it anymore because that darkness kept me alive long enough to come back to you."

Turning her around slowly, I grabbed her hands and splayed them on the tiled wall. Her back arched as I ran my fingers down her spine and grabbed her hips. Hot water continued to rain over us. Lust caught me around the back of the throat as I dipped my fingers between her legs and found her drenched.

I choked on a snarl. "You're so wet, *aşkım.*"

Her hips rocked back. She whimpered under her breath. "I always am around you."

Testing her, I dipped two fingers deep inside before pressing my thumb on her clit and grabbing my cock. I fingered her while stroking myself, driving us into that dark tangle that made us reckless and wicked.

"Aslan…" Her head tipped forward, her hair streaming with water. "Please…"

The latent need in her voice. The sinuous grace of her spine. The magnetic charge between us that transcended distance and time.

It was too much.

It wasn't enough.

It struck a match to my darkness and filled me with savage desire.

Removing my fingers from her core, I smeared her arousal over her hip as I pressed myself between her legs. "I missed this." I rubbed my cock through her drenched folds. "I missed you." I angled myself to nudge against her opening. "I missed fucking you." My voice strangled, deep and smoky.

"Do it," she gasped. "Fuck me. Please."

I shuddered as I pushed inside her.

Slowly.

Possessively.

She cried out as I filled her, thickly, slickly, not stopping until my hipbones wedged against her ass and her fingers clawed at the tiles.

Just like that time on *The Fluke* when she asked me if I could come without moving, I felt the tingle, the pressure. All it would take was a kiss to her spine, a lick of her skin, and I'd spurt so fucking hard inside her.

"Do you still love me, Neri? Knowing what I agreed to. Knowing what I'll have to do?"

She groaned and shifted on my cock. "I love you more. I love you with everything that I am."

I withdrew only to spear back inside. "I want you to come with me to Turkey. I want to show you my old home and build a new one with you here and there. Everywhere. As long as I'm with you, I'm happy. If you've figured out how to live beneath the sea while I've been gone, I'll happily live there. Or if you want to fly away to the moon, that works too."

I rocked into her, withdrawing until I almost popped out before sinking fierce and fast.

She pressed her forehead against the tiles, wet hair sticking to her shoulders. "I don't care where we live. Like you told me when I was seventeen, I love you here, there, and everywhere. It's physically impossible for me not to love you, Aslan. I don't care what our address is. I don't care if you're now some lord of deceit and crime. You're still you, and I love you."

I chuckled low. "Does it turn you on? Knowing I have power? Knowing I'm no longer that penniless refugee you found clinging to a shipwreck?" My pumps turned shallower, quicker, riding her from behind as my balls tightened and my blood sang with sensitivity.

"Everything about you turns me on. The man you are now and the boy you were before. Avci and Kara. I love you both."

I couldn't get enough.

I'd never tire of her confessing how she felt about me.

I wanted to hear those words every day for the rest of my life.

Folding over her, I wrapped my arm around her chest and fondled her breast. "Good answer. And here's mine in response."

Wedging my forehead against her nape, I gave in to her. "I've loved you every day of my existence, and I'll love you every day to my death. I'm never letting you go again, Neri. Never. You're mine. I'm yours. No secrets. No lies. No more pain or fear."

Pressing a kiss on her shower-slick shoulder blade, I gave into the devout appetite of my starving soul.

I wanted to consume her.

Possess her.

I wanted to remind her all over again who she belonged to for the rest of our days.

"*Sen benimsin, Neri. Sonsuza kadar.*" (You're mine, Neri. Forever).

Words slithered from my mind as I gave in to the carnal calling between us.

My lips pulled back.

My breath turned to grunts.

I fucked her like she was my queen.

I made love to her like she was my ever after.

Because she was.

We were one.

One heart, one soul, one life.

And for the first time in my existence, I didn't have the cold kiss of a guillotine pressed against my throat. I didn't fear that she could be taken or horror that I could be stolen.

I was free.

Free in ways I'd never hoped or dreamed for, and I gave this woman everything.

I fucked her hard and deep.

I groaned as she came around my cock, fisting me, milking me, sending me spiralling into heaven.

And when I let go, I roared and quaked and marked her forever as mine.
My wife.
My soulmate.
My home.

"Wakey, wakey."

I groaned and swatted at something soft poking my cheek.

Comprehension muddied with dreams, doing their best to keep me asleep.

I groaned as something heavy suddenly squashed against my belly followed by a worried whisper-hiss. "No, moonbeam. Don't touch him when he's sleeping. He might hurt—"

"Neri?" I blinked and looked down my chest where Nerida lay sprawled sideways over me, her hands locked around a tiny girl's wrists. A girl with dark eyes, dark hair, pink nightgown, and a stern twist of her lips.

How long had I begged to wake to safety?

How many mornings had I longed to wake with Nerida in my arms only to find the stark, cold walls of a cave?

But now that it'd happened, I fought a dark chuckle.

I was free and back in Nerida's bed, but this wasn't quite what I expected.

"Hi." Neri smiled shyly, still lying over my middle. "I, eh…Ayla tried to wake you up, and I panicked." Letting her daughter's—*our* daughter's—fists go, she slowly sat up. "I'm used to you being a tad…violent when you wake."

I sat higher in the sheets and reclined against the pillows. "It's prudent to protect her from me, and obviously I can't promise I won't have another nightmare, but…I've lived them all. I have nothing left to haunt me. Nothing else to fear. I've let Emre, Jale, Afet, and Melike go. I truly don't think I'll wake with that sort of emotional pain again."

Neri never took her eyes off me. A gleam of wonderful love lit up her blue gaze. "Have I told you I adore you this morning?"

I stretched and drank in my sleep-fuzzy wife. "Have I told you that this is the best morning of my life?"

My heart kicked.

She sucked in a breath.

Our moment was shattered by a little finger poking me in the side, over and over, finding each and every scar from the electrodes. "What's that and that and that?"

I waited for the urge to cover up or to shut down but all I felt, all I *incredibly* felt was joy. Untarnished, unblemished *joy*.

"A few things hurt me, but I'm okay now." I held out my arms. "Do you…would you like to join us?" I flicked a look at Neri, who sat up in a lacy nightdress. "Is it okay if I pick her up?" We'd finally fallen asleep sometime around dawn, and judging by the light, it wasn't that much after, but I wasn't tired.

I was buzzing.

Tingling with life and newness.

"Of course, it is," Neri said. Glancing past me at Ayla, she added, "Do you want to come snuggle with Mummy?"

Ayla crossed her arms and scowled at me. "Depends."

"Oh?" I raised an eyebrow. "On what?"

"On who you are, silly. Why're you in my Mummy's bed?"

"Ah, well. I'm…I'm—"

"I've got this," Neri murmured before sliding out of the blankets and padding toward Ayla. Dropping to her haunches, she took Ayla's tiny hands in hers and said softly, "You know all those stories I told you about the lion being your father? The painting on your wall and—"

"The kitty on your arm?" Ayla poked Neri's tattoo.

"Yes." Neri nodded. "Remember how I told you he had to go away but he was never truly gone?"

"Uh-huh." Ayla nodded and flicked me a look of intense concentration.

"Well…that lion came back. He's right there." She laughed under her breath. "I should probably read a parenting book on how we're supposed to do this, but…Ayla…" She stood, grabbed her daughter, then deposited her on the bed right beside my prosthetic. The metal foot with its mechanical toes and carbon pylon poked out of the sheets. Unable to tell the temperature difference, I hadn't been aware I'd stuck it out. Then again, it'd been the first time I'd slept with it on, and surprisingly, it didn't ache.

I wouldn't make a habit of it, and I supposed a part of me was still a little nervous about showing Neri my leg without the metal attachment, but…even that worry didn't affect me.

I'd never been so fucking free. So in the moment. So *grateful*.

"Ayla, this…this is your dad. Aslan."

"You are?" Ayla's little eyebrows crawled up her face. "You don't look like a lion."

"Well, you don't look like a cub." I grinned. "Or moonlight, considering that's what your name means."

"Huh." She frowned. "Suppose that makes sense." She shifted to her knees, using my false leg as an anchor. Her serious stare shot straight to where she held me. The one place I couldn't feel. Her mouth fell open. "Oh no, did you lose a leg like Scuttle?"

"Scuttle? Who's Scuttle?"

Neri snorted and did her best not to laugh. "She means the seagull we've been feeding when we go out on *The Fluke*. It has semi-adopted us and has a missing leg."

"I named it because it's a mermaid," Ayla announced proudly.

I chuckled, utterly bewildered but completely bewitched. "Neri? Care to translate again?"

She laughed, running her fingers through Ayla's pretty hair. "She means we stole the name from the neurotic seagull in *The Little Mermaid*. She's addicted to Disney."

I smirked. "So, let me guess. She wants to live beneath the waves, just like her mother?"

Neri reared back with mock shock, planting a hand over her heart. "What on earth are you implying?" She fluttered her eyelashes with innocence. "Are you saying I have an ulterior motive to ensure my daughter is part fish, so she willingly moves to the Coral Sea—if and when we make it a possibility?"

"That's exactly what I'm saying. Couldn't have her being like her father, could you? Stubborn as hell about never stepping foot in the ocean."

"Well, I got him in the water eventually." Her cheeks pinked. "In fact, I happen to remember the first night he swam with me was one of the best nights of my life."

I stilled. The light-hearted conversation faded as I remembered why I'd gotten into the sea with her and why I'd pledged my soul to hers as I sank inside her that first time.

Ethan.

My first kill but not my last.

That was my only regret in this new world of light. I'd killed. How many I didn't want to think about and none by choice. But I was still responsible for taking lives, and eventually, I would have to accept and move on. I would do my best to make up for my sins by ensuring I helped instead of hurt.

For now, though, I was just grateful I'd woken up, untethered from everything that'd haunted me.

I felt...*reborn*.

"You know I can fix you," Ayla chirped, interrupting the tangled stare between Neri and me. "I'm gonna be a doctor." She knocked on my metal shin, then fiddled with the single adjustable strap around the base of the coupling where it attached to my body. "I'm gonna be the best doctor in the whole wide world."

Neri sighed, love glowing from her every pore. "If I was a bleeding heart when I was little, Ayla is ten times worse." She leaned over and planted a kiss on our daughter's cheek. "She wants to fix everyone, don't you, moonbeam?"

"Moonbeam?" I asked quietly, my heart skipping a beat as I bled with too much affection. How was it possible that I loved this kid with every part of me when I barely even knew her? I would raze the world for her. I would do unthinkable things to keep her safe. I stood by what I said to Neri: I would always love her above everyone else, but Ayla…fuck, my damaged heart expanded so there was enough room to adore them both.

"Yep." Ayla puffed up her chest. "Everyone calls me that."

Never looking away from her depthless brown eyes, I whispered, "*Ay'ı seviyorum. Annen ve benim için çok özel.*" (I happen to love the moon. It's very special to your mum and me).

Her little nose wrinkled, mulling over her second language, understanding me and blowing me away with her quickfire intelligence.

She beamed. "That means I'm special too?"

"Beyond special." I nodded. "And I have no doubt you'll make a great doctor."

"I better start saving." Neri chuckled under her breath. "With her inheriting your IQ, she'll be enrolling into medical school when she's twelve."

"My IQ?" I asked, smiling as Ayla investigated how the toes moved and the ankle mechanism worked on my prosthetic.

"Your father told me of your family trait. He finally gave me the name for the skill you have that makes math come so easy to you. She has the same gifts. She got into a heated debate with her day-care teacher that colours aren't named after numbers just because she sees them in different shades."

I winced. "She has synesthesia?"

Ayla interrupted. "I know that word. It's when the rainbow comes, and numbers go all pretty."

"Huh." I studied the intelligent, inquisitive girl who'd somehow taken all of my good and some of my bad.

What other traits did she inherit?

It seemed there was a piece of Cem in both of us, even now.

The door to Neri's bedroom suddenly swung wide from where it'd been pushed open by Ayla's sneaking. Apparently, we'd forgotten to lock it after we'd returned from our shared shower and now had the entire household in Neri's bedroom.

Sitting taller against the pillows, making sure the sheets covered my nakedness, I stiffened as Teddy stuck his head in.

He caught my eyes, then Neri's. "Eh, I'm terribly sorry to interrupt, but I'm looking for moon—" His eyes fell on Ayla as she knocked her knuckles on my knee, learning what was flesh and what was carbon. "Ah, there you are, you little slippery eel. I told you to eat your orange and not to disturb your mother."

Ayla stuck her tongue out at him. "But Daddy's here."

Teddy shot me a look. "You told her?" His eyes instantly filled with tears. "Oh God…that's…wow." Leaning out the door, he yelled, "Eddie, get your ass in here right now."

Footfalls came running before a second man crowded into the doorway.

"What? What is it?" His hazel eyes fell on me, a faint blush dusting his cheeks. "Morning, Aslan. Sorry to disturb." He pinched Teddy in the side. "What the hell are you doing barging in here with these two love-birds? Jesus."

"I was looking for Ayla." He pointed at her still playing with my leg. "She's the one who disturbed them. Not me. Then again, we heard the shower going mighty late last night, so I'm guessing they weren't exactly catching up on beauty sleep."

He winked.

Neri groaned.

My heart squeezed.

Teddy rested his head on Eddie's shoulder. "Guess what? They told her. Ayla knows. How freaking awesome is this?" Standing straight, he suddenly clapped and announced, "We're celebrating. Right now. Get up. Both of you. Champagne breakfast coming right up!"

"Oh God." Neri laughed. "You're insane. You made me vow that we'd save that bottle for when we finally break ground on Lunamare."

"Seriously, Nee?" Teddy crossed his arms. "Who cares about that? You'd rather save a four-hundred-dollar bottle of champagne on a business venture that will probably never happen over the fact that your lover has come back from the dead?" He rolled his eyes dramatically. "And you call yourself a romantic. I take it back. You don't believe in miracles. You're just deluded."

A pillow went flying as Neri tossed it at his face. "Careful. I could still cut you out of the company."

"The penniless company." Teddy waggled his eyebrows. "Come along. Less arguing, more drinking. Aslan...I want to hear everything."

With a dip of his chin, Eddie murmured, "I apologise for my husband. He's just a tad excited. We both are. We've never known someone to come back from the grave before."

Teddy suddenly yanked Eddie out of the door and down the corridor, his voice trailing back. "Neri, go raid our wardrobe for your reincarnated man. He can't wear that stuffy shirt and pants on a hot morning like this. Ayla, come help me make pancakes for your dad. Aslan, get dressed and come join us!"

"Wait for me!" Ayla scurried off the bed and charged after them.

The peace after the sparkling energy of their presence made the silence between Neri and me all the more potent. Our eyes met and held.

For the longest moment, we didn't say anything, but finally, she crawled into my arms and kissed me.

I cupped her cheeks and kissed her back, licking her bottom lip, losing myself to her like I always did. When she finally pulled away, the blankets had tented above my waist and the last thing I wanted was pancakes.

"Are you okay?" She nuzzled my nose with hers. "Is this all too much? Say if you need more time. You were so supportive and wonderful when I was healing after what Ethan did to me. You knew when I was hurting and gave me things I needed, despite your wishes. It's my turn to protect you. And if you'd rather stay here, processing that you're not being hurt and everything is better now, then they'll understand."

The seriousness of her question wasn't lost on me.

The history between us and the darkness in which we'd swum swirled around us. I took a moment to figure out how to give her the truth.

A truth she probably wouldn't believe because even *I* didn't believe it.

After a lifetime of fighting the black smog of depression. Of living with a cloud constantly hovering over me, I hadn't gotten used to the sunshine in my soul. The endless happiness that didn't just come from her, or this, or freedom…but *me*.

I was happy, despite everything that'd happened.

I was happy *because* of everything that'd happened.

The reasons were scrambled in my head. I struggled to put them into comprehensive sentences, and while my mind figured out the puzzle of what I needed to say, I grabbed her around the waist and shifted her over my lap.

I sucked on my bottom lip as she straddled me, rocking herself over my hardness. Her breath caught and her nightgown rose up, sending me straight into lust.

The blankets between us drove me fucking crazy, and the heat and weight of her threatened to push me to an edge that was always far too easy to fall over whenever she touched me.

"*Seni tekrar istiyorum,*" I whispered. (I want you again).

Flicking a look at the corridor, Neri leaped off my lap, darted across her small bedroom, closed the door, engaged the lock, then pulled her nightgown over her head.

Fuck, she's stunning.

Every curve.

Every shadow.

Tangled words flew from my head.

With shaking hands, I tossed back the covers, revealing my cock, weeping and painfully hard. "Come here," I growled. "Sit on me before I have a heart attack from needing you."

"You cured me through sex," Neri whispered as she moved to my side of the bed, kneeled on the mattress, then resumed her place over my lap. Her belly flexed as she straddled me. Her breasts bounced as she soared upward on her knees. Her mouth captured mine as she grabbed my cock, angled me upward, then sank down excruciatingly slowly. "If I can do the same for you, then I will be at your beck and call, Aslan."

I groaned as she kept sinking, her body hot and wet, the pressure of her around me reverting me to something primal and oh, so fucking needy. "I wouldn't say that if I were you," I grunted, my hands landing on her hips and pushing her harder over me. "You'll spend the rest of your life with me inside you."

"I wouldn't complain," she moaned as I spread her completely, sinking in the final delicious inch. Our eyes dropped to where we were joined. It blew my fucking mind that a part of me was inside her. Imprisoned by her strength. Fisted by the flutters of her pleasure.

I swallowed a growl. "Fuck, I'm so close, and you haven't even ridden me yet."

Her eyes flashed. "Do you want me to ride you?"

"Is that a trick question?" I gasped as she rose up a little, then sank back down. A stream of Turkish curses escaped me as she clenched her inner muscles, sending every cell in my body to snap between my legs.

I could come far too easily.

We were expected at breakfast far too quickly.

But I had to answer her question. Had to give her the same peace of mind that I had so she wouldn't worry or search for signs I wasn't coping. I'd driven myself mad trying to help her after Ethan. Fear had made me reckless, and I'd forced her to fight me off in her room on Christmas all because I was so fucking terrified of losing her.

I didn't want her to go through that.

I didn't want her to think there was any chance that I would leave because she was stuck with me until death did us part.

"Wait." I choked as she rocked her hips, fucking me with intoxicating rhythm. "Stop. Just…let me say this."

She sat heavily on my lap, her arms thrown over my shoulders, her fingers knotted in my hair. Her gorgeous eyes met mine, and I reached up to cup her cheek.

"What? What is it?" she breathed. Her inner muscles fisted me, keeping me locked inside her.

Joined by body, mind, and soul, I murmured, "You know I've always struggled with letting go. You called me out on being sad in the past and begged me to get help to somehow be free of my ghosts. I wasn't able to back then because…I didn't feel safe. I was living in a country that wasn't my own and loving a girl I wasn't allowed to keep. I now know there are two types of trauma: physical and emotional. And I've lived most of my life trapped by both. The wanting you but knowing I wasn't in a position to keep you? That was a direct threat to my life, just like the storm, the shipwreck, and everything that Cem did to me.

"My body has been through hell, *canım*, but so has my heart. I'm not going to deny that. I'm sure there will be days where I will miss my leg and I will remember all the moments that I wish I could forget…but…that is where my pain ends, Neri. I don't know how to explain it any better than that. Whatever trauma I've endured is finally over. Everything that worried me before is gone. I have money. I'm legal. I have the ability to go home to Turkey without the fear of being slaughtered. And...I have you."

"You have me forever." She kissed me.

I kissed her back, then pulled away.

Catching her stare, I murmured, "You made my world a thousand times better when my life was temporary. You kept me present even though being present is what made me afraid. My mind wanted to find happiness, but in a way, I suppose I disconnected. I put barriers up because I'd already lost so much and I wouldn't survive losing you. But...then that happened. The worst thing imaginable happened, and I spent five fucking *awful* years missing you.

"But...I survived. The physical pain is forgotten. What he took from me is forgiven. My past is in the past, and my future?" I cupped her breast, grazing my thumb over her pebbled nipple. "Well, I've never looked forward to something so much. I've never been more connected to life because it's *my* life, and no one can take it from me again."

I clenched my stomach muscles, sending my cock twitching inside her. "I'm connected to you, Neri. Body and heart. I'm safe now. I'm anchored. It's like I'm finally waking up from a nightmare that no longer has any hold on me."

I arched up and kissed her.

I licked her.

Nipped her.

Then I pulled away and breathed, "I need you to trust that I'm okay. I'm not lying. I'm not pretending. I'm truly, *honestly* okay. I'm okay because I'm safe. I no longer need to run or hide. Cem taught me that I can survive anything. I'm strong enough. I'm powerful enough, and that sense of safety within me is astounding. It's liberating. It's utterly freeing. So fucking freeing that I can say, here and now, you don't need to worry about me. Because for the first time in my life, I mean that word. Those four little letters that are used so blasély."

Flipping her onto her back, I pinned her against the bed and thrust. "I'm okay." I drove in deep. "I'm okay." I increased my pace and fed her every inch. "I'm going to be okay for the rest of my life."

Her hands landed on my cheeks, holding me above her as I thrust and claimed her. She didn't speak for the longest moment. Her eyes flaring with passion every time I rode her. But then tears welled and rolled from the corners of her eyes, soaking into the sea-scented pillow beneath her.

"*Tamam, Aslan. Tamam.*" (Okay, Aslan. Okay).

Our mouths locked.

Our tongues danced.

And when we came, we tasted true, endless happiness.

Chapter Fifty-Two

ASLAN

(Heart in Spanish: Corazón)

THAT FIRST MORNING BACK IN AUSTRALIA WAS spent in a borrowed pair of shorts and a pale green t-shirt—courtesy of Teddy (slightly too tight but gratefully received)—and the four-hundred-dollar bottle of champagne went well with fresh strawberries, pancakes, and copious amounts of whipped cream, thanks to Ayla being in charge.

Jack and Anna joined us.

The table outside barely held all of us as we spent the day talking, drinking, eating, and soaking in the fact that things were exactly as they should be.

Neri helped me tell a heavily redacted tale of abuse and imprisonment, revealing my leg and scars. I brushed over how I'd been able to return to Australia and had no doubt questions would come once the shock of my miraculous appearance wore off. By then, I would have a better story. One that would keep my new job a secret and protect everyone.

At some point after lunch of cheese, biscuits, and hastily made cucumber sandwiches, Ayla disappeared into the house and appeared in a bathing suit. She begged and begged until Neri changed too and opened the childproof lock on the fence around the pool.

I stood on the sparkly pavers while Ayla dove as deep as she could before shooting for the surface. My heart overflowed as Neri asked me to do something that'd been a nightly ritual for us.

Almost shyly, she'd passed me her old stopwatch and I'd timed her breath hold, giving her a kiss that'd turned into something definitely not suitable for children when she popped up four and a half minutes later.

The metal of my leg glinted in the setting sun, obvious thanks to the pair of shorts I wore, and Jack pulled me aside to check, man to man, how I was doing. The tears in his eyes spoke of guilt and pity, but I had nothing to blame on him, and I definitely didn't need his pity.

I was the happiest man alive.

I could walk, run, jump, and love.

I hadn't swum yet, but I'd already had a blade fashioned to fit the socket of my leg by my doctor in Turkey. There were multiple attachments—a fin to swim with, a blade to run on, even one made of high-grade silicone that looked exactly like my own leg—airbrushed and haired to be as natural as possible.

Funny that that didn't interest me.

I wasn't trying to hide that I was now an amputee. I'd hidden all my life as a refugee, and I was strangely proud of my carbon replacement. It represented everything I'd overcome and proved that I was virtually unkillable.

By the time we'd all tucked into a reminiscent dinner from Nemo's and I'd devoured a fish burger and salty fries, Jack and Anna vanished into the bathroom to bathe Ayla, and Teddy, Eddie, and Neri guided me down the road to the beach.

The waves welcomed me back with their ever-constant song and the sun slowly went to bed while the stars slowly woke up. Teddy toasted me with the beers he'd brought for all of us and leaned over to bear hug Neri. "Best. Day. Ever."

She chuckled and gave me a soft smile from his arms. "Best day ever."

Eddie raised his bottle to the silver half-moon. "To dreams that do come true."

We all toasted.

Teddy finally sighed and pulled away from Neri. "So, I...I have a confession to make. I didn't want to say anything with Aslan's return, but...now is as good a time as any." He grinned my way. "Goes without saying that you're welcome to move in with us, mate. It's a full house, but Neri is part of our family, so is Ayla. It would mean the world to me and Eddie if you stayed...if only for a little while. We need time to adjust to the idea of no longer sharing our life with our two favourite girls."

Eddie looked away, trying to hide his sudden sniff, doing his best to camouflage how deep his grief went at me taking Neri and Ayla away.

Fuck, I hadn't even thought about that.

Neri had found salvation with them.

They'd helped keep my wife alive and my daughter happy. I owed them the biggest debt of gratitude. What right did I have to swoop in and steal them?

The part of me so used to having no money and no ability to put down roots flared. I wanted to do something for them, but what—

You know what.

I stiffened.

I was a Kara now.

I was obscenely fucking wealthy—

"What is it you wanted to tell us?" Neri asked quietly, cutting off my thoughts.

"Ah, yes, well." Teddy shrugged. "I applied for a job opening at a local architect firm in Brisbane. I can work remotely, so I don't have to move down there, but…I was offered the job, and I'm gonna take it."

"Oh." Neri's face plummeted.

Eddie flinched. "But what about Lunamare? We're so close."

"We're bankrupt," Teddy muttered, taking a swig of his beer. "We have all the theory done, but we have no way of building it. Not past leaky prototypes anyway. We don't even have the money to get planning permission to build on the reef that Jack and Anna have been planting out for us."

"I understand," Neri said. "I can't expect you to work for nothing. We all need money to survive. Bills don't stop just because we're trying to change the world on a shoestring."

"It's only temporary." Teddy dug his bare feet into the sand. "I promise. I'll only work there until we can get another investment injection."

"I have two podcasts next week." Neri grinned, optimistic and bright-eyed. "I'm sure the more we get the name and our mission out there, the more people will be intrigued enough to—"

"I'll invest," I said, taking a sip of ice-cold beer.

Three sets of eyes shot to me. "Say what?" Teddy asked. "How on earth would you do that? You're as penniless as we are." He laughed under his breath. "Unless you're going to get your old job back working for your previous landlord, Griffen Yule, in Townsville?"

"No. They're not allowed to leave yet, remember?" Eddie said, shuddering. "I need time to say goodbye to our little moonbeam. Not sure how I'm gonna cope not hearing her darling voice in the morning."

Neri gave him a hug. "We're not going anywhere yet, Ed. You have my word. Aslan can move in with us and—"

"Reject the job, Theodore," I cut in. "Stay with Lunamare." I tried to fight my smile but couldn't. "How much did you say you needed? To start breaking ground on building whatever pods or bubbles you've designed?"

Eddie and Teddy shared a frown before bursting into laughter. "Why? You got a spare couple of million lying around, Aslan?"

"Ha, good one." Eddie snickered and tapped his bottle with Teddy's. "Wait…don't you mean ten million? It's easily gonna be north of—"

"Done." I crossed my arms. "Ten million to start with. More when you need it. I'll have the funds transferred in the morning."

"Wait…" Neri froze. "What…what do you mean? How…how is that possible?" She swayed on the spot and tripped toward me. "Aslan…?"

Chuckling under my breath, I pulled out my phone from my borrowed shorts, pulled up the app for Cem's bank accounts—*my* bank accounts—and put in the password I had yet to change.

Cem had been nothing but nostalgic and had used my birthday as the log-in. Hardly secure and it was on my very long list of things to change but it was also rather…sweet.

For all his short-comings and all the pain he'd put me through, he'd given me everything he'd ever created, and in a way, that made my forgiveness far easier to give.

"It's not dirty money. Actually, that's a lie." I passed my phone to Neri, the blue light of the screen etching her face. "It's laundered, sure. But it can't be traced back to the illegal ways he got it. And you have my word the rest will be clean because I'm not running the same business he was. I understand if you'd rather not touch it—considering where it came from, but I'd like it to be used for good, even if it came from something bad."

I shot Neri a look, making sure she remembered not to say what shady businesses I meant or what I'd promised to do in return for my visa to be granted and access to Australia reinstated.

Her eyes dropped from mine, glued to the phone, then snapped closed as if she'd pass out. "Holy shit, I-I can't breathe."

I shot forward and scooped her into my arms. Taking the phone, I chuckled. "Did you think I'd returned to you like you'd first found me? Shipwrecked with nothing in his pockets?"

"H-How many zeroes did I just see?" She blinked and shook her head. "I-I'm in shock."

"Nine."

"Hold up." Teddy raised both his hands. "Nine zeroes? You have a figure with *nine* zeroes behind it?"

"It clocked from eight to nine last week."

Eddie's face went white. "You're telling me you have over a *billion* dollars?"

Neri's legs buckled. I gathered her tight and kissed her forehead. "*We* have a billion dollars."

"I-I can't take it," Neri whispered. "It-It wouldn't be right. That money is yours."

"No. It's his. But I'm happy to take it for what he put us through. And I seem to remember that I'm on those business documents for Lunamare. So…as the fourth member of this company, I say I want to invest. Ten million, a hundred million, I don't care. Every penny is yours, *canim*, because I believe in you, and you believe in this, and I have no doubt that one day, we will all be living under the sea…exactly where you belong."

Two months later...

We waited until sunset, welcoming both the sun and the moon to bless us.

Ayla appeared first, skipping and twirling down the shell-bordered pathway, her bare feet kicking up sand, her pale-pink dress full of frills and rhinestones. She scattered yellow rose petals as she came, her hand diving into the little basket before tossing another flurry of lemon.

I couldn't take my eyes off her.

My heart tripped over itself, a symptom of too much electricity and far too much love.

The waves licked up the shore of Low Isles, lapping over my right ankle and foot.

I'd changed my prosthetic to a simple ergonomic blade. The slight curve and clever engineering was salt-proof, waterproof, and flexible enough that I found walking on sand far easier than a carbon pylon.

Behind me, the lighthouse turned on as the sky bled with crimson, peach, and lilac. The sunset was almost as pretty as the aurora australis that'd presided over our first marriage and consummation.

"Did I do it right, Daddy?" Ayla skipped into my arms as I bent to catch her and placed her beside me beneath the driftwood arch complete with white ribbons, shells, and sprigs of cherry blossom.

I hadn't gotten used to having money, but...I had become adept at spending it. It pissed me off that so many doors that'd been firmly closed to me when I had nothing were now flung wide as a billionaire. Those standards weren't fair. The way society treated those less fortunate than others' grated on my temper.

Our wedding was a good example of the powerful being favoured over the poor.

All it had taken was a phone call to the custodians of the lighthouse and a hefty donation to the upkeep of the island. Within a few days, we had permission to wed on the shore, sleep on the beach in luxury tents, and rent the entire space until dusk tomorrow.

No one else.

Just us, our celebrant, and our loved ones.

Anna smiled at me as she blew a kiss at Ayla beside me, her tiny hand tucked safely inside mine.

Teddy and Eddie held hands.

Honey and Billy blinked back tears.

My skin prickled, and my heart fisted, ripping my head up to the end of the sandy aisle as Neri and Jack appeared.

I would always know when she was close by. Always sense her. Feel her. Hear her soul and know her spirit.

Our eyes met across the short distance.

No music apart from the constant lap of waves, chirp of roosting birds, and swish of palm trees.

No one spoke as Jack led my moon-given wife toward me. He looked dapper dressed in black shorts and silver shirt.

Beach smart had been our dress code for everyone.

I wore the same: black shorts and white shirt with my cuffs rolled up to my elbows, revealing two bare forearms. Next week, I had an appointment with the same artist in Townsville who did Neri's lion. I would get my second replica, and then…we were catching a flight from Brisbane to İstanbul. I was needed back home and would spend a few weeks wearing the Kara crown, striking the fear of obedience into my generals.

Part of me had no interest in playing that role, but the other was fucking excited at taking Neri and Ayla. I could finally show them my home. Show them my culture. And I knew I'd fall even harder for them as they spoke like locals and fully stepped into their bilingual belonging.

Jack and Anna hadn't wanted me to take Neri and Ayla with me, but…there was nothing to fear anymore.

I was the one to fear.

I had no intention of taking them to Cem's mansion, where I'd spent five years being tortured. I'd fly them to İzmir where I'd lived happily with my Avci family. I'd take my girls to the sea there and walk on the sands of Diamond Beach. I'd show them the bazaars and introduce them to my people and pile their plates with every delicacy.

My thoughts fell quiet as I drank in Neri. Her bare feet and elegant ankles vanished and reappeared beneath her white gown as she padded toward me. The heavy silk rippled from her shoulders like spilling moonlight, following her curves, shimmering over her belly and breasts. The bow secured behind her neck trailed down her back with the ends sliding through the sand behind her.

Her gorgeous chocolate hair had caught some sun over the past few weeks of spending time together on *The Fluke* and the loose waves were the same salt-teased tangle that I adored.

Anna let out a quiet sob as Jack finally stopped before me, kissed Neri on her cheek, then passed her hand to mine. He gave me a nod as I squeezed my wife's fingers, then he stepped back to join Anna.

I didn't speak as I fell into Neri.

What was there to say?

What was there to do apart from stand in this wonderful moment and fall head over fucking heels all over again?

We'd opted for a simple beach wedding rather than follow any Turkish or Western traditions. To us, this was just an affirmation of the vows we'd already said.

But that'd been before Jedda—Neri's godmother and the woman who'd tried to save my life at the hospital—had visited last month when Anna told her I'd survived and was back home.

She'd overheard our wedding plans. She'd mentioned she was a celebrant as well as a nurse, and offered to wed us in the spirit of Australia. An honour that both Neri and I could not refuse.

Ayla let my other hand go so I could take both of Neri's.

Our daughter giggled under her breath as Neri sighed heavily, tears sparkling on her eyelashes.

A heavy hush fell over us as Jedda raised her hands, gathering everyone's attention. She stood before Neri and me, short and grinning, her brightly painted dress somehow capturing the wind and ocean in its swirls.

Her husband, Coen, sat beside Eddie and Teddy and her voice carried ancient promises as she said, "We gather here tonight to witness Nerida Avci and Aslan Kara's love. A love that struck young, held fast, and overcame death itself."

Lowering her hands, she smiled at both of us. "The land owns us, the sea guides us, the stars teach us, the sun watches us. When the wind blows, we breathe. When the moon glows, we heal. We are all connected. We are all one."

Neri shivered, and I sucked in a breath as Jedda came forward and placed her hands over ours. "We carry a spark of souls all while living in bodies of soil. You found each other and turned separate into whole. You are now the rain to each other's growth and the shelter to each other's successes. It is not words that bind you but fate. Fate that knows. Fate that designs. Fate that will one day guide you into the divine where, fate willing, you will find each other again."

Ayla shifted beside me, slipping her hand into the pocket of my shorts where my shell was firmly back home.

I glanced at the little girl Neri and I had created, and my pulse skipped with awe as Jedda passed Neri a gold band. Pulling her hands from mine, Neri splayed my fingers, kissed my knuckles, then slid the wedding band onto my left ring finger.

"I wed you years ago on this very beach beneath this very moon," she whispered. "I've loved you since I found you, and I'll love you until I lose you. I vow to continue finding you for the rest of my existence."

Tears lodged in my throat as I accepted the simple gold band from Jedda and repeated what Neri had done to me. I lingered over the kiss on Neri's knuckles, inhaling her gorgeous frangipani scent, schooling my hiccupping heart that wanted so much to be alone with her.

Sliding the ring beside her engagement diamond, I whispered, "I fell in love with you in this very ocean and became yours beneath this very sky. I only exist to love you, Neri, and I'm honoured to be yours forever."

Jedda wiped away a tear, bent down, and picked up two smooth stones just out of reach of the tide. Passing them to us, she said, "Face the sea."

Together, Neri and I accepted the small rocks, then shifted to wade a little deeper into the shallows.

Ayla came with us, staying glued to my side with her hand in my pocket, fingering my shell, linking our past, present, and future.

The sea lapped around my leg and blade, teasing at that phantom awareness that said I could feel the coolness of the salt even though I had no foot to sense it.

"Do you, Aslan Kara, agree to love Nerida Avci until your last breath?" Jedda asked. "Do you promise to protect her, adore her, and forsake all others for as long as you both shall live?"

My hand shook. "I do."

"Do you, Nerida Avci, agree to love Aslan Kara until your last breath? Do you promise to protect him, adore him, and forsake all others for as long as you both shall live?"

"I do," Neri whispered.

"Then cast your stones and offer your love to the sea. Let your rocks sink with commitment and settle beside one another, content together while life ebbs and flows around you."

Neri caught my eyes, her blue gaze catching the steel-coloured dusk.

We threw on the same breath, watching the small splashes, hearing the quiet plops.

Only once the ripples had faded did Jedda say, "Now kiss as one because that is what you are."

I didn't need telling twice.

Scooping Neri into my arms, Ayla laughed as I planted my mouth on my *legally* married wife. A girl I'd proposed to countless of times, married twice, and pledged my soul to every fucking day.

I didn't stop kissing her as we spent a lovely evening sharing a simple barbecue on the beach, indulged in sticky raspberry and vanilla wedding cake by firelight, then retired to our private tent with its heavy canvas walls, king mattress on the sand, and a thousand pillows in reds, oranges, and golds.

Our daughter bunked with her grandparents.

Our friends knew not to disturb.

And that night, Neri and I didn't go to sleep.

We consummated our marriage a hundred times, ensuring the world knew that this was it, and we were one, and nothing on earth or in the heavens could ever tear us apart.

Eleven months later...

POP.

Ayla skidded back as the cork from the replaced champagne bottle went flying.

"That was loud!" She grinned, her dark hair braided down her back with a baseball cap keeping the relentless sun off her beautiful little face. "Again. Do it again!"

I laughed and turned to fill everyone's glasses. "Have to drink this bottle first, *tatlım.*"

"Have I told you how much I love hearing you call her sweetheart?" Neri said softly, her eyes alight with love.

"*Bana kocam demeni sevdiğim kadar değil.*" (Not as much as I love hearing you call me your husband). I completely forgot about everyone else. It was a curse. A gift. A compulsion to trip into Neri headfirst with all my being.

She licked her lips.

I instantly hardened.

"Get a room." Ayla smirked, picking up a line she'd overheard Jack saying. He'd finally called us out on the wicked few weeks Neri and I had enjoyed while they'd been in New Zealand all those years ago. I didn't know how he found out, but one night last month, when we'd popped round to theirs for homemade pizza night, he'd casually informed us that it was about damn time we bought them a new couch, dining room table, and probably a kitchen sink, considering what we did on them.

Neri had choked on her pizza.

I'd exploded into laughter.

And Ayla had looked between us all with a scowl, trying to get in on the joke.

"I agree, little moonbeam." Teddy squished my daughter into his side. "They're sickening, aren't they?"

I chuckled and struggled to tear my eyes off Neri.

"Nah, they're cute. Like puppies." Ayla smirked. "I like puppies."

"Gee, thanks." I rolled my eyes and tore my attention off my delectable wife. Resuming my job at filling people's glasses, I said, "I would prefer being called a lion, but you know…whatever."

"Rawwwwr." Teddy chuckled and held out his glass. "Thanks, mate." Bouncing on the spot, he grinned. "I can't believe it. I can't believe after all this time, it's actually happened."

"This is insane." Eddie chugged back his champagne before I'd even finished pouring. With a shaking hand, he held out his glass for more. "Someone pinch me. It doesn't seem real."

"Sapphire!" Ayla yelled, bolting to the side of the sparkling brand-new, two-cabined boat we'd named *Denizatı* after the Turkish word for seahorse. "She and her pod are here to celebrate with us!" Her small hands went to her turquoise dress, ripping it over her head as she danced around in her navy one-piece. "Hi, Bubbles. Oh yay, Rocket is here too! Wait for me!"

"Ayla Kara, you stop right there," Neri barked. "You're not going swim—"

SPLASH.

"Bloody hell." Neri rolled her eyes. "She's a menace."

Jack chuckled. "Payback is ever so sweet." He went and kissed Neri's cheek. "Now you know what it was like trying to keep you out of the water, little fish."

"I was never that bad." Neri chuckled, quickly slipping out of her calico sundress and revealing the ever-present Lycra beneath. Today's choice was a plain black bikini with glittery ebony thread.

I could see my wife naked a million times.

I could taste her, touch her, thrust inside her, yet I would never stop being stunned stupid by how absolutely gorgeous she was.

"Close your mouth, Aslan. You're drooling." Teddy snickered.

I gave him the finger as Neri threw me an apologetic grin. "Be back soon."

Before I could reply, she sprinted for the railing, leaped up to the top rung, and swan-dived into the ocean.

"You sure they're not part mermaid?" Eddie laughed. "I swear I saw scales on Ayla's legs in the pool last week."

"The minute my wife grows a tail is the day I finally understand why she's so intuitive. If she ended up being a mystical creature, it would explain a lot of things." I grinned even as my heart skipped a few painful beats, reminding me that for all the perfection of today, my heart wasn't perfect.

Not anymore.

Not after Cem's machine.

It was the one and only secret I kept from Neri.

In the dark, alone in our bed, on the nights when she worked up the courage to ask me about my leg, the caves, and the electrocution, I was nothing but honest. Probably too honest.

But I never told her that for all my happiness and lack of nightmares. For all my gratefulness and completeness, my heart was the only part of me that let the past affect it.

"You guys truly did it." Jack grinned, ending my slight worry and toasting Anna as I filled their glasses again.

"I'm so proud of all of you," Anna said, her eyes covered with huge sunglasses. "I can't wait for the tour."

"Well, that won't be till next year, I'm afraid," Teddy said with a smile. "Today marks the momentous occasion of finishing our first anchor. The prototype will be transported here next week and assessed on interaction with the environment, water-tightness, and other necessary functions for a few months. Then…if it proves as successful as we hope, we'll begin the permanent hub."

"I just love that you found a way to encourage coral to grow on the spheres." Anna sighed in awe. "You're not just putting foreign buildings into the reef, you're giving wildlife a brand new habitat."

"I know." Eddie sipped his champagne. "That was a stroke of genius on Nerida's part. And the reason we finally got planning permission to try. Even the anchor points are sprayed with micro-cells that will eventually encourage kelp to sprout, and the way we've fashioned the architraves around the windows are perfect homes for eels, seahorses, and crabs."

Only half listening, I padded barefoot to the side of our new boat, *Denizati.*

Not only had I invested heavily into Lunamare, but I'd also bought Neri this craft so she didn't have to rely on *The Fluke* to pay visits to the new work site. I'd also given Jack and Anna twenty years' worth of grants so they could study and research whatever the hell they wanted without having to wait for aquarium donations or bid for jobs. They'd hired another assistant called Tina and only worked four days a week instead of seven like they used to.

I'd enlisted contractors to paint their house and replace their deck and had gotten rather addicted donating to charities that helped misplaced people, animals, and those needing somewhere safe to call home: animal shelters, refugee organisations, medical programmes for the underprivileged, and schooling for children falling through the cracks of poverty.

All those mansions of Cem's, dotted around the world—estates that I'd visited in a fugue of reconditioned despair—were now half-way houses for broken families. Homeless men, abused women, orphaned children…they were all welcomed into houses full of luxury—luxury created from the suffering of others.

I couldn't save those Cem had hurt but I could save others. I could repent for his crimes by protecting those who had nothing and no-one, just like Jack and Anna had done for me.

Last time we'd been in Turkey, I'd visited Cem's grave. In his last will and testament—the same one giving me everything he owned—he'd requested to be buried next to my mother. A woman I'd never met. Neri had taken Ayla for a stroll around the tombstones while I told my psychopath of a dead father that all his wealth was now used for good instead of evil.

I imagined him yelling at me for spreading around the same wealth he'd wanted so desperately to protect and keep in the family. But I also wondered if he'd be proud in his own twisted way. Proud that I was the king of his empire, walking in his footsteps, even if we wore different shoes.

Everything we donated went under our second non-profit company, Cor Amare, and we encouraged emails, suggestions, and nominations, happily helping those needing a hand and opening those doors that had remained firmly shut until money greased them open.

Between Lunamare and Cor Amare, we employed close to thirty people, and were only getting started. We'd travelled to Istanbul four times in the past year, and so far, the secret international operation I worked for had shut down three trafficking rings dotted around Saudi Arabia and the Mediterranean.

No one suspected the Kara empire as the one who fed such contacts and whereabouts. My generals settled into their loyalty for me and continued running the many side businesses without issue. More and more, the wealth I made came from legitimate investments into startup companies and taking risks on those ready to prove themselves rather than things that could destroy lives.

After hiding most of my life, I was now making a difference in others, and it was the best thing I'd ever done.

Apart from finding Neri, of course.

My eyes tracked my wife as she swam beneath the surface with Ayla. Both of my girls were surrounded by darting dolphins and flashing flippers.

They duck-dived with the pod, kicking and spinning, making their way to the platform bobbing in the distance. The platform with the first official letterbox of No 01 Coral Sea. That platform would eventually be the dry porch for those arriving and the location for the lift down below. It would grow, transform, and become fundamental to this new community, delivering its residents to an underwater world perfectly pressurised so no one felt the effects of long-term exposure of living fifteen metres below the surface.

If the prototype held up in a tropical storm and the anchoring system with its ability to spool out and in so the spheres could sway like seaweed instead of fight against unfightable currents worked, then the next stage would be all the technology to recycle air, waste, and power.

I sighed with a mixture of lust and love as Neri suddenly vaulted from the ocean and leaped onto the platform. She sprayed the logo for Lunamare—a crescent moon and a crashing wave—with seawater from her hair, sending a hundred tiny rainbows into the sky.

Ayla sprang up beside her, spinning around with her hands in the air, yelling, "This is gonna be my new bedroom, and I can wave to Sapphire and Bubbles every morning!"

"We can fall asleep to turtles and anemone." Neri laughed.

"I can have the best sleepovers. My friends are gonna be so jealous!"

Neri laughed and grabbed Ayla's hands. Together, they danced around the platform before diving off and disappearing into the blue with the dolphins.

My heart swelled.

My fingers curled around my champagne flute.

I toasted the love of my life and the life we were building together.

Two years later...

"If I wasn't madly in love with my husband and slightly afraid of your wife, I'd kiss you," Teddy muttered, his eyes round, his knees visibly jerking beneath his shorts as he stepped into our new house.

Not that it could really be called a house.

"I don't...how can we...I mean...I had *no idea* this was your plan all along."

I grinned. "You did say you'd be lost if I took Neri and Ayla away from you. And to be fair, your house was getting rather cramped."

I flinched, remembering all the moments Neri and I had almost been caught fucking in the shower or during the quickie we'd indulged in in the pool. We'd always had a taste for impromptu, rough, delicious sex, and having two adult housemates and a nosy daughter meant we were playing with fire each time we touched each other.

We needed more space.

We all do.

"Yes, but...they're yours," Teddy argued. "We get that. We'll accept our new role as the annoying uncles eventually. Besides, we see each other every day at Lunamare."

"If you'd rather stay at your place, you are more than welcome," I rushed, only now seeing how pompous this might seem. "I merely wanted to show you that I love you both, and I'll always be in your debt for looking after Neri and Ayla when I couldn't."

They thought this was a surprise? Wait until I showed them the paperwork in my back pocket. Neri and Ayla were in on it, but Teddy and Eddie didn't have a clue.

Nerves struck me.

Perhaps they wouldn't like that either? Maybe I'd overstepped—

"Strewth, you built a house big enough for all of us?" Eddie choked, swaying on the threshold of the sprawling living room with sunken linen couches, gas fireplaces, and Turkish décor of bright colours and lamps blended with the subtle elements of the seaside.

"Aslan…I have no words, mate." Eddie wiped his mouth, drifting toward me, almost drunk on shock. "I-I literally have no words."

"When you invited us for your first official night in your new home, I didn't expect this," Honey said, gawking at us as she and Billy appeared through the Bali-inspired front door.

They'd flown up from Sydney last night to join in our housewarming. "This is absolutely mental." She blinked at the U-shaped house replacing four dilapidated bungalows along the coast above Port Douglas.

We'd moved out of town, but not by much…just enough to have access to the beach, a lush tropical garden, and an infinity pool.

Neri hadn't known I'd bought the four blocks. I'd enlisted a local building firm to knock down the bungalows and an architect from Turkey to design the stone house I'd always wanted in İzmir. Granted the stone houses in my homeland were a twentieth of this size, but…it wasn't just one family moving in here.

"Holy shit, this is nuts." Billy scowled at the huge skylights above us and the polished concrete floors flowing out into the garden—a garden flanked by two wings of the massive house. One wing with its four bedrooms, four bathrooms, yoga room, sauna, and spa was for me, Neri, and Ayla. The other wing with its mirror image floorplan was Teddy and Eddie's.

Neri was the only one who didn't say anything as our friends drifted throughout the space, running awed fingertips over black marble countertops in the kitchen and opening the many stacking doors leading to the garden. The glass conservatory with banana plants, paradise palms, and sweet-smelling fruit trees added a riot of green against the sparkle of blue from the ocean beyond.

I sucked in a breath as Neri slowly slipped her hand into mine and squeezed. "You are the most generous, most amazing man I have ever met."

I bowed my head and kissed her. "And you are the most special woman in the world."

"Jesus Christ!" Eddie's shout found us before he did. He bolted into the lounge with Teddy on his heels, his mouth scrunched up with emotion. "This is real? You want us to move in with you? You're not just pulling our leg?"

"We just saw our room. The welcome letter on the bed and the monogrammed towels." Teddy bowled into us, wrapping his arms around Neri and me. "Are you sure? *Truly* sure? Last chance to say no."

Neri chuckled. "We're sure. In fact…" Untangling herself from one of our best friends and business partners, she gave me a look. *The* look. "Shall we show them the rest?"

My heart kicked, and I couldn't tell if it was from genuine concern or past abuse. "No time like the present."

"Ayla!" Neri yelled. "Where are you?"

"Here, Mum!" Ayla skipped into the lounge, her bare feet trailing water from the pool. It was because of my two water sprites that I hadn't approved carpet anywhere in this house. Living on the beach was an invitation to lose both sirens to the sea forever and leave a trail of salt in every room.

"Do you want to do the honours, moonbeam?" I asked softly, pulling the paperwork from my jeans back pocket.

"Sure." Ayla tucked her chocolate hair behind her ear and her soft brown eyes warmed. "They're gonna flip the freak out."

"Honey, do you mind pouring a few shots of vodka." Neri chuckled. "Your brother is gonna need it."

"Why? What did you do?" Honey asked.

"Yeah. My question exactly." Teddy scowled. "Too many surprises for one day. I can't handle any more. I just learned that your crazy-ass, mega-rich, very handsome husband just invited us to live with you for all of eternity. I'm gonna need a minute."

"You're such a drama queen." Ayla giggled.

"Drama king, I'll have you know." Teddy tickled her as she spread the paperwork on the recycled jarrah wood dining table. "What's this?" he asked suspiciously.

"Read it and find out," Neri said, pulling me closer to the table, the click of my blade loud on the concrete. I no longer needed a cane at all, but I preferred the blade rather than a metal limb; I found it far easier to run on.

Billy and Honey gathered closer, and Eddie read over Teddy's shoulder. Ayla buzzed with energy, watching all of us, waiting for the explosion.

It didn't take long.

Just a skim of a document they already recognised.

A crumpling of faces.

A gasp of hearts.

"Well, fuck." Teddy let out a puff of air.

Eddie choked on a sob.

And both men grabbed my daughter, squeezing her in the biggest hug. Raining her in kisses, they let her go, then launched themselves at Neri and me, trapping Ayla in the middle.

They didn't speak.

We didn't either.

There was nothing to say.

While sorting out things to move—after I finally told Neri I was building us a house—I'd come across the adoption paperwork that Neri said Teddy and Eddie had drawn up when I was at Cem's mercy.

They'd done it to free Neri to come find me. To give her the peace of mind that Ayla would always have love and safety.

Safety.

That'd become the greatest gift of my life.

It was tragically underestimated and was the keystone to every happiness.

No one could be truly happy unless they felt safe.

And through that epiphany, I'd found peace.

I'd never had another nightmare or dark cloud in my head. Darkness didn't surround me anymore, just light, and I wanted to ensure Ayla would always feel that. Always know how much she was cared for and protected.

Therefore, the smart decision, the *only* decision was to ensure that Ayla had more than one set of parents. She already had four. She'd had four since she was born.

Now...it was official.

Over the heads of my family, I smiled at Neri's and my signature on the adoption paperwork.

As Ayla's biological parents, we'd willingly shared custody of our wonderful child.

Teddy and Eddie were legally her guardians.

In the eyes of the law and always.

Four years later...

I found her lying in her favourite spot in our sphere.

The chaise lounge had been one of the first pieces of furniture we'd brought into our underwater home, and the pale-blue velour mimicked the dappling of the moonlight spearing through the water above.

Fluorescent pigments of corals and other cnidarians glowed with faint greens, yellows, and pinks. The nightscape of the reef looked as wonderous as the aurora lights when we'd married the first time. Lazy fish swam while sleeping, and inquisitive octopuses waved tentacles in hello, recognising us and becoming friendly through the marine glass.

Our bedroom, off the main bubble, had the biggest window. The construction of the spheres had been kept simple with exposed beams, bamboo screens instead of doors, and the all-important massive windows. The ability to extend the anchor cord to bob on the surface or retract to lock on the seafloor had been an ingenious idea, and the more spheres we added, the bigger our community had grown thanks to photos online of bubbles bouncing on the waves, looking like alien ships or some strange kind of jellyfish.

I sighed in wonder as a fever of moon dappled manta rays soared past, and two peacock mantis shrimp snatched at scurrying crabs.

Neri lay on her stomach, eyes wide at the glowing reef before her, her legs raised and crossed at the ankles, her chin in her hands as she peered into the inky sea.

Two years we'd spent our weekends in this bubble, and each Sunday, when it was time to return to shore, both of us were becoming more and more reluctant. For all my stubbornness of never stepping foot into the sea, I was now as addicted as my wife.

"Oh, wow," Neri breathed as two wobbegong sharks darted up the glass, following the contours of the curve. Her endless fascination with this world never failed to punch me directly in the chest.

She belonged down here.

With me.

I stopped on the threshold of the living room. The space wasn't overly large with a comfy couch, chaise, and kitchen. No TV. No computers. When we were down here, we wanted no sign of the human world. No way for others to find us. Up there, we were a power couple. Nerida Avci and Aslan Kara, entrepreneurs, visionaries, and philanthropists.

But down here…we were just *us*.

Two souls stripped of wealth, importance, and endless to-do lists.

Down here, we were nothing more than two people in love.

I clenched my jaw as I drank Neri in. I'd come to get her. She'd said she'd come to bed the minute she'd finished sipping her chamomile tea, but it seemed she'd gotten distracted.

Again.

I'd known she'd be unable to ignore the song of the sea, especially after we'd been staying at our second home in Turkey for the past month.

We'd purchased a house in İzmir a few years ago.

Ayla had come house hunting with us, and in some strange twist of fate, we'd bumped into Çetin—Cem's old doctor who'd removed my leg and kept me alive. He'd returned to his family in İzmir after I'd taken over, and when he'd spotted me on the waterfront, strolling hand in hand with Neri and our perfect daughter just up ahead, he'd cut us off and bowed.

He apologised for his role in my torture.

He kneeled for cutting off my tattoo.

He cleansed his soul of all the things he'd done against his wishes.

And I'd forgiven him.

I knew how hard it was to resist Cem's convincing.

Çetin wasn't a bad man. He'd just been…persuaded, like me.

Ayla bombarded him with medical questions, and somehow, the family vacation I'd promised after a week spent in İstanbul with my generals turned into Ayla's first initiation into the healing profession.

The only dark spot on our reunion was the whispered conversation I'd shared with Çetin just before we left. He'd asked how my heart was after the endless shocks Cem had given me.

I pressed a hand to my familiar aching chest and stepped away from my wife and daughter. Once we were out of hearing distance, I said, "Is there something I should know, Çetin?"

He flinched and said quietly, "Did Cem tell you the truth about what happened the night you passed out before the raid, or did he say it was nothing more than a panic attack?"

I stilled. I dropped my hand. I didn't like where this conversation was going because I'd always suspected it'd been so much more. "What's the truth?"

Çetin winced harder this time. "I can't be sure, as I didn't have the equipment to do an echocardiogram, but…in my trained opinion, I believe you suffered a silent myocardial infarction."

"What the hell is that?"

"A mild heart attack. Normally, most people aren't aware of them. That's why they're called silent. But…your system was under immense stress. It had been for years. I'm not surprised you passed out."

"Wait. You think I had a *heart attack*?" I stumbled back and shot a look at Neri and Ayla strolling out of listening distance behind us.

"Only mild. You're young and strong and will most likely be fine, but…I wouldn't be doing my duty as a doctor if I didn't warn you that the excessive use of electricity could have caused permanent scarring on your heart. Next time you're back in Turkey, come to me, and I'll run some tests. I work at the local hospital now. You need to be aware of your risk of stroke or future health complications—"

"I'm fine." I sliced my hand through the air. "We won't mention this again."

"But—"

"I said, *I'm fine.*"

He'd nodded, gone to say farewell to my wife and daughter, all while I trembled with fear.

It'd been my dirty secret until last year when my left arm had gone numb, and I'd lost my balance that I prided myself on. Considering I was well used to hopping when others walked and stayed in shape with strength, cardio, and weight training, my power didn't protect me from the slam of dizziness as my heart twisted strangely in my chest.

I'd fallen over in the kitchen.

Neri had come running and called an ambulance.

I'd cancelled that nonsense, but Teddy insisted on driving us to the hospital, which involved numerous tests and meeting with cardiologists.

Turned out, Cem *had* ruined me…just not in the way he'd hoped.

Mentally, I was stronger than ever, but physically, I had a weak spot. Just one.

The very thing that existed to love Neri was the one thing that would end up killing me.

Neri had withdrawn from me for a little while, absorbing the ramifications of living with a soulmate that had a dicky heart. Any moment, it could stop. I could live for decades, or I could die tomorrow.

No one could predict my future.

No one could say if the random palpitation attacks might one day be the episode that eradicated me. All they could do was recommend drugs—which I wasn't interested in taking. And suggest a healthy, stress-free lifestyle—which I was already living.

I'd fallen so deeply down the rabbit hole of health that I now freedived with Neri often (because breathwork and cold-water exposure were scientifically proven for longevity). We had daily saunas (because same thing) and ran on the beach most mornings, my blade cutting through the sand as effortlessly as Neri's two feet.

Teddy and Eddie knew, and I was insanely grateful we had paperwork that meant Ayla would always have two other fathers to step in if fate decided I'd had my dose of allotted happiness.

Outwardly, I was still the same unkillable refugee turned billionaire. Inwardly, I valued my life all the more. I surrendered to every day and everything in it. I never grew angry because time was too short. I let go of my temper because I preferred total bliss. I was free in ways that no fear or worry could find me.

Thanks to her.

She was my anchor.

My heartbeat, my breath, my blood.

As long as I had her, I would live forever.

"I can feel you watching me, you know," Neri whispered, turning onto her side and catching my eyes across the sphere. "By the way, my heart skipped just before. Was I sensing you, or am I just getting carried away with the view again?"

I chuckled and headed toward her, the click of my cane the only sound as I hopped across the small space. I'd already taken off my prosthetic to sleep and no longer had any qualms about my physical appearance.

Neri loved me.

Whole or in pieces, dead or alive.

All my blissful happiness stemmed from her unconditional love.

"I'm going to say your flutters are caused by your obsession with this reef and have nothing to do with me. My heart has been quiet as a mouse lately."

"Promise?" She shifted until she sat cross-legged. "Because you know you can't lie to me. I still keep my heart journal. I still feel you, and I'll know if you're lying."

"That both mystifies and terrifies me." Sitting beside her, I cupped her cheek. "You and your knowings, *canim*. You worry me because what will you

470

feel when my time truly ends?"

"I don't care because I'm going with you."

I stiffened and shook my head. This argument wasn't new. She vowed it each time I had an episode. "We've spoken about this. If I go, you're to stay. That's non-negotiable. I'll just be patient until you come to join me. When it's your turn, Neri, and not before."

Sitting up on her knees, she straddled me and pushed away my cane. Running her fingers through my hair, she whispered against my mouth, "You're forgetting I already know what it feels like to live when you are dead. It almost killed me the first time, and I swear on both our lives, I won't let it happen again." Pressing a fierce kiss to my lips, she pulled away, her eyes full of blue flames. "Do you hear me, Aslan? We live together. We die together. *That's* what is non-negotiable."

My heart tripped over her words, picking itself up in a regular beat. "You're a sea witch. Did I ever tell you that?"

The fire in her gaze warmed to molten ocean. "Maybe once or twice. Perhaps that's why you love me so much." Her tongue ran over my bottom lip, making me jerk beneath her. "I put a spell on you."

"It explains why I can't keep my hands off you." I ran my fingers over her bare arms, across her tattoo, and gathered up the silky material of her champagne-coloured night slip.

My own inked arm caught the soft light. The lion and its siren, scribed over my scars, binding me to Neri with the same permanence I'd always felt. We might wear rings and had promised eternal vows, but having my tattoo redone had completed me.

A full circle of before and now. Darkness and light. Tragedy and triumph.

Running my hands over her bare thighs, I couldn't hold back my throaty groan. "You made me wait in bed while you were out here. I think you need reminding why you shouldn't do that, *especially* when I have something to give you."

"Something to give me, huh?" She fluttered her eyelashes. "What is it?"

"Get on your hands and knees, and you'll find out."

Her teeth clamped on her bottom lip. The air crackled with lust and the moonlight spangling through the sea lit up the sphere with silver streaks and dancing glows.

She'd never looked more stunning with the sea sparkling all over her, reminding me of the Turkish word *yakamoz*: the beautiful phenomenon of shimmering moonlight on water and the blue glow of bioluminescent plankton.

Two things currently framing her in my view.

Two things that embodied Neri in one perfect picture: a creature of spirit and stars, dwelling on the seafloor with fish and dolphins.

Tugging her forward, I nipped her ear. "Get off me, get on your hands and knees, and lift your nightgown. I won't ask again."

She shivered.

I waited to see if she'd disobey—I almost wanted her to because part of me needed to chase, discipline, and punish her for making me love her like this—but then a coy little smile twitched her lips, and she did exactly as I asked.

Our sex life had only gotten better as we'd gotten older.

I was no longer afraid of letting go.

We played with toys.

We shared our fantasies.

Not a day went by that we didn't seduce each other with dirty promises.

I often joked that if my heart was going to stop beating one day, it would be when I was balls deep inside her because she always took my breath away.

Moving off my lap, she kneeled on the chaise lounge. Her eyes remained locked on the radiant waterworld beyond, and with a flick of her wrist, she flipped up the short skirt of her silky nightgown.

The globes of her ass.

The glisten of her arousal.

The pinkness of her pussy.

I groaned as my hard cock popped out of the waistband of my boxers.

Without fail.

Every single time.

She bewitched me body and soul. I could barely breathe as I kneeled behind her, tugged my boxers down, and grabbed her hip with my left hand.

"Are you wet, *aşkım*?"

She moaned and hung her head. "For you? Always."

I feathered my fingers over her core, finding her heat and slick invitation. Hissing between my teeth, I sank two fingers inside her, stretching, claiming. "Do you need me as much as I need you?"

"God yes," she whimpered, pushing back against my hand. "Don't tease me, Aslan. Not tonight."

"Why shouldn't I? Why shouldn't I make you writhe?"

"Because tonight is the anniversary of the first day I found you. My head's been swimming all day with a boy who looked so lost, so broken. A boy who stole my heart with a single stare."

"Fuck," I grunted, my heart rampaging through my ribs, drumming its own possessive beat. "How many years has it been, Nerida, since you fell for me?"

"Twenty."

"Twenty *wonderful* years."

"I want twenty more. A hundred more."

"I can't promise you that." I withdrew my fingers and wrapped them around my erection. Spreading her desire over me, I reared up behind her and notched myself in that perfect spot. "But I can promise you that I'll love you for every day I'm alive and beyond."

I thrust.

Hard and punishing, sending her falling to her elbows.

She moaned.

The reflection of us on the glass painted my mind red with lust. The vision of her on her knees, ass up, and me rocking behind her made the urge to come slam through me.

Only her.

Always her.

A reef shark glided past as I withdrew, then plunged back in.

A bloom of jellyfish floated nearby, their tentacles trailing like glitter-string as I bent forward and placed my hand on her nape.

The coral glowed brighter.

The moonlight dazzled.

And Neri gasped beneath me.

I lost myself.

To my wife.

To our love.

I fucked her.

I worshipped her.

Together, we said no to death and yes to life.

Yes to a life worth living.

Chapter Fifty-Three

NERIDA

(*Love in Spanish:* Amar)

THE SILENCE FOLLOWING MY VOICE SOAKED UP our story and hoarded it in the shadows of the conservatory. The house that Aslan had built for us huddled around me, almost as if it didn't want our secrets being shared.

But it was too late.

I'd confessed every shred of truth.

I'd spoken until dawn.

My throat was scratchy and dry, no matter how much lemon water I sipped. My eyes burned and blurred from exhaustion. And my old body was no longer used to all-nighters when I longed to return beneath the sea and the reef where I truly belonged.

It'd been a long time since we'd lived in this house on the shore. This wonderful house where Teddy and Eddie still lived and Ayla now dwelled with her husband and their two daughters.

Aslan and I had been too busy with creating Lunamare and running his empire in Turkey to spy time to have another baby, but we'd gotten the joy of grandchildren in our later years.

Needless to say, Teddy and Eddie had been beside themselves to have yet more children to dote on, and I had a sneaking suspicion that Melike and Bella preferred those two grandfathers to the one-legged one and strange Nana who lived beneath the sea.

Dylan shared a look with Margot.

I rubbed my eyes, doing my best to stay coherent for a little longer.

I hadn't expected this to take as long as it did, but I was grateful I'd done it.

Grateful that our love story was told because that was my biggest legacy, my greatest lesson, triumph, and tragedy. Dropping my hands, the image of the two reporters before me was jarring after sharing the last moments of the romantic interlude in our sphere so many years ago.

I'd loved Aslan for twenty years at that point. An eternity for some. Yet for us, it'd merely been our beginning. Now I was seventy-two and had loved him for sixty. And I would keep on loving him because it was physically impossible to stop.

"Wow..." Dylan finally muttered, rolling his shoulders and forcing his body to wake up. "That...that is quite the tale."

Margot grabbed a fresh tissue from the box on the coffee table, dabbing her eyes for the thousandth time. Ever since I started telling them what Aslan had suffered with his leg, the electrocutions, and the barbaric ways Cem Kara had tried to make him obey, she'd sniffed and cried and forgotten to write a damn thing.

I hoped their tape recorders had enough memory to record everything because...I would never repeat it.

This was a one-time thing.

It was done.

I was happy to have shared, but now...the urgency to leave pressed far too insistently.

Tossing the blush blanket off my legs, I stretched and swallowed a moan of discomfort. "Thank you so much for staying all night." I smiled and reached for the armrest of the couch. I didn't need a walking stick like Aslan did sometimes, but I wasn't nearly as nimble as I used to be. Especially after sitting for eighteen hours. "I'll walk you out."

"No, wait." Margot scrunched up her tissue. "But you haven't told us the rest."

"The rest?" I frowned, staying sitting. "There is no rest."

"Did Zara always keep Aslan's secret about what he did to Ethan? Did she marry Cooper? What about Joel and—"

I held up my hand, stemming her questions. "Zara and I patched up our friendship when Aslan returned to me. We see each other once a month for coffee. And yes, she has always kept the fact that she saw Aslan knocking Ethan out by her rubbish bins a secret. She has never betrayed us, and I will always be grateful to her. She did marry Cooper, and they have two lovely sons who have given them four grandchildren. As for Joel, he married a woman from Samoa, and they live there together, running a boutique hotel."

"Did Aslan remain head of the Kara empire?" Dylan asked, consulting his notes. "You mentioned he was going to dismantle it when he'd helped whatever government he was working for clean up a few messes."

"He did." I folded my hands in my lap. "He officially shut down every aspect of his inherited business when he was forty-four." I winced, remembering why but not willing to share.

Unfortunately, Margot noticed and said, "It was because of his heart, wasn't it? He stopped straddling the law of right and wrong because his heart needed less stress?"

I narrowed my eyes and chuckled under my breath. "Even after such a long day, you're still shrewd."

"I have to be." She shrugged. "I'm invested in your story, Nerida. Wait—" Her eyebrows knotted together. "You go by the name Nerida Avci. All your biographies mention you as Avci."

"I'm sure there's a question in there somewhere." I smiled.

"Why did you never change it to Kara? After all, that's who you legally married."

I looked into the distance, forming a suitable answer. "I suppose my first marriage to Aslan was the one that solidified my true purpose. I married him as Aslan Avci. I loved him with all my heart and soul. I was grateful he shed his demons and ghosts, but a part of me wanted to keep loving that tortured boy even though the man was free. I always wanted Aslan to know that I loved both sides of him. The good and the bad. The dark and the light. In Turkey, our friends and extended family we've reached out to over the years and reconnected with all know me as Nerida Kara. Ayla goes by Kara, or she did until she married Harry.

"I suppose, if I had to put my finger on the *exact* reason I stayed an Avci, it's because Cem never deserved Aslan as his son. Yet Emre and Jale Avci, kind people who raised him during his most formative years, did. He learned his love of math from them, even if his synesthesia was genetic. He learned how to love and protect from them, even if they weren't originally his to love and protect."

"That's beautiful, Neri," Dylan said softly.

"Thank you." I did my best to hide my impatience for them to go but Margot once again picked at a sore spot. "I didn't give you a chance to answer my other question...the one about why he shut down the Kara empire."

I sighed.

I wanted to refuse.

It was a little too close to home and the reason I was now desperate to leave.

But...I'd given everything else away, so I suppose I couldn't hold on to the final pieces.

"You're right that Aslan dismantled his holdings and trades in Turkey to protect his health. The legitimate companies we'd invested in remained, but the illegal stuff was handed over to the operation that only ever met Aslan in secret.

"I never truly knew what he had to do for them because it was safer that I didn't. And Aslan never put us at risk because although the deal he'd made had allowed him to return to Australia, he would never put his family in danger.

"We came first. Above everything."

"Do you still come first, or…are we speaking past tense again?" Margot winced.

Taking pity on her, I tampered my impatience and gave her what she needed to hear. "Do you want me to say the words that Aslan Kara, my most wonderful husband, is still alive?"

She melted into the couch. "Oh, would you? Please. That would help me sleep tonight. If you don't, I'll always imagine him keeling over while you enjoyed your twentieth anniversary in Lunamare."

Glancing at Dylan, then back to Margot, I sucked in a breath and told her the truth and nothing but the truth. "Aslan is still alive. Forgive my use of dramatics for the article, but I stand by what I said. I never saw Aslan Avci again because he was ruled by shadows and grief. Aslan Kara is light and faith itself, even after everything he'd endured."

"So…he's okay?" Her voice was nothing but a whisper.

"He's still alive." I nodded, skirting her question. "I've been honest, so I'll continue being honest. When he was forty-three, his heart skipped a little too badly at dinner. Luckily, Teddy and Eddie were there to break all the speed limits and get us to the hospital. Turned out, he had another attack. Only mild, but enough for the doctors to come up with more rules and restrictions.

"Time lulled us into a false sense of security, and we spent almost seven years with only a few palpitations before…" I swallowed hard, struggling to remember that time without great lancing pain. "He had a stroke when he was fifty."

"Oh no," Margot exclaimed. "Is he…did he lose—"

"For a time." I nodded matter-of-factly. "He lost sensation in his left side, which meant walking on his prosthetic was hard. If it'd happened to any other man, losing part of his ability to speak and move might've broken him, but…it only made him more determined."

I didn't tell them why he was so determined to survive because if I did, they'd know exactly what I had planned after this.

"It took him close to four months to fully regain his strength. By the time he was speaking clearly again, with no signs of what he'd gone through, he'd learned Spanish. The doctors claim his recovery was so swift thanks to his eidetic memory and the many neurons firing in his brain."

We let them think that.

No one ever knew the vow I'd made to him and the threat that kept him living.

I looked back now on the many incidents when his heart tried to take him from me and each time, I'd dragged him back. Not because he was ready to leave me but because he wasn't going anywhere without me.

It was his duty to stay.

His soul-bound oath to exist while I did.

You die, I die.

It'd been a promise.

A threat.

A vow.

"You have to understand, Margot, this is our life story. It's a love story, yes, but most importantly, it is the truth. No one's life is perfect. No romance lasts forever. As of today, you can honestly finish your article with the words 'And they lived happily ever after' because we are still wed, still very much in love, and still very much alive."

"Why do I sense a but coming?" Dylan asked quietly.

"Because...if you follow any romance for long enough, they all end in tragedy. Every single one. Eventually, someone dies or gets sick or falls out of love. Even the tales about immortal gods and goddesses all end at some point. There is no such thing as immortality because time marches on and everything always changes. The only thing a love story truly has is the promise that if it was *true*...if that love was the one you were destined to find and you adored that mate with all your wretched soul, then...that part *is* forever. Those are the tales that last a lifetime because love *exceeds* all lifetimes."

"I don't know if that comforts me or hurts me," Margot muttered. "I think I prefer the Disney version where you close the book or turn off the movie and believe that their happily ever after lasts an eternity."

"Love does. Bodies don't." I shrugged. "That's irrefutable. And...in a way...it makes our time on earth all the more precious because it isn't infinite. It's far, far too short, and why waste it being unhappy or sad or angry? Why bicker and stress? Why pout and play games? The only point of existence is to love and be loved as wildly and as freely as possible."

She gave me a smile and a nod. "You're a wise woman, Nerida."

"It took a while and a fair few mistakes, but I try." Standing stiffly, I smoothed down my dress and glanced at the garden drenched in colours of dawn. The sand twinkled with rubies; the waves glittered with sapphires.

My time on land had come to an end, and the sea was calling me home.

"Gather your things. I'll walk you out." I smiled to take the sting out of my order to go. "I'm truly ever so grateful you spent so much of your time with me. I'm aware of how precious every moment is, and it's an honour to have claimed so many of yours."

"Not at all." Dylan stood and packed away his microphone, pens, cords, notebooks, and devices. "It was our pleasure."

"Yes." Margot stood and slung her satchel over her shoulder. "I've loved every moment of it. Even when you were deliberately ripping out my heart."

I smiled. "I'm glad. I'm happy to have shared it with you. Hopefully, your readers will like it."

"I'm sure they will." Dylan swiped a hand through his manicured beard.

"To have a tell-all tale by Nerida Avci herself will bring the science world to its knees."

I went to reply, but Margot interrupted, "But what about the other scientific discovery you made? Did that get filed in science or spirituality?"

"I don't follow." I scowled. "Lunamare is my life's work. I never—"

"Your heart journal. The moments you felt Aslan when he was being electrocuted."

"Ah, that." I clasped my hands and walked toward the main lounge and the open foyer beyond. The reporters followed me in a sleepy shuffle. "If you truly want to know, research my legally married name of Nerida Kara. You'll find a paper called 'The Study of Soulmates and Proof They Do Exist.'"

"So your palpitations *did* line up with Aslan's?"

"They did."

"That's...that's..." Margot shook her head as I slowed and opened the front door. "That blows my mind. Did you ever get tested for psychic abilities? Did you train your intuition?"

"That's a tale for another day." I sighed. "Let's just say, I've been blessed with a sensitivity not unlike Aslan's. His is physical. Mine is spiritual. We both learned to live with our gifts the best we could."

Tiffany had gone to bed. Teddy, Eddie, Ayla, Harry, and the grandkids were all snoozing.

I wanted to be gone before they woke.

"Thank you again," I said quietly, glancing into the forecourt with its seahorse fountain and the two cars the reporters had driven. "Safe journey home."

Dylan spun around on my sweeping sandstone stoop. "Oh, will you be around in the next few days to ask any follow-up questions?"

I held his stare.

I resisted the urge to shake my head.

Instead, I smiled at both of them, stepped back into my home, and said, "Goodbye."

Chapter Fifty-Four

ASLAN

(*Heart in Korean:* Ma-eum)

I SENSED HER COMING.

I supposed, after living with her for so long, her little knowings had finally rubbed off on me. There wasn't a moment that I wasn't aware of her, in-sync with her, in awe of her.

She still helped Teddy and Eddie oversee their hordes of managers and hundreds of staff for Lunamare. She still went on podcasts promoting the need for action to protect our seas and creatures. She was tireless and wonderful, and it kept me up at night that a woman such as her—a woman with so much life that she could last centuries—had shackled herself to a man like me.

I was one month away from celebrating my seventy-seventh birthday. By most counts, I was still a youngish man. I'd lived through things most people couldn't dream of and existed in a state of happiness that not many were privileged to find.

Yet...I was getting tired.

It wasn't every day, and it wasn't all the time, but the ache in my chest had become a constant companion. A companion Neri could feel.

I'd never willingly lied to her, but now...it was physically impossible.

She knew.

She always damn well knew.

And she knew that my latest heart attack—another mild one but not mild enough to keep me out of the hospital for a few days—was increasing the speed on the ticking bomb in my chest.

Eventually, it would stop, and I honestly couldn't stomach the thought of it happening when I was holding one of my granddaughters or making passionate love to my wife.

I didn't want to go out on my heart's terms.

I didn't want to suffer another stroke and lose the ability of words and numbers.

After everything Cem had done to me, that had been the worst.

A living fucking nightmare being trapped in my body and housed in a mind that no longer worked the way it should.

It could happen again.

One day, I could see rainbows in my head while helping Bella with her math homework, and the next, I could be a fucking vegetable.

To think of Neri having to care for me?

To think of my family seeing me that way?

No.

Just...*no*.

I wouldn't let that happen, and the only power I had over not allowing my body to forsake me was picking the time for *me* to forsake *it*.

Standing stiffly from the weathered bench swing we'd set up years ago to watch the water, I dug my cane into the sand and stepped toward her. Dawn-light caught her pretty seafoam-green dress, shimmering with reality and myth, making it seem as if she appeared from the ocean itself.

Our eyes met.

Our lips smiled.

No matter how many years passed, I would never get over the tingling sensation in my blood whenever she returned to me.

Home.

She's home.

"Hello," I said softly, not wanting to disturb the dawn. "You were a while."

"Aslan, what on earth are you doing still waiting for me?" She marched toward me with balled hands. "I texted you to go on board *Stardust*. You should've been resting."

"I can't sleep if you're not beside me."

She winced and slotted into my arms. "And you think I can?"

"I know you will."

"I'm not having another fight with you, Aslan. I said my piece before I left you for that interview. You know I can't sleep without you either, and I never intend to."

I sighed and kissed her before letting her go. "Not this again, *canim*. I thought we'd settled it before you left this morning. Well, yesterday morning now."

"We did. We settled everything. Where you go, I go."

"And I said that's not happening."

"And I said, bite me."

A chuckle escaped me, smothering my frustration. "You don't know what you're asking me to agree to."

Her eyes met mine, the blue catching flecks of new sunlight. No matter the age that stamped its relentless time into us. No matter the white hairs and wrinkles. I only ever saw her as the girl I fell madly in love with. My little water sprite, my sexy siren. She still had a power over me that made lust an insatiable force. Still made my heart kick and palms sweat. Still made me adore her.

"I do know what I'm asking," she whispered. "I knew the moment I felt your first heart flutter that this was how it would end. It's always been you, Aslan. Just you. Don't ask me to give you up because I won't."

Prickles darted down my spine. Ever since I'd woken with a splitting headache last month and my right eye went blind for the day, I'd feared I'd had another stroke. We never went to the doctor because I was already on everything they could pump into me, but it solidified my plan: I refused to be at the mercy of pain again.

I'd endured enough.

I'd accepted my limitations.

I'd embraced the changes in my body and learned to love myself despite them.

But…I would not live through more.

Not now.

Not when the next one might steal who I was. Take my mind. My life. My *love*.

Ice rolled down my spine as a blizzard replaced my bones.

That was the worst thing imaginable.

To forget Nerida.

To forget all the moments we'd shared and all the triumphs we'd accomplished.

I might be a dead man walking, but I planned on walking beside her, cane, blade, and all until *I* said stop, not my heart.

I didn't speak for the longest time, glancing out to sea where our yacht, manned with four staff, five luxury cabins, and a helipad, waited for us to climb aboard. We'd named it *Stardust* after the brightest spritz of the milky way that'd become a firm friend while living out to sea. With no light pollution and our nightly ritual of swimming around our sphere, we'd often floated on our backs and contemplated the meaning of all of this.

We were just a speck.

The tiniest piece of dust among the stars.

Which was why…I was okay with my choice.

Why such decisions of taking charge of my destiny might be frowned upon by society, but it wasn't a decision I took lightly.

Neri's gaze drifted to *Stardust* too. The windows twinkled, her lines beautiful and railings polished. The sleek speedboat waiting to take us to her bobbed on the seashore. The yacht was fully stocked for months at sea. We'd always said we'd go around the world on a voyage, but that had never happened.

Lunamare took up too much time, and I was still active in charities for the underprivileged.

Despite our years, we hadn't slowed down, and a part of me regretted that. Regretted the chance to travel with Neri with no destination or itinerary. Just us and the sea, following the moon wherever it took us.

Wrapping her arms around me, she pressed her ear above my heart and murmured, "I'll make you another vow, Aslan. The one I made has kept you alive this far. You know when you die, I die. It's made you fight to remember how to walk again. It's forced you to speak again. It's kept you strong and healthy, and I don't care if it's unfair of me to put that burden on you when I know what you struggle with.

"I know you're afraid of losing yourself like you did when Cem broke you. I know you're afraid of becoming someone you don't know and fearing you might never find your way back to me. You're more afraid of losing me that way, of forgetting me while you still live, than you are at losing me through a grave. And I get it. More than you probably know because I know *you*. And so…"

Pulling away, she cupped my cheek and rose on her tiptoes to kiss me. Unhurried.

Unexpectant.

Our lips touched, and our tongues grazed, and by the time we stopped kissing, the sun had breached the horizon and blinded the world in newness.

"My second promise is…I will do it."

My eyebrows flew into my salt-and-pepper hair. "Do what exactly?"

"If the day comes that you don't remember me. If your heart makes you weak or your mind turns you simple. If there is no chance of bringing you back, I will set you free."

I reared back. "I-I could never ask you to do that."

"You're not asking. I'm offering." She took my hand and squeezed hard. "I'm telling you, I will be there to say goodbye, Aslan. In whatever way is needed. I love you enough to kill you."

A half-choked, half-strangled laugh fell from my lips. "I-I don't think anyone has ever uttered that sentence before. And…somehow, it makes me love you even more."

She smiled. "In return, all I ask is that you stay. Let's go on that voyage. Let's go travel the seas. Let's swim in the arctic and let icebergs cure our ills. Let's chase the orcas and find the narwhals. Lunamare doesn't need me anymore. Ayla is on the boards of your charities and can continue your donations.

"Let's go, Aslan. Together. Right now. Let's disappear so we can live with no fear…until that time comes for this life to end."

Her voice caught, and tears shot to her eyes. "I told our story, you know. I told them everything. It wasn't planned, and I probably shared too much, but…I needed to love you one last time. I wanted to relive every moment we shared because I knew you intended to kiss me goodbye today. I knew you were going to walk into the surf and not return. And, you stupid, *stupid* man…you thought I would let you."

She scoffed and shook her head. "Where you walk, I walk. Where you swim, I swim. Where you sleep, I sleep. I was prepared to die today with you, *kocam*. I have said my goodbyes and tasted what it will feel like to no longer be in this world. I shared our tale with two reporters so our love would live on. I asked myself a thousand times if there was the tiniest piece of me that would rather stay than go.

"But…each time I envisioned living without you. Each time I imagined my bed empty of you and my heart hollow and my love gone, I knew I was making the right choice. The *only* choice.

"I know you want sovereignty over your body. I know you don't trust your heart, and I get that. I get it because I don't trust it either. But I trust *us*." She tapped my chest and hers. "I trust that we share that same heart, Aslan, and you cannot ask me to live without it. You cannot expect me to survive without it. I lost you for five years, my darling, and it broke me in ways I will never be free of."

Smiling sadly and brushing away her tears, she whispered, "So the choice is yours, Aslan. We die today, together, right here like you planned, with the dawn on our faces and the tide around our ankles…or you trust me to free you if your body forsakes you. If that day comes when you are lost to me, I will let you go and then I will follow. Just like I know if I went first, you'd chase me. We can't do this alone, my love. It's just not possible."

I blinked at my wife.

At the woman who made me whole while somehow carving me into pieces.

My damaged and scarred, besotted and obsessed heart fell firmly into her grasp.

I'd never had someone give me their everything before.

Never loved anyone as much as I loved her.

I'd been lucky enough to own her in every way for six decades.

Every part of me shook as I cupped her cheek and kissed her forehead with utter reverence. "You always were and always have been my life's purpose, Nerida Kara. What would I be without you? Where would I go without you by my side? What would I become without you there to love me?"

"Make the choice, Aslan." She kissed my palm. "Today…or someday?"

I pulled back.

I held her stare.

I didn't answer for an eternity.

I skimmed through the scenarios of another stroke, another heart attack.

I weighed up the pain and the loss against the moments we could still have. All the happiness we could still gather. All the love we could still share.

Was that worth the pain?

The fear?

The not knowing when it would end?

Yes, my heart thumped.

Of course, my blood sang.

Always, my bones ached.

Slowly, I ran my knuckles beneath her chin and tipped her mouth to mine.

I kissed her deeply, longingly. I worshipped her with every molecule in my breaking and failing body.

I *trusted* her.

I trusted that she would put me out of my misery if it came down to it. She wouldn't go back on her promise.

She was brave enough to do what needed to be done.

I ought to feel horror at putting that on her but…it only gave me peace. Safety. Freedom.

Freedom to stay and enjoy every moment.

Safety to continue loving her.

Gathering her in a bone-crushing hug, I pressed my mouth to her ear and fed her a vow of my own. "Someday…but not today."

She shivered in my arms.

I kissed the soft skin behind her ear, nuzzling into her time-whitened hair. Even now, it smelled of salt and ocean. Of waves and eternal sea. "Let's go on that cruise, *canim*. Let's get lost. Let's explore. Let's be selfish and say goodbye so it's just us. Like it's always been."

She moaned as I kissed her deep.

No guilt for how others would grieve us when that day came.

No fear for how it would feel to slip from this existence into another.

This was *our* choice.

The only choice.

Because our heart was one, just like it had always been.

"I love you," she whispered against my mouth.

"I adore you," I breathed into her soul.

She teased me and tempted me and repeated a phrase that would become a mantra to us. A prayer of togetherness and forever. "Someday, but not today."

I pulled away and took her hand, leading her to the speedboat. "Someday…but not today. Today, we live. Today, we love. Today is all that matters."

Epilogue

NERIDA

(Love in Korean: Salang)

ASLAN LAY SPRAWLED BESIDE ME, SOAKING in the last rays of sunshine.

A sudoku book rested on his trim belly, black-framed reading glasses perched on his nose, and his pen was still stuck in his fingers even though he napped with his salt-and-pepper hair flopping over his forehead and his delectable lips slightly parted.

Four years ago, I'd given a tell-all interview about love, grief, and adversity. Four years since we'd stepped foot on Australian soil, not because it was safer to remain in international waters now that the article and numerous blogs had been published, but because we were living our life the way we wanted to.

Ayla and Harry often visited us with the girls, flying to whatever port we were currently visiting and catching a local helicopter to land on the helipad on the upper deck. Teddy and Eddie regularly video chatted us, and we'd spent Teddy's birthday with him and Eddie, Honey and Billy in Cuba.

The article that Dylan and Margot completed included what Aslan had done to Ethan, and none of our friends batted an eye. They all knew Aslan had a past. All felt the power running in his veins, all saw his ruthlessness in keeping me safe, but they also knew he was one of the most loyal, trustworthy, and generous people on the planet.

In hindsight, I might not have been quite so honest if I'd known I wouldn't be wading into the ocean with Aslan on that dawn and swimming to our death like I'd envisioned. But after I'd left Aslan the day before—thanks to a heated argument that he couldn't take another stroke and that he was done waiting for his heart to finish him—I'd made him promise to wait for me.

To wait to say goodbye.

For me to do the interview I couldn't cancel, then I would kiss him farewell and watch him vanish beneath the waves, just like he was about to do amongst the shipwreck all those decades ago.

Silly man.

Stupid soulmate.

Of course, I would never let him go anywhere without me.

If he wanted to die, it was a joint activity.

Living through five years of loss had permanently scarred me, and I would *never* live through that again. The day Aslan Kara passed away was the day I did too with absolutely no regrets and a heart full of gratefulness to have loved him.

But…apart from a few hiccups with his heart and a few doctor visits around the world, he was still him. Still bright-eyed and sharp-witted. We hunted for super foods and took local medicines. We were open to nature as well as science, and I'd begun noting my findings on the latest therapy or longevity secret on my website.

I didn't know if anyone read my ramblings, but…if some of the information I gathered—thanks to the freedom and money to visit far distant places and travel to hidden oases—helped those who weren't in such enviable positions to try such things, then I was glad.

Aslan had stayed alive for four more years.

Four *wonderful* years.

Four years and counting…

The captain stepped over me, casting a shadow from the setting sun. "We're weighing anchor for the night, Mrs Kara. Dinner will be in an hour in the dining room."

"Can you have Harriet set up the table on the back deck, Ben? I'd like to drink in the sights of Karon."

"Of course." He nodded and headed back to the captain's cabin above us.

Aslan stretched and sat up, tucking his pen behind his ear and giving me a lazy smile. His lion tattoo flashed me, slightly weathered with time, partly faded from sunshine. It never failed to bring a glow of happiness as I dropped my stare to my own. Even in death, our bodies would always wear that permanent mark. A picture of two hearts becoming one.

Catching my eyes as I looked back up, he gave me the sweetest grin along with a suggestive quirk of his eyebrow. "Want to get another?"

"Another?"

"Tattoo." Leaning forward, he cupped my breast beneath my cream dress with familiar possessive fingers.

I gasped and leaned into his touch.

Society would say we were too old for lust and longing. But society was an idiot. Despite our years, our need for one another had never dampened.

"I think my name inked right above your heart would look extremely fetching," he purred.

"Fetching, huh?" My heart kicked of its own accord, leaping from love, and not his faulty rhythm.

"We could pop into Thailand tomorrow and find an artist."

"We could." I smiled. "But if we do, I get to put my name right above yours too. It's only fair."

Sighing, he dropped his hand, his eyes burning with coal dust. "It's been yours since I was born, Neri. It's defective and damaged and only beats because you command it to, but if you want to autograph it, then by all means."

"You've got yourself a deal then," I whispered. "I'll ensure it beats for another decade."

"Knowing you, you'll find a way to make that happen."

He could live for a millennium, and I would still find new parts of him to love.

Still obsess over how handsome and kind and amazing he was.

Still want a thousand more years with him.

Looking toward the tourist beach in the distance, he took off his glasses and closed his sudoku book. "Another port." He grinned. "Another night."

"Another day." I put my hand in his as he reached for me.

"Someday...but not today," he whispered, squeezing my fingers and pulling me to my feet.

I smiled as he kissed me.

I laughed as he waltzed me around the deck, the slight clack of his blade in contrast to our bare feet.

Someday, but not today.

What a wonderful life.

What a fabulous love.

What an incredible day.

Today was not that day.

Tomorrow might not be, either.

But when someday came, we would face it together.

We would leap into the void.

We would swim into the stars.

And there, with the moon to guide us and the sea to carry us, we would find each other...

...all over again.

Thank you so much for reading!

I truly hope you enjoyed this story. When Neri and Aslan popped into my head, they took over my entire world, and it's an honour to share them with you. If you like this type of read (in the genre I've nicknamed Dark Sparks) then please make sure to check out THE RIBBON DUET. I also have another duet planned for later in the year that has the same feels so subscribe to my newsletter or keep an eye on my socials.
Thanks again so much.

Pepper
x

Other Upcoming Titles...

Ruby Tears
(Dark Romance)
Find out more at:
www.pepperwinters.com

"Ten thousand dollars.
That pitiful sum changed my entire life.
It bought *my entire life.*
A measly ten thousand dollars, given to my boyfriend by a monster to fuck me.
He took it.
The monster took me.
And I never saw freedom again."

I'm the bastard son of a monster.
My other half-blooded siblings have their own demons...but me?
I truly have the devil inside.
I try to be good.
To do my best to ignore the deep, dark, despicable urges.
But every day it gets harder.
I thought family could help.
I reached out to my infamous half-brother, Q, begging for his secrets to
stay tamed.
Instead, he gave me an ultimatum to prove I'm not like our father.
Infiltrate The Jewelry Box: a trafficking ring of poor unfortunate souls, kill
the Master Jeweler, free the Jewels, and don't lose my rotten soul while trying.
Only problem is...my initiation into this exclusive club is earning a Jewel
all of my own.
She sparkles like diamonds, bleeds like rubies, and bruises as deep as
emeralds.
She's mine to break.
I can't refuse.
If I want to prove to my half-brother that I'm not like our sire, I have to
sink into urges I've always fought, plunge into madness, and lose myself so
deeply into sin that the only one who will be breaking is me.

WOULD YOU LIKE REGULAR FREE BOOKS?

Sign up to my Newsletter and receive exclusive content, deleted scenes, and freebies.
SIGN UP HERE

UPCOMING BOOKS 2023

Sign up to my Newsletter to receive an instant 'It's Live' Alert!

Please visit www.pepperwinters.com for latest updates.

OTHER WORK BY PEPPER WINTERS

Pepper currently has close to forty books released in nine languages. She's hit best-seller lists (USA Today, New York Times, and Wall Street Journal) almost forty times. She dabbles in multiple genres, ranging from Dark Romance, Coming of Age, Fantasy, and Romantic Suspense.

For books, FAQs, and buylinks please visit:

https://pepperwinters.com

DARK ROMANCE

Goddess Isles Series
Once a Myth
Twice a Wish
Third a Kiss
Fourth a Lie
Fifth a Fury

Monsters in the Dark Trilogy
Tears of Tess
Quintessentially Q
Twisted Together
Je Suis a Toi

Indebted Series
Debt Inheritance
First Debt
Second Debt
Third Debt
Fourth Debt
Final Debt
Indebted Epilogue

Dollar Series
Pennies

Dollars
Hundreds
Thousands
Millions

Fable of Happiness Trilogy

SEXY ROMANCE

The Master of Trickery Duet
The Body Painter
The Living Canvas

Truth & Lies Duet
Crown of Lies
Throne of Truth

COMING OF AGE ROMANCE

The Ribbon Duet
The Boy & His Ribbon
The Girl & Her Ren

Standalone Spinoff
The Son & His Hope

STANDALONES

Destroyed – Grey Romance
Unseen Messages – Survival Romance

MOTORCYCLE CLUB ROMANCE

Pure Corruption Duet
Ruin & Rule
Sin & Suffer

ROMANTIC COMEDY written as TESS HUNTER

Can't Touch This

CHILDREN'S / INSPIRATIONAL BOOK

Pippin and Mo

FANTASY ROMANCE

When a Moth Loved a Bee

UPCOMING RELEASES

For 2023/2024 titles please visit www.pepperwinters.com

RELEASE DAY ALERTS, SNEAK PEEKS, & NEWSLETTER

To be the first to know about upcoming releases, please join Pepper's Newsletter (she promises never to spam or annoy you.)

Pepper's Newsletter

SOCIAL MEDIA & WEBSITE

Facebook: Peppers Books
Instagram: @pepperwinters
Facebook Group: Peppers Playgound
Website: www.pepperwinters.com
Tiktok: @pepperwintersbooks

ACKNOWLEDGEMENTS

I'm both elated and sad that The Luna Duet is finished.

I have lived and breathed Neri and Aslan, and they will always be a part of me. I'm ever so grateful to you for taking the time to read this book. Like Neri, I am aware how precious every moment is and it's an honour to borrow so many of yours.

I have the following people to thank:

Rowan, Cyn, Melissa, Rochelle, Danielle, Heather, and Effie for beta reading.

Another massive thank you to Betül from Silence is Read for her incredible Turkish translations and her huge help at making Aslan as authentic as possible.

I owe another massive thanks to Tor Thom and Fiona Clare for the impeccable narration.

Valentine PR, Nina, Kim, and all the fabulous girls for epic promotion.

Jenny for her wonderful edits and eagle eyes.

Cleo for the absolutely gorgeous covers (all three versions!).

Christina for the awesome final proofread.

Sedef for the sensitivity read to remain respectful and authentic.

All the incredible bloggers, tiktokkers, instagrammers, and facebookers who helped review and share.

And…you!

Thank you so much for reading and allowing me to share a small piece of my imagination with you once again!

Pepper

x

TURKISH WORDS & GLOSSARY

Aşkım: My love
Canım: My life, my soul (everyday word for family, friends, even acquaintances)
Güzelim: My beautiful/handsome one
Sevgilim: My darling/lover
Hayatım: My life (used to express affection for someone significant in one's life)
Meleğim: My angel (used to express love or admiration)
Güneşim: My sunshine (used to express affection or admiration)
Çiçeğim: My flower (used to express admiration or endearment)
Or Kuzum: My lamb (used to express tenderness, gentleness, and affection)
Tosunum: My bull calf (used for young boys or chubby babies by doting loved ones)
Aslanım: Brave (used to signify brave, strong, heroic people)
Kahretsin: Dammit (curse word when things go wrong)
Kafami sikeyim: Fuck my head (curse word that is commonly used. Loose translation: 'fuck me')
Birtanem: My love (used to express a loved one, my only one)
Seni çok seviyorum: I love you so much
Seni seviyorum: I love you
Özür dilerim: I am so sorry
Teşekkür ederim: Thank you (formal with polite meaning)
Teşekkürler: Thank you (informal)
Defol: Get lost, go away (loose translation)
Karıcığım: My wife
Kocam: My husband
Lanet olsun: Damn or Damn it
Efendim: My lord / my master
Patron: Boss

The most common terms of endearment are *Aşkım, Güzelim, Sevgilim, Hayatım, Canım.* These are made extra affectionate by adding *benim* (ben means me and benim means mine).
Aşkım benim.
Hayatım benim.
This intensifies the phrase between close loved ones.

Thank you to Betül for this amazing list and for all her help making Aslan as authentic and as culturally respectful as possible. And to Sedef for reading early and ensuring I was sensitive to the amazing country of Turkey and its people.

I am now head over heels for everything Turkish and can't wait to jump back into Aslan and Neri's world in Cor Amare.

Any errors are mine.

Thank you so much for reading.

Printed in Poland
by Amazon Fulfillment
Poland Sp. z o.o., Wrocław
20 July 2023

54645924-39b4-42e9-9d44-ed05cb27b608R03